Uncle Arctica

Drew Harmon

Trespass Island Books
trespassislandbooks.com

Formatting by Polgarus Studios
polgarusstudios.com

ISBN 978-0-692-48589-7 (print)

Acknowledgements

I'd like to express my gratitude to the following people for their support, encouragement, and inspiration in writing Uncle Arctica:

My beloved wife Karen, who has stuck with me through the victories, and the capsizes.

My son Ian, who gave me honest feedback and kept a watchful eye on my typos.

To Kelly and Rowan, who always gave up the computer whenever I asked.

Beth and Roger Lovell, who couldn't get enough of Uncle Arctica.

Della Jules, my manuscript consultant, who suffered the endless barrage of my loony voicemails, yet told me to keep calling.

Naomi Mueller and her dog Buck, who lent his name to one of the characters in this book.

My beta readers: Beth Lovell, Mark Cudworth, James and Arthella Lacey, Karen Harmon, Rhonda Parr, Jerry Purvis, Rachel Swaim, and Jason Work.

And all the great old sailors who made the Indianapolis Sailing Club the stuff of legend, in my mind.

In memory of
Burl Albert Harmon
Who left me the legacy of sailing

Preface

I suppose that after this six-year voyage with *Uncle Arctica*, I should take a moment to write a preface. The idea for *Uncle Arctica* began to take root while I was working as an academic advisor in a call center—in the ninth ring of Hell. I think that all call center jobs should be rated by the ring of Hell to which they belong. I'd typed enough meaningless schlock into the customer service database to sink the proverbial ship. I knew I had to start writing something with color and direction before the *S.S. Drew Harmon* hit the rocky bottom. Between calls I started writing short accounts of the sundry adventures I'd had in recent years, then moved on to odd little scenes which eventually birthed the characters and incidents of *Uncle Arctica*.

Then something wonderful happened. I lost my job! I escaped into a blissful two-year period of unemployment. I promptly fell under the delusion that this was early retirement. That's when *Uncle Arctica* really took off. My wife would hear me reading it to friends on the phone and cackling. After a couple of weeks of this she finally inquired as to just what was going on. My explanation was something on the order of "a novel about Kids. Sailing. Mayhem. Criminal misuse of fireworks." She figured it was something to do with my childhood.

Indeed, I did grow up sailing—mostly racing with my dad. Sometimes it was fun—oftentimes not so much. Sometimes it was terrifying. Service was involuntary in the Harmon Family Navy, and there were only three ways to escape: grow up and move to the other side of the continent, as did my sister; become too pregnant, as was my mother (carrying yours truly,) or have a near-death experience while sailing, which is how my brother and I mustered out of our tours of duty on the old red boat. I gladly received my honorable discharge at sixteen. But yet, bribed by the promise of reward, I was not wholly unwilling to be "pressed" back into occasional service. I returned to day-sailing with my father in the late 1980's, and intended to start racing with him again, as soon as I could leave the world of TV production and establish my bodywork business. But it didn't happen. When Dad and I pulled the boat out and packed her up for the winter of 1993, it would be our last time.

I inherited Lightning 8679 in early '94, renaming her *Weirdly Manor*. For crew, I shanghaied my wife, and many friends. We raced that boat like maniacs for the next ten years. Dad was always a by-the-book man, and it won him a lot of trophies. I have always been the "by-the-seat-of- your-pants" type. For a long time after his passing, Dad would turn up in my dreams complaining that I was a reckless skipper. My reply was always that it was fun, and it got results (usually being madcap situations and harrowing predicaments, in lieu of trophies—but I didn't tell *him* that!)

Uncle Arctica takes place against the backdrop of an inland sailing club. A good bit of the geography and a few other features of the story will be familiar to anyone who has been part of life at the Indianapolis Sailing Club. This story is about much, much more than sailing. It's about by-the-seat-of-your-pants madcap situations and harrowing predicaments. It's about fear and fun. It's about friends and jerks—and folks who are a little of both. It's about love and abandonment. It's about being a kid. It's about summer at the lake.

Table of Contents

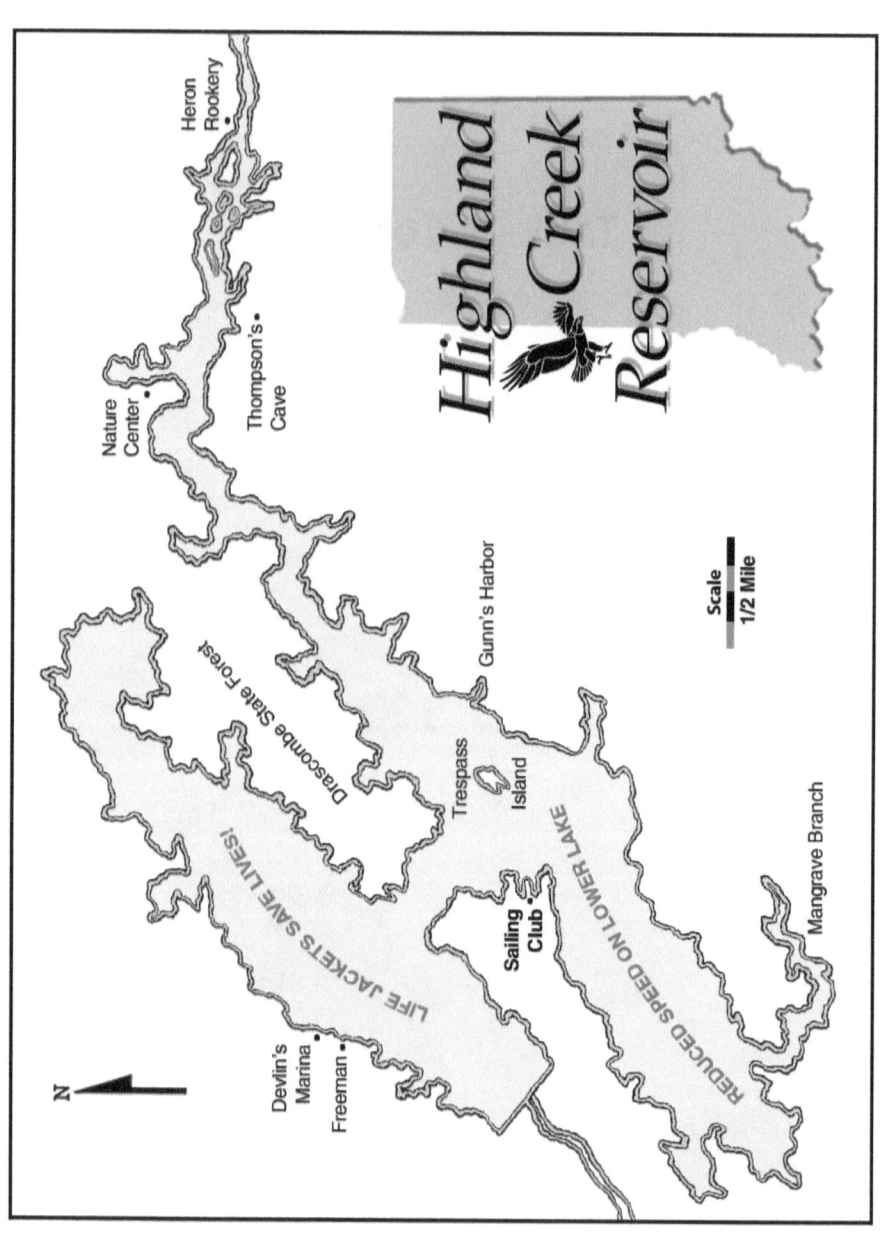

Highland Creek Reservoir

N

Heron Rookery

Nature Center

Thompson's Cave

Diascombe State Forest

Gunn's Harbor

LIFE JACKETS SAVE LIVES!

Devlin's Marina

Freeman

Sailing Club

Trespass Island

REDUCED SPEED ON LOWER LAKE

Mangrave Branch

Scale
1/2 Mile

Part I

Uncle Arctica

Chapter 1

"It's the kind you feed *rats*, it's so big," said Agatha, adjusting her very black sunglasses. Her twelve-year-old brother scowled through his own reflection in the car window. Tears of hate and fear welled in his eyes.

"I know you're listening, Blake," she continued. "I heard you sniffle."

"Oh shut up," he said weakly, face close to the glass.

"Blake, we don't say 'shut up,' do we, honey? You know that," interrupted Mother, sweetly.

Her eyes darted to Father, whose knuckles were white on the steering wheel. It was the typical Barber family road trip: a sort of tepid hell of borderline car sickness and bickering siblings. And as always Father was simply trying to prevent jets of steam from shooting out of his ears while he struggled to keep the car between the lines. Agatha waited a second.

"Too bad you can't go to Europe with Mom and Dad, and me. Hope you have fun out here in the boondocks with weird old Uncle Arctica."

"His name is Uncle Carson."

"*I'll* be touring castles and meeting royalty and enjoying gourmet meals. *You'll* be working jigsaw puzzles with Nanna Urquart all summer!"

"You're so *stupid*," Blake said. "You just pick on me because you're jealous!"

"Blake, we don't call people stupid; honey, you know that! Mean well, speak well, do well," said Mother. Father's face reddened.

Agatha cocked her head. "Why would I *ever* be jealous of a little

3

pipsqueak like you? Name *one* thing!"

"Because *I* can stand up to pee, but *you'll* always be a dirty squatter!"

The car swerved sharply, knocking Blake's forehead against the glass. "Blake Alan Barber!" Mother gasped, "Where did you ever learn to say such a thing?"

"Sunday school!" Blake replied.

Father made a strangled wincing sound in his throat like a steam pipe about to burst. He was superintendent of the children's Sunday school at Pine Terrace Christian Church.

Without delay came the blowback from the driver's seat. "If you two don't shut up I will stop this car and so help me I'll knock you both from Sabbath to Sunday!" Father could shout louder than any other on earth. The shock and awe usually left its victims in stunned silence for at least thirty minutes. This time it only lasted ten before Agatha went for it again.

"That giant tarantula Uncle Arctica has? Well, it got loose in Nanna's house," she murmured, like a wicked Siamese cat.

Blake bit his lip and glared out the window. It was an unusually chilly and blustery day for mid-May. Towering cumulus clouds heaped up in the sky, their tops curling over like cosmic tidal waves. The trees swayed in wild rhythm, leaves blown back, shaking their white undersides like pagan worshippers in a demonic frenzy. It only added to his anxiety and sense of his own smallness.

"Think of it. A spider *so* big it eats rats," Agatha had her victim right where she wanted him. He was almost thirteen and she could still make him cry. She could see he was starting to sob. She savored it. "And guess what? He trained it so that just before it bites, it taps out 'Shave and a Hair Cut' with one hairy leg!" She tapped it out on her window—tap-tappa-tap-tap! "Shave and a hair cut! Shave and a hair cut!" she whispered with ghastly drama. She rapped it out on the door—knock-knocka-knock-knock! Shaaave and a hairrrrr cuuut!" She lunged and pinched her brother's arm savagely and shouted "Two Bits!"

Blake jolted and let out an ear-piercing shriek. The car swerved, and shuddered to a halt. He and Agatha lurched forward then whipped back into their seats. In the blink of an eye Father coiled completely around, arm cocked to swing. Mother caught the stinging slap in her palm before it could sweep across the faces in the backseat. There was a reason Agatha always sat behind the driver's seat when Father was at the wheel.

The remaining miles were covered in complete silence except for the occasional sniffle. Blake glanced over his shoulder at his father and sister, then leaned his forehead against the cold window. *At least I'll be away from you two. Maybe I'll get lucky and die while you're gone.*

***

Blake struggled to wakefulness. The car had turned and they were in a forest. They passed through a big gate and instantly the forest gave way to a wide gravel parking lot and then a forest of a different kind: one of straight, limbless trees, wire, and rope. There were rows of sailboats in every shape and size, some on trailers, some on dollies, up high and down low, on blocks, and on timbers. In the distance beyond the grove of masts Blake could only see more woods. *The Black Forest,* he thought. On the right was a big hill. Wide timber-and-brick steps led upward. It looked like there might be a big house or something at the summit. Lock-studs popped up. Seat-belts clicked free. Doors opened. Fresh air rushed into the car. Finally, after one hundred and fifty of the longest minutes that ever ticked away, the Barber family had reached its destination.

Gravel crunched under Blake's feet. The chilly wind still howled, the leaves still rustled and hissed. The gusts whistled shrill and ghostly through the wire stays that braced the masts up. It banged countless halyards and fittings against them in an endless, eerie rhythm—like a cacophony of xylophones played by skeletons. There wasn't another soul in sight. Blake felt that this must be the loneliest, most remote place on earth. It made his stomach tighten into yet one more knot. He waited for Agatha to start in about Bigfoot or the Wendigo. But she didn't.

Father glanced around impatiently, trying to dislodge the wedgie of the century. "Well, where is he?"

"Let's go up top and see if the groundskeeper knows, and everyone can visit the necessary room," Mother answered.

The Barber family ascended the grand staircase. Blake was impressed with its brick-and-timber construction and its short lamp posts. He wondered what it would look like all lit up at night. They passed through a semicircle of spruce trees at the crown of the hill and crossed a circular, blacktopped drive. In the center was a little flower garden surrounding a boat anchor, half again as tall as Blake. The clubhouse loomed large before them. The great gambrel roof and blue-gray shingled sides made it seem to Blake like a regal barn with shutters and dormer windows. The door was unlocked and Father led the way in. Blake forgot the staircase and anchor immediately. He left his mother's side and weaved between tables and chairs to reach the wall of windows on the opposite side of the big room.

He stood wide-eyed and took in the panorama. Sunlight shot down in shafts through endlessly shifting mountains of cloud and swept across rolling water. It painted the lake with shifting patches of turquoise, silver, sapphire, and jade.

A sparsely wooded peninsula with a ridge of its own stretched out ahead for a quarter of a mile. The furious wind drove white-capped waves up the lake and into the harbor. Blake was transfixed. *We must be forty feet above the lake!* He thought. For a long minute he forgot about the car trip, his family, and Europe lost. He turned around and found himself alone. His family had vanished into the restrooms.

He tore himself away from the window to visit a glass case full of trophies, memorabilia, and model ships. He glanced around at fleet bulletin boards papered with pictures, score sheets, protest-forms, and crew-wanted notices. There was a wall of portraits of past club commodores, and a huge stone fireplace. Over it hung a painting of two old sailing ships engaged in battle. *The Constitution versus the Guerriere, no doubt*, he thought. The whole place exuded an ambience of manly adventure. It stirred in him latent aspirations of being something or somebody, someday. It was a place, he thought, to which he would like to become accustomed. But the spell of fascination was broken by his father's voice. "Don't touch a thing! This is not a place for little boys!" Suddenly everything seemed alien and intimidating again. Father looked out the same window that Blake had. He scanned the grounds and shoreline. "Looks like there's some activity down at that garage by the water" Father said. "I wish we'd driven up here."

"Why don't you go down and ask about Carson? I'd like to walk to the point with the children," said Mother. Father agreed and they went their own ways.

Father reached the bottom of the hill and meandered through rows of trailered boats to reach the garage. A motorboat bearing the words "HCSC Safety Patrol" on its side sat on blocks of orange foam in front of the open overhead door. "Hello! Anybody here?" He called, tenuously.

"Yeah! Who's there?" answered a rough but friendly voice. A man emerged from the garage wiping his hands on a grease rag. Gray-bearded and burly, he could have passed for a startled grizzly.

"I'm looking for Carson Urquart. Is he around here?"

"Well, I think he said he was gonna be down the lake workin' on someone's dock. He was supposed to help *me* with *this* sonofabuck this afternoon. Figured he'd be back by now. I'm Ray, by the way." The grizzly pulled a paw from the rag and extended it to Father. He shook it and to his displeasure got his hand back reeking of gasoline.

"Sorry. I'm James Barber. Carson's my brother-in-law. We were supposed to meet him here this afternoon."

"Aah, he'll turn up. He's good for his word."

"I hope so. We're kind of on a schedule here," James said, more to himself than to Ray. "Thanks."

"Sure!"

On the point it was all that Blake, Agatha, and Mother could do to face the gusts and stay on their feet. Blake saw it as a positive thing, as it seemed to keep Agatha's mouth shut. The mossy ground was damp and squishy. Not only did the wind roar but waves splashed against a protective apron of shoe-box-sized limestone chunks that bordered the shoreline, filling the air with spray. Agatha hid herself as best she could behind a tree trunk, her back to the wind. She was miserable. Blake stood half behind his mother so as to keep warm yet still maintain a clear view down the lake. Father waddled up, shoulders hunched, hands in his pockets. Mother was squinting westward, lips pressed into a tight smile, her curls blowing every which way.

"Well, that werewolf wasn't any help. Carson was supposed to be back hours ago. Now what?"

"He'll be here soon. Just wait," said Mother, still squinting into the wind.

"What makes *you* so sure?"

Mother pointed to an indefinite spot in the distance. "Look, *there!*"

Father could make out something red, bobbing a half mile away.

"That's him!" beamed Mother.

Blake watched intently as the bobber became a thin red line and eventually a seemingly empty canoe. It drifted sideways, its length parallel to the waves. As it lolled over each swell, he could see that there seemed to be someone lying in the bottom. He thought the enchantment of the entire scene was lost on everyone but himself: the raw power and primal chaos of wind and wave, light and color, dark and shadow, a family huddled against the storm, and a mysterious figure carried in on the surge like an apparition from some epic sea story.

Finally the little craft and its mysterious cargo reached the mouth of the harbor. Without warning the figure in the bottom of the canoe sat up and paddled furiously across the whitecaps. To Blake's alarm, his mother broke loose from his grip and trotted down to one of the narrow docks along the shore. He followed but stopped in his tracks at his father's terse command: "Stay!"

The man in the canoe tossed a rope to Mother as he approached. She caught it handily. Blake watched as she made loops in the end of it and jerked it tight around one of the poles that supported the dock. She knelt and grabbed the edge of the bobbing craft and stopped it from banging against the dock. Blake was astonished to see her performing these tasks with speed and skill as if she had done them a hundred times before. The man slid out onto the dock on his behind and stood up. He was not tall, but was powerfully built. Waves of dark red hair crept out from under a black stocking cap, complimenting a long, thick mustache that bracketed his chin. His smudged sweatshirt made it obvious that he'd been painting. Mother released the canoe and sprang into his arms, the dock wobbling precariously beneath them.

"Carson!' she exclaimed, "Big bro!"

"Hey Ava!" They trundled off the dock single file.

"Blake, Agatha, come say hello to Uncle Carson! Car, it's been so long you won't even recognize them!"

Blake took a step forward and greeted the man with a cautious wave. Agatha remained behind her tree, but to avoid being seen had slunk around it to the windward side.

"My goodness, you *have* sprouted into a fine young fellow!" he said. "Now, where's your sister, Agony?" Carson cast about for Agatha and called "Agony, oh Agony, it's safe to come out! It's only your Uncle Arctica!" his voice seemed a little nasal and had more than a hint of drawl.

James, impatient, interrupted sourly. "Her name is Agatha, and we need to get going. Where can we leave Blake's luggage?"

"Clubhouse is fine, old boy! And I say, good to see you too, James!"

James stared in silent aggravation for a moment then turned his back and called to Agatha.

"Come on Agatha dear, we're leaving." Agatha jerked herself from the other side of the tree and trailed the procession back to the clubhouse.

Blake was filled with wonder at what kind of man this Uncle Arctica might be who within five minutes had transformed his mother, insulted his sister, and completely annoyed his father. He couldn't help the impression that he was a living jack-in-the-box who would spring out on you just as his rinky-tink music had you hypnotized.

"Sorry I'm late, Sis," he said. "I was working on someone's dock down the lake and my mooring slipped."

"You tied a hitch instead of a bowline, again. Didn't you?" asked Ava.

Carson looked back at Blake and said, "She got me, kid! The lazy man must do his work twice. That's what the Russians say!"

"Well I certainly hope you won't be as careless with our son," sneered

James.

"Don't worry, Jim, I'll be the *right* kind of bad influence."

***

Carson leaned against the front door of the clubhouse while Ava said goodbye to her son. Blake heard the car doors slam shut and the engine start at the bottom of the hill. The time had come and the reality of it hit him with a force that pressed his stomach toward his feet and his heart into his throat.

"Why can't you stay here, Mom, while *they* go to France?"

"Oh sweetie, who would watch your sister while your daddy is working?"

"She's old enough, she could stay at the apartment and do her homework."

"For twelve weeks? No, you know I have to go." She caressed his teary cheek. "Besides, Nanna has some wonderful things planned for you this summer. She'll pick you up in a couple of days. And I know you'll get along just fine with Uncle Carson in the meantime. This is such a neat place!"

"What if he's really a pirate, like Father says?" Blake countered.

"Better a pirate than a werewolf!" Ava smiled softly, but her attempt at irony didn't help.

She knew Blake hated the way his father labeled anyone he considered below himself a pirate, werewolf, heathen, outlaw, or pagan. It only made the world seem more lurid and dangerous than it already was to a sheltered boy of twelve.

The family car crested the hill and stopped in front of them. Father emerged, leaving the car door open, the engine running, and the "door ajar" bell dinging impatiently. He gave Blake a little hug which Blake did not return. "Be good for your Nanna and stay away from the water while you're here. Mother will call as soon as we're settled. Bye-bye." He climbed back into the car and slammed the door.

"It's time for me to go, sweetie. I love you so much!" said Mother, tears streaming and voice quivering. She wrapped her arms around Blake and held on for a long time. "Remember, trust and go forward." Finally, she managed to wrench herself away. "I know you'll take good care of him, Carson. Love you!"

"You know I will. Love you, Sis!"

James leaned across the front seat and shoved the passenger door open. The impatient dinging resumed.

"Bye-bye, sweetheart." She kissed Blake on the cheek and retreated to the car.

Blake and Carson watched them arc around the circular drive, Ava waving the whole way. As they turned to drive down the hill Agatha craned her head over the back seat, nose in the air, and stuck her tongue out as far as it would go. And then they were gone. For a moment there was only the sound of the wind, the car fading into the distance, and a boy's quiet, sorrowful moaning.

Carson stepped forward. "That girl is made of pure snot," he said. "*Pure* snot."

And then between sobs of repressed anguish, Blake gasped "I... hope... their plane... crashes...I...hope...they die...I hate...I hate...them all."

Carson drew a deep breath and took a long moment to gauge his response. "I know," he said, earnestly. "C'mon, let's get your stuff squared away." He opened the clubhouse door. "You like hot chocolate?"

There was no response. "Well, I'm taking your bags down to our quarters. On the ridge. We passed them on the way up."

Blake turned around slowly.

"You mean... that... that *mini-barn*?" Blake produced a wad of old Kleenex from his pocket and swabbed his nose then dried his cheeks on his sleeves. "Mom said we were staying in the assistant groundskeeper's quarters."

"Yeah, that's it. The *unofficial*... assistant...groundskeeper's quarters."

"*Un-* official? Let me guess. There is no *official* assistant groundskeeper and you just live in the tool shed for some very *un-official* reason?"

Carson's face drew into a crosswise smile. "That's pretty close, kid. C'mon, I'll explain everything. It's cozy. You'll like it."

***

Evening had fallen but the gale of wind had not let up. Now rain was beating down on the roof. The unofficial-assistant-groundskeeper's-quarters creaked like an old wooden ship on its last passage around Cape Horn. Blake huddled on a canvas cot, a blanket around his shoulders, sipping hot cocoa. A Coleman lantern cast stark, shifting shadows at all angles around the shed. The plywood walls were decorated with vintage regatta posters. An old, orange spar-buoy bearing the number four stood in one corner. A plastic mermaid figurehead wearing a Highland Creek Sailing Club tee-shirt leaned in another, a stash of old trophies piled around her tail. Overhead, laid across the joists, were life jackets, paddles, hanks of rope, poles with curious brass fittings, and several red duffel bags bearing stenciled labels: Spinnaker, Main, Jib. Directly across from his cot, staring back from a shaving mirror tacked to the wall, was the face of a pale, apprehensive little boy. *Church mouse,* he thought. *Scared little church mouse. Pathetic.*

He took a gulp of his hot cocoa. "Why does my sister call you 'Uncle Arctica'?"

"Oh, one time when she was little, maybe five or six, she was teasing me. She said 'I know all about Antarctica, but you must be *Uncle* Arctica!' It was cute, so it stuck. She wasn't always so hateful, once upon a time, you know."

"Until about the time I was born, I suspect."

"That'd be about it."

"So, why don't we ever see you?"

"Circumstance, I guess." Carson dragged a thumb and forefinger down his bushy moustache.

"When you were born I was in the Navy. Then Dad died, so I spent a lot of time down at Mom's taking care of her place. Haven't owned a car since who knows when and that makes it a long way up to Fort Wayne from Pemberton. That and the fact that your Dad doesn't exactly harbor the warmest feelings for me."

"I guess it's the same for us," said Blake. "Dad's always so busy with work and church, and Mom is always tangled up with Agatha's school stuff."

"So, where do you fit in?"

"The cracks."

Carson burst out with a loud laugh then stopped himself abruptly.

"What's so funny about that?"

"Boy you don't take prisoners, do you? So why ain'tcha in France, kid?"

"Oh. Dad's company is doing a thing where they trade their people with their sister company for a while. They'll send three family members all expenses paid and put them up in a company apartment. Three people. Anyone else costs lots extra."

"I see. And you just happen to be?"

"Lots extra, as usual. Dad can afford to send *one* of us to a private Christian school, but not *both* of us."

"And so you're home schooled."

"Exactly. Agatha won't wear second-hand clothes."

"So, you get Goodwill."

"Salvation Army, actually. Dad thinks the Goodwill is a Communist front organization."

Carson raised a bushy eyebrow.

"The point is I'm extra—extra money, extra effort, extra trouble. I was an accident. I'm not supposed to be here."

"Now, where do you get away with an ungrateful idea like that?"

"Well, when your dad introduces you to people as 'the little accident' right in front of you, you kind of get the idea."

"Yikes! I guess you would. Well, France ain't all it's cracked-up to be, anyway."

"Dad says the French are all snotty, snail-eating perverts."

Carson snorted and nearly spewed cocoa. He set his mug down very deliberately, leaned forward and put his elbows on his knees.

"Trust me Blake, your father is mistaken about a great many things, especially about *you*. And expected or not, your mother *adores* you, your grandmother is *always* thinking about you, and I'm *enjoying* getting to know you."

Blake tensed-up at his uncle's words but never broke eye contact. Carson noted this. He relaxed back into his lawn chair.

"As to the French and their likes, I'd say they're no better or worse than anyone else. As to their attitudes, however, I will only hazard to guess that Agatha will probably feel quite at home there."

It took a second, but a smile of comprehension flashed across Blake's face.

Carson picked up a harpoon-like boathook and began jabbing intently at something unseen, up in the shadows. "Ray's cooking breakfast for us tomorrow on account of your being our honored guest. Then you and I are being shanghaied by the ancient mariner himself, Daniel Tripper Gunn, to serve the day on his slave galley, the *Terrapin*. So, you better finish your cocoa then we can make one last visit to the facilities."

"Do we have to go back out?"

"Well, you can pee out the door if you want. But I have to go up top."

"Ugh! No way! I'll get my toothbrush."

That night, Blake dreamed of pirates fighting werewolves in the creaking, cramped hold of a ship called the *Terraphim*. He cowered in a corner behind red sail-bags and could hear his uncle shouting in the distance. And then suddenly Carson was standing in front of him, prodding the ceiling with a harpoon. Wind roared through the hold and there came a banging from above like cannonballs dropping on the deck: Bam bamma bam-bam! Splintered bulges erupted wherever they struck. Carson began jabbing the bulges back into place and then with a roaring laugh, looked at Blake and said, "You saved the ship, kid! You saved the ship!" The hold lurched violently, then rolled slowly over onto its side with the inexorable sensation of vertigo, as all faded into dizzy blackness.

Chapter 2

The morning was cool. The wind had spent its fury and now just blew reasonably. Blake had never smelled air so sweet with lilac. After breakfast, he and his uncle hiked down to the last dock on the peninsula.

"Should we really be going out on a boat? My father said he didn't want me near the water."

"I suppose he should have taken that into consideration before he left you with a guy who makes his living on a lake! Can you swim?"

"Surprisingly well."

"You don't have any other clothes with you? No tennis shoes?"

"This is it. Pretty much just black pants and white shirts."

"What's up with that? Your father grooming you to be a funeral director or a Mormon missionary?"

"It's a Chet Allworth thing. You wouldn't understand," Blake lamented.

"Oh, the Chet Allworth Organization! Now that explains some things. Everything neat as a pin, all your ducks in a row, triumphal music before work every morning, Pledge of Allegiance. Does he play the music?"

"John Phillip Sousa, 7:00 a.m. every day. I hate it. But don't tell my father."

"Don't worry, kid. I don't have any affection for Mr. Allworth and his Baptist business empire."

They passed the end of the ridge, walked through a grove of trees, and finally arrived at the planked pier where the red canoe was still tied up. A big bluish bird with legs like stilts, a long neck and a beak like a sword stood at the end of it. Startled, it made a noise halfway between a screech and a squawk and leapt into the air on the biggest wings Blake had ever seen.

"Was that a heron?" he cried. "That thing was as big as I am!"

"Great blue," Carson chuckled. "But the swans are a lot bigger and they don't scare. Keep that in mind. And there's our boss, now—coming around Trespass Island. Looks like Mr. Gunn wants to get on with his morning!"

Just to the right of the island, in the golden morning light, was a square, reddish-brown sail over a boxy white hull. As the boat rounded the island, Blake could see that it also carried a triangular sail on a pole out over the water in front of the boat, and a tall triangular sail at the very back. On each side of the hull, about midway down its length was a large paddle-like board that stuck straight down into the water. The boat looked like something from another time, something from one of his history books.

"She seems to be a cog or a sloop of some sort," Blake declared authoritatively.

"That's the *Terrapin*. She's a shoal-draft micro-cruiser based on a Bolger stitch-and-glue design: twenty-six feet at the waterline, thirty-six overall, and Yawl rigged, which means her mizzen mast is aft of the tiller. Her main is lug rigged. Tripp added the jib on a jury-rigged bowsprit to balance her helm a little better."

Not to be out-bantered, Blake countered, "Why doesn't Tripp flip over to the leeway and pick up some more speed if he's in such a hurry?"

"Blake, what is 'leeway' and why would it make him go faster?"

"Um, I guess I forgot. It must be the other way."

"What other way? Kid, Mr. Gunn knows what he's doing. And you will too, eventually, if you only talk about things you know about and stop trying to impress everyone with what you don't. Understand?"

"Yes," Blake snipped.

"Now listen up, the old fellah can be a little thorny sometimes— that's just his way. But he's a darn good man. You do right by him and he'll do right by you. You just have to keep your mouth shut and ignore the prickly parts."

Blake felt certain that this meant there would be more of the non-stop taunting that he could get at home. In fifteen minutes the *Terrapin* reached the harbor, entering on the far side. Gunn steered in a wide U-turn toward their shore.

"Get ready to step aboard, mate. He won't be stopping!"

Blake's eyes widened at the news. As the *Terrapin* approached the end of the dock, her sails emptied and began to flutter noisily. "On three!" prompted Carson. The bowsprit and jib passed, then the bow. "Three!" Carson pulled Blake along as he stepped onto the moving deck.

"All hands and the cook! Ready aboot and hard-ah-lee!" boomed a deep Scottish voice from the back of the boat. "G'mornin', Mr. Urquart!"

Carson took hold of the mast and Blake knelt instinctively to grab a fitting on the deck as the *Terrapin* veered away from the dock. The sails rattled and shook to the left side of the boat, then suddenly snapped taught, full of breeze. The boat leaned and picked up speed.

Carson assisted Blake across the top of the cabin and down into the cockpit.

"Morning, Tripp! Say hello to my nephew, Blake Barber."

"Welcome aboard, Blake. Mother Carey's chickens, he's the spittin' image, Urquart!"

"Ain't he?"

"Make yerself at home, lad. Yeh can have a look around if yeh like."

"Thanks," said Blake, timidly—still wondering what the old man had meant.

Carson took a seat on one of the benches that ran the length of the cockpit. Tripper Gunn was tall, old, and rugged. He had sparse white sideburns down to the bottom of his square jaw, and big, ugly, yellowed teeth. He wore wire-rimmed glasses and a black boonie hat. Blake peered down the companionway into the cabin and lowered himself onto the first step. The cabin was packed with bags of concrete, tools, buckets, rope, paint brushes, and stuff of all sorts. He remained there, where he could keep a cautious eye on the old ogre.

Soon the harbor and the point were out of sight and the nearest shore was a half mile away. It was captivating the way the *Terrapin* rocked, creaked, and sploshed as she cut through the water. With great rust-colored sails above, a cabin full of gear below, and two rugged sailors in the cockpit, Blake could not help but imagine that he was standing in the heart of a pirate ship, two hundred years ago. He imagined that the *Terrapin* was on a mission of high adventure. There would be swordplay, loot, cannon fire, and fair maidens to rescue! And he would be the hero! These fantasies were all contraband in his homeport. For that moment he felt...big. He felt...thirteen.

This reverie was interrupted by the ominous shadow of a black-bottomed cloud. It blotted out the sun and the breeze chilled instantly. The waves turned from blue to silver. Everything felt like it had been doused with a bucket of November.

"Do you think maybe we should turn back?" Blake said. "That looks like a rather threatening nimbus!"

"A threat'nin' wha?" Gunn laughed. "Yeh gotta talk plain to an auld Highlander, lad! Threat'nin' nimbus indeed!"

"It means rain cloud..." Blake said, but his explanation was not appreciated.

"I know what a nimbus is, lad! But that's cumulus and the only thing it threatens is fair weather! Did yeh teach him to talk like that, Urquart? Threat'nin' nimbus, indeed."

Carson could see that Gunn had torpedoed his nephew's spirit. "Don't worry about it, Blake. Tripp's just testy because he never learned to speak English!"

"Hah! Gaelic's the pure tongue! Lad, make yer threat'nin' self useful and haul that threat'nin' mainsail, will yeh?" Gunn commanded. "It's threat'nin' to luff! It's that threat'nin' red and white rope right there!"

Blake glared straight ahead for a moment then stepped up into the cockpit. He snatched the mainsheet and gave it a respectable jerk. It wouldn't budge.

"C'mon lad! Put some threat'nin' effort into it! Yeh have to brace yer foot against the bench and haul the threat'nin' thing!"

Blake, burning with humiliation, turned sharply, stomped one foot onto the bench by the companionway and poured all of his anger into the effort of pulling that rope. He hoped to tear the pulley straight out of the deck or put his foot through the bench, anything that would damage Gunn's boat. But the *Terrapin*, he discovered, was made of tougher stuff. Anyway, he liked the boat. It was Daniel Tripper Gunn he was beginning to hate. He strained every muscle in his body and groaned through clenched teeth. Suddenly the thick rope slid through the jaws of the cam-cleat, the pulley-block made a ratcheting sound, and the boom swung in a little way. The *Terrapin* heeled over a little more and picked up speed.

"That's it, man!" Gunn cheered. "She's still lifting. Haul in another foot!"

Blake strained at the sheet again. Once more the cleat's jaws opened, the block ratcheted, the sail came in, the boat heeled and gained speed. "Haul it again, man! Bring that boom all the way in!" cried the skipper. Blake did, again and again until his shoulders ached. At last the boom was over the cockpit and the *Terrapin* was heeled over so far that he had to brace one foot against the bench on the low side and hang onto the trim around the companionway. He still wasn't comfortable with the idea that a boat was supposed to lean over that far, but it was exhilarating all the same. And the thought that his father would have a stroke if he could see him now went a long way to bolstering his courage. The boat went tearing along, throwing cold spray each time her bow crashed over a wave. Finally the cloud cleared off and once more all was green and blue and bright springtime.

Gunn smiled and winked at Carson. "There may just be a sailor in that lad!"

"Just like his mother." Carson looked up at the mainsail. "And his granddad."

Gunn studied his friend's expression. "Aye. To be sure."

***

After an hour under sail the *Terrapin* and her crew neared their destination. "There 'tis lads!" said Gunn, pointing to the hilly shore, still a good way off. "Mr. Urquart, show yer boy how to get the sails down."

Carson clambered over the cabin top to the small, open compartment which formed the bow—where Blake was now ensconced. He loosed the halyard from a cleat on the mast and began to lower the jib. "Gather it in there, kid. Keep it out of the water if you can. Now get up here and help me with the main."

It took considerably more effort to bring the main sail and its heavy lug down without breaking anything or killing anybody.

"Up the leeboard!" said Gunn.

Carson and Blake scrambled over the cabin and back into the cockpit. Together they hauled on the line that swung the big "paddle" up to a nearly horizontal position alongside the hull. Gunn finished furling the mizzen sail around its mast in the stern. With one swift yank he started the outboard motor and puttered the boat up to a shady cove. Bright green duckweed swirled in their wake. Gunn reversed the motor for a moment then killed it. The *Terrapin* drifted up to an old floating dock that looked like it might have been used by Noah. "Put your fenders over!" Cylindrical air-filled cushions were pulled from the storage lockers under the benches, looped around horn-cleats, and put over the side of the boat to keep the hull from rubbing against the dock.

As the *Terrapin* slid up alongside the gray-green raft, Carson grabbed a rope which was attached to the bow of the boat and jumped out. The dock plunged under his weight, sending him to his hands and knees. He regained his balance and, bringing the *Terrapin* to a stop, tied the bowline to a rusty horn-cleat.

"Parks department is reopening this recreation site and they've hired us for a little patch up," Gunn said. "Break out the bookits, the concrete, and the trowels. Tomorrow we pick up a new dock from Devlin's and tow it down here."

While Gunn unloaded supplies, Blake made his way onto the precarious dock and followed Carson across the narrow strip of gravely beach. He stopped and watched his uncle ascend the decrepit stairway that disappeared up a dark hillside. The cove seemed altogether foreign and creepy. The air was still and stale. Everywhere, gnarled roots snaked their way out of the grooved, dirt bluffs. Dead branches stuck up out of the water, clouds of midges annoyed constantly, and that mossy dock threatened with every step to plunge him beneath the green water to whatever tentacled-horror undoubtedly lurked below.

"Lad!" Gunn called from the boat. "This is for you, then!" He stood ready to toss a big white bucket to the beach. "While we're up top setting concrete, yeh pick up all the trash and glass and bottle caps yeh can find, and put 'em in the bookit. But yeh save aside all the fishing lures and bobbers, anything else that may be of value."

"What about buried treasure?" said Blake.

His insolence was not wasted. Gunn stiffened, thrust the bucket down on the bench with a loud whack and shouted "Stoof it in yer pookits!" The old man tossed the bucket to the beach then turned and went into the cabin, growling to himself. He emerged with an armload of tools, gained the dock and headed up the stairs.

Blake clenched his fists. Anger coiled up in him like a sickening, burning snake. It exploded in all of the roar his twelve-year-old lungs could muster. In the quiet that followed he heard Gunn say, "Carson, that lad's got an anger problem!" Blake snatched the bucket and flung it up the bluff with all his might. It bounced off, flew back over his head, and splashed down ten feet out in the water.

"Don't let that sink, Blake!" called Carson, like the voice of conscience.

For a moment he contemplated the slowly sinking bucket, then clenched his fists again and shouted "Stoof it in yer pookits!"

***

Blake sat hunkered-down in the white trapezoidal cell that was the bow compartment, all the way back to the sailing club. As the *Terrapin* approached the peninsula Gunn noticed a long flag of red and white vertical stripes, flying from the pole on the point. "Yeh've a phone call, Carson, there's the answering pennant!"

"Now, who could that be?"

"It's Jack, lookin' fer yeh to throw his bail, like as not!"

"He can rot! Give 'em some time to think things over."

They sailed on until they were near the mouth of the harbor.

"Do an auld man a favor, will yeh? Strike the canvas. I don' feel like doin' it all myself, tonight."

Carson set about lowering the sails, being sure to drag the jib across Blake's cubby hole. Gunn furled the mizzen sail around its mast and started the motor. Finally the *Terrapin* made its familiar u-turn in the harbor and coasted up to the dock from which their journey had begun.

"All ashore that's goin' ashore!" Carson said. "We're here kid, let's go!"

Blake decompressed himself and rose awkwardly from the little compartment. He hopped over the side onto the dock and stormed for shore without looking back.

Gunn gave Carson a disapproving look.

"Don't say a word."

The old man maintained the expression and gestured toward the dock.

Carson disembarked. "See you tomorrow, Mr. Gunn."

Blake was well ahead, tromping up the trail that ran along the edge of the peninsula. He snarled, kicked up gravel and occasionally flailed a fist in the air with a grunt. At length, he scooped up a potato-shaped rock with his foot and launched it with a sidelong kick. It flew a good twenty feet and struck the safety latch on a winch-head. The winch kept a sailboat safe and snug, high out of the water on a kind of carriage. The hand-crank whizzed angrily and spun so fast that it was almost invisible. The carriage rumbled down its track, on its way to launching the sailboat. Blake froze in helpless horror at what he had just set in motion.

Carson flew past and leapt down the embankment to the dock. He seized the runaway boat by its side-stays. His feet slid down the planks as if he were struggling to hold back a charging bull. He stopped two inches from the end of the dock.

Blake was dumbfounded.

"Don't just stand there," Carson shouted, "winch it up! Hurry up! The boat's still lashed to the dolly, she'll float it off the track and then we *will* be in trouble!"

Blake took the crank with both hands and struggled to turn it around.

"Put the safety latch back on! If you slip, the crank'll whip around and break your arm!"

Now Blake was truly frightened. That handle had spun like the propeller on a plane. He flipped the latch in to place and began to labor with the crank. The latch made a rapid clinking sound in the braking gear.

"C'mon! C'mon! Crank it!"

The dolly-carriage made its way back up the track, rising slowly beneath the boat. As soon as the weight of the hull came to bear, the boy's efforts ground to a stop. Carson returned to the trail and took Blake's place at the winch.

"I'll be up top in a minute," he said, and began to crank furiously. Blake took the hint and resumed his journey up the gravel path. Completely drained and feeling very sorry for himself, he trudged up the tiring hill to the clubhouse.

Carson secured the boat and tied its bowline to the winch post. He drew a very deep breath and, as always in such moments, ran his fingers down his bushy mustache and thought for a while.

Blake was sitting on a bench in the men's locker room when he heard the back door squeak open and thump shut. To his surprise, his uncle didn't come looking for him. He got up and cautiously peered out into the main room. He could hear Carson mumbling faintly to himself somewhere, then dialing a touchtone phone.

"Hi, Mom! Yeah…okay, I guess. A little stormy this afternoon, but I suppose that's to be expected."

Blake slunk out of the locker room to a place where he could eavesdrop more effectively.

"So, you're still in Charlotte? That means you'll be here Friday then, right? *How* long? Well, do you want me to send him by bus or by plane?"

Blake's heart was in his throat again.

"Ahhh, that wasn't the plan, Mom…now, just wait a minute! Well, you *know* that means I'll have to leave Jack at your place all summer…That's fine? Are you sure? You don't quite understand what I've got on my hands here, Mom…Alright, alright. Does Ava know? We'll see how it goes. Love you too. Tell Gabby I said take it easy…okay, bye."

Carson emerged from a little alcove just inside the hallway to the women's locker room only to meet his nephew, who now stood in plain view.

"What was that all about, as if I even need to ask?"

"I'll give it to you straight, kid. Your Nanna is taking care of a sick friend in North Carolina. Doctor says the old girl ain't gonna make it—your Nanna's decided to stay with her 'til the end."

"Well how long will that be? Now I have to go to North Carolina?" Blake huffed, on the verge of another tirade.

"I don't know kid, three days, three weeks, three months? Point is you're stuck with me."

"Stuck with you? Here? In that shack? I heard what you said. Sounds more like you're stuck with me!"

"Blake, you sit yourself down in that chair right there and you listen to me," Carson growled, barely containing his temper. He steered Blake by the shoulder with one hand and plunked him down in one of the canvas deck chairs, looking him sternly in the eye. "I know things aren't very pleasant at home. I know how betrayed you feel about being left behind. I'm truly sorry that you feel so unwanted. You deserve better. But I can't change it. There is nothing we can do about what has happened. But I *can* tell you about the way things are gonna be. We do not have the time nor are we inclined to spend our summer coping with this angry struggling of yours. Look out that window, boy—tell me what you see."

"Trees."

"What else?"

"The lake."

"What else?"

"The sky! The grass! The sun! Is my psychiatric appointment over now?"

Carson pointed out the window. "Do you see your father out there?" he asked, with equal intensity. "Do you see Agatha out there? Do you see anything from your life back in Fort Wayne that has followed you here? No! Nobody could have foreseen your Nanna's decision to stay in North Carolina. Now I can put you on a bus and have you down there by midnight tomorrow, if that's what you want. You can spend your summer helping your grandmother empty bedpans and learning how to administer tube feedings. But that don't sound like much fun to me."

"I'm not allowed to have fun."

"That's horse crap!" Listen, you know what sounds like fun to me? Having the two people that make me miserable climb on a jet plane and fly clear to the other side of the Atlantic Ocean for the summer! Fun sounds like being twelve years old and left to enjoy what amounts to a twenty-acre private park with a lake! You've got beaches, islands, and more adventure than a boy can shake a stick at! There's swimming, sailing, hiking, fishing, wildlife, weenie roasts, staying up late, and just about anything else you can think up! You've got a library upstairs, a box of Legos the size of Wyoming, and a crazy uncle who wants to see you enjoy every last bit of it. Do you think you could take a minute and wrap your head around that?"

"Do I still have to pick up trash everywhere I go?"

"Does it hurt to help out once in awhile? Just take a minute and let it sink in, Blake. Look what you have here. What twelve-year-old boy has all this within his grasp? You can't tell me you've never dreamed of something like this? The Almighty's given it to you—take hold and do something with it! Look, you don't have to go with us tomorrow. It's going to rain all day. C'mon, let me show you the library and where the Legos are. I know you'll have fun if you just give it a chance!"

Blake glanced around at the big room that had so impressed him at first. "A box of Legos the size of Wyoming?"

"Maybe Texas."

"Alright. We'll see how it goes."

Chapter 3

Carson's weather forecast was dead on. The next morning it poured buckets. Carson and Gunn sat by the blazing fireplace eating eggs and pancakes, and playing cribbage. To avoid the old Scot, Blake holed up in the library on the second floor. He surveyed shelf after shelf of sailing manuals, books on knots and rigging, racing tactics, and back-issues of boating magazines. To his delight he discovered a small section of nature books and a surprising number of literary titles. He pulled down *White Jacket*. The cover of the book depicted a man in a high-collared white coat gazing warily into a storm-torn sky—below him, a square-rigged warship on a raging sea. The man bore an uncanny resemblance to his uncle. After reading half a page of thick prose he put it back. He spotted *Treasure Island*. He read the back cover and decided that a tale about a boy stuck in a life-or-death adventure with an old pirate warranted further attention. He settled into a comfy wing-back chair. An oversized volume entitled *The Birds of Indiana* lay open on the coffee table before him. He leafed through the pages and had just stopped at the entry for the blue heron when he heard someone laboring up the stairs. Aside from Agatha, it was the last person he could have hoped for. He heard the door to the dorm room open.

"Yeh in there, lad? Nope!"

Gunn came across the hall and looked into the library. "There yeh are! Rain's lettin' off. We're gonna give it a go. Like the birds do yeh? Well look at this." He stepped into the room and planted a gnarled finger on a wall map of Highland Creek Reservoir. "Yeh got some of the best bird watching in the state, right up here in the wetlands." Blake sensed an unsolicited lecture coming on as Gunn continued. "And there's a Heron rookery here, a cave here, and something we call 'The Castle' here, and…" He paused and adopted a serious tone. "Here lad, this yeh'll need to know aboot."

"What is it?" asked Blake, tenuously.

"This is where Yaegerstown *used* to be: in the channel between the upper and lower lake. There's a moonster lurks here, lad!"

Blake hadn't paid much attention to the map but now he was riveted. The lake was shaped vaguely like the capital letter "H" turned diagonally. "It'll reach right up and tear the guts out of yer boot!" A chill ran up Blake's spine.

"Aye, the Yaegerstown bridge piling! When the state built the lake there was a little town right here. They bought up all the property, demolished the houses, and the bridge. But for some reason, Heaven knows why, they left one of the bridge pilings. Twenty-foot concrete column. Three feet wide, twenty feet long in this direction." Gunn moved his fingertip back and forth, parallel to the shore line. "It's no a problem *most* of the time. But after a long dry summer, the top of that pillar is just two feet beneath the surface. And woe betide the skipper who d'know where it is!"

Blake was relieved to hear that the "moonster" amounted to nothing more than a seasonal shallow spot. "Wow, thanks for telling me about that," he offered, in hopes that Gunn would feel gratified that he had imparted some of his ancient wisdom to the younger generation and shove off. But no such luck.

"Here lad, on the shore. There's a fat stump with a big rusty chain 'round it. When yeh can see that straight abeam then look straight to your southwest and sight the big flag pole, then you're right over it."

"Wow, thanks!" said Blake. He desperately wished Gunn would just get the drift and leave.

"The big flag pole is a cell tower, makes a right angle with the stump, like an 'L.'" Again he illustrated, making the shape with this thumb and forefinger.

"I know what a right angle is," replied Blake, in exactly the wrong tone.

"Oh do yeh, then!" snapped Gunn.

"But I appreciate you telling me about it. And the herons!" said Blake, too late to assuage the offense. "What's a rookery?"

"A nestin' ground. Read it in yer book. I've work to get to!" Gunn stalked out of the library.

Blake waited until the stairs began to creak then pulled his chair over to the wall. He stood on the seat and poured over the map for the next twenty minutes.

By early afternoon the rain had stopped and wedges of sunlight illuminated a vast Lego battlefield in the foyer outside the library and down the stairs. Ray, the groundskeeper, brought him a deli sandwich and chips through enemy lines.

"May I go down to the point?" Blake said.

"I wouldn't go further unless you can swim!"

"Then it's okay?"

"If it's okay with your uncle, it's okay with me. Make sure you get all those little pieces picked up. I go barefoot around here, sometimes."

***

Blake tromped down the hill, *Treasure Island* in hand. The clouds had cleared but it was still chilly. A gleaming white keelboat with *Eclipse* painted on her sides was tied-up along the main, floating dock. She was much larger than the boxy *Terrapin*. Her lines were sleek and gave a sense of speed even though she was sitting still. But what really caught Blake's attention was that there was a girl sitting on the foredeck, reading a book. He changed course toward the shoreline and sauntered across the gangway to the big floating dock. The girl did not look up. Her hair was an ebony cascade of natural curls flowing out of the depths of a purple hooded sweatshirt. Blake thought she looked about his sister's age.

"Watcha reading?"

"A book," she said, without looking up.

"Oh, yeah. My sister reads those. Well, see you later." He headed back for the gangway.

"Why are you dressed like you're going to church?"

"Why are you dressed like you're going to Hell?"

"You should stick around, I might decide to like you. Seriously, are you Amish or something?

Blake stopped at the gangway and looked back over his shoulder. "It's just what I've got. What's your excuse?"

"This is the way we dress around here in the summer."

Blake walked back to the *Eclipse*. "Technically, summer doesn't begin until June twenty-first. You have weeks until the solstice."

"Then it's how we dress in late spring, Mr. Professor. You know, there's some crazy guy on the lake who wears a white shirt like that all summer, but with the collar turned up. Makes me think he should be wearing a tuxedo. You're not his kid are you?"

"No, my dad's in France. I'm staying with my Uncle Carson."

She squinted in disbelief. "No way! Herr Bum-meister is your uncle?"

"He's not a bum! And he's the only family I've got right now."

"Well, I wouldn't let my dad know. Your uncle and that crabby old Scotsman spend half the year bumming around the lake in that shoebox, stealing our business!"

"How could they do that? They just fix up campsites, and people's seawalls, and stuff."

"And they fix boats, and they mend sails, and build docks, and paint, and do motor repair, and they do all of it 'to-your-door.'"

"So what?"

"Soooo, my dad owns the marina!" she droned, rolling her eyes. "Hellooo! Does Devlin Marina ring a bell?"

"Competition is healthy for the local economy."

"What *ever*! How old *are* you, Mr. Professor?" The girl demanded.

"Thirteen, almost. And my name is Blake, Miss Devil-woman, if that really is your name!"

"Dev-lin, Mia Devlin."

"Age?"

"Six. Teen."

Blake heard the back door of the clubhouse thump shut.

"Here comes my dad. You'd better go."

A man appeared at the top of the stairs and stopped to open a can of something. It foamed over in his hand and he returned to the clubhouse.

"So, have you made a decision, yet?" Blake said.

"What are you talking about?"

"Have you decided whether you like me or not?"

"I don't know. You're pretty annoying. Let me give you some advice, Tux: if you're going to be around awhile, get yourself some new clothes, blend in, and *whatever* you do, steer clear of my brother. Now go on, get out of here!" Mia rose from the deck and picked up the towel she'd been sitting on, then made her way back to the cockpit, signaling the end of her audience.

Blake had half a mind to cast off her moorings and set the *Eclipse* and her mistress adrift, but thought better of it. He headed back for the shore, tantalized by the thought that Mia had liked him enough to give him advice. He thought he might turn his collar up the next time he was out on the water. He pondered her warning as he headed up the ridge. Why did there always have to be some lousy, lurking doom?

***

Evening had settled over the harbor with a pleasant warmness. Blake watched the sunset from the point. The last rays of golden splendor slipped behind the forest's silhouette and the lake flowed together with the deep indigo ocean of the sky. All around, the sounds of night rose in a whirring crescendo. The serenity of the harbor, the sweet night air, the outline of the far shore, and the gently fading daylight—so warmly golden—stirred him, unsettled him. It was like a longing, a yearning in his core to melt into this scene, to live in this moment forever. He stood for a long time feeling as if he might cry. Then something in the water caught his eye. V-shaped ripples spread silently. He couldn't believe it. It was a beaver! Before long another

V rippled past, and then a third. In the distance, the ghostly call of a loon quavered from the cove on Trespass Island. All the things he'd ever read or seen in books were now right here in front of him. Until that moment they might as well have been science fiction.

His thoughts wandered to Mia—where she was, what she might be doing, if she had watched the sun set, and if she had felt the same way that he had. He wanted to tell his mother about the beavers and the loon. Now the beautiful solitude began to turn to loneliness. Blake realized with alarm how dark it had become and hurried back to the sail shed. He jogged nervously up the foot path through the shadowy grove and was on the verge of panic until he saw a light high ahead on the ridge. His uncle had both doors of the shed wide open and the Coleman lantern glowing at full strength. There was something deeply welcoming about that bright little shack on the dark hill, something that made him feel that just as long as he could see that light he was home and safe.

"Well there you are!" said Carson, looking over the top of a magazine.

"I heard a loon!" Blake flopped down full-length on his cot. "And I saw three beavers! I can't believe it! Real beavers!"

"It's a great place, ain't it kid? So, you had a better day?"

"Yes, actually I did. I played with Legos, and I talked to a girl down on the main dock."

Carson closed the magazine. "You talked to a girl?"

"Apparently her dad is your competition."

"Wow, Miss Devlin spoke? You didn't tell her we're bunked-out in here, did you?"

"No, I didn't. And it's none of her business anyway. Why, what's wrong?"

"Well, her daddy's the commodore this year. He wouldn't think too highly of our choice of digs. Best to keep a low profile where the Devlins are concerned. By the way, we're going to town tomorrow for supplies. Your Nanna left me a debit card and told me whatever you need or want is to be provided—within reason."

"*Really?*"

"Really."

"Summer clothes. If I'm going to keep a low profile, I can't go around looking like it's always Sunday morning."

"That's within reason. So, I'm guessing that you came with instructions for care and feeding?"

Blake dug into his suitcase, produced a thick envelope, and handed it to his uncle. Carson opened it and mumbled over the first of several typewritten pages.

Daily:

7:00 a.m. Rise

7:45 a.m. Breakfast

8:15 a.m. Academics

11:45 a.m. Lunch

12:15 p.m. Bible Study

1:45 p.m. Bible memory verse

2:00 p.m. Nap

2:35 p.m. Academics

5:15 p.m. Dinner

6:00 p.m. Chet Allworth Christian Family Hour

7:00 p.m. Bath

8:00 p.m. Bed

No fraternizing with heathen children, especially girls.

No television, except Chet Allworth Christian

Broadcast Network.

No worldly music.

No computers or video games.

No heathen toys.

No soda.

No sweets.

Carson handed the stack of papers back to him. "Hold it up, by the bottom corner."

Blake held it as instructed. Something went "scritch!" And before he knew it a flame raced up the left margin and spread across the pages.

"Whaaa! What do I do?" Blake yelped.

"Get rid of it before you burn the place down!"

Carson cackled as Blake hastened to toss the blazing manifesto out the door. Carson held up his hands and in a preachy voice declared, "And Moses said: 'At his right hand was a fiery law!'"

"That was my…but, my dad…Now what am I going to do?"

"You've got all summer to figure it out, kid!"

Chapter 4

Blake sat on the cabin roof, reclined against the furled main and boom. The *Terrapin* droned along under motor. "Still don't see why we just don't drive," he said, over the noise of the outboard.

"Lad, it's three miles down to the bridge, four miles across, and five back up to Freeman. Now, how far is that?" said Gunn.

"Twelve miles. Twenty-four round trip."

"My old van gets twelve miles to the gallon on a *good* day. Gas is $3.50 a gallon. How much is it to drive to Freeman?"

Blake thought for a moment. "Wow, seven dollars!"

"Yeh've got a head for figures, lad. And since it's no even three miles up the channel, we take the ol' barge for a buck fifty!"

"And like I said," added Carson, "it's our way of life. We work on the lake, we play on the lake, we come and go on the lake. It's our world. This life's a journey, Blake, and for the time being the Almighty has blessed us with a situation that allows us to amble along and enjoy the scenery as we pass through."

Carson's mention of scenery jogged Blake's memory. He sat up, looked to the southwest horizon, and there it was: a giant flag hanging limply from a white tower. He began to scan the shore off the left side of the boat, searching for the tell-tale stump. He spied it, not far ahead. It was all that remained of a huge sycamore—white, streaked with gray and tan, girdled with a rusted chain.

"Mr. Gunn!" Blake called out, anxiously.

Gunn, who had been watching the boy closely, only smiled. He held up his right hand, fingers in an "L" shape. He let go of the tiller and pointed back at the cell tower with his left arm and straight across the boat at the shore with his right. He swung his right arm forward to point at the stump then tracked it back to point straight across the boat. Blake got it: a ninety-degree angle between the tower and the stump, with the *Terrapin* at its vertex. He signaled his understanding by repeating Gunn's pantomime, then pointing straight down. The old man gave him a deep nod and a satisfied smile. Still, though, Gunn didn't alter course and Blake watched with apprehension as the stump drew ever closer. At the last second, Gunn pushed the tiller over hard then hauled it back, dipping the boxy *Terrapin* around the submerged hazard.

Blake nearly slid off the cabin roof and let out a loud "Heeeey!" in protest.

"All hands and the cook!" Gunn cried, over Carson's chuckling.

"Very funny! I could've fallen in, you know!" Collecting himself, Blake climbed down into the bow compartment and continued his sightseeing from the front of the boat.

"Hey, when we come out of the channel," called Carson, "look to your left. I think you'll be impressed."

As the *Terrapin* passed into the upper lake Blake looked left. An enormous, sloped, gray wall gradually came into view. It spanned the far end of the lake.

Blake was astonished. "Is that the dam?" he called aft.

"Watch yer mouth, lad!" Gunn said, grinning impishly.

"I said *dam!*"

"Hey kid! We don't talk like that around here!" said Carson, returning Gunn's smile.

Blake climbed back over the cabin shouting "No, I mean dam! Dam!" He discovered the men snickering boyishly in the cockpit and realized that he'd been had.

"Well, if yeh don't curse like a preacher's son!" Gunn laughed.

Blake tried hard to be angry, but surprisingly the rage just wouldn't come—instead, just an embarrassed urge to giggle. Despite his efforts to keep them turned down, the corners of his mouth drew upwards as if by buccaneers hauling up the Jolly Roger. He jutted his jaw, squinted, and in a Scottish accent said, "Stoof it in yer pookits!" He hopped down into the cockpit and knelt on the bench. "It looks like the Great Wall of China!"

"Always reminds me of Jericho. That's still a mile and a half down the lake. Wait 'til you see it up close," said Carson.

"Or at night," said Gunn.

"Amazing! So, where's Devlin's Marina?"

"Over there, close by the grand Freeman waterfront. What do yeh know of *him*?"

"Nothing. Just wondered."

The lighthearted atmosphere seemed to evaporate. Gunn gave Carson a look of disapproval, to which the mate only shrugged. All along the north shore as far as the eye could see, there were giant mansions stacked up the hillsides—looming one over another—resplendent on their immaculate lawns, flaunting their waterfalls, pools, tennis courts, their boat houses and docks showcasing jet skis and powerboats.

"What is all of this?" said Blake.

"Money. And lots of it," said Carson.

"Money is ugly."

"Money for money's sake sure is."

"There are plenty of good people up there," said Gunn. They chugged along without saying anything more for several minutes.

"I bet this is a total zoo on the weekends," said Blake.

"We call it the Devil's toilet-bowl," said Carson. "Anything goes up here, and it goes fast. But the channel and the lower lake are like one big no-wake zone. Only sailing club safety and Department of Natural Resources patrol boats are allowed to go above 10 miles an hour. Houseboats, fisherman, and the occasional sightseers are all you'll get on our side."

"And the headwaters are on the lower lake. The outlet's up here, at the dam" said Gunn. "So most of their stink stays where it belongs."

The *Terrapin* neared the Freeman Public Marina. Three long floating docks stretched to welcome them. An overlook and elevated promenade fenced in green wrought-iron presided over the shore-walk. Gunn brought them alongside the dock, across from a gleaming white power boat. It was a seventeen-foot Boston Whaler sporting Indiana DNR insignias on her sides and a red and blue light bar above the cockpit. Blake deployed the fenders as his uncle hopped onto the dock and secured their moorings. Gunn wrestled a folding cart from the cabin and heaved it up to Carson. Gunn stopped to regard the DNR craft with admiration.

"Brand spanking new!" he pronounced. "There's finally a fitting use for yer tax dollars!"

"If I paid taxes," Carson mused.

Blake glanced back as they passed by and was amused to see the name "*Moby*" stenciled on the transom.

They left the dock and ascended the ramp to the overlook. A wide brick walk extended far along the shore in either direction and also northward through a well manicured park. The crew took this middle path, passing a huge gazebo in a grove of catalpa trees. They emerged on the far side of the park at the edge of town.

"Yeh fellows do what yeh come for," said Gunn. "I'll hit the hardware store. Meet you at the parlor for lunch and then we'll do the shopping."

"Alrighty!" said Carson. "C'mon kid, let's get you some clothes. Then we'll hit Vance's Army Surplus and really see what kind of trouble we can get into."

"I'm in!"

Blake felt it would be a different kind of day—a day out with the guys. No one discounting him, deriding him, or humiliating him—being in the company of grown men who enjoyed his company and treated him like one of their tribe. It was indeed a new world and a new way of life. Change was in the air. He was almost thirteen. The summer was his—and it was exhilarating.

***

Blake made out well at the thrift store. He and his uncle each emerged with a big plastic bag full of clothing slung over their shoulders.

"Is it all antique shops and restaurants, here?" Blake asked as they walked down the street.

"Pretty much. Freeman lives and dies on the tourist trade. There ain't a box-mart super-store for twenty miles. The beauty of it is that in spite of all of the new money on the lake, the locals haven't let it go to their heads. They manage to keep it all pretty real."

They turned a corner and trundled down a steeply inclined street past a barber shop, a bowling alley, and a pet shop. "See, there's three basic kinds of people around here," Carson said, "lakers, locals, and shore birds."

"And we're lakers!" said Blake, proudly.

"*I'm* a laker. *You're* a visitor."

They arrived at a big red missle standing on its fins outside the entrance to Vance's Army Navy Surplus Store. The place smelled odd to Blake—a musty mix of canvas, dirt, and vulcanized rubber. Carson chatted with a young man wearing a burr haircut and a drab, green tee-shirt. Blake left his sack with his uncle and explored the cavernous establishment. It was a jungle of camouflage, tents, and tank netting. He perused a rack of books, then moved on to headgear. He tried on a WW II storm trooper helmet in front of a mirror, turning his head to consider the faded swastika on each side.

Carson passed by with an armload of stuff. "Let's go, little Hitler!"

"Good grief, what is all of this?" said Blake.

"Everything a boy your age needs to get himself into the appropriate kinds of trouble! Compass, foul weather gear, binoculars, Swiss army knife, waterproof walkie-talkies, BBs, shirts bearing offensive patriotic messages, cigarette lighters, and enough class C fireworks to sink the *Bismarck*."

"You know, you're crazy. But I think everyone should have an Uncle Arctica!"

Carson smiled. "Well, it takes all my time," he said. The buzz-cut clerk rang up the sale. Carson collected two big bags of loot and said to the clerk "Thanks, Chief!"

"Semper Fi!" said Buzz-cut, as they exited the store.

"What did he mean by that?" said Blake.

"Semper Fidelis. He's a Marine, I'm Navy. Military folks share a common bond, whoever they are, wherever they go. Man, we should've brought that dang cart with us," Carson groaned. "We've kinda got a load here! C'mon kid, let's go find the old man!"

They lumbered back up the hill and turned left again. "Wait! There he is! Hey Tripper Gunn!" Carson shouted. Not far up the walk, the tall old man stopped and then turned his whole body around. "Bring that cart back here!"

Gunn beckoned with a gesture as impatient as his expression. The two jogged up and plumped their awkward loads down on the two-wheeled cart.

"Holly have everything we need at the hardware store?" said Carson.

"Yup. Had it delivered."

"Delivered where?" Blake said, not thinking.

"China. No! The boat, where else, lad?" said Gunn.

Carson shot a glance over his shoulder to catch Blake's quizzical scowl. He replied by making a face and shrugging in a way that seemed to say *Let it go, kid. He's buying lunch and he's our ride home!"*

Blake tried to remember when things had gone sour that day. Everything had been light and fun until, when? The mention of Devlin. That's what had done it. Blake made a mental note to ask his uncle about it, and to never mention it—or anything else for that matter—to Tripper Gunn, ever again.

Much to his surprise his guardians parked their cartload outside the Emporium Eatery and Ice Cream Parlor and went in—something you'd never do back home. He was about to ask about it but decided to hold his peace. The Emporium was as much a curiosity shop as it was an ice-cream-and-burger joint, with plenty of eccentric atmosphere. Antique knick-knacks and old photos, the mundane and bizarre, farm implements, and taxidermied game of all sorts adorned the richly paneled walls. A sign hanging over a pair of swinging doors at the back of the dining room warned: *You must be 21 AND have a note from your mother to enter!*

A pretty young woman, her golden hair up in a loose bun, hurried to meet them. "Hey boys!"

"Sit us down somewhere soft, Treva" said Gunn. She showed them to a quiet booth with luxurious red leather seat cushions. A plaque bearing old German lettering graced the wall over their table. They settled in and before long were feasting. Blake pondered the plaque. It featured a drawing of a mischievous-looking child on a riverbank, with a water wheel and mill in the background. He was determined not to ask about it, but eventually the bodily resources required to digest a double cheeseburger, fries, and root beer float dulled his wits and loosened his tongue. "That must be some sort of blessing from the home of a pious German pioneer," he said.

Gunn smiled slyly at Carson. Lunch had improved his humor. Carson shifted in his seat and grunted through a suppressed grin. Gunn cleared his throat. "It says 'the mayor has decreed that Thursday is beer-brewing day, so please—after Wednesday don' pee in the creek!'"

Blake's face flushed red as the seat cushions. Again, he wanted to be angry for having been caught talking out of his hat but instead only found himself fighting to suppress the strong urge to giggle. He'd be sure to tell the guys back at Sunday school about this one.

The waitress returned, flirted with Carson and Gunn while she counted out the skipper's change, cleared the table and left.

"Will that hold yeh 'til yeh get to a restaurant, young fellow?"

"Indeed! I hope we can come back here again. Thank you very much, Mr. Gunn!"

"Alright. To the grocery, lads!" groaned the old Scot as he shifted himself out of the booth.

They made a short work of the grocery shopping and drew the customary greetings, honks, and waves of town familiars as Carson towed the now outlandishly-piled cart down the sidewalk. The *Terrapin* was stuffed to the gills as they pulled away and started for home. Blake slithered into the cabin and sank comfortably onto the big bags of clothing. The droning motor, the rocking hull, the warming afternoon, and the occasional whiff of pungent exhaust were a powerful sedative that was not to be denied. Blake was overcome and took, or rather was taken by, a pleasant nap.

***

Another fine evening fell upon Highland Creek Reservoir. Carson put Blake to work gathering twigs and log-rounds to build a fire in the grove. He gave his nephew some instruction in the art of fire crafting, then set out for the clubhouse to fetch their dinner from one of the big refrigerators in the galley kitchen. He was pleased to find that Blake had a small blaze going by the time he returned.

"Nice work, kid! You're a regular fire bug as my dad would say. I tell ya, I'm kinda beat after all that tramping around."

Blake smiled at the approval. He fed twigs into the gaps between burning logs. "What's on the schedule for tomorrow?"

"Friday—moving day!"

"Moving what? Who?"

"Us! People use the shed on the weekends, so we move into the attic over the dorms. Then we move back Monday morning when they're all gone."

Blake chuckled. "We're like homeless people!"

"Now you have an idea of what they face on a daily basis."

"I guess I never considered that. So, what happens here on the weekend?"

"This weekend is the Spring Fling Regatta. The fleets race in the mornings and afternoons. Lunch'll be provided both days. There'll be a big dinner and party Saturday night. Your dinner is already paid for," he said, skewering a beef-brat and handing it to him.

Blake looked puzzled. "Aren't you going to be here?"

"I'll probably show for dinner. But Saturday's the Sabbath and I visit my friends in the nursing home all day. You're welcome to join me if you like."

"No thanks, I don't like those places."

Carson opened a can of beans and poured them into a cast iron pot.

"You think the old folks do?"

"And the Sabbath is on Sunday, anyway—unless you're...you're not...Jewish are you?"

"I challenge you to find anything anywhere in The Good Book where the Sabbath is *anytime* but sundown on the sixth day to sundown on the seventh day!"

"But!"

"*You* find it and show me, Blake!" Carson said with a grin. "Find it for yourself!"

"So, what church do you go to?" said Blake, reluctantly.

"I don't! Like The Good Book says, pure religion in the Almighty's eyes is visiting the orphan and the widow in their time of need, and keeping uncontaminated by the world. So, I try to behave myself, I take care of mom—when she stays put long enough—and on the seventh day I quit what I'm doing and visit the old folks." He stirred the beans with the beef-brat on his skewer. "And if you ever do go with me I will introduce you to Korbin Dubois, who is an improbable one hundred and eight years old!"

"That's impossible!"

"Impossible, yes, but true!"

Blake carefully turned his skewer over the fire. "I guess I sort of count as your orphan, huh?"

"Don't let it haunt you, kid. They'll be back."

"But what if their plane crashes? I cursed them. I said I hated them, I said I hoped they'd die!"

Carson had not anticipated this turn in the conversation. He was quiet for a moment then said gently "What is said is said. You'll have to live with it. But I don't think it's the first time you've ever said it, either. Tell the Almighty you're sorry for cursing your family and ask him to watch over 'em, and to bring 'em back home safely. He'll forgive you."

Blake remained quiet, cautiously wrapped a bun around his sizzling bratwurst and pulled it off the skewer. "Could I ask him to find Father and Agatha a nice home over there and just send Mom back?" he said, with a half-hearted half-smile.

"Don't joke with your Creator, Blake. You take Him seriously and He will pay attention to you."

Blake cocked his head a little, as if straining to hear something. He stood up and looked out toward the channel. A low rumbling was growing in the distance—the sound of a stout engine.

"What's the matter?" said Carson.

"Something's coming." Blake walked down to the shoreline.

Carson pulled the pot off the fire and ambled down to where his nephew was standing.

A quarter of a mile away a monstrous, purple and yellow cigarette boat crawled out of the channel and into the lower lake, running lights gleaming in the dusk. Its hull was a long sleek curve on the water, from its slanting transom all the way to its pointed bow.

"Now what is *that* doing down here?" said Carson, annoyed.

Blake found it a little unsettling that Carson did not refer to this craft with the usual nautical 'she.'

"What is *that*?" he asked, eyes still locked on the garish motor yacht.

"Just all of the sound and fury a half-million dollars can buy, that's all."

"Seriously?" Blake said, flatly. "A half-million dollars?"

"That's what they say. *Tantrum II*: Daddy Devlin's claim to fame. His son Hunter thinks it's his, though. He just dreams of being able to run that thing a hundred and forty miles an hour down the length of the Lower. Probably out giving a bunch of cheerleaders a ride."

"A hundred and forty miles an hour? That's more than two miles a minute! You could run the whole lower lake in three minutes!"

"And he would if it weren't for *Moby*! There are a *few* things even the Devlins can't get away with. Though I hear he made a hundred and ten on the Upper without getting caught. It just eats him up to have all that power in his hands and not be able to use it."

Tantrum II rumbled along for a few minutes then swung in a wide arc and headed slowly back to the channel.

Carson returned to the fire. Blake shook his head in disbelief and mumbled, "A half-million dollars and a hundred and forty miles an hour."

Chapter 5

Blake was amazed that there was yet another level to the clubhouse. He stood at one of the dormer windows and relished the commanding view. *Like a castle overlooking the Black Forest,* he thought. *Must be a good seventy feet above the water!* The early morning sunlight crept slowly across the row of docked boats that stretched endlessly down the point—their bright blue canvas covers creeping out of the shadows, chrome mast-spreaders glinting. There was still plenty of mist drifting over the flat harbor and rising from the roof of the forest across the lake. Killdeer wheeled and piped over the water and a flotilla of Canada geese came ashore to graze on the hillside. Blake began to feel a lot less like he'd been cheated out of Europe.

Carson dropped the last of his things and left to begin mowing the vast, rolling grounds of the Highland Creek Sailing Club. The attic was a single gallery and very much an enormous version of the sail shed. Blake set up his cot in the middle dormer and stuffed his suitcase and a red sail bag holding his new clothing underneath. He spread his blanket on it, and smoothed out the creases.

Blake wasn't accustomed to wearing shorts or tee-shirts; it still felt like going out in public dressed in his pajamas. Barely a week had passed since his arrival and he had hardly had time to count the number of things he'd experienced or done that his father would never have allowed: sailing, sleeping in a shed, peeing outdoors, building fires, performing manual labor, reading fiction. While they were mostly circumstantial and beyond his control, this wearing of shorts and tee-shirts seemed an act of willful disobedience, almost a declaration of rebellion. It played havoc with his conscience.

Blake repented somewhat by changing into a red Hawaiian shirt with buttons. He folded the yellow tee-shirt dutifully and slipped it neatly back into the sail bag. He paused then pulled it back out. He contemplated the coiled snake and the motto emblazoned beneath—*Don't Tread on Me.* He frowned and put it back. At his core he only wanted to please his father and his father's god. James Barber's god was not a terribly angry god, but certainly an uptight and picky one. He hoped that the buttons would atone for the shorts and hiking sandals. *But they wore sandals in the Bible, didn't they?* he thought.

He sat on the edge of his cot and stared down the attic gallery. Dusty shafts of golden sun streamed in from the three eastern dormers, illuminating every crack and knothole in the dull, planked floor. He thought back on the week's events and realized that he really was having a good time and it looked like it would hold out. *But there has to be a catch,* he thought. *Just like there always is. There has to be another shoe, and it has to drop. Just as soon as I'm having a really good time, Father will find out and job or no job, Atlantic Ocean or not, he'll come swooping back ASAP to snatch me out of this unacceptable, highly improper situation.*

That familiar tightness returned to the pit of his gut. *I might as well put my Sunday morning clothes back on, curl up on this cot and wait for them to show up.*

As if on cue, the faint hum of a vehicle coming up the hill caught his attention. He went to the window overlooking the circular drive. A van rolled up and parked right in front of the clubhouse. An older lady exited and lugged a big purple storage tub out. With it she swayed and staggered up the steps. Blake rushed to the great room and hauled the door open.

"Hoh! Why thank you!" she said, wide-eyed. "Open sesame! I sure didn't expect that. I thought the door was opening all by itself!" She staggered in and dropped her burden on the nearest table. She leaned on the tub and panted for a moment.

Blake stayed quiet, ready to run for help if she keeled over. "Is there more to bring in?" he asked.

"Oh heavens yes, the van is full. It's all stuff for the party tomorrow night!" she said, as if he should have known. "But you don't..."

"I'll get it!" Blake trotted back to the van and toted three more tubs in before he too was huffing. The last couple of tubs they had to haul in together.

The woman wore a floral-patterned blouse of black and teal. She sat down in the closest chair.

"Thank you so much! What a nice boy you are. Are you one of Ray's grandchildren?" she asked in that warbley a-little-too-loud kind of grandma voice.

"No."

"Is your family here for the regatta?"

"No."

"Well are you the paperboy, then? I haven't ever seen you around here."

"No," he repeated, not realizing that he was being annoying.

Her eyelids narrowed. She leaned forward and stared a stormy stare at him. But the clouds of exasperation parted and the light of dawning comprehension broke through. "*Yooou* look like an Urquart!"

Blake's jaw dropped.

"Yes, indeed, you are an Urquart! You can't be Ava's little boy, can you?"

"That's my mom. I'm Blake Barber. How did you know that?"

"Oh my goodness sake! It's Blake! I can't believe it! It's so good to meet you! My name is Beverly Maitland. Is your mother here?" She gushed.

"No, she's in France. I'm staying with my Uncle Carson," he explained.

"In that shack? Why aren't you staying with your grandmother in Pemberton?"

"I was supposed to. Nanna is taking care of a sick friend in North Carolina. You know about the sail shed?"

"Well of course! It's the worst kept secret on the lake! Everyone knows but the commodore which, by the way," she put her hand by one cheek and feigned a whisper, "is the best laugh on the lake!"

Blake instantly liked this woman. "But how do you know my mom?"

"Well, my goodness! She and your Uncle Carson grew up here! I remember them when they were just babes in arms! Why your granddad, Declan Urquart, is the reason this whole place exists. He and Tripper Gunn!"

This revelation hit Blake like a ton of bricks. *Why don't they ever tell me these things?* he thought. Probably for the same reason, he surmised, that no one had ever explained to him until he was nine years old that his uncle was his mother's brother and his Nanna was his mom's mother. They were too busy or assumed that it was common knowledge. Blake now felt that maybe he needed to sit down, too.

"Tell me about it. All of it. I want to know."

Beverly related how Declan and Tripper had been best friends in the old country and had come to the United States after World War II to attend college. His granddad had become an architect and Tripper Gunn had gone into engineering, though boatbuilding was his great love. They had shared a vision for creating a state park and a sailing club on the newly completed Highland Creek Reservoir and eventually convinced the Indiana Legislature to set aside the land.

"Your granddad designed this clubhouse and Tripper laid out the grounds and supervised the construction. That was about 1958. But the water company retained ownership of the upper lake. When the developers finally made it out here in the 80s, they bought all the land and built palaces for the shore birds. And didn't they make a pretty penny, hmmmm?"

Beverly asked about his family and Blake, in turn, recounted the details as he had to Carson that first blustery night in the sail shed.

"My goodness! You poor boy. Well, now you're here with us where you belong, Blake Urquart!"

Those words would echo for days in the hollow parts of Blake's soul. Beverly was the club's historian and they spent an hour or more up in the library, poring over old Highland Creek Sailing Club yearbooks.

"Now, who are these two, I should wonder?" she said, pointing out a pair of teenagers posing proudly with a trophy.

"Is that Mom? And Uncle Carson?"

Beverly nodded. "Umm-hmm. About fifteen years old, I'd say. Now, who's this?" she asked, turning the page.

Blake looked at the next picture. "That's Nanna and that must be my granddad and—no way! Tripper Gunn?"

She leaned away and surveyed his features proudly. "And don't you favor your granddad!"

I have a history, he thought. He felt as if he were a long-lost heir who had just returned to his ancient ancestral estate.

Blake and Beverly spent the rest of the afternoon moving tables in the great room, hanging decorations and strands of colored lights. Occasionally his uncle would appear over the patio railing as he swept across the hilltop, seated on the big lawnmower.

***

As they settled into their cots that night, Blake was all questions and chatter. His exhausted uncle was hardly in the mood to answer at length, but he did his gracious best.

"Why didn't you tell me?" said Blake.

"I figured you knew. I'm surprised your mom never talked about it."

"We never talk about anything at home except when will I have my homework finished, and when will I unload the dishwasher, and when do we have to pick Agatha up here, and when do we have to take Agatha there."

Blake asked about the trophy picture, and about his grandfather, and Tripper Gunn. Then he went on to ask about Carson and Ava's home life, growing up. This was the opportunity for which he had been waiting.

"So, did you have any pets?"

"Aw no, I mean we had dogs and cats like anyone else. Mom had a bird when we were really little."

"Is that all? You never had anything exotic like lizards or snakes or…scorpions?" Blake's eyes were fastened on the shadowy form in the cot across the room, alert for anything that might betray the truth, if he didn't get a straight answer.

Carson yawned expansively. "Nah, we caught frogs and snakes and stuff, but we always let 'em go. Never kept 'em." Blake began to see his opportunity fading with his uncle's consciousness. "Never went in for the creepy-crawlies…giant cockroaches…millipedes…" Blake hung on every slurred syllable. "And spiders…hooo!" Carson shuddered. "I *hate* spiders…ooooh! Do I *ever* hate spiders!" His head rolled back and a muffled final "hate 'em" was heard before he began to snore.

Relieved, Blake settled back into his own cot and gazed through the dormer-window at the stars. His thoughts drifted to the grandfather he never knew, who had built this place for everyone—never knowing it would become a refuge to his own children and children's children. But maybe he had. Something curious surfaced in Blake's mind. It was *Behold, I go and prepare a place for you, that where I am, there you may be also.* He didn't know what to make of it. Pondering its depths he sank into a dream.

Chapter 6

Blake was roused from his slumber by banging and thumping from the dorms below. He got up and opened the window across from his cot. The cool air was fresh with the smell of the cedar trees that ringed the driveway below. And though he couldn't see beyond them, the sounds drifting up from the parking lot told of a flurry of activity—rumbling, crunching, clanking. Farther in the distance, whirring and clicking, revving, rattling, and shouting. His uncle was still dead to the world. Blake chose a blue and white Hawaiian shirt, fastened his sandals and headed downstairs. He stopped by the galley. Ray's wife, Elsie, gave him a bagel, an apple, and a bottle of water. He hurried out the front door and over to the grand staircase. From there he surveyed the whole scene. It looked like an invasion! The desolate lot that had received him only six days before was now occupied by an army—or maybe a navy—of people who had come to sail in the regatta. Blake could now identify the foreign sounds he'd heard from the attic window: boats on trailers being trundled across the gravel, their loose stays and halyards clanking against their metal masts. Farther in the distance he heard the hoists whirring and clicking as they lifted those boats and lowered them onto the water. He saw their empty trailers being rattled back to the parking lot. He recognized the revving of outboard motors as safety-boat crews got under way. Greetings and laughter bounced between old friends and competitors. Families set up tents around the foot of the hill. The entire place vibrated with energy and enthusiasm. A white forest of sails was springing up all along the floating docks near the hoists. And that is exactly where Blake headed.

A line of boats on trailers waited their turns at the yellow hoists. Countless crew members wandered on and off the docks. Two Boston Whaler safety-boats puttered by, towing huge inflatable orange buoys in their wakes. Near the cinder-block garage a large pontoon boat capped by a red awning lay moored. Blake took a bite of his apple and sauntered over that way. Old Glory fluttered from a mast on her foredeck along with several signal flags on a crossbar below. Her crew was busy with all manner of things. Ladies filled out forms. A man talked on a CB radio and drew on a map. Another arranged square placards with numbers on them, some red and some green, in a display rack hinged to the side of the boat. This was the Race Committee.

Someone called out to him from the big pontooner as he passed by.

"Hey you! You're just the fellah I'm looking for!" A blond boy in a straw cowboy hat with curled-up sides leapt off the Committee boat and extended a hand.

"Griffy... Griffy Williams!" he beamed. "They call me the "Mad Cowboy!"

"I'm Blake...Barber." he clasped hands with Griffy only to experience a disturbing, wriggling sensation on his palm. Blake realized Griffy was tickling him with one finger—a favorite gag of his own father's.

"Good to meet ya! Good to meet ya! Pardon the growth, get it from my mother's side! Pardon the growth, please!" Griffy had all the energy and bluster of a snake-oil salesman.

Blake withdrew his hand and shook it as if he'd touched something unclean.

"You from out of town? I haven't seen you around. You sailing today?" said Griffy.

"Yes, nothing, um, I mean I'm new, I'll be here all summer, and I don't know how to sail."

"I knew it, just the guy I was looking for! Hey Mom! I got a crew, will you let me go now?"

"Hey, wait a minute!" said Blake.

"You'll love it, I promise! I've got my own Laser. Mom says the wind is coming up later and she's afraid I'll dump the boat and get in everybody's way, but with your kiester on the rail it'll be a cinch!"

"Griffyn Williams, hold it right there!" yelled a woman from somewhere under the red awning. She made her way to the railing of the sunlit foredeck. "Young man, did you agree to crew for my son of your own free will? It's okay if you don't want to."

"I guess I don't mind." Griffy began to do a little victory dance for the benefit of his mother. "I'll have to go get a lifejacket and tell my uncle. When do we have to go?"

"Harbor gun is in thirty minutes. You have plenty of time." she said. "I'm Judy, by the way. I appreciate you going out with him. Griffy's a good sailor. But don't let him twist your arm into doing anything you don't want to do."

"Thanks Mrs. Williams, I'll be back!" said Blake. He looked at Griffy. "If you're lucky!"

"You're a winner! I could see that right off! You're a champ!" said Griffy. "See you back here at the signal."

Blake headed off for the sail shed, following the shoreline along the Interlake fleet's boardwalk across little Pram Point, past a short stretch of beach, a medium sized mini-barn, and finally down the peninsula. There the crews of the Lightning fleet were launching boats and hoisting sails. The sail shed was wide open and it sounded like there was a grade-school riot going on inside. He stepped in to discover several roughhousing children, much younger than himself, wrecking the place.

"Hey! Stop that! What do you think you're doing!" He shouted with such authority that there was a temporary cessation in the pandemonium. Once the brawlers saw that the commanding voice did not belong to an adult they mocked him and went right back at it.

"A bum lives in here!" cried one.

"Yeah, we're gonna find his stuff and throw it in the lake!"

"I'm gonna fire up his smokes and drink his whiskey!" another shouted, to the delight of the others. They all had a hold of each other and ran in a tight circle, squealing and hooting.

"He's not a bum, he's my uncle! And we use this shed, now get out of here!"

"He's not a bum, he's not a bum, waaaah!" they mocked, "Get out of here! Get out of here!"

An older voice, smooth as oil, stopped everything cold. "Maybe if he'd get a job and find a place to live, people wouldn't call him a bum."

Blake spun around. With the sun at the intruder's back Blake couldn't make out his face, but it was clear that he was taller than Carson, and very muscular. He hung in the doorway, hands on the lintel above.

"He does have a job. He works on the lake." said Blake.

"I suppose you could say that, if you call stealing our business a job!"

"Well, who died and made you king of th…you, you're Hunter Devlin!"

"Yes I am," he said coolly. "And I *am* king of this lake." Blake's eyes had adjusted and now could make out Hunter's smooth, swarthy features and arrogant smile. He projected a vibe of domination and cruelty like none Blake had ever encountered. Hunter Devlin hung in the doorway like a python over a nest of fledglings. Wilting fear began to drain Blake's resolve and he hated it. And that hate was the only thing he'd ever found that allowed him to cope with the fear. With it he could stir the specter of his own anger into a coiled serpent of rage. He locked his eyes on the Hunter's very black sunglasses and stared stubbornly.

Someone called from down on the gravel footpath. "C'mon Hunter, it's ten minutes to harbor gun and were not even rigged, man!"

Hunter smiled, satisfied that he had completely petrified every living being in the shed. "Look at the fire in those eyes!" he said. "I can tell we're gonna have some fun this summer, aren't we, Sparky!" Devlin spat to the side, chuckled smugly and walked away. Blake, heart still in his throat, realized that he was now alone, though there were no other exits in the shed.

"You can come out now, he's gone." Sail bags and piles of tackle on the floor began to shamble aside as the children emerged from hiding.

"He talked back to Hunter Devlin? Man!" said one.

"And lived!" said another.

"Yeah, and if you don't get all this picked up by the time I come back, I'll tell Hunter you were making fun of him behind his back." said Blake, to test this newly earned credibility.

It was all hands on deck—clearing, stacking, and straightening. Blake took a life jacket off of a hook in the corner and headed down the hill, nerves still rattling. He passed a boney man in a Jolly Roger tee-shirt lying in the grass, scratching a thin scruff of black beard that barely concealed angry red acne. This one called to his mate, a pale, flabby young man basking shirtless on a dock between two Lightings. "Hey Jack, 'bout time, isn't it?"

Jack didn't answer but just lay in a daze and ran his stubby fingers through long, greasy, black hair.

"Hey Jack?"

"Tom-Tom! Man the winch!" That familiar Scot's brogue seemed to sound out of nowhere.

Tripper Gunn came up the path. He reached the dock and announced "I'm taking yer boot, Jack! get off yer back and get aboard! Yer making us look like fools! And put on a shirt—yeh look like a bloated, leprous maggot lying there on my dock! There's Blake Barber! Yeh coming Caddugin? I can leave Jack ashore!" Jack didn't protest.

"Maybe next time, Mr. Gunn. I've been shanghaied already."

"Good for you, lad!" Gunn cheered, as he carefully climbed aboard. "Who tied granny knots in those jib sheets! Jack! Of all the slop! You're an embarrassment! Tom-Tom let fly! And you, Jack, tie figure-eights in there like you should'a in the first place!" He waved to Blake who was very much amused to see Gunn in such good humor and taking it all out on this deserving slob, Jack. "Good luck lad!"

Tom-Tom let the winch handle go and the *Darby McGraw* rumbled down her track and sloshed into the water. Blake jogged back up to the clubhouse to find his uncle. He couldn't help thinking that Jack must owe

Tripper Gunn an awful lot of money to relinquish all rights to his property and person without so much as a whimper.

He found Carson eating breakfast by a window in the great room, a Bible open on the table. Blake received permission, with a disconcerting smile from his uncle, to crew with Griffy Williams. A horn sounded long and loud from the waterfront. He could see the ponderous Race Committee boat crawling away from her mooring, the big outboard motor blowing swirls of blue-gray exhaust over the churning water. The forest of sails was now gradually spreading into the harbor. "That's your cue!" said Carson.

Griffy waited by a gently rocking sail. Blake could barely see the boat itself over the edge of the dock. "C'mon, hurry up! I thought you'd bailed on me!"

Blake stopped and raised his eyebrows at the small, glittering, red boat with the Laser insignia on its sail. Its white deck sat barely eight inches above the water and sported a very small cockpit.

"Where are the sides?"

"It's got sides! This ain't no pleasure craft, sonny, it's a high performance racing dinghy! C'mon, get in! Sit down on the dock, put your feet in the boat and sort of slide in."

"But what if we capsize? What if I fall overboard?"

"You'll get wet, big surprise! Now get in!"

Blake complied, settling awkwardly into the shallow cockpit while Griffy untied the bow. He towed *Cherry Bomb* down the long dock and around its end. "In case you don't know, port is left and starboard is right. Remember, port and left both have four letters."

The Mad Cowboy adjusted his straw hat and boarded expertly. He instructed Blake to shove the bow away from the dock. Griffy gave the helm a sharp jerk. The bow swung slowly to port. Blake felt the breeze flow across the starboard side of the boat. The sail filled and the little Laser slipped away smoothly. It felt very different from the *Terrapin*. The big square boat had a stability, a solidness about her, but *Cherry Bomb* was lively. She dipped and heeled with every change in the breeze, every wave or wake she crossed, every shift in the weight of her crew.

The view from so low on the water intrigued Blake as they made their way through the flotilla. The harbor was streaked with rippling reflections from hulls of every color. A dozen swallows zipped and skimmed over the water's surface, snatching insects off the ripples with absolute precision.

"Okay, what am I supposed to do? I know 'trim' and 'ease,' and 'ready about, hard a'lee.' I've just been out on the *Terrapin* a couple of times. That's all the sailing I've done."

"The shoebox? Give me a break!"

"Why does everybody call it that? It's a good boat."

"No, *this* is a good boat! Look, your job is to watch out for traffic, call the puffs, and hike out."

"Okay, you lost me after the traffic part. Speak English please."

"Look dude, sailing has its own language! You gotta learn the lingo, you savvy? Puffs are gusts of wind. They make dark patches that move across the water. More wind means we start to tip, so you hook your feet under this strap here and hang out of the boat to hold 'er down. It's a blast, you'll love it! I'll show you when we get out there."

Blake was not completely convinced. "So, what do we do if we capsize?"

"I hate to tell you but it ain't *if*—it's *when!*"

"What is that supposed to mean?" Blake was beginning to feel that Griffy was avoiding this question.

As the Committee boat reached the harbor's mouth her skipper throttled up and began a wide turn, sending a sizable swell through the fleets in her wake. *Cherry Bomb* crested it and rolled a bit, her captain and crew taking a little of the lake across their backsides.

"Oh man, my behind is all wet!" whined Blake.

"Lasers are wet boats!"

"I wish someone had told me that! I hate how wet underwear feels. And don't tell me I'll get used to it, either."

"You won't. You have to get used to ignoring it. Wear swimming trunks next time."

They passed out of the harbor and caught a little more breeze.

"Here we go!" said Griffy.

He trimmed the sail in a little and adjusted course for maximum speed. *Cherry Bomb* seemed to leap to life. Blake grabbed the deck's edge as he felt it tilt and hooked his feet under the long padded strap on the floor of the cockpit. Griffy hooted and yelled "Hike!"

It was one thing when the *Terrapin* heeled over—she had high sides and the lake always appeared safely outside the boat, where it belonged. But now *Cherry Bomb*'s deck was at a forty-five degree angle and Blake was looking straight down at rushing, churning water surging along the low side, which occasionally slurped into the cockpit. He was terrified.

"Hike!" cried Griffy. Blake looked back to see the young skipper, feet under the hiking strap, his entire body from just above the knees suspended out over the water. He still had the tiller in one hand and the mainsheet in the other. "C'mon! Hike, dude! It's awesome!"

"Okay, I think I want to go back now." cried Blake. "You were right, I belong on the shoebox. Just make it flat again!"

"No way! You're my ticket to the silver fleet, man, I just know it!"

"Please, Griffy! What if the strap breaks, what if we capsize, what if…"

"Who cares? You're wearing a life jacket, it's not a big deal! We just pick up and go on!"

"But Griffy!"

"But What? What if the bird of paradise flies up your nose? What if my head explodes and your ass catches fire?" The imagery and sheer shock of that statement hit Blake in exactly the right spot. He wasn't sure how the ticklish sensation in his brain was going to manifest but, after a moment of stunned silence, it began to spurt out in burbling giggles and finally burst into a belly laugh. When Blake regained control of himself, he resituated and began little by little, to lean backwards out of the boat.

"That's it buddy! Look at you, you're awesome!"

"I can see the leeboard under the water!" exclaimed Blake "That is so cool!"

"You mean the dagger board! Sometimes, I hike out so far I can look through the bailer and see the bottoms of my tennis shoes!"

"You're a liar!" laughed Blake. "Can I touch the water?"

"I don't know, can you?"

Blake reached down and plowed his splayed fingers into the lake. They furrowed the surface and shot ribbons of spray. It was exhilarating. Blake was hooked. The breeze dropped off and *Cherry Bomb* slowed. She leveled out enough that the boys could return to an upright position.

"Well look who it is!" said Griffy. They had caught up to the *Darby McGraw* and were about to overtake her on her leeward side.

"Hey, anybody hurt in that wreck!" jeered Griffy.

"Just Jack's pride, what's yer excuse?" said Gunn, without looking.

"I'm stuck with your greenhorn castaway!"

Gunn leaned down and peered under the boom. "Blake! Yeh did'na tell me you were shipping with that gimp! Yeh need a rescue, lad? I can chuck Jack over!" Jack did not protest.

"I think I'll be okay, Mr. Gunn. Thank you."

"Yeh stick with him and you'll learn how to sail, for sure. And *you*, Cowboy!" he said, pointing at Griffy sharply. "Yeh could learn a little aboot decency and respect from this fellow."

"I'd rather learn to be a geezer from you!" Griffy returned.

"I'm no a geezer, lad, I'm *The* Geezer! Now get yerself over to the Committee boat, I think I hear yer mother calling. Hard a'lee, Jack!" Gunn pushed the tiller toward the low side of the boat and tacked away.

Blake gave Griffy a serious look. "You really should show a little more respect to your elders, especially Mr. Gunn."

"Whatever, man! Ready about and hard a'lee!" The boys slid to the opposite side of the boat as Griffy tacked. "You need to know a few things before the start. First, never touch anyone else's boat, even if they're going to bump us. That's a seven twenty—we have to do two penalty circles. Never touch the buoys—that's a 360. If you see the boom swinging toward you, never reach out to stop it—that's a broken arm. Always duck, no matter what—never reach for it. You keep a lookout under the boom and let me know when anyone is going to cross us. Did you get all of that?"

"Yeah. Keep your head down, your hands to yourself, and always look to see if someone's coming. Sounds pretty much like my Sunday school."

Another horn sounded from the Committee boat and Blake observed a strange transformation in his skipper. Suddenly he was quiet and focused. He continually looked this way and that, behind, ahead, and under the boom, now at his watch, now at the masthead signals on the Committee boat. The rest of the Laser fleet was congregating in the starting area, as well. The competitor that really caught Blake's attention sported a curvaceous black-and-white pattern and a savage, red maw on the bow.

"Is that supposed to be a killer whale? That's cool!"

"That's Hunter. Get ready, we're running the line." They circled around behind the Committee boat and as they cleared her stern Griffy started his stopwatch, trimmed the sail, and headed for a spherical yellow buoy two hundred feet ahead. "Hike 'er down!" he commanded. As they passed the small, yellow ball Griffy announced "That's a thirty second line. Hey, when you're crossing the boat when we tack, you want to be in the center just as she levels out, and on the other rail as the sail fills. Ready about, hard a'lee." He tacked, coaching Blake through the maneuver. He continued to turn, easing the sail far out. He pulled a short grease pencil out of a pocket in his life jacket and wrote 1 2 7 1A P in a smooth spot on the deck.

"What's that?"

"The course, of course!"

Blake started to ask the obvious, then stopped himself. He looked ahead to the Committee boat and spotted the same numbers on red placards, posted in the rack on her side. "It's buoy one, then to two, then seven," he recounted, pointing in the direction of each marker, in the distance. "What's the rest mean?"

"Finish at temporary mark one. Red means round that mark with it on the port side of your boat. Green would mean on the starboard." Griffy had the tiller and mainsheet in one hand, finger on his watch, and expectant eyes on the Committee boat's masthead. A horn sounded and a flag with the laser insignia went up. He started his watch. "Three minutes 'til we start!" As they headed back toward the big pontooner, Blake watched the other twenty Lasers perform the same "running of the line" ritual. The other fleets were milling all around the vicinity waiting for their starting sequences to begin.

Everything was in continual motion, going in every direction, without brakes.

"How does everyone keep from hitting each other?" Blake asked.

"They shut up and pay attention."

"Why are we the only ones with two crew?"

"We're not. It's a single-handed racing class. The race committee allows juniors under a certain weight to have two crew, so welcome to the underweight weenie class. Now, shut your pie hole and pay attention!" Another horn sounded and a blue flag with a large white square in the center went up to join the Laser Flag.

"Two minutes, dead on! Looks like the pin end is favored, so we want to hit the line with about twenty-five seconds to go." Griffy might as well have been speaking Chinese to Blake. "Where's Hunter?"

"I don't see him." Blake replied.

"Good. He stinks in a big start but he makes it all up by the second leg. Thirty seconds—It's time to get in the way! Jibe ho!" *Cherry Bomb* started into a turn, but it didn't feel like the usual tack.

"What?"

"Duck!"

Blake hit the deck as the boom swept violently across the boat and slammed to a stop on the other side.

"Are you crazy!" screamed Blake.

"Sorry! Jibe means duck or die! I should've told you. My bad." Griffy was now trimming the sail in as fast as he could and *Cherry Bomb* was picking up speed. Several competitors had slipped into place ahead of them. The horn sounded and the blue flag came down. "One minute!" Griffy looked absolutely grave. The rest of the fleet had fallen in behind them.

The Committee boat and starting line were coming up fast. "Are those boats ahead going to beat us?"

"Nope. They've blown the race already. They'll be over early."

"How do you know?"

"'Cuz I know! Now shut up and get ready to hike!" As they passed the Committee boat Griffy glanced at his watch, smiled and trimmed the sail the rest of the way. *Cherry Bomb* heeled and the boys hiked out farther. For some seconds the only thing Blake heard was the sound of hulls cutting through the water and a few squabbling skippers. Griffy started a countdown. "Five, four, three, two, one!" The horn sounded exactly on cue and the Laser flag came down. Two short blasts of the horn sounded and a voice came over a loudspeaker announcing several long numbers, followed by the words 'over early!'" The five competitors ahead peeled away and sailed back for the starting line. "Awesome start! Ha, I told you! Now they've got to go around the ends. That hurts!" said Griffy.

A couple of minutes passed as Blake watched the Committee boat shrink into the distance.

He felt the boat turn to port a little.

"What are they doing behind us?" demanded the skipper.

"A lot of boats are tacking. Should we?"

"No, we just got a little header and they spooked. It's gonna lift big in a minute or two and then we'll be in business!"

"I'll take your word for it." Blake sat up from hiking to give his aching abdominal muscles a rest.

"Wind shifts, dude! Lifts are good, headers are bad. On a good day they happen like clockwork. I was testing them on the way out while you were screaming like a little girl."

Blake ignored this unkind reminder. "Wait! There's Hunter, he didn't tack. What's his boat called?"

"*Grampus*. How far is he?"

"I don't know, as long as the starting line was, maybe farther. Looks like three more behind him."

"Bader, Hopkins, and Rexroat. Those idiots! Find the mark for me."

Blake scanned the distance diligently and spotted the orange tetrahedron. "There!"

Griffy gave a quick glance over his shoulder. "Here's our lift!" Griffy followed the shifting wind, turning *Cherry Bomb* to starboard by twenty-five degrees. "Huge! Let's hope it gives out when we're ready to tack back."

While Blake had enjoyed the excitement of the starting sequence, he couldn't help feeling that most of the race was going to be fairly boring and he said so. The skipper concurred. "Yep! Racing is hours of sheer boredom, highlighted by moments of sheer terror. Look, Hunter hasn't gotten the lift yet!"

Blake looked back and noticed that though *Grampus* was directly astern and had gained on them quite a bit, the killer-whale-with-a-sail seemed to be pointed a little more to port. He projected that if they both kept sailing on their present course, Hunter would end up farther away from the buoy than they would when it was finally time to sail toward it. The idea of playing the wind shifts began to make sense. He admired, if not envied, Griffy's knowledge and skill.

"Dang it, we're almost to the lay-line. Come on wind, shift, will ya?" said Griffy.

Blake was still watching their pursuer, somewhat mesmerized, when *Grampus* veered to starboard. It took a moment to register, but he snapped out of it and reported. "I think Hunter just got it!" Almost simultaneously, he felt *Cherry Bomb* veering to port.

Griffy gave the command to tack and coached Blake through crossing the boat. "Wait... now to the middle, now on to the rail. Good tack, buddy! Watch under the boom and tell me what's going on."

Three more fleets had started by this time and a white wall of sails now stretched from the starting area to almost the point where they had just tacked. The rest of the Laser fleet was strung out close to the far shore. It appeared that they would all converge at a point just to the right of the buoy.

"Get ready to meet the family!" Blake peered under the boom. They were on a collision course with their competitors, who were drawing closer by the second. He wondered nervously what kind of mad maneuver his cowboy captain would pull next. Griffy called for the tack and suddenly the entire fleet was twenty yards behind them, with Hunter and the rest falling in line halfway between.

Griffy let rip with a big "Yeehaaaah!" as they rounded the bobbing orange pyramid. "Congratulations! We're first around the first mark, buddy! Two more to go!"

It was the first time Blake had ever been first in anything and he felt an ambiguous sense of accomplishment. Griffy eased the sail out three quarters of the way and *Cherry Bomb* simply got up and ran away. In their wake, colorful spinnaker sails blossomed out of all of the larger boats. Griffy managed to keep the lead for the entire lap but Hunter had closed the gap between them to just a few boat lengths.

They rounded the second mark. The best sailors of several fleets had caught up and there was now an armada of various boats hot on the heels of *Cherry Bomb*. The breeze had increased a little and both of the boys had to hike all of the time. Griffy could see Blake's fatigue and handed him the mainsheet for something to hold onto. "Trim like a maniac as we go around the next mark!"

Blake was astounded by the fact that this brashly obnoxious kid, who couldn't be any older than himself, had maintained first place in a race against an armada of seasoned adults—for almost an hour—around a three mile triangle. And as experts often do, he made it look easy. It made Blake feel inferior and unaccomplished, and disgusted with himself.

They rounded the last mark, still in the lead. "Trim, trim, trim, trim!" piped Griffy. Hunter and several Lasers tacked after rounding the buoy. Griffy did not.

"Hunter and a bunch of others went the other way." said Blake.

"Tell me everything they do exactly when they do it! I hate the last leg!"

"Why, what do you hate about it?"

"You have to be perfect! One little thing and you can lose it all!"

Blake began to worry about what that one little thing might turn out to be. He came to his senses again and cried "They're tacking!"

"Go! Hard a'lee!" Swift as an eagle, *Cherry Bomb* pivoted ninety degrees, Griffy coaching Blake through the tack. "Hike!"

Blake's heart pounded as he realized that *Cherry Bomb* and Hunter's pack were on a T-bone collision course. "We're not going make it!"

"Yes we are!"

"No, we're not, they're coming too fast!"

"I know something you don't!" They were seconds away from piling into *Grampus*. Griffy filled his lungs and shouted "STARBOARD! STARBOARD!"

Shouts of panic erupted from the oncoming pack of Lasers. Hunter tacked *Grampus* away, *Cherry Bomb* rushing past her with mere inches to spare. Bader and Hopkins turned down and went behind them as they passed. "Hard a'lee!" shouted Griffy. "Take that, you damn swabs!" Hunter tacked back but was now three boat lengths behind, again. The Committee boat and finish line were just ahead.

"You're allowed to do that?"

Blake couldn't believe it—they were actually going to win! He was exhausted. His gut ached from hunger and hiking. He couldn't wait to eat, and collapse on his cot in the dormer. Then something caught his eye—a familiar movement which, even without comprehending it fully, evoked a deep and instinctive revulsion. A couple of feet away he spotted the *one little thing*. A long-legged water spider had splashed up on deck and was making its way to the high-and-dry side. Blake shrieked and instantly backed himself into the skipper who, between Blake's cries of "get it away from me," began shouting obscenities. The arachnid continued to advance. Blake turned around and tried to clamber over Griffy. Then to add to his panic, he sensed that everything around him felt completely wrong.

Cherry Bomb slewed around violently, her deck suddenly vertical. Blake felt himself falling backwards. He was swallowed up in a splash of cold darkness. His lifejacket returned him to the surface instantly. He watched in complete shock as the black and white bottom of *Grampus* flew past, Hunter's mocking laughter looming above. *Cherry Bomb* was on her side, sail and half of her deck under water. She was beginning to go belly up. Griffy was nowhere to be seen. Boats passed to either side, their skippers and crews offering encouragements, condolences, and even jeers.

"Griffy?" Blake called, on the verge of tears.

"Get over here you idiot, before she turtles!" Griffy shouted from the other side of the hull. "I can't believe it! Three boat lengths from winning the best race I ever sailed and you go psycho on me? What is wrong with you?"

Blake made his way around the transom and found his skipper just pulling himself up to a sitting position on the end of the skyward-rising dagger board. "Your hat's not wet!" he observed.

"Hang on the board, idiot!"

Blake struggled to reach the blade-like plank which stuck out the bottom of the glittering, red hull. His body was beginning to register just how cold the lake really was. "There…was a big…sp-sp-spider," said Blake, between gasps and whimpers. "On the…deck" His skipper was not interested.

"Go on, put your weight on it!" Blake did his exhausted best. Slowly, under their combined weight, *Cherry Bomb*'s belly began to roll back toward the water. He heard the submerged sail slosh out of the lake with the sound of a rainstorm. Griffy threw a leg over the side as soon as it reached a convenient angle and slid over on to the deck.

Blake realized the hull was now rolling on its own and was going to come down on top of him. *I deserve it.* he thought. *It would be a fitting end.* But he thrashed himself clear and the boat finally rocked upright. Griffy was now situating things aboard. "Get in here, c'mon!" He helped his forlorn crew struggle over the transom and into the swamped cockpit. The angry young skipper trimmed the sail and got under way again.

They crossed the finish line. The Principle Race Officer announced the number on their sail over the loudspeaker and added that there were still five Lasers behind them. It was little consolation.

Griffy's mother was on the foredeck waiting her turn. "Awesome job Griffyn Williams! I'm proud of you too, Blake! Are you alright?" Blake held up a hand and let it fall. "Griffyn, I want you to take him back to the club right now. Look, he's shivering! He's exhausted!" Griffy didn't so much as give his mother a glance but tacked the boat without a word, eased the sail and headed for the harbor.

Blake slid down into the flooded cockpit and stared hopelessly at the deck. Griffy pulled a black, rubber drain-stopper from the floor. Within minutes the cockpit was dry.

Blake didn't wait for Griffy to tie up when they arrived back at the club's marina. As soon as the sail luffed and the hull bumped the dock he took the first handhold available and extracted himself from *Cherry Bomb*.

He staggered stiffly across the deserted launching area intent on making it to the clubhouse before Griffy could catch up. Mrs. Williams had radioed ahead and Elsie was waiting at the door. She followed him up to his attic sanctuary with towels and a plate of hot food. The aroma of the cheeseburger and fries carried him up the final two flights of stairs. Elsie pulled an old cable spool over for a bedside table and put the plate down on it. He picked up the hamburger, gave thanks, and stuffed his face. Elsie smiled and headed down the steps. "Please lock the door and don't tell Griffy where I am. Don't tell anybody." From far out on the lake he could faintly hear the Committee boat's signals. The second race was beginning.

***

Blake napped solidly through the lunch hour in spite of the boisterous mob on the patio below. He awoke sometime in the mid-afternoon. Sitting up, head still thick with sleep, he leaned against the window and stared through his reflection at some children playing on the hill.

I had so looked forward to seeing the regatta—from the sidelines. He thought. *Why did that pushy kid have to snag me? Why did I ever agree to go with him? And why did that lousy spider have to show up—in the middle of the lake, of all places? I'm undoubtedly the laughingstock of the entire Highland Creek Sailing Club, now.*

So he sat, prisoner to his own embarrassment, locked in the castle attic all afternoon. But by late afternoon, hunger and loneliness were conspiring powerfully against his pouting. He watched Ray fire up the big grill while Elsie and several other ladies set out bowls of snacks and filled tubs with ice and cans of soft drinks. A band was setting up in the gazebo at one end of the patio deck. There came a knock at the door and a friendly voice at the foot of the stairs. It was Beverly Maitland.

"Blake, are you up there, dear?" Blake hurried down the stairs and unlocked the door. "Well yes, here you are! We'll be serving dinner soon and I wanted to be sure you had your ticket. I haven't seen you all day, have you been up here this whole time?"

He explained things in brief. Beverly reassured him that everyone in the club had done something similar at some point in their sailing career and though he might have to endure some good-natured ribbing for a while, he would live it down. "The best way to do that is just laugh and go right back at it like nothing happened." She gave him his meal ticket and reminded him there would be apple crisp and ice cream for dessert. That was all he needed to hear. He *would* venture out.

Blake decided to test the water with a preemptive foray. This would be better than appearing suddenly before everyone and having the whole club receive him with mocking laughter and ridicule. He slunk downstairs to the great room and, to his surprise, the few people on hand took little notice of him. He found almost the same reception out on the patio, where those who spoke complimented him on the job he and Beverly had done with the decorations. He also inquired discretely as to Griffy's whereabouts and found that he had gone back out as crew with someone in the Y Flyer fleet. He scooped up a handful of chips and nuts, a few pickles, and walked down to the point. When he saw that the fleets were returning to the harbor he retreated once more to his attic refuge, and read *Treasure Island* until he dozed off.

By the time that the hungry sailors began lining up for steak and baked potatoes, Blake had mustered enough courage to go back downstairs. No one said anything about the capsize. Beverly caught sight of him and pulled him into the serving line ahead of herself.

"Do you like Celtic music?" she asked. "Because that's what we've got tonight! And Irish step dancers, too. I think you're really going to enjoy them, they're marvelous!"

"Sounds neat," he replied, fully intending to return to his dormer once he'd filled his plate.

But his elderly companion had different plans, steering him to a table near the gazebo. He situated himself with his back to the crowd. Beverly talked a blue streak about random things, pausing only to swallow, and wave at parties behind him. She flagged someone down and beckoned them over to their table.

"Good evening Ms. Maitland, who's yer friend? Caduggin! I should've known." Gunn groaned as he sat down. "I'm getting too auld for this sort of thing. Well, every time I caught sight of the two of yeh, yeh were leading the pack. How'd it wind up?"

"Upside-down fifty feet from the finish line." Blake didn't look up from his plate. "I capsized us."

"How could yeh manage that when yeh were just crew?"

"Oh Tripper, one of those nasty water spiders popped up on deck and startled him. He feels just terrible about it." said Beverly.

Gunn chuckled. Blake drew a deep breath and prepared for the worst. "Yer granddad sank us that way once. We'd just gone around buoy number four in first place, at the very far end of the course. He'd hoisted the spinnaker and I was puttin' up the pole. Declan was standing in the back of our Lightning with the tiller 'tween his knees, spinnaker sheet in each hand. One of those blasted things went right up his leg! He twisted this way, the tiller went that way, the boot went straight across the wind. Knocked us right over. Folks said they'd never seen a Lightning go down so fast!"

"See!" said Beverly, "It happens to everybody, once in a while."

"I remember looking at the pole as we went over and thinking 'I wonder if this thing floats?'"

"But he said I ruined his best race." said Blake.

"Don' yeh worry, lad. That boy'll win his share of races before it's all over. He wants to beat Hunter every time, that's what's burning in his gut. Well, yeh've been through the worst of it anyway. And now yeh know! A capsize isn't anything to worry aboot as long as you're wearing your lifejacket and the water's no too cold."

"I told him he should go right back out there, tomorrow." Beverly concurred.

"When yer ready, lad. They can always use a hand on the safety boots."

"I think I'll just stick to the *Terrapin*."

"I saw yeh hiking out there with yer hands in the water, lad. I think yeh'll go back. Just wear a hat. This old thing here's got more spider guts in it than a wasp's nest!" he said, motioning to his own headgear.

The band took their seats in the gazebo and tuned their instruments.

"I really like this group, Tripper. I'm glad you could get them again this year." said Beverly.

Before long a lilting jig was in the air and three young women were clogging away on the open deck in front of the ensemble. They kept their hands at their sides the entire time. Blake inquired about this. Gunn explained that "in the auld country it wasn't considered lady-like to dance with the hands in the air."

Finally, the music began to replace the worries of the day and Blake relaxed and enjoyed himself. After the first set, the two root beers he'd downed with dinner began to make demands. Blake excused himself, fully intending to return and claim his share of dessert. Halfway through his plan, however, things went awry. On his way back, almost to the patio door, someone flung an arm around his shoulder and steered him off course.

"Hey ol' buddy! I've been looking for you all over, man! We're going back out tomorrow right? Look, I found a flyswatter you can take. We had Hunter by three boat-lengths!" Blake was relieved that Griffy wasn't holding a grudge, yet thought maybe it would be better if he was.

"Is your dad a used car salesman or what?"

"No, fertilizer. I can't believe how well we did! We beat everybody as far as I'm concerned."

"He sells fertilizer?"

"No, I mean he *is* fertilizer. Worm feast. Pushin' up the daisies. He's dead, Jim. Thanks for reminding me! We capsized and still beat five boats! Outrageous! It'll be ten to fifteen tomorrow but we can do it. You were awesome, you *gotta* go back out now!"

Blake, thoroughly shaken by Griffy's callous revelation, was trying to figure some way to escape his clutches when came another familiar voice from a table just ahead.

"Hello Tux." Mia Devlin sat with her feet propped up on the window ledge, leaning her chair back on two legs. "I see you took my fashion advice, but now we have to talk about your choice in friends."

Griffy didn't miss a beat. "She's completely right. You wanna stay away from girls like that they ruin your reputation!" He would have swept him along to the side door but Blake stopped dead in his tracks.

"I hoped I'd see you again. How have you been?" he said.

"Okay. I was working at the shop. Dad came straight here. I didn't have a choice. Tell me you're not sailing with the Mad Cowboy?"

"Yeah, as a matter fact he is, and we had Hunter and everyone else by three boat-lengths at the finish!" said Griffy. Before he could get another word out, heavy hands dropped from nowhere, clasping the boys like a bird-of-prey snatching two rabbits—each by a shoulder.

"Until Sparky here just couldn't wait for the honeymoon and attacked his boyfriend!" laughed Hunter. Blake kept his eyes fixed on Mia. Long black curls framed her hard, dark eyes. Hunter went on. "You should've seen it little sis! Sparky just went completely gonzo-spastic and climbed all over Cowboy, here. They beat the *entire* club and flushed it right at the finish! And all in the name of love!" He squeezed their shoulders harder, his voice suddenly assumed a sinister, nervous edge. "Isn't that right, Sparky?"

"He's not my boyfriend." said Blake.

"Oh, did I have it backwards, Sparky? Backwards? You're *his* boyfriend?"

"Maybe he's *my* boyfriend." said Mia, with a stern glare. She now had everyone's undivided attention. "Hey Hunter, Jenny Hopkins is down on the point."

"Nice try, sis. You haven't even been to the point."

"No, but Bader has, and he just told me that Jenny and the Cheer twins are down there all alone by the fire. At least they will be until that *molester* gets down there." She stared at her brother, poker-faced. He was sure she was bluffing. He glared back, gauging whether he should chance it. "He was headed that way in an awful hurry!"

Hunter blinked. "Not allowed. Denied!" Releasing his captives he exited out the side door.

Blake headed straight for the stairs. Griffy stood rubbing his aching shoulder. "Sheesh, is he off his meds or what?"

"He doesn't take meds, that's part of the problem." said Mia. "*You* can go now."

"I think *I* will!" he sneered.

She hefted a backpack from under the table, slid it on, and went out to the patio.

***

Mia returned to the clubhouse and searched the second floor for Blake. She balanced a heaping bowl of hot apple crisp and ice cream in each hand. He wasn't in the boardroom, the library, or the office. The dormitories were empty. The only door left was to the attic, and it was locked. She put one bowl down, stood on her toes and felt along the top of the dusty lintel. Success! The key was there. She quietly unlocked the door, put the key back, and proceeded cautiously up the stairs. Blake was sitting on his cot staring blankly out the window.

The middle dormer was larger than those on the ends of the attic gallery, and it made a cozy nook. Mia set the desserts down on the spool-table without a word. She slipped out of her backpack and opened the window to let the music in. Blake didn't move. She brushed a ribbon of hair out of her face and sat down on the floor

"Your ice cream is melting."

He remained silent. A minute or two passed.

"That's the *Swallowtail Jig* they're playing. I can play that on my violin. I suck at it, though."

Two more songs went by. The sun was now sinking behind the trees on the ridge, and the attic was painted with golden rays and long shadows. The next song began. "Oh, now that's *Wayfaring Stranger*," said Mia. Blake's blank expression drew into a frown as he strained to recognize the tune.

"That's *Wayfaring Stranger*?" he said, just above a whisper.

Mia began to sing. "I am a poor, wayfaring stranger, traveling through this world of woe. And there's no sickness, no toil or danger in that bright land to which I go." She had a nice singing voice.

"I don't know the rest."

"That's a church song. My mother's favorite song." said Blake. He listened intently and shakily picked up the chorus "I'm going there to meet my mother, she said she'd meet me when I come..." Mia could see the anguish welling up in him and as he reached the end of the phrase, the tears were streaming. His face wrenched with sorrow and he began to sob. For a moment Mia wasn't sure what she would do. But compassion got the better of her. She sat down behind Blake and put her arms around him. He leaned back and rested his head against her shoulder.

"I know." she said. "My parents are separated. I go between two big empty houses on the lake. I stay with Dad when Mom's mad at me, and Mom when Dad's mad at me. When I want to go do something for a few days, I just tell them both I am at the other one's house and nobody ever checks up. I could be dead for months and nobody would notice. You know what's worse than knowing someone hates you, Tux? Knowing that someone doesn't care."

They were quiet for a few minutes. Blake calmed a little.

"I want to go home, but I hate my home. I want to stay here, but I have to worry about Hunter and Griffy and spiders every time I turn around—and I'm just going to have to leave it all in the end anyway."

"Look, Hunter usually never sets foot over here except for Sunday races and regatta weekends."

"Usually." Blake sniffled.

"You're just going to have to toughen up Tux. Take things as they come."

"How come you're so strong?"

Mia didn't answer. She sat Blake up, drumming both hands on his back as she rose from the cot. She retrieved her backpack. "That apple crisp is awfully good. Do you know how to play Backgammon?" She unzipped the pack and pulled out a leather case. Blake shook his head in reply. "I'll teach you."

Sharing a game over dessert with a new friend, the fading light and the live music from the patio made the evening pleasant again, even welcoming.

"So, where is your uncle?"

"He visits the nursing home in Freeman on Saturdays."

"All day?"

"I guess so. I haven't seen him since this morning. He says there is a man there who is a hundred and eight."

"I'd like to meet that guy."

"I'm going to, next week. You could come along."

"I don't know. We'll see. Roll the dice, it's your turn."

"Mia, you won't tell your dad we're staying here, will you?"

"Why would I do that, Tux? Roll your dice."

They heard the attic door open. The light over the stairs came on. After a moment the stocky form of Carson Urquart emerged from the stairwell. He spotted only his nephew at first.

"There you are!" he said. "Let's shed a little light on the subject, shall we?"

He flipped a wall switch at the top of the stair, flooding the center section of the gallery with warm, yellow light. Then he saw Mia. "Well, hello Miss! There's still food to be eaten down there, if y'all want seconds."

"There's still steak?" said Blake.

"I'll go get you another plate. I hear you had a heck of a day! You, Miss?"

"I'm good. Thank you."

"The last set is starting, by the way." called Carson as he trundled back down the stairs. "We'll want to hit the hay pretty soon after they're done."

Mia rolled her dice and moved her pieces. "Your uncle seems like a nice-enough guy. We'd better finish our game so I can get going. The last thing we need is for my dad to find us all up here."

"When will you be back?"

"I think I should probably show up for the last week of school. So, I don't know. Maybe next weekend. Sunday. Maybe before."

"I never know when I'll be out with Mr. Gunn and my Uncle. But we usually get back by four. And I can always stay behind if I know you are going to be coming."

"We'll just have to play it by ear, Tux."

Blake rolled double sixes and removed his last four pieces from the backgammon board. Mia congratulated him with a pouting smile and mussed his hair.

"You're stronger than you think, Tux. Hang in there. Learn to say 'no.' I'll see you around."

Mia packed the game away and vanished down the stairs. Blake looked for her from the dormer window but she didn't appear on the patio. He went to the window at the end of the attic. He could see her making her way down the dark hill to the main dock where a dozen keel boats were tied up. He pondered her statement about saying "no." It seemed so easy, so sensible. He would just start saying no. He reviewed the day's disasters which he would have been spared if only he had said no. *I wouldn't have gone with Griffy or run into Hunter. I wouldn't have encountered the spider, I wouldn't have been embarrassed and humiliated. I wouldn't have spent all day hiding in the attic.* He stared at his own reflection in the glass and realized: *I wouldn't have discovered that I could hang off a boat upside-down and put my hands in the water. I wouldn't have discovered the power of being on starboard tack. I wouldn't have discovered that capsizing isn't such a big deal. I wouldn't have had this evening with Mia. 'No' is a two-edged sword.*

Chapter 7

The club's big Boston Whaler banged across the choppy waves. It was one of three on safety patrol for the second day of the regatta. Blake sat next to Carson and held onto the dashboard with both hands. They towed three six-foot orange tetrahedrons behind them and had both a yellow and a green sphere buoy taking up most of the space in the bow. Carson explained the basics of sailing as they set up the starting and finishing lines, the windward, leeward, and the jibe marks.

"See, you can't sail straight into the wind. You have to go at it at an angle. That's called 'beating' or being 'close hauled.' You have to zig-zag to get where you're going. The first mark in a race is always straight upwind." He had to shout to be heard above the motor, the wind, and the hull banging on the waves.

"So, that's why we do all that tacking?"

"Right! Then between the first and second mark the wind is off the back quarter, usually. That's called a 'broad reach.' That's actually your fastest point of sail. Sometimes it's dead behind, and that's a run. In either case that's when you put the spinnaker up and really go!"

"I remember seeing them do that."

"Then, at the jibe mark, you shift the sails to the other side and head for the leeward buoy. That's where you drop the spinnaker, hoist your jib again and start beating back to the finish—if the race is a one-lapper."

"You make it sound so easy!" Blake laughed.

"Practice, boy, it just takes practice. I sure could use an assistant when Junior Training starts in a couple of weeks."

"What would I be doing?"

"Helping other kids feel comfortable with the boats and just kind of coaching them. It's fun."

"But I don't know how to sail."

"We'll fix that, soon enough. Just think about it and give me a yes or a no in a couple of days. I'll teach you everything you need to know."

Blake thought about it for a moment. He remembered what "no" would have cost him the day before. "Yes" would mean new friends. Some of his friends at home had bicycles and were allowed to ride wherever they wanted. Blake had always envied their independence. He imagined being able to explore Trespass Island, and going to the Emporium by himself or even better—with Mia. And he just plain liked sailing. Somehow it seemed natural to him.

"Yes, I want to learn how to sail this week! And I want to help with Junior Training."

"Alright! There's a good book in the library. *Start Sailing Right*. The Red Cross puts it out. Start reading that."

They had just set the last buoy when another Boston Whaler zoomed past. It bounced from wave to wave, red and blue lights flashing. The conservation officers aboard waved as they headed for the channel.

"There goes *Moby*! I wonder what that's all about?" said Blake.

Carson cut the wheel to the right and throttled up. Blake held on tightly to the windshield with one hand, the back of the seat with the other and braced one foot against the inside of the driver's pulpit. He saw they were headed right into the big wake that *Moby* had thrown up. Then it occurred to him that his crazy uncle was going to jump it. He couldn't imagine that they would land right-side up. But just before the fateful moment Carson cut back to the left. Blake felt the boat heave upward; suddenly they were surfing diagonally along the ridge of that wave! Carson let go with a tremendous "wahoo!" It felt like they were flying forward and sideways at the same time, three feet off the water. His uncle kept them perched precariously aloft for a half mile.

"I want to learn how to do this too!" Blake shouted.

They spent the rest of the morning assisting capsized crews, towing their swamped boats back to harbor, as well as readjusting the position of the windward buoy before each race. By lunchtime, the wind had strengthened to the point that the Committee boat couldn't make headway into the breeze. Carson and Blake towed her upwind several yards to slacken her mooring chain just enough to weigh anchor. While the other two safety-boats shepherded the fleet back to the harbor, they collected the race buoys.

Back on the patio, everyone had settled in for lunch. The fleet scorekeepers completed their tallies and handed them to a man in a black blazer jacket. He donned a white, naval officer's hat bearing the sailing club's emblem, and appeared at the trophy table. Commodore Lawrence Devlin picked up a microphone. Blake thought he looked about Carson's age, but with much grayer hair, and deeper lines in his face than a man his age should have. He called out the top three finishers from each fleet, one crew at a time. His jocular air barely disguised his bored insincerity. Skippers and crews rose and claimed their trophies, and everyone applauded. Many skippers took the time to thank their crews, the race committee, safety patrols and, to Blake's irritation, the 'wind gods.'

"Lightning, third place: Tripper Gunn. Not shabby for a man of eighty five!" said Devlin. Blake caught the condescension in his tone, but was otherwise delighted. Gunn rose and ambled to the trophy-table unaccompanied.

"Thank you, Mr. Commodore. And Tom-Tom."

"Snipe fleet..." Devlin began, before Gunn had even collected his trophies.

"Hold on! Beg yer pardon, yer highness. Do yeh mind?" Gunn motioned to the microphone. Devlin relinquished it with obvious reluctance. "When Declan Urquart drew up the bylaws for this club, he included an article specifying that any of his direct descendants, and mine as well, should they wish, be granted lifetime membership in this club for as long as it exists. I'd like to introduce you, if yeh've no met him already, to our newest legacy member, Blake Urquart. Stand up lad!"

Blake felt his face flush. He rose to his feet bashfully, taken completely off guard. Commodore Devlin fixed his eyes on him, his expression betraying his displeasure, but quickly smiled and clapped with everyone else. Blake immediately had him pinned for a snake. Somewhere in the back, Hunter and his gang drummed their hands on their table and mocked "Yay Sparky" in deep bellows.

"When I get *that* lad for crew, you'll see what a man of eighty-five can do." Gunn returned the mic to the commodore with a casualness that bordered on contempt.

"Well, welcome Blake! We look forward to reviewing your application," said Devlin, with the same smug, liar's smile that Blake had seen on his pastor's face—the time the man had promised to put an end to his son's bullying. He dished out the remaining trophies, announced the upcoming board meeting, made a few concluding remarks, then made himself scarce.

"The board meeting is a week from Tuesday night," Carson explained. "So, don't make any plans. We filled out all the membership paperwork for you."

"Okay. I don't even know what to say. No one even asked me," said Blake.

"You have a point there, Sonny. Do you want a membership in the Highland Creek Sailing Club, free of charge for the rest of your life, courtesy of your dear old granddad?"

"Well…yes. Of course! I guess it's just a little unexpected. I'm kind of overwhelmed."

"Some men are so generous that they continue to give long after they're gone."

"Can I ever be kicked out?"

"Only if you really goof up. Outside of burning the place down the only thing you could do is bring public shame to the club, like assassinating a head of state, or robbing a bank and running off with the commodore's daughter. Something akin to that, you know?"

"Do you think I shouldn't be associating with Mia, then?"

"Nah, I didn't mean it like that! It's really nice that you two are getting to be friends. Well, I have to go deflate the buoys and put the Whalers in the shed. Why don't you lend a hand up here?"

"I'd kind of planned to."

"It's your club, now. Get involved!"

Carson finished off his soda and left. Blake took a hopeful glance down at the main dock. *Eclipse* was long gone from her berth. The crowd on the patio had thinned considerably. Up in the dorms people packed their things. At the foot of the hill tents collapsed and at the waterfront hoists whirred and clanked. Masts came down, hulls were lashed to trailers and rumbled back across the lot. Within two hours the club was empty, save for those faithful few who remained to help clean up. Griffy eventually appeared and helped Blake clear tables, and pick up trash. Griffy never stopped talking. Blake wondered if it might ever be possible to lock him in a room with his sister, Agatha.

Chapter 8

Clean up extended into Monday morning. Blake picked up trash along the entire point and stuffed it into overflowing garbage barrels, which Carson hauled away on a flatbed trailer. When the chores were completed, Carson departed with Tripper Gunn for welding work somewhere on the lake. Elsie showed Blake her favorite trail in the woods behind the keelboat parking lot. They began near the main gate and, after twenty minutes, emerged at the end of a narrow asphalt lane—in the club's junk yard. As they walked on toward the hoists they met with a flock of Canada Geese grazing along the lane.

"I bet Ray'd pay you ten bucks a week to keep those flying poopinators off the property!" Elsie said. "They're cute when they're little but all that goose-grease—what a mess!"

"Sounds like a career opportunity to me," said Blake. He opted to stay and watch the flock. Elsie returned to the clubhouse. Ray stood on the patio, scowling grimly down the hill. *Tantrum II* lay moored along the main dock. She took up a full forty feet.

"Hunter you know you can't park that here!" Ray roared as he ambled down the steps. He stopped at the first landing. Hunter Devlin and Thad Rexroat had just come ashore and were headed for the boathouse.

"What?" said Hunter, with a sarcastic grin.

"You heard what I said! You know it's against club rules, you can't tie that up here! Now get aboard and shove off!"

"Tell it to the commodore, old man! Oh yeah, my Dad is the commodore, I forgot!"

"If you don't get back on that boat and cast off, I'll cast it off for you!"

"Rexy, eggs!" Hunter pointed to a pair of Canada geese nesting nearby. "You can just stop right there, Griz! That nervous edge cut its way back into Hunter's voice.

Ray started down the hill again. "You just try and stop me!"

Rexroat ran the geese off and returned to his master with an armload of large eggs, just as the main flock waddled their way around the bottom of the hill. Blake gently herded them from behind. He was just in time to see Ray dodge the first egg. The two geese were now back on their nest in a squawking fury, making short, hissing, sorties against their plunderers. The young men were oblivious to the situation developing behind them. Eggs continued to fly as Ray cussed and dodged.

Blake spread his arms, bent low and started urging the flock forward. "Come on guys, go, go!" he pressured, keeping his voice low, "Go! Don't fly, don't fly! Wait for it, c'mon goosies go! Go!" Blake managed the flock masterfully, bringing them to a full panic just as they reached the boathouse, mere yards from Devlin and Rexroat. Then he lunged at the trailing ganders. The air erupted instantly in a cacophony of honking geese and beating wings—mixed with the confused cries and curses of Hunter and Rexroat. The bellowing laughter of the groundskeeper blasted through it all. When the pummeling, thrashing, thumping and scratching had ended, the two villains lay facedown in the grass.

Ray was still laughing. "Hey, don't look up with your mouth open!" he guffawed. Blake was nowhere to be seen.

"Laugh it up, Yogi!" Hunter sneered. "We'll see who's filing for unemployment after the next board meeting!" His tee shirt and face were one big smudge of grass stain, green goose poop, feather down, and bloody scratches.

"Aw, that's all right, Hunter! It's all worth it. I'll be laughing about this for the rest of my life! In fact, I feel so good now, I'll give you five minutes before I call the police!" Ray headed back up the hill, laughing to himself the whole way.

"It was that kid!" said Rexroat. "I saw him, he was chasing the geese toward us."

"You mean my little buddy, Sparky?" Hunter called loudly to the empty grounds around them. "C'mon, he can't be too far away." They circled the boathouse completely and stopped in front of a long storage rack of stubby, square, training prams. The little boats stood on their sides, each overlapping the bottom of the next. Hunter thought for a moment. An expression of satisfaction disguising repressed anger spread over his face.

Thad whimpered apologetically. "I don't get it. I was sure I saw him!"

"It's okay Rexy. We'll get him. In fact, we'll get him and the bum at the same time. Somebody needs to teach those low class, mooching legacies a lesson."

"Yeah? What do you have in mind?"

"It just so happens that the bum and Little Orphan Andy are camping in the sail shed up there on the hill. Looks very unsafe to me, perched right on the edge of that steep slope."

Rexroat was tantalized. "Go on!"

"Tonight. Midnight. A few anchor chains and a little tug of war."

"Awesome, dude, I'm in! Oh, but wait…"

"Don't worry Rexy, the trees'll stop 'em. They won't even roll over. But they'll get bounced around good and hard, and take the blame for destroying the shed!"

"Man, you're an evil genius! I'm in. I'll get Hopkins and Bader. Pick us up at my place?"

"I'm feeling gracious—why not?"

Their reverie was broken by a shout from the clubhouse. "You got sixty seconds, Hunter!"

"I hear you, old man! We're just leaving!" Hunter called back.

Blake peeped out from his hiding place between two prams. *Tantrum II* rumbled to life, crawled out of the harbor and rounded Boy Scout Point. Blake slithered out from between the prams, stretching and rubbing the cramps out of his joints. But his physical discomfort didn't compare to aching realization of what he had just done.

"Doesn't set foot over here. *Usually*," he grumbled.

"I think you've started a war, son!" said Ray, tromping down the hill. "And you won the first battle, score a point for you, Blake Barber!"

"I'm afraid you're right. And I mean afraid!"

"Aw, Hunter's just a big spoiled jerk! Here, have a root beer." Ray offered Blake a brown bottle.

"Yeah, but now he's coming back with his friends!"

"Sure he is!"

"I mean tonight! I overheard him tell his friend. They're coming back with chains. They're going to pull the sail shed off the cliff. I think we should call the police."

"And tell them what? This is just a squabble between kids to them, Blake. And even if they did come out here and catch Hunter at something, his old man's in tight with the Freeman police chief."

"Then what are we going to do?"

"You're gonna stop whining, for starts! You know his plan, that gives you the upper hand! You just have to put that information to work. Now you go up there and look the situation over. Figure out where they'll come ashore, what they'll do. Then come up with a plan of your own. You tell your uncle when he gets back and if he has a better idea, go with that."

"I still don't know what to do!"

"You knew what to do with those geese, boy! Ha! That was the best thing I've ever seen, hands down! I know you don't know what to do. Just think about what you *would* do and see if you can make it work. Imagine it's pirates coming ashore to destroy your fort. It's the same thing! Man didn't get to the moon 'cuz he already knew how. He got there because he imagined what it would be like if he could. Now, go on up there and start imagining!"

***

The midnight sky was deeply black and glassy, buoyed by sharply shining stars. The slightest breeze rippled the lake's surface, which sparkled with

May's waxing crescent. The sweet, night air whirred with crickets and peeping tree frogs. But in the distance there rose that rhythmic rumbling as *Tantrum II* made its way through the channel, barely above idle. It crept past Boy Scout Point, past the sailing club's harbor, around Highland point, and into Thistle Bay. There the pilot carefully turned her stern toward the wooded bluff and backed the big boat into the shallows as far as he dared.

Three young men went over the side. They waded ashore towing a heavy chain behind them. Meanwhile, Hunter shackled it to a tow ring on the port side of the transom. Two invaders stealthily scaled the bluff, one stopped halfway up, the other waited at the top, behind the sail shed. The chain was passed from one man to the next until there was no more slack. Together, they looped the big chain once around the shed, made a clumsy overhand knot and secured it with a hook shackled to its end. The work done, they scrabbled back down and took to the water.

On the other side of the ridge, two figures emerged from the picnic deck and trotted silently to the shed.

"Okay," whispered Carson, "hold the end while I loosen the knot... pass the hook through here... now take it around!"

Blake took the end of the chain back around the shed while his uncle kept tension on it, to keep it from rattling. Then he ran three laps around the sturdy trunk of an oak, tied a hitch with the last few feet and snugged the hook into the last wrap.

"Good job! Now, let's go watch the fun!" said Carson.

The pair made their way down the hill to the little beach at the bottom of the bluff. Ray was waiting for them. "Just in time," he said. "They're getting the last man aboard, now."

Rexroat scarcely had time to drip on the deck before Hunter grabbed the wheel and thrust the throttle forward. The engine thundered and *Tantrum II* lunged forward. The chain slashed up out of the water and snapped taught. An abrupt cracking split the air as the tow ring and its bolts tore from their foundations in the big boat's hull. Fiberglass shards rained down. Devlin killed the throttle and turned the bow toward the open lake.

"Hey Dev, there's like a whole corner ripped out of your dad's boat, man!" said Bader.

Hunter ground his teeth and growled. He throttled up and roared back for the channel. The triumphant trio watched them pass out of sight.

"The Almighty does catch the clever in their schemes!" said Carson, with a satisfied grin.

Ray snickered, lighting a cigarette. "He won't fix that with duck tape!"

"Well, let's go collect your prize and get to bed, sonny."

"What am *I* going to do with all that chain?" said Blake.

"Sell it at the Freeman flea market. Tripper has a booth."

Chapter 9

The next week passed placidly. Hunter didn't return for revenge as Blake feared he would. He was still looking over his shoulder and he didn't like to be alone on the grounds for too long at a time. And, in spite of Carson's insistence, he steadfastly refused to move back into the sail shed.

He was, however, settling into the daily routine of his guardians: early to rise, with a stout breakfast including coffee and a game of cribbage; work on the lake; learn to sail in the afternoon; enjoy some free time; build the fire for dinner; wash the dishes; read in bed. It was a far cry from life at home and that suited him just fine.

Carson taught him to sail in the club's boxy little Optimist Prams. He became proficient with his boat handling skills. He understood when and why to ease the sails out and when to trim them in, and how to stop the boat and remain in place. He learned how to rescue a man overboard and, above all, how to recover from a capsize. Blake practiced *that* exercise repeatedly. He made sailing his own. He read all that he could on the subject, practiced knot tying, maneuvering, used the lingo, and generally showed off his new knowledge until it was almost all Carson could swallow. Except for raising and lowering the mainsail, which required his uncle's assistance, he took over all of the sail handling aboard the *Terrapin*. Tripper Gunn quietly ate it all up.

The trio spent the better part of the second week of June rebuilding the pit-toilet facilities at another recreation area. Blake got his first experience swinging a hammer and using a paint brush. He put his math skills to real use, measuring and marking lumber, and calculating the volume of the concrete needed for the project. Friday arrived before he knew it and the new pit toilet was done. Blake was dog tired but all of this learning and hard work made him feel useful.

It wasn't a pyramid but it was something; and he had helped build it. He thought a small brass plate just above the sink, inscribed with *Built by Blake Barber & Company*, might be in order.

"This is the way things used to be," Carson explained as they loaded the last of their tools aboard the boat. "A young fellah was apprenticed to a tradesman or followed in his daddy's footsteps. That's how he learned his job. Nowadays they've got everybody fooled into believing you've got to go to college and get a degree to get a job. And you just about *do* —Blue collar America is all but gone."

"My dad went to college and it got him a good job," Blake said.

"Sure it did. But is he happy? I mean, in marketing? Why invest four years and a hundred thousand dollars just to learn how to spend the rest of your life making someone *else* a lot of money? I'm just saying. Be interested in everything. Find what you love and figure out how to make it your living."

Although Blake wasn't fond of his father, it sounded like his uncle was taking a swipe at him, and he wasn't going to stand for that. "Well, I guess if building outhouses makes you happy."

Carson bristled. "I was a Navy diver! That's what I loved and I still do! Would've been my career, too—were it not for some genius opening the wrong valves and purging the ship's sewage tanks on us while we were in the water."

"Thanks, I think I'll vomit, now!" said Blake.

"Tell me about it! They gave us about every vaccine known to man. And I still got sick! Probably from the shots, like as not. I was sick for so long they ended up giving me an honorable discharge. And that was the end of my diving career. The moral of the story is: sometimes life takes a big poop on you and you have to change your plans."

Gunn boarded the *Terrapin* through a v-shaped opening in her stern. "Lad, with that head for figures yeh've got, yeh *should* go to university! I was an engineer all my life. My love is boot building. The two go together. There's a beauty and an art to the both of them."

"Yet some of the greatest figures in history were self-educated," said Carson.

"And one of them ended up turning valves on a Navy destroyer!" said Gunn.

"Look, I'm not telling him *not* to go to college, I'm just saying do something that makes sense, that's all!"

"And I'm just saying he's got a head for mathematics and university *makes* sense. Yeh don' have to get all bent out of shape! Now push us out and get aboard." The *Terrapin* lay in sandy shallows. Carson put his shoulder against the square bow and shoved the boat into deeper water, climbing over the side as she began to float free.

"Make sail, Caduggin!" said Gunn.

Blake hoped the momentary distraction of getting under way would cool the men's tempers. He really hadn't intended to get them riled but it was gratifying to have someone sticking up for him, for once. The bickering continued at low broil all the way back to the sailing club. This time it was Carson who made for the shore first, leaving the old man and the boy looking at each other.

"I'll drop the sails if you want to motor home, Mr.Gunn."

"Thank yeh, lad. I'll get 'em. Yeh better go. Yeh got a fire to start, don' yeh?"

"I think I already have."

"Just let him be. He'll cool down soon enough. I hear yeh want to get out of Dodge, Sunday? Why don' yeh drop by the flea market, help me peddle that chain of yers!"

Blake jumped at the idea. "Pick me up?"

"Nine o'clock. Let your uncle know."

Blake climbed out and gave *Terrapin* a good shove off. Her sails filled and she cruised away toward Trespass Island. He had the fire built and the beans cooking before his uncle turned up again. Carson filled his plate, mumbled a prayer of thanks and retired to the sail shed to pass the evening by himself.

Chapter 10

Blake's nose wrinkled at the first hint of diaper-pail bouquet which lingered in the air of Golden Grove Nursing Home. He had second thoughts about going along with his uncle, but the mere notion of a chance encounter with Hunter was enough to change his mind. He had tried to imagine what a man of a century and eight years would be like. He had settled on the image of a boney, little, white-haired man with a whispy voice. Each open door they passed framed a new picture of quiet despair—grim, lonely, and grotesque. Somewhere, someone cut loose with mad wailing and was answered by jeering, cursing neighbors.

"There goes poor ol' Betty," said Carson. "We'll stop by and see her later on. Poor ol' gal."

Blake wanted to run out the nearest exit. He couldn't imagine how Carson could spend all day in a place like this. Carson knocked on a closed door. "Come awn!" boomed a big voice from within. Blake noticed the name 'Dubois' on the door as they entered. He wondered where the man with the whispy voice was.

"Korby, I brought someone I'd like you to meet," Carson announced.

As Blake stepped out from behind his uncle he was astounded by the man before him. Black, large-framed and very tall, Korbin Dubois lay stretched out in his recliner.

"Whatcha say, Caw? You caught me with my eyes closed." His voice was strong, deep, and resonant.

"I say I brought someone who wants to meet you."

"Well who is it?" said Korbin, attention fixed on Carson.

Carson pointed at his nephew. "Right here!"

Korbin glanced down and his dazed expression gave way to excitement. "Aw, now who is this? Who is this?" He fumbled with the controller to his chair and reached out to Blake as it slowly rose upright. "Come here son, let me take a look at you!"

Blake stepped to the edge of his chair and said "Hello."

Dubois held one big, trembling hand against Blake's face. "Aww, awww now! Who is this boy? I know! Don't I know that face! But you don't have a son, Caw? Aw, but you're an Uh-quot, just the same!"

"I get that a lot, lately."

"I bet you do, son! Who are you?"

"I'm Blake. Carson is my uncle. Ava is my mother."

"Ava! Aw now! Sweet little Ava! Son, I worked with your great-grandfather on the B and O Railroad in Washington, Indiana in the nineteen-twenties! Aw now you orta be outside playin' ball with your friends! What do you want to come see a stinky ol' man like me for? You orta be outside, not in this stinky ol' place! Come to see a stinky ol' man like me!"

Blake was mesmerized by the old man's deep, crooning voice. There was something about him—a power that seemed to emanate from his core. Blake could not think of a word to describe it. The closest he could come was *holy*.

"I wanted to meet someone who was one hundred and eight years old."

"Did you, now?" He straightened a bit. "I was born in nineteen hundred and three, the very year the Wright brothers took to the air. Up in the air! From horse and buggy and bicycles, up into the sky! I was just about your age when the First World War broke out. I worked at the roundhouse and I built boxcars, and laid track through the Great Depression, and then cooked my way all over this country on a kitchen car—right through the Second World War. Didn't see much of my family then, no sir. I saw the day come when we could wipe out a whole city with one bomb. I saw the day when we could take one man's heart and put it in another man's chest. I saw the day when a man set foot on the moon. But I don't really believe he done it! I've seen the coming of the computer, and more wars and disasters in the last ten years than the last hundred put together!"

"Wait, you don't believe our astronauts landed on the moon?" This was simply astounding to Blake. It made Korbin Dubois seem authentically from another planet. Carson took a seat on the bed and smiled to himself.

"Why no, I don't believe they done it! That's too close! Too close to the Throne! He's not gonna let a mere man come that close! No sir!"

"But they teach it in school. It's in my history book. I've seen TV shows about it."

"What else do they teach in schools? I bet they teach you man come from a monkey, don't they? You don't believe you come from a monkey, do you?"

"They do in public schools. But I don't go to public school. And no, I don't believe we came from monkeys."

"Do you believe men walked with the dinosaurs? I believe Noah had dinosaurs on the ark!"

The phone rang. No one moved to answer it. It rang again. "Aren't you going to get that?" Blake said.

"No."

"Do you want my uncle to get it?"

"No."

The phone was still ringing and Blake fidgeted. The old man and Carson seemed absolutely at peace. "Do you want me to get it for you?"

"Not at all."

"But it's ringing!"

The ancient black man smiled. "Just because it's ringin' don't mean I gotta answer it!" The bit about the moon-landing had been flat-out heresy, but this was simply mind-blowing anarchy. Who ever heard of not answering the phone?

"You're not one of Pavlov's dawgs are you, son? Somebody rings a bell and you slobber all over yourself?"

Blake would remember those words for the rest of his life: *Just because it's ringin' don't mean I gotta answer it!* He would run them over and over in his mind for days before he fully comprehended their full meaning.

Korbin took stock of Blake's expression. "Aw, look what I done. I upset you. Now, you didn't come here for that! Stinky ol' man talkin' crazy to a fine young boy. What kind of way is that for an old man to talk, huh?"

"You're not upsetting him, Korby, you're making him think!" Carson said.

"Naw, now I'm sorry young fellah. You orta be out playin', 'stead of standin' around this stinky ol' place. Now, Cawson you take him on out and get him some ice cream down to the Emporium, and go play ball, and leave an old man be."

"But I enjoyed meeting you, Mr. Dubois. I hope we can visit again sometime," said Blake, not sure if he really meant it. But he wasn't about to pass on the get-out-of-jail-free card.

"Awright, then. You come back sometime and we'll talk about anything you want."

Carson, still grinning, escorted Blake out into the hall. "You got your watch on? I'll meet you at the *Darby McGraw* at two o'clock—take you back to the club."

"That's okay, you don't have to do that just for me. I want to go to the library and the pet shop."

"Okay, make it five. But if you want to go back, you know where to find me. Just tell folks you belong to me or Tripp and they'll take care of you."

And Blake did just that. Almost anywhere he dropped their names he was instantly treated like royalty. That is until the owner of the pet shop laughed and said, "Oh yeah, you're the kid that busted up old man Devlin's boat! Let me shake your hand, son!"

Only three people on his end of that chain, plus Gunn, knew what happened to *Tantrum II* that night. Two of them had good reason to keep it quiet.

"Did Ray tell you about that?"

"And the geese, I never laughed so hard! All the fellahs at the pool hall call you the 'goose whisperer!'"

The panicked words of Moses suddenly rang in Blake's mind: *Surely this thing is known!*

A title at the top of a magazine rack caught his attention and made him shudder: *Spider Fancy*. "May I ask you a question?"

"Sure, anything—shoot!"

"Do…" He could hardly bring himself to speak of it. "Tarantulas ever get big enough to eat rats?"

"Oh sure, the Goliath! South American. They call it the Bird Eating spider. You want me to get you one?"

"Nooo thank you. Just curious. You sell many rats?"

"Oh yeah, but not for spiders. Boas and pythons, mainly." The man blabbed about spiders and snakes, monitor lizards and piranhas for the next twenty minutes. "Say now, I have a question for you. Have you ever seen the White Hound?"

"No, I don't think so. Why?"

"Oh, for years folks on the Lower been talking about seeing a big white dog roaming the edges of the woods—they say he looks like a wolf! Sometimes they hear him howling, but only before bad weather rolls in. They say he calls the thunder. Sounds like you've got a gift for animals. Thought maybe you could make friends with him, if you saw him."

"I'll keep an eye out. Thanks for letting me look around."

Blake hit the sidewalk, his mind reeling. The pet shop owner had been a real talker and it was pure relief to find out that his uncle wasn't a regular rat customer. But, he was staggered by the thought that the chain-gang incident was local news. And not only were people laughing about it, they were putting him up as the hero. To top it all off, he'd gained yet another nickname. He still had an hour to kill and he wanted to find somewhere quiet where he could recover his wits. The storage space below the foredeck of *Darby McGraw* was just the spot, made comfortable by a pallet of life jackets and safety cushions, with a fat dock fender for a pillow. Blake listened to the muffled hum of ski boats and stared blankly at the white walls of his fiberglass cubby hole.

Chapter 11

Sunday morning, Tripper Gunn unlocked the chain-link curtain that shrouded his booth.

Blake surveyed the inventory. *So, this is what he does with all of the stuff he has me picking out of the lake!* he thought. "What was this place, originally?"

"An auld warehouse. What do yeh think now that you've had a look around?"

"I think if I were going to name it, I would call it 'Acres of Junk!' I also think there are more tattoo artists than dentists in these parts." He took a fishing lure from a display-board and examined it. "These are neat! Do they really work?"

"Oh, some are better than others I suppose. I think they catch more fishermen than fish, though."

He nicked himself on one of its treble-hooks. "Kind of like Matchbox Cars with hooks?"

"That's exactly what they are, lad." Gunn seemed much more relaxed than usual, almost cordial. "What are we going to do aboot all this," he said, kicking the first in a row of four milk-crates full of chain.

"I have no idea. Where did Hunter get all that, anyway?"

"Dunno. It's no my concern. It was abandoned on club property and, what's more—it was being used to commit a crime. If I had to guess, it probably came out of the auld man's salvage locker. If he's no gonna keep his son under control, that's his loss."

Blake wasn't exactly sure that Gunn was standing on high moral ground, but he had learned where pushing the matter would probably lead. "How much is it worth?"

"That's five-sixteenths galvanized, no rust, hardly used. Yeh'll pay five dollars a foot for a new chain like that."

"A thousand dollars worth of chain?"

Gunn lifted his eyebrows and nodded. "The money's all yours. Price it to sell, lad. I'd go half off."

"I don't know, Mr. Gunn. I'm just not sure I should, if it was stolen from Commodore Devlin's shop." It was out of his mouth before he knew it. Gunn sat down and studied him in stony silence. Blake was sure he'd just flushed the whole day.

In a moment the old man nodded. "Yer folks raised yeh right, lad. We'll just ask the commodore at the board meeting Tuesday night." Blake wasn't sure he liked that idea, either. "When yeh go for lunch, yeh stop by the Police Department and ask if they have any reports of missing chain. Tell 'em yer inquiring on my behalf. In the meantime let's move it all under this table, here."

Blake checked with the police on his way to the Emporium and found that no reports of missing chain had been filed. It occurred to him that Gunn had been testing him—and that he had passed, thanks to his parents—of all people.

The Emporium was crowded and noisy. Blake got in line for his carry-out order. The antique carousel organ had just finished its noontime rendition of *Garryowen* when he noticed a group of teen-aged girls in a booth snickering among themselves. Their snarky leers washed over him in a wave of self-conscious embarrassment. He tried not to look back at them. *Does everyone in this town know who I am?* he thought. *I wonder if Trespass Island is uninhabited on weekends. Better yet, that cave.*

"Hey kid, where's your girlfriend?" said a tall, drop-dead-gorgeous red-head. She seemed to be the ring-leader.

Blake took a quick glance out of the corner of his eye.

"Does she kiss on the first date, Sparky?" said another girl.

He heard the name "Jenny" amid the mocking giggles. Face flushed and fists clenched, he turned and approached them. There were six girls and to Blake, every one was Agatha.

"Oh my god, he's actually coming over here!" said two girls, in unison.

"Jenny Hopkins. And you two must be the Cheer twins. You don't look much alike but you're each about as ugly as the other. I can only assume that your nickname is a euphemism for a decided lack of morality."

Their expressions changed like masks in a Greek drama—catty mockery gave way to bare viciousness.

"Wow, was that Shakespeare, little man? Listen up smart-ass! You better stay away from her, if you know what's good for you."

"If you're referring to Mia, I think…"

"I don't care what you think!" snapped the redhead. "It doesn't *matter* what you think, *little boy*! What matters is you're nothing but lake trash. She's one of us and we look out for our own. Get it?"

"Hey," said one of the twins, "did this little runt just call us sluts?"

"Let me give you some advice, *little boy*: go back to wherever you came from before somebody squashes you like a bug." She slapped her hand on a ketchup packet, splattering Blake's shirt and shorts. There was a brief, shocked silence, then shrieking laughter.

He was just about to lay into them with both fists when Treva hurried up from behind. She filled his hands with more sacks than his order could possibly require. "Don't worry about it, honey. It's on us," she said, looking over her shoulder at the girls. She shepherded him to the door and quietly let him know it would be a good while before the 'silver-spoons' would get their order.

He figured out why, when he and Gunn opened the sacks. Treva had given him the girls' order as well as their own.

"Lightning rod, that's what yeh are, lad! Yeh kicked the hornet's nest!"

"I came over here to *avoid* trouble. Turns out the whole world knows what's been going on."

"That's how it is with trouble. Once it's stirred up, it comes looking for yeh wherever yeh go. I understand yeh come from a pious family. Maybe you should talk to God aboot it?"

"God's got better things to do than listen to my problems."

"Like what, lad? What's he got to do?" Gunn smiled. "He's omnipotent isn't he? That means he can do as much as he wants, all at once, if he so chooses."

"So I should just turn the other cheek and let Hunter kill me?" Blake sneered.

"Watch yer tone with me, lad. I'm no saying that at all. Hunter's a bad one and we've needed to be rid of him for a long time. And the club would'na suffer any by saying farewell to his auld man, either. Yeh read yer Bible and yeh'll see that God brings his people *through* their troubles. He does'na just yank 'em out and drop 'em in the promised land all fat and sassy. Remember, Daniel went *into* the lions den and his friends went *into* the furnace."

That wasn't really what Blake wanted to hear. "How far away is that cave?"

"It's no very hospitable. Ye and yer uncle can come and stay at my place any time. And he knows that."

The Sunday crowd finally made a show of strength and it turned out to be a good day for selling fishing tackle and dock fenders. One couple decided that they couldn't live without the ten-foot fiberglass shark that hung from the rafters above Gunn's booth. It went home to fill the void over the bar in their double-wide trailer.

Chapter 12

Blake was both pleased and worried to see *Eclipse* moored at the main dock when he awoke. He dressed quickly and tip-toed down the stairs, listening at the attic door before easing it open. There was no one in the foyer. Neither could he hear anyone in the great room, so he crept on downstairs and out the front door. At the west end of the clubhouse he jumped down the retaining wall where the entrance to the groundskeeper's apartment was cut into the hill, and ambled down to the secluded trail that ran along Thistle Bay. He followed the shoreline all the way to the bluff below the sail shed, swishing a stick around to clear his path of spider webs. He emerged in the little grove and jogged to the point. She was there, sitting on the picnic table, her back to him.

"Good morning, Mia. I hoped you'd be here."

"There you are, Tux," she said with a casual air. "Don't worry, Hunter's not here. Did you run into my Dad?"

"No. Where is he?"

"Probably in the office on the second floor." That stirred a few butterflies in his stomach.

"I hear you almost started a riot at the Emporium, yesterday."

"How does everybody know every move I make? I hate this!"

"I have my sources. Treva told me you were about to go mad-dog at the cat show. By the way, she made them wait until they got fed up and left."

"Really? I hope her boss doesn't find out."

"Who do you think told her to do it?"

Blake shook his head. "I feel like I've started a civil war in this town! I can't stay here because I'm afraid of Hunter, I can't go to town because the shore birds hate me, I can't go to my Nanna's because there's a… Because my uncle doesn't drive. There's no escape!"

"Welcome to my world," she said. "They're none too happy with me, either."

"Crap. Sorry!"

"Hey, don't hold back on account of me, buddy!"

"I just want to go someplace where there isn't anybody at all. Do you want to go sailing?"

"Sorry, Tux. I don't sail."

"You don't *sail?* You live on the lake! What do mean you *don't* sail?"

"I mean I *don't* sail. My *Dad* sails. Everything he does is sailing. His business is sailing, and when he isn't working, his hobby is sailing, and when he takes a vacation, he goes somewhere else and sails. And when it's my weekend to be with him, I work in his sailing shop. And when he isn't doing any of that, he gets to play commodore for the sailing club this year. Sailing split up his marriage, sailing split up our family, and the only reason he pays any attention to my psycho brother is, you guessed it, my brother sails. So, why would I sail, Tux?"

Blake stood in stunned silence for a few moments, soaking in Mia's confession. He genuinely felt her pain. He realized that it was the first time he really understood someone else, and the first time he really felt a little less alone. Something ached in his heart for her sake. He so wanted to express that to her. He wondered how to say it.

"My Dad doesn't pay any attention to me, either. If he isn't at the office he's working on church stuff, or doing something for my sister's school." He paused for a long moment. "But in spite of that, I still believe in God, I still go to church. So, maybe you could still sail."

"Nice try, Tux. But my Dad's life *is* sailing. And in *spite* of *that* I *don't* sail." She drove those words home, like nails in a coffin.

Blake remained quiet a while longer. "My uncle told me about some neat places around the lake. I'd like to go check them out but when the wind kicks up I'm too light. I can barely even hold down a pram." This wasn't remotely true.

Mia didn't take the bait. In fact, she got up and stretched as if she had somewhere to be and was about to get on her way.

Blake couldn't help it now. He needed to open up to someone so badly that he swallowed his almost-thirteen-year-old pride and gambled against his fear that she'd surely slaughter him in this vulnerable moment. "Truth is, I'm afraid to go that far alone. I can't even go out to Trespass Island without getting nervous. I hate it. I'm such a chicken, I never really feel safe anywhere except … never mind, I'm so stupid." His face flushed and his heart pounded. He was sure he had done it again—offered himself up as the cosmic doormat.

There was more silence. Mia didn't attack. She didn't leave. Instead, she took a couple of steps toward the water, stretched again, and gazed out on the lake with a far-away expression. "You can't get to most of those places in a sailboat," she said. Too shallow, too many stumps. No breeze in the coves, tree limbs snag your rig, shred your sails… Nope, you either take a canoe or a kayak and canoes are too much work if you ask me."

Blake's heart half sank with disappointment. Still, his gamble hadn't ended in emotional evisceration—yet. But then she spoke again, slowly building anticipation or perhaps still making up her mind. "Which is why…" She paused and turned around. "We will have to take my kayak."

Blake couldn't believe his ears. "Really? We'll go?"

"Nine a.m. tomorrow. Pack a lunch and bring water. I'll pick you up down here. And not a *word* to anyone, d'ya hear?"

"You bet! I mean, I can tell my uncle, can't I?"

"Him and him alone. Got it?"

"Got it. Thanks!"

"I gotta go. See you at nine," Mia started back for the *Eclipse*.

"Yeah, see you! Thanks again! I really…"

"You're welcome, Tux. Don't grovel, it's not dignified."

He stood and thought about that for a moment. That was the word for Mia: dignified.

Blake returned the way he had come. As he skirted the foot of the clubhouse hill he heard the automatic gate clacking into action. He made his way through the woods all the way to the edge of the parking lot. He heard the car's door slam. He darted across the gravel to an island of tall cedar trees. Fifty feet away a big black tank of a car creaked and hissed.

He pondered just what kind of oddball would park a black car in the middle of the sun-baked lower lot, then labor up to the top of the hill where there were plenty of shady places to park. Then he caught sight of the driver, slogging up the grand stair. Black combat boots, cut-offs, and a mangy black tee shirt. It was Jack. As soon as he was out of sight, Blake slunk over to his car. It was dirty, and blazing hot even at a short distance. He wiped a spot clear on the dusty passenger-side window and peered in. It was a total pig sty. A sleeping bag, wadded up clothes. Trash from fast food joints filled the foot-wells clear up to the seats. A copy of the *Pemberton Patriot* newspaper lay folded in the middle of it all. A headline on the front page read "Discovery of Missing Chihuahua Raises More Questions," but the article itself was on the other side of the fold. The doors were locked.

An outboard motor started up in the direction of the main dock, signaling the Devlin's departure. Blake decided to pursue Jack. He ran up the hill and cut through the clubhouse. A pile of mail lay half scattered on a table by the back door. He looked at the name on one of the envelopes: Clarissa Urquart. Jack had delivered the mail. He sifted through bills and advertisements until he uncovered a postcard. He stopped and stared. It featured the Eiffel Tower at night. He picked it up and flipped it over.

Hi Sweetheart!
Hope you are having fun with Nanna! Agatha's been sick since we got here, Daddy's at the office all the time. My college French sure isn't what it used to be! Sis is feeling lots better, today-so I think we'll get out this week. I can't wait to get home to my big boy!
I Love you!
Mom

The card was postmarked just a week earlier. Blake's lower lip quivered. He was a dozen kinds of confused. He read the card twice more, or rather heard his mother reading it to him. He came to his senses, slipped the postcard into his back pocket and continued his hunt for Jack. As Blake approached the grove on the point, he heard a familiar voice. He drew as close as he dared. Carson and Jack were sitting by the fire pit.

"Well, did you try setting traps?" said Carson.

"Nah. Waste of time if you ask me." Jack kept rubbing his right hand. When he paused, Blake could see a patch of red, irritated skin between the middle knuckles and down the fingers.

"Mom wants this taken care of, Jack!"

"I hear ya. I told you it will be. I left your mail up top."

Blake retreated up the path as the scroungy young man got up to leave. He ambushed him at the edge of the parking lot, stepping out from behind a big oak.

"Why have you been living in your car?"

"Why is it your business?" Jack retorted, without breaking stride. Blake stayed in front of him, walking backwards.

"Because you're supposed to be staying at my Nanna's and taking care of her house. What's in the house, Jack? Why don't you want to stay in the house?"

"I set off a flea bomb, okay? So, I spent the night in my car. Now get off my back, punk."

"There's a week's worth of laundry and trash in that car. Where did the fleas come from? Nanna doesn't have any pets."

"I brought a stray kitten home, alright? The thing had fleas and they've gone gonzo crazy berserk. I had to flea-bomb the place for four days and still didn't get 'em all, alright? Are you satisfied with that, Sherlock? Now leave me alone!" Jack pushed his way around his interrogator and headed for his car.

"What did you do to that Chihuahua?" Blake jeered, not knowing quite where it came from. Jack tripped over his own feet, but kept walking.

***

Blake grilled Carson that evening before bed. Carson backed the story up and even described flea traps and said he'd point them out the next time they hit the hardware store. *Plausible enough.* Blake thought. He wanted to believe it. He pulled out the postcard and read it three more times. *Mom went to college?* he thought. *She can speak French?*

Chapter 13

Griffy? thought Blake, looking out his dormer window. The cowboy skipper stood at the end of the main dock. *What is Griffy doing here at eight-thirty on a Tuesday morning?* Blake grabbed the watertight bag he'd packed the night before and hurried down the other side of the ridge. He found Mia waiting in a lawn chair by the fire pit in the grove.

"Good morning! Are you ready?"

"Good morning yourself! You in a hurry, Tux?"

"I don't know why, but Griffy is here; so if we want to keep this…"

"Hey there you are!" called Griffy, coming down the gravel path.

"… *Quiet.* What are *you* doing here?" Blake said.

"Mom's working from the beach today. What's your excuse? *You're* getting an early start."

"Well speaking of that, c'mon Tux," said Mia. She got up and started for the point. Blake followed.

"Cool, I'll get rigged and catch up to you!"

"It gets kind of shallow where we're going. You won't be able to keep your board down far enough to beat effectively," said Blake.

"What? When did *you* start talking like that?"

"It's true, Cowboy, whatever it means!" added Mia.

"Gotta learn the lingo, buddy!" said Blake, pleased with himself.

"Oh, I see how it is! Thanks a lot."

Mia stopped suddenly, and shouted an angry "Hey!" at someone or something ahead. Three figures burst off the last dock and bolted straight for them, yelling like Viking marauders. Blake knew instantly who they were and ran for the ridge. Griffy sped for the gravel path. Mia charged straight for the invaders. Gauging the perfect moment, she planted her left foot, pivoted to her side and pounded her right foot square into the deeply tanned chest of a shirtless young man. He hit the ground without a molecule of oxygen in his lungs. His compatriots continued their pursuit.

"I told you what would happen if you ever laid another hand on me, *didn't* I, Bader? *Didn't I?*" She shouted, jerking him up by his cowrie-shell necklace. He could only stare in quivering, visceral panic and gasp like a suffocating fish.

Griffy knew he couldn't outrun Hopkins on solid ground, much less a gravel path. He made a desperate leap down the riprap embankment to a dock, ran its length and dove in. Hopkins stopped to pick up an armload of fist-sized rocks.

Blake flew through the grove and up the ridge toward the sail shed without any sign of slowing. He darted behind the little building, Hunter almost on his heels. Devlin came to a screeching halt at the bluff's edge. Blake was wrapped around a tree trunk, well out of reach.

"Ohhh Sparky! You're up a tree without a paddle, buddy!" said Hunter, with a satisfied chuckle.

"Miaaaa!" cried Blake.

"Save you're breath Sparky, Bader's keeping Sis company, now. You know, you are the fastest kid I have ever had to chase down! You really are amazing!" He knelt down and peered under the sail shed. I tell ya, I am really impressed—there, that's the ticket!" He pulled out an old bamboo tiki-torch. "And you must've jumped six feet to make that tree. You could've been the school track star if you'd just stayed home." He removed his tee-shirt and wrapped it around the end of the pole.

Blake had little doubt about what was next. He looked down. Every wiggle or shimmy he made sent cracks running through the crusty soil around the dead tree's roots. He wondered how long his sweaty hands could hold onto the smooth, barkless trunk. Hunter produced a cigarette lighter from his pocket and set the shirt on fire.

Each of Hopkins's lobs shot a plume of water up like a depth charge. Griffy dove and changed direction with each throw, until he surfaced in the middle of the harbor, out of range.

Hopkins laughed to himself and was about to return to shore when he spotted Mia on the far dock. "Oh, no you don't!" he said as he leapt back up to the path and sprinted for the point.

Griffy saw her too, and raised the alarm. "Mia! Look out!"

She finished tethering the pirate's canoe to her two-seater kayak and snatched one of the canoe paddles. Hopkins thundered onto the dock, stopping just in time to save his bare belly from catching Mia's home-run swing. She recovered and lunged, attacking with the paddle in a high brace. He seized it at the ends, caught his balance and laughed, "Gotcha!"

Mia looked him in the eye and smiled a hateful smile. She stabbed a heel like a dagger into the bridge of his left foot. He yelled and relaxed his grip. She jerked the paddle free and slammed the wooden shaft into the bridge of his nose. The haft of the paddle cracked. Hopkins went down backwards. He didn't get up.

Blake shimmied ten feet up the bare trunk, but could still feel excruciating heat of Hunter's makeshift torch. He held it just low enough to be painful, without doing real damage. The tree swayed even more precariously now and there were popping sounds from the ground below.

Blake was frightened nearly to the point of paralysis and was crying "Mia! Mia, Help!"

Finally the torch went out. "Too bad, the barbecue's over. Oh, I'm *sorry*, things a little warm up there for ya, Sparky? Let's cool ya down, whaddaya say?"

He braced the bamboo pole against the tree trunk and gave it a shove, then another until it was swaying rhythmically. With each pendulum stroke the tree traveled farther out until, with a final mighty push, Hunter sent it past the point of no return. Now there was the continual sound of snapping roots and cascading dirt. To add to Blake's terror, a deep creaking vibrated through the entire tree as it slowly canted out over the water. Hunter stood at the bluff's edge watching with sadistic delight.

"Please God, don't let it fall, don't let it fall! Please help me, please!" Blake pleaded, eyes fixed on the water, twelve feet below.

"Hang in there Tux, help is on the way!" Mia paddled into Thistle Bay with all of her might, with a very large, green canoe in tow. "Get ready!"

"Ready to what? I can't get down!"

"No!" howled Hunter, hastily looking for an easy way down the bluff. "Mia stay out of this, you little witch!"

"Get ready to drop, Tux! I'll count you down." He slipped around and hung from the underside of the steadily descending trunk. The creaking and popping was getting louder. Larger, deeper roots were snapping.

"Hurry up!" he cried.

"Three, two..."

Mia deftly maneuvered her kayak under her dangling friend and just as the bow passed below him she called "Drop!" He fell five feet and landed in the forward cockpit, legs and arms splashing over the sides. Just as the kayak cleared, the big canoe drifted under the timber. An astounding crunch resounded from the shore. She tossed the tow line over her shoulder. Blake looked back just as the tap root gave way. Freed from its earthy bonds, the now horizontal tree plunged through the middle of the canoe, folding its halves up vertically like the jaws of a monstrous snapping turtle biting a broomstick.

"Mia! You little witch! That's it! You're on my list, do you hear me? You're on my list!"

"Better bring more help, that's all I can say, Junior. Try some girls, next time!" she retorted. "We need a little more horsepower here, Tux. Your paddle is under the deck. The two halves snap together and lock in the middle."

He managed to assemble the paddle and began to stroke with every thing he had.

"You'd better call Rexroat and get those guys to the ER! Consider yourself warned, Junior!"

As they glided swiftly out of the little bay, Mia's taunts reminded Blake of the other two pirates, and Griffy. Scanning the point, he located Bader. He was on his knees, clutching his ribs. Farther down, Hopkins staggered to a tree, leaned against it and puked.

Blake cast a bewildered glance back at his rescuer. She shrugged. "We're trust-fund kids. Hunter buys golf clubs, and gas for the boat. I bought a violin and Karate lessons. Don't worry, Cowboy got away."

Blake didn't say anything, but resumed his furious paddling.

"You're getting to be an expensive friend, Tux."

"I don't want to know."

"That canoe was a classic. All wood. Century old."

"Don't tell me, please."

"Eight thousand dollars."

Blake groaned.

"And that little job you pulled on *Tantrum II?* That was brilliant, by the way. That was six thousand!"

"Don't forget the anchor chain," Blake added, reluctantly. "A thousand, new."

"Awesome! And then the hospital bills for those morons, but that won't come out of Daddy's pocket. You're already into my old man for fifteen thousand dollars, and how long have you been here?"

"Just over two weeks," he moaned.

"You know what, Tux? I've decided I really *do* like you!"

Judy Williams watched the bright, yellow ski boat roaring away from the point, throwing up a wake like a tsunami. Her son was nowhere to be seen. This wasn't unusual but her intuition told her otherwise. She descended the steps to the foot of the hill and called for Griffy. From the woods across the harbor she thought she heard the sounds of someone thrashing their way though the underbrush. She hurried across the beach and called again, "Griffy Williams is that you?"

"I'm coming!" was the distant but clear reply. Griffy finally emerged directly across from his mom.

"Griffyn, what are you doing over there? Are you alright?"

"Don't worry about me! Blake and Mia are in trouble! Hunter and his pals jumped us."

"Griffy, find the trail and walk back, don't swim it. I'm going down to the point." She ran the entire way, making it to the end of the peninsula just in time to see a tandem kayak disappear behind Trespass Island. She pulled out her cell phone and activated the speed dial.

It rang twice. A woman answered, "Freeman Police Department. Is this an emergency?"

***

When they reached the other side of the island, Blake stopped paddling.

"You're going to wear yourself out." said Mia. "Take a break, Tux, we're okay now. I'll show you how it's done, in a minute."

"I'm done, alright. It's over. I'm going to have Uncle Carson put me on a bus and send me down to my Nanna in North Carolina."

"You could do that. And you could inherit a whole new set of problems while you're at it."

"At least I'd be safe."

"And bored to death. At least you've got *excitement* here!"

"Ha ha. Very funny. What I've got here is fear—constant fear. Even when I'm out working with Mr. Gunn and Uncle Carson, I've always got it in the back of my head that Hunter, or a big spider, or a werewolf is going to come out of the woods, or a storm is going to blow up. Seems like fear's all I've ever got, anywhere I go."

She paddled in silence for a moment. "Tux, there are two kinds of people in this world. People that make things happen, and people that things happen to."

"Guess which one I am?"

"How you handle it makes all the difference. You want to be a victim? Go on being one. The world loves victims. Eats 'em right up. You want to be a hero? Stop whining about being a victim and go make something happen."

"Simple as that?" Blake snapped.

"Almost. You know what? Mark Bader is twenty years old. He

outweighs me by fifty pounds. He's an athlete. Lance Hopkins, too. I just sent them both to the hospital, I guarantee it. See, I figured out early on that Hunter and his baboon friends were a big threat. Sure, I was afraid. But when I saw no one was going to stand up for me I knew I was going to have to do it for myself. So, I enrolled in Karate. I took it seriously, worked hard at it. Today it paid off. They won't ever mess with us again. Hopkins and Bader anyway."

"You think Hunter is going to come back after us, today?"

"Not by a long-shot. Believe me, he has his hands full, now. He has to get the guys to the hospital and come up with an alibi for the shape they're in—and the canoe."

"What do you think he'll say?"

"Oh, I know what he'll say. He'll say that they were paddling around, minding their own business when you set that tree on fire and pushed it down on them."

"What? I can't believe this!"

"Well that's what he's going to say, so be ready for it. Or you can just sit around and cry about how life sucks and how picked-on you are. Think about how you are going to defend yourself and then do it. Then get on with making the things happen in your life that you want to have happen. Am I making any sense here?"

Blake had a natural resentment for self-improvement lectures. He didn't say anything.

"*Blake*, what do *you* want?"

"You don't understand!" He exploded. "Every time I speak up for myself or fight back I get in even more trouble. I never win, I can't ever win. It's not allowed!"

"Speaking up and fighting back aren't always the best ways to win. You have to pick your battles. And just because you lose one or have to compromise sometimes, it doesn't mean you've lost the war. Sometimes the best thing is to back off and find a way *around* the opposition."

"What best-seller did that come out of?"

"Mr. Haraguchi, my Karate sensei," Mia said, a little offended. "Look, why don't we just turn around. I'll take you back." She shifted her weight to tilt the kayak and began a turning stroke.

Blake grabbed the sides. "No, I don't want to go back."

"Then what do you want?"

"I want to see the heron rookery."

"Then make it happen. We've got three and a half miles to go. Now, let me show you how to paddle a kayak."

Once Blake got the hang of it they made good time. He had twice been up as far as the soaring highway bridge aboard the *Terrapin,* but never beyond. Here the lower lake narrowed down to a quarter mile. He stopped paddling as they passed beneath the span and stared straight up in wonder. Light danced and rippled like silver flames on the towering piers. Swallows chittered and zoomed back and forth to their mud nests on the arches. It seemed like the great vaulted ceiling of Notre Dame Cathedral. The hilly shore rose sharply on either side now, giving way to high limestone walls. Soon the lake made a hairpin bend to the right and then back to the left. They had not spoken a word since passing under the bridge.

"It's only about three feet deep from here to the headwaters," Mia said. "Too many stumps and rocks to risk a wake boat. You're safe up here, Tux. Just try to relax and enjoy the rest of the day."

That helped. But still he worried about what was going to happen when he and his uncle faced the commodore and the board of directors at the meeting that evening. It burned in his mind like the tormenting heat of Hunter's torch, for the rest of the day.

"Hey, see if you can touch bottom with your paddle," said Mia.

He leaned over and thrust his paddle straight down into the cool water. Sure enough, it bumped and dragged along the silty lake bed. Blake was amused by the idea he could now actually walk to shore, even from the middle of the lake.

Soon the beige, stone outcrops gave way to retreating hillsides, then to reedy flats dotted with little muddy mounds. The marsh drew closer and closer, constricting the lake into a channel a few hundred feet wide. Ahead, a narrow strip of island split the stream. On its end, two black, shaggy-looking things sat, each in the top of its own spindly tree. As the kayak drew near, the vultures raised their wings in unison, spreading them into great arcs over their heads like guardians of the gate of the underworld. They held them up until the interlopers were well past.

The effect was not lost on Blake. "That was…ummm…"

"Ominous?" said Mia.

Cattails and reeds loomed on either side, the stream was now a mere twenty feet wide. A few crickets still serenaded and cicadas whirred in the distance. It made Blake's bladder claustrophobic.

"Isn't this cool? All you can see is the water, the cattails, and the blue sky. I love it here," said Mia.

"So, what's the most dangerous creature out here?" said Blake. "Besides you."

"Snapping turtles. Look there's one!" She smacked her paddle on the water, splashing him.

"Hey! Wait that actually felt good! Man, I am so thirsty. You're going to kill me, but I left my pack back at the club."

"I got it. It's in the aft hatch. If you can wait fifteen minutes we'll pull out and have lunch."

The stream split again and they took the left branch. The wetlands suddenly parted and the kayak glided into a little lagoon at the foot of a wooded slope.

"It's deep here" Mia explained. "That's why the marsh falls away. We're going in that little cove, right there."

The shady cove was nestled between two ridges. Massive limestone shelves jutted out from black soil and leaf litter. They formed a mossy staircase in the "V" where the steep slopes met. Everywhere, water dripped from the bottoms of the slabs.

"There's actually a little waterfall here when there's enough rain," she said, working the kayak sideways to the bottom shelf. They climbed out and pulled the boat up onto the ledge. Mia popped the round hatch cover off and peeled the neoprene liner away.

"Here you go!" She tossed Blake's pack to him. "That's awful lumpy.

Whatcha got in there?"

"Two bottles of water, a deli sandwich, chips, a waterproof walkie-talkie, binoculars, a compass, and a little Gideon's Bible."

"Well you never know where *that'll* come in handy! What's the range on your radio?"

"It's supposed to be five miles. I should be able to get Ray at the clubhouse. I guess it depends where *Moby* and my Uncle Carson are, whether I can get them or not."

"Let me see it." She held out her hand. He forked the radio over. She switched it on. "Hey Grizz? You copy? Hellooo clubhouse?" She switched frequencies. "Bucky boy, you out there? Mueller, pick up da phone!" She tossed it back to him. "I'd rather have a night scope."

Mia extracted her own backpack and a rolled up blanket. She replaced the hatch cover. "C'mon. We'll eat on the ridge."

They climbed out of the ravine onto to a faint path which went deeper into the forest. Blake began to feel small again, as he contemplated the terror of becoming lost under this endless, towering canopy, miles from any familiar territory.

"These trees just go on forever, Tux. They're just there. They'll always be there. And they don't care. If I died right here, they would just go on standing there and the sun would keep beating down through the silent blue sky. Nature is indifferent."

Her philosophy instilled in him a feeling that surpassed insignificance. It boldly opened a shocking new realm of crisis for his consideration—meaninglessness. As they topped the next ridge the stillness of the forest gave way to a distant commotion. They crossed a shallow valley and topped the next ridge. The indistinct ruckus grew into a cacophony of boisterous squawking, chattering, and screeching blue herons.

The rookery occupied the trees on the opposite bank. Everywhere, the big beautiful birds were continually taking off and landing, tending nests, feeding young, courting mates, and chasing rivals. The racket they made was incredible.

Blake grinned at the pandemonium. "I forgot that the book said that they roost in trees! They look so funny, you don't expect to see big, leggy birds like that standing around in trees!"

"You're looking at about a hundred twenty-five nests. That's what a park ranger told me. And that's Highland Creek down there." Mia spread out the blanket and they sat down.

"Why didn't we just come up the creek instead of going the long way around?"

"Because the long way is easier than paddling against the current and you don't really want to be right under all those birds do you? Think about it, Tux. What's the main dock at the sailing club got all over it?"

"Looks like somebody spilled a bucket of white paint."

"That ain't paint, buddy."

"Ohhhh yuck!"

"And that was just one bird. Here, you like pudding? I brought tapioca."

"You are not even funny, Mia!" he laughed. "What do you have in *your* pack."

"My lunch, laminated nature guides, a map of the park, pepper spray, a whistle, and a roll of toilet paper. You are here." She pointed to a spot at the right extremity of the map. "And this dotted line is the trail we're on."

"Okay, wow, it goes all the way between park headquarters, clear to the channel."

"And if you weren't exhausted from the six mile trek, you could swim the last half mile home to the sailing club."

Blake stared at the map pensively.

"What are you thinking about, Tux?"

"Home. I don't know where home is," he said. "It's funny. I feel like the sailing club *is* kind of my home, now. They're supposed to do my lifetime membership at the board meeting tonight."

"Congrats."

"But if they believe what Hunter says, they won't let me in. In fact, they'll probably kick me out and my uncle too."

"You'll just have to stand up for yourself," she said.

"But wait, you and Griffy were there, you guys could…"

Mia peered into the depths of her pack and rooted around for nothing in particular.

"I'm afraid I'm not in a position to help you with that one."

"Why not?" Mia could see the hurt on his face. "Because I'm just lake trash?"

"Where did that come from? I didn't say that! Are you touchy or what? Do you think I'm just a stuck up shore bird?"

"No! I don't think of you as a shore bird at all. You act more like a laker."

"Watch it, buddy! You've only been here two weeks. How would you know anyway?"

"I dunno, I guess because I spend all my time with lake people? You know, like Mr. Gunn and Uncle Carson, Ray and Elsie, and Beverly Maitland? And what's wrong with lakers anyway? They made this place their own because they loved it. The shore birds bought it all up just because they wanted to own it. My Grandfather was a laker. Did I tell you he built the sailing club?"

"No. Are you kidding me?"

"It's true. My Granddad and Tripper Gunn. They're the ones who got the State to make the park and they set up the sailing club. Designed and built it all from the ground up. Nineteen-fifty-eight. They wanted this place to be for everyone."

Mia was quiet for a moment. "I'm sorry I snapped at you. But you have to understand something. If I show up at that meeting with you…Let's just say that "hellish" only scratches the surface of what my life will be like. But there may be something else I can do to help. We'll just have to see."

"I'm sorry for snapping at you, too. I guess I'm too sensitive. You don't still think my uncle and Mr. Gunn are stealing your dad's business do you?"

"I guess I was just being defensive about that. The old guy is still crabby as all-get-out, though."

"He can be. But I'm starting to see he has a good side to him." Blake unwrapped his sandwich and opened his chips. "You want some?"

They broke bread together and looked over the field guides. On the map Mia pointed out Thompson's Cave, and where the egrets roosted, and a place called Stone Hollow. Then they waded upstream from the rookery and spent a while catching tadpoles and crawdads, and scooping up minnows with their hands.

Once back in the kayak, they rode the creek's gradually diminishing current for a half mile before bothering to paddle again. In an hour and a half they were in home waters. As they skirted Trespass Island, Blake spotted a mother mallard negotiating the lily-pad shallows with a dozen brown, peeping fuzz-balls in tow. She led her brood into open water then circled back around and quacked impatiently at the edge of the lilies. Two more peeping fuzz-balls popped out of the green maze and joined their siblings. Mama gave a couple of scolding quacks and they continued on their way.

Nature, Blake thought to himself, *is not indifferent.* However heartwarming the reunion of the ducks may have been, the cold reality of the excursion's end lay directly before him.

"Take me back to Thistle Bay. Let me off below the clubhouse," Blake said. He was alarmed to see that the shattered halves of the canoe had been pulled up on the little strip of beach and lay neatly beside one another, their varnished ribs glinting in the sun like the dried carcass of some giant fish. He retrieved his pack from the hatch. "Well, thanks for everything. I guess this is probably goodbye."

"Don't give up so fast, Tux. Don't back down. If it doesn't go your way, find a way around the opposition and come back with a vengeance. You can do it."

"Thanks for believing in me."

Mia smiled. "I've gotta get going. I have a few phone calls to make. It was a great day." She made it sound as if all of her days began with hand-to-hand combat.

***

Blake was a bundle of nerves. Carson was nowhere to be found. Ray and Elsie were still away, as Tuesday was the groundskeeper's day off. It was highly unusual for the club to be so completely deserted this late in the afternoon. He wondered if the commodore would bring Hunter and maybe the police. He'd heard the bogey-man stories at church—about kids being snatched away by Child Protective Services at the mere hint of neglect made by some false accuser. Where would they go if they were kicked out of the club? Nanna's house in Pemberton. His stomach was in knots again.

The hot and stuffy attic offered no solace. Blake switched on a huge exhaust fan at the north end of the gallery. The breeze helped, but he was still sweaty, gritty, and miserable. An hour and a half still remained before the dreaded meeting. He decided a cool shower would be just the thing.

Blake shoved the little spool table aside as he pulled his suitcase from beneath his cot. Out of the corner of his eye, he caught something pop out of the hole in the table's center. Instinctively, he shrieked and leapt backwards six feet, still grasping the unzipped suitcase. Underwear flew everywhere. The knots in his gut liquefied. Salty sweat stung his eyes. There, in the middle of the table, sat a meaty black arachnid. He drew a deep breath and let go with a furious cry. He lunged at the table and slammed the suitcase down. It echoed like thunder through the gallery. Blake clubbed the table mercilessly, though the spider was obliterated by that first wild swing. He shouted every curse-word he'd ever learned on the playground after Sunday school.

Blake staggered back a few steps, red in the face. With the last bit of his rage he flung the suitcase clear to the other end of the attic. He was absolutely staggered by what he'd just done—what he had just accomplished. He gathered up his wardrobe, tossed it in a pile on the cot and went downstairs. He was right: a cool shower was just the thing.

***

Gunn scrutinized a long scoring-sheet on the Lightning Fleet's bulletin board. He looked over the tops of his glasses and poked a gnarled index finger from place to place on the chart as he hummed to himself. Blake carried his dirty clothes out of the locker room, wrapped up in a damp towel. Gunn turned around with a sort of shuffle, shrugged his broad shoulders and spread his hands in the air. "Where is everybody, lad?" he said, smiling.

"I don't know. They were gone when I got back."

"I hope they'll show up soon. Otherwise it'll be life or death on a lee shore for us both, Caduggin!"

"I guess you've heard, then?"

"I heard the fan going' upstairs. Yeh go switch it off and open the registers. Get that place cooled down."

"But…"

"Don't come down 'til six o'clock. And here, stoof this in yer pookit, and bring it with yeh." He winked and tossed Blake a piece of mangled metal, like a big chrome pretzel with two long, bolts protruding from one end. "That's your insurance policy. Don' forget it! Now get on with it!"

"Yes sir." He ascended the stairs, realizing that this pretzel was a souvenir from the chain-gang incident.

***

Board-members rolled into the parking lot in a steady stream. Chatting and laughing they sauntered into the clubhouse like the last grains of sand in an hourglass. "Here's the jury, now where's the judge?" Blake whispered to himself. He found the answer at the opposite window. Commodore Devlin was securing *Eclipse* to the main dock. He was alone. Blake studied the twisted tow-ring, turning it every which way. Devlin, in white hat and black blazer, ascended the hill. Blake glanced across to Carson's empty cot and down the gallery where red sail-bags hung in dusty sunbeams. The back door squeaked open and thumped shut. The hour appointed had finally come.

He tried to remember all the advice that Mia had given him, that *anyone* had given him. "Father in Heaven," he said, "Be thou my help."

Fifty people milled about the crowded great room. The tables had been moved to the far end and the chairs arranged in rows before which a long table with four laptop computers had been set up. Another man in a black jacket gave a brass ship's bell, mounted over the galley door, several ear-splitting clangs. "Lets come to order, people! We have a lot of ground to cover this evening!"

Everyone found their seats, many still gabbed over their shoulders as they sat down. From the stairs Blake spotted Gunn in the back row. The old man motioned him to an empty seat between himself and Beverly Maitland.

"Where on earth is your uncle, Caduggin?"

"I was going to ask you."

The commodore brought the meeting officially to order and began the tedious process of calling the roll and determining if a quorum was present. He did not notice Blake in the back row.

"Mr. Gunn, what's going to happen?"

Gunn only put a finger to his lips. Beverly smiled that knowing, grandmotherly smile at him and patted him on the knee.

"In light of today's shocking events," began Devlin, "I move that we address old business after the present situation is resolved." A hushed murmur rippled through the crowd. The butterflies in Blake's stomach turned into bats.

Someone in the first row raised their hand and said "I second the motion!"

"All in favor?" said the commodore.

"Aye!" replied the crowd.

"Opposed?" No one answered. "Motion carried unanimously."

Gunn gave Blake a sidelong glance and whispered "Did yeh bring it?"

"It's in me pookit."

Gunn snorted approvingly.

The commodore stood up. "What I have to say is so difficult that it will not be easy for many of you to believe. This is indeed the most awful day in the otherwise proud history of our club. As some of you may know, my son and his two friends, Lance Hopkins and Mark Bader, were the victims of a violent and cowardly attack, on club property this morning."

Another murmur, less restrained, rolled through the room.

"They were paddling their canoe in Thistle Bay when someone set fire to a dead tree on the bluff and pushed it down on them."

Shocked exclamations splashed the air like giant waves against a seawall.

"Luckily my son was not injured but Mark has three cracked ribs and Lance suffered a concussion. And our priceless Yukon Voyager canoe was also destroyed in the incident." Gasps of disbelief followed.

"Yes, I know. But don't worry—the guys are going to be okay. I know this is all terribly shocking but I am afraid it only gets worse."

"Here it comes, lad. Just sit tight." said Gunn.

"The Highland Creek Sailing Club has had the pleasure of entertaining a guest for the past few weeks. Many of you know Carson Urquart's nephew, Blake. We had hoped to welcome him this evening as our newest legacy member. But I am sorry to have to tell you that this will not be possible, because—it was Blake Barber who nearly killed our three young men this morning.

Now a tumult of disbelief and horror erupted in the room. Several calls of "Order!" were required to quell it.

"I have filed a report with the Freeman Police Department. Officers will be here shortly to take the boy into custody." Blake's heart skipped a beat. The anxiety was unbearable, more so even than when his mother left him on the porch in the howling wind.

"As I said, Highland Creek Sailing Club is a proud and storied institution. But times and people are changing and not for the better. In light of today's tragedy I believe this is an appropriate occasion to review the relevance and fiscal sensibility of maintaining the outdated policies of legacy and lifetime memberships. It also saddens me deeply to say that, ultimately, Carson must be held responsible for his nephew's actions, and we will have to call his future with the club into question as well."

Devlin paused to allow the crowd to soak up the tragedy in full measure. Lively chatter began to fill the air.

As if on cue, the front door opened. Blake was relieved to see Carson enter but a wave of cold panic washed over him when he saw that his uncle was followed by a burly man in uniform. It was a state park police officer.

Commodore Devlin smiled, smugly satisfied with his performance. His computer chimed and softly spoke the words "You have an important message." He ignored it and prepared to quiet the room and deliver the final, triumphant blow. The phone in the alcove rang. Carson trotted into the side hall to answer it. He returned, waving a hand to get the commodore's attention.

"That was for you!" he shouted over the crowd. "Some lady from the PD says you need to check your email, right now!"

Lawrence Devlin looked down at the screen. A sudden expression of urgent concern seized his face. He sat on the edge of his chair and read the subject line under his breath. "Freeman Police Department Official Business?" He opened the message.

The vice commodore noticed he'd gone as white as the muck on the main dock. "Is everything okay, Larry? It's not about the boys, is it? Larwrence?"

Devlin startled. "After all I've done. Sold me out," he mumbled in disbelief.

Carson sat down next to Gunn and winked at Blake. Beverly Maitland stood up and raised her hand.

"Order!" called the secretary. Devlin continued to stare at the screen. Puzzled by the commodore's distress, Vice Commodore Trudeau took over. "Beverly you have the floor."

"Thank you, Vice Commodore. I have asked Lieutenant Buck Mueller from the park police to come and address the board, concerning his department's investigation of today's events."

Devlin slowly closed the lid of his laptop and with lips drawn tight as bowstrings, consented. "By all means. The Chair recognizes Officer Mueller."

The big man stood by the club officers' table. "Ah, like Mrs. Maitland said, she asked me to come and make a statement about our investigation into the alleged incident this morning. The Freeman Police Department received the original report that there had been a battery with multiple injuries on sailing club property this morning."

Everyone was riveted to the officer's words. Lawrence Devlin's color had returned, but more deeply red than usual.

"Now, you probably know that the FPD would normally handle this sort of thing, because the sailing club is private and not park property. But we received a report from a Ms. Judy Williams this morning and another anonymous report this afternoon advising us that part of the alleged incident took place on the lake, which *is* our jurisdiction. When our agency contacted FPD about the issue we discovered that Ms. Williams had also filed a report with them, as well. So, the chief asked us to take it over, in the interest of preventing confusion and duplication of effort."

"Thank you for you time, Officer," said Devlin.

"You're welcome," he replied, "but I haven't made the report yet." There was an uncomfortable silence. Someone cleared their throat. Blake straightened up to get a better view of Devlin and Mueller. It seemed as though something miraculously good might be happening.

"Ms. Williams reported that her son alleged that he and two friends had been talking at the foot of the ridge on your peninsula, when they were attacked by three assailants which he identified as Mark Bader, Lance Hopkins, and Hunter Devlin. Ms. Williams' son escaped by jumping into the lake and swimming away. It is not known what happened to the other two youths. After FPD turned the case over to our agency, we conducted an investigation on your grounds and found evidence that there had been a struggle on your property and that a tree had been pushed down, requiring considerable effort, and that it showed signs of exposure to fire, but had not actually caught on fire, and had apparently struck and destroyed a large wooden canoe in the cove adjacent to the south shore of your peninsula, known as Thistle Bay."

"Thank you." said the commodore again, shifting in his seat as if he were about to rise.

The officer smiled wryly. "Hold on, sir. I'm almost done. Happy hour still has thirty minutes!" There was snickering in the audience. "We received an anonymous tip this afternoon by someone who said they witnessed one of the victims trapped high in that tree, being menaced by an assailant with a torch, who then used it to push the tree down. The fire damage to the tree trunk is consistent with that report, so we are taking it as a credible witness. We are now in the process of obtaining statements from the young men who were injured on your property and are still trying to locate your son, Mr. Devlin, and Blake Barber for questioning." All eyes shifted to Commodore Devlin.

"My son left this afternoon for a three week golf clinic in Florida. I will have him contact you as soon as I can reach him." Devlin stood up and addressed the astonished board members, whose faces clearly showed their readiness to hear how he was going to explain *this* one. Officer Mueller retired to the back of the room.

"I do not know what to say. Clearly, I have been misinformed. I owe you all an apology. When your child calls you from the hospital and tells you that he and his friends were nearly killed, your first instinct is to believe him. I am deeply hurt to have been deceived by my son in this way and shamed by his behavior."

"Aha! Plausible deniability. He's one cool cat!" whispered Carson. Gunn grunted in agreement. Blake was just trying to keep from laughing for joy. He was sure he knew the name of that anonymous caller.

"I know that I can continue to count on your support as we work together to get past this unfortunate situation. I really must excuse myself now. Vice Commodore Trudeau will conduct the rest of this meeting. Bill?"

Beverly sprang to her feet. "I think you need to apologize to Carson and Blake, Mr. Commodore!"

He froze. There were several cries of "here, here!"

"I didn't realize that the boy was here! Well, I...am...truly sorry," he said, nearly choking on the words.

"Ask him aboot the chain, lad." Gunn urged Blake. "Go on, stand up and ask him!"

Now it clicked. Blake understood why Gunn had given him the

mangled souvenir. Devlin had turned to pick up his notebook and the vice commodore was about to speak when Blake stood up and said nervously, "Mr. Commodore, I think I have something that belongs to you."

Devlin turned around and strained his eyes to recognize the shiny object that the boy was holding up. "What are you talking about? What is that? Is this some kind of joke, young man? This is what I mean about kids, today."

"It was shackled to the end of two hundred feet of anchor chain. We found the other end wrapped around the sail shed."

"I don't know what you're talking about, son. That's not mine, whatever it is." He turned again to pick up his notebook.

"It's got purple and yellow paint on it, so I thought it might have come off your motorboat. It's in the shop for repairs right now, isn't it? Your big, noisy, one hundred forty mile per hour, *purple-and-yellow* motor boat?"

Carson was grinning deeply, Gunn beamed with pride. Beverly got their attention, pointed at Blake and mouthed the word "lawyer!"

"That's not mine, kid," insisted Devlin, making his way to the door.

"What should I do with the chain?"

"Keep it!" was the commodore's terse reply as he left the building. There was a mixture of applause and cheering from the commodore's less-ardent supporters. The vice commodore allowed it for a minute, then called for order.

A motion was made and carried to proceed with the immediate review of Blake's membership application. Mr. Trudeau called him to stand before the remaining officers.

"Blake, we've never met. But Mrs. Maitland has told me a lot about you and I think you will make a fine addition to our club. But membership in the Highland Creek Sailing Club carries with it a certain amount of responsibility. There are rules and regulations. Do's and don'ts. There are standards of personal conduct you will be expected to maintain. Do you understand that?"

He felt the eyes of everyone in the room upon him. "Yes sir."

"And do you agree to abide by those rules and always behave in a way that honors and builds respect for our club in the community?"

Blake thought for a moment, gathering his courage. Gunn watched intently, grasping his chin with one hand. Carson ran his fingers down his mustache.

"Will Hunter Devlin be held to the same standards, Mr. Trudeau?" he asked, respectfully.

Carson cringed a little. Gunn nodded to himself. "Good job! That's the way, lad." he whispered.

"Well, Blake, that is a fair question and I will tell you that you are not the first person to ask it. We expect everyone to follow club rules. Even if you see that someone else is not. Even if they seem to be getting away with it all the time, you are still responsible for playing by the rules. You have to trust that the officers of this board and the directors of this club will do the right thing and deal appropriately with the bad actors." He looked to the assembly, fixing his gaze on certain individuals here and there. Raising his voice, he asked, "Isn't that right?"

There were many calls of "here, here!" and some clapping.

"And it is our responsibility to demonstrate these values to the next generation of club members, is it not? Because they are the future of inland sailing." There was more vocal approval and applause.

"What Commodore Devlin said was true. Because of your age, your sponsors—Carson and Mr. Gunn—are responsible for your conduct. If you get in trouble, they get in trouble. So, do you still want to be a member of the Highland Creek Sailing Club, Blake?"

Blake thought hard for a moment. "I really want to, Mr. Trudeau," he said. "But honestly, I don't think we've seen the last of Hunter Devlin. He'll come after me again and I don't want Uncle Carson and Mr. Gunn to take the blame for anything that happens."

Trudeau smiled a proud, fatherly smile. "Blake, are you up for adoption?" The crowd chuckled warmly. "You leave Hunter to us, Blake. Ladies and gentlemen, based upon personal interviews and the references presented on this application, I move that Blake Alan Barber, grandson and legacy of our founder Declan Urquart, be accepted as a lifetime member of the Highland Creek Sailing Club."

"Second!" cried Beverly Maitland.

"All in favor?"

"Aye!" roared the majority.

"Opposed?" There was silence.

"Abstain?"

A dozen hands went up with the low moan "abstain."

"Motion carried, Thirty-eight in favor, none opposed, twelve abstentions. Welcome to the club, Blake!"

Almost everyone in the room stood and applauded. Vice Commodore Trudeau, the secretary, and the treasurer all shook his hand in turn, as did everyone on the way back to his seat.

Carson met him at the back row with a firm hand shake. "Good job kid. You did yourself proud!"

Beverly gave him a big hug over the back of her chair. "You are just amazing, young man!"

Gunn patted him on the back. "First rate, Caduggin!"

"You keep calling me that. I've been wanting to ask you what that means?" he said, from the depths of Beverly's unrelenting embrace.

"Caduggin? It's Celtic. Means 'battle victory!' Mrs. Maitland, when yer done smothering the lad, I think the officer would like a word with 'im!"

Vice Commodore Trudeau again called for order, motioning to the sergeant-at-arms to clang the bell by the galley. The board members settled back into their seats.

***

Carson shut the leaded glass doors of the library. Blake took to his favorite wingback chair and closed the large, bird book on the coffee table.

You've had quite a day, I hear," said Buck Mueller, as he sat down. "It must have been terrifying."

"That was the scariest thing that has *ever* happened to me."

"Blake, I don't know if you understand this, but several of the things that happened this morning are serious crimes. We intend to get to the bottom of this and prosecute the guilty parties. We need your help to do that. I need you to tell me everything you can remember about this morning's events. As much detail as you can remember—what people did, what they said, the clothes they were wearing, every little thing is important. Don't leave anything out, okay?"

Blake gave a careful account of the morning's attack and the incidents that led up to it, while Officer Mueller wrote busily in a notebook.

"Blake, do you know how Lance Hopkins and Mark Bader sustained such serious injuries?"

Mueller leaned forward and looked particularly attentive. Blake wilted.

"Um, I only saw them running toward us. I turned and ran. I didn't see them again until Mia and I were on our way out of Thistle Bay. Bader was crawling, holding his side, and Hopkins was stumbling around throwing up."

"You don't have any idea what happened to them? Your girlfriend didn't mention anything?"

"She's not my girlfriend! I mean, we're just friends. She had her kayak tied up to the last dock. Maybe they hurt themselves trying to get to her."

"Three broken ribs and a concussion?" Carson said, squinting suspiciously at his nephew.

"Blake," continued Mueller, "Mia is not in trouble—anything but. If she was defending herself, we need to know. They could say she attacked them, just like they did you."

"Honestly, I don't know what happened, down there. She told me later that…" He shifted his gaze from his uncle's increasingly stern expression to the Officer's countenance of courteous, professional patience. "She said that Hunter and his friends were a threat to her safety and she knew nobody would protect her, so she enrolled in Karate lessons."

"Anything else?" asked Mueller. Blake looked as if he were about to cry.

"Now either you've said too much, or too little, Blake," Carson prodded. "What is it?"

Tears rolled down his cheeks. "I don't know. She just acts like any little trouble she gets in is going to cause big problems for her at home. I think she means with her mom."

"But what else did she say?" said Carson.

"She said she…sent them to the hospital, guaranteed. That's all."

Mueller closed his notebook and leaned forward. "What you, Griffin Williams, and our anonymous caller have told me matches up perfectly. We have a warrant out for Hunter's arrest. If he really is in Florida we'll have to extradite him, and that could take awhile. His old man probably has three lawyers running interference already."

"You sound like this isn't the first time you've done this," said Blake, wiping his nose.

The officer chuckled. "Not hardly! But it's never been anything like this before. Blake, you should be proud of yourself. It took a lot of courage to do the things you've done today. We'll need you and your friends to testify when we finally bring this guy to court. If you think of anything else, no matter how insignificant it may seem, you give me a call, okay?" Mueller handed Blake a business card. "In fact, if you ever need anything, just give me a buzz."

Officer Mueller stood and shook hands with Blake and Carson. "How would you and your friends like to take a ride in ol' *Moby*?"

Blake brightened up. "I *would* like that!"

"You're on! Oh, did you say Mia takes Karate lessons?"

"And violin," Blake remembered, before he could stop himself.

"Excellent. In town?"

"I don't know. *Honestly*," Blake said, glancing at his uncle.

"Blake, I need to talk to Mia and I may have to pay her a surprise visit to do that. That might not work so well if she knows that I know where to look for her. Do you understand?"

"Yes sir," he replied. He felt like he'd just betrayed his one and only friend.

***

Blake re-folded the last of his shirts and tucked them into his suitcase. The embers of another glorious sunset were fading over the horizon. The light over the stairs flicked on and the steps creaked under the weary feet of his uncle. Carson emerged from the stairwell, carrying his shaving kit.

"How did *you* know?" he said, almost sneering.

"Know what? I dumped my suitcase. I was just picking up."

Carson threw his kit bag down on his own cot in disgust. "Just as well. We have to leave."

"Leave? When? Why?"

"We're not exactly maintaining a low-profile, kid. They can't just keep on turning a blind eye. Oh well, I told 'em I'd be out of here three months ago anyway." Carson collapsed on the cot.

"What did they say?"

"Trudeau cornered me and let me know that he and the directors appreciate everything we've done for the club but, considering current circumstances, it would be best if we weren't squatting here. I told him we'd be out in the morning."

"Where are we going to go?" Then it dawned on him. "We're not going back to Pemberton are we? I mean, I like it here! All my friends are here! I just got used to it, now we have to leave!" he rattled out, in a near panic. "I don't...just...do we *have* to go to Pemberton?"

Carson scratched his head. "Umm, I was thinking plan 'A' might be to get a tent and rough it at one of the Drascombe campgrounds."

Blake contemplated that for a moment then remembered to breathe. "Okay, that sounds like a good idea. How about Blue Rock Recreation Area?"

"Hmm. Interesting choice. We just rebuilt the johns, there."

"And I painted the monkey bars and the merry-go-round. And there's a white-sand beach, and a pier where Mr. Gunn can pick us up."

"Alright. I'll have Tripp take us over to Freeman tomorrow and we'll get a tent. I'm beat. It's time to assume the horizontal."

Carson wriggled to get comfortable, more exasperated than exhausted. Blake couldn't help but feel that he was somehow to blame. His insecurity drove him to make small talk. Yet Blake had discovered that you could get the best information out of Carson just before he dozed off.

"Why does Mr. Gunn call me 'Caduggin?'"

"Hah, Caduggin! Biggest, meanest, orange-est shop-cat you ever saw. Used to have his own cushion on a whiskey barrel, just inside the front door of Tripp's old boat shop. If he didn't like you when you walked in he'd flatten his ears back and growl like the devil at you. Good judge of character, that old cat! He either hated you or loved you the minute you walked through the door. Those guys that worked for Tripp back then used to torment him something awful—but could that cat ever dish it right back to 'em. Gunn made those guys buy their own first aid stuff, they went through so much of it! I had a girlfriend back then. She ran the office. Caduggin would bring her mouse heads and bird guts all the time. I remember Tripper walking in one day and here's the cat on her lap, and he growls at the old man himself!"

Carson gave a snort and added, "After Dad died, Caduggin became Tripper Gunn's best friend and closest companion. Long time ago. Long time. Hit the lights, kid."

Blake turned out the attic lights and laid himself down to contemplate this curious revelation.

Chapter 14

The *Terrapin* cut a zig-zag course up the channel, Blake at the helm. Tripper sat on the low side of the cockpit, giving orders and instructing him on the finer points of boat handling and sail trim. Carson skulked in the cabin, only emerging to tack the jib when Blake would call "ready about! hard a'lee!"

Within forty minutes they struck sail and Gunn motored them up to the Freeman waterfront. Blake was first onto the dock and secured the *Terrapin* to her berth with spring lines fore and aft. He basked in Gunn's glowing approval.

"That's good, lad! Yeh run on, now; I need to talk to yer uncle. Mind yeh be back here by ten-thirty."

"Um, okay," he replied, looking to his uncle for final permission.

"Whatever, kid. I guess Tripp's calling the shots today," said Carson, visibly annoyed.

Blake jogged off the dock, up the steps to the overlook, and vanished into the park.

"What was *that* all about?" Carson said.

"Carson, I like that boy. I've never seen a better boy than that."

"What are you getting at, Long John?"

"Urquart *you* need to cultivate that child."

"I don't get you." Carson backed into the companionway and put one bare foot down on the step.

"He's been uprooted and cast out from everything he's known. Now he's wanting to put down roots here and grow again. Yeh need to cultivate that."

"What are you talking about? He's got everything a kid could want here! Comes and goes as he pleases, he's got friends, and I gave him every dangerous toy a boy his age should have. What more does he need?"

"That's what I'm trying to tell yeh. He needs family. It's fine to play the indulgent uncle for a few weeks, but he needs to feel like someone's investing in him."

"Well good luck with that one." Carson retreated into the cabin. "Where are my sandals?" He rummaged around for a couple of minutes. "Besides, it'd serve his dad right if I sent the kid home looking like a biker." When he returned to the cockpit it was to face the stony scowl that was the old Scotsman's trademark.

"Yeh'd no ruin that lad Carson and yeh know it. But he's becoming a young man and looking for his place in the world. He's trying to find where he fits in and it's only natural for him take to yer lead. Yeh rest assured if you don't, he'll start taking his cues from that girl or worse— Griffy."

"Now just what's wrong with Griffy?"

"He's a smart-ass, he's disrespectful, he does'na face up to responsibility. And his mother lets him get away with it just because his father died!"

"Just what are you saying about me?"

"I'm no saying anything aboot *you*! I'm talking aboot Griffy!"

"No, I don't think you are. Look, Blake's a great kid but I didn't sign up for this!"

"Yeh've no signed up for anything since the Navy!"

"You do not know what you are talking about!" shouted Carson.

"And yer impossible to reason with when yer in a mood! Get the hell off my boot!"

"It ain't *your* boot!"

"Then get the hell off *yer* boot!"

"Well, I don't mind if I do!" Carson hopped up on the bench and leapt over the side onto the dock. "'Scuse me!"

The old man set his jaw and sighed.

Blake slunk through the park, keeping well off the beaten path. He nervously avoided the main drag at all costs, choosing to take a side street into town. He hurried along for several blocks, not sure where he really wanted to go. He paused in front of the public library to take his bearings. Two carved stone monks squatted weirdly on either side of the arch above the entrance, each perusing a nameless stone book. He stared at them blankly for a moment. Someone shouted "Boo!" right behind him.

Blake gave a startled yelp and spun around. "I figured it would be you!"

"Relax, Tux! Hunter's in Miami," said Mia, biting into an apple.

"Are you sure?"

"Sure I'm sure. I got an email from my cousin this morning. My uncle has him stuck away on one of his resorts. He won't be able to make a move without me hearing about it. C'mon, let's go inside. You *could* offer to carry my violin for me, if you'd *like* to," she said, handing him the black case.

Blake took the case, embarrassed at missing the cue. He trotted up the steps and held the door for her. She rewarded him with a lovely smile. They settled into an overstuffed loveseat in a little reading nook on the main floor. Mia sank into one corner facing Blake, an arm across the back, one leg on the cushion. He sat with both feet on the floor, arms crossed.

"You still look a little uptight about something, Tux. What's eating you?"

"Mia, I need to… But, I can't…"

"Yes?" she replied, with raised eyebrows and an expectant smile.

"I… Officer Mueller…"

"Is going to intercept me before my violin lesson for a round of questioning, this morning?"

"He did? I didn't mean to tell him. I didn't want to tell him about the Karate either, but he's the police and my uncle looked so mad at me."

"I didn't tell you *not* to tell, did I? Don't sweat it. We had a nice talk. I told him everything he wanted to know."

"Really?"

"Oh, I ratted on Junior, but good. I've been waiting for this for five years, Blake. And now that he's eighteen it isn't going to be so easy for him to get off the hook. I hear that Daddy has three lawyers on the job already, but I think they'll get him this time."

"Seriously? Three? Where does he get *that* kind of money?"

"The old-fashioned way. He inherited it."

"What if he does get off the hook? How long before he shows up here again?"

"A month, give or take a week. So, better enjoy it while it lasts!"

"At least he won't know where to find me."

"How's that?"

"My uncle and I can't stay at the club, anymore. Because of all the trouble. I think we're going to camp over at Blue Rock. That's why we're here, my uncle is buying a tent."

"That's not too far out of the way. I'll find you. I'd give you my cell phone number but I never have it turned on. Best way to get hold of me is to call Treva at the Emporium, leave a message."

"Thanks! You know, I…" He looked at her with a soft expression, "I've never had a friend like you."

"You're a really nice boy, Tux. But I have two rules. Don't be a suck-up and don't fall in love with me."

His face flushed a little and his almost-thirteen-year-old pride bristled, but he kept a lid on it.

"I'll see what I can do," he said.

"Hey, what do you say we go over to the Emporium? They make the best sticky buns in the world."

"I've got to be back at the boat in an hour. Is there enough time?"

"There's always time for sticky buns!"

***

The clatter and clink of the breakfast rush filled the Emporium's dining room. The smell of coffee and pancakes, sausage and syrup blended into a rich aroma that soothed the soul like a cozy blanket on a rainy Saturday morning. Mia and Blake had scarcely stepped through the door when Mia called out "Hey Blondie!"

"Hay is for horses!" said the waitress from the far end of the dining counter. "I've got two for you right here, hon. Let me get 'em cleaned off. Buns and tea for two?"

"Make it snappy woman!" said Mia cheerfully.

They sat down on the swiveling counter stools. Blake loved the place and had begun to tell Mia about the German plaque when he noticed who was sitting next to her. He stopped mid sentence and stared. She looked to her left.

"Nice to see you again, Miss Devlin!" said Buck Mueller, leaning on his elbows, sipping coffee.

"Good mornin' lass!" said Gunn, over Mueller's shoulder.

"Miss Treva," said Mueller as she returned with the tea and buns. "They're on my ticket."

"Thank you, Buck," said Mia, blushing.

"We're just goin' now," said Gunn, rising to his feet. "Take yer time lad. Yer uncle'll be anguishing over tents for another hour. Oh, and I've got a business proposition to discuss with yeh, so don' let me forget."

Mueller tucked a five dollar bill under his mug and accompanied Gunn to the cash register at the far end of the long counter.

"That was odd," said Blake.

"Very."

"You're on a first-name basis with Officer Mueller?"

"So?"

Treva returned with a plate of eggs and hash browns, setting it down in front of Blake. "Is this for me? I didn't order anything."

"Boss says a growing boy needs to eat. You don't want to upset the boss, do ya?"

"I guess I'd better not! Please tell him I said thank you." He was beginning to feel a lot less guilty about accepting the royal treatment.

"You bet, hon! You got the day off, girlie?" Treva said, turning her attention to Mia.

"Yup! Permanently."

"No! What happened?"

"Rosaria told me that Dad called this morning and said I didn't need to show my face around the shop anymore."

"You're kidding me?" gasped Treva. She leaned on the counter and asked in a hushed tone, "This doesn't have anything to do with Bader and Hopkins, does it?"

"And Junior. I think he's done it, this time. We'll see."

"Tell me everything! I want to hear every detail! How many lawyers?" she said, with a hungry grin. "How are those eggs darlin'? You want a glass of chocolate milk? Charlie! Brown Cow, here! Now, start at the beginning."

"Order up, Treva!" called a voice from the kitchen. "Treva! Work now, gossip later!"

"Ahh, Charlie doesn't know what he's missing. Catch up to me tonight, kiddo!"

"See you later, Blondie."

"She's really nice," Blake said.

"Heart of gold."

"So, is Rosaria your mom?"

"Get serious! My mom wouldn't answer the phone if she ever *was* home. Rosaria is the head of our housekeeping staff."

"Staff?"

"Yeah, staff. You don't think I'm going to vacuum nine-thousand square feet of house, do you?"

Blake mouthed the words "nine-thousand" silently to himself. "What does your mom do?"

"Real estate. One of the most successful agents in the region. Probably in Chicago right now. Rosaria is part of my spy network. Half of our staff is related to my dad's staff. Anything interesting that happens at Dad's house goes from his people to mom's people, to Rosaria, to me."

"You spy on your dad, too?"

"You bet. I'm going to get them both, one day," she said, in a cold, convincing tone.

Blake looked down at his eggs. He had long dreamed of seeing his sister get what she deserved and of escaping his own father's loveless, obsessive control. But his conscience never let him fully enjoy those fantasies. His mother had taught him too well: *Repay not evil for evil; Vengeance is mine, saith the Lord.* he thought. *Thou shalt honor thy father and thy mother.* That one was the hardest to comprehend—the father part, anyway.

"What did you say?" said Mia.

"Huh?" said Blake, with a start.

"You were spacing out, then you said something about "mother and father."

"Oh yeah. I was just remembering the Ten Commandments. Thou shalt honor thy mother and thy father."

"The ten what?"

"You don't know the Ten Commandments? You know, as in Moses, God, the Bible?"

"Nope, I can't say that I'm familiar with them. We've never had anything to do with religion."

Before he could elaborate, Mia nudged him and said "C'mon eat your eggs and we'll play some pinball!"

***

Blake and Mia meandered through the towering cottonwoods and catalpas of Waterfront park. The leaves rustled and branches swayed. By the time they reached the green iron railing of the promenade, dark clouds had crowded out most of the blue sky. Blake picked out the *Terrapin* from several houseboats now berthed at the long dock. "There's Mr. Gunn!" He waved his arm over his head. The old man waved back from the cockpit. "I guess Uncle Carson isn't back yet."

"Please, just let it rain!" Mia pleaded to the sky. "We haven't had a drop for a month. My beautiful marshes are drying up."

"Yeah, Ray finally had to turn the sprinklers on. The hill was becoming a fire hazard. I hope it doesn't storm." As if on cue, a distant rumble sounded in the southwest. His stomach began to tingle. White strobe lights flashed from atop cell towers scattered along the horizon and from the dam's intake turret, as if warning of things to come.

"Is there anything you're not afraid of?" she said.

"Just you!"

"You'll learn, kid. I love storms," she said, unconvincingly. "But I think it's just going to rain."

"No, this is a definitely a gust front, there's bound to be a squall line brewing up behind it."

"Whatever, Mr. Professor. And you know this how?"

"I came, I saw, I read a book. You should try it some time."

"In that case, give me my violin. I want to get home before it lets loose."

"Not shipping in that square boat there, are ye?" Called a haggard voice from down the sidewalk. A thin, stubble-faced man with a mane of gray hair and nose like a shark fin ambled up. His blue-jeans were ratty, his white dress shirt was wrinkled and untucked. He pointed an accusing finger at the *Terrapin* as he approached.

"The shoebox! The boat with no ends?"

"Yes, I am. So what?" said Blake. He hoisted the black violin case up to his chest. "Who are you, anyway?"

"Call me Kalijah, son! Not signed with the old Scot, have ye? Not shipping with old Gunn?" he said, still advancing. Kalijah was close enough to smell now. "Have they told thee how he built this lake and owns half the souls upon it? Doesn't own thine yet, does he? 'Who needs one,' says ye!"

Mia and Blake began a slow, backwards retreat toward the landing.

"How many times do I have to tell you, Garvey? Beer isn't just for breakfast anymore!" said Mia.

"Did they tell thee how he cheated the Devil? 'No, of course not,' says ye! Here ye be with the Devil's own daughter! Have ye seen the white hound, son? Heard him howl for the thunder and the hail? I saw him just this morning, heard him call to the Almighty for judgment on the unrighteous! Mark my words son, it'll hail like cannonballs and the boat with no ends will go down!"

Finally, they reached the landing. Blake, mesmerized by the spellbinding vagrant, backed into Mia who had stopped at the top of the stairs.

"Thank you, Captain Nutwhack," said Mia, firmly. "You may *go* now!"

Kalijah stopped in his tracks. "What be thy name, son?"

"Blake Urquart! I mean Barber."

Kalijah straightened up and took a step away, as if warded off by a talisman. He tilted his head back and regarded Blake circumspectly. With affected courtesy and a strange smile he continued to back away toward the park. "Good day to thee, Master Urquart, good day! Good day to thee, Miss Devlin. Good day! Good day!" Finally, the grove gathered him in and he was gone.

"*That* was the freakiest thing that has *ever* happened to me," said Blake.

"Yup. I'd say that was his best performance yet. Even had me going for a minute." Another low rumble, longer, louder rolled across the lake. They looked at each other and listened as it faded into the distance.

"I think you're right about the weather. Give me my violin I want to get home before the rain gets here." Mia reclaimed her case and trotted down the stairs, Blake in tow.

"Hey, hold on!" Blake said. "He had a white shirt. His collar was turned up. *That's* the guy you named me for?'

"He's a hard act to follow!"

"Hey, when are we kayaking again?"

"I think Friday's the day." She walked away briskly. "Don't worry, I'll track you down, Tux!"

He stood and watched her for a moment until a sudden gust pushed him off balance. He thought he felt a sprinkle and headed for the boat.

***

"I see yer lass has got yeh totin' for her, now?" Gunn sat in the middle of the boat, hand buried in his tobacco pouch.

"She's no me lass!" protested Blake, as he climbed aboard the bobbing *Terrapin*.

"And yeh've no found you're uncle anywhere, have yeh?"

140

"No, and we were all over."

"Ah, well, yeh got acquainted with the town kook, anyhoo."

"Yeah, is that guy cracked or what?"

Gunn gave a little nod and hoot of agreement as he cupped his hand around his pipe and attempted to ignite his lighter.

"That's what a drama degree and paint fumes'll get yeh!" He puffed out rivers of white smoke which vanished away in the breeze.

"I don't follow you."

"That's Garvey Woodhead, lad. Goin' on twenty year ago, down comes Garvey to my place with his merry band. They wanted to paint boots. But it was no painting they wanted, 'twas the paint fumes. If I took my eye off them for two minutes they'd have that shop closed up tighter than a drum and every can of thinner open. Middle o' summer mind yeh."

"They were getting high on fumes? Doesn't that wreck your kidneys or something?"

"Aye, Does'na do yer brains any good either! So I fired 'em! Figured they'd kill themselves or blow my place up—or both."

"Why do people do stuff like that?"

"Who knows, lad. He came from a good family. Was keeping with bad company, I s'pose. They came back that night and stole a little boat and a couple of cans of paint and five gallons of thinner. You'll see him sailing it 'round once in awhile."

"You didn't report him?"

"No, lad, I did not."

"But he stole a boat, that's piracy in the truest sense!"

"Aye. But his father was a good friend. And ol' Garvey forgot one important thing." He puffed through a cheerful smirk. "He'd brought his own boot into the shop. It was worth far more than that little plywood sharpie he made off with. His father was more than happy to sign craft and trailer over to me. And that brings us to the business I mentioned to yeh."

The sky rumbled, closer this time. A few large drops of rain spattered on the deck. "Let's below, Caduggin, 'fore we melt!"

They hurried into the cabin. Blake sat on his suitcase. Gunn squatted on a tall plastic bucket turned upside-down. He pulled the sliding hatch cover over the companionway as the rain began to fall in earnest.

"You're a natural born sailor, Blake, that's for certain. And a sailor needs a boot. I'm offering yeh a Laser II, trailer, sails, and five hundred dollars in cash in exchange for all that anchor chain yeh won.

Blake was excited, disappointed, downcast, and hopeful almost simultaneously. "Yes! I don't know… where would I keep it? I don't think my dad… did you say *five hundred dollars in cash*?"

Thunder cracked over head. Wind swirled in through the companionway and the bulkhead vents made a low moan. The white cabin was beginning to feel much smaller. Blake drew his feet up and wrapped his arms around his shins. He tried hard to hide his nervousness and not to think about Kalijah's prophecy.

"What *is* a Laser II? Is that like Griffy's boat?"

"Aye, but a bit longer, fourteen and a half foot. Carries a jib, spinnaker, and a trapeze, big cockpit. It's more fun than three kids should be allowed to have on a windy day!"

"That would be neat! But I'll just have to give it up at the end of the summer. And I'm sure Hunter is going to come back."

"Yeh leave Hunter to us, Caduggin. As far as the boot goes, yer a lifetime member of the Highland Creek Sailing Club. Yeh can leave her there 'til kingdom come. And I'll keep an eye on it while you're away. We'll sign the title over to yer grandmother until yer of age. But no matter what, she's yer boot."

Blake thought about it for a moment. A blinding flash illuminated the elliptical portholes, followed instantly by a booming avalanche that sounded like the Heaven itself had exploded. Blake yelped and flinched. Gunn didn't budge. A grin spread across his craggy face.

"What'll yeh call her, Caduggin?"

"*Seven Thunders!*"

***

The driving rain had finally slacked off to a shower, the nerve-rattling thunder softened to low groans in the distance. The wind had let up and the *Terrapin* settled into a gentle rocking by the dock.

"*Treasure Island* is one of my favorites," said Gunn. "But if yeh want some real action close to home, read up on the Battle of Lake Erie. Oliver Hazard Perry—now *there's* a hero!"

Blake was about to reply when his uncle's werewolf-angry face suddenly appeared in the porthole—he yelped, instead. Gunn looked over the tops of his glasses at the ceiling, as the creature boarded and tramped across the cabin roof. There was a considerable amount of thumping, bumping and grouching on deck. Gunn bit one corner of his lower lip. "Oh lad, I'll hear it aboot that spar," he lamented. The mast creaked as it pivoted in its tabernacle. "Here comes another squall, Caduggin. We're aboot to get it!" Gunn ducked his head a little and peered cautiously out of the companionway. Blake leaned forward to do likewise. The main-mast was slowly descending over the cockpit, coming to rest horizontally alongside the lashed-up lug, mainsail, and boom. Carson hopped down into the cockpit.

"Are you out of your mind, old man? You two sat that storm out with the mast up? Are you completely stupid?" he shouted. Gunn only shrugged, lifted his palms and averted his gaze. Blake withdrew to the safety of his suitcase in the corner. "You didn't even have a grounding chain over the side! What were you thinking?" Blake thought that the rain and wind seemed to be picking up. Carson, still ranting turned his attention to starting the motor. He leapt onto the dock once more and freed the spring lines. He wadded them carelessly and tossed them into the boat. He hopped back in and motored away from the dock in full reverse; then it was all-ahead full, in a hard, heeling turn toward the channel.

"They did'na have a tent?" said Gunn, after a long silence. Carson glared ahead through the rain, drenched and grim.

"I was just telling the lad the door's always open at my place." Still, there was no response from the helmsman. Gunn took note of Blake's expression. "Well there's only one thing for it. You take the boot for awhile.

I've got mosquito nets, hammocks, and you can use my camp stove."

"That's *my* stove," Carson said, barely audible over the growling motor.

Gunn waited awhile, then suggested "You could berth up in the backwater of the harbor, there. You'd be out of sight, sort of off Club property and still have access to the fridge and the privy." He produced a deck of cards from his pocket and dealt out a hand. "My crib," he said to Blake, who handed over two cards, face down. Gunn added them to two of his own and slipped them under the toe of his shoe.

A full ten minutes passed. "I think that'll work," said Carson.

Gunn turned over a jack. He smiled and gave Blake a knowing wink. "Nobs!"

Chapter 15

Morning's first light crept through the portholes. Carson lay awake in his hammock, staring blankly at the collection of winged insects that had accumulated on the mosquito netting over the companionway. He ignored the nagging need to go on deck and threw a gritty forearm across his sweaty brow. He shifted his gaze to the white ceiling. The crickets and peepers still whirred away in the shadows and a kingfisher chattered from the masthead. Blake slept soundly on an old chaise cushion on the starboard side of the cabin.

At length Carson found the urgent resolve to roll out of his hammock. His appearance on deck touched off a mad evacuation of wildlife that squawked, splashed, flapped, and cackled in a frenzied dash out of the quiet little backwater. Then all was idyllic solitude again. Carson shuffled his way to the open transom and paused there awhile. His mission completed, he shuffled back to the cabin. He stopped in his tracks at the companionway. The cabin roof was covered by a constellation of little, brown, eight-legged stars.

"Shoo!" he puffed at them. They didn't move. He thumped his hand lightly on the roof. The entire constellation moved in unison exactly one quarter-inch to the left. Carson furrowed his brow and thumped the deck again. "Git!" he hissed. Again, the hundred little spiders moved as one—exactly one quarter-inch back to the right. "Hmmph! I'll fix you!"

Carson ducked into the cabin and fetched the big, white bucket.

Blake began to stir. "What are you doing?"

"Nothing. Go back to sleep." Carson returned to the cockpit.

Blake heard the bucket clatter, a small splash and a choice word from his uncle. He propped himself up on one elbow and with a sleepy grin called, "Don't let that sink!" There was more fumbling, followed by a huge, plunging splash that doused the porthole and set the *Terrapin* rocking. The few remaining mallards took to the wing.

Blake emerged from the cabin and looked over the starboard side. Carson bobbed in shoulder-deep water, glaring up at him. "This ain't gonna work, kid."

"Why not?"

"I didn't get a lick of sleep, last night" he griped, treading water to keep his feet off the mucky bottom. He worked his way around the end of the boat and chucked the empty bucket into the cockpit. Carson hoisted himself up through the transom and sploshed down on the bench.

Blake picked up the bucket. "I slept fine."

"I know *you* slept fine, that was half the problem! Between you shifting around and snoring and talking in your sleep."

"What was the other half?"

"I dunno, maybe it was the hundred-percent humidity, or the bugs, or the owl, or the belching bullfrogs from Hell."

Blake giggled.

"Or the pack of coyotes."

"There were coyotes? We've got coyotes here?"

"I'm surprised you didn't know! Now, look behind you. Cabin-top."

Blake turned around and winced. He realized what his uncle had been doing with the bucket. He considered doing the same until he turned back around and saw him prop his feet up on the opposite bench and smile sourly.

"Go ahead," said Carson. "Get'cha some water and wash 'em off there!"

Blake knew what his uncle had in mind for him, were he foolish enough to lean over the side.

"It's alright. They're just little ones. It would make the deck all slippery anyway."

"Okay then, go up there and untie us. I want to get out of this swamp-hole," said Carson. He grinned with cunning expectation.

"Sure!" Blake took a deep breath and turned once again toward the cabin.

"What're you waiting for?"

"I'm just trying to think what Mia would do." Suddenly he disappeared down the companionway and reappeared with his water bottle. He popped the squirt-top open and spritzed the cabin roof with a steady sprinkling that sent the little spiders scurrying for the edges. The way cleared, Blake went across the cabin top to the bow compartment and freed the *Terrapin's* bowline from an overhanging branch.

"Mooring's clear! All aback full!" he called, in triumph.

"Well done," murmured Carson. "Little smart-alec."

Blake retuned to the cockpit as Carson lowered the motor. "Are we just going to stay in the boat, over at Blue Rock, then?"

"No. We're gonna go back to Mom's and make sure Jack hasn't burned the house down. We'll pick up a tent down there and come back in a couple of days."

"Nanna's! No! I mean, you said it wasn't very far. Why don't I stay here and you just come back later today?"

Carson sat back down with a squish. "Because, I'd like to enjoy a couple of nights of air-conditioning. Why are you so dead-set on staying here?"

"I don't know, I guess I finally got used to it. All my friends are here, the fishing just got good, and most of all I planned to get Griffy and learn how to sail my new boat, tomorrow."

"Well, like I always say, sometimes life takes a big dump on you and you have to change your plans."

"Mr. Gunn said I was welcome to stay at his house whenever I wanted. Couldn't I stay with him while you're gone?"

"Cut the crap Blake! Ever since you got here you've been in mortal fear of going to your grandmother's. Now, why is that?" Carson said, with that angry stare. Blake's lower lip began to tremble. "Out with it!"

"Agatha told me that you let a big tarantula loose in Nanna's house. She said you feed it rats."

Carson's bearing softened. Yet Blake had noticed something in his uncle's expression at first—what was it? A fleeting look of... surprise? Guilt? Or was it *fear*?

"Now I see. Look, when I called your mother to make final arrangements for picking you and your sister up, Agatha answered the phone. She was being a snot. I thought she was staying at Mom's, too—so I told her the story about the spider to give her the heebie-jeebies. And here you've been anguishing over it this whole time. I told ya straight, kid—I hate spiders!"

Blake breathed easier. "Would you mind if I stayed with Mr. Gunn?" He ventured, meekly.

"Well, let me tell you about life on the Gunn estate. Tripper is the undisputed lord of his castle and when you're on his turf he never lets you forget it. He's got something to say about every little thing you do, whether it's the time you get up in the morning or what you put on your hamburger. And heaven help you if you don't agree."

"Do you think Nanna would mind? Just for a couple of days? You could call her and find out."

"She doesn't care, kid! Go stay with the old badger if you want!" Carson snapped, loudly. Tears started to well up in his nephew's eyes. "I meant to say that she won't mind. I'm your guardian right now, anyway. You can stay with Tripp if you want."

Blake sniffled and mustered a meek "Thank you. I think I'll take the trail over to the club." He made his way back to the bow and hopped down onto the shore. He put his shoulder against the square bow and pushed with all his might. The *Terrapin* slipped free and drifted backwards into the cove.

***

Blake took his time on the short trail but, instead of following it all of the way to the club gate, he cut through the woods and emerged in the keelboat lot. There he lurked among the big boats, which loomed on their trailers like a herd of sleeping dinosaurs. Someone had left a ladder leaning against a craft called *Vantage*. He ascended to the deck and made his way to the bow-pulpit. Before him the gravel parking lot spread out like a white sea and right in the middle of it swam the big, black monster that was Jack's car. *That was fast,* he thought.

The front door of the clubhouse squeaked open and thumped shut as always; but Jack took no notice. He sat alone in the shadowy part of the great room, chair balanced on two legs.

"Hello, Jack!" said Blake. Jack stared straight ahead. "Hey, Jack?" He stood directly in front of him, yet he did not respond. Blake could see his dim reflection in Jack's very black sunglasses. The chair creaked slightly as he rocked in a slow, steady rhythm, one hand on the table beside him. He seemed to be in another world. "Jack! Do you have our mail?"

Blake reached for a thin wire that ran across three red sixes on Jack's black tee-shirt, up through a necklace of scorched pork ribs, and into his greasy ears. Blake gave it a sharp yank. Two gunky buds popped out. Screeching noise pulsed out of the little speakers. A growling voice tore through the metal cacophony:

"Blood on the Altar!

Blood on the knife!

Hail the season

Of the sacrifice!

Hear the screaming of the sacrifice!"

The bobbing stopped "Not cool, little dude." Jack droned, in a quiet, creepy monotone.

"Why are you wearing those bones around your neck?"

"Because if I wore them anywhere else, I couldn't sit down."

"Do you have our mail?"

"Do I look like the mailman, little princess?"

"There was a postcard for me in the last batch you left. Are there any more?"

"Talk to your uncle."

Recalling Jack's apparent spinelessness in past encounters, Blake slammed his right fist on the table and shouted "Where is our mail, you pagan freak!"

Jack merely gave a burbling chortle from barely parted lips. Blake thought hard about hooking a foot under one of the front legs of Jack's chair and jerking him over backwards. He reconsidered when he imagined the trouble that would result if Jack cracked his skull on the floor.

"You better watch yourself, little dude. I'm the voodoo man! I just bought a tsantsa." He murmured smugly.

"Aren't you a little old to believe in Santa?" said Blake, a cunning gleam in his eye.

"I said tsantsa, punk! I might just use it on you if you're not careful!"

"I doubt it. That's not what they're for." A little twitch disturbed the shaman's smile and Blake knew he had called Jack's bluff. "Hope you kept your receipt!" he said, crossing to the back door.

"You don't even know what it is, you little liar!"

He grasped the doorknob, paused and hung his head.

"See, I knew it! I'll put the whammie on you, kid!"

Blake looked over his shoulder and smiled. "It's a shrunken head. I have to read Christian missionary stories for home school. Some of them are almost as perverted and vulgar as you!" Jack dropped his chair flat on the floor. Blake exited onto the patio feeling victorious. From the railing he spied Carson coming off the main dock, duffel bag on his shoulder. He met him halfway up the hill.

"So, you'll be back Saturday?"

"Probably Sunday," said Carson, as he passed by.

"Did Jack bring the mail?"

"Why would he? I'm going down there."

Blake began to feel the chill blowing off his uncle's cold shoulder. He stopped "Are we just going to leave the boat at the dock? How am I getting over to Gunn's?"

"You know how to run the motor now, drive her on over there," said Carson, continuing up the hill.

"I don't now exactly where he lives, I don't think I could find his cove."

"Then give him a call. He'll come get you."

Blake stood and stared up the hill. His uncle disappeared behind the patio railing. A familiar anguish began to seep into his heart. *I will not cry.* He thought. *I am almost thirteen. I will not cry.* He heard the back door whump shut.

"Wait! I don't even know Tripper Gunn's number!"

Blake sprinted up the hill and burst into the clubhouse in a panic. They were gone. He raced out the front door, leapt down the steps and dashed to the edge of the hilltop. Car doors slammed in the parking lot below, the engine was already running. "Wait!" he wheezed. His sides felt like they would split open. "What did I do? What is wrong with me?"

The great black beast slithered out of the parking lot.

***

Blake stood in the phone alcove, thumbing through the back of the HCSC yearbook. He mopped his cheeks on one shoulder then other. "There it is!" he said to himself, feeling a little encouraged. He dialed the number and, to his great relief, the unmistakable voice of the old Scotsman answered the phone. Blake explained his sad predicament.

"Don' yeh worry yerself, Caduggin." Gunn replied. "I'll be there presently. We'll take our lunch at the Emporium, we'll do the shopping, then we'll see if this boot yeh bought lives up to yer expectations."

***

It seemed as though there wasn't anything a cheeseburger, fries, and a root beer float at the Emporium couldn't fix—or at least take the edge off of. Treva exchanged a little gossip with Gunn and promised to pass Blake's whereabouts to Mia. In fact, she did nothing *but* talk about Mia and the adventures she and Blake were having together—as if they'd been at it for years. She left Blake with an interesting piece of advice:

"Don't you let her fool you with that hard-nosed front she puts up. You're good for her, Tux—that's such a cute little name! Make no mistake about it, sweetie—she needs you. Now, you don't say anything or I'll have the devil-woman to pay!"

***

By early afternoon they were stowing groceries in the cabin and making sail for Trespass Island. The sky was hazy blue. A moderate breeze made the temperature perfectly comfortable. Blake manned the helm while Tripper enjoyed a smoke.

"It'll be good and hot for yer junior training. Hope yer wind holds out," said Gunn, between puffs.

"Me, too."

"Yeh know, with a yawl rig like this, sometimes you can trim your sails 'just so,' and let the tiller go. She'll balance out and hold her course."

"Hmm? Oh."

Gunn let a couple of minutes pass before speaking again. "It's no yer fault, yeh know—the way yer uncle's acting—yer no to blame for it. And neither am I."

Blake only nodded.

"See, he resents me, lad. I remind him too much of his father. And now he resents himself because he knows he should be a better example to yeh. But he does'na think he has what it takes. And that's no any of yer doing."

"I guess I understand."

"I know, but it does'na make it feel any better does it?"

Blake shook his head. "Can you show me how to balance the helm, like you said?"

"Certainly! Where's the wind and what's our point of sail?"

"The wind is from the southwest and we're on a beam reach."

"Now, let go the tiller and see which way she wants to head. That'll tell us which sails to trim and which to ease."

Blake was amazed to find that the *Terrapin* could be made to steer herself. He walked all over the boat, keeping a watchful eye on the unattended tiller. Finally he settled down on the cabin roof, delighted.

"We're halfway doon the channel, lad. What should yeh be looking

152

for?"

Blake sighted the cell tower and the sycamore stump, and pointed. "Yaegerstoon Moonster, Cap'n, off the starboard quarter!" he replied, in a convincing brogue.

Gunn grinned, blew smoke and nodded.

"I hate to burst yer bubble, lad, but what'll happen when the wind shifts?"

"We'll have to trim the sails again to keep her balanced?"

"That's it, Caduggin! And the wind shifts mighty regular around here, don' it? Out on the ocean, it stays pretty steady and yeh don't have to fool with it so often. Yeh practice keeping her trimmed up 'til we pass the island."

The lesson proved an excellent diversion. Blake's spirits had lifted considerably by the time they rounded Trespass Island.

"Take us due east, lad." Gunn directed.

"Aye," Blake replied, "trim yer main and jib! The wind's abeam again, Mr. Gunn."

"Yeh do that accent fair justice, Caduggin!"

"You don't mind, do you?"

"Imitation is the sincerest form of flattery, so they say. But there's a fine line between it and mockery. Be sure yeh know where it is."

They covered the last half mile to the southeast shore of the lower lake. Gunn dropped the mainsail and jib. "Fire the ol' widow-maker up and round this point into the inlet—all ahead slow!"

Blake carried out the orders and the *Terrapin* puttered into what, to Blake's surprise, turned out to be a bay, every bit as big as the club's harbor, if not more so; hidden from the rest of the lake by a low ridge that formed a cape. Farther down, the bay narrowed into a channel crossed by a low causeway.

"There's good fishing on the other side of that little bridge. Take us over that way—that dock over there."

A long, dilapidated building seemed to emerge from the woods with what appeared to be a two-story house stuck to the far end. The hull of a wooden motor boat, long out of style, lay rotting on the shore. Drab keel boats sat in a weedy side-yard, paint bleached by years in the sun instead of the water.

"Man, this place is a disaster area! I mean a *total* dump? Somebody ought to be shot for this mess!" Blake said.

"I know. State's been after me to clean it up for years."

"Why aren't we working on it?"

"It's no exactly a paying job. It's the owner's responsibility."

"Well, who does it belong to?"

"That's my place, lad! The auld marina!" Gunn chuckled.

Blake swallowed hard and blushed.

"Yeh called it right, Caduggin! All-stop and coast us in. Lay us long— starboard side." Gunn put dock fenders out as Blake shifted the motor into neutral and steered a graceful arc into the dock. It looked unnervingly similar to the one they'd removed from the creepy cove his first day out.

In fact he was certain that it was the same. He tossed his suitcase and duffel out first. The dock didn't even creak. He held his breath and stepped gingerly—one foot at a time onto its weathered planks. Surprisingly, it didn't sag wildly as before. Bands of bright orange peeked between the boards in several places, betraying the addition of large blocks of Styrofoam floatation.

"We'll stow your dunnage up in your room. Then yeh get the grand tour. Here!" Gunn handed up the collapsible shopping cart and began to pass bulging bags to Blake.

"I get my own room? I mean I'm just staying a couple of days, right?"

"No more of this sleeping in sheds and attics and boots. That's no proper for a lad, is it?" It seemed more a declaration, than a question. Blake's mind ran straight to his father and then to Carson's warning.

"I kind of…" he caught himself about to voice his affection for the attic. "Like the idea of having my own room."

With the last of the cargo unloaded, Gunn reached out his right hand. "Give me a boost, lad!" Blake took the old man's rough hand and steadied him as he stepped up on the bench, over the side, then down onto the dock.

***

The big workshop door rumbled aside with squeaking complaint, admitting a flood of daylight into the first work bay. Blake peered in and wondered at the odd, tarp-covered shapes that stood like tombs and monuments here and there.

"Devlin's got four times this space," Gunn mused. "Let's get the next one." They strained at the next door. It slid aside, gradually illuminating the word "*Sophia*," emblazoned ornately on the transom of a keel boat high on her trailer. "One more, Caduggin!"

The third portal yielded in like manner. Gunn strode to the middle of the bay where another tarped mystery stood like a bishop's crypt in a cathedral catacomb. "Roll it up!"

Together they turned back the heavy canvas, fold by fold. Slowly the deep blue and white hull of *Seven Thunders* emerged. Blake's eyes darted back and forth over her deck, cleats, and lines, wondering how he would ever learn their purposes, ever be able to skipper this boat.

"Sails are up in the loft. The top of the stairs on the right. I'll fetch yer spar."

By the time he returned, tubular sail bags dragging behind, Gunn had the mast standing upright, next to the boat. "Get on deck and keep it steady while I drop it in the step."

The mast installed, Gunn solemnly guided Blake over each connection, each line, and each knot until finally the time had come to set her afloat. Together they carefully backed her trailer down the launch ramp.

"Mind the slime, lad. That algae is slicker than greased snot on a doorknob!"

Blake took her bowline and leapt onto the dock. He guided *Seven Thunders* gently off her trailer as if leading a mare from a stall. He secured her to the dock and slipped aboard. He pushed the boom aside, put the dagger board into its slot and shoved it down all the way. He stood with his feet spread to the edges of the cockpit and began to rock the hull harder and harder. Satisfied with his little stability test, he took the main-halyard in hand.

"Now, I want yeh to stay fairly close for the time being. Yeh may go between here and the Club and round aboot the island." He groaned as he pulled the trailer back up the ramp. "Don' stray too far either way and stay out the channel. Yeh understand, me lad?"

"Aye. The club and the island. Wait, you're not coming?"

"That's no a boot for an auld man like me! Yeh call Griffy when yeh get to the club. Yeh'll never be rid of him, now!"

"I don't know his number."

"How'd yeh find mine?"

"Simple, I just looked it up … Oh. In the club directory." He hauled on the main halyard. The sail went up a little at a time, rising like a great white cobra teased from a snake-charmer's basket.

"Remember, yeh can always ease out, or drop one or both of yer sails if it gets to be too much," Gunn advised, as he lumbered down to the end of the dock. "And one more thing…"

Blake paused from his labors and looked up attentively at his new guardian.

"*You*—are skipper of *this* boot. *You.*" He pointed a finger of unquestionable authority at him. "*You* are responsible for the safety of everyone aboard and everyone around yeh. What *you* say goes. Anyone who won't obey yer orders yeh put ashore at first opportunity. And yeh don' have 'em back!"

Blake stood under the weight of this command for a moment, nodded, and returned to hoisting. As soon as the jib went up, Gunn knelt down and freed the boat from her mooring.

"Be back by six, d'yeh hear?"

"Six, aye."

Gunn tossed the line into the cockpit. Blake sat down on the port side and pulled the tiller close. *Seven Thunders* drifted in a backward arc until her sails filled and snapped into shape. She surged forward decisively. Blake checked the telltales, trimmed for a broad reach, and slipped across Gunn's harbor with all of the eager nervousness of a boy on his first date. In less than five minutes he reached the open lake and turned toward Trespass

Island. He surveyed the cockpit, which was shallow like *Cherry Bomb*'s, but larger. And the lines! Griffy's boat had five but the Laser II, it seemed, was a veritable tangle of colored ropes—not to mention that trapeze thing! Blake stared at it all.

The sails began to rattle a little, prompting a quick check of the telltale yarns on the jib. He trimmed the sails until the yarns were streaming straight back. Without warning, Blake felt his side of the boat pitch skyward. Water sluiced over the low side into the cockpit and *Seven Thunders* began to turn sharply into the wind. Blake flung himself back to hike and cried "no, no, no! Please no!" Then he remembered—and jerked the mainsheet from its cleat. The boom swung out. The sail dumped its wind. The boat leveled with a slosh. He pushed the tiller all of the way to lee and settled *Seven Thunders* into the 'safety position.' He sat and panted, casting nervous glances in every direction. The water in the cockpit lapped over his ankles.

He'd capsized in the prams a hundred times, so why did this seem like the end of the world? Because if the little, square Optimist Prams were Shetland ponies, then this was a wild mustang. Not to mention that he'd never ventured very far in any direction from the point—and now he was alone in the middle of the sprawling lower lake, in a boat that would be the boss if he didn't show it what he was made of.

He brushed a wave of hair from his eyes. "Note to self," he gasped out loud, "keep an eye on the puffs!" He caught his breath and found the resolve to press on. He opened the bailer and resumed his course toward Trespass Island, keeping a wary eye out for those dark patches sneaking silently across the water.

A hundred coots bobbed in the shallows around the east cove of the island. Blake was about to charge down on them and put them to flight, when the boat lurched then suddenly slowed as if caught in the clutches of some awful demon of the deep. A horrid scraping-grinding-thudding rumbled through the entire hull. He leapt to a half standing straddle over the dagger-board and desperately tried to pull it up without letting go of the tiller. It wouldn't budge. In a panic, he scrambled to release the main and jib sheets, one foot braced against the low side of the cockpit. *Seven*

Thunders began to pirouette on its muck-mired dagger-board. "We are *not* going over!" he groaned, straining with all his might. Grudgingly, the lake-bed surrendered its hold and two feet of the board slid up through its slot in the floor. Blake plunked back down on the rail, gave the tiller several sharp jerks to windward and raced toward deeper water.

"Note to self. Pay attention to the shallow water buoys!"

The sight of Highland Harbor, a half mile distant, along with a favorable shift in the wind's direction buoyed his courage. Now he would be able to beam reach all of the way across to his destination; an easy thing—if he kept a vigilant eye out for marauding gusts. But the wind shifted back and gradually his leisurely reaching turned into spirited beating. Twice more he took water over the leeward rail and rounded up into the wind. But each time it seemed a little less frightening and by the third blow he was beginning to bring all of his pram-practice together with his book-learning. Blake hiked hard and eased the mainsail rapidly. He let the boat round up a little, to rob the sails of just enough of their remaining power. It all went together to keep the situation manageable and allowed him to put her back on course again.

At last, perched proudly on the high rail, Blake brought *Seven Thunders* into the harbor. He tacked for the point and once safely sheltered by its wind shadow, assumed a parallel course to the shore. He eased the sails all of the way out. *Seven Thunders* relaxed and settled into a gentle amble. He took a deep breath and watched the scenery roll by for a moment. He looked aft. In his wake, the vast reservoir spread into the distance. Something welled up in him. What was the feeling? It spread across his face in a broad smile of pride and awe, and the satisfaction that every sailor feels when he returns to his home port.

Blake tied her up at the main dock, in the exact middle of Commodore Devlin's favorite berth.

***

It took Griffy no time at all to find a ride to the sailing club. He trundled down the gangway onto the dock, barely able to contain himself. "No freakin' way!" You're joking me! The old man just *gave* you a Laser II?"

"There it is."

"Geezer don't giveth nobody nothing—he taketh away!" Griffy brushed curly blonde hair out of his face, resituated his camo-green headband, and consumed *Seven Thunders* with his eyes.

"It was a trade. The boat and five hundred dollars for all of Devlin's anchor chain."

"You got the boat *and* five hundred bucks? Seriously? You ought to be slapped!" he said, as he slipped into the cockpit. "You got the harness?"

"In that bag. You know how to use it?"

"Sure, my girlfriend has one!" Griffy snickered.

"Don't be vulgar."

"I don't know, Blake," Griffy said, donning the strange rig and adjusting its straps. "I think this boat may be too much for you."

"I got it over here, didn't I?"

"Beginner's luck. No offense, but a boat like this needs a real sailor at the helm."

Griffy's careless words hit Blake like a punch in the gut.

"I can sail!"

"Prams? Oh, please! They're like baby versions of the shoebox!"

"Well then I'm sorry," Blake said, squatting down on the dock, "that you came all this way just to *look* at my boat."

"Hey, no offense, man! I'm just saying…"

"And I'm just saying if that's your attitude, you can get off *my* boat."

"Alright, alright! Let's go see what she can do. Cast us off!" Griffy took up the mainsheet and tiller.

"No, *you* cast us off. *I'm* skippering," Blake replied, in a commanding tone. "And another thing—If I do let you steer, Mr. Gunn wants me to stay between the club and his place, and around the island. Got it?"

"Aye aye, captain!" Griffy gave a sharp, mock salute. "Damn the torpedoes, full speed ahead!" He started straightening lines, adjusting the trapeze and, to Blake's secret alarm, preparing the spinnaker for launch.

"So, you and Devil Woman really beat the hell out of those guys the other day, huh? What did you do to them?"

"Please don't call her that. And I don't know what happened to them. Hunter… I'd rather not talk about it."

"I hear his old man's hiding him 'til he can get him off the hook. Hopkins is still in the hospital."

"Get ready to close-haul the jib when we clear the point."

"I don't know man, this is a lot of boat," Griffy said, flipping the jib sheet this way and that.

"Yeah, but with your fat kiester on the rail it'll be a cinch, right?"

"Whatever, dude."

Blake was quiet for a moment, calculating. "The original Lasers were just really prototypes, weren't they?"

"Prototypes? What are you talking about?"

"You know, like a first attempt. Just one sail, not many controls, little cockpit. It's like just a…practice design that they didn't perfect until the Laser II?"

"Practice design? Kiss my butt!"

Blake trimmed the mainsail all the way in as *Seven Thunders* cleared the point. The boat heeled over and sprinted forward. "Trim yer jib, Mr. Williams!" he commanded, in his best Scots accent. Griffy complied. He wasted no time in clipping his harness to the trapeze. He backed himself off the edge of the deck until his feet were under him, then he pushed his entire body out over the water. He couldn't help but let out a wild, war whoop.

"Keep her on the wind, dude! Watch your luff!"

"What are you talking about?"

"The luff of your jib! I thought you said you knew how to sail! Keep pointing up and as soon as you see the leading edge start to cave in, you back off a little. Keep doing that when you're beating and you'll never have to look at the wind vane again."

"Awesome! Where did you learn that?"

"The old man who taught me to sail."

"What old man?"

"The Geezer, of course! Who else?"

"Tripper Gunn taught *you* to sail?"

"And to race. He's a wiley old fart, that's for sure! Now pay attention to your luff!"

"You better watch how you talk about him!"

"Oh come on, lighten up! Now, keep her on the wind!"

"Nobody badmouths Mr. Gunn on my boat!"

"Or *what?*" sneered Griffy, defiantly.

Blake let the mainsail fly out then hauled it back in. The high side of the boat—and Griffy—plunged suddenly, then lifted again.

"Crap! Hey, what's the idea?" Griffy yelled.

"I *said* nobody badmouths Mr. Gunn on my boat!"

"Oh boo hoo! Little buddy's gotta stand up for grandpa!"

Blake let the mainsail go again and Griffy plummeted.

"Dammit! Stop that!"

"You don't curse on my boat, either!"

"What? You know, I was right? This boat *is* too much for you! Why don't you go back to the baby boats so your momma can keep an eye on you, little boy!"

Blake bit his lip and sucked in a breath, then shouted, "Hard a'lee!" He thrust the tiller away and dove to the other side of the cockpit. Griffy barely had time to swing into the swiftly turning boat and free himself from the trapeze, before his side of the deck plunged. Rushing water swept him overboard. He surfaced in the spreading wake of *Seven Thunders*. The nearest land was a quarter mile away and Blake had not turned about to pick him up.

"Get back here, you jackass! You'll never hold that boat down by yourself!" But the boat continued on, her skipper apparently unconcerned. "Well don't expect me to come to the rescue when you dump it on the next gust!"

As if on cue, the breeze rose. Griffy watched in gleeful anticipation as *Seven Thunders* heeled excessively, her skipper hiking to the fullest of his ability.

"Goooing once! Goooing twice!" chanted the castaway. "goooing…Huh?" His delicious expectation melted away as the imperiled craft weathered the gust and returned to a manageable angle. "Lucky dog!"

To Griffy's further amazement, Blake executed a flawless "figure-eight" man-overboard maneuver and returned to him, parking his boat twenty feet away. "Crikey! I guess the kid does know how to sail," he muttered to himself.

"Hey! Are you trying to kill me or what, moron?" he shouted, for the sheer sake of shouting.

Blake leaned down to look under the boom and shouted back. "If you want to sail on *this* boat, you don't badmouth Mr. Gunn, you don't curse, and you don't treat me like a little fool. I can get *that* at home!"

Griffy began to swim for *Seven Thunders*. "Why are you such a goodie two-shoes?"

Blake trimmed the mainsail, sailed another twenty feet and parked her. "I dunno, why are you such an obnoxious loudmouth? I've never seen anyone like you! You never shut up! You never take anything seriously, except racing. And you never treat anyone with a shred of respect. Why do you think nobody wants to be around you?"

Griffy stopped swimming and scowled for a moment. "You'll still need someone to fly that spinnaker for you."

"I'll find someone, unless you agree to my rules. Oh, and that means you stop calling Mia 'devil woman,' too."

"We're going to keep sailing?"

"Depends on you."

"We're gonna fly the chute—today—right? It's not too windy. I think you can handle it."

"No cursing, badmouthing, or belittling. Think *you* can handle that?"

"C'mon, let me aboard. The minnows are nibbling my nuggets." He started to swim for the boat, again. Once more, Blake moved her off another twenty feet and parked.

"Do you accept my rules?"

"Okay, okay, I accept your blessed rules!"

Blake stood up, pushed the mainsail out, and held it against the wind. *Seven Thunders* backed up to retrieve her lost crewman. He eyed Griffy warily as he pulled himself up onto the aft deck and crawled into the cockpit.

"Welcome aboard, Mr. Williams! Yer gittin' me boot all wet!"

Griffy collected the jib sheets and readied the trapeze wire.

"Close haul yer jib. We'll beat to the shore, then run back on the spinnaker!"

"Well you're gonna have to listen to me when we put up the chute or we'll both be breathing water."

"Yeh jest tell me what to do, Mr. Williams!"

"You can stop talking like the Geezer, for starters."

Blake paused from trimming the mainsail, cocked a disapproving eyebrow and glanced quizzically at his dripping crew.

"I mean like…Tripper Gunn," Griffy grumbled, trimming the jib even with the edge of the deck.

Blake smiled. A few shoves on the tiller and they were back on the wind.

***

The blue and yellow spinnaker fluttered madly as it went up. The sheet block ratcheted like an angry cicada as Griffy reigned it in. Suddenly the sail filled and snapped taught with an impressive thump. *Seven Thunders* streaked away faster than Blake imagined a sailboat could go.

"Oooh yeah!" cried Griffy. "Just wait 'til we do this in some real air! It'll jerk the boat right out from under ya!"

"Where do you want me to go?"

"Keep her pointed at the tip of Boy Scout Point. You jibe the boat with me on the wire and I'm a dead man!"

"Seriously?"

"Serious as a heart attack, now pay attention!"

Blake imagined the boom sweeping across the boat and slamming into Griffy's midriff. It would be like getting hit by a car. Gunn's words about a skipper's responsibility rang in his head.

"Griffy, are you sure you want to do this? I don't want to mess up and get you killed."

"Hell... Heck yeah! I've watched you, you know what you're doing! Just don't panic. Focus on that point."

That affirmation was balm to Blake's sore ego. He committed himself to hiking and keeping his eyes on Boy Scout point. Then it occurred to him: Griffy was in racing mode: serious, focused, giving straight answers.

"What if the wind shifts?" he asked, testing this hypothesis.

"If it shifts up, trim in but hold you course. If it shifts down, then go with it and ease if you have to. Anything to avoid a jibe!"

This was a breakthrough. You could actually communicate with Griffy Williams when he was in this frame of mind. He let a couple of minutes pass. The harbor was fast approaching and beyond it, the forbidden channel. If he was going to ask, it would be then or never.

"Hey Griffy?"

"I know! We have to drop it soon. You're doing fine!"

"Griffy, what happened to your Dad?"

"Cancer. Died on my birthday. I was seven."

Blake was totally unprepared for the weight of that revelation, but he had no time to ponder it.

"Okay, ease out slowly, put the wind behind us. Get ready to drop it!" Blake held his breath. Griffy hauled the big sail around in front of the boat. He swung into the cockpit and disconnected from the trapeze in one smooth motion. Then he let the sail swing back around behind the main and jib, snatched it by a corner and gathered the bottom in as fast as he could. "Drop it!"

Blake released the halyard and, like a genie returning to its lamp, the mighty spinnaker surrendered its power and disappeared into to its bag.

"That—was unbelievable!" Blake said.

"You think that was something? When it's really blowing, like fifteen or more, the whole front of the boat comes out of the water!" Griffy took down the spinnaker pole. "It's a total rush! We'd need three for that though. Let's do it again! You want to ride the trapeze this time?"

"Uh, I think I need to practice my helmsmanship a little more."

"Ahh you didn't do bad! C'mon, one more time?"

"Alright, Mr. Williams, let's come about. Trim for a beat!" Blake swung *Seven Thunders* in a wide turn, both boys trimming their sails in unison until the boat was hard on the wind and Griffy was flying over the water. "Now, you're the Flying Cowboy!"

"You bet I am!" Griffy Laughed. "The mad, bad, totally rad Flying Cowboy!"

Blake decided to try his luck again. "How long have you known Mia?"

"Since we joined the club."

"When was that?"

"After I was seven. Watch your luff, you're pinching, bear off a little!"

"Did she ever sail?"

"Don't jerk the tiller when you steer! Small, smooth movements! Feel the boat, it's talking to you!"

Blake was about to restate his question, when Griffy piped up again.

"We need to practice tacking. You have to give me time to get off the wire before we go. I'll call the tacks 'til you get the hang of it. Ready about!" the Flying Cowboy swung back into the boat and released the harness as he called "Hard a'lee!" Blake pushed the tiller over and they slipped under the boom and took up their positions on the other side. Griffy was back in the air by the time the turn was complete.

"Awesome job, man!" Blake's spirit soared with the praise. They repeated the maneuver five times. "You know what you're doing, man! I think you may be a natural! You call 'em now!"

Three more tacks and they were ready to turn back for another spinnaker run. Griffy hooked the pole to the topping lift, then to the spinnaker guy-line and finally to the mast. "Don't let the speed scare you," he said. "Watch the point like last time. Now, haul it up!"

Blake stood up, held the tiller between his knees, and hauled the halyard like there was no tomorrow. The spinnaker reminded him of a giant kite.

"One hundred and ten square feet of sheer terror, baby!" said Griffy. "You're basically running a windward-Leeward race course, you know?

Once you learn how to start, I bet we could really kick some butt!"

Griffy's 'one more time' stretched into five more times.

"What do you say we do a lap around the island and call it a day?" Blake suggested, hopefully.

"Really? Okay, I guess."

Griffy swung back into the cockpit, and disconnected from the wire. Blake was relieved to find a gentle reach in the shadow of Trespass Island. The cruise assumed a leisurely pace that made the heat of the afternoon very apparent. Griffy was completely dry now. The tolerable Flying Cowboy transformed back into the familiar Mad Cowboy once more, fidgeting and flipping the jib sheets this way and that.

"Have you ever been to the island?" said Blake.

"Yeah. What a bore. You walk around. It's hot. Things bite you. On second thought, why don't you just take me back to the club."

"I can do that." Blake wasn't sure what to make of this sudden shift in mood.

"What time do you want sail tomorrow?" said Griffy.

"Um, sorry, but I'm busy tomorrow. And Saturday. Maybe Sunday?"

Griffy slouched down into the cockpit and trailed his left arm in the water. "Sundays, I race."

"Are you okay? You seem so down all of a sudden."

"Nah, I just get bored easy."

They cleared the wind shadow of the island and sailed into the breeze. Griffy scrambled instinctively backward to the rail as the deck tilted rapidly, the water rushing by at his feet. *Seven Thunders* had turned away from the harbor and was beating hard for the southeast shore. He looked back at the skipper, puzzled. Blake only smiled and hiked out. Griffy's spirit leapt like a child who had just gotten a bike for his birthday. He was on the trapeze and flying again in five seconds flat. They kept the spinnaker up all the way into the harbor, dropping it at the last possible moment. Finally, *Seven Thunders* moseyed up to the main dock.

"You're alright, Blake! 'Cuz you get to sail with me, of course! Lemme tighten the outhaul. That'll take some fight out of her on your trip back."

166

Griffy made the adjustment, shed the harness, and climbed out onto the dock. "Thanks for the ride! Don't forget Sunday! I'll get online, see if I can scare up some competition. Maybe we can start a Laser II fleet, or host a regional regatta or something! We'll whip 'em all!" He rattled on, walking backwards toward the gangway.

Blake was glad to see Griffy back to his usual, jabbering self.

"Try to think of a third crew so we can go out in heavy air. Maybe your uncle?"

"I'll ask him! See you!"

Blake already had a third in mind, but she didn't sail. And she didn't hold Griffy in very high regard, either. He planned his return course carefully. An easy reach in the shelter of Trespass Island, around the far end, to a manageable close reach into Gunn's harbor. He tied up at the mossy dock opposite the *Terrapin* at precisely five-thirty. An old red tractor sat at the top of the ramp, with his boat trailer hitched and ready.

***

The top stair creaked as Blake entered the living room. Gunn snorted awake in his recliner.

"Yeh caught me kippin', lad! I though yeh were the pizza man." He sat up and put on his glasses, and breathed heavily. "Yeh like deep-dish?"

"I'd like about anything in a dish, right now!" Blake said with a smile. He sank into the coolness of the big leather couch.

"Lads like you are always hungry as sharks!"

"That would be Long John Silver at the Spyglass Inn. You must've read *Treasure Island* a *few* times."

"Yeh might say that. Made my old Dad read it to me over and over when I was yer age. Griffy behave himself?"

"Once we got going he kind of settled down."

The old man chuckled. "That's giving him the benefit of the doubt! I saw what yeh done to him. And that was a fine bit of seamanship, Caduggin!"

Blake wasn't sure how to take that news, but he was sure it would be important to remember: *Gunn is watching.*

The doorbell rang. "Speak of angels, hear their wings!" Tripper pulled a fold of bills from his shirt pocket and held them out. "Here's forty dollars, go pay the man. Tell him to keep the change."

Blake labored cautiously back upstairs with their order. The heavy pizza boxes made a scorching-hot foundation for a precarious tower of salad, soft drinks, bread sticks, and cookies. He wondered if Gunn hadn't invited someone else to dinner. After an hour of leisurely dining, Blake slouched at the table, one hand on his belly. He was prepared to become intimately acquainted with the entire length of the couch. But those dreamy, burgundy cushions would have to wait.

"What'll it be first Caduggin? Billiards or darts?"

"I've never played."

"We'll start with Eight Ball then. A clearer demonstration of physics and geometry yeh'll never find." Gunn shuffled over to the cue rack. "That's the beauty of billiards."

Blake hoped he could keep his eyes open and his mouth shut during the impending lecture. But things turned out better than expected. The game was enjoyable and the nuances of spin, force, and angle fascinated him. Then quite unexpectedly, a new understanding began to unfold on the green felt. In the paths of the rebounding balls he began to see the paths of boats, the fundamentals of racecourse geometry. Suddenly "lifts" and "knocks" made perfect sense. After the game, which he narrowly lost, he placed the One, Two, and Three balls in a triangle, and presented a couple of sailing scenarios to Gunn. He laid a cue stick on the table, its butt-end next to the number One ball, its tip six inches from number Two.

"So, I'm going from buoy one to two, on a beat. The pool cue is my course. I would end up here, but I get a lift," he pivoted the cue so the tip swung three inches toward ball Two. "And it puts me here, closer to the next mark."

"That's positively brilliant, lad! And if yeh get a knock it goes the other way. Yeh try to stay on the lifted tack as much as possible." He went to the mantel and returned with a little model boat, which he placed on the pool table. "Use that, it'll make even more sense." Gunn went to the refrigerator and retrieved a red, arrow-shaped magnet. "There's yer wind." He tossed it on the table. They went on setting up examples and what-if scenarios for another forty minutes.

***

Blake awoke on the couch, a throw blanket half draped across his chest. The house was dark. The sounds of the night lake seemed much louder and clearer than they should have. He realized that the big bay windows were open. Then the window bench creaked and he noticed Tripper Gunn sitting furtively in the shadows. Blake sat up. The old man held one finger to his lips. "Looks like yeh got someone's attention today," he whispered.

Blake took up a position on the other side of the window-seat. Down on the water, just entering the harbor was a white boat with pointed ends, its lateen sail reflecting ghostly moonlight. The skipper moved to the middle bench, unshipped long oars, and began to row for the dock.

"Good evenin' Mr. Woodhead. Yer going the wrong way!" Gunn called down.

The rowing stopped and a throaty voice answered. "I've come to claim what's rightfully mine, Gunn!"

"I've got nothin' of yours, Garvey, but I do recognize that sharpie yer sailing. I thought yeh might be bringing it back to me?"

"I saw her with my own eyes, Scotsman! With all her canvas stretched out, flying over the waves with Master Urquart at the helm!"

"Aye, and he is her master, now! And you'll leave him alone, or else!"

"Are there any *normal* people on this lake?" said Blake.

"Aye, but they only show up on the weekends."

"The eyes of the Lord are upon the wicked!" roared Garvey. "Give back what you've stolen!"

Gunn motioned to Blake. "Behind yeh lad. Hand me that brick o' Cat's." Blake turned to the roll-top desk and picked up the only object matching the description. It was wrapped in a kind of flimsy wax paper. The yellow label sported the hissing countenance of a black cat.

"I d'know aboot the Lord, Mr. Woodhead, but the Bishop of Smith-and-Wesson has his sights trained on yer arse aboot now!" The rowing stopped. Gunn pulled three packets from the end of the brick and tore notches in one side of each of them. "Yeh come aboot now and get out of my harbor, or there won't be enough left for Buck Mueller to scoop out with a tea cup!

"Ye would do violence to my *Covenant*?" And in like manner they killed the prophets!" Garvey bellowed. He resumed rowing. "Whether it 'tis nobler in the mind to suffer the slings and arrows..."

Tripper flicked his lighter and three sparking packets flew out the window. The quiet darkness erupted into rapid bangs and fierce flashes. With one mighty sweep, the oars spun the *Covenant* one hundred eighty degrees on the spot. The skipper began to pull like a galley slave, shouting curses and dire warnings on his way. As the trespasser made his escape, Blake couldn't help but notice that the hull of the boat was now black.

Gunn laughed mischievously. "That's the last we'll see of that fool for awhile, I suspect."

The smell of burnt gunpowder wafted into the living room. "Smells like the fourth of July," said Blake.

"That means someone has a birthday, soon, don' it?" Gunn returned to his recliner and switched on a floor lamp. Blake glanced at the old mantel clock over the fireplace. It was nine forty. Behind the clock hung a large rectangular mirror, five feet wide.

"On the first. I'll be thirteen."

"That's four weeks from tomorrow. Who will yeh invite to your party?"

"Pardon me for asking the obvious but, what party?"

"Well we can no just let yer thirteenth roll by without a celebration, can we? Aye, we'll get the clubhouse and yeh invite whomever yeh like. Griffy, that girl, Beverly, Ray and Elsie."

It was such a new and pleasant thought, that Blake smiled. He'd never considered the idea.

"That reminds me. Yeh've had a couple of phone calls today. Judy Williams sent her gratitude for amusing her son so mightily and Treva called and said yer to meet the little girl on our dock at nine tomorrow morning. Where are you two headed?"

"I think she was interested in going to someplace called Stone Hollow."

"That, yeh'll like. You mind the ladders, though; and watch your footing."

"*Ummm okay*, sounds like an interesting place," Blake said. He went and stood before the hearth, eyeing a myriad of mementos and curiosities that flanked the aged time-piece and ran to the ends of the mantel.

"Go ahead, step up there, lad. Lots of intriguing things to look at."

Blake stepped up and froze. Staring back at him was the reflection of a boy he almost did not recognize—tan and lean with brown hair that hung over his blue eyes, and showed a hint of red and a little wave. He looked down at his Hawaiian shirt, khaki cargo shorts, and bare feet. He pondered the new strength his body had earned climbing hills, swinging a hammer, hiking out, and trimming sails. He wondered when he had become this person and where the miserable, timid, church-mouse he knew four weeks ago had gone.

"Oh, and yer grandmother called, too. Yeh can call her anytime yeh want, by the way. Talk as long as yeh like."

"I *would* like that! I haven't talked to her in a long time."

"She said, uh… that she wanted yeh to stay here with me for the foreseeable future."

The boy in the mirror suddenly looked familiar again. "But Uncle Carson will be back with the tent on Sunday, won't he?" he said over his shoulder.

"We'll see what he does, Caduggin."

"Why wouldn't he come back? What did I do?"

"Not one blessed thing, son. Yer uncle gets in a mood once in awhile. If he's feeling cornered or he thinks too many folks are expecting too much of him, he makes himself scarce for a spell. So, don' blame yerself."

"It's kind of hard not to."

"Pitch me that little green pouch from up there, yeh see what I'm talking aboot? Right in front of the clock."

Blake gently tossed it over. From it Gunn took something the size of a silver dollar, huffed hot breath on it and polished it with the pouch. Finally he handed it over. Blake supposed it to be a coin, at first, but closer inspection proved otherwise. He blushed.

"That, lad, is the Urquart Clan badge. Yer clan. Yer grandfather would have wanted yeh to have it."

"My family's symbol is a woman with a sword, a palm branch, and no shirt on?"

"Well," the old man smiled impishly, "It's better than a boar's head!"

Blake clothed the woman with his thumb and read the inscription around the edge. "Mean well, speak well, and do well."

"That's yer clan motto."

Blake's jaw dropped.

"Yeh Urquarts have a battle cry, too. 'Trust and go forward."

Mom! Blake thought. *So, that's where... that's why...* "What's yours?" he said.

"Do unto others, then split!"

"Oh, it is not!"

Gunn half laughed, half coughed. "Yeh no believe me? I'm crushed! Nah, it's 'stand ready for peace or for war.'"

"Thank you very much. By the way, there's a letter or something behind the clock up there. I saw it in the mirror."

Gunn leaned forward a little. "I know there is, lad. That's for yer uncle's eyes only, d'yeh here? And he *knows* it's there."

Before he could catch himself he asked "Who is it from?"

Gunn raised his bushy eyebrows and looked at him sternly over the tops of his glasses. "It's from his father." He sat back again. "I don' suppose yer ready for bed now that yeh've had yourself a nap? Why don' yeh fetch your book and I'll read yeh a chapter or two."

Blake ran the errand with eagerness. He settled on the burgundy leather. Gunn adjusted his glasses and read "Chapter Thirteen. How My Shore Adventure Began."

Chapter 16

The coots and mallards couldn't figure out which way to go. The mixed flock swam this way and that, trying to second guess the kayakers' course. Blake stopped paddling for a moment and watched them. He thought they seemed much more nervous than usual. He took a large pair of field binoculars from his lap and scanned the far shores for a particular sail and a particular boat which, at any given moment, might be white or black. He had learned that Hunter was still in Florida. And for the moment the coast seemed clear of his newest adversary.

"What do you know about Garvey Woodhead?" he asked, resuming his stroke.

"Pot-head loser. Creeps around the lake in a double-ended rowboat with a sail."

"Tell me something I don't already know."

"Gets lost in the hills hunting mushrooms on a semi-regular basis. And I don't mean the kind you put on your pizza. Used to have a big, white dog. The usual suspect when anything goes missing."

"Guess what I got yesterday?"

"A sailboat." Mia replied, glibly.

"How'd *you* know?"

"I heard about it."

"How does everyone know everything about me? I hate this!"

"I told you, I know everything!"

"Then did you know it was Garvey's old boat?"

She stopped paddling. "Come again?"

"You heard me. He stole that sharpie from Mr. Gunn, after he got fired from the shop. Completely forgot he'd left his *own* boat in the yard. Now, she's mine."

"And let me guess—you're afraid he's going to come looking for it?"

"Already has. He's been warned."

"*Interesting!*"

"I thought you knew everything?"

"I do."

"Then what did I name her?" he demanded, tossing a taunting smile over his shoulder.

"I'll play your silly little game, what did you name your cunning vessel?"

"You said you knew everything?"

"You asked!"

"Liar!" he laughed and flipped a little water off the end of his paddle at her.

"Alright, c'mon! What did you name it?"

"*Seven Thunders!*"

"That's good. Powerful. I like that."

"It's from the book of Revelation. Hey, I never asked this—what did you name your kayak?"

"I haven't. It's just a big plastic tube I get around in. I don't have to name everything like guys do."

"I bet you have a secret name for it!"

The voyagers passed out of the cool shadow of Trespass Island into the full morning sun.

"You know it's getting really shallow all the way out here?" he said.

"Yeah, well you'll be able to walk all the way from the Island to Grandpa Gunn's place, if we don't get more than a shower every couple of weeks."

Blake took a breath to begin his protest but Mia cut him off at the pass.

"I know, he's not your grandpa. And I'm not your girlfriend either, *right?"*

Blake couldn't quite figure her tone. Was that last part a statement or was it a question? Was this a test?

He waffled. "If you say so."

"I say so!"

A series of loud whistles and chirps rose from the wooded island. Blake looked back. The coots and mallards became silent. They crowded around the shore, under trunks and branches, and overhanging bushes, seeking any cover they could find. The song of chirps repeated.

"What is *that?*"

"Wow, *you* actually don't know something? We *actually* stumped Mr. Professor?"

"Why does everyone call me that? I just like to read a lot of interesting stuff. I don't have much else to do back home in Fort Wayne."

"It's an *osprey*. A pair showed up a couple of days ago. They're big…"

"Ohhh, that's why all the ducks are so nervous! I never imagined a big raptor like that would have a pretty chirp. You always think of them screeching like hawks!"

"Thank you, Mr. Professor!" She smiled mischievously and flung water at him. He giggled and squirmed, then settled with a sigh.

"*Cry of the Osprey*—that'd be a great name for a boat."

"Dibs!" Mia exclaimed.

"On *what?*"

"I called dibs. That's the name of my kayak. *Cry of the Osprey.*"

"What?" Blake said, in disbelief.

She giggled. "That was the secret name of my kayak. It was so secret I didn't even know it. And you guessed it!"

"Bah! I can't believe this. Help! Thief!" He laughed loudly as she splashed him again.

"Thanks for naming my boat, Tux! I love it!"

"Glad I could be of assistance," he said, rolling his eyes.

***

The trip across the lake was easy enough, but hauling *Cry of the Osprey* ashore and into the woods was a chore. Blake was not, Mia had reminded him, the only one with enemies on the lake. They hiked twenty minutes up a trail into the lush, green forest to a sheer bluff, one hundred feet high. Mia stopped at the foot of a stout, wooden ladder which disappeared into a vertical crag in the cliff wall. She slipped out of her backpack and began to pull her curly hair back. Blake gazed up at the ledge for a moment and then stared at her, vacantly. She noticed and smiled.

"Wake up, space cadet!"

"I was just estimating how high up that is."

"Twenty-three feet. The next one is twelve and the last one is ten. You're going first. Don't look down."

"I'm not acrophobic. Um, I mean afraid of heights."

"Um, I know what it means," she said, with an unusual air of friendliness. "I learn a few things at school—when I show up. I'm ready, let's go."

Blake mounted the ladder and had climbed halfway up when it occurred to him. There was no one on the rungs below. He paused.

"Keep going, Tux. Don't look down."

He heard Mia take a deep breath and let it go. Then he felt the ladder jiggle and knew she had begun her ascent.

"Just go on to the next ladder. I'm right behind you," she called up to him as he dismounted.

"You don't want a hand?"

"I'll be alright. Just keep going."

He had nearly reached the top of the second ladder when, from below, he heard nervous panting, and what sounded like someone scooting across the limestone outcrop on their behind. Still, repressing his curiosity, he pushed on without looking back. Finally his hands reached the last of the thick, square rungs on the third ladder. Instead of coming out on top of some pinnacle overlooking all of creation, Blake found himself peering *up* into a magnificent canyon. Walls of algae-streaked limestone towered above, hung with ferns, and roots, and emerald mats of moss, crowned by enormous oaks. The green canopy revealed only the merest hint of the blue world above it. He finished the climb and stepped into this primal realm.

"This is *awesome*!" he called. "There ought to be dinosaurs up here!"

"Welcome to my refuge. Have a look around!" A full five minutes passed before the third ladder began to creak. By the time Mia peered over the top rung, Blake had wandered ahead to a block of tan stone the size of a mini-van. He leaned against it with one hand and ran the other over it from place to place, face aglow with utter delight.

"Crinoids! Here's one with its calyx! Brachiopods! And this is fan coral! Did you know these fossil beds were probably laid down during the flood of Noah?"

She ambled up, a little winded, and slumped her backpack to the ground as if *it* were filled with fossils. "You mean, as in Noah's Ark?" She pulled out a water bottle, took a long swig and rinsed her knees and hands. "I hadn't heard that one."

"What took you so long?"

"Hey, safety first! Right?" she said, pleasantly. She seemed almost determined not to be short with him. She let go a long deep sigh and gazed all around. Blake couldn't help but notice that some of the hardness seemed to have melted from her eyes. "Tux, you're staring again! Are you blushing?"

"No, it was the climb. I'm just winded, that's all."

"I bet you say that to all the girls. Remember the rules, guy! C'mon, wait till you see Stone Hollow."

"You mean this isn't it?"

Mia took up her pack again and led the way with renewed vigor. And then she did something Blake never expected—she began to sing.

***

"Not again?" Mia turned around, fists on her hips. "Will you come on, we're almost there!" Blake was on hands and knees engrossed in yet another fossil bed.

"Hold on, I'm looking for trilobites!"

"I've been coming up here for years, I've never seen one."

"You know what a trilobite is?"

"Uh, duh! Doesn't everybody?" she said. "I even know a little about Noah, too."

"Did you know that almost every ancient culture has a global flood story?"

"There's going to be a *cannibal* story if we don't get up to the hollow and get some lunch! Hop to it, kid!"

The canyon floor became rockier and harder to navigate, the farther they hiked. At last the two adventurers made their way up to a narrow, vertical fissure in the wall. Mia slipped into the crack sideways, holding her pack on her head with one hand. Blake followed suit. "Glad I'm not claustrophobic!" he said.

After what seemed to Blake like an eternity of squeezing, sliding, and shuffling they reached a spot where the crevice began a steep rise. Mia chucked her pack up into the rift, wedged her feet and hands into familiar cracks and hoisted herself up. "No graceful way to do this, but at least there aren't any ladders!"

"So, does this lead out of the canyon?" said Blake, heaving himself up after her.

"Not exactly. Pretty rugged, though, huh? You having fun?"

"This is totally cool. My Dad would split a gasket if he could see me now."

"Too bad he can't,"she said, testing her footing and making another short ascent.

Blake was struck by the underlying malice in her statement.

"Here!" She offered a hand. "Give me your pack. Put your foot in that crack there, and haul yourself up."

They continued to thread their way slowly upward, working around boulders, over outcrops, along ledges. Finally the rift widened enough for them to walk single file. He donned his pack and wondered what invisible imp had filled it with rocks. A strange growling gurgled out from somewhere ahead. Blake stopped in his tracks. Before he could speak, Mia slapped her belly and laughed.

"Oh my gosh! Did you hear my stomach!"

"That was *you*? Man, I thought we were about to be attacked by a bobcat or something."

At last the narrow passage opened into a circular, sun-dappled hollow, like a giant bowl in the limestone, forty feet in diameter. Mia dropped her pack and laid out a beach towel. She sat down at one end, leaving plenty of room. Blake stood, looking up at the forest canopy. A tree trunk, long ago fallen into the pit, offered the only means of reaching the forest floor, twelve feet above.

"Hey you!" She patted the towel next to her. "Sit! Eat!"

Blake sat down and leaned wearily against the wall. He closed his eyes and let out a long sigh.

"Well, what do you think? This is my secret place. Where all my best ideas are born."

"You come up here alone? I'd be scared to death!" He opened his eyes. "But I guess that goes without saying."

"What'd you bring me to eat?" She unpacked oranges and two halves of a foot-long sub.

"Cold pizza, assorted gourmet olives, feta cheese, croutons—the big ones! And cookies," he said, as he unloaded his goodies and added them to the pile between them.

"Looks like someone's been to Nick Tyner's Pizzeria!" Those were the last words spoken for the next fifteen minutes.

***

Blake slouched languidly against the cool limestone, head back, eyes closed. Mia scooped the last of the orange peels and olive pits into a zip-close baggie and stuffed it into a mesh pocket on her pack. A sweet fragrance caught Blake's attention. *What is it?* he thought. *Not the oranges. Very Familiar. Slightly chemical.* It washed over him with a gentle feeling of comfort. It smelled like—mother. Her shampoo. But it was *Mia's*. He heard her settle back against the wall and bite into an apple.

"Want one?" she asked.

A new wave of that scent wafted over him. He inhaled until it filled every corner of his consciousness with pure euphoria.

"No. Thanks, I'm stuffed." *She is so pretty,* he thought. *And she actually likes me.* He wanted to take her hand in his. Then he felt *her* touch. Lightly at first, on his shoulder, then slowly and smoothly downward to rest on the middle of his chest. He kept his eyes closed. His pulse quickened, his thoughts raced to near panic. *What is she going to do? What should I do? What if she...* Trembling, he struggled for words, then said, "Are... are you going to put me in a head lock, or are you going to kiss me?"

"Is there a preference?" she giggled. "That has got to be the best pick-up..." Her abrupt stop spoke volumes. "Keep your eyes closed, Tux."

He whimpered faintly. "What is it?"

"Well, the good news is, it ain't a spider. But it *is* the biggest one of its kind I've ever seen. Tux, how do you feel about..." Blake opened his eyes and gave a short, sharp gasp. "*Snakes?*"

A serpent lay like six feet of black ribbon down the wall, over his shoulder and across his chest. He gulped and darted a pleading look at Mia. She was smiling impishly and slowly inching away.

"Get it off me...please?"

"Go ahead, Tux, catch him!" She pulled her legs up and shifted onto her knees. "Wait 'til he's close to your hand, then grab him right behind the head!"

Blake went pale at the suggestion. The snake descended another six inches.

"Relax, will you? It's not like it's a...wait, don't tell me! Even *I* know this one! How many kinds of poisonous snakes live in Indiana?" she droned.

"Four," he peeped.

"Riiight! And only *one* kind lives anywhere close to these here parts. Does that look like a timber rattler to you, Tux?"

He wobbled his head in reply, which prompted the snake to slide precipitously onto his lap, piling itself like a thick black rope thrown carelessly on a dock.

"Yup, what'cha got there is a good ol' black rat snake! Think about it Tux—if you caught that snake you could put it under Griffy's boat cover, or in your uncle's sleeping bag; personally, I'd feed it down the deck hatch on my dad's boat while he's wining and dining the mayor's wife. Hey, are you still breathing?"

Blake strained his eyes downward, only to meet those of the serpent, staring back. To his relief, the reptile shifted a large loop of its body onto the ground and appeared poised to make its escape. Gathering all of his courage, he twitched his right leg a few times. Shimmering black coils cascaded over his left hip as the serpent fled for the crevice that led down to the canyon. Blake got to his feet and watched the last inches of the creature vanish into the gap. He caught his breath. Gone were the dreamy aromas of orange-peel and flowery shampoo. Now the musty odors of damp earth, rotting wood, and his own sweat filled his nostrils.

"You know, I've heard of a 'whiter shade of pale,' but…"

He turned to face her. She was still smiling. "Well, I'm glad you think it was funny."

"Panic never got anybody anything but killed, Tux."

"I'll try to remember that, thank you very little."

"F.E.A.R. False Evidence Appearing Real!"

"Is this going to be a lecture?"

"Will you relax? You knew in your *head* that that snake wasn't poisonous."

"Venomous. There's a difference."

"Now see? There's my professor using his head! You knew it wasn't a rattler, but you let yourself believe the F.E.A.R. and totally spazzed out!"

She stood up, took a long drink and popped the nozzle on her bottle shut with a smack. "It's all in your head, Tux. You get hold of your head and you can control your body. Just like handling a snake."

"And it's all just that easy," he sneered, donning his backpack.

"No. It's *not*, Blake. It's *hard*. But it's either that or go around being a scared little boy all of your life." Mia crossed to the other side of the hollow. He scowled at her as soon as her back was turned. "I bet you're not afraid to climb this log up and out of here." she said.

"No, who would be?"

She didn't answer, but mounted the log and worked her way up the makeshift ramp slowly and carefully, never looking down.

***

Blake hauled himself over the lip of the pit and got his bearings. Something was missing. "Where's the trail?" he said, glancing around, nervously.

"We blaze our own!"

"We won't get lost?"

"You can go back the way we came if you want. I'm sure your scaly little friend would appreciate the company."

"But we won't get lost, right?" he said, looking down into the hollow, weighing whether he had the courage to make the trip back alone.

"Don't panic, Tux! I've been this way like a million times. Look, what's this?" She pointed to a heavy line on the map."

"The fire road, a quarter mile from here, northeast." He thought about it for a moment. That's like from the clubhouse to the point. That's not far at all."

"It's pretty hard to miss. So, you ready?"

He stared at the map. "You won't leave me, will you?"

Mia looked annoyed, but then a little more of hardness melted from her eyes.

"No Tux, I won't leave you. Get your compass!"

Blake kept them on course and in fifteen minutes they reached a narrow gravel road.

"Looks like there's a fire tower in the direction we're going. Are we allowed to go up in it?"

"Yup."

"Awesome! It says it's the highest point on the lake!"

"That, it is," she said, without enthusiasm.

Another fifteen minutes and the forest backed away to expose the hill's summit to sun and sky.

Mia wiped her brow and surveyed the one hundred fifty foot observation tower.

"Race you to the top!" Blake challenged, as he wrestled his big binoculars free from the jumbled contents of his pack.

"I paid my dues back at the ladders, buddy. But don't let me stop you." She dropped her pack and thrust a hand inside.

"What are you going to do?"

Mia extracted a small roll of toilet paper and a zip-close bag. She lifted her eyebrows at him and walked toward the underbrush.

"Lookout for poison ivy!" he said, under his breath.

"I heard that!"

***

Blake leaned against the rail and scoured the lake like a pop-eyed owl perched on the pinnacle of Drascombe Heights. Everywhere, vacation season was in full swing. Wave runners and ski boats churned the upper lake into a watery chaos worthy of the name 'Devil's Toilet-bowl.' Giant houseboats, sixty feet long, chugged lazily from cove to cove on the lower lake. He was tracking three bass boats up the channel when a familiar sail caught his eye—that of a lateen-rigged sharpie, her black hull cutting over the wakes. Blake rested his elbows on the railing and adjusted his focus. Her white-shirted skipper, stood in the stern, his collar turned up. He steered with one hand and shielded his eyes with the other, as he himself scanned the distance for something of importance. Blake stamped a foot as he recognized her shirtless crew, slouched unmistakably across the middle of the boat. It was Jack, sure enough—rib-bone necklace and all. There would be another late-night inquisition when Uncle Carson got back, Blake promised himself.

"Whatcha staring at? Mia called from the foot of the tower. "You finally find the nude beach?"

"Ha ha. Nothing. Just a pagan and a pirate."

"The *Covenant*?"

"In black and white. Looks like they've got a big duffel of some sort on board. They're just turning down on the lower lake."

"Shroom hunting. It's always the same. Two go out, one comes back. There'll be a party in Pemberton next weekend."

"Drug smugglers? Pirates, thieves, *and* drug smugglers!" Then it hit him. He lowered his binoculars. "Did you say Pemberton?"

"They call it Voodoo Jack's Party Shack."

"Dang it!" he roared, and pounded his fist on the wooden rail repeatedly. "Dang it! Dang it! Dang it!"

"Wow, do you kiss your mother with that mouth?" she said, sarcastically.

"That's my Nanna's house, you idiot!"

"Hey you don't have to call me names!"

"Well what would *you* do?"

"If that's the way you're going to treat me…" Mia picked up her pack and started walking.

"Wait! Blake yelped, as he ran to the opposite side of the platform. "Wait! You said you wouldn't leave me! I'm sorry I lost my temper, but those freaks are in my Nanna's house doing who knows what!"

She paused. "So, what are you going to do about it? Two kinds of people Tux. Which one are you going to be?"

He stared down at her, lips clenched between his teeth. He looked back at the lake and drew a long, pensive breath. "The one that *makes* things happen," he decreed resolutely.

"That's my Tux! C'mon Crusoe, we've got two miles ahead of us."

***

The trail wound on and finally began to descend toward the channel. Blake marched a few steps behind Mia and fumed quietly. "You still back there, kiddo?" she said over her shoulder.

"How do you know so much about those two?"

"I told you. I know everything. This is my lake. I make it my business to know."

"I suppose being cozy with Officer Mueller helps a lot."

She stopped abruptly and faced him. "I don't think I like the way you said that!"

"I didn't mean anything by it," Blake stammered. "It just sounded wrong. I'm sorry. I was having a great time until I spotted the *Covenant*."

She gave him a long, hard stare. "Alright." She started walking again. "Buck's had his eye on Voodoo Jack and Kalijah for a while. Thinks they might be connected to bigger fish."

"What bigger fish?"

"Don't know. Maybe that's why he's keeping an eye on them? Ya think?"

Blake made a face at the back of her head.

"Hey you hear that?" she said, and stopped. "There it is again. Sounds like… something crying like… a sick squirrel."

Blake hitched his pack up and jogged around her, toward the bend in the trail. "It sounds like a little kid to me!"

Mia followed, without picking up her pace. "Don't get too close, it might have rabies!" When she rounded the bend she found Blake doing his best to console a bawling child.

"Hey little guy? Don't cry, we'll help you! What's your name?"

"Good luck with that. I don't think he can understand you."

"He looks old enough to talk."

"Yeah, but he don't exactly look like his folks speaka da English. Try Spanish."

"I don't know Spanish. I thought you did"

"Why would I?"

"You've got Mexican housekeepers."

"Like I said, why would I? They're just the help."

"Here, amigo, you want some water? Uh, agua? Agua?" He offered the child his water bottle. But the sniffling tot looked only the more frightened to hear familiar words coming out of this strange, white boy and began to cry again in earnest.

"Man, you gotta get him to stop. I can't stand babies crying. It gives me a migraine."

Blake reached deep into the front pouch of his pack and produced a little red flashlight and big chocolate-chip cookie.

"Hey amigo! Check this out!" He pretended the light didn't work then shined it into his own eyes. He groped at the air in clownishly pantomimed blindness. Amigo throttled back on the bawling and looked ready to give up a giggle.

Blake repeated the show twice more to unbridled bubbly laughter.

"Brilliant performance. Honestly, how do you lose something that big? Where could his parents be?" she said.

"Ta-dah!" Blake offered him the flashlight and the cookie. Amigo reached incautiously for the cookie but pushed the light back to Blake.

He looked Amigo up and down. "Beach. They're at a beach."

"How do you know?"

"Well just look, he's got sand all over him!" Blake savored the moment and added "Ya think?" He zoomed the flashlight around Amigo's head like an airplane.

"I hate to inform you, Sherlock," she said with a self-satisfied smirk. "But there are a hundred little coves with beaches all down the channel."

"Ah ha! But this is the *fine*, white stuff. You only get that at the State Recreation areas. And on this side of the channel that can only mean Blue Rock SRA."

"How do *you* know all that?"

"I work on the lake. Why wouldn't I?" he replied, smiling at the child.

***

Blake stopped for the umpteenth time to pull his hat down over his eyes and bounce his piggyback passenger into a more comfortable position. The cool green canopy had given way to blue sky and blazing sun. Motorboat-chop lapped sloppily at the weedy shoreline, punctuated by the occasional piping cry of a killdeer. Now he wished he'd been wrong about that fine white sand. It poured like white-hot grit into his sandals. The little castaway clung to his back like a steamy, damp towel covered with cookie crumbs.

Mia schlepped along, sleeves of her tee-shirt rolled all the way up. Both backpacks swung rhythmically from either end of a makeshift yoke, balanced on one shoulder. "Well Chico, you see anyone you recognize?" she said, as they plodded down the beach.

They passed a dozen families who played in the water, lounged on towels as big as rugs, or rummaged through coolers. No one seemed to be looking for anything but sunscreen, much less a lost child. Ahead, two fat gray gulls squabbled over a huge, half-eaten hot dog. Wary of the approaching humans, they moved their frenetic flap-and-squawk away, a few feet at a time. The less distracted bird skewered the meat and took to the air, inches ahead of his enraged antagonist. Blake was watching them wheel out over the water when, like echoes of the shrieking pursuit, sounds of a new squabble drifted up the beach. The dead-weight on his back stirred to sudden life and began calling out sleepily, "Abuelita! Abuelita!"

Blake dropped to his knees and disembarked his sweaty burden.

"Look at you," said Mia, "you're drenched, Tux. Must be why they call them 'wetbacks!'"

"You sound like my dad," he said without looking back. "Go get 'em Amigo! Where are they?" But the little boy still clung to his arm with one hand and continued to call for Abuelita. "Where's Ab…Ab… Oh just show me, come on!" He took Amigo's hand. Without hesitation the little boy dragged him in a half stumbling run across the burning sands, straight for the sounds of the quarrel.

At the waterline, standing in front of a sixteen foot, flat-bottomed motorboat, a woman of grandmotherly deportment was hysterically berating a wilted girl—whom Blake guessed to be about Mia's age. Two gray-haired men stood waist-deep in the lake and watched gravely from either side of the uncovered motor.

"Hey!' Mia shouted. "Does this belong to you?" The woman kept right on raving in Spanish, but one of the old men took notice. His somber expression turned instantly to elation. he slapped his companion on the shoulder and directed his attention to the approaching trio. They abandoned their stations, and charged out of the water shouting in joyful recognition of the little boy who, though now equally excited, still refused to release his grip on Blake.

"Gracia a Dio, gracia a Dio!" The older, potbellied man cried, scooping the child up in his arms. Amigo began chattering a mile a minute.

The other man, aged, yet lean and muscular, turned his attention to Blake. "Muchas gracias! Muy muchas gracias, mi hombre!" He patted Blake on the back so hard that he knocked him off balance.

"Salma!" he shouted to the ranting woman, whose tirade had not abated for one second. "Salma! Aqui! Salma!"

She stopped and searched with an imperious glare for the poor soul who had dared interrupt her. When her eyes locked on the little boy she gasped, burst into tears and charged up the beach wailing "Marcelo! Mi monito!" She seized her 'little monkey,' clasped his head to her chest and wept. The strong man made some explanation to her, which resulted in Blake being swept into her tear-drenched embrace and showered with kisses.

Mia circumnavigated the blustery family reunion and approached the boat. Backpacks slumped into the sand. She planted her fists on her hips. "Number six," she said, in disgust. "We meet again."

"Is big problem motor," said the girl at the bow.

"Ya think?" Mia said, hopping over the side. She made her way to the stern. "You got a screwdriver or anything, Chica?" She turned around and pantomimed a twisting motion with her hand. "Screwdriver?"

"No."

Mia pointed. "My pack."

The girl raised her eyebrows. "You pack? Is bueno. So what."

"Por favor, Señorita?" Mia sneered.

"My name is Sylvana," she said, solemnly. She fetched the pack and pitched it back to Mia. She produced a multi-tool from a side pouch, unfolded a screwdriver, and bent over the motor.

Sylvana made her way around the boat to get a better look at Mia's tampering. "My name is Sylvana."

"Mia."

"Thanks for bring my brother, Mia."

"Thank Tux. He's your hero." She gestured toward the huddle on the sand, which was now making its way to a well-laden picnic table. The muscular man began to shout toward the forest through cupped hands, then toward the campground.

Mia extracted a little metal cylinder and blew hard through it. Sylvana caught a glimpse of Blake and gave a little wave.

"Su novio? You boyfriend?"

"No, no es mi novio," Mia replied, without thinking.

"You speak Spanish, *good.*" Silvana cast a suspicious glance over her shoulder.

"Nope, no habla, Señorita." Mia re-installed the cylinder and made a couple of adjustments, squeezed the bulb on the fuel line twice, then moved to the driver's seat. She made sure the throttle was in neutral, lifted the choke lever and turned the key. The starter whirred and the motor struggled to life.

The huddle stopped in its tracks and stared in delight as if that gurgling, popping, smoking engine were singing the happiest tune they'd ever heard. Mia shut it off, grabbed her pack and hopped out of the boat.

"Get your gear bud, let's get the *Osprey* and get out of here."

"I think they want us to stay and have dinner with them."

The potbellied man ambled down to the boat, smiling in disbelief. He spoke to Mia and then glanced at Sylvana.

"Mi grandfather say thanks for fix the boat. He say how you know fix boat?"

"De nada. It belongs to my father," she said. "Tell him I'm sorry Daddy gave you the clunker. Numero ses is muy malo. Remember that, next time."

Sylvana relayed the message. The old man chuckled, said something in reply and returned to the picnic table.

"He say you should work for you father."

Mia bit her bottom lip, shifted her pack and trudged up to the picnic table, which now sported a banquet. Several more relatives joined the party, all fawning over little Marcelo and glad-handing Blake. The strong man beckoned Sylvana to join the family once more.

"You ready to go?"

"If we don't stay they'll be insulted."

"You found their kid, I fixed their boat and they'll be insulted if we don't stay for tacos?"

"I'd kinda like to stay, just a little while."

"Is okay," interrupted Sylvana. "We take you. Tio say is no problem."

"Gracias, um, I'm Blake."

"My name is Sylvana." She smiled sweetly and brushed a shelf of hair out of her eyes. "Thanks for bring Marcelo. Is big problem for me."

"Um, you're welcome." His cheeks flushed. "I guess I'd better go. My ride is leaving."

"No, we take you. Tio say is no problem."

Blake looked to Mia. "Would you mind?"

"Fine with me. Saves me a mile of paddling."

"Hey, Sylvana," called one of the young men at the table. "Como se llama su novio?"

"Blake!" she replied with a giggle. "No es me novio!"

"You can call me Tux," Blake added.

Mia shot Sylvana a look. "I think I *will* stay, Tux. I'll take one of those orange sodas."

Chapter 17

Blake kept one hand pressed firmly against his stomach and rolled his window down with the other. He pushed his face into the wind as the rust-scarred, blue van jostled and squeaked its way over the brick-paved side-streets of Pemberton. Tripper Gunn lounged casually behind the wheel steering with the thumb and forefinger of one hand and with his opposite knee. He hummed tunefully and puffed thick clouds of smoke from his pipe.

"You don't think Nanna will mind that we changed the locks on her house, do you?"

"No doubt aboot it! She'd demand it, if I know her—and I do! What's wrong with yeh, lad? You're a little green around the gills."

"I get carsick. Maybe we should postpone until we can call Nanna?"

"Called this morning. No answer. She turns the ringer off so her patient can sleep—which is most of the time."

Blake admired the ornate, old houses and thickly wooded lots until they passed a lady walking a Chihuahua.

"This sure is a neat neighborhood. If Uncle Carson is here, maybe he can help you with the locks and I could look around?"

"I don' want to disappoint yeh lad, but he'll no be there. He left his keys at my place like he always does. That's how we're getting' in! I'll need yeh 'round for a bit. Yeh can explore after we put Jack's effects on the curb."

Blake's stomach made a silent but strong protest. He swallowed hard and regretted his resolution on the tower, the day before. It had been easy to look down from that lofty vantage and declare war on the tiny pirates and their tub-toy boat as it sailed into the distance. But now he was invading their territory, their very headquarters. *But it's Nanna's house!* he thought. *But why can't the grown-ups just handle these things? Life is just beginning to settle down, why do I have to be the one to throw the match into the powder keg—especially when Uncle Carson might be in it?*

"Yeh know how to run a lawnmower don't yeh, Caduggin? We'll have to come down here every week, now that we're putting the supposed groundskeeper out on his ear."

Gunn slowed the van and turned into a long concrete driveway, lurching over the curb on Blake's side.

"Well, there 'tis Caddugin" He switched off the ignition. "When was the last time yeh were here?"

"I don't remember. Maybe when I was five."

"I'll go open it up. The tools an' such are in that bookit in the back."

Blake let his gut settle for a moment while he surveyed the chocolate brown bungalow.

"C'mon Lad!" Gunn called from the porch. "If yeh want time to look around, yeh better get moving. I want to stop by the club in time to repossess the *Darby McGraw*. Jack's defaulted on his contract and she's rightfully mine now!"

Blake closed his eyes tightly and groaned.

***

The screen door might as well have been a brick wall. Blake stood at the top of the steps and peered uneasily across the porch. He could see Gunn lumbering into the dining room, the hardwood floor creaking with each step.

"Here's the mail. I would'na doubt but there's a postcard in all of that!" he said loudly, for Blake's benefit. "C'mon Caduggin, there's nobody here but us chickens!" The creaking resumed as Gunn vanished into the depths of the house.

His pounding heart echoed in his ears. He lugged his right foot forward, then his left. He held his breath, jerked the screen door open and darted to the dining room table only to be confronted by a mountain of envelopes, ads, and Pemberton newspapers. He looked for a horizontal surface onto which he could sort the heap. Gunn reappeared from an adjoining hall.

"Leave that. We'll bag it up and take it with us." He went into the kitchen. "Does'na look like he's even staying in the house! Let's go check the garage."

The opportunity to escape the house had just won out over the aching desire to hear something from his mother when he spotted it. Just a glossy, red corner of a card but he knew exactly what it was.

"I need to use the bathroom, I'll be right there."

"If yeh insist! It's through the hall, there," replied Gunn, already at the back door. Blake waited for the whack of the screen door, snatched the card from the pile and dashed back out onto the front porch. It featured a French Revolution-era guillotine. He turned it over and his mother's voice filled his head.

> Hi sweetheart,
> Sis and I saw Notre Dame, today! It was simply breathtaking.
> The French have been very nice to us.
> I hope you get to spend some time at the lake!
> Sis says to tell you "Shave and a Haircut!"
> (Guess who chose the card?)
> I Love you,
> Mom

Then he noticed there was a line through the word "hair." He moved to a sunny spot between two columns at one corner of the porch and squinted at it closely. It wasn't a line at all, but a short rusty brown bristle. Stymied by the weird coincidence, he scrutinized it even more closely, tilting the card this way and that. The whack of the back door startled him and he puffed the hair off the card and into oblivion. "No! Dang it!" he winced. He darted back through the house, and met Gunn in the kitchen.

"Sorry I took so long. I was just coming out."

"I thought yeh fell in! Come look at this."

The garage-door opener moaned balefully. The varnished wooden door-panels clacked and chunked the way up their tracks, slowly revealing what surely was a den of iniquity.

"That's Voodoo Jack's Party Shack, if ever I saw it!" said Gunn.

Two mangy couches flanked a low, concrete birdbath. Upon it stood a neon-purple hookah, with four smoking stems. Above that, a mirrored disco-ball glinted meekly. A vast pile of trash and garbage flowed out of an overstuffed barrel like a refuse-vomiting Vesuvius.

"Tell me that's not on our list, today?"

"Nope. It's on yer uncle's. Get the bookit, Caduggin. We'll start here."

***

Blake's stomach rumbled loudly, as he slid the lock-core into the deadbolt on the front door. The job would be finished in a matter of seconds and he was counting every one of them. That is until the last screw stopped half way home, and stuck fast.

Gunn stood on the porch, relighting his pipe. "Let me have a go at it." He shooed Blake back into the living room. His eyes darted back and forth, scrutinizing every nook, every corner and cranny, every fold, every place in which an eight-legged abomination might conceal itself. He contemplated the mantel which, like the old Scotsman's, was a museum of memorabilia. Yet, there was something conspicuously different, here. In the middle, there was a large gap where a clock might have been expected. He bent over and strained to see into the dark recess of the brick fireplace, then hopped up and down several times to make sure there was nothing alive up on the mantel. He steeled his nerves and stepped up on to the hearth.

His suspicions proved to be correct. An area of dustless wood, perfectly square, told the tale. Next to it, stood a framed photo of his grandfather, posed in a kilt, sporran and all. An eighteen inch dirk hung at his side and he leaned on a hiking stick with its top carved into Scottish thistle. Something twinged between two toes on his right foot. He wriggled them together, which helped for a moment. Gunn, hunched over the lock, grunted unintelligible curses then finally huffed out to the van.

Blake stepped off the hearth and approached a bookcase across the room. Warily, he opened its latticed door. It was filled with old books and pieces of decorative china, all ordered and positioned just-so. On the middle shelf, sitting slightly askew, there was an empty wooden rack, six inches wide. It looked as if it were designed to hold something long and flat. The van door slammed and Blake realized he was about to lose his chance to escape to the porch, a chance he did not waste. Safely outside in the sun and breeze, he leaned against one of the columns and rubbed his toes vigorously. Gunn ascended the steps, armed with a little can of penetrating oil and a new screw, and returned to his battle with the lock.

"Treepah!" called a cheerful, if distinctly non-local voice. Blake half turned on one foot, trying to see who was coming, as he struggled to get his sandal back on. A short, wiry Asian man with a mop of salt-and-pepper hair, was coming up the walk.

"Haraguchi!" Gunn returned, with equal aplomb.

"Gesundheit!" said the man, with a chuckle. He stopped and placed one foot resolutely on the first step. "Hey, this your kid? He look like trouble!"

"He will be if we raise him right! This is Clarissa's grandson, Blake."

"Hello, Blake. My name Haraguchi," he said, extending a hand. Blake hurried to the steps and shook it.

"Pleased to meet you, sir." Then it dawned on him. "Wait, *The* Haraguchi?"

"Wow! You hear that, Gunn? *The* Haraguchi! I must have got famous sometime! Maybe I put that on my dojo in big letter: *The* Haraguchi!" He stretched the words in the air with an expansive pantomime. "How you know my name?"

"My friend, Mia, is one of your students," he said, quite annoyed.

"Ohhh! Mia Devlin? That girl intense! Wait, you Mia's friend? You must be Tux?"

"Yeah, that's what she calls me."

"You got good heart, Tux. She need friend like you."

"I don't think she needs anybody."

"She very hard on outside. Inside—different story. You strong, inside—here, and here," he said, tapping a forefinger to his temple, then his chest.

"I'm not so sure about that."

"Hey, you got bully problem? You come down my Karate dojo, I teach you how kick everybody ass! Haha! No, not true! I teach Karate for self defense only. Treepah, Doris get angry if you don't come for lunch."

"Well, we'd no want to anger the Empress, now would we? What needs fixin' now?"

"Twelve o'clock, you come and find out. She got big fat list, this time! He laughed himself all the way back down the walk. "Don't be late Treepah!"

"What a merry little fellow. Not at all what I would have expected," said Blake, standing on his left foot and rubbing the middle toes of the other, again.

"Mind your manners, lad." Gunn replied, casually. The new screw went in perfectly.

***

The school of koi sped across Mr. Haraguchi's pond like a salvo of multi-colored torpedoes.

"They see me coming mile away!" chortled Mr. Haraguchi.

"Those are huge fish! That guy must be three feet long!" Blake said.

"Those not fish! Those hogs with fins! Eat me out of house and home! Why you think I gotta go work every day!"

Blake crouched down at the edge of the pond. It was a churning frenzy of fish heads that splashed and shoved, their mouths gaping for anything that might be close enough to gulp down.

"Don't fall in, we never see you again!" he said, appended with a customary chuckle. "Here!" He pulled the lid off a coffee can and handed it to Blake. "Give them some of that, they go crazy!"

He scattered a handful of pellets across the water and watched the chaos.

"How long you know Mia?" said Haraguchi.

"I don't know. About a month."

"She tell me all about Tux."

"Is that a good thing, or a bad thing?"

Haraguchi squatted down next to him. "Blake, you know difference between a trip and a journey?"

Blake threw another handful of pellets and stared in wide-eyed delight at the kaleidoscopic feeding frenzy. "One's longer than the other, would be my guess."

"Man leave home, take trip some place; stay awhile. Come back home. Nothing different. Home same, people same, man same. Man on *journey* leave home, maybe long time. He visit many place, his eyes open. He see new things, he meet people, learn about new ways. Some day he go home, but nothing same. Home change, people change—everything different. He cannot stay there. Why?"

Blake pondered for a moment. "Because everything at home *was* still the same. The man changed."

"You are young man on journey Blake. But, remember, some people never change; but we still try to love them."

Blake scooped up another handful of pellets, but did not throw them.

"I go see Empress about lunch," Haraguchi said, slapping his thighs and rising. "You stay here, give names all these fish."

"How many do you have?"

"I don't have any. But look, my pond is full of them!"

***

The *Darby McGraw* rocked gently by the dock, as night spread over Gunn's harbor like a cloak. Blake sat in the bay window, reading his postcards for the umpteenth time. The raid on Nanna's house had yielded a total of four more. He sequenced them by their postmarks and filed through them; first staring at the picture, then flipping the card and reading his mother's message, one after the other, over and over. They *seemed* to be from his mother, yet not from the one he thought he knew.

On the front of the third card a big, glass pyramid, glowed in the Paris night. On the back he read:

> *My Dearest Blake,*
> *Daddy has to work in another city for three days!*
> *I'm taking Sis to the Louvre today and tomorrow.*
> *It makes me want to paint again!*
> *I hope to hit Versailles Palace the day after.*
> *I know Nanna is taking you to some great places*
> *too!*
> *I love you so much,*
> *Mom*

A pouting gargoyle graced card four, chin resting on its hands, its tongue stuck out at the world.

> *How is my sweetheart?*
> *Sis has been awful, so today I paid a street*
> *artist to sketch her—as a gargoyle!*
> *Then I dragged her on a tour of the catacombs!*
> *She blubbered the whole way. I thought you might*
> *appreciate that! (It was really creepy, though!)*
> *You're my Hero!*
> *Love,*
> *Mom*

The last card featured an old painting of a sailboat crewed by several children and a man, obviously having the time of their lives.

> *Sweetheart,*
> *It seems like it's been forever. You're probably having*
> *so much fun that you've forgotten all about us. I*
> *wouldn't blame you. It's great to be back in France,*
> *but I'd trade it all to be with you!*
> *I miss you so much, I cry at night.*
> *Love,*
> *Mom*

He looked at the irritated spot between his toes. Gunn had given him some ointment and now it only itched a little. "*Back* in France?" he wondered, aloud. What did that mean? What had come over her? She never would have defied Father's edicts at home. Yes, she bent his rules for Blake—often. But *this* was, to use Father's favorite word, rebellion. Had she changed, or was this who she really was? He pondered Haraguchi's words. Was mother on a journey, too? Would they be so different to each other, when she came home? Would she still love him, then? It had been a stressful couple of days, almost more than he could cope with. He pressed his palms against is face, took a deep breath, and resolved that he would not cry.

Chapter 18

Blake speared a wedge of syrup-soaked waffle and poked it into one cheek. He slapped his cards on the table with a triumphant flourish.

"Fifteen two, fifteen four, a run of three makes seven, aaand…" He counted the points off on the Cribbage board with a red scoring peg. "The Jack of Heels makes eight! Aaand I win. Aaagain!" He stuffed more waffle in his mouth and smiled smugly.

"Hah! I should'a stood in bed!" Gunn huffed. He unfolded a copy of the *Pemberton Patriot* and snapped it taught between them. "What's on yer plate today, Caduggin?"

"I thought I'd ride over to Freeman with you. Maybe visit Mr. Dubois."

"Fine. Yeh want to race with Griffy, this afternoon? I forgot to tell yeh he called, yesterday."

"I guess." Blake, sipped his coffee and let his eyes run over the back page of the newspaper.

"And you're taking lunch with your new señorita's family, tomorrow?"

"She's no my señorita," he replied, vacantly. He was engrossed in the Crime Watch section. "Anna June's Auntie-Q's reported a heavy, black, opera cape was stolen from the shop."

"That's weird," said Gunn, not giving it a second thought.

Not for a weirdo, Blake thought. "What's the date on that paper?"

"Last week's."

Blake retrieved the stack of *Pemberton Patriots* from the kitchen counter.

He ordered them by publication date and then scrutinized the Crime Watch section of each one. "Graffiti...public intoxication...skate boarding...Wow, listen to this one! Catfish head—Donny and Hazel Winslow reported that the preserved head of a prize-winning catfish was stolen out of their garage. The record-breaking, *seventy-pound* catfish was hauled out of Highland Creek Reservoir by Mr. Winslow in 1965."

Gunn lowered his paper. "I remember that! Zebco company gave him all sorts of free tackle for hooking it with their gear. Put his picture on their packaging and everything!"

"Seventy pounds?"

"Aye, and there's one bigger. I saw it with me own eyes ten year ago, down the Lower. Just come straight up and sucked a mallard down in one gulp!"

Blake was not comforted by the notion that he had been swimming, blissfully unaware, in a lake that contained a catfish of those proportions. He checked the date on the paper. "It was stolen about three weeks ago."

"Eh, people'll take anything. It'll probably turn up at our flea market, sooner than later."

The clock on the mantel began to chime sweetly. Blake stared over his shoulder at it until it finished. "I think *we* may have something to report. What happened to my Nanna's mantel clock?"

Gunn knitted his bushy, white eyebrows together. "I don' follow yeh, lad."

"Nanna's mantel clock—it's gone."

"I don' remember as she ever had one."

"There's a big gap in the middle of all the stuff on her mantel and a clean place where something square used to sit."

Gunn pursed his lips and wracked his memory. He heaved himself up from the table and lumbered over to the bookcase. He returned, thumbing through a sailing club yearbook from 1977. "Here 'tis," he said, folding the cover back and laying it on the table.

It was a picture of Blake's grandfather in a tuxedo, being handed a large, loving-cup trophy. It was mounted on a cubical, wooden base. Blake read the caption aloud. "The first Declan Urquart Service Award is presented to its namesake at the Commodore's Dinner Dance."

"Yeh say it's gone?"

"Aye. And there was something else, too. Out of the bookcase. There was a little wooden rack with nothing on it."

The old man drummed his knuckles on the table and scowled at the picture.

"We should ask Uncle Carson. He's due back today, right?"

"Go brush yer teeth, lad, then we're off!"

***

"Mr. Dubois?" Blake called, quietly. He stuck his head into the shadowy room. "Mr. Dubois?" He knocked tentatively on the doorframe. Still there was no stirring, no shift, nor snore from the old man in the recliner. Blake crept to the edge of the chair and stopped. Korbin lay stretched out and motionless, mouth agape, narrow white crescents shone like grotesque voodoo-moons through half open eyelids. Blake strained his vision in the dimness and struggled to catch the slightest rise or fall of shirt-buttons. He turned an ear and listened for the faintest whisper of breath, for any sign that the spirit of life still animated this ancient ebony vessel, but he could not. Panic and sadness at once began to swell up from his chest into his throat. He had never been in the presence of the dead before and it terrified him.

A dietary aide swung into the room, loaded down with a full lunch tray. She practically shouted, "Lunchtime Mr. Dubois!" Blake screeched and spun around. The dietary aide shrieked and launched the tray into orbit. Its contents crashed to earth in a cascade of china and tableware sufficient to wake the dead—Korbin revived with a holler and clamped a big hand on Blake's belt. He screeched again. The aide followed suit.

"Box car's on fire! Jump!" boomed Korbin.

The light went on. The woman, finger still on the switch, glowered in disgust. A crowd of muttering gawkers slowly collected in the door behind her like flotsam washed up by motorboat chop. "Just who are you little man and where do you belong?"

Korbin came to his senses and discovered he had a boy by the britches. He shook his captive, feebly. "Speak up now, who is this?"

"It's me Mr. Dubois. I was trying not to wake you." Blake's voice quavered.

"Aw, now! Now, now! It's the prince of Uh-quot! Missy, you clean all that up and get me my lunch, you hear? And bring this boy an ice cream cup! And a real spoon, not one of those splintery, sawed-off tongue depressors!"

She turned on her heel and huffed out the door, yelling for the housekeeping staff.

"Where's Cawson, boy?"

"I was hoping that you would know?"

"Haven't seen him all week." The motor on Korbin's recliner started to whir. The entire chair rose and tilted forward, lifting Dubois to his feet. He was taller than Tripper Gunn and towered over Blake. "He ever tell you how he joined the Navy?" He seized a four-footed cane and ambled stiffly toward the bathroom. "Flyin' a kite! Just a minute, here."

Housekeeping arrived and began the cleanup operation: sweeping, mopping, sponging, grumbling, and tossing unfriendly looks Blake's way. He tried not to make eye contact. A stormy flushing sound heralded the return of Korbin to his electric throne.

"Sit down in that wheelchair boy, make yourself at home." Blake complied, happy to have his back to the housekeepers.

"See, boy, life just happens to some people. Least that's what *they* think. And Cawson is one of those people. You follow?" he said, as the chair returned to ground-level.

"I think so."

"Couldn't wait to get outta his daddy's house and on his own. So, on his eighteenth birthday he packed up and hitchhiked all the way to California. Well, one fine day he's thummin' along the highway when he spies a fifty-foot dragon kite, dancing in the blue sky—one of those silver ones made out of Mar-lon."

"Mylar?"

"That's it! Well, he saunters on down that hillside to make the acquaintance of the fellah holding the string. And old boy hands the string to your uncle and says he'll just go up to his truck and get 'em both a beer."

"Now, you're wondering how this all leads to the Navy?" Something behind Blake caught Korbin's attention. "Say, there, young lady! Where this boy's ice cream? And where's my lunch? A fellah get's hongry!" Blake glanced over his shoulder. The cleaning crew had just finished swabbing up and stationed a yellow 'wet floor' cone in the doorway. Korbin continued. "So, no sooner had that fellah pulled the brew outta his cooler and what you think happened?"

Blake shrugged.

"The wind quit! Down come that old silver dragon, oh-so-graceful over one of those giant, electric towers!"

"No way!" Blake chortled, in disbelief.

"Cawson hadn't let go that string and taken ten steps 'fore it hit those power lines and boom! He was flat on his face listenin' the sound of squealin' tires!"

"The guy just took off and left him?"

"Well, he wasn't alone for long! 'Bout the time he collected himself and got to the top of the hill, here come a jeep up from the naval base, just across the way. An officer and a couple of M.P.'s the size of grizzlies."

"What did they want?"

"Just wanted to alert him to the fact that someone had just blacked-out half o' Orange County and Summit Naval Station." Korbin suppressed a laugh. "That and if he'd ever seen the inside of a Navy brig!"

"So, how did he get out of it?"

"They made him an offer he couldn't refuse. Next thing his folks knew, they were gettin' postcards from the Persian Gulf!"

"How long after that was the sewage accident?"

"Few years, I reckon. Course his Daddy died before that, while he was away in the Gulf. Where is Caw?"

"He's supposed to come back today. But Mr. Gunn doesn't seem very optimistic."

"Then Cawson's in one of his moods, again, huh? Well, they're like that, those two."

The sudden voice of the dietary aide echoed in the hall, accompanied by the loud clip-clop of platform heels.

"Aw, here comes Miss Clydesdale."

The dietary aide entered the room with a middle-aged woman in a business suit. "There he is!" she said.

"Mr. Dubois, do you know this young man? Were you expecting him?" said the administrator, with calm condescension.

"What? Well of course I know this boy! I knew his great grand-daddy thirty years before you were even born!"

"We were just concerned, Mr. Dubois," she said, in a patronizing tone. "There was a laker boy who set fire to a big boat and put three young men in the hospital last week. We just wanted to be sure it wasn't him."

"Concerned my foot! This old bovine busy-body come bargin' in here a' bawlin' like she lost her calf! Scared us outta our skins and decorated the walls with my lunch! Now, where's the ice cream I ordered for this boy?"

"Coming right up, Mr. Dubois!" said the administrator. "Chocolate or vanilla, young man?"

Blake melted into the seat of the wheelchair. "You know, I think I've really got to be going, anyway."

"And a real spoon, Bessy!" shouted Dubois.

Blake wondered just how wide the window would open.

***

The sun punished the eyes harshly, after the dimness of Korbin's room. Blake pulled the brim of his boonie hat down and walked aimlessly along a street of little shops. He thought about his uncle, and what his father could have done to alienate him, what Gunn had done, or moreover—what Carson himself had done. But soon his mind was drawn back to the mystery of the cape, the trophy, and the giant catfish, and tsantsas, magic mushrooms, Voodoo Jack and Kalijah—the usual suspects. He stopped at the next intersection and squinted at a sunflower-yellow cottage on the opposite corner. Electric-blue letters painted across the shop's big picture-window announced it as the Nirvana Book Nook. The door chimes jingled pleasantly, as if to apologize for the portentous creaking of the door. The air was cool and reeked sharply of sandalwood incense and musty books.

"Looking for something in particular?" asked a mountainous woman seated behind a bamboo sales-counter. It looked like something out of a tiki bar. She had a ragged sandwich in one hand and a romance novel in the other, and couldn't have sounded less interested. "Graphic novels are right over there." She leaned over to meet the sandwich on its way up and chewed a bite out of it, without giving her customer so much as a glance.

"Um, yes. Do you have missionary stories?" Blake said.

She gulped, then dabbed the corner of her mouth with her wrist.

"Boys your age usually want Manga."

"I'm sorry, I don't know what that is. I'm also looking for, um… do you have books about mushrooms and witchcraft, and things like that?"

Her penciled-on eyebrows rose in great brown arcs above her red-rimmed half-glasses.

"In there. Little room, under the stairs. Not many folks looking for that sort of thing. You don't exactly look like the type."

"I wouldn't know" he countered. "What *does* the type look like?" He edged his way over to the archway into the next room. "Maybe a turned up collar, or pork-rib necklace? Tattoos? Shrunken heads?" he said, thinking himself sly.

"Could be. They friends of yours?"

"Quite the opposite, I can assure you."

"Most of what we had is gone."

"Stolen?"

"Gone," she said, sternly. Blake noticed she was wearing a necklace made of long, purple crystals.

"I'll need a Spanish dictionary, then. If you please."

"Foreign Language. End of the hall on the right. Stay out of the room with the bead curtain."

Blake thumbed through the meager collection of Spanish books on the shelf, which seemed to be mostly raunchy novels and completely free of dictionaries. He settled on a well-used paperback edition of *See it and Say it in Spanish.*

As he returned through the hall he could hear the corpulent woman at the counter talking to someone. He stopped and tried to make out the muffled words. She was on the phone and obviously trying to keep from being overheard. Then, as if sensing his presence, she proclaimed loudly, "It's awful quiet back there! You better not be in the adult room, little boy!"

Startled back into motion, he returned to the counter and presented his purchase. "It should be one dollar and thirty-five cents, with tax," he announced, uneasily. A cell phone lay on the counter, its display glowing.

She jabbed at the keys of a small cash register. Blake produced the exact amount from his billfold.

"You still accept cash, I presume?"

"Only with proper ID, smarty pants." She shoved the book into a plastic bag.

"May I have the receipt? In case it's defective."

Her lip curled. "All sales final. Bring your parents with you, next time."

***

Chase Street led away from the book shop and directly to the flea market. It was the border between the business district and Freeman's eastern neighborhoods. Blake had barely passed the first side-street when he heard a bicycle whiz around the corner, behind him. He glanced over his shoulder. A short, lean teenager with bright orange hair hunched over the handle bars of a BMX bike like an orangutan, carelessly swerving his ride to and fro. He gave Blake a little nod and a snarky smile. Blake picked up his pace, slipped the handle of the bag around his wrist and gathered its top in his palm. As he crossed the next street, another cyclist whizzed from out of nowhere and joined the other. He sported huge tubes in his earlobes and a green, buzz-cut Mohawk. They chatted in low speculative tones and laughed in unsettling cackles. Blake was sure he heard one of them say "bookworm."

From ahead came a growing rumble, a scraping, rattling crescendo of small wheels on asphalt. Two more lanky teens swooped into Chase Street on long skateboards, one in a baggy knit hat with black and white stripes and rings in his lower lip. The other had sleeves of colorful tattoos. They cruised back to meet the riders.

False Evidence Appearing Real...They're okay. They just look different, he thought. *Don't judge a book by its cover. That's what Mom would say. Trust and go forward.*

"Hey bookworm!" one of them called. "You sure ask a lot of questions."

"You got some Shrooooms?" said Orangutan, in a goofy voice. They all cackled like demented mallards.

Blake was on the verge of panic. *Two kinds of people, Tux. Gotta make something happen!* He whimpered in his head. *Gotta make something happen!*

"Hey Wormy! You gonna put the spooky on us?" said Mohawk.

"I'll pay you five bucks to put the spooky on my girlfriend!" said Tattoo.

"Unga bungaaaa!" proclaimed Ring-lips, in a deep resonant groan that echoed down the street. Tattoo answered with a raucous belch. After another outburst of cackling, the tribe followed suit, chanting "Unga bunga! Unga bunga!"

Father in Heaven, he pleaded in his mind, *I know I haven't been very good. But please, let me run like Elijah!*

A sudden up-tick in the rumble of the long boards and a "Yeehaa!" from Orangutan set Blake to flight. The riders flew past the skaters, Orangutan jumped the curb onto the sidewalk. The other streaked ahead to cut Blake off at the next side-street. Blake broke right, just as his pursuer surged up to his heels. They blew full tilt across a broad lawn, Blake hurdling a hedge of white peonies. Orangutan made the jump but skidded-out in the grass. Blake was nearly to the street before the simian was up to speed again. He changed course and charged straight for Mohawk, who was coming in at top speed from the left. He veered back, drawing his pursuer behind him as he darted across the street. Blake sprang aside to reveal a mailbox, which Mohawk had not foreseen. In a feat of acrobatics the rider abandoned his bike. It wrapped itself around the mailbox post. He made a spinning, three-point landing in the gravel driveway and sprinted after his prey on foot.

Blake tore through the side yard between two houses. He vaulted the chain-link fence and ran hard for the next obstruction—an eight-foot privacy wall. And now there was new footfall behind him—something in primal pursuit. Pure instinct took over, sending a super-charge of adrenaline into Blake's boiling blood. He heard the first fence shudder as Mohawk came across. Blake leapt at the wooden wall, planted his toes on the middle rail and clutching the top edge, launched himself skyward. The yard exploded with booming barks and savage screams as he slammed into the ground on the other side. He lay panting in a grassy alley. The rumbling of the long boards and shouts from the next street put him on his feet, and he took off in the direction of Chase Street. Orangutan skidded into the intersection. Blake diverted across yet another lot. He burst out of the front yard and into the next street—fifty feet behind the skaters. He sprang across a ditch and plunged into the next property.

"Flea Market! Flea Market!" Orangutan shouted, as he pumped like a powerhouse back to Chase Street. The skaters dismounted, grabbed their boards and dashed between the nearest houses.

Blake stormed through a little wood—a gauntlet of slapping, slashing, and stabbing underbrush. He jumped a log and shot into the wide-open space of the Freeman Flea Market's parking lot. The side entrance was two hundred feet straight ahead. Orangutan reached the corner of the lot two seconds later. Blake knew that Pythagoras was on his side and he'd make it, if he didn't let up. He sprinted and managed to wedge in just ahead of two men carrying a coffee table though the double, glass doors.

Inside, it took a second to get his bearings. His lungs were on fire and someone was sewing big X's up his sides. His legs were jelly. He struggled and staggered between shoppers, who were now but mere obstacles. Something kept thumping him in the knee He looked down. The bag still hung around his wrist. Then a glimpse of black and white stripes bobbing at the far-end of the aisle revived his senses. He charged down an aisle to the left. Then left again. Then right—into a deserted aisle of empty booths.

"Almost there, almost…" He trudged on with hopeful determination. That was, until Ring-lips stepped into view at the end of the aisle. Blake shuddered to a halt. Orangutan turned the corner behind him, his smile snarkier than ever. Blake's eyes filled with tears. He was exactly halfway between them. Ring-lips took hold of the chain-link curtain that cordoned off an empty booth and began to shake it rhythmically. Orangutan did the same. Slowly they worked their way toward their quarry, shaking the metal curtains.

Blake's fear coiled into that hateful fury. He took a step back and sprang up the curtain in front of him. Before his stalkers could summon the speed to seize him, he had scrambled up the metal mesh and slithered onto the cement block partition between two booths.

Tripper Gunn was arranging dock fenders and life jackets on his front table when something smacked the concrete floor behind him. He turned to find Blake in a squat, leaning on his finger-tips, gulping air like a giant toad. Gunn was speechless. He turned back around as Ring-lips, Orangutan, and Tattoo bustled up from opposite directions.

"Well, well. Mr. Ryrie, Mr. Scofield! Whose personal property are yeh peddling today?" said Gunn, a grim edge in his voice.

"That kid, he has something that belongs to us!" huffed Ring-lips, attempting to peer around Gunn. Orangutan tried to push past. Gunn repelled him with a surprisingly stout shove.

"It would'na be this, would it?" Like a flash of lightning, the gleaming blade of an eight-inch buck-knife locked straight and glinted uncomfortably close to their noses.

"Any of yeh touch that lad and I'll cut off yer gas and water." He menaced them with the knife and shouted, "Security! Booth thirty-eight!"

The tribe of stalkers evacuated, immediately.

Gunn turned himself around. "Nice of yeh to drop in, Caduggin. Yeh look like Hell!"

***

The *Terrapin* eased into Highland Harbor under full sail. The docks and grounds bustled with the customary activities of the Sunday race crowd.

"What did yeh expect, walking in there and asking questions like that?"

said Gunn.

"I don't know. I guess she didn't seem like a bad person."

"Yeh know better than that, lad. People aren't usually what they seem."

"Mia said that Jack and Kalijah were connected to big fish. I didn't know she meant literally. "

"Ha! Edna's a big one, alright. And yeh just about ended up Jonah to that whale. Yeh'd best lie low 'round town and mind yourself on the lake for a while. We've captured their castle and it looks like yeh just poked their dragon in the backside."

"And here comes the court jester, now," Blake sighed, with a resigned look. Griffy was coming down the main dock to meet them. Tripper made the customary U-turn into the wind as Blake lowered the jib. He tossed the bowline to the Mad Cowboy.

"Hey, you'll never guess what! Old-man Trudeau has a Laser II and he wants to race us!" said Griffy, in high spirits. He secured the bowline to a cleat on the dock and boarded the *Terrapin*. "Hey, where's your boat?"

"It's at home. I mean Mr.Gunn's. Help me get the main down."

"I told him you were organizing a regatta and he said it was a great idea! Said he'd do whatever you needed to make it happen!"

The two boys strained at the halyard and slowly lowered the mainsail.

"Have you seen my uncle, today?"

"I bet we could start a fleet! Hey, you springing for lunch today, Skipper?"

"I'm gonna spring *you* in the mouth in a minute!" said Gunn, furling the mizzen. "Now get up there and catch this stern-line."

Griffy traipsed along the edge of the cabin like a squirrel on a clothesline and leapt from the bow. He caught the line and pulled the *Terrapin* alongside the dock.

"So, are we going to pick up *Seven Blunders*, after lunch?"

"I thought we'd just sail your *Hairy Bum*."

"Ha! That's awesome! C'mon, I was going to start teaching you how to skipper a race today. Not up for the thrill of the chase, huh?"

"I've had my share of thrill and chase, thank you," Blake said as he disembarked. He turned to give Gunn a hand up.

"Hey Tripp, you're in the commodore's spot, man!"

"As long as I'm gone by Happy Hour he'll no be the wiser, will he? Caduggin, yeh both get whatever suits yeh for lunch. Tell Ray to put it on my tab."

Griffy sprinted away. "Last one up the hill packs up the boat!" He reached the top of the hill and looked back, only to see Blake and Gunn ambling off the gangway.

"It's your choice as to how yeh spend yer afternoon, Caduggin. Yeh never committed to anything. Yeh can accept or yeh can decline. Remember that."

***

No one had seen Carson since Thursday. Not Ray, not Elsie, not Beverly. Ray had even called Nick Tyner to see if he had turned up in his usual haunts—the pub and the pool hall—but he had not. Blake sat and brooded while Griffy stuffed his triple cheeseburger in his mouth, and jabbered endlessly about regattas, racing tactics, strategy, and their chances at winning the season if Hunter and company didn't return.

The mention of Hunter brought Blake back to the moment. "You know," he said, "I don't feel like racing this afternoon."

"We're gonna win! We'll take *Cherry Bomb*—you can skipper. Just do everything I tell you and we'll win. It's a cinch!"

"That would be fun, but…" He teetered on the edge of the decision, gathered the will power and politely finished his sentence. "I decline."

"You *decline*? Oh, c'mon! Who talks like that? What about tomorrow?"

"I'm booked."

"Tuesday?"

"If Tripp doesn't have anything planned, I'll commit to Tuesday," Blake replied. He rose and went to the galley and returned with a to-go box for his meal. He hadn't touched a bite.

***

Blake lurked in the attic. He was beginning his tenth circuit in a window-to-window procession around the great gallery. He paused at each one and scanned the lake and grounds for anything that might signal the return of his prodigal uncle.

The faint ringing of a telephone from the second floor interrupted his vigil. He tried to ignore it and went on to the next window. But like a baby bird demanding its due, the phone kept up its insistent cry. At the next station it was barely audible but, somehow, all the more maddening.

Blake stalked back to the stairs. "Alright, alright!"

He tracked the phone down in the boardroom. It sat in the middle of a long, polished table the size of his boat. He snatched the receiver off of the cradle.

"Highland Creek Sailing Club," he said, almost politely.

"Dang, Tux, I thought you'd never pick up! Were you stuck on the john or something?" said Mia.

"I was up in the attic. How did you know I was here?"

"Where else would you be? You wanna ride?"

"Well, I'm kind of hoping that my uncle will show up here this afternoon. He's supposed to, anyway."

"What about tomorrow? I was thinking of showing you Thompson's Cave."

"That would be really cool, but uh, I'm sort of booked tomorrow and Tuesday."

"You got a job with the big Gunn?"

"No. I promised Griffy that we'd sail on Tuesday."

"So, what's the big secret about tomorrow?"

"I was invited to lunch, that's all. It'll probably be an all-afternoon thing."

"I see. You don't have to tell me," she said, with a frosty curtness.

The feeling that he was disappointing her was crushing. "You won't be angry, will you?"

Mia added the silent treatment to the guilt trip.

Blake let out a little huff of defeat and confessed. "Sylvana's family asked me to spend the afternoon with them."

Apparently this was not enough, for the punishing wall of silence did not come down.

"Are you still there?"

"I'm here."

"I just want to go someplace where I don't have to keep looking over my shoulder all of the time. They're like the only people on the lake who don't want to kill me right now."

"Give 'em time. Have fun!"

The line went dead.

"Mia? Mia?" He crammed the handset back onto the console. "I'm sick of your snot, anyway!"

Chapter 19

Sylvana's grandmother had spared no trouble in preparing a feast on the beach, for her new hero.

"Mas! Toma mas!" urged Abuelita.

"She say 'have more.'" said Sylvana.

"I got that," Blake replied. "Muchas gracias, Señora."

"Oh!" said Abuelita, covering her heart with her free hand. "Escucha! El habla muy bien!"

The entire family had gathered: uncles and cousins, grandparents and brothers. They all made sure Blake felt that he was the guest of honor and fawned continually over his efforts to respond in Spanish. But none with such passion as Abuelita.

Little Marcelo sat close on Blake's left, flying his food around and making airplane sounds. Sylvana sat close on his right—so close that eating became difficult without leaning forward and putting his elbows on the picnic table.

A young man came to the table. "Hey Tux, te gusta futbol?"

"My brother mean do you like soccer?" said Sylvana. "His name Cezar."

"I've never played. I can run fast though."

Sylvana answered Cezar, who approved. "My brothers teach you after lunch."

"So, are you the only one in your family who speaks English?"

"Yeah. My father too, but he's not here. He's look for work."

"Then where did you learn to speak English?"

"Oh, boys mostly." She took a bite of watermelon and looked away from him. Blake's eyes widened as he felt something slither up his thigh— but this was no snake.

"What's your dad do?" His voice cracked and he half choked on his food.

"Sylvana! Manos!" snapped Abuelita. She smiled maternally at Blake and put a little cluster of grapes on his plate. The girl leered slyly at him and folded her arms in front of her.

"Ah, we do work for the yards. Cut the grass, cut the weeds, clean up stuff."

"Landscaping? Like groundskeepers? So does my uncle. He's supposed to be staying here. I wanted to check the primitive campground later, if we could?"

"Sure! We can go primitive," she agreed, with a lusty wink. She hooked her foot around his.

Cezar excused himself from the banquet and returned with a soccer ball.

"Listo, amigo?" he said, spinning the ball up on one finger then bouncing it on his head.

"Listo mean 'ready'" Sylvana advised.

"I know!" said Blake, disentangling himself from his hostess. He stood and hastily followed her brother. "Si, muy listo!"

"Oh, wait! Please, watch my boat," he said, gesturing toward *Seven Thunders*. "Piratas!" There was hearty laughter all around.

"Serioso! Bad people want to steal my boat. Sylvana, tell them. Watch for a guy in a white shirt. He keeps his collar turned up. He sails a boat that's black on one side, white on the other. My boat used to be his. And there's a guy that wears bones around his neck. He's a real diablo."

Sylvana interpreted and the hilarity died down. Looks of honest concern spread across the faces of the family.

"No preocupada, hombre. Guardo su barco. Va, juega futbol!" said the pot-bellied, old man.

"He mean don't worry, you go play soccer. My grandfather say he watch you boat."

After two hours of soccer in the sand with Cezar, Romero, and some cousins, Blake was ready for a break. It was the break Sylvana had been waiting for. She brought him a cold, green soda as the sweaty young men dragged themselves back to the picnic table.

"You ready go find you uncle?"

"Maybe your brothers might like to go sailing?"

"No, they too tired. Come on!"

They wandered through the primitive campground, then the modern. They checked with the registration station, but nobody named Urquart had rented a site.

"Hey, Tux, I know short cut back to the beach! I show you."

The detour took them into the woods and to a small picnic pavilion.

"Let's stop here, sit down a minute." She took his arm and escorted him to one of the picnic tables. She sat down next to him and shook out her hair with a dramatic sweep of her head. "You think I'm pretty, Tux?" she purred, as she combed an impossible shelf of hair out of her eyes.

Blake inched away. "Yes, very."

"I think you're guapo. That mean handsome. How come you don't got a girlfriend?"

"I don't know. I guess I just don't know many girls."

She slid nearer. "You ever kiss a girl, Tux?"

"Just my mom." He scooted over more, leaving handprints in cold sweat on the bench.

"I got a surprise for you. It's nice." She took his arm and sidled up. "Close you eyes."

"Do I have to?"

"C'mon. It's okay. Close you eyes."

Reluctantly, Blake complied. In a moment he sensed something nearing his face, felt her hand on his shoulder, her breath on his lips. He held his.

"Romeo y Julieta, eh!" Boomed a big, angry voice. Her presence was suddenly torn away as if she had been snatched by a condor.

"Poppi! You back!" she cried.

If Blake had suspected that his uncle was a werewolf, there was no question about this man. He was all of that with plenty of scorpion and cobra thrown into the deal.

"What you doing with my little girl, boy?"

"Nothing!" Blake yelped.

"Poppi, is no his fault. He never even kiss a girl before!" Sylvana pleaded, tugging his elbow.

"Well, he never gonna kiss another one again, when I get done!"

Blake went white as a sheet. He was too terrified to breathe, much less make a break for it.

"Poppi, this the boy who find Marcelo! He fix the boat for us!"

Those seemed to be the magic words. He tilted his head back a little and took in a hissing breath over lips drawn tight as drum-skins.

"You find my little boy?"

"Si, Señor. In the woods," Blake squeaked. "Very far! I carried him on my back. The whole way."

"Ohhh. And *you* fix the boat motor, *too,* huh?"

"No Señor, that was my friend. It was her dad's boat. He owns La Marina. No es mi novia."

"How long you speak Spanish?" he asked, suppressing the faintest smile.

"Since lunchtime," his voice squeaked again.

"You find my little Marcelo. We call it even."

The man took two steps backward, turned and walked away.

"Sylvana, I tell you to stay away from the boys, no?"

"I didn't know you mean the white ones, too!"

"Señor?"

"What you want, Romeo?"

"Sylvana says you do landscaping "I may have some work for you."

The man turned around and looked frighteningly severe again. "What, little Rico don't wanna mow his lawn, so gonna get a Mexican to do it?"

"Rico mean rich," offered Sylvana, placidly.

"I'm no rico, Señor. I'm just staying here this summer. My friend, he's old and he needs help cleaning up his place. We can't do it by ourselves. It's the old marina."

"How you think you gonna pay me?"

Blake considered for a moment. "I have four hundred dollars, cash."

"You no rico, but you got four hundred cash? Why don't you buy you a motorcycle or video game, or something like that?"

"I don't care about that stuff. I've got a boat that's getting me in enough trouble, as it is. I thought it would be a nice surprise for Father's Day. Is four hundred enough?"

"You gonna pay me four hundred for a present for you friend?"

"Si, Señor."

The man's face seemed to wrench a little, as if he were fighting back some insistent emotion. "Sylvana, go! Let me teach you something, amigo. You don't never tell nobody how much cash you got. Especial a stranger. You understand? You get yourself killed. And my little girl? Ay Chihuahua, she trouble! She like the boys to fight each other for her. Trouble maker. So you better stick with that little rica from la marina, you understand me? Sylvana big trouble for you."

Blake nodded.

"You come back. Mi Madre, she like you. I tell my boys. They keep Sylvana away for you."

"Muy muchas Gracias, Señor um…."

"Pagán."

"Señor Pagán?" Blake wasn't sure if he heard right.

"Si. I know—everybody think we are Pay-gan. But we are Christian."

"Oh."

"But hey, es better than Bastardo! That's Luis my brother-in-law. My sister, she is Pagán. So you know what that makes their kids?" Señor Pagán smiled wryly, inviting Blake to say it.

"Um, little…pagan…bastards?"

"That's it! But don't let Abuelita hear. She kill you and me both!"

Chapter 20

Mia flung her gym bag against the wrought-iron fence, like a minion that had failed her for the last time.

From the overlook above the Freeman docks she surveyed her dominion: the cracked muddy banks of the far shore, the bleak gray embankment of the dam and its tower, here and there the fading foliage of thirsty trees on Drascombe Heights. She glared at the sun and sky, wind and water with rank disapproval.

Haraguchi had annoyed her all through Karate class, continually ribbing about Tux. When she complained to Treva about it, she earned a lecture on not treating Blake like her personal property. She'd waited for Buck Mueller to show up at the usual time, but he hadn't. But Rexroat and the Hellcats had— bearing unwanted news, at that. Now they bobbed lazily in a lemon-yellow wake boat in the middle of the sparkling upper lake.

It was a gorgeous, breezy day—perfect for sailing—but in a kayak it would be a long paddle back from anywhere. By all accounts, it had been a crappy day. The real source of her black mood, however, had just tacked out of the channel and was sailing fast toward the floating lemon.

Her eyes narrowed to slits. "Just. Don't. For once." As if on cue, the little sailboat tacked away from her collision course. Mia could make out the crew now. A boy in a straw cowboy hat at the helm and a boy in a Hawaiian shirt riding the trapeze. "Thank. You. Moron."

But then they tacked back. "Ugh. Today's forecast: scattered idiots with a 100% chance of *severe* stupidity."

***

"I'd really rather stay off the upper lake," said Blake.

"You're doing great on the wire, man! Think of it! A three-mile spinnaker run on a day like this!"

Griffy peered under the boom. The wind had been on his side and allowed him to keep *Lemon Drop* and her crew out of Blake's line of sight—while hiding their own identity from the bobbing sunbathers.

"Hellooo Rexy!" Griffy chortled to himself. He kept bantering at Blake, giving it his all to keep him up on the trapeze for the last hundred yards of the approach.

"All right, come on in, I think we may need to jibe in a second!" Blake swung back into the boat.

"Jibe? Here? I thought we…"

Griffy let the main fly out two feet and steered to starboard. *Seven Thunders* slowed hard for a second, as if the lake-troll had seized her by her dagger-board again. A thump vibrated through the hull and the boat sprang free of the denizen's invisible grip. Angry shouts erupted from the other side of her sails.

"Jiiibe ho!" cried Cowboy. Blake ducked just in time to miss having his head staved in, as the boom slashed across the cockpit and slammed to a stop at the end of the mainsheet.

They were careening past the *Lemon Drop*, barely six feet from her gleaming, yellow hull. Thad Rexroat stood up and shouted "Hey!" cold horror gripped Blake by the throat. He quickly turned away.

"My bad, man, I thought that was Fisherman's Wharf, with all that blubber on deck!" Griffy cackled.

"That's a sweet bucket, punk! How long did you have to nurse your mommy to get that?"

Griffy swung *Seven Thunders* around the wide back-end of *Lemon Drop*, trimmed the main, and headed back up the other side. "It wasn't my mommy! It was yours!"

"You twing my anchor line again and that'll be the last boat you ever own."

"I don't own it. He does!"

Griffy rounded the bow and skillfully thumped *Lemon Drop's* anchor-line, again. Blake turned around to see Jenny Hopkins and the Cheer twins rise from their basking.

"This was not my idea!" Blake declared, in earnest regret.

"Rex, its Mia's boyfriend!"

"Did he like, just call us fat?" mused one of the twins.

Rexroat was thrilled. "Guilt by association, Gooseboy!"

"Please! I had no idea! I was on the trapeze! I couldn't see!"

"No apologies once the truth is known, pal. And I owe you one, too." He followed *Seven Thunders* back down the starboard side of his boat.

"I've got some news for you, buddy. Old lady Devlin is sending Mia away. But don't worry, I know someone who wants to take care of *you*, Goosie!"

Blake's jaw dropped.

"That's right and he's on his way back, right now!"

Griffy rounded the transom again and started another lap.

"We're not afraid of psycho boy! Are we, Tux?" Griffy laughed.

"Don't do it Cowgirl, I'm warning you!"

"Griffy, tack away! that's an order!" Blake demanded

"You know I've gotta do it Rexy!"

"Tack away!" Blake shrieked. The girls mocked him with shrieks of their own and laughed scornfully.

Seven Thunders rounded the bow and the anchor line thumped a third time.

"Jenny, pull the anchor!" Rex ordered, turning the ignition. It gave a shrill, electronic whine and then died with a loud click. All three girls struggled with the anchor-line. The ignition whined again.

"Still haven't gotten that fixed?" said Griffy.

"Get out of the way!" In one move, Blake wrenched the tiller from

Griffy's hand and shoved him to the other side of the cockpit. He pointed *Seven Thunders* back toward the channel. "Ease the jib, and get the pole up, you idiot!"

"We can't fly the chute without me on the wire, and you're wearing the harness, genius!"

Blake glanced back. *Lemon Drop* was still riding at anchor, the ignition squealing at regular intervals. He scanned the lake and brought *Seven Thunders* onto a broad reach, her fastest point of sail and fled for the shallows at the mouth of the channel. Griffy hiked out, hands over his head, hurling insults, and laughing at his own defiant abandon.

"Ease your jib 'til it dances, then trim up a little," barked Blake.

"I know how to trim for reach, man!"

"Shut up and do it!"

Griffy took note of their course, then saw the look on Blake's face. "You're headed for the shallows?"

"Ease your jib!"

"Lighten up, man! I think we're gonna make it, tack back!"

"Why should I listen to *you*?"

"You gotta trust me on this. We'll make it to the channel!" Griffy pleaded.

Lemon Drop's engine turned over with a roar of triumph, interrupting the squabble. Rexroat helped the girls pull the anchor out of the muddy bottom. As soon as it was rinsed and stowed, he sprang to the driver's seat and throttled up. *Lemon Drop* made a swooping turn, like a giant, yellow bird of prey wheeling on one wing-tip.

"Stay out of the shallows Blake! Alright already! I'm sorry! Get back to deep water, please!" he pleaded, frantically.

"Shut up and hike!" Blake yelled. Get ready to pull the board!"

"Are you freakin' stupid? Tack, now!"

Blake looked back. Their pursuers were eating up their wake by the second. Jenny Hopkins' red mane blazed in the breeze. "Pull the board!"

Griffy howled with rage and pulled the dagger-board almost all of the way up. They were now over the shoals, in three feet of water. The drone of

Lemon Drop's motor faded away as Rexroat throttled back to idle. The bow of the motorboat settled into the waves at the edge of the shallows. Blake was just beginning to think they *had* made it when Rexroat stood up and shouted

"I warned you what would happen the last time, didn't I, Bronco!"

Blake glared at a bewildered Griffy. "You've done this *before?*"

Lemon Drop roared to life again, plowing a tight circle nearly on her side. The girls clung to the rail and screeched like delighted banshees on a roller coaster from Hell. Round and round and round—the wake that the boat threw up was enormous, but when those mountainous swells rolled over the shallow shoal, they heaped in to titanic, six-foot breakers. Blake had navigated large swells before but could not comprehend how to deal with these sheer-faced cliffs of water. Griffy gripped the deck's edge and braced one foot against the daggerboard.

"What do I do?" cried Blake.

The first wall of water surged up from behind. The stern pitched skyward. The bow plowed into the lakebed. Blake seized a thin line on the after-deck, as *Seven Thunders* stood on her nose and whipped hard around. Griffy leapt onto the mainsail as the boat went over on her starboard side. The hull now lay parallel to the waves. The next crest tossed her up and drove her masthead a foot into the mucky bottom. Griffy sluiced down the sail like an otter on a water slide and body surfed the last hundred feet to shore.

The next trough slammed the hull down on the lakebed, then heaved her up again. The line cut into Blake's palms and broke his death-grip. The tsunami sucked him under and rolled him across the bottom. Something jabbed him bluntly in the belly and then he wasn't rolling any more. The water was still trying to drag him shoreward, but he was fixed in place. The hull boomed against the lakebed like a cannon, just a few feet away. A trough passed over him and the murky, gurgling grave turned to clear sunshine and a quick gasp of life. Then the lake heaped up and piled down, burying him anew. The hull boomed and another trough followed.

Blake came up on his knees this time and saw that he was the prisoner of a branch that had skewered his harness ring. He went down again. Something slashed sharply across his face. He became aware of a droning— *Lemon Drop* was still at it. He struggled to dig his feet into the squishy lake-floor and push against his captor. *Seven Thunders* boomed and he emerged into the air, straining at the branch. The force of the next wave tuned him upside-down. There was a muted crunch and the sensation that he'd been punched in the gut and suddenly he was being swept across the shoal again. The next wave deposited him, wrapped in prickly lake-weed, on a little beach of coarse sand.

Another torrent inundated the beach and another, but with fading ferocity. Blake dug his fingers into the gravelly sand and let them wash over his back. He breathed long hard breaths and listened to his heart pound in his ears, as if echoing *Seven Thunders* booming in the surf. *Lemon Drop* hummed away in the distance. The breeze rustled lively in the trees, the crashing waves diminished to loud sloshing. He gathered his strength, rose to his hands and knees, and threw up.

Griffy came squishing up a little fisherman's trail, zipping his shorts, cursing and ranting to himself. He still had his trademark hat and there wasn't a scratch nor a spot on him. He stopped when he saw Blake and thrust out an accusing finger. "I told you that boat was too much for you! I told you to stay out of the shallows! Well you got what you deserved! Next time you decide to commit suicide, do me a favor and try not to take everyone else with you? Go back to nursing your mom and leave sailing to people who know what they're doing!"

Griffy was staring right at Blake, yet so consumed with his own tirade that he never saw the scraped, scratched, muck-smudged, sandy-faced maniac coming at him. Blake flew off the beach in a fury and slammed into the Mad Cowboy, landing him flat on his back. After five minutes of solid pounding, Blake staggered to his feet and surveyed his handiwork. With a split lip and bloody nose, Griffy looked almost as good as he did. Blake turned the straw cowboy hat inside-out, punched through the top and threw it back at his victim for good measure.

Griffy crawled to the trail, hoisted himself up with a moan and stumbled away. Blake staggered back to the water-line and collapsed. He sat without a thought in his head and stared vacantly at *Seven Thunders* bobbing on her side, Trespass Island in the sunny blue distance and a pretty young woman with curly black hair, paddling a tandem kayak toward him.

***

"Here. Hold this right here and keep pressure on it," said Mia, folding a large square of gauze into quarters. She pressed it against his forehead.

"How bad is it?" Blake said.

"How many fingers am I holding up?"

"Your voice is shaking. Now how bad is it?"

"How many fingers?"

"How bad?" Blake shouted.

"It's bad! How many fingers?"

"Three!"

"Thank you! How's your vision? Things look fuzzy?" She produced a little flashlight and shined it in one eye, then the other.

"Ow! Crap! Now I can't see anything!"

"Pupils are normal, that's good. Oop! Keep the pressure on that! She pressed on his hand as a scarlet stream ran down his forehead and poured off his right eyebrow.

"Anything hurt anywhere else?"

"No."

"Hey, where's Griffy?"

"Who cares?"

"I said where is he? Oh my god, he's not under the boat is he?" She turned and dashed into the water.

"Relax. He didn't even get a scratch. I'm surprised he even got wet. He took the trail back."

"We need to get you somewhere where they can sew your head up." She eyed him cautiously, then waded out to the shipwreck. "That mast is stuck in the mud pretty good. I don't think I can get it out by myself. You couldn't sail her home alone in the shape you're in, anyway."

"Leave it, for all I care. I'm not sailing anymore."

Mia waded out and heaved against bow with all her might. "We'll have to call Gunn."

"I said leave it, I'm not sailing anymore!" He flung a rock.

She waded to the stern and tugged on it, to no avail. She trudged back to the end of the mast and tried to lift it out of the mud. It might as well have been set in concrete.

"Quit ignoring me!" said Blake.

"You know, you almost made it? I watched you tear across that channel. You had her up on a screaming plane most of the way. That's real skill. You were awesome."

"Shut up."

"A hundred feet, Tux. You almost made it. Nothing to be ashamed of." She washed her hands and waded back to the beach. "I don't know what I would've done, if it had been me in the *Osprey*."

"I almost drowned! I got hung up on a stick and I almost died! I can't do anything on this lake without being chased, or attacked! Your brother's on his way back, and my uncle left because of me!"

"Don't forget the gaping, blood-gushing laceration on your forehead."

"It's not funny! What did I ever do? I didn't ask to be here. Every time I try to make the best of things and start to enjoy myself, something bad happens and it just keeps getting worse! Why does God hate me?"

The air-horn from a passing pontoon boat bleated, as if to announce the answer to his timeless question. It was one word, stenciled in eloquent, red cursive on her aged, gray sides—"*Quitcherbitchin!*"

Mia snatched a whistle from her pack and blew it wildly. She waved her arms over her head. The Pontoon boat throttled down and turned carefully into the shallows. Blake was put aboard by a pot-bellied, balding retiree and his unnaturally sun-baked, bleach-blond wife. Blake thought she looked liked a creepy, brown mermaid whose leathery clutches might well have had him pinned to the bottom of the lake, twenty minutes ago. Mia rigged a harness using the mainsheet and, taking the helm of the pontoon boat, gently extracted *Seven Thunders'* mast from the muck. She righted the boat, dropped the sails, and tethered her with *Cry of the Osprey*, behind the pontooner. The unlikely flotilla made for Gunn's Harbor.

***

"All hands and the cook! What happened to yeh, lad—and yer boot?" said Gunn, as *Quitcherbitchin* puttered up to the dock.

Blake disembarked and pushed past. "I'd rather not talk about it. I need to call Nanna. I'm going to North Carolina. Tomorrow."

Mia accepted the towline from their portly rescuer and stepped on to the dock. Gunn looked to Mia with a bewildered expression. "Miss?"

"Three words. Griffy's. Big. Mouth." She pulled the gunky and bedraggled *Seven Thunders* up to the dock. Gunn looked the boat up and down.

"Mother Carey's chickens! And where is *he*?"

"Walked back to the club and called his mom, I guess. Mr. Gunn, Blake needs stitches."

Blake had just set foot ashore. "Stitches! No! You put a butterfly bandage on it, that's good enough!"

"But I didn't clean it out! You've got mud, sand, and who knows what else in it."

"She's right lad, yer head'll swell up and burst like a road-kill haggis."

"No! It just needs some Neosporin on it."

"You will go in that house right now and get changed and then we are going to the ER," he said, shaking a finger. "Go on! Now!"

Blake stiffened and scowled defiantly before he turned and stalked up to the house.

Gunn turned back to Mia. "Miss,"

"I'll go with you."

"I'd consider it a personal favor. Can yeh drive an auld tractor like that one?" He pointed to the ancient Ford sitting on the ramp, hitched to *Seven Thunders'* trailer.

"Sure. You want the boat around back?"

"Just put 'er in that end bay and close the door—yer kayak too. Lock

228

'em up." He regarded the pontooners as their engine clunked into reverse. "Maynard, Shelby I'm in yer debt. Yeh drop 'round for a beer, sometime."

***

Blake groaned with each throbbing bump in the road. A sudden swerve to miss a deer toppled Mia from the inverted bucket she was sitting on and sent a milk-crate of tools crashing across the metal floor of the van. A pile of mail cascaded off the dash into Blake's lap. He squinted through the brain-banging headache and read the topmost envelope: County Department of Health—Final Notice.

***

The exam room was dark, cool, and quiet. It suited Blake just fine. Gunn was at the Nurse's station making phone calls while Mia explained the incident to the doctor. A young woman with close-cut hair and raspberry scrubs that matched her acne, knocked on the door.

"Hi there! Are you Blake?" She hovered over him and brushed blood-stiff hair off his forehead. "Ooh, that's a doozey! Let me guess—saber duel, right?"

"Boating accident. I nearly drowned."

"Yowee! Well you'll have to tell me all about it while I'm sewing you up. My name's Tamzon. I just have to get a few things together first and then we'll get started."

The doctor—a short, young man—joined them. He, too, came and hovered over Blake's forehead, while the nurse rummaged through various cabinets, assembling supplies on a small tray. He inspected the gash with a little flashlight, pointed it into one eye, then the other. "Follow the light with your eyes, Blake. Right, left, right. Good. No blurred or double vision? Are you sleepy?"

"No. Mia already did all that."

"Yeah, that's what I hear! Tamzon, you ought to encourage his girlfriend. She'd make an excellent triage nurse," he said perusing papers on a clipboard. "Well, buddy, Miss Mia took pretty good care of you.

Tamzon's going to numb you up real good so you don't feel anything, then she'll clean out the wound and sew you up. I'll come back with your post-op instructions and a prescription for antibiotics. The biggest thing you'll have to remember is not to get it wet. Ok? You're a brave kid." He patted Blake on the knee and left the room.

Tamzon sat down next to the bed and began opening packages and arranging their contents on a little rolling table. Gunn appeared in the doorway, blocking most of the light from the hall.

"Yeh alright, Caduggin? Yeh know, she could put a bonnie zipper in there for yeh. Make it easier to change your mind!"

"Did you call Nanna?"

"Aye, I spoke to your grandmother."

"When does my bus leave?"

"Ahhh, well, Gabby's taken a turn for the worse, see. Clarissa said those homecare folks are in and out at all hours and she's so busy making arrangements and what not, that, uh..."

"That what?"

"Well, she would'na have time to take care of yeh, much less that wound of yers. And entertain all of the friends yeh have such a talent for making. Frankly, I don' a think North Carolina's ready for yeh!"

"Ooh, North Carolina! That's where Blackbeard's treasure is buried, isn't it?" Tamzon said. "I bet you love pirates, don't you?"

Blake glared at the nurse. "Don't you have work to do?"

"Keep a civil tongue lad."

"I'm going to North Carolina," Blake snarled.

"And I'm going down to the coffee shop and call Mrs. Williams. Your grandmother will be back soon enough, then yeh can move on down to Pemberton, if..." Gunn became pensive. "Ah! Here comes the girl."

Before Blake could react, Gunn shuffled away and Mia swung in the door. "How's it goin', Tux? Anything I can do for you?"

"As a matter of fact, there is something you can do before I go."

"I didn't know it was *that* serious!" Mia smiled and inspected the implements on the tray.

"To Nanna's, you goofus."

"Gunn said she's coming back soon."

"He's bluffing. I'm leaving. I've got some money I want you to take to Sylvana's father. Tell him it's from me. Tell him where Tripp's place is. He'll know what to do. You've been a good friend, I'll miss you."

"Read my lips, Tux—you are staying."

"Even if I was, you're leaving."

Mia looked at Tamzon with a puzzled expression. "What did you give him? He's speaking in mysteries."

The nurse shrugged. "Nothing, yet. I am ready to get started, though. You want to watch?" She prepped a syringe with a long, bent pipette. Blake's eyes darted around the room. He wriggled nervously.

"Sure! So, pal, where am I supposed to be going?"

"Rexroat said your mom is sending you away and Hunter is on his way back."

"Hmmm. Mom must have gotten my report card in the mail. That or the social-worker called. I just found out about Junior, myself—and not from my ring of loyal spies."

The nurse rolled her stool around to the head of the bed.

"Okay, I'm just going to get some anesthetic in there to numb things up. It may sting a little to start" She turned on a blazing light overhead.

"Could you numb *that*?" Blake groaned.

"You want me to be able to see what I'm doing, right? Hold still."

She inserted the pipette into the gash and started to work it around under the flesh, injecting medicine as she went. Blake clenched his teeth and squirmed. Mia clasped Blake's hands with her right and held his legs down with her left. "Hold on buddy, you're doing fine," she said. "Just a minute and you won't feel it at all."

Tamzon extracted the syringe, reloaded it, and went back to work. "I heard your triage assessment was pretty good," she said. "Doc Feeney thinks you'd make a good nurse."

"Really?" said Mia. "The doctor said that? About me?"

"Gotta have the grades, though. Nursing school is really competitive.

Med school even more so. Okay, let's let that soak in, then we'll rinse it out and start suturing."

Mia released her gentle grip on Blake and sat down on the edge of the bed. Blake did not relax.

"Tell Officer Mueller I caught his big fish."

"Honestly, what's in that stuff?" said Mia. "What *are* you babbling about?"

"You said Buck Mueller thought Voodoo Jack and Kalijah were connected to bigger fish. I caught his big fish."

"Well, don't keep us in the dark!"

Blake allowed himself a smug smile. "That fat lady at the bookshop."

"Mount Edna?" the girls chorused, in disbelief.

"How do you know?" Mia said.

"I asked too many questions. She sic'ed a pack of circus freaks on me. I barely got away."

"Ryrie, Scofield and company? How did I miss that connection? My intelligence network is getting pretty dumb, these days. I know their old man deals in stolen goods. Been locked up a few times. But the Fat Lady, Voodoo Jack, Kalijah, and the Freeman Freaks? Together? That's something to ponder."

Tamzon filled a new syringe from a large bottle of sterilized water and began rooting around in Blake's forehead with it. "Here, put on some gloves and you run the suction."

Mia pulled on the purple gloves with an enthusiastic snap and took the suction tube.

"Just suction around the edges as it overflows."

"What are we going to do about that bunch, Tux?"

"What do you mean we? I'm leaving. *Tomorrow*. Hey, watch that you don't suck my brains out with that thing!"

"Tomorrow? I thought I'd come over and help you clean up *Seven Thunders*. Then we could play games or something."

"What's *Seven Thunders*?" said Tamzon, refilling the syringe.

"His sailboat," Mia said, before Blake could reply. "He's a darn good sailor, too. Just needs better crew, that's all."

"How long you two been together?"

"We just met a couple of weeks ago, we're..."

"Thirty-four days," Blake interrupted.

Mia blushed. "We're not really together-together. Just friends."

The nurse grinned. "You sure bicker like it! Finish that up, then pad his forehead dry with this. I think it's quit bleeding."

Mia gently padded Blake's forehead with a large square of gauze. Tamzon prepared the suture.

Gunn shuffled into the doorway. "What's this, a quilting bee? Sew 'im up right so he has a good scar to brag aboot!"

"Scar?" whined Blake.

"I got a question for yeh, Caduggin. What do yeh tell a cowboy with two black eyes?"

"Who cares."

"I'll bite!" piped Mia.

"Nuthin'! Yeh done told him twice a'ready!"

"I thought you said he didn't have a scratch on him?" said Mia, hanging over and looking Blake in the eyes, upside-down."

"Heeey!" reprimanded the nurse. "You wanna get hair and boogers in the wound!"

"Whoop! Sorry!"

"He *didn't* have a scratch on him," said Blake. "Until he started yelling at me. I suppose I'm in trouble now."

"Actually, Mrs. Williams sends her apologies *and* her gratitude for putting her son in his place. Although yeh came just short of sending him here."

"Hold his head steady," said Tamzon. She began the first stitch. Mia watched her every move. Blake felt nothing.

"Yeh sure you won't change yer mind, lad?"

"I'm going."

"He's staying," said Mia, without looking up.

"I'm going. And that's final."

Gunn sagged. "I'll call yer grandmother back when we get home. I'm going out front, for a smoke."

"That's so cool, the way you wrap the thread around the grips and pull the needle through to make the knot!" said Mia.

"Yeah sweet, huh!" Tamzon said.

"Tux, he *wants* you to stay."

Blake remained silent.

"I still haven't shown you Thompson's Cave."

Tamzon started the third stitch.

"Or the ibises."

The nurse made the fourth suture.

"Or the nature center."

Blake stared into the light.

"Which is totally awesome."

The fifth stitch was tied off and cut.

"It's gonna be boring without you."

Number six went into Blake's brow.

"You want me to stay? Sail with me."

Mia's jaw dropped. The nurse paused in her work and gave her an expectant look.

"You... *know*... how I feel about sailing, buddy."

"I'll pick up a snake."

"What did you say, my trippy little friend?"

"I said I'll handle a snake."

"And why?"

"I'll pick up a snake if you sail with me."

Mia glanced at Tamzon, who pursed her lips trying to suppress a smile. Mia swallowed. She was on the spot, now. "You really want me to sail *that* badly?"

"No. I want you to sail with *me* that badly."

The nurse glowed with sentiment. Mia sighed deeply.

"A snake? A real snake?" she said, almost with regret.

"A real snake."

"A real, big snake."

"Put it around my neck."

"Constrictor, then?"

"Bring it on."

"When."

"Tomorrow."

There was a long silence.

She sighed again. "Will Gunn let us take the shoebox, or should I plan to pick you up on my scooter?"

Chapter 21

Sun streamed in through glass walls of the nature center's conservatory. A mosaic of orange and white scales slid smoothly through Blake's palms. He smiled in wonder. "It's gorgeous. An albino python! I'd seen pictures, but they really don't do it justice." The snake hung comfortably around his neck, tail wrapped once around his left arm. It nuzzled Blake under the chin. "I think it likes me!"

"Eve's a pretty laid back snake. But they're not affectionate like mammals," said the park naturalist, as she changed the water in the snake's display case.

"They don't have *that* part of the brain, right?"

"That's right! You're pretty smart."

"Too smart!" Mia said. "We had to remove part of *his* brain, as you can see."

"Yeah, what's that all about?" The woman motioned to the gauze patch on Blake's forehead.

"They had to take out the part of my brain that controls anger, so that I can stand to be around *her*."

Mia lifted her eyebrows and smirked appreciatively in a way that said *touché. I'll get you later!*

"Hey Tux, if you kiss the snake and eat a spider, I'll marry you."

"I'd take her up on that!" said the woman.

"Have I satisfied my obligation to our agreement?" Blake said, raising his serpent-laden arms.

The naturalist lifted the python from Blake's shoulders. "I bet you're home schooled!"

"I'm satisfied, Tux. You win."

"A wager, Hmmm?" said the woman, eying them both.

"We have a lot of work to do on your boat, first."

"We've got all day!"

"A night sail would be romantic!" crooned the naturalist. "If your parents don't mind."

The two locked eyes. "We don't have parents," they declared, with one voice.

"The old gentleman who dropped you off, that wasn't..."

"You're new here, aren't you?" said Mia.

***

"I recognize that Contessa!" Mia declared, hands in her back pockets, as she admired the graceful lines of the yacht in Gunn's workshop. "Love that full keel."

"Yeh ought'a recognize her. I won her from yer Father in a legal dispute. That's my *Sophia*."

She smiled to herself, wheels turning in her head. "A boat like that belongs in the water, Mr. Gunn."

"Agreed. Been too long. Put the oil in there like I showed yeh, Caduggin."

Blake fuelled the power washer. "Have a look inside."

Mia contemplated the twelve-foot ladder propped against the side of the boat. "You ought to dress her up for the Fourth of July flotilla." She sauntered over to Blake. "You all ready there, Tux?"

"Just one more thing!" He pulled a pink shower cap from his back pocket and stretched it gingerly over his forehead. "Doctor's orders."

"Let me get upstairs an' shut the windows, before yeh fire that thing up," said Gunn, ambling off.

Mia wheeled the washer out to the head of the ramp, where *Seven*

Thunders sat in the blinding sunshine. Blake followed up with a hose. He connected it and turned on the water. Mia gave the starter cord a wicked yank. The motor fired up without argument.

"So, how do you use this thing?" Blake shouted, carelessly brandishing the spray wand.

"You never point it at me—that's instant death!"

"Should I be using something that powerful?" He looked at the wand suspiciously.

"No, I mean if you spray me I will kill you without hesitation!" she said. Mia seized the business-end of the sprayer and pointed it at *Seven Thunders*. "Point and shoot, Tex!"

Blake blasted mud and sludge away in violent surges, revealing a hull largely unscathed. Mia spread the sails in the grass and sprayed them clean. When she finished, she hopped aboard and began untangling lines. "You know," she said, "there are a lot of people who'd ditch my dad and come over here if Gunn opened the place back up."

"He's retired. Why would he?"

"Dunno. Save him the trouble of tramping all over the lake looking for business."

"He likes that. He's got no help for the shop, anyway."

"What about your uncle?"

"Too temperamental, I guess."

"Crap. The main halyard's jammed up. Well your cunning dinghy is none the worse for wear. How's your head?"

"It pulls a lot. Feels creepy," he answered, delicately removing the shower cap.

"You probably don't feel much like sailing tonight."

"No I'm fine! Let me get a nap and some ibuprofen. I'll be good to go! I'll ask Mr. Gunn if you can stay for dinner."

"Thing is, I have to drop in on Treva. We'll see what tomorrow night brings. Don't worry, I promise I won't welch on you."

"It'll have to be Friday. We're painting someone's boathouse over the next couple of days."

"Alright, Friday."

"Hey, could you do me a big favor? You remember Mr. Pagán?"

She raised a skeptical eyebrow. There was a long silence. "Are you seriously prepared to owe me, big-time?"

Chapter 22

Gunn opened one of the bay windows and called down to the dock, "Come on up, Lass. It's no locked!"

Mia waved in reply and finished tethering her kayak. She made her way around several paint buckets and a stack of tarps piled by the *Terrapin*. She strolled up to the front door, mopped her brow and slogged up the stairs to the living room. The air conditioning was on, full blast. It gave her goose bumps.

"Anybody home? I thought I'd come by a little early so I could check Blake's stitches."

"Make yourself at home, Miss. Caduggin's in the shower. He got more paint on himself, the last two days, than he did on what he was painting!"

Mia sank into the cool, middle cushion of the big couch. "You guys sure had a hot one."

"Hotter than the hinges in Hades! That's what me dear old mum would say. Yeh like Chinese? We're expecting Ping's, any time now."

"I Love Yu Ping's! But will there be enough?"

"Be certain," he snorted, "with that lad in the house, yeh order double everything—or yeh starve!" He slapped his thighs and rose to his feet with a groan. "Where are my manners? Can I get yeh a Coke, Miss?"

"Please. That would be really nice." Mia stood up and smoothed her shirt and shorts. She glanced at the mantel as she retied her hair. A black and white portrait in a silver frame caught her eye.

Curiosity got the better of her and she went over to the fireplace. A tall young man and short young woman. The young woman looked over her shoulder at him, radiant with happiness.

"Is this your wife?" she asked. "I'm sorry, it's not my business."

""No worry, lass," Gunn replied, shuffling back into the room with two glasses of soda. "That's my Sophie."

"I didn't know you were married."

"We weren't. Mr. Hitler saw to that. But—she's still the love of my life," he said, gazing at the photograph. "Aren't yeh, Sophie?"

Mia accepted her glass. Gunn returned to his recliner. "That was nineteen-forty-three. We were seventeen."

"I'm sorry," she said, softly.

"Time heals all wounds, Miss Devlin." He smiled wistfully. "Almost."

Mia sank back down into the couch, this time at the end nearest him.

"So, who's teaching Junior Training this summer?" she said.

"Fair question, seeing as someone put our two prime candidates in the hospital and the other two've gone A.W.O.L."

"Yeeeah. Sorry about that."

"Why? Girl's got to protect herself, don' she?"

"That, she does, Mr. Gunn. That she does."

"There's usually only eight or ten kids in a session, anymore. Used to be packed. Just like the Club. Members and their families spent the whole weekend there: racing, fishing, swimming, cooking out. Wall-to-wall kids. But now there's Nascar and every kind of little league sport, and satellite TV, and football, and basketball. So many choices. And sailing is just another choice."

"It must have been something to have been a member then."

"Well, the old Club is just fadin' away. A fact not lost upon your father, either," he said, fastening his gaze upon her.

She drew one leg up and wrapped her hands around the shin. "I'm not really on speaking terms with my dad, these days."

Blake's voice drifted out from the depths of the house. "Hey is dinner here, yet?"

"Make sure you're decent, before yeh venture out, Caduggin! Yeh've got company!" The smile returned to his face.

Blake entered the room, combing his wet hair back. "You're early!"

"I wanted to check your stitches. Sit down."

Blake complied.

"Looks good. Keeping your hands off it?"

"Yeah, mostly. I hate the shower cap though."

"I can fix that!" She produced several packets from her pocket. "I brought you some Tegaderm patches. "Slap one of these puppies on there and you can swim, shower, whatever!"

The doorbell rang a dozen times, followed by riotous banging on the door below. It sounded like storming a castle gate. "There's Yu Ping!" Gunn said. "Better get down there before she beats the bloomin' door in! She's got the funny notion that I'm deef!"

It took both kids to haul the sacks of Chinese food up stairs.

"You guys eat all of this in one go?" said Mia.

"Sometimes."

"I thought you were beefing up a little."

"We're going to watch *Master and Commander* while we eat," said Blake. "Mr. Gunn said it will inspire me."

"Dinner and a show—you guys really know how to treat a girl!"

***

Seven Thunders ghosted along in the moonlight. Blake steered for the looming silhouette of Trespass Island.

"He didn't think he could do it?" said Blake, puzzled.

"That's what he said," replied Mia, as she coiled the main halyard, then the jib.

"I don't get it. They're landscapers. I offered to pay up front. Why doesn't he think he can do it?"

"I think he means that he can't just take four hundred dollars in cash from a kid. I have to admit, that's more than I gave him credit for. You mind cluing me in?"

"The county's been after Mr. Gunn to clean his place up. He just ignores the warnings. I found a final notice in the van the other night."

"Got a plan B?"

"No. Ray and Elsie are too busy with the club. They're the only ones I could think to ask. I wish I knew where Uncle Carson was."

""What about… *Me?*"

"You'd help?"

"Are you asking?"

"Would you please help me?"

"No!" she said, plainly. "Just Kidding! But don't get *too* used to it. You *really* owe me now!"

"Start Sunday? Early, before it gets hot."

"We'd better! Sounds like we only have a couple of weeks."

He glowed with hopeful gratitude. "Thank you."

Mia dug into her backpack, "Hey, wanna see something cool?" She produced a rectangular object. "Look through this end. Press this button."

"A night-scope? Cool!"

Blake looked into the eyepiece and activated the scope.

"Now, look up."

"Whoa! I thought you could see a lot of stars out here in the country, but it's like the sky is carpeted with them."

"In the desert, or on the ocean, you don't even need the scope."

"So shall your offspring be!"

"Come again?"

"God promised Abraham that his offspring would be as many as the stars of heaven. It didn't sound like such a big promise until just now."

They were quiet for a solid minute. Blake scanned the sky. The wind shifted a little and he caught the flowery scent of her shampoo. He breathed it in slowly and gently.

"Do you believe in God, Mia?"

"I guess," she said, sliding down into the cockpit. "I dunno."

"I used to be mad at God."

"Mad at God, eh? How'd that work out for ya?"

"I used to beg him to kill me, because I hated my dad so much," he said, almost absently.

"Wow. I just ran away. I mean, it would've been running away if anyone had noticed I was gone. Don't you ever act up to get attention?"

"I try not to." He placed the scope in his lap and rubbed his neck. "I just try to keep it all inside. For my mom's sake."

"That ain't good! You've got to let off steam somehow or you'll split a gasket!"

"I know, but God says thou shalt honor thy father and mother. I want to do what God says."

Mia cocked her head, her expression halfway between a question and a sneer. "Let me get this straight. Your god sticks you with parents that neglect you and totally treat you like crap, and then says you have to respect and obey them? I mean..." She looked straight at Blake. "What the hell, Tux?"

"My *mom* loves me," he said, in a tone that sounded more like he was reassuring himself than answering Mia.

"She doesn't stand up for you?"

"Dad's the head of the family. She has to do what he says."

"I'm sorry, *that* is just whacked up. I mean that's plain screwed."

"Any more than your family?" he said, softly.

There was silence, again. "Touché. A family broken together is just as bad as a family broken apart," said Mia.

"Broken is broken."

Mia sighed deeply. "So, what made you change your mind? About wanting God to kill you?"

"I finally got what Uncle Carson was talking about. What kid my age has a lake, a club, a sailboat...a friend? And my dad can't take any of it away. He can take me away from it. But he can't ever take it away from me. It's mine."

"Well, he'd have to get in line, at any rate," said Mia, stretching. "Dad's after the club, Hunter thinks the lake is his, Garvey wants your boat, and my mom is planning to lock me up in some convent in Outer Mongolia."

"A pretty girl once told me that there are two kinds of people."

"Yup. Vikings and victims."

"So, what are we going to do about it?"

"Who are you really and what have you done with Tux?" she purred. "*Master and Commander* must've gone to your head. What are you, little Lord Blakeney, now?"

"Why not? The kid loses his arm in battle and by the end of the movie he's leading a boarding party of grown-ups and saves his ship! That's the kid *I* want to be!"

"I think you should do what Gunn says and lay low for a couple of weeks. At least until that gash is water-tight."

The breeze freshened a little and *Seven Thunders* responded enthusiastically. They reined her in and cantered her in to the lee of Trespass Island.

"Pull up in the cove," said Mia. "I have to make a pit stop."

Sails rattled down, the board slid up, the boat was beached and the duo went ashore. Blake stood on the hard, weedy dirt and watched as the beam of Mia's flashlight disappeared up a little path.

The symphony of night was in full swing—bullfrogs belched their love-songs in time with the tree-peepers' castanet-clicking, the crickets supplying the string section. Something large splashed in the middle of the cove. Blake remembered Gunn's catfish story. He fidgeted in the inky solitude until nature got the better of him, too. He resorted to the bushes and began nervously watering the weeds. Something fluttered in the underbrush. A strange whine crescendoed into a piercing phantom wail that split the ears and turned courage to jelly. It seemed to last forever. He shrieked and fell backwards across the deck of the boat. Then all was silent, save for the sound of Mia trotting back down the path. The moonlight opus faded back up to full volume. He hurriedly zipped his shorts.

"What are you doing?" she chortled.

"Watching for meteors. What else?" he panted, still flat on his back. "What the heck was that?"

"A ring-necked loon. You got too close to his territory."

"Oh, Is *that* all it was?" He raised himself up.

"Come here. You'll want to see this."

***

They stood silently among the dark trees along the north shoreline. Blake adjusted the scope and scanned the distance. "Wait, there—a sailboat. The *Covenant!*" he hissed.

"Notice anything weird?"

"Yeah, look how low she's riding in the water. Jack scrunched up in the bow, like there's no room in the boat."

"Nobody's bailing, so she must not be leaking. Get down."

They crouched behind some cattails as the *Covenant* passed. Barely fifty yards away, she was showing her black side. Voodoo Jack was crammed in the bow like a sulking troll. Kalijah stood at the helm, white shirt and sail glowing eerily in the moonlight. Filling the entire space between them was a large, tarp-covered hump.

"What *is that?*" Blake whispered, as he handed the scope to Mia.

She squinted into the eyepiece. "Big. And apparently very heavy."

The spectral boat cleared the island. "Hey look! Beavers!" Blake said, standing up.

Indeed, in the *Covenant's* wake were several v-shaped ripples, heading straight for them.

But as soon as they reached the shallows, the ripples erupted into great black figures which wrestled up out of the lake, splashing and gamboling, and leaping toward the shore like giant dervishing-demons.

"Oh crap!" cried Mia, jerking a petrified Blake behind a stout tree trunk. Ten huffing, snorting shadows bounded and smashed though the underbrush, all around them. Mia and Blake remained wrapped together, hearts pounding. They listened to the herd of monsters crash its way across the island and splash back into the lake on the far side.

Mia swallowed hard and started to laugh. "Deer! Stupid.... flippin'... Deer!"

Blake caught the bug and started laughing, too. "I had no idea they were

246

recreational swimmers!" They disentangled themselves from one another.

"I bet you're ready to call it a night, huh?" she said, in a way that almost seemed a suggestion.

Blake gazed down the lake. He could still see the phantom sail. "No on your life, lass. I want to know where they're going. Jib oop, board doon, Trim for a beam reach!"

"You do that so well, it's scary! Well, c'mon, your ship awaits, Captain—or is it Master, or Commander?"

"Please. *Just* call me Tux."

***

Seven Thunders gained on the *Covenant* handily. When they were within five hundred feet, Mia eased the sails to match their quarry's speed. They tailed the black-and-white sharpie for forty minutes. Finally, Blake handed the tiller over to Mia and went on deck. He focused the night-scope.

"What's the report, Cap'n" Mia whispered.

"They're turning to starboard. Ducking... there's the jibe. They're headed for shore."

Mia let the Mainsail all the way out. *Seven Thunders* slowed to a gentle crawl. Blake turned to protest, but Mia cut him off.

"This is where we turn around, skipper. They're headed down the Mangrave branch. Nothing good *ever* happens down there."

He stepped to the bow, took hold of the forestay and resumed his surveillance. His blood ran cold: Kalijah turned and waved.

***

The breeze faded away. The lake was smooth as glass; a perfect mirror for the shining lights of the sky-ocean, save for the gently spreading wake of *Cry of the Osprey* and the few ripples from Mia's expert strokes.

She rested for a moment and let the *Osprey* glide under the stars and the setting moon which was just beginning to wane from fullness. She pondered Blake's question. His blind devotion to an ancient decree from an invisible deity. His dutiful willingness to suffer self-destruction for the sake of his mother. Mia frowned to herself in the dark and resumed her paddling. She was tired. Gunn's offer to drive her home drifted to mind. She blew a mosquito out of her face and worked to paddle harder, as if trying to leave the evening behind. But try as she might, the memories swirled and eddied in her mind like the little whirlpools off the ends of her paddle. They stirred strange feelings that she was not altogether comfortable with.

What was it? Breaking bread with people who actually cared about each other? Gunn's understated concern about not liking the thought of "a young lass crossin' the lake alone, this time o' night?" Or was it Blake's innocent goodnight hug? Cared for. That was it, she thought. She felt cared for. And nobody expected anything in return. She wasn't quite sure what to do with that.

Here and there along the shadowy shores of the Lower, little campfires gleamed warmly. Ahead, the dazzling lights of Gold Coast mansions bled down the channel. In the distance, a massive houseboat hummed along, windows dark, kids in bed.

Highland Harbor lay to her left, the marina murky and brooding. A solitary fire glowed on the sailing club's peninsula. She found new vigor and covered the half mile to the point. Mia adjusted her night-scope. A blaze—a tent—a short stocky man with a bushy Fu Manchu mustache.

Chapter 23

The Sunday morning edition of the Freeman Gazette fluttered and rattled over the breakfast table like a giant newsprint butterfly. Gunn snapped it taught, and folded it into a size manageable for one hand.

"Best. Waffles. Ever. Hands down," Mia said as she stuffed another chunk in her mouth.

"It's the syrup. Get it at the State Fair every year," said Gunn, scanning the paper.

"No, it's the waffles too. Better than the Emporium's! Uh, don't tell Charlie I said that," said Mia.

Gunn snorted absently and gave a little chuckle.

Blake laid his cards on the table and counted the score. "Fifteen-two, fifteen-four, fifteen-six, a double run, the Jack of Heels and...And?"

"Go ahead, say it Caduggin."

"I win!"

"I'm no sure why I taught him to play this infernal game! He still has'na bested me at darts though." Gunn gave Mia a wink. He pushed his cards to the center of the table. "Well, let's see what evil men have wrought whilst we slumbered." He opened the paper up and folded it over the other way. "ah-tah-dee, ah-ta-dahhh—Look at this! Lucky's been pinched! If God lived down here, people'd break his windows!"

"Who or what is Lucky?" Blake inquired.

"Lucky's Catfish Cove, up the highway. Lucky's the mascot."

"You mean that stupid, plastic catfish with a chef's hat?" Mia said.

"Resin, actually. Must weigh four hundred pound if he weighs an ounce!"

"When was he stolen?" Blake said.

"Friday evening, right after closing."

Blake and Mia locked eyes.

The doorbell rang. "Now, who's that, first thing on Sunday morning?" said Gunn. He rose with a groan and shambled off to the stairs.

He opened the door and was surprised to greet a burly Latino man, sporting a crew cut.

"If you're recruitin', my lad's a bit young for the Marines."

"Mister Gonn, sir?" said the man, almost bashfully.

"Aye."

"Mr. Gonn, my name is Pagán. I am sorry, I hope I am not intruding?"

"How can I help yeh?"

"I'm sorry, Mr. Gonn, but Tux hire me and my family to clean up your place."

"Hired you, did he?"

Blake and Mia lurked just out of sight, eavesdropping at the top of the stairs. Blake was grinning ear-to-ear, with a look of astonished euphoria.

"Ah, yes sir. He say is for the Father's day. A gift for *you*."

Gunn looked pleasantly surprised. "Master Urquart!" he called up the stairs. "Your contractors are here!"

The eavesdroppers rumbled down the stairs to the little foyer.

"Thank you so much for coming, Señor Pagán!" Blake said. "I hope you don't mind, Mr. Gunn. Happy Father's Day!"

"I did'na know I was a father, but thank yeh lad! Yeh better go and show your crew what's what!" Blake slipped out the door and jogged across the weedy, gravel parking lot to Pagán's big green pick-up truck.

"I'll clear the table and be out in a minute," said Mia. She went back upstairs and resumed eavesdropping.

"Mr. Gonn, may I have a word with you? I want to say that Tux, he is very fine boy. He offer me four hundred cash for this job. I ask him why he don't buy a nice videogame or a bike. He say he don't care about them things. He just want to help his friend. I tell him I can't do it. He even send his girlfriend with the money and I tell her I can't do it." He paused and ran his hand over his bristly hair. "Mr. Gonn, I am very hard man. But I tell you, this touch my heart. My little boy, he was lost in the woods. You know Tux, he find my little boy and bring him back to me? What I'm try to say Mr. Gonn, is we not going to charge Tux nothing to clean up your place. If that's okay with you."

Mia's eyes misted up. She crept back to the table and sat quietly.

"Well, Mr. Pagán," Gunn said, thoughtfully, "I'd be honored. I hope you will allow me the pleasure of providing lunch for your family."

"Thank you Mr. Gonn, you are most gracious."

Gunn looked past Pagán to the beehive of activity surrounding the truck. "I see you've brought the auld folks. Send 'em upstairs here, where it's cool."

Sylvio Pagán beckoned Salma and the old men, who were laughing and making over Blake.

"Miss Devlin! When you're done bussin' the table, put on another pot o' coffee, will yeh?"

Mia flinched at the sudden order and thought *What the Hell?* She sucked it up and replied "Alright Mr. Gunn!"

***

Weed-whackers whined like angry hornets, a lawn tractor growled about the property, and a chainsaw ripped through old, wooden hulls. A pillar of smoke rose in black billows from a raging pyre in the back lot. Periodically, Gunn would appear in an upper-story window to direct the workforce, like a captain from the quarter deck.

Mia had not yet managed to get back outside, where she wanted to be. Gunn kept her busy playing waitress and gopher, while he sat at the dining-room table with Salma. The old men played billiards. She put up with it partly for Blake's sake and partly for her own reasons; and yet, much to her own surprise, because she kind of wanted to. Now and then she would make it to a window to keep tabs on Sylvana, who was not giving Blake a moment's rest.

"Ah Miss, another pot o' coffee when yeh've a moment. And I need yeh to call in an order to Nick Tyner." He waved a menu-flyer in the air.

For a second, she looked as if she'd been asked to clean the toilet. "Sure, Mr. Gunn." She fetched the menu, Salma looking on with royal satisfaction. "I want to put on a right feast for these folks. Yeh call Nick and tell 'im how many we've got, and he'll fix us up. Spare no expense."

"Okay." She started for the phone.

"Wait! There's folding tables and chairs in the shop. Get those lads to haul 'em out and set 'em up for yeh. Make sure yeh wipe 'em down."

"I'll handle it," she replied, restraining her natural urge for sarcasm.

Blake thought he had finally found a spot to work where Sylvana wouldn't find him. He was at the end of the long shop building endeavoring to pull a lead pipe out of the ground when something caressed his behind and quickly wandered into forbidden territory. "Hey!" He yelped with a squeak.

"Es okay, Tux; you girlfriend no see us."

"Don't touch me like that! Y no es mi novia!"

"I could be you novia, Tux," she moaned and cocked her head seductively.

"No you *can't.* Your poppi said so."

"Come on Tux, I want to show you something. You gonna like it." She seized his hand and dragged him across the back lot at a run.

Mia called Tyner's from the kitchen phone, dumped the coffee grounds and prepared a new pot. She spotted Sylvana, hapless Blake in tow. Mia threw open the window as if she were escaping a fire and shouted.

"Hey, chica! Necesita ayudar, imediamente!"

Sylvana stopped in her tracks. Blake reclaimed his hand and stalked away, in disgust.

"Yeah? What for, Miss ' *I don't speak-a no Espanish?*'" Sylvana sassed back.

"Sylvana!" Came a stern shout from within the house. "Haz lo que esa chica se dice!"

Sylvana shot Mia a dirty look and answered "Si Abuelita! I'm help, I'm help!"

**

Blake dragged a huge bundle of dry pine branches to the fire and began to manhandle them into the blaze. The inferno flared hotter and higher. Blake dodged away from the unbearable heat. He rubbed stinging smoke from his eyes, and when his vision cleared he could not believe what he saw. On the crest of the ridge that shielded the property from the lake stood his uncle.

Bare chested, thumbs hooked in the belt-loops of his cut-offs, he surveyed the clean-up operation.

"Uncle Carson!"

Carson turned and walked back over the top of the ridge.

"Uncle Carson! Wait!" Blake sprinted across the boatyard with all his might. Mia heard him yell and followed after. She caught up to him at the edge of the bluff, overlooking the lake. The red canoe was almost to Trespass Island.

"Come back! Please! What did I do?" He bent double, hands on his knees, struggling to catch his breath. Three minutes passed and the canoe disappeared behind the island. "What the hell did I ever do to you!" He flung a rock.

"Good arm," said Mia, joining him. Blake stood and fumed for a minute. He stared into the distance. Far down the lake, sails sat like white napkins folded on a flat blue tablecloth. The sound of the Committee boat's horn drifted up to them in three muted blasts.

"Race cancelled. No wind," said Mia.

Still, he did not answer. He turned his attention to two white swans, as they preened by the cape.

"You think our little pirate friends made off with that stupid catfish? That thing's as tall as I am!" she said.

She put her hands in her back pockets and scuffed a rut in the crusty earth with one foot. "Listen. I don't mind helping out but Gunn's really getting on my last nerve, ordering me around like a galley slave."

"It's just his way. Probably just testing you," Blake said, quietly. He threw another rock. "He did me. Don't let it ruin your day."

"Yeah well, if I wanted tests, I'd stay in school."

"I'll try to say something. We better get back. Lots more to do."

***

It took everyone to unload the food from Nick Tyner's delivery truck. Tyner himself sat behind the wheel and chatted with Gunn. Gunn called Sylvio over and introduced him.

"Mr. Pagán, here, is not only a landscaper but a carpenter. Does cabinets, specifically."

"How about pools?" said Tyner.

"Oh yes. My son, Cezar, he's pool expert—pomps, plumbings, the chemicals, cleaning."

Tyner nodded, approvingly. "Cabinets, huh?"

"Oh, yes Señor. That is my occupation. In my country I am cabinet-maker. The very best. Very fine coffins, too."

"You hear that Gunn?" Nick winked. "Mr. Pagán, I'm renovating my rental properties and it just so happens I need new kitchen cabinets. Why don't you come 'round my restaurant for lunch tomorrow and we'll talk about it."

"Thank you, sir. I have a few tools but, cabinets—I need a shop."

"We'll let Gunn solve that problem. You show up for lunch tomorrow. Bring your family."

Tyner put his truck into reverse. Sylvio stepped forward. "Mr. Tyner, we are legal, I show you." He reached for his wallet.

"Don't bother yourself. Gunn's recommendation is good enough for me. Be talkin' to you, Tripper!" He turned the truck around and drove away.

***

The clean-up was thorough and far-reaching and finally it was done. Scrap metal was loaded into the bed of the truck. Firewood cut and stacked, the pyre burned down and extinguished. Trailers, sunk in the earth up to their axles had been exhumed, the tires re-inflated. Every weed on the property cut down and incinerated. The banquet was packed away. The Pagán's tail lights disappeared up the long dark drive. The pole light at the water's edge flickered to life. Mia sat on the dock, feet in her kayak.

"Yeh sure you'll no let me drive yeh home? Yeh look awfully beat," said Gunn, ambling up.

"Thanks Mr. Gunn, but I have a stop to make on the way back. I'll be fine."

"It's come to my attention that I've been treating one of my honored guests like a common scullery maid. I owe yeh a debt of thanks for today. Yeh really went the extra mile."

She smiled shyly. "Thank you Mr. Gunn. I enjoyed it."

"And I appreciate yeh lookin' after that lad." He turned to face the house. "Caduggin! The girl is leaving!" he bellowed. "I still wish yeh'd no cross that lake after dark." He ambled back to the shore.

Blake came down from the house. "Man, you've still got enough oomph to paddle home?" He sat down next to her.

"Girl's gotta do what a girl's gotta do!"

She gave him a little hug. "You're a good guy, Tux. I better be careful. You'll wear off on me." She slipped into her boat and got situated. Blake untethered the bowline and watched her paddle out of the harbor.

***

Again, Mia found herself pondering beneath the waning moon. The work had been exhausting, but not without its rewards. Lunch from Nick Tyner's was a reward in itself. She wondered at how gracious and generous Tripper Gunn had been to the Pagán family; how he entertained the elders all day long without speaking a lick of Spanish; the way that Cezar and Romero had treated Blake like a little brother. It was all very powerful, puzzling, and painful at the same time.

And then there was Carson's appearance on the ridge. Aloof. On the outside, looking in. *Like me.* She thought. *That's me. Always on the outside, looking in. Always on guard.* All of her life she'd felt there was something missing. And now she'd gotten a glimpse of it—and it made a hollow ache in her chest and throat and a tingling behind her eyes. Ahead, she could see a solitary campfire flickering through the grove on Highland point. She was glad to see it—because it made her angry. It cleared her mind. It gave her the strength to paddle on.

Carson slouched in his camp chair, flipped an empty beer can into the fire and opened another. He took a long swig and then stared blankly into the night.

A young woman materialized like an apparition in the rippling heat, above the flames.

"I figured you'd show up. What kept you?" he sneered.

"I'm a little tired. Could've used some help today."

"You got something to say or did you just come here to haunt me?"

"Blake really didn't need that little stunt you pulled, today."

"'Scuse me, I didn't know he was still around. Figured he'd had another meltdown and been sent packing by now."

"Could you blame him? Dumped by his parents, abandoned by his uncle, attacked by every psycho-freak on the lake? He's twelve flippin' years old, for the love of Pete!"

"Life's rough."

"Tell him about it. He's got seven stitches in his head to prove it."

"I rest my case." He took another long swig. "What am I supposed to do about it?"

"He needs to know that he's not to blame for *your* behavior. He's driving himself nuts trying to figure out what he did to make you angry at him."

"I ain't."

"Would it be too much trouble to let him know that?"

"Are you done?" he shouted, fiercely.

"You know, I have to admit that I was totally wrong about Gunn. But I had you pegged right, you passive-aggressive horse's butt!" She turned and stalked off into the darkness.

Carson struggled to sit up and jeered "Why don't you come back sometime when you can't stay so long?" He guzzled the last of his beer, dashed the can into the fire and slumped back into his chair in a dejected funk.

Chapter 24

Blake lazed under the covers, arms over his head. He watched with vacant contentment as a patch of harsh sunlight crept across the swallow-tailed sailing club pennant he'd tacked up on his bedroom wall, and eased onto a large map of the reservoir. It was not that he was too tired to get up, but too cozy—snug as a bug in a rug, according to his mother.

Eventually, he had to rise and do what a boy must do. He wandered through the silent house to the big bay window and spied Gunn aboard the *Terrapin*, exchanging gas tanks and stowing the folding cart in the cabin. A snarling from his belly turned him back toward the kitchen. The clock on the stove read 1:00. The storm door in the foyer banged.

"Caduggin? Are yeh vertical?"

"Just getting something to eat, Dad," Blake said. "I mean, Mr. Gunn!"

"Then get dressed and grab a snack. We'll have luncheon in town."

***

Blake sat with the tiller in one hand and a slice of cold pizza in the other.

"Whoever invented cold pizza was a genius!" he said, over the droning of the motor.

Gunn, puffing clouds of white smoke from his pipe, gave a little nod and winked. "Mind your helm lad and always keep a weather-eye on the traffic. Keep to starboard, as we go up the channel."

"If I see *Lemon Drop*, can I ram her?" Blake asked, jokingly.

"You'll no even talk like that," Gunn barked. "It's foolishness. Don' even think it! You are responsible for the safety of everyone around yeh when yer at the tiller. Boat, bike, car, or bloomin' roller skates. You avoid a collision at all costs."

"I understand, sir."

"Aye, the sailing rules let yeh bump your competitors when you're luffing. But I never much cared for the hitting game."

Blake scanned the lake for traffic, adjusted his course, and let Gunn puff away in silence for a few minutes.

"I was looking at the map," Blake ventured. "What's down the Mangrave Branch?"

"A lot of nasty people. They're territorial and they play for keeps. I'd suggest yeh no go down there."

"Mia says the wetlands are drying up."

"Everything is. Yeh'll be able to walk to town, before long. Which reminds me—mind the bridge piling on the way back."

"I guess Mia probably told you that we saw Uncle Carson, yesterday?"

"She did not!"

"On the ridge. When I called to him, he just turned around and left."

Gunn's eyes narrowed, his jaw jutted, and he stared into the distance for a moment.

"What are we going to do about Junior Training if Uncle Carson doesn't come back?"

Gunn remained silent a little while longer. "It'll be you, me, and Griffy. Yeh think that girl'd help? Pays ten bucks an hour."

"It pays?"

"Aye. Yeh've got yourself another job."

***

Blake lurked in the section closest to the library's computers. He peered furtively between bookshelves, his heart racing. Not ten feet away, Voodoo Jack slouched in front of a computer, surfing the internet. Blake ran all of the contingencies through his head and bided his time. Finally, Jack leaned over to scratch a red, bumpy patch on one calf. Blake ducked a little lower. On the screen was a single, blood-dripping word—Dagon.

"Can I help you?" Asked a lady librarian. Blake nearly dove through the books. "No, I'm fine."

"Doing a report?" she said, with a smug smile.

"Just browsing."

"We usually want kids to have a grown-up with them, in this section."

Blake scanned the books on the shelves. Every last one had the words *sex* or *sexuality* in the title. Blake turned three shades of red.

"I see… Well, I've got to get going. Thanks for the assistance!" he said, backing down the aisle. He sneaked another glimpse between the shelves. Jack was still glued to the screen, white wires trailing from the buds in his ears. Blake slunk around the perimeter of the main room and escaped out the front door. "Mueller," he thought. I've got to find Officer Mueller." He checked his watch. "Time to get back to the boat."

Blake rounded the big gazebo in the middle of the woodsy Waterfront Park. Just ahead, trudged a familiar figure; grunting rhythmically as he massaged his lower back with both hands.

Blake darted off the sidewalk and into the grove. Kalijah continued on his way until, seemingly from nowhere, came a boy's voice with a Scots accent.

"Where have ye been, Mr. Woodhead?"

Kalijah stopped and cast about, looking more dazed than usual. A wry smile spread across his face. "Walking to and fro on the earth and going up and down in it!"

"Mooch hairt are ye, Mister Woodhead?"

Garvey hobbled in the direction of the voice and popped around the closest tree.

"Gotcha!" he exclaimed, to no one.

"Lift wi' yer knee's, no wi' yer back; 'tis what they say, is it not?" teased the voice, now from the direction of the lake.

Kalijah groaned his way around the next big tree. "Ha!" he cried, but he surprised nobody.

"Spiriiit!" he moaned in a low crescendo.

"Nay, but ye been fishin'! Were it a *Lucky* catch?"

The shabby pirate flinched, his eyes grew wide. One last time he sought the voice, but found only solitude. Blake snickered to himself, then turned and darted straight into a wall of body odor and a pork-rib-necklace. He fell flat on his rump and was immediately seized by one arm and yanked back up.

"Found your ghost, Kalijah!" yelled Jack. "Think you're pretty smart, don'cha, kid? I told you I'd put the whammie on you!"

"You still trying to get that tsantsa to work? Should'a gotten a refund while you had the chance," Blake chided through clenched teeth, as he struggled to escape his captor's iron grip.

Kalijah shambled into view. "Jack, be kind! We are glad that the Dauphin is so pleasant with us," he said with sardonic graciousness.

Blake ceased his wriggling and jerking. *F.E.A.R.* he thought. *Panic— never got anyone anything but killed.* But then an odd phrase floated into his mind: *Surely I have calmed and quieted my soul.* He gathered his courage, began to assess his predicament, and resolved to wait for the decisive moment.

"Release the Little Prince, Jack," Kalijah requested, gazing at Blake with mock affection.

"Not on your life. You know how fast this runt is? I say we take him now."

"Jack, you would spoil everything. If you love something, set it free. It will return, if meant to be!"

"Why wait?"

"Everything in its appointed *season*! He will return to us," he said, with eerie reasonableness. "Now release the Little Prince, Brother Jack."

"What have you done with my Granddad's trophy? What did you steal out of the bookcase in the living room, Jack?"

Jack shook him angrily. "I've got a few questions for you, myself, pal! Where's Carson, huh? Why'd he change the locks, huh? What happened to my *stuff*, huh?"

Blake lifted both feet. Jack hauled up on his arm to compensate. Blake stomped down on the bridge of his booted foot like a drop forge. Jack hollered and relaxed his grip. Blake broke free, caught his balance and began to sprint—but Kalijah snatched him as he tried to sidestep.

"Not so fast, Master Urquart!" groaned Kalijah, through his pain. You haven't answered Jack's questions!"

Jack struggled to stand straight and put weight on both feet, again.

"I don't know where my uncle is," Blake shouted. "But if you want to know who changed the locks, it was me! And if you're talking about that bag full of stinking fungus, check with the sewage department."

"You flushed my shrooms?" roared Jack.

"*Our* shrooms, Jack!"

"And notified the police! I wouldn't show my face in Pemberton any more, if I were you!"

"Most uncharitable, Master Urquart."

"You're bluffing!" Jack said with a guttural rumble. He lunged, fist raised.

"Touch not the Lord's anointed, Jack!"

Blake saw that it was now or never. He planted his best kick solidly between the goal-posts. Voodoo Jack hit the lawn with a strangled "hooomp," which welled up from the depths of his groin. Kalijah caught a flying elbow, like a steel-spike in the solar plexus. He tottered under the sudden loss of breath and spreading pain in his back. He slowly crumbled backwards into the cool grass.

"Caduggin!" came a most welcome shout from the sidewalk. "Leave off tormentin' that scabby lake-trash and get yerself down the boot! Yeh got cargo to stow!"

"Yes sir!" Blake replied in delight and jogged after him as innocently as if he'd been playing with puppies.

***

Blake lounged on his bed and stared up at the wall map. He had learned at the Emporium that Mia would not be by tonight—she was moving in with

Treva. He was absolutely itching to tell her about the day's events, sure she'd be proud of his victory in the park. Though at first it had been harrowing, there was also a lot of satisfaction in drubbing those two. It almost seemed fun when he looked back on it. But on the other hand, just when things seemed to be settling down, he had gone and kicked the hornet's nest yet again.

But *their* days were numbered, Blake reassured himself. As soon as Buck Mueller could be apprised of the situation, he would track them down, catch them with Lucky and the Urquart family heirlooms and pack them off to jail. And that would be that.

"Caduggin!" Gunn called down the hall. "Dinner's here. Hurry up, We're watchin' Hornblower tonight!"

Chapter 25

"Can I help you?" said the secretary, doing her best to ignore the kids at the service desk. "Nature center and conservatory are downstairs. Maps are in the lobby. Coke machine's by the restrooms."

"We know," said Mia.

"You need fishing licenses?"

"We need Buck Mueller," Blake said. "If you please."

The secretary's expression dripped condescension. "*Buck* Mueller, eh?"

"Just tell him that Mia and Blake are here," said Mia.

"What's it concerning?"

"We have critical information on persons of interest," said Blake.

"I *see*," she droned. The secretary picked up the phone and dialed two numbers.

"Officer Mueller, Mary and Frank are here, they say they have *critical* information on *persons of interest.*"

Mueller peered through a gap in the curtains that covered the glass wall of his office. "Heh-heh! Send Mary and Frank in."

"Go on in," said the secretary, irritated that her determined efforts to be unhelpful had been thwarted.

Mueller sat behind a huge desk, laden with piles of paper and file folders. A stuffed great horned owl loomed high on the wall behind him—wings outspread, ever poised to swoop. With unblinking vigilance, its giant, yellow eyes seemed to drill straight into anyone who stood before the desk.

"How you kids doin'? Staying safe? Wearing your life jackets, right? I heard about your little scrape the other day. How are those stitches?"

"I get them out in a few days."

"Well, how can I help you two? I'm due on patrol in a half hour and, as you can see, I'm buried in paper work," he said with a sweeping gesture.

"Blake thinks he knows who stole Lucky."

"Catfish Cove's Lucky? Didn't know he was gone."

"It was Voodoo Jack and Garvey Woodhead," said Blake, with all the self satisfaction of a hanging judge.

"Okay, I'll buy that for a dollar. But that's not Drascombe business, that's Freeman PD's jurisdiction."

"Friday night we saw them hauling something huge down the lake. I think Lucky's on park property," said Blake.

"We tailed them as far as the Mangrave Branch," Mia added, hoping Mueller would deliver a lecture on the merits of avoiding it.

Mueller shifted in his seat, uneasily. "Well…"

"They attacked me in Waterfront Park, yesterday!"

"That's Freeman PD, too, I'm afraid."

"You *are* going to check it out, right?" Blake said. "We could go with you on patrol and show you. You *did* offer me a ride in *Moby*, remember."

"Look, it's a good tip but I can't follow up on it right now. I've got the Freeman Freedom Festival coming, the fishing tournament and a dozen other things I have to chase down before the end of today. It's a back-burner priority, Blake. I'm sorry."

Blake's heart sank. He could hear the hornet's nest buzzing angrily.

"I see your uncle's set up camp over at the J. Parrish Primitive. On the 'outs' with Tripper again?"

"We don't know what his deal is," said Mia. "We better let you get back to work."

"I'll keep what you said in mind, it's a good tip. If it leads to an arrest, there'll probably be a reward. Let me know if you see anything else suspicious," he said, with an air of finality. "Hey, I've got something for you." He reached into a desk drawer and tossed them each what appeared to be a fishing lure, without hooks. "Flash drive! Pull the head off and plug it in!"

"That's awesome! Thanks Buck!" Mia chuckled.

"Yes, thank you, Officer Mueller," said Blake, puzzled at the green, plastic fish with *Drascombe State Park* stenciled on one side.

"Call me 'Buck,' son. Give my regards to Tripp."

***

Cry of the Osprey coasted beneath the highway bridge. Blake's voice echoed off its massive concrete piers.

"I can't believe he didn't jump right on that! I thought you said he'd been watching them. I figured that was the break in the case he'd been looking for. American justice has gone to the dogs. My dad was right about that much."

"Look, at least he made time for us. You made your report, found out where your uncle is and got a cool-swanky flash drive. Look at the positives."

"I don't even know what a flash drive is."

"You're kidding me! I figured you'd be a computer wiz."

"Nope. Dad won't allow us to have one in the house. My sister gets to use them at school."

"Your little fish is a storage device that plugs into a computer. You can save all your pictures, music, and stuff like that on it. When you're done, you just unplug it and take it with you. I've got a laptop. I can teach you all about computers if you want."

Blake sighed and began to paddle. "There have got to be drag marks, or something. If the wind was right, we could go down the branch, spot where they went ashore, and fly right back out with the chute. With that kind of evidence Officer Mueller'd *have* to go check it out."

"*We* ain't doin' any such thing! I may be dumb, but I'm not stupid."

"But now they're *really* going to be after me!"

"You would be, too, if some kid shut down your clubhouse, flushed your drugs *and* beat the crap out of you. I mean that was kind of adding insult to injury, wasn't it? You need to learn when to keep your head down."

Blake fumed silently and watched the swallows as they dipped and wheeled from their mud-ball nests, picking tiny insects from the air.

"Just watch your step. I'd forget about Lucky and concentrate on patching things up with your uncle."

"Where's J. Parrish?"

"Not too far from where you thrashed the Mad Cowboy."

Griffy, he thought. The wheels began to turn. *Surely, Griffy!*

"Want to have lunch in the Hollow?" she suggested.

"Sure! Then we could go swimming back at Mr. Gunn's. We're watching the Horatio Hornblower series with dinner, wanna stay?"

"You guys and your high seas adventures! The guy that plays Hornblower's pretty cute, though; you might be able to talk me into it."

***

"Caduggin! We're startin' without yeh!" Gunn yelled down the hall.

"Be right there!" Blake answered, from his bedroom.

"A south wind," he muttered to himself, "I'll need a south wind." He planted a finger on the map, zig-zagged it from his home port, down lake, and into to the Mangrave branch. "Then we escape under spinnaker. No way they could catch us, then," he assured himself, tracing a rapid arc out of the branch and back up the lake.

"C'mon, Tux! Can't you smell the popcorn?" called Mia.

He tore himself away from the wall map and returned to the living room.

"Mr. Gunn, you ever sail *Sophia* in the Wednesday-night Keel boat races?" said Mia.

"Nope. I have not. I s'pose it's no out of the question, though."

"Does Griffy's mom sail her Catalina on Wednesday nights?" said Blake.

"I believe she does. Are we ready to start the show?"

"Fire it up!" said Mia with an expectant smile.

"Here we go." Gunn started the DVD and regarded them both with a suspicious eye.

Chapter 26

Griffy sat at the table with the best view of the harbor and watched the keel-boats heading out to race. He perched his chair on two legs, toes hooked under the window ledge as if he were hiking out on his Laser, skimming along in the breeze and spray.

"Ooh, how ye wish ye were oot thair! Eh Cowboy?" came that annoying accent, from behind.

Griffy dropped his chair flat again and set his jaw. Blake slipped into the chair opposite him.

"I'm in need of a crew Mister Williams. And I think ye can help."

"You need to go die in a fire." Griffy snarled.

"Oh, nay man! Don'a hold a grudge! Ye got but bruises, *I* got stitches!"

"You hit your head pretty stinkin' hard, didn't you."

"What if I could get yer mother to let ye off the hook? Would ye go then?"

"Go to Hell."

Griffy looked as if two wolves were fighting in his soul. One wanted to kill Blake, the other desperately wanted to sail.

Blake smiled slyly. "Think of it, man. Tomorrow. Ten knots oot the south. We beat doon lake and broad reach with the spinnaker all the way past the bridge, and thee on the wire the whole way."

Griffy was beginning to wag his head slowly in denial, and breathed in short, audible puffs through his nose. Finally, he broke.

"You think you can really get me off the hook?" He scowled at his own reflection in the window. He'd sold himself out, once again.

"Aye!"

"I'll go."

"There's me lad!" cheered Blake, rising and heading for the door.

"On one condition!" Griffy said loudly. "You quit talking like the Geezer."

"I'll see what can be done!" From the harbor, twin diesel-horns blared the half hour signal.

"That's me cue! If ye'll excuse me, I'll be shipping oot!"

"With *who*? Who are you crewing for?"

"Who else? Yer mum!"

Chapter 27

Blake covered the woman on his clan badge with his thumb and read the inscription: Mean well, speak well, do well. At that moment the Gunn motto seemed more agreeable to his conscience: Stand ready for peace or for war. He slipped the badge into its pouch and put it back on his dresser. He picked up *Treasure Island* and flipped to chapter twenty-two. He read Jim Hawkins' words again: "I was a fool, if you like, and certainly about to do a foolish, overbold act. But I determined to do it with all the precautions in my power." Blake stared at himself in the dresser mirror for a minute. *Honor your Father and Mother,* he thought. His chest tingled. He combed wavy hair off his forehead, peeled open a packet and carefully plastered a Tegaderm patch over his wound. He took the Highland Creek Sailing Club pennant from the wall, folded it and slipped it into his red sail bag, along with a six-pack of bottled water and some sunscreen. Into his cargo pockets he crammed a compass, buck knife, disposable camera, three packs of Black Cat firecrackers, an air horn, and an energy bar. He slid a lighter into his pocket. "All the precautions in my power," he whispered to himself. "Get in, look for clues, fly back on the chute."

Gunn had taken the van and gone to town to meet with Tyner and Pagán. Blake started the old tractor and backed *Seven Thunders* down the ramp. He moored her across from The *Terrapin* and gazed up at the empty house, the lonely yard, and silent harbor.

Blake stood on his toes and rigged the HCSC pennant to the port side-stay. He glanced back at the empty *Terrapin*, gleaming white in the noonday sun. "What are *you* looking at?"

***

Griffy paced the length of the main dock, arms folded, the brilliant day reflecting from his mirrored sunglasses. "Didn't put the jib up, huh?" he said, watching as Blake swooshed up and made his u-turn into the wind. *Seven Thunders* slowed to a stop alongside the dock. Griffy plunked into the cockpit.

"Didn't need to! Here's the harness." Griffy hoisted the jib, pushed off, and they were away.

Blake called "Ready about! Hard a'lee!" as they passed Highland Point. *Seven Thunders* tacked and rounded the peninsula. She heeled over and took off. They beat all of the way to the south shore, Griffy flying on the trapeze and Blake hiking out. But contrary to Griffy's expectations, Blake did not turn back and head north.

"We're not going to run the chute up the channel?"

"Mr. Gunn wants me to stay out of the channel, after what happened," Blake said, comforting himself that this was not entirely untrue. We'll beat down lake then come back broad the whole way. A broad reach is the fastest point of sail, after all."

"I think I liked you better when you didn't know how to sail."

It took forty minutes, but at last Griffy relaxed and slipped into "race-mode." Blake took full advantage.

"You ever sail with my uncle?"

"Just when he crewed with Geezer, back when I was learning to sail. Pretty cool guy."

"Why does he hang around that loser, Jack?"

"Uncle Creepy? His mom's a friend of your family or something. Thieving lake-trash, if you ask me—even if he is from Pemberton. We're lifting! Watch your luff, like I taught you."

Blake compensated for the wind shift. "It's kind of hard to see the jib through your fat kiester! So, did Mia ever sail?"

"Like a maniac! Unbeatable."

"What happened? Why did she quit?"

"I don't know. The old man gave Hunter all the attention, I guess. He was the golden-boy at all the regional regattas. You *know* why she keeps you around, right?"

"Because we're friends."

Griffy laughed scornfully. "Devil-woman doesn't *have* any friends. She likes *you* because you're the only boy on the lake who doesn't want to get her alone in the back seat of a car." That was like a bucket of cold water in the face. "C'mon, man! A hot, Karate queen like Mia and a choirboy like you? How naïve can you be? Please!"

Blake hiked out farther and stared hard ahead. The gaping maw of the Mangrave Branch yawned just off the port bow.

Griffy railed on, but Blake wasn't listening. His heart pounded in his ears like jungle drums. He asked himself if he was really going to do this. At the far side of the opening, he steeled his nerves and made his decision.

"Man, if you think this *boat* is too much for you, Mia Devlin…"

"Ready about, hard a'lee!"

"What are you doing man? Where are you going?"

"I just want to see what's down here. Then we'll put the chute up and fly away home!"

The branch narrowed the farther along they went. Blake tacked again, mid channel. "Ease out for a close reach. Let's take it easy for a minute." Blake squatted in the cockpit, peered under the boom.

"What do you think you're doing, doofus?"

"Looking for drag marks. Broken branches. Anything that looks like something heavy's been lugged ashore through the brush."

"Hey, where the? We're sailing up Mangrave Creek? Are you totally out of your freakin skull?"

"Yes, I am! Now shut up and help me look. The faster we find it, the faster we get out of here."

"Turn around, now! My mom will sooo kill me if she finds out! Please!"

Blake scanned the shore intently. "What's everybody freaked out about?

It doesn't look any different than the rest of the lake."

"It's not the place, stupid! It's the people!" Griffy began to bounce nervously on the trapeze and cast about like a neurotic monkey in boa country. "A conservation officer was murdered down here a few years ago. They never caught his killer."

"That explains a bunch," Blake said. His anxiety level ratcheted up another notch.

"Not to mention the druggies from that crap-hole town up the creek."

"Do-it-yourself tattoos? No teeth?"

"Mangrave meth zombies. One time, I saw this dude—no choppers, sores all over his face, and a tattooed swarm of bees swirling out of his butt-crack and up his boney back."

"I saw that guy at the flea market!"

"Yeah, so why didn't your girlfriend come with you?"

"I guess she's smarter than that," Blake said, trying to lighten his own spirit.

"See what I mean? Even she has enough sense not to come down here!"

Blake was determined not to chicken out in front of Griffy, especially since he was certain that Griffy would tell everyone and make himself out to be Captain Courageous in the process. Then he saw it.

"There it is!" He eased the mainsail out and headed for a low mud bar blocking the entrance to a cove. His fears melted away.

"Okay, so can we go now?" said Griffy, almost pleading.

"Hold on!"

"Don't lee-shore us, Bozo!"

Blake brought *Seven Thunders* across the wind and let the sails luff. "Dang, look at that rut! No wonder Kalijah's back hurt. they must have portaged the whole boat over that bar!" He stood up on the afterdeck and craned his neck to see over the high grass that topped the bank. Something on the far side of the cove glinted in the midday sun.

"There's something back there! I knew it!"

To Griffy's relief, Blake trimmed the main and jib and got the boat moving again. Until he swung them into a swampy little inlet a hundred feet past the mud bar.

"Pull the board."

"Oh my god, you are NOT going ashore?"

"You can stay and guard the boat if you want. But I'm taking the rudder with me." He beached her in silty, leafy muck. "I came here to prove that they stole Lucky," he said. Blake stretched across the afterdeck on his belly and fiddled with something on the transom. "So Buck Mueller can put them in jail and get them off my back, once and for all." He slipped something into his pocket. "And that's exactly what I'm going to do."

"Don't take the rudder! I'll go—but if you see that flippin' catfish do you promise that we'll leave?"

"Promise. C'mon."

They tramped through cattails and brush. Blake forged incautiously up a faint trace that led into the woods.

"Hey, slow down! Be careful, you idiot!" Griffy hissed.

Blake could see that the trace opened into a clearing just ahead. He left the path and made his way in a squatting scuttle to the tree line. Griffy followed, cussing to himself the whole way.

Blake grinned. He pulled out the camera and snapped two pictures. Fifty feet away on a weedy, sun-baked mud flat stood a man-sized statue of a catfish wearing a chef's hat. A heap of ashes in a stone ring lay between it and the waterline. Lucky seemed to look cheerfully over the dismal, stumpy lagoon, presenting the day's menu to all who swam, slithered, or slunk in its icky emerald waters.

Griffy parted the weeds like a curtain and peered through. He was speechless, if only for a moment. "Man, it's bad luck just to *see* something like that!" he murmured. "Alright, you've seen it. You promised. Let's get out of here."

"Hold on!" Blake replied, and crept out onto the flat.

"If you don't get back over here right now, I'm leaving without you," snarled Griffy though clenched teeth.

"Not without the drain-plug, you're not!" Blake said, patting his front pocket as he strode across the flat. He met Lucky, face to face.

Griffy hurried warily to catch up with his skipper, who was totally engrossed with snapping pictures of the catfish.

"What the crap is that pukable *stench*?" Griffy glanced around. "Why are there dead catfishes nailed to the trees?" He swatted at enormous flesh-flies that buzzed malevolently around his head.

"Witchcraft. Plain and simple," Blake said, eyeing the dark stains that streaked Lucky's glossy white belly. "Look at these glyphs." He pointed to the chalkboard. "Phoenician, I should think."

"Good job, Mr. Spock. And why are there white feathers all over the water?"

Blake pondered for a moment. "Of *course!* The fish-god of the Phoenicians," he said to himself. "Blood sacrifice! They're worshipping Dagon, the fish-god of the Phoenicians."

"It freaks me out that you even *know* that."

"Only one thing left to do." Blake got behind Lucky and began to rock him back and forth. "And when they arose early on the next morning, behold…" Blake grunted, shoving rhythmically with all his might. Lucky swayed forward precipitously, balanced for a second, then crashed face-down into the fire pit. "Dagon was fallen upon his face to the ground before the ark of the Lord!"

There was a startling splash in the middle of the lagoon.

"Did you see that!" cried Blake, astonished at the plume of water.

Griffy only stared past him in cold horror.

"Sacrilege!" boomed that hollow, theatrical voice.

Blake spun around and there was Kalijah, twenty feet away. Then it registered: he was holding a walking stick with a green and purple thistle carved on its top. Without warning, something exploded from the nearby brush. It was a blur of black billows, white blubber and a guttural cry. Like the demonic fury of the idol itself, the ghastly catfish-headed monster bounded straight for Blake, arms open wide for the fatal embrace.

The boys screamed as they sprinted for the trace. Griffy caught a toe under a root and hit the crusty ground hard. Kalijah was on him in an instant. Griffy began to bleat like a goat on its way to slaughter. Blake darted to the right and tore through the woods, the caped catfish in hot pursuit. He flew up a steep slope. But the beast could not keep up. It began to stagger and fell against a tree, gasping. It pulled off its head and became Voodoo Jack. He huffed heavily back to the lagoon, lugging the mask under one arm.

"Kalijah, go for the boat! Leave him to me!"

Jack took custody of the squirming, cussing, crying cowboy. Kalijah headed for the trace. "*Our* boat, you moron! He'll be halfway to the lake by now!" he roared.

Kalijah skidded to a stop, then loped off in the opposite direction. He tossed the walking stick to Jack and cried, "Bind him, well!"

Blake ran until breath escaped him. He collapsed. His pulse crashed in his ears. A sizzling buzz surged in his brain and rattled his last fearful thought into nauseous blackness.

***

Dog breath. Hot, panting dog breath in his face. And nose. And ears. Slobbery licking on his mouth and cheeks and forehead. Daylight leaked back into Blake's brain. Whining. More dog breath and licking. He rumpled up his nose and opened his eyes. A large white dog stood over him. It gave a hearty bark of approval.

"Shhhhhhh!" Blake scolded. The dog left him and trotted up a nearby rise. He barked into the air. Blake belly-crawled after him and peeked over the edge. Down a steep slope, in a small clearing, stood the drab ruins of a cinder-block garage. Its window panes were gone from their casements, the ruined roof caved in and overgrown with clumps of moss. Varnish peeled in curls from its buckled overhead door. Next to it stood the rotted jamb where the front door once was.

The White Hound barked twice more.

The hideous face of the catfish appeared in the window and shouted "Shut up, moron!"

Blake could hear Griffy's muffled protests and pleadings. The White Hound barked three more times. "Shut up Moron!" echoed angrily out of the concrete lair. He licked Blake in the face and returned to the spot where he had lain and began to sniff around, enthusiastically. He found the camera and snapped it up in his jaws. The hound drew Blake's attention with a beckoning whimper. "Hey, thanks!" Blake whispered in amazement. "Bring it here boy!" He slid away from his vantage and crawled toward the dog. The hound dropped the camera, hunkered down on his front paws and barked once, tail swooshing expectantly.

"Shhh! Hey, I need that! *Bring* it here!" The hound barked again, snatched up the camera and disappeared into the woods. Exasperated, Blake returned to his lookout. Low groans now emanated from the lair and a sharp smelling smoke drifted from the window and wafted up the slope. *I can't believe this. What have I done? Who do I think I am, Little Lord Blakeney?* he thought. He studied the building. *Viking or a Victim. Lord Blakeney. I have calmed and quieted my soul. I beat them once.*

Voodoo Jack began to chant with renewed intensity. Blake spotted the walking stick. Jack had left it outside the door. The white hound reappeared down in the clearing. He loped around the perimeter of the garage, camera still in his jaws. He stopped short of the smoking window and whined at the scent. The dog dropped the camera, looked up to the ridge and barked mischievously. The catfish appeared at the window again and chucked a brick at the dog. "Get out of here! Go on! Git!" The white hound growled at him and ran off. Jack left the window and returned to his chanting.

Blake followed the ridge down to the clearing and stole up to the back wall. He pulled the firecrackers from his pack, tore the wrappers, and twisted the fuses together. He made his way stealthily along the side of the garage, collecting his camera as he went. He ducked under the window. Blake eased the lighter from his pocket, ignited the fuse, and tossed the Black Cats through the casement. He scurried to the front corner of the garage and took up his grandfather's walking stick. Two seconds later, it sounded like the building had been set upon by Israeli commandos.

Blake wielded the walking stick like a Louisville Slugger. The high priest of the catfish cult came shrieking out of the door in a stumbling leap, like a drunken dancer from the undead ballet company. Declan's staff whistled through the air and caught Jack across the upper thighs. He landed facedown in a screeching heap, rump in the air. Blake hauled back and gave him a whack across the gluteus maximus. The writhing priest wailed again and keeled over.

Blake cautiously peeled the cape back with the end of his staff. Dangling from Jack's waist was an eighteen inch dagger in a red, leather sheath. On its hilt gleamed the Urquart clan badge, in miniature. Blake seized it, drew the blade and cut the leather thong that held it around Jack's fat waist. He backed up, slid the scabbard under his own belt, then proudly sheathed his grandfather's clan dirk.

The interior of the hideout was shrouded in a choking mix of sandalwood incense and sulfurous smoke. At the far end of the dim room Griffy, bound and gagged, squirmed in midair. Blake coughed and rubbed his eyes clear. His friend was hanging by a rope tied to the ring on his trapeze harness and thrown over a rafter. When he noticed Blake, his expression of frozen mortal terror melted into hopeful relief, then steamed into seething anger. Blake untied the line and lowered his friend to the ground, in front of a crude altar made of limestone slabs. Blake's jaw dropped. There, on top, gleaming like the Holy Grail was the object of his quest: his grandfather's trophy. Below it, a framed document, and an old family picture of his grandparents, mother, and uncle.

Griffy struggled and growled through the gag. "Hold on," Blake mumbled. He stepped over Griffy and picked up the trophy as reverently as if it were a sacred artifact. Outside, the shaman groaned and struggled to get to his feet. Blake returned to his senses. He took up his staff and, to Griffy's grunting protests, went back outside.

Griffy could barely see Jack through the front door. Jack had managed to get to his hands and knees before the hiking stick smacked him across the shoulders. Griffy flinched. The caped figure slumped face first into the leaf litter. The end of the stick jabbed, then ground into the shaman's ribs. Griffy could hear Blake interrogating him, but not clearly. Something about his family, a curse, his uncle. Jack only responded in sinister, pained giggles. Blake ground the walking stick harder and said something about prison. Jack groaned. He regained his breath and sneered "Not without your boat!" He laughed contemptuously and spat, which earned him a stiff kick in the side. Griffy was shocked. For a kid who had never played video games, this church boy had the brutality thing down pat. Blake returned to the smoky dimness of the garage, drew his dirk and cut Griffy free.

Before Griffy could get the gag out of his mouth and release a hurricane of verbal abuse, Blake pointed to the altar and commanded calmly, "shut up and get my stuff." He took the rope and went back outside. Griffy emerged into dappled sunlight, clutching the heirlooms. Jack was tied hand and foot and tethered to a nearby tree.

Blake looked at Griffy, who seemed strangely tame and contrite. Blake finished the last knot. He stood up and looked Griffy in the eye. "I am really sorry, Griffin. Are you ready for that spinnaker run I promised you?"

A single trail led away from the hideout and, as Blake anticipated, it took them straight out to the mud flat where Lucky lay facedown in the fire-pit.

"What if the boat is really gone?" said Griffy.

"Then we'll find the *Covenant*. She's got to be around here, somewhere."

"What if…"

"Then we'll hike to the mouth of the branch and start a signal fire."

But the boat *was* there. They pushed her off and hopped aboard.

"Wait! The drain plug!" Griffy remembered.

Blake smiled apologetically. "It's in the transom. I never had it to begin with."

Griffy answered with a look of grim disgust and began to paddle them out into the branch. At last, *Seven Thunders* was under full sail, streaking toward the freedom of the lower lake. Griffy rode the trapeze, flying the spinnaker with expert diligence.

A startling bang echoed across the water, followed closely by another. Something shrieked through the air ten yards ahead and even more closely behind. They exploded in two nerve-rattling bursts, a hundred feet to starboard. Blake hiked lower, to see under the boom. The black and white boat was descending on them from the headland.

"It's the *Covenant*!" Blake said.

"Crap! How could he get the drop on us in *that* tub?"

"He came down in our blind spot! He's reloading! Jibe the chute!"

Griffy swung in and dove for the spinnaker pole as Blake ducked the boom in its sweep across the boat. Double reports cracked like howitzers. Another pair of firework shells screeched fore and aft, trailing spiral curtains of sparks. They detonated in blinding flashes that spewed shimmering white fire-fish which wriggled and twirled through the atmosphere.

As fast as *Seven Thunders* was, with the wind now at her back it felt as though they were crawling.

"Mother Carey's chickens! That was close!" cried Blake.

"He'll get us next time!"

"Drop the chute!" Blake ordered, looking over his shoulder. They had clear view of the *Covenant* now. She sported a cardboard mortar tube mounted horizontally in each oar-lock.

"No, You're nuts!"

"He's almost loaded! Get the chute!" Blake popped the halyard out of its cleat with a thump. Griffy gave a shout of disgust, reached out and snatched billows of feather light sail into a duffel-bag.

"Trim up hard and get on the wire!" Blake put *Seven Thunders* back on the wind and pointed her bow straight at the *Covenant*. Griffy turned white.

Kalijah did too, when he looked up from loading and saw his opponent swiftly bearing down on him like a hawk on a rabbit. He hastily ignited the fuse on each cannon. "Fire in the hole!"

"Fire in hole!" Griffy repeated.

Blake hiked and bit his lip. "Get ready!"

"Blake…Blake?

"Ready…"

"Blaaake!"

"Hard to lee!" Blake shoved the tiller over. The makeshift cannons banged. *Seven Thunders* sliced through the tack so fast and effortlessly, that it felt like she would slip from beneath their feet and leave them standing on thin air. Twin trails of spiraling smoke whooshed well astern and slashed the sky with crackling scimitars of golden fire.

"Hard a'lee!" Blake shouted.

"We're almost to the lake! We can make it!" Griffy objected, as the boat swooped through another tack.

"This ends now! Trim for a reach!"

Kalijah was struggling to reload when he heard *Seven Thunders'* sails rattle and snap taught. Again the hawk was swooping down on its prey, eating up the yards between them with each passing second.

Blake looked up at the fluttering pennant on his side stay and let out a confident battle cry. Kalijah fell against his tiller and hauled in on his mainsheet. The *Covenant* made a graceful arc, heeled, and began to trot away on a beam reach. Kalijah cast worried glances over his pointed stern and struggled to open something with his free hand. "I warn you, Master Urquart! I have not yet begun to fight!" he bawled.

Griffy's heart leapt in hopeful elation. "He's running! You won, lets go!"

It was no race. *Seven Thunders* caught up to the fleeing craft in less than a minute. Blake cut close behind *Covenant's* stern and slid along her lee side.

"What are you doing?" cried Griffy.

"No quarter given, Master Urquart! I warn you!" bellowed the pirate. Blake could hear the fear in his voice.

"Get ready to take the tiller," said Blake.

"Say what?"

Blake slammed *Seven Thunders* hard against the *Covenant*, the hulls colliding with a deep thud. He kept the tiller hard over and drove both boats straight into the wind. The sails rattled themselves empty and fluttered violently in the breeze.

"Keep us in irons!" Blake commanded. He grabbed the short, wooden paddle and leapt into the enemy vessel, with a hearty yell. Kalijah was standing at the helm, frantically attempting to light an eighteen inch

Roman candle. Blake lunged and swung his paddle-axe. Kalijah deflected the blow and seized the boarder. The firework plunked into the lake, his lighter clattered into the bottom of the boat.

The shabby pirate struggled to keep his balance in the narrow quarters of the stern, while Blake did his best to push him overboard. "I knew you'd come back, boy! Hand over the boat and the booty and I'll let you swim home!" he snarled, finally finding his anger.

"Stoof it in yer pookits!" Blake barked in his face. A well placed head-butt sent Blake crashing backward over the middle bench. Kalijah grabbed another Roman candle and scrabbled madly in the bilge for his lighter.

"Blake! Get up! Get him!" Griffy cheered.

"A little help would be nice," Blake snarled, as he pulled himself, belly up, onto the bench.

Griffy lifted the starboard mortar gun out of its mount and chucked it in the lake. "How's that?"

Kalijah's fingers closed around the little plastic cylinder. He grinned and sprang to his feet. Blake braced himself on the bench and delivered a sturdy kick to the knees. Kalijah toppled back howling and landed on his side, across the stern. Blake leapt up and began to batter him pitilessly with the flat of the paddle.

"Mercy! Oh mercy of God!" Kalijah wailed pathetically. "Daddy Don't! Don't hit me, Daddy! Please! Oh please!"

Blake relented in mid-swing, confused by unexpected pangs of guilt and compassion.

Then he heard the unmistakable *skritch!* of a cigarette lighter.

"Ohhhh, Master Urquart," Kalijah smirked with mocking satisfaction. He pointed a smoking, sparking tube at him, "you fell for it!"

Blake dodged, but landed a glancing blow to the tube just as it made a sharp 'pop!' A brilliant, red fireball zinged past Griffy's face.

The pirate kicked him backwards, sat up, and took aim again. Blake grabbed the boom as he fell. It swung inboard under his weight and cracked Kalijah in the side of the head. The tube popped again. A blue fireball scorched a black streak across the *Covenant's* canvas sail. Griffy took note and began to work *Seven Thunders* forward. He grabbed *Covenant's* bowline and let her trail aft. Kalijah was still seeing double when Blake landed on him, but managed to hold on to the candle with an iron grip. Sparks spurted, stung, and singed as Blake wrestled to turn the maniac's aim. Pop! A green ball bounced off *Seven Thunders'* after-deck and plunked into the lake. Pop! Griffy watched another red flaming star skitter up the *Covenant's* canvas and slide back down into a crease in its foot.

"Blake! Blake!"

"I'm kind…of busy…right…now!" he groaned, trying to force the tube away from his own sails. His traction gave way and—bam! He was across the middle bench, once again—facedown over a bucket full of firework shells.

Kalijah pulled himself up, but not before another jet of sparks belched two meteors up his sail and back down into the crease. Blake rolled over and kicked. The tube flew out of the pirate's hand and splashed into the water. It was then that he saw a smoldering, brown blotch spreading along the foot of the sail above him.

"A most scurvy Monster," cried Kalijah. He snatched the paddle, "I could find in my heart to beat him!"

The pirate wheezed and raised the paddle-axe over his head. Blake hollered "Fire!" just as the foot of the sail burst into flames.

"Blake! Get out of there! Blake, you're burning!" Griffy shouted. "Blake jump! I'm coming around!"

Kalijah plunged to the rail with a panicked yelp and started to sling lake-water at the flaming canvas. Blake, directly under the blaze, curled over the bench and dove into the stern. His right hand slid beneath the aft bench and happened over a cool metal handle.

The sail roared into an inferno, the heat instantly intolerable. Kalijah gave a cry and flung himself over the side. Blake lifted the handle and gave it a solid yank. He sprang up and bounded off the little wedge of after-deck, just as Griffy cut *Seven Thunders* across the *Covenant's* stern.

He landed in the cockpit, flat on his rump.

The bucket of explosive shells went supernova. A white-hot pillar of shooting stars jetted skyward. The fury of relentless detonations deafened like the hoof-beats of the four horsemen on Judgment Day. Flaming paisleys screamed out in all directions. Cascades of gold and silver sparks crackled down in an avalanche of heavy smoke that stung the eyes and smacked of rotten eggs.

"Man! That was just like the movies!" Griffy beamed.

Blake came to his senses and searched the waves intently. "Where's Kalijah?"

"He was on the starboard side!"

"There!" Blake pointed. The pirate bobbed, barely visible in the pall of smoke, a dozen yards from his boat. He watched as the last shreds of canvas burned and smoldering rigging fell.

"What took you so long, anyway?" Griffy inquired, with a smile.

"Souvenir hunting!" Blake held up a drain plug with a long chrome-handle.

"Ha-haaa!" Griffy looked back and indeed, the *Covenant's* stern was riding much lower in the water than before. "We need some theme music. Somebody play the Star Spangled Banner!"

"I don't think he has any flotation aboard," said Blake. "We'd better leave him a life jacket."

"Is that a suggestion?"

"Ready aboot, Mister Williams, hard a'lee!"

***

The clock on the mantel chimed four as Blake and Griffy topped the stairs. Gunn sat in his recliner, behind a curtain of newspaper.

"Where have yeh been, Caduggin?" he said in a tone of grave displeasure.

Blake swallowed hard. "Down lake, sir."

"He means Mangrave, Tripp."

Blake gave Griffy a dirty look.

"Griffin Williams, what an unexpected pleasure, seeing as how you're no even supposed to be thinking aboot sailing 'til you're thirty."

"He talked my mom into it. Just about got me killed, as usual! I'm gonna need *therapy*."

"I've given yeh a pretty long leash, Mister Barber. Would yeh mind explaining your disobedience?"

"Disobedience…sir?"

"I told *you* to stay out the Mangrave Branch."

"Technically speaking, you just *suggested* that I not go there," he said, meekly.

Griffy was amazed. Once again he had underestimated the church boy.

"Don't play sea-lawyer with me, lad!" roared Gunn, dropping the paper flat. "All this blessed whining aboot trouble always finding *you*. Now, why would yeh go runnin' after it?"

"Because it had my stuff," Blake said, holding out the red duffel with one hand. Gunn stared. Blake approached the recliner and set the bag down so that it clanked. Griffy tossed him the hiking stick. Blake planted it on the floor with a thump.

Gunn was taken aback. "Declan's stick?"

Blake reached into the bag and produced one article after another.

"His clan dirk!"

"That's what was missing from the bookcase," said Blake.

"The folks and the kids, and the *trophy*! And…"

Blake revealed the large, framed document.

"The *benediction*!" he whispered, in awe.

The phone rang. Gunn dug a cordless handset from a pouch on the side of his chair.

"Gunn. Buck Mueller? Imagine you calling, just now! Aye, they're here. Hurt? Are yeh lads hurt? No, they say they're fine. Boot? Boot okay, lad? Aye, fine. Fire? Really, yeh don' say." He eyed Blake, noting the little holes burned all over his shirt and hat. "Gladly! Ninety minutes, tops. Tell 'im Woodhead's in custody? Ah-right."

"Tell him we found Lucky," Blake interrupted. "Oh, and we left Voodoo Jack tied up, back there. He probably needs medical attention."

"Yeh get that, Buck? Aye, he said medical attention!" Gunn was now completely bewildered.

"I've got pictures!" Blake waved the camera before the old man.

"Aye, he'll bring 'em. Goodbye." He switched the phone off.

"Officer Mueller says he does'na know whether to give yeh a medal, ground yeh for life, *or both*. I tend to agree with the latter."

"Oh, one more thing!" Blake pressed his advantage. "I brought you something." He produced the *Covenant's* drain plug and handed it to Gunn. "Souvenir!"

"I got one thing to say to yeh, lad." Blake held his breath. "Put another tank of gas in the *Terrapin* and fetch the grapple hooks. Griffy, you'll help me launch the work barge. We've got salvage."

***

Evening fell lazily over Gunn's Harbor. The *Terrapin*, the work barge and the scorched hulk of the *Covenant* were all rafted together by the dock.

Gunn plunked a brown bottle of root beer in front of Blake and took his seat on the other side of the dining-room table.

"I suppose I bear part of the blame," Gunn sighed. "Filling your head with Treasure Island, and Cap'n Jack Aubrey. Horatio Hornblower." He twisted the cap of his own bottle. "Good thing I did'na show yeh Tintin!"

"I wanted to see that!"

"What am I to do with yeh, lad? Do yeh know some fisherman video'd the whole thing on his cell phone—it'll be all over Facetube or what ever yeh call it, by morning! What will I tell yer grandmother? She's bound to see it!"

Blake shrugged and stared sheepishly at the label on his bottle.

"Oh, yer insufferably pleased with yourself; don' bother hiding it! No doubt yer granddad would be *fiendishly* proud of yeh, as well. Yeh done that auld school, I'll give yeh that."

"I guess you should punish me," Blake murmured.

"Aye, I should! But how could I, lad? We demand yeh kids grow up, but how we scold when yeh do something manly! The bottom line is this: yeh misrepresented yourself to Judy Williams and put your friend and yourself in mortal danger."

"I apologized to Griffy."

"And yeh'll apologize to Mrs. Williams."

"Yes, sir."

"Yeh vanquished your enemies,"

"Voodoo Jack got away. I still haven't figured that one out."

"Yeh vanquished your enemies, yeh rescued your family treasures. Do yeh *think* you could stay out of trouble 'til your folks collect yeh?"

"Hunter's due back in town anytime."

Gunn stared in exasperation, then rose and stalked off. "Where *did* I put those Tintin books?"

Part II

Local Hero

Chapter 28

Twenty-one sweating junior sailors fidgeted and shuffled their feet in the roasting sands of Turtle Beach. Griffy swaggered before them on a half grounded dock, delivering his welcome address.

"Okay newbies, listen up! As the repeat offenders will tell you, we have a long-standing tradition here at the yacht club."

The repeat offenders moaned. "Not pirate names, again?" said a chubby boy.

"You guessed it, Pirate names!" Griffy hopped down to the beach and thrust his hand into a paper lunch-bag. "I was up all night combing the nautical dictionary for these little gems, so show a guy some appreciation."

He pulled out a strip of paper, glanced at it and presented it to the first sailor as if it were the Congressional Medal of Honor. "You're Deadhorse!" He continued down the line: "and you're Futtocks; Baggywrinkle; Monkey-Blood; Fantail; Scuttlebutt; Soojee-Moojee; Beakhead; Wait, you're Twins? This calls for the *personal* touch. Scurvy and Rickets!" He moved to a skinny, freckle-faced girl with stringy hair. He glanced at the slip, smiled sheepishly, and showed it to her. She slapped his face.

"It's okay. I probably deserved that."

"Do I get a new name this year?" whined the chubby boy.

"Well *let's* see!" Griffy, grinned fiendishly and plunged his hand into the bag. "Wow! Amazing!"

"Oh no. Please?"

"What a coincidence! For the fourth straight year! You're Poop Deck!"

Griffy handed out the rest of the names and leapt back to the dock.

"I think we should get to give you a name." said Poop Deck.

"Sorry, ordinary seamen don't have a say."

"Unless there's a mutiny." said a boy with a Scots accent. Blake sauntered up behind the group.

Everyone looked. Hushed recognition rippled through the class. "That's the kid who whooped Hunter" said Scurvy.

"And blew up that boat in Mangrave!" said Rickets.

"And drownded in the channel!" said the girl with stringy hair.

"Mutiny? Never happens!" said Griffy. Now, the next order of business,"

Twenty-one expectant faces turned back to Blake. *You're kidding?* he thought. *This is better than the geese!* "Don' look at *me*! Get 'im!"

A frenzied cry broke out and the languid assembly burst into an angry mob. The mutineers thronged onto the dock, swept Griffy up, and carried him like a tidal surge to its end. They pitched him headlong into the drink. He surfaced amid a flurry of paper slips, which fluttered down like cherry blossoms in the spring.

Blake pushed through the cheering rowdies to make sure Griffy was alright. A car door slammed. The mutineers turned as one and stared. An SUV pulled away, leaving a scarecrow of a young man standing at the end of the gangplank. His head seemed too large, jaw too square and jutting; nose too flat and arms too long and gangly. He curled his upper lip and wrung his hands.

"*You're kidding me?* thought Blake.

"A retard?" someone whispered.

"Shouldn't he have a helmet?"

"Grotesque!"

The scarecrow flapped his hands, stamped his feet and bleated excitedly. The mob shuddered as one and drew together. He flapped his hands again and tromped happily onto the gangplank, lolling his head and blathering with his tongue hanging out.

The mob shrieked and compressed itself at the very end of the dock. Griffy grinned and hastily swam backward.

The scarecrow let go with bawling laughter and stormed down the planks flailing his arms like a crazed toddler descending on a cornered puppy. The panicked horde cascaded off the end of the dock in a human waterfall. He strutted to the end and surveyed his handiwork. The scarecrow smiled wryly, cleared his throat, and struck a theatrical pose. "To be, or not to be: that is the question! Whether it is nobler in the mind to suffer the slings and arrows of outrageous fortune, or flap my hands at a bunch of ignorant morons and chase them off a cliff like the stupid cluster-brained lemmings that they are!"

I hope he'll accept my apology, thought Blake.

"But seriously folks, I'm not retarded but I do have genetic issues. Yeah, both my parents are extremely ugly! When I was little, they tied a pork chop around my neck so the dog would play with me. He went kosher on the spot!"

Blake looked to Griffy, as if seeking permission to laugh.

"Tell 'em about the tree, Kaz!" said Griffy.

"Hey Griffy! I couldn't tell if that was you, or somebody forgot to flush! When I was little, I fell out of the top of the ugly tree and hit every branch on the way down!"

"Kyle Kazdorf, ladies and gentleman!" said Griffy. "He'll be here 'til Friday. Be sure to tip your waitress!"

Blake swam to the ladder on the end of the dock and hoisted himself out. Kaz lent him a hand. The class chose to wade ashore.

"Blake Barber," he said, "but everyone calls me Tux. I'm sorry about all that."

"I'm used to it. Griffy told me all about you. I saw your video. You're gonzo crazy."

Poop Deck slogged down the dock. "Do I *have* to sail this year? Hunter always let me stay in the clubhouse."

"Hunter's not here. Everybody sails." said Blake.

"But I'm too big! I can't balance the boat. Besides I'm sensitive to the sun and I can't…"

"You're sailing."

"What if I capsize and the boat turtles and my foot gets caught in the hiking strap? I'm afraid of storms—what if there was a tornado,"

Oh, tell me I wasn't like this! Blake thought.

"I have irritable bowels, what if,"

"What if my head explodes and your ass catches fire?" Blake said. "What if? See that kid there? He's only eight. He's going to sail. He's not crying about it, is he?"

"He's little! I'm too fat for the Prams."

"We're gonna need a bigger boat!" said Kaz.

"Very funny," said Poop Deck.

"You want to be called Poop Deck all your life?" said Blake.

"Heck no!"

"You want to lose the name by the end of the week?"

"How?"

"Earn it. You learn to sail, tie all the basic knots. You sail to Trespass Island and back and I'll make sure nobody calls you Poop Deck again."

"But…"

"In fact," Blake continued loudly, "Anybody who sails to the shallow water mark at the island and back to the harbor gets to ditch their pirate name immediately! Now, who's ready to learn to sail?"

A cheer went up from the soggy mutineers.

"Alright you guys," said Griffy, striding out of the water and onto the beach, "over by the swings. We're going to learn how to rig things up. Tux'll teach you the 'circle of sail' during lunch, then we hit the water this afternoon."

The class gathered around a Flying Junior while Griffy delivered his demonstration. The air was humid and sweet with an intoxicating blend of shampoo, sunscreen, body lotion, and deodorant. It smelled like bath-time. Blake was floating in the memory of his cozy, terry-cloth robe when something—light as a feather—traced a ticklish line up the small of his back. He twitched and glanced around. A round-faced girl with a luxuriantly braided pony-tail cracked her gum and winked at him. Another, with electric-blue bangs peeked slyly around her. The girl with stringy hair inched closer and leaned against him, casually. He was surrounded by girls. He noticed for the first time how nicely wet, clingy clothing emphasized the curvy differences between the sexes.

"Wow, its hot!" he said, pressing the back of his hand to his forehead. It felt like the morning's heat was now radiating from his face. "Pardon me," he said. "I better go check on the safety boat situation." Blake backed out of the crowd, stiffly. He disappeared between two racks of windsurfers and awkwardly adjusted his shorts.

Mia had just docked *Safety Patrol 3* when Blake walked up. Gunn sat in *Safety Patrol 1*, in the shade of the shed—which was really just an open-sided lean-to, sheltering the safety-boat dollies. He tampered with the radio.

Mia pulled the keys out of the ignition. "Hey Tux, who's your shadow?"

Blake stopped. The stringy-haired girl bumped into him. He looked over his shoulder and startled. "Do you *need* something?"

"Nope." she said. "What's that?"

"A patch to keep my stitches dry."

"Bet it leaves a scar. My cat has a scar where they took out her plumbing."

"Caduggin! Come over here and put me in the water!"

"You better get back to class." Blake gladly escaped to the shed and manned the winch controller. The winch screeched and the Boston Whaler jostled its way down the ramp. The motor chugged to life with a cough of blue exhaust. Blake turned and ran straight into his shadow.

"Could you *not* do that?"

"I'm Natalie."

"Hi, Natalie. Go back to class. Shoo!"

Blake side-stepped her and marched to the dock.

"Are you going to the Fourth of July in Freeman?"

"He's got a date!" said Mia, as she slid a large cooler into the bow of her Whaler.

Gunn chugged up to the dock. "Who's yer assistant?"

Blake grabbed the handrail and guided the bow to the nearest cleat. "Natalie." he replied, with irritation. He tied the bowline off, stood up, and backed straight into her. Blake spun around, ready to tell her off, but tripped on the cleat. He plunged backward into the lake. Natalie silently exited stage left.

Blake had squished halfway across the boatyard when he was met by the winking gum-cracker. "Oh, there you are! The other kid said to tell you he was done. My name's Gretchen."

"He's got a date!" said Natalie, appearing from behind.

"Will you *stop* that?"

"Oh with *you*, I suppose?" said Gretchen, with a withering scowl.

"With me!" said Mia, as she strode past. "C'mon Romeo, you can flirt with the chicks later."

"*You*," he said to Natalie, "stay six feet away from me at all times. Gretchen? Is that your pirate name?" said Blake, departing. Gretchen cracked her gum with a half snarl.

Blake reached the top of the hill when he was met by Blue-Bangs. "Hi,"

"He's got a date." said Gretchen and Natalie, bringing up the rear.

***

At last, crew assignments were handed out and boats launched. Everyone seemed to be relieved to finally be doing something that didn't seem like school. All except Poop Deck. He stormed down the dock, whipped his life jacket down on the planks and screwed up his face. The class watched in embarrassed silence as he stamped his feet and bawled like an enraged toddler. Everyone held their breath as the old Scot loomed up behind him. He seized Poop Deck by the upper arm and turned him with a vicious jerk.

"Straighten up! Stop embarrassing yer mates! Yer a shame to yer parents! Now get yer blubber in that boot before I take a strop to yer arse! Do I make myself clear?"

Poop Deck nodded faintly.

"Then hurry up!"

The boy oozed out of Gunn's grip and slunk away to his boat on all fours.

"Dang, can he do that?" said Deadhorse, sinking low in his cockpit.

"Just did." said Natalie.

"What was *that*?" said Soojee Moojee, brushing her blue bangs aside.

"That," said Kaz, "was old school."

Chapter 29

The clock on Gunn's mantel chimed four. The old man snored in his recliner. Blake stood and stared at the young man in the mirror. Wavy auburn hair, long enough to give his father apoplexy, hung in one eye. It stuck to the skin where the Tegaderm had been. The scar still bristled with stitch-ends, like a pink caterpillar crawling across his tanned forehead.

He reflected on the aggravations of the last couple of days: of how, on Tuesday, another dozen sailors enrolled. How the girls continued to flirt and hit on him—and how it was beginning to feel a little exciting. On Wednesday Mia helped three crews of his nubile admirers trundle their boats to the launch-ramp and waved as they sailed away. He found out later that her back pocket was full of drain plugs.

He brooded on how the tiny training staff was totally undermanned and overwhelmed. Gunn was clearly not taking sweltering heat well and did little but drive the Boston Whaler from one sinking boat full of girls to the next, while Griffy did the real rescue work. Gunn brought the *Darby McGraw* over, which put six sailors in one boat; but still it was not enough. Blake's resentment toward his uncle smoldered.

One of the new kids had a driver's license. Despite his inexperience with motorboats, Gunn assigned him to the small pontoon and put Blake in charge. Poop Deck, defying instructions as usual, had managed to take to the water in the club's one remaining old-style pram—the one without any flotation. He sailed just beyond the point and capsized it in the light breeze.

He also managed to loop the main sheet around his neck, twice. Blake's rookie helmsman came up too fast and reversed the throttle too late. He parked the pontoon boat directly over the shrieking boy just as his pram went under and the noose began to tighten. Blake grimaced at the fingernail he'd bent back, trying to open his knife before he shed his life jacket and leapt over the side. He remembered praying that Poop Deck wouldn't drag them both to Davy Jones.

He felt bad for the helmsman. The young man was still shaking uncontrollably and screaming "Oh my god! Oh my god! Oh my god!" as Blake boosted the erstwhile drowning victim onto the aluminum deck, like a beached manatee. It took ten minutes to get the rookie calmed down and the threat of violence to get Poop Deck to shut up. With the Pagán's cabinet building operation in full swing down in the workshop, Sylvana was always around. He felt like a prisoner in his own home. *None of it would have happened if Uncle Carson had been there,* he thought. His eyes landed on the letter behind the clock.

Someone rapped on the front door. He grumbled as he slogged down. He peered through the peephole. It was Slyvana.

"What do *you* want, chica?"

"You got the mail!" she said, holding up a sheaf of envelopes. "Big card. Looks like it's from Francé."

The front door flew open and Blake burst out with such force that Sylvana jumped back.

"Give it to me!"

"What, you no say 'por favor' in America?"

"I say stay out of Mr. Gunn's mailbox." He lunged and snatched the mail out of her hand.

He went back inside filing through the envelopes and shoved the door closed with his behind. Indeed, there was an oversized postcard, bearing a portrait of Napoleon Bonaparte on a rampant, white stallion. Blake seated himself halfway up the stairs and consumed his mother's tiny printing.

My Dearest Blake,

Sorry I keep missing you. I've only been able to call a few times. You and Nanna are always out! I bet you've been to the zoo and all the museums in Indy. You're probably in Chicago by now! I just realized I never gave you my return address! No wonder you haven't written me!

Blake, it is so hard to be away from you. Daddy just found out his project has been extended until late September. Agatha is terribly homesick. Daddy hates the French, the food, everything. It is all so very hard. But plans change and I guess you just have to roll with the punches, and go on as best you can. Say a prayer for us! Give Nanna and Uncle Carson my love!

I love you, my brave heart!
68 Rue Haricourt
Paris, France
Mom
P.S. Sometimes Carson needs a little cheering up!

Dear Mom, Blake thought. *Zoo? Museums? Chicago? No, Mom. I've been fighting pirates, werewolves, and psychopaths. I've done fifteen-thousand dollars in damage and got seven stitches to prove it. I've got a job. I've got pretty girls who keep grabbing my behind and one who says she's not my girlfriend but is still crazy jealous of all the others. Uncle Carson walked out on me like the rest of my family, but I've been adopted by an ancient Highlander who let's me do just about whatever I want—as long as I speak respectfully, stay out of the Mangrave Branch, and come home by 11:00. None of which I have managed to do. And if Carson need's some cheering up?* "I'll give him some cheering up," he said, and ascended the stairs.

***

A small fire burned in a stone ring, littered with beer cans. The screen windows of the dome tent were open and the door-flap was unzipped, but there didn't seem to be anyone vertical inside.

"Uncle Carson?" Blake said. "Uncle Carson?"

He rubbed stinging salt-sweat from his eyes. "I need to talk to you."

There was a long silence.

"Well, if yer gonna talk, yer gonna talk," Carson said, without sitting up.

"We've got thiry-two kids in Junior Training. We can't cover it with just two safety-boats."

"Sounds like a problem for the J.T. Committee."

Blake clenched his fists. "We can't find anybody to help. We really need *you*."

"I've got a fear of commitment. What can I say."

"You were supposed to be the main instructor, remember? That was the plan."

"Like I say, sometimes life takes a big dump on ya and ya gotta change your plans."

"Yeah, but you just stopped *making* plans!"

"You better quit while you're ahead, buddy!"

"You had an accident. You just quit."

"I'm warning you kid."

"Then your dad died and you just stopped making plans."

"Yer a snot-nosed brat and I don't have to take that crap off you!"

"After Hunter, Kalijah, and Voodoo Jack, you think I'm afraid of a drunken uncle who won't even sit up and talk to me?"

"You never knew your granddad, so you can shut your mouth about that matter."

"I've got a letter from him right here."

There was a malevolent quiet.

"You better not have opened that."

"It wasn't sealed."

"If you read one-single word…"

"I don't know how long I can hold this without dropping it," Blake said through clenched teeth.

Carson sat straight up in front of the flap. Blake strained to hold the envelope above the flames as high as he could, but the heat stabbed his hand like red hot daggers.

"You take that back and put it where you got it!"

"Take it back yourself. It's time you read it!" His hand wavered violently. He cried out in agony.

Carson flew out the tent and slammed into his nephew. Blake hit the hard dirt six feet away and skidded four more. Carson missed the grab and the envelope landed on the coals. He snatched it out with a growl and a four-letter word. The stench of burnt hair filled the air. Carson returned to his lair and collapsed on his cot.

Blake crawled to a utility post and hoisted himself to his feet, then stalked down to the beach and found his Uncle's red canoe. He flung its paddle, cushion and life jacket as far into the lake as he could, then he set the craft adrift with the best shove he could muster with one good hand.

***

Seven Thunders was halfway down the channel when the wind quit. Blake straddled the bow, gripping the paddle with his burning, lobster-red hand; each agonizing stroke powered by his road-rashed arm and aching shoulder. The wakes of passing boats came in long, low swells, one after the other. The bow bobbed over their blue crests and rolled into their troughs in an endless cycle; bathing Blake in bath-warm water, challenging his balance every second. Headway was out of the question. The battle was just to keep from being swept into the shoals. The boom and main slammed back and forth with a maddening clatter. His brain throbbed in the merciless heat. It sloshed. It stung. It felt like a nauseous puffer in a fishbowl two sizes too small.

The last of the waves passed under him and *Seven Thunders* settled. Blake lay back on the deck, covered his face with the blade of the paddle and just breathed for a couple of minutes. The sound of thrashing rock music and the moan of another boat drifted up the channel. He sat up and squinted. It was *Lemon Drop*, poking along with a wake-boarder in tow.

"So, this is how I die," he said. He realized that he didn't even care.

Lemon Drop passed a hundred feet away, headed for the upper lake. Blood and adrenalin rushed back into Blake's head as he recognized the man in tow. Hunter stood so deep in the wake and displayed such a casual air that had he worn a laurel and carried a trident he could have passed for the son of a sea god, surveying his kingdom from behind his heliotrope steed. No one took notice of Blake; not Rexroat, not Hunter, nor the Hellcats—whose adoring gaze never strayed from their bronze deity. Blake whispered a quiet word of gratitude and paddled for home.

Chapter 30

That familiar patch of sunlight crept over the window frame and onto the bedroom wall. It was finally Friday, July first. Blake was thirteen years old. He looked his hand over front and back. It still stung like crazy but, thankfully, it hadn't blistered. He'd been able to conceal it from Tripper Gunn and that guilted him. But not like taking the letter. That burned in his conscience with a searing agony all of its own.

Blake ran a finger lightly over his scar. The Vice Commodore, Dr. Trudeau, had dropped by the club yesterday and declared that the sutures could come out. He supervised contentedly while Mia, to everyone's horror, snipped and pulled the stitches with implements from her multi-tool.

The day had gone pretty well. The Juniors were reasonably proficient at boat-handling. Mia had consolidated the crews so that there were now only a dozen boats on the water—which was still barely manageable with two safety-boats. But it couldn't keep Blake's mind from grinding over Gunn's inevitable discovery of his breech of trust. Mia listened sympathetically between assistance runs and yelling at Poop Deck. Her advice was all over the map. Call the cops on Carson for child abuse; confess to Gunn outright; or just keep a low profile and hope he wouldn't find out until Blake was safely back in Fort Wayne.

"I could never do that. You don't understand," he'd told her. "It's killing me! "He trusts me and I broke that trust. And that would kill *him*."

"Trust doesn't mean much in my family," she'd said. "So it's a little hard for me to relate. We just pretend what we did was everyone else's fault, slam doors, and forget about it."

He lay there and thought about what she had said. *If Carson had kept his commitment, this wouldn't have... No. If I hadn't gotten angry this wouldn't have happened. No one to blame but myself. I've ruined my own thirteenth birthday. Idiot.* He dug his nails into the palm of his tender hand until the pain flushed all thought from his head.

***

"Cheer up will ya?" Mia sat perched on the back of the driver's bench and scanned the fleet for signs of trouble. She swigged from her bottle. "You're the guest of honor tonight."

Blake moped on the bench in front of the driver's pulpit. "I feel like such a hypocrite."

"You learn to live with it."

"I've got to tell him."

"A fellah's got to do what a fellah's got to do." She seemed a little too blithe for his temperament. He waited until she took another long swig.

"I forgot to tell you I saw Hunter yesterday."

Mia spewed water into the air. "*What* did you say?"

"Wake boarding up the channel."

"That's important! How could you just forget to tell me?"

"I guess I just had other things on my mind." He allowed himself a snarky smile. "I was barely a hundred feet away. He didn't see me."

"Crap! Well, we knew it was coming. I wish you had told me. I've got to warn Treva."

The radio crackled to life. "Alright yeh two, the last buoy's set. Let's get these kids racing!"

The ignition whistled as Mia started the motor. Blake stood up and looked at her through the windshield. "Mia, what are we going to do?"

"Finish this job then throw one heck of a party, tonight. We'll worry about the complications tomorrow."

***

The last of the sails were rolled and hulls rinsed. Boats were dollied back and parked. The last covers were zipped up and tied down The class assembled in the shade of the big oak at the bottom of the hill. Tripper Gunn handed out hearty congratulations while Blake, Mia and Griffy distributed tee shirts. Blake took a moment to examine one. It was emblazoned with the club logo on the front. On the back, a boat flying a plaid spinnaker and a crew of two playing the bagpipes. The caption read "I Survived HCSC Sailing Camp!" The first session of Junior Training was done.

"One more thing," Gunn said, as the sailors milled off toward the line of cars that waited at the edge of the parking lot. "There'll be a party here tonight to celebrate Master Urquart's thirteenth birthday. You're all invited!" Gunn said merrily, as he headed for the dock.

A cheer went up and at least three replied "Thanks, we know!" Mia and Blake exchanged puzzled, if not suspicious glances. Griffy vanished.

"That was random!" said Mia.

"I can't go to the party feeling like this."

"Then you'd better catch him!"

Gunn was halfway to the hoists. Blake stood, stuck in a quagmire of fear and indecision.

"Tux, he's getting away! That old guy can really move when he wants to."

"Oh, dirt!" he huffed, then jogged away.

"Mr. Gunn," he said, catching up.

"They did alright didn't they?"

"But wait,"

"Don't worry, lad. There'll be plenty of food. They all signed up for second session, yeh know? And I dunno how we're gonna handle *that.*"

"Mr. Gunn, I need to talk to you."

"Have to wait, Caduggin." Gunn lumbered down the dock to the *Terrapin.* I have a couple of errands to run before tonight. You two help Ray and Elsie get the place ready. Band'll be here aboot six. Tyner delivers aboot seven."

"Band?"

Gunn boarded and started the motor with the customary, punishing yank. "Clear my moorings!"

Blake got the message. For whatever reason, Gunn was cheerfully stonewalling. He loosed the spring-lines and tossed them aboard with an air of resignation. "Well, you can't say I didn't try."

***

Blake held the door for yet another carload of teens bearing pizzas, cake, and two-liter bottles. Already there were several rows of cars in the lot and the patio and great room were bustling with people that Blake had never seen before.

He found Mia helping the band set up in the Gazebo at the far end of the patio.

"Is Mr. Gunn back, yet?"

"Haven't seen him. Did he invite the whole freakin' world, or what?"

"I don't get it. The last group came from Cincinnati. I saw a car with Michigan plates in the parking lot."

"Hey you?" Mia said to a bystander. "'Scuse me. How did you hear about the party?"

"Facebook. But I'm cool, I RSVP'd! Happy birthday, man!"

"Translate, please?" Blake said.

Mia's eyes narrowed to slits. She made her way through the crowd, searching for certain faces. She spotted Soojee in the far corner, sketching on a notepad. "Hey, Blue Bangs! You got your tablet?"

She pulled her iPad out of her shoulder bag and brought it. Mia's fingers pecked and swiped over its screen. "Son of a gun, you do have a fan-page!"

"What the! Who…why…how is this possible!" said Blake. "Where did they get my picture?"

"There's the announcement," Soojee said.

Mia scrolled down the screen. "Tux Urquart's 13th Birthday Bash!

Come one, come all! Admission: 1 pizza, 1 cake and 1 case of soda per carload. Party starts at 7! Highland Creek Sailing Club, Highland Creek Reservoir, Indiana. Click here for map and directions."

"Check the RSVP page," said Soojee.

Mia's eyes bulged. "O.M.G!"

"What? What is it?" said Blake.

"O.M.G! Four hundred seventy five!"

Blake had never seen Mia so close to panic. "Four hundred seventy five what?"

"People, Blake! Coming! Here! Right! Now!"

"Who did this, how did they get my picture?"

"Who cares? This is a total flippin' disaster, don't you understand that?"

The crowd parted for a moment and Mia's eyes landed on someone like an osprey on a carp. "You! Kazdorf!" she barked.

Kaz startled as he came out the back door. "Oh hey! Y-y-you guys better quit playing Angry Birds and get back to work!"

Mia flipped the tablet over so he could see it. He froze. She cocked an eyebrow.

"I didn't have anything to do with that!"

"Bullroar!" said Mia, advancing like a panther. "But you know who did, *don't* you."

"I'm invoking my fifth-amendment constitutional rights."

She backed him right up to a picnic table. He plunked down hard on the bench.

"Who did it? Who took this picture?" said Blake.

"I think you can guess! He used my computer. I told him it wasn't a good idea. Give me some credit, I made him put in the part about the pizza and cake!"

"For that, I'll let you live," Mia said. "You understand this *is* Armageddon, right? You have to have special permission from the Board to have more than seventy-five guests for a private event. They have to *vote* on it. And they *never* allow events on a Friday before a club regatta. Mr. Gunn conveniently ignored that rule. And what's tomorrow, moron? Oh yeah!

The Independence Day Regatta! This entire place has got to be spotless before nine A.M. You know what it's gonna look like after five hundred party animals are done with it? You understand that we'll probably all be kicked out for this, right, Kaz? Me, Tux, and Gunn, and Griffy, and his mom? There'll be a meeting Tuesday and don't think my dear old Dad won't get right on it."

Blake's heart began to sink with comprehension, but was buoyed up by a rising current of anger. He took a deep breath and straightened up.

"What are we going to do about it," he said, trying to keep his voice from cracking.

"I dunno. What do *you* think we should do, Tux?"

He ignored her surly retort. "Vikings or victims. What do you want to be?"

"I vote Viking!" said Soojee.

Mia glared at them. Blake raised his hand. "Viking."

Mia turned back to Kaz. "You keep an eye out for Griffy. As soon as you see his mom, you tell her Tripper Gunn wants to see her ASAP. If you don't, I will gouge out your eyes with stale pizza crusts and pack the sockets with habanera flakes. Do you understand me?"

Kaz wilted. "Yes ma'am."

"You may go!"

Kaz slithered away.

"Where is Gunn?" Mia hopped up on the picnic table and scanned the crowd. Ray spotted her and lumbered over to the table.

"Uh, we can't do this! There's a regatta tomorrow!"

"We know, Griz," Mia hopped down. "Give us something we can use!"

"I hate it when you call me that. Just cuz I work here doesn't mean you can treat me like a darn peasant, you know."

"Griffy flash-mobbed us," said Soojee. "Posted the party on the net."

"I'll lose my butt over this! I'm gonna kill that kid!"

"Get in line," said Blake. "Got any suggestions?"

"First thing is how you're gonna control this crowd. This sorta thing can get outta hand real quick."

Mia scratched her head and thought. "I'll call the Freeman PD. See if they have any off-duty cops willing to do security for us."

"Who's payin' for that?" said Ray.

"Griffy's mom."

"What if we gave everybody a club brochure and membership form?" said Soojee. "Turn it into a publicity event for your club?"

"I think I might like you," said Mia. "You know how to run a photocopier?"

"Who doesn't?"

"Tux, get a membership app, take Soojee up to the office and run off five hundred copies. There are boxes of brochures in one of the cabinets."

Ray pulled on his long, graying beard. "Your band'll be your best bet for keeping everybody focused. It's a Cajun band, have'm teach everybody to two-step and waltz. Keep 'em dancing."

"Brilliant!" Mia purred. Blake thought she looked a little hopeful. "If we're going down, at least it won't be in flames. Battle stations everybody!"

***

"All hands and the cook! What is this?" said Gunn, as he escorted Beverly through the packed clubhouse to the patio. A wall of Cajun sound swept countless couples along, swaying and dipping with its chatty accordion cadence. The man playing it sang:

"Poor me! Pour mi! What's a fellah to do?

Quelle Damage, c'est un Grande ménage!

My baby won't be true!"

"C'est les fin des haricourts! That's what I say to you!

Poor vous, pour you— Now, whatcha gonna do!"

Blake and Mia came twirling by. "Oh hey, Mr. Gunn! Don't worry, we've got it under control!" Mia said.

"Almost!" added Blake, as he spun in and out of view. They vanished into the river of dance.

The number finished to laughter and applause. "Thank you! I am Jean Paul and we are Poor Vous!" said the man with the little red accordion.

"Okay we gotta another snappy number featuring the fiddle, here! How's everyone down by the water? Nobody fall in I hope, eh?"

Blake and Mia made their way back to Gunn. "So, you've probably already guessed…" said Mia.

"Do I even want to know?" he replied.

"Griffy flash-mobbed us on Facebook," said Blake. "That's why everybody's been signing up for Junior Training. He put that video of me sinking the *Covenant* on the internet and posted that I was looking for a girlfriend."

Gunn crossed the dance floor and gazed out over the grounds. Picnic blankets were spread everywhere. People covered the hill, the ridge, the beach, and the lower lawn. He came back. "We're gonna hang for this, yeh know. Every bloomin' one of us."

"Tripper!" Vice Commodore Trudeau came out the back door. "Um, this is a little more than we agreed on. I hope you appreciate the position this puts me in."

"Aye, Bill, I do. I'll let the kids explain."

"Facebook. Prank. Griffy Williams," said Mia.

"At least we have a scapegoat," said Trudeau. "That leaves us room for damage control."

"We've got two Freeman cops working the crowd," said Blake. "Plus Buck Mueller brought two conservation officers in uniform. We had Jean Paul announce it."

"Soojee and Deadhorse are sticking brochures and membership forms on all the windshields." Mia continued. "Tyner's delivered and they're coming back with more."

"And I've got the Pagáns and half a dozen others committed to cleaning up," concluded Blake.

"You know, sometimes I worry about the future of this club," said Trudeau. "You kids give me confidence. All I think we need now is to give boat rides and we'll be able to bill this as the biggest open house in the history of the Highland Creek Sailing Club. Mia, tell your emcee to announce half hour cruises from the main dock starting in fifteen minutes."

Mia went to speak to Jean Paul.

"*Sophia's* already down there," said Gunn.

"That's two with my *Serengeti*. Mrs. Maitland, would you be willing to bring *Scaramouche* out and make it a fleet?"

"Well, I hadn't planned on it, but anything to save our hides!"

"Mr. Gunn, could I talk to you for a minute?" said Blake.

"You go help Beverly get rigged up. I'm sorry aboot all this. Happy birthday Caduggin!"

***

Judy Williams stood in a daze, Griffy at her side. The entire multitude had just finished singing *Happy Birthday* to Blake. Griffy snickered at his epic mischief.

"You! I oughta break your scrawny neck!" Ray came roaring out of nowhere.

Griffy took one look at his lava-red face and bolted from his mother's side. Without even glancing, she shot forth her hand and snatched him by his golden curls.

Ray grabbed him by the collar and hauled him so close that he could smell his beard. "You're gonna be making one of the two major trips to the vet—I haven't decided which one yet!" He snarled through clenched teeth.

Judy released her grip. "He's all yours Ray. Try not to leave any marks," she said without emotion, and walked away.

"Looks like I got me a new janitor! You know what you're gonna do, punk? You're gonna plunge, clean, and flush every crapper in this place—every time it's used! And so help me, if the thing backs up, it'll be you going in the septic tank with the pipe-snake, not me!" Ray slammed the business end of a wet plunger against Griffy's chest.

Blake thanked his fans graciously and handed the microphone back to Jean Paul. He turned and almost ran into Judy.

"I am so sorry Blake. So sorry."

"We're making the best of it. We'll probably all be kicked out, anyway. But hey, I just had five hundred people sing Happy Birthday to me. Who can say that?"

She gently brushed the hair off his forehead. "You got your stitches out."

"Mia pulled them yesterday."

Judy winced. "Is there anything I can do, Blake?"

"Could you rig up your Catalina and give rides? We're trying to spin this as an accidental public relations campaign of monumental proportions."

"You know what? *You* are my hero, Blake Urquart." She bent over and kissed him on the head. "Happy Birthday, sweetheart. I'll go get my boat."

The band broke for a 'oui oui' break, as they put it. Blake gazed over the crowd on the grounds, on the patio; he smiled. Then he spotted Sylvana prowling through the throng. He hopped over the rail and slipped into the woods. He was pleased to see that the shoreline trail had not yet been discovered by his guests. Blake hurried halfway down the peninsula to the bluff. He sat down on a stump and took in the view. The sun was a red disk hanging flat against lavender haze in the west. The sails of the evening cruisers slipped silently across silver and orange ripples, their red, green, and white running lights gleaming like jewels. Across Thistle Bay, a little flock of coots muttered and tweeped in their sweet, silly way. A joyful contentment settled over him.

"Father in Heaven, thank you for my life. Thank you for this place." He was silent for two full minutes, soaking in the gorgeous solitude. "I am sorry I took the letter from Mr. Gunn's. I keep trying to tell him, but it never works out. It's torturing me. Please help me. Please let him understand."

He looked down for a moment. At his feet lay a foot-long shard of purple fiberglass.

Crunching footfall, as stealthy as a rhinoceros walking on hot coals, interrupted his reverie. "Malditos espinas! Ay! Yow!"

Blake wasted no time scaling the bluff. He emerged from behind the sail shed and dashed between picnickers, down to the grove.

"Sparky! Is that you!" laughed an all too familiar voice. Hunter and his royal entourage were holding court around the fire pit.

"Hey! Hi!" Blake said. *Be casual, be ready,* he thought.

"Did I get it right? This is *your* birthday bash?"

"Uh, yeah. Thirteenth! Having a good time?"

"Are you kidding me? This is awesome! Cajun? Who'da thunk it? Did you hear that? Thirteen!" He made a sweeping gesture toward the Hellcats. "Put 'er there young man!"

Blake shook his hand.

"I hereby declare that you are officially a young man, with all the rights and privileges!"

Blake brushed his bangs out of his eyes.

"Hey, what happened here, Sparky?" Hunter said, squinting at Blake's scar.

Rexroat shifted uneasily.

"I got swamped in the shallows. Big wake. Pitch-poled the boat. I was trapped underwater, nearly drowned. Seven stitches."

"Kee-rap buddy! Did you see who it was?"

The Hellcats glanced at Rexroat in quiet panic.

"Um, it was *Lemon Drop.*"

"Rexy! Did you do that to this fine young fellow?"

Rexroat threw up his hands and averted his eyes. "Hey, Cowboy had the stick. That's all I'm sayin'"

"Ahhhh! Did bad ol' Cowgirl thump your anchor-line again?"

"Three times."

"Now see, He's been warned about that," said Hunter, turning back to Blake. "That's rule number one: never, *ever* give Cowgirl control."

"I understand that now."

"Sorry you had to learn the hard way."

Jenny snickered. Hunter rounded on her. "Something funny, Jenn? Let me tell you something: Sparky is the fastest, smartest, bravest young man on this lake! Isn't that right little buddy?" He was starting to get that spooky edge in his voice.

"Well, except for you, Hunter," said Blake.

"You see!"

"Hey Tux! There you are!" Sylvana came swishing down the hill, picking burrs off her clothes.

Hunter saw Blake's eyes roll back. "Hey, who's the Jeanie Beanie?"

Sylvana came up and threw an arm around Blake's waist. He jerked away. The band started to play again.

"Say, I gotta get back up there. Hunter Devlin, Sylvana Pagán. Sylvana, Hunter. Glad you're enjoying yourselves!" Blake beat a hasty retreat out of the grove.

"Hey, you good lookin'! How long you been working on that tan?" She threw her hair back with a snap of her head.

"Long enough, Jeanie Beanie. You better run along. Your boyfriend is getting away."

"Nah, he got a girlfriend. That little rica from la marina." Sylvana sauntered away. "She's getting kind of fat in the belly," she said, with a casual air. "I don' know. I think maybe he give her a *baby*!"

The Cheer twins dropped their jaws. Jenny whistled in delight and almost licked her lips over that delicious morsel of gossip.

"Whoa, you gonna let him get away with that?"

"Whaaat?" said Hunter, with a sneer. "She's just a jealous little beaner. My sister'll be a virgin eight days after she's married! Hah! Cajun— I'd never have guessed him for Cajun!"

***

Blake found Soojee and Deadhorse dancing close and slow beneath a tree near the patio. They seemed unaware that everyone else was doing a lively two-step up on the deck.

"Hey, I hate to interrupt, but have you seen Mia?"

Someone swooped up from behind, snatching him by the arm.

"Yeah, she's right here! Where ya been!" Mia whisked him up the steps and into the dance.

"I need to tell you something!"

"Pay attention to the beat, stop tromping on me!"

"But Mia...hey, did I just see Haraguchi?"

"Yup! And Treva and Charlie, the police chief, some bikers, and a nun." Mia seemed to radiate an energy that Blake was not fully acquainted with. He couldn't bring himself to tell her who he'd just been talking to. He twirled her through the two-step and then the band started a slow, haunting waltz.

They swayed under strings of naked lights, the air was humid, and sweet with the smell of pizza spice, and people, and Mia's flowery shampoo. Just when he expected the dance to end, the tempo picked up. The singing, though he couldn't understand the French, seemed sadder, more desperate. Mia led him into a swinging step and they swirled around as the band took it from waltz to a steady pounding cadence. Bystanders stomped and clapped in time with the music. Mia and Blake spun faster and faster, until everything was a whirling tornado of sound and color and light. They were alone in that dizzy blur, waves of curly black hair flew around her fine, tan face. Her dark eyes glowed with an inner light. She was living in the moment, unguarded and happy. He gave himself over to it and forgot everything, everyone but her. People were now shouting with the thunderous stomping. The music reached a fever pitch. Something in Blake anticipated that in a moment it would explode and burn itself out. When it did, they released each other and flew apart with an exuberant cry. The crowd went wild, laughing and cheering.

He wanted to draw her close like Soojee and Deadhorse, and collapse in her embrace.

She ran back to him and gathered him up in a hug as warm his mother's, kissed him on the cheek, then fled away.

Blake staggered backward a little and bumped into someone. "Oh, sorry!" he said, turning to apologize. "Uncle Carson!"

Blake threw his arms around him and held on tight. Carson patted him on the back, a little embarrassed. "Happy birthday, kid!"

Blake finally released his bear-hug and took a step back. "Uncle Carson, is it too late to put the letter back?"

"Letter? Oh you mean this one?" Carson grinned and produced the scorched envelope from his back pocket. He held it in the air as if beckoning someone's attention across the deck. Blake looked over his shoulder. Tripper Gunn had finally returned and was enjoying a slice of pizza with Beverly, at a table by the railing. Gunn took notice and scowled hard for a moment. But then one eyebrow went up, when he saw what was in Carson's hand. His head bobbed in approval and he turned his attention back to Beverly.

"Don't need to, now. Well, I better go make up to the old man." Carson started across the patio.

"But wait,"

"Don't worry, kid. I picked it up on the way over here. Sometimes the Almighty lets you off the hook. Now, go enjoy yourself!"

Jean Paul started another number. Mia appeared at Blake's side with cold sodas.

"Whatcha thinkin' about?" she said.

"Grace." Blake took a long draught from his root beer. "What's this song called?"

"Retourne de Loup Garou."

"Translation?"

"Return of the Werewolf, I think," said Mia.

"You've got to be kidding."

Chapter 31

"Quit kicking my bed!" Blake grumbled. He shielded his eyes as the radiant, morning sun invaded his consciousness.

"Wake up! Elsie says come get something to eat before she shuts down the galley," said Ray, gruff from the long night.

"What time is it?"

"Time to eat!"

"I slept outside?" He rose up on one elbow, then slumped back in the chaise lounge.

"At least *you* got some sleep!" said Ray, tromping across the patio.

Blake remembered chucking the last black bag onto a mountain of garbage bags, just as the sun came up. He only half recalled sitting down on the chaise. He wandered into the galley. "Where is everybody?" Soojee and Deadhorse dragged in behind him.

Elsie handed a plate of pancakes and eggs over the counter. "Home, in bed!"

They ate breakfast on the patio, at a table with a good view of the lake.

"It's unreal," said Deadhorse. "Eight hours ago, this place was wall-to-wall party. Now it's all gone. It's like it was a dream."

"Except for the energy," said Soojee. "It's still here. You can almost see it."

Mia trudged up and dropped her plate on the table. "Best. Party. Ever."

"That was the most amazing night of my whole life," said Blake.

"Hands down."

"Ditto," said Mia.

"I got news for you," said Soojee, "It was for a whole lot of people. You're what's trending on Facebook right now."

"What are we going to do about that fan page?"

"I made Kaz give me the login and password. I made a personal page for you, then gave you ownership of the fan page."

"People are tagging pix and posting videos like mad," said Deadhorse.

Blake chuckled. "I don't even know what any of that means!"

"You're amazingly popular. That's what it means," said Soojee.

The Vice Commodore shambled up. "Kids, I'm here to tell ya, there's only so much that Red Bull can do. My crew welched on me. Any volunteers?"

"Me and Horse'll go!" said Soojee.

"Much appreciated. Blue Lightning, halfway to the grove. Shove off with the half hour gun."

Blake caught Deadhorse sneaking a glance at Mia. She saw it too and flicked her eyes away. Deadhorse dropped his gaze and feigned interest in his hash browns.

"You'll have to show me how to do that Facebook stuff, Sooj," Blake said, keeping a furtive watch on her boyfriend.

"I'll take care of it," said Mia, through a mouthful.

Deadhorse's expression betrayed his disappointment.

"Too bad you don't have something to sell, with all this traffic. You should at least do a blog," said Soojee.

"Which is?"

"Like an online diary. You could write about all your adventures. People would love it!"

"Bad idea," said Mia. "With court cases and pending arrests? You really want to admit to the whole world that you disabled Jack *then* tied him up, *then* beat the crap out of him with a stick and *then* kicked the puke out of him?"

Soojee's jaw dropped.

Blake shrugged. "He's twice my size! He was torturing Griffy! He still wouldn't tell me what I wanted to know."

"It's creepy to think he's still lurking around here somewhere" said Soojee.

"I just wish I didn't always have to keep looking over my shoulder. At least Hunter's being civil to me. Uh I mean..."

Mia's face flushed pink and she nearly choked on her orange juice. "Say what?"

"Uh...You were having such a good time!"

"Hunter was *here* ...last night?"

"And Rex, and the Cats. Down in the grove. Hunter even stuck up for me."

"And you didn't tell me? That's twice!"

"I tried too! I said I needed to tell you something and you told me to quit tromping on you. Remember? And then we were spinning like mad and you looked so happy, then Carson showed up, and I was so happy. It just felt like everything was going to be okay. I've never felt like that before."

Mia held her breath and scowled.

Blake steeled himself up for one last defense. "It's not like we didn't have seven cops here, anyway."

"And Haraguchi," she said, calming down.

"*And* a nun!" said Deadhorse.

Blake saw her let a shy little smile escape, like the time Buck Mueller paid for their breakfast.

Deadhorse saw it too and then noticed Blake's expression. "Well, I think I'll go down and help the skipper rig the boat."

"I'll be there in a minute. I mean," said Soojee stuffing another bite In her mouth, "after seconds!" She rose and headed to the galley. Blake and Mia were suddenly alone.

"Nice guy," said Blake. "How old is he?"

"Seventeen. Just got his license. I hear he's going to be on staff for J.T.-two." She was silent for a while, looking at the blue lake. "We have to do something about Junior." She paused again."You still hang with that old guy at the nursing home?"

"Yes."

"Lets go see him."

***

"Young man! *Young man!*" called the administrator, clopping down the hall as fast as her platform heels would allow. "All visitors must sign in at the front desk and wear a badge. That's the new policy." Blake and Mia stopped and waited for her to catch up. "Oh, its *you!*" She halted and shot an accusing look over the top of her half-glasses. "Visitors are also required to leave by the approved exits, not out of the windows. Do I make myself clear?"

"Yes Ma'am," said Blake.

"You two go sign in and I'll ask Mr. Dubois if he's feeling like visitors."

The administrator clop-clop-clopped down the hall. Blake and Mia returned to the front desk. She stuck a paper badge on her shirt and gave Blake a quizzical grin. "Out the window?"

"It was totally justified."

The administrator called back up the hall "Mr. Dubois will see you now!" She clopped into another wing of the building.

Dubois' voice boomed into the corridor. "Giddy-up, Nelly!" A chorus of whinnies echoed out of the surrounding rooms.

Blake knocked lightly on Korbin's open door. He slipped cautiously into the shadowy room, Mia in tow. "Mr. Dubois, may we come in?"

"Come on in now!" Dubois said, his brow furrowed. "Where you been, boy?"

"Sorry it's been so long."

"You take to one of your moods and have it out with the old man, again?"

"Mr. Dubois, it's me, Blake."

"You ain't Caw?"

"I'm Blake Urquart. Ava's son."

321

"Ava? Ava's here? I haven't seen my little Ava since she married."

"No, Mr. Dubois, my mom isn't here. Remember? I'm staying with Uncle Carson and Tripper Gunn."

Dubois took a spoonful of ice chips from a Styrofoam cup and sucked on them a moment. "Now I recall. You're the Prince of Uh-quot. I just get things a little mixed up sometimes."

"I brought my friend, Mia. She wanted to meet you."

"Well hello, Missy!" he said, extending an enormous hand. She smiled apprehensively and shook it.

"She's a pretty one!"

"She'll do," said Blake.

"I don't know why you'd want to come see an old man. Don't know what the interest is. I s'pose you want to know if my folks were slaves?"

"Um," Mia glanced at Blake for help. "Were they?"

"My great, great, great, great grandfather Hezekiah came to Indiana in eighteen hundred and eleven. He was the slave of a Methodist preacher from Virginia. Well, not long after, the greatest earthquake this land has ever known—the New Madrid—shook folks up pretty good. They were all in a panic thinking it was the wrath of God, so they did all sorts of things to buy him off. That old preacher gave Hezekiah his freedom. We've been Hoosiers ever since. Indiana abolished slavery in eighteen hundred twenty, anyhow."

"That's amazing," said Mia. "So, speaking of God, Blake says that God expects us to honor our father and mother."

"That's right. First commandment with a promise. Thou shalt honor thy father and thy mother, that your days may be long upon the land which Yahweh your God giveth thee."

"But what if your parents don't care about you?"

Blake nearly swallowed his tongue.

"What do you mean, don't care about you? You look cared for!"

"Oh yeah, I'm set! But my parents couldn't care less about me. Same story with Blake's dad. How are we supposed to respect that?"

"Your folks gave you life! Changed your stinky diapers and they go to work everyday to put a roof over your head and food in your belly. You might owe 'em a little respect for that much!"

"I was born because my mom's hay-fever meds interfered with her birth control meds. I was nothing but a career killer to her, so I've been raised by nannies, and baby sitters, and housekeepers all my life."

"Now, hold on!"

"Mia," said Blake, weakly.

"And Dad already had the son he wanted. He's never lifted a finger to protect me from him or his pervert buddies!"

"Mia, please?"

"Now wait just a minute! I don't know about all that! Folks think just 'cause a fellah lives to a ripe old age he's Moses or something! I don't have all the answers!"

"Hey, my birthday was yesterday!" said Blake.

"Seems to me a person in your situation orta behave in a fashion that'd make your folks proud—in such case as they ever *do* get their heads screwed on straight."

"I turned thirteen!"

"Huh? Thirteen! Why that makes you about a young man! With all the rights and responsibilities! You have a big party?"

"Mia and Mr. Gunn put it together. Five hundred people showed up!"

"No! That's a power of people! They all sing Happy Birthday to you?"

"Yup. And Uncle Carson showed up."

"Well how about it! I was thirteen in the year nineteen hundred and sixteen. That year the Cubs played their first game in Chicago. Half a million or more of Europe's finest perished in the Battle of Verdun. You remember that? My uncle was one of the Buffalo Soldiers. Tramped all over old Mexico with Black Jack Pershing, chasing Pancho Villa. Say, you remember when that fool hung that dead chicken from the traffic light, down home in Lick Skillet?" He laughed. "Drove through that intersection in the middle of the night, knocked the windshield clean outta my Model T! Now, let me tell you, don't get tangled up with ol' Malva Winters. You know who I'm talking about, don'cha?" He gave Blake a wink. "You know! You'll have to pay the doctor a visit, if you do!"

"No...I don't..." said Blake, giving Mia a worried look.

Dubois yawned long and loudly. "'Bout naptime. Seems like all I ever do lately. You send Caw around, you hear? I want to see him before I move on. It was nice to meet you, Miss Mia," he said, as he lowered his recliner.

"Thank you for sharing your stories with us, Mr. Dubois." she said.

"Glad you found 'em interesting. Send Caw on around here!"

***

Blake pulled his boonie hat down over his eyes. They ambled along the blazing sidewalk, toward town. "I'm kind of worried about Mr. Dubois," said Blake.

Mia donned her round, mirrored sunglasses. "I'm not buying it."

"Buying what?"

"That God sticks us with these buttholes and expects us to honor them after they screw us up, abuse us and drive us crazy. For no other reason than they had the hots for each other at some college party."

They walked in silence for another block.

"Provoke not thy children to wrath, lest they become discouraged," said Blake.

"Do what?"

"It just came to mind. I've heard my mom say it to my dad. I think it's a Bible verse. Provoke not thy children to wrath, lest they become discouraged."

"Too late. Let's get carry out and go up to the Hollow. I need to do some thinking before the regatta dinner, tonight."

"Oh wow. I totally forgot," said Blake.

"Another dinner, another band, another party! Then we do it all again day-after tomorrow, with the whole town and mega-fireworks."

"Sounds like a riot!"

***

Blake spotted the *Terrapin* as she motored into the harbor. He jogged down the hill to meet her at the main dock, hopping aboard eagerly to fetch the spring-lines.

"Where've yeh been all day, Caduggin? Yeh manage to get any sleep?"

Blake jumped back to the dock and secured the boat to her moorings.

"Aye. Mia and I spent the afternoon up in the Hollow. I got a good nap."

"Probably the coolest place on the lake. It was a hundred-one in the shade at my place. Lad, take this." Gunn handed out a large picture frame—the one Blake had recovered from the hideout in Mangrave.

Blake read it aloud.

"Benediction:

Almighty Creator, maker of Heaven and Earth,

Who is like unto thee in the splendor of thy handiwork?

Having made bird and beast, fish and the creeping

Thing of the earth; who hath made man in his own image

And given him dominion over all the works of thy hands;

We bless thee this day and praise thee

For thy wonderful works, and for thy

Salvation.

We ask that thy blessing be always upon this place,

And all who visit here; may they find thy peace under the

Spreading boughs of its trees, thy serenity upon its waters

May they comprehend thy majestic glory in every season and

In the starry canopy of night.

Grant, O Lord, this place as a refuge for the sons of men

And for all thy creatures.

Amen

Declan Urquart

Upon the Dedication of Highland Creek Sailing Club

July 2nd Nineteen Hundred Fifty Eight"

"You read that well," Gunn stepped out onto the dock.

"Fifty-three years to the day?"

"What are the chances, lad? Let's go put that back in the boardroom where it belongs."

"It belongs downstairs where everyone can see it," said Blake.

"Agreed. But to some, it's just an embarrassing relic."

"Are they really going to kick us out of the club?"

"No doubt Commodore Devlin will have a go at us." They left the dock and began the long climb up the hill. "But it takes a special inquest and a seventy-five-percent majority of the board of Directors—and the board of governors—to revoke a lifetime membership. But, inquest or no, Judy and Griffy are goner's for sure."

"I'm sorry. It's all my fault."

"Stop talking that way! It's Bill Trudeau, Ray, and me—we wantonly flaunted the Friday-night rule—we're the ones on the hot seat. Maybe your friend's little plan will work and it'll all blow over."

When they reached the patio, Gunn mopped sweat from his brow and waded through the dinner crowd to a nearby keg, seated deep in a barrel of ice. Blake recognized a number of faces from the night before as he waited for Gunn to draw a glass of beer.

Carson ambled up from behind. "Whatcha got there, kid?"

"It's the Benediction," said Gunn, blowing the froth off his brew. "Jack, that dirty primate of yours, stole it. Your nephew took it back. Show him where it belongs, will yeh, man?"

"Your demand is my command! Follow me, sonny. I want to hear all about this."

Blake tailed his uncle across the great room. "And I want to hear why on earth you're friends with that guy."

"Who said I was? His mom's a friend of your Nanna. She thought I'd be a good influence on him. So I got him to crew with me and the old man. Seemed alright, at first."

They made their way to the boardroom with the big, polished table, on the second floor.

"He made a deal with Gunn to buy the *Darby McGraw*, then got behind on his payments. I hired him to watch the house for a few weeks. Had no idea he'd gone so far around the bend."

"Wait 'til you see the garage."

Carson hung the frame on the wall at the end of the table.

"So, where's your acid-tongued little girl?"

Blake squinted at the Benediction. He tapped it on opposite corners until it was straight.

"Don't know. She dropped me off. Said she had some things she needed to take care of. Are you coming back to Mr. Gunn's?"

Carson drew a deep breath and ran his fingers down his moustache. "We'll see, Blake. It's probably best if I don't, right away."

"Is it me?"

"No it ain't you. The universe don't revolve around you all the time, ya know? Look, your Nanna and the old man expect me to be some sort of father-figure to you, but I don't know how to do that."

"Then don't. Just be my uncle."

"I'm afraid I haven't done a very good job of that, either."

"Then just be around." Blake gave him a wry smile. "Just be… Uncle Arctica. Like when I first got here."

"You forgive me?"

"As my favorite uncle once said, sometimes the Almighty lets you off the hook."

***

Blake walked down the gravel trail until the brassy sounds of Swing Dream and the noise of the regatta party faded into the night. He passed under the peaceful boughs of the grove and on to the end of the point. He stood at the waters edge, looked up at the starry canopy and breathed in its majesty. His reflection floated serenely on the surface of the mirror lake. Then, in the familiar strains of the night choir a new, unsettling voice drifted across the water. He held his breath, there it was again—the faint but unmistakable howling of a dog. Out of the distant, dark west rolled a muted peal of thunder.

Chapter 32

It rained. Not much. Not enough. But it finally rained. Blake sat in the bay window and filed through his postcards. The *Hebrides Overture* rolled and surged on the stereo. He stopped and watched absently as heaven filled the harbor drop by drop. He thought about the birthday party and took a long deep breath through his nose—breakfast, fabric softener, pipe smoke. He smiled. It was another cozy, homey Sunday morning at Gunn's—not at all like the hectic fuss-and-rush to church back home.

The phone rang. Blake bounded to the recliner and dug the portable handset out of the depths of its cushions. "Gunn residence."

"Hey Tux, anything weird happen over there last night?"

"Do you always start conversations this way?"

"Ha ha. All the alarms went off at my mom's house last night. Police dispatched and everything."

"Hunter?"

"You can bet on it. Someone came prowling around Treva's, about one."

"Yikes. What are you going to do about it?"

"I haven't decided. But it calls for extreme action."

"Get some pepper spray. There's a guy who sells cayenne-pepper bear foggers at the flea market."

"I was really thinking of a *different* kind of extreme."

"You going to the club, today?"

"No. Got traps to run and plans to make. See you tomorrow afternoon, Tux."

"Okay. See you tomorrow, love you." It was out of his mouth before he knew he'd said it. "Um…you still there?" The line was dead. *How did that happen? I only say that to mom…ever…period!*

The gray harbor brightened suddenly, then darkened, then brightened. The rain stopped.

"Weather's breaking, Caduggin! Go rig up the *Darby*," Gunn called from the laundry room. "Your uncle and I got three races in yesterday afternoon. If they run four today, we can throw out the two we missed yesterday morning. We've got a shot at a trophy!"

"Where are the sails? And is Uncle Carson crewing?"

"We'll meet him at the club. Jib's under the deck; main's on the boom already."

***

Blake entered the clubhouse in search of his uncle. He saw Soojee just heading up the stairs. He caught up to her on the second floor.

"What'cha up to?" he said.

"Hey Tux! Where's your woman?"

"I don't know. Where's Deadhorse?"

She brushed blue hair out of her eyes. "Down at the boat. I came up to get something I left in the dorm. What are you doing up here?"

"I was just … looking for my uncle."

"So, how long have you and Mia been an item?" she said, as she walked into the girls' dorm and sat down on the first bunk. Blake leaned against the doorframe.

"Well, we're not really an item."

"Oh, yes you are!"

"Well not according to her, anyway."

"Uh oh. An un-girlfriend! Do you guys kiss and stuff?"

"No!" Blake chortled nervously. He noticed her innocent smile and how her dark blue eyes complemented the electric blue of her bangs. He didn't find her repulsively seductive, like Sylvana.

"How come? Horse and I kiss. He's really good!"

"Well, um…"

"Sit down here. I can teach you how!"

Blake felt wave of heat wash over him like a fever. The sweet, casual way she offered surprised him more than the offer itself. For a moment it seemed like a nice idea.

"What about Horse?"

"He won't mind. We're just friends!"

This girl was beyond Blake's comprehension.

"Um, I think I heard the half hour signal. We should probably get to our boats."

"Okay. I'll be down in a few. If you ever want to make out, just let me know!"

Blake stopped halfway down the stairs, sure that his face was incandescent by now. He was trembling. He felt ashamed because he *had* wanted to sit down with her. He felt like he'd betrayed Mia, un-girlfriend, or not.

The rain had not cooled things down. By the time racing started, the atmosphere was positively soupy. On the *Darby McGraw*, temperaments were as tense and hot as the little breeze that ghosted them across the glassy water. Gunn gave Carson his orders in abrupt tones of disapproval. Carson's replies were snide and inflammatory. Gunn insisted on heeling the boat over so far that Blake was sure that one false move and they'd be belly up. He was wedged between the two roasting, sweaty curmudgeons on the low side of the cockpit, for two hours. He tried to ignore the cramped discomfort and focused on the fact that they were gradually gaining on Trudeau, Soojee, and Deadhorse in the *Itasca*.

Blake was about to ask if he could swim back to the club, when he heard excited chatter erupt from the boats ahead. Suddenly everyone was trimming sails, moving to the high side and tacking. The wind had come up!

"Get up to the rail! Go!" said Gunn.

Carson and Blake groaned and struggled stiffly through the two-foot gap between the centerboard trunk and the boom. Blake barked his shins as he crossed. They reached the high rail just as *Darby's* sails caught the breeze. Gunn didn't budge. Water rushed along the rail, splashing across his back. He held the mainsheet in one hand, the tiller in the other. He leaned out and peered ahead sharp-eyed, fearless, and determined. *That's the guy I wanna be when I get old,* thought Blake.

" Ready aboot! Hard a'lee!" said Gunn. He tacked the boat, the crew crossed again and now all three were hiking together. It was still horribly hot, but the excitement seemed to transform everyone's dispositions. *Itasca* was just three boat-lengths ahead, with the windward buoy coming up fast.

"Get the chute ready, lad. Carson, get the pole up!"

"There'll be a squall behind this!" said Carson, rigging the spinnaker pole to the mast.

"Like as not! But we'll get two more races and we'll beat Trudeau." Gunn winked at Blake.

When the *Darby McGraw* crossed the finish line for the fourth time, a black pall was spreading over the southwest horizon. No one wasted any time in getting back to the harbor.

***

Sailors assembled on the patio deck and engaged in raucous conversation while they waited for the regatta results. Blake lurked at the railing and nervously anticipated the weather. Angry thunder rumbled across the lake. As usual, Commodore Devlin worked his way through the fleets announcing the winners and presenting trophies.

"Fourth-place Lightning: William Trudeau with... Soojee... Moojee, and Deadhorse? Seriously?" Customary applause followed, with not a little snickering at Devlin's dismay. Carson and Blake whistled and cheered as Trudeau and crew approached the trophy-table.

"Thank you!" said Trudeau. "And thanks to my gallant crew! You're going to see a lot more of these kids around the club and on the water. Sebastian's family is in the application process and Kiki, sorry—Soojee's folks are talking about joining up, too. This is because of the absolutely amazing job that Tripper Gunn, Blake Urquart, and Mia Devlin are doing with Junior Training. So, give them a special hand when they come up to claim their prize. Remember, kids like these are the future of this club and the future of inland sailing!"

The crowd responded with enthusiasm. Commodore Devlin got on with his duties.

"Third-place Lightning: Tripper Gunn, with Carson, and Blake Urquart."

A generous "Hurrah!" went up as they crossed the patio. The two teams high-fived and razzed each other as they passed.

Gunn took his prize, a replica whale tooth decorated with a magnificent scrimshaw of the *U.S.S. Constitution*. Devlin did not shake his hand. Blake and Carson each received a drinking glass bearing the club logo.

"You all need to be at the meeting, Tuesday," said Devlin, discreetly.

"What did *I* do?" said Carson, his voice full of challenge. "I haven't set foot around here for weeks."

"You and the boy. Gunn. Tuesday."

"And what did the lad do? This all comes down to me and Bill," said Gunn. He turned to the crowd. "Thank you! I second the V.C.'s sentiments. But only because I beat him! Because of this lad's popularity our J.T. enrollment has been phenomenal. We need at least two more instructors with driver's licenses. If yeh know anyone, give 'em my number."

"Can we get on with it?" said Devlin, looking up at black, lowering clouds. "I'd like to get out of here before this thing puts down a funnel."

I hope Mia's safe, thought Blake. *I wonder if he even cares?*

"Second-place Lightning, Treat Cudworth with Shirley and Joe Herrmann. And in first for the Lightnings is Burl Albert, and his son Andy."

Lightning split the air directly over head with a deafening crack, followed instantly by a boom that rattled the clubhouse windows. The patio cleared in seconds. Rain swept into the harbor and up the hill like a white wall and pounded the deck, windows and roof. Packed into the clubhouse, the regatta crowd didn't seem at all flustered by the furious tempest. They cheered carelessly with each blinding flash, with each explosion that slammed the clubhouse, with each malevolent blast of wind that whipped torrents of white water against the windows. The Commodore resumed the awards ceremony in the great room. Blake found Gunn and Carson seated with Trudeau and his crew. Soojee was curled up in a ball, face buried in Deadhorse's chest, his long arms wrapped around her. She shuddered with each crash of thunder.

"Can you imagine being caught out in this?" said Blake. He had to shout to be heard over the crowd and the roaring wind.

"I'd rather not!" said Gunn. "I hope the roof at the flea market holds up."

"Why the flea market?" asked Blake.

"'Because I own the blasted place!"

"You own the flea market?"

"Aye. And a half dozen other properties in town. I'm worried aboot our Mexican friends. And your little girl."

A large blue and yellow object came flying out of the squall and plastered across three windows.

"I do believe that's my tent!" said Carson.

"Yeh know, they put those stakes in the bag for a reason, man?"

"Is *that* what those are for?"

"That *is* your tent! Shouldn't we be taking this a little more seriously?" Blake said, trying to hide his terror.

"Aye. Quite right. We'll take a salvage cruise once this blows over. Yeh always find the best stuff after a good blow."

Hail the size of marbles began to tap on the windows like the insistent claws of a demonic horde.

"The wise man sees danger and hides himself," said Carson, "but the simple pass on and are punished!"

Thunder cracked. Blake flinched. The power went out. He pulled a small flashlight out of his cargo pocket. "I'm going down to the boiler room." Soojee uncurled and followed him. Deadhorse stayed behind.

Blake hung the light from a nail on a joist and sat on the floor against the wall, facing the huge rusty boiler-tank. Soojee plunked down next to him and quivered violently. He thought she wore the most fearful expression he'd ever seen. Tears glinted in the faint light and ran down her trembling cheeks. She flung her arms around him and held on tight. He held her awkwardly for a moment. Her hair smelled of harsh, bitter chemicals. Blake's heart pounded in great hollow thuds, but not because of the storm. Then she kissed him. And again. And again. Longer with each embrace. *I shouldn't be doing this! I shouldn't be doing this...I...I ...* Somehow the storm and the fear, the rough cinderblocks at his back and the cold, concrete floor—everything—melted away. Her face and mouth against his were all that existed in that desperate moment. Then she pressed her face against his neck and whimpered. He wondered if he and Mia would have kissed in their fear, too.

Fifteen minutes later, a single, bare light-bulb flickered to life above them. A merry cheer went up in the room above. Blake would have ventured to the top of the stair but Soojee wouldn't let go.

"It's all over, you can come up now!" someone called down.

"Let's go. It's okay. Storm's over," Blake said. *Or is it just beginning?* he thought.

Chapter 33

"Am I glad to see you!" called Blake, jogging down the dock between *Sophia* and *Terrapin*. "Did you get caught in that storm, yesterday?"

Mia paddled *Cry of the Osprey* across Gunn's Harbor. "Uh, *yeah!* I was up in the Hollow! I had to wedge myself in a crack to keep from being pulverized by the hail. Where were you?" She coasted up to the dock and tossed him her bowline.

"We barely made it back to the club. I went down to the boiler room. Hey, we got third place!"

He helped her onto the dock. "Did you grow, over the weekend? I swear I was taller than you on Friday."

"Something's wrong with that kid." Carson emerged from the cabin of the *Terrapin*. "He's shot up at least two inches and put on ten pounds since he got here and his voice has dropped an octave."

"Who are you, really? And what have you done with Tux?" she watched Carson brace his shoulder under the horizontal mast and heave. The tabernacle creaked as the counterweight sank into the bow compartment. The gleaming wooden spar pivoted slowly to vertical and locked into place. The '76 Stars and Stripes flew from a pole fixed to the masthead.

Mia turned to the *Sophia*. "Ready to do some decorating?"

By the time they set out for the Parade of Yachts they had dressed *Sophia* up in red, white, and blue bunting, a long Stars and Stripes pennant from the masthead and Old Glory on the backstay.

Mia covered *Cry of the Osprey's* cockpits and tethered her to *Sophia's* stern.

***

"Slow boats to the back of the fleet, Gunn, you know that!" shouted Commodore Devlin. The *Terrapin* met the *Eclipse* leading the keelboat fleet out of Highland Harbor. The rusty red sails eased out as she turned onto a broad reach. A huge yellow Gadsden flag trailed proudly from the leech of her mainsail and a blue United States Navy Flag from her mizzen. Devlin could now see the skipper clearly.

"Anybody hurt in that wreck, Larry?" said Carson.

"Urquart, I'd hoped you wouldn't embarrass the club with that floating… sarcophagus!"

Carson dug into a pocket in his cut-offs and produced a small screw and washer.

"Don't take it personal-like Larry, but that boat makes your butt look big!"

Carson turned into the parade behind the *Eclipse* and a little to windward, revealing the *Sophia* in his wake.

"Hi Daddy!" called Mia from the bow pulpit. "How do you like my new boat? Looks a lot like that old Contessa you used to have, doesn't it?"

Carson took advantage of the distraction and threw the screw high into Devlin's mainsail. It zipped down the Dacron, plinked off the aluminum boom, then ricocheted around the fiberglass cockpit.

"What the heck was that!" Devlin snatched it up and scrutinized it, then stared hard at the masthead in near panic.

"Speaking of old contessas, where's Brigita, Daddy?"

"You're dead to me!" he said, his attention divided between his daughter's taunts and the rigging.

"I was dead on arrival, Daddy!" The *Sophia* assumed a course parallel to *Eclipse*.

Carson threw the washer. It slid down the sail, pinged off the boom and hit Devlin on the nose.

"Youch! Terrence!" he said to his crew. "Don't just stand there! Rig the bosun's chair and see what the hell sprung loose up there. And *you* don't need to show your face around the club anymore, little runaway!"

A clevis pin skittered across Devlin's deck.

"It's not running away if no one cares you're gone!"

"Terri, get the main down before we lose the mast!"

Mia hauled on a halyard and a big "Liberty or Death" banner went up the port side-stay.

"A'right you two, break it up!" said Gunn, from *Sophia's* stern. He steered into the lead as *Eclipse* dropped her sails and started her motor.

"Slow boats to the back of the fleet, Larry!" said Carson, as *Terrapin* passed.

Mia made her way back to the cockpit.

"Yeh said yer peace. Now, are yeh satisfied?"

"Sorry. Didn't mean to embarrass us," said Mia.

Two blasts from a diesel horn startled everyone in the fleet. "Oh, lass we have'na seen embarrassing just yet," he said looking over his shoulder. "But don' worry, its aboot to rear its ugly head!"

A small cabin cruiser with shabby, stained sails and patchy paint in various shades of faded green, skirted along the windward flank of the squadron. The Confederate flag rippled from her backstay, the Jolly Roger from her masthead. Strings of Stars and Bars fluttered from her shrouds.

"Is that Ray?" said Blake.

"Behold, a pale horse!" said Gunn. "And a redneck!"

Ray chugged along under sail *and* motor, standing shirtless in the stern. He blasted his horns and shouted rhetoric at everyone as he went. "The South had the right to secede! The War of Northern Aggression wasn't a *civil* War!" He coughed and spat over the side. We should'a freed the slaves *then* fired on Sumter! The South *will* rise again!"

"Keep your distance, Skipper. I think that boat has a disease!" said Mia.

As *Southern Stars* overtook the *Sophia*, Ray shook his fist at her patriotic finery and cried "Extremism in the defense of liberty is no vice!"

"I love Independence Day," said Gunn with a wink and a smile. "Turns

Ray into an absolute hooligan!"

The diesel horns blasted and Ray sang "Sweet Home Alabama" as he headed up the channel.

"Yeh kids know the difference between liberty and freedom?"

"I always thought they were the same thing," said Mia.

"Liberty has boundaries. Yeh are at liberty to do whatever the law permits. But freedom has no rules. It leads to anarchy and destruction."

The thirty yacht fleet passed onto the upper lake and took the lead of an armada of motorboats. Together, they cruised the length of the Gold Coast from the east bridge to the dam in the west, then back to the Freeman Waterfront. People waved and cheered from their lawns and balconies and inflated bouncy houses. They launched fireworks and played music as loud as their stereos would go.

"John Philip Sousa. Wouldn't you know." Blake scanned the motor fleet with his field glasses. "There's *Tantrum II*." He handed the binoculars to Mia.

"Junior, Bader and Hopkins, Rexroat, the Hellcats and a handful of assorted wannabees."

"Where's *Lemon Drop*?"

Mia smiled slyly. "Her engine was running a little sour. Somebody poured a couple gallons of corn syrup in her gas tank to sweeten it up."

"And how do you know that?" He looked at her suspiciously.

"I told you, I have my spies. Speaking of that, I may need to disappear occasionally, tonight; don't be offended if I take off without warning. Check this out." She ducked into the cabin and popped back out with her backpack. "I got a new camera."

"I thought your phone was a camera?"

"Needed a longer lens and better low-light performance."

"Is that a film camera?" said Gunn.

Mia chuckled. "Those are about all gone. Look." She flipped it over and popped open a little door on the bottom of the camera. "Just push in and let go and boink! Here's the memory card!" She handed Gunn a little, square of black plastic about the size of a postage stamp.

"Amazing. Sixty-four Gigabytes? How many pictures can yeh put on that?"

"More than I can take in a day. And a ton of video, too."

"Amazing," said Gunn. "Still, there's nothing like film. If I get a picture of yeh two, can yeh get a print?"

"Sure! Any drugstore can do it," said Mia, replacing the card in the camera. "Just hold the button down. It'll focus and shoot when it's ready.

The waterfront was one packed mass of humanity. Live music and the smells of vending-cart food drifted through the trees in the park. Festival goers picnicked, swam, and played volleyball. Children with painted faces ran this way and that with helium balloons.

"This is like my birthday party ten times over!" said Blake, as they made their way to the gazebo.

"It's like this all the way down Main Street. And there's a carnival at the flea market!" said Carson.

The mayor, a well-groomed man with sleek, silver hair had just taken the mic at the gazebo. He welcomed everyone to the Freeman Freedom Festival, thanked the sponsors and introduced the band.

"Thank you! We are the Mutineers!" said the leader, adjusting his red bandana. He wore a blue-striped shirt and a gold ring in his left ear. "You know, America has a great maritime tradition. So great that we still use the expressions that our sailing forefathers used. 'Fair and square, ship shape, three sheets to the wind!'" The crowd cheered, lustily. "They left us their stories in the form of old sea shanties. From the great oceans to the Great Lakes they sang of shipwrecks, and lost love, of backbreaking toil, of joy and disaster. Our first tune is based on a tale told to me by my old friend Buck Mueller and it's dedicated to one of Highland Creek's very own."

Blake looked at Mia. "No way…"

The man turned a couple of tuning pegs on his twelve stringed guitar, then started strumming. A recorder, concertina, and bodhran drum joined in.

"I'll tell you a story of a sailor named Tux,
a young pirate hunter and here is the crux:
He rode *Seven Thunders* across Highland Lake
to take on the Cov'nant in a battle first rate!
Derry down, downnn! Down Derry Down!
He boarded her broadside, he struggled and brawled,
He whacked Voodoo Jack, now Kalijah would fall;
He bested her skipper, that dirty old skunk
Set fire to her sails, and laughed as she sunk!
Derry down, downnn, down Derry Down!
He leapt off the deck, our young hero so bold,
The powder went up with a bang so I'm told!
He pulled out the plug and left her to sink,
Her loot in his hold, her crew in the drink!
Derry down, downnnn, down Derry Down!
So all of you pirates, who prowl Highland Lake,
Smugglin' and stealin', your living to make;
You better beware for Tux will find out,
And he'll hunt you all down and rout you right out!
Derry down, downnn, down Derry Down!"

The tune rolled into an instrumental break. Carson mussed Blake's hair. "Don't let it go to your head, kid. Keep a low profile and don't get hassled by the man. I'll be at Tyner's, if you need me."

"Grab that bench over there!" said Gunn as he ambled off. He returned five minutes later with an arm load of chili-dogs and soda.

When the set ended, Mia stood up and stretched. "C'mon Tux, I want one of their CD's. We'll get him to autograph it."

"Here Caduggin, get me one too." Gunn handed him a wad of cash. "You two blow the rest on the festival. Be aboard after the fireworks. That'll be aboot eleven-thirty. Missy, make sure he stays sober. And *no* tattoos!" He shuffled into the crowd.

"Weird. I'm getting to like that old guy," said Mia.

"He kind of grows on you."

At the next break they collared the singer, who happily autographed their CD's. Blake was signing copies for the Mutineers when suddenly there was a bright light in his eyes and a microphone under his nose. A lady in a red polo shirt started talking to a man with a video camera.

"Thanks Bob! Daley Dunright, here for the Channel Three Action Report! I'm here at the Freedom Fest and as you can see people have come from miles around to celebrate Independence Day. I'm talking with local legend Tux Urquart about his recent adventures fighting crime on Highland Lake's notorious Mangrave Branch. Tux, tell us…"

Blake was frozen like the proverbial deer in the headlights. Mia snatched the mic and pushed her face in front of the camera. "My client can neither confirm nor deny these or any other allegations! Any questions you have may be directed to my client's legal counsel. And by the way, we're both minors, so if even one frame of that video hit's the air, there *will* be immediate consequences!"

The spotlight on the camera went out. "Young lady," said the reporter.

"Does the word *harassment* mean anything to you? How about Double and Krossler Attorneys at Law? Now get lost!" said Mia, ferociously.

Daley Dunright put up her hands and slowly backed off. Mia winked at the astonished Mutineers and towed Blake away.

"I'm guessing you've done that before?"

"You don't grow up in my family without learning a little courtroom drama. Here, put this in your pack. And don't turn it off." She handed him a cell phone.

"I don't know how to use one of these."

"You don't have to. Just put it in your pack. If it rings, push the green 'answer' icon, and talk. Here's what's cool—see this map icon? Touch that." A map of Freeman appeared on the screen. "There's an icon for me and one for you."

"It tracks where we are?"

"Yup! If you need to find me just launch that App. Here's how you dial. But I probably won't answer tonight."

"Dare I as ask why?"

"Ask me no questions and I'll tell you no lies! I told you, I have some recon to do. I'll have mine set on silent."

They meandered along, browsing the booths and tables of local shops, artists, and craftsmen. Blake noticed that Mia checked her own phone regularly and occasionally grimaced and smacked it on the side.

"Something wrong with it?"

"Battery's fritzing out."

"Why don't we just trade?"

"Nope. Yours is only set up to track me." She looked at hers and smiled. "Okay, score! Do you hear barking? Why don't you go up there and check that out? I'll be back in a while." Mia adjusted the settings on her camera and took off on her mission.

***

The sign over the table read:

A-paw-stolic Animal Rescue
Friends of Saint Francis
Third Order—Episcopalian

A pair of women whom Blake took to be nuns, owing to their long headdresses, oversaw a pen of a dozen assorted canines. "Hey you! I know you!" he called to one in particular. The White Hound woofed, then bounded over to meet him. He stood up with his paws on the fence-rail and licked Blake in the face.

"Long time no see!"

"Is this your dog?" said the younger of the nuns.

"No, we're—well he saved my skin once. He's kind of a local legend." Blake scratched the hound behind the ears and hugged him. "How did you get clear up here, pal?"

"Does he belong to anyone?"

"Sort of, but he'll be in jail soon if we're lucky."

"Would you be interested in adopting this dog?" said the older nun.

"He seems to like you."

"I'll have to ask Mr. Gunn or my uncle. I'm just here for the summer."

"Tripper Gunn," she said, making a sour face. "I see. Sister Elizabeth, you are needed at the far table."

"Yes, Sister Solomina." Sister Elizabeth smiled apologetically and returned to her duties.

Blake became aware of someone standing very close.

"Don't you think those little chocolate Easter eggs look like rabbit turds?"

He jumped. "Natalie!"

"They don't taste like rabbit turds. They taste just like dogfood."

"Don't tell me how you know that!"

"I don't think dogs should be penned up like that. Most dogs come home good on their own."

"Did you do something to your hair?"

"Papaw paid the water bill, so I got to take a bath this month."

"Young man? Here!" The old Sister handed him a packet of adoption paperwork. "Is this the young woman?"

"Which young woman?" said Blake.

"The mother-to-be? So young. Such a tragedy." She glared at them with a look of withering disappointment and returned to the adoption tables.

"I saw Deadhorse. He asked if I'd seen your girlfriend."

Blake checked the tracker. Mia was on the move, several streets away.

"Nice to see you, Natalie. I gotta go."

***

Mia perched deftly on the edge of a concrete planter, lens pushed between two tall, evergreen bushes. She snapped picture after picture of a romantic couple on the patio of *The Tryste Sidewalk Café*. Though they maintained a discreet distance and propriety, the woman glowed with affection. She was impossibly beautiful—ruby lips, platinum blond hair, icy blue eyes. Her ruggedly handsome companion, Lawrence Devlin, worshipped her with every longing gaze. Mia, ready for the decisive moment took her final image—her father planting a quick kiss on the blushing cheek of his adoring paramour. He left the patio, hurried down the sidewalk straight past a hedge of strangely rustling bushes. Mia hopped down, brushed herself off and headed straight for the gorgeous blond at the corner table. She made herself at home.

"Hi! Is that your boyfriend? He's cute!"

"My Lawrence?" she said still looking in the direction he'd gone. "Is… a friend."

"Your accent, you're Croatian?"

"Eh… yes! You have been to Croatia? It was the most beautiful place. Before the war."

"No, I haven't. I wish I had your hair. It's fantastic!"

"Thank you. But you have a lovely face and a gorgeous head of hair, I think surely you must be after something more than mine. Do you want to take my picture?"

"How well do you know *your* Lawrence?"

"How well do we know anyone?"

"Exactly. How would you like to know more about him?"

The woman crossed her arms and smiled politely. "What could *you* possibly know?"

"Plenty. Intriguing isn't it?"

"I suppose you know things about me, too?"

"You're Brigita Dragana Rozik. You're Croatian, thirty-three, you're great at tennis and unbeatable at chess."

"Impressive! So, you've seen my Facebook page. Tell me something the rest of the world doesn't already know."

"You have a big birthmark on the top of your left foot, which is why you always wear socks; you like frilly blue satin nighties; and you have a cute little dragon tattoo on the right side, well below the neckline."

The woman took a deep breath and shifted in her seat. Mia suppressed the urge to smile.

"I should slap that pretty little face right off your skull," she said with aristocratic dignity.

"But you won't, because you're hungry for what I've got."

"And what will you offer me for an appetizer? And what is the cost?"

"Well now that you mention it, I do need a favor. Your Lawrence is going to a meeting tomorrow night. And he's bent on getting a lot of really good people in a lot of trouble. And I'd really like for that not to happen."

"Well, well. You play chess, too."

"Backgammon's my forté."

"Ah, then you are a gambler. I don't see how I can help you."

"But you're married to the mayor, right? You must have some power or influence?"

"Yes, but,"

"But I need Lawrence to miss that meeting or lay off my friends. One or the other. And I need him not to know that we spoke."

"One of your great American authors once said that it is the easiest thing in the world for someone to seem like they have some great secret in them. So, tell me little girl, some great secret."

"Lawrence is healthy and wealthy, but he ain't that wise. Lousy decisions and misguided priorities have put his empire in danger."

"Hmm! Is that all?

"Oh, there's more."

"What is my mother's maiden name?"

"Novak. Dragana Zrinka Novak. Born June 3rd, 1949."

"You are a presumptuous little brat." Brigita stood up and straightened her skirt.

"Ain't I though? Runs in the family. Do we have a deal?"

"I suppose you will find out tomorrow night. And what if I don't help your friends. What then?"

"I guess *you'll* find out tomorrow night! Good evening, Mrs. Mayor."

Brigita strutted off like an offended tigress. Mia savored her success and was about to get up when someone sat down next to her.

"Hi Mia!"

"Horse?"

"It's Sebastian, please. Where's your sidekick?"

"Actually I was just going to find Tux and get some ice cream."

"Allow me! We could have dinner."

"Thanks Horse, but no." She looked at her phone for a moment. "C'mon Junior, where are *you*? Turn on your stupid phone."

"I'm really excited about working with you during Junior Training."

"Well, it's not like we'll be on the same safety-boat. You, me, Gunn, and Carson Urquart, we're all drivers. I figured Soojee would be *your* partner," she said, while she reviewed her handiwork on the camera's display screen.

"Whatever works out, I guess. Um, nice camera. Bet you like art, too?"

"It's overrated."

"Have you been to the Lovell Center for the Arts?"

"Duh! I grew up here."

"So, what's your favorite painting?"

She looked at him with a straight face and said "*Jean Paul Marat, Dead in His Bathtub.*"

He sat for a moment in stunned silence.

"We could walk over there. I bet they're open."

"Don't you ever give up?"

"Mom always said that persistence pays off!"

"Was she ever wrong? You want to know what I'm going to call my next picture? *Sebastian: Dead Horse on the Sidewalk.* Look, Tux'll be here in a minute. Thanks for saying hello."

Deadhorse stood up before Mia could and stepped behind her chair. He leaned over and planted a little kiss on her cheek, just as Blake appeared on the patio and spotted them. He stopped in his tracks. The look on his face said it all. Mia thought about giving Sebastian a flying elbow in the ribs for his efforts.

"I was just coming to find you. Horse is going to treat us *all* to ice cream!" She pushed the table forward and joined Blake.

"Uh, well actually I think I'm going to head on over to the carnival," said Deadhorse.

"Fine with me Horse," said Mia, she locked elbows with Blake and left

Deadhorse standing at the table.

"Sebastian, remember?"

"Whatever works."

"Where you want to go, bud? The Emporium or the Lil' Dipper?"

"Lil' Dipper."

They walked for a block without speaking. "Guess who I saw?" said Blake. "The White Hound! Oh, and Natalie. But she stayed behind with the dogs."

"With the rest of the strays, huh?" said Mia, her attention fixed on her phone.

"I think her family must be really poor."

"Sorry, say what?"

"Nevermind." *You wouldn't understand.*

The Lil' Dipper was doing a brisk business, it took ten minutes just to get to the counter. Blake stewed over the thought of Deadhorse wooing Mia. As they made their way out of the little storefront, Blake caught his foot on something and tripped. Mia managed to save his dark-chocolate-dipped waffle-cone as he went down.

"Better watch where you're going, smarty pants!"

"Oh, excuse me I'm so sorry!" said Blake. Then he recognized that whiney, nasal voice. Mount Edna stared down at him with a haughty, if not vengeful, glare. She gave him a light jab in the ribs with her thick, strangely-carved walking stick.

"Don't be," said Mia, helping Blake to his feet. "Is that the ugly-stick your dad beat you with?"

"My boys are gonna get you, Speedy."

"Then they better learn to sail," said Blake.

The enormous woman made an odd waving gesture with her hand, tapped her stick on the floor three times and mumbled something unintelligible.

"Thanks," said Mia, as she ushered Blake toward the door. "A two-bit Juju curse from a bloated porn-dealer. Just what we needed."

"Don't forget to name it after *me*, honey!"

"You bet! Hindenburg has a nice ring to it. See you later Jumbo."

The sun hung low over the western corner of town, the sky was hazy pink. Chimney swifts raced above the rooftops and cicadas chorused loudly.

"Fireworks start in about an hour. We have time to hit the carnival?" said Blake.

Mia smacked her phone. Blake craned his head to see the icons on the screen.

"What are you doing" Mia chuckled.

"I saw four icons. Who are you following?"

"Don't worry about it! You wouldn't approve."

"Deadhorse?"

"Now you can just put that idea out of your head."

"I saw him looking at you Saturday morning."

"Lots of boys look at me. It's annoying!"

"You smiled at him."

Mia stopped and faced him. "Look! What the? Are you jealous? Is that what this is?"

"Why shouldn't I be?"

"Because, we… I…uh," her phone chirped. She glanced at the display. "Crap! Look, I don't have time for this! I'm trying to save our butts, here. Can we talk about this later?"

"Griffy says the only reason you keep me around is because I'm the only guy on the lake who doesn't want to get you in the back seat of a car."

"Is there something wrong with that? Can you blame me? And by the way, that's not the reason I *keep* you around. It's the reason I *like* being around you. Think about that for a while. I have to go. Meet me at the boat at nine thirty. I'll call you if I need you sooner."

She stormed off. Blake thought she looked far more hurt than angry. Giant arcs of purple and yellow neon turned slowly in the twilight above the nerve-jangling cacophony of the midway. Blake wandered aimlessly down an endless avenue of garish booths, ignoring the barkers and hucksters.

"Yo, Tux!" Deadhorse was just exiting the go-cart track.

"Go away."

"Sorry, man. I heard you two weren't an item."

"Would it stop you if we were?"

"You don't have to be insulting! But she is a lot older than you. You ought to hang with Soojee for awhile, 'til you learn the ropes."

"I don't think Mia is really interested in you."

"We'll let time be the judge of that," said Deadhorse.

Blake spotted one of the last people he thought he'd ever be glad to see. "Hey Horse, you speak Spanish?"

Sylvana stood in line for the roller coaster. As they walked by, Blake reached behind Deadhorse and tugged one of her belt loops.

"Hey, watch it muchacho!"

"Sylvana! Que pasa, chica!" said Blake, feigning innocence.

"Tux, what you doing here!"

"Eso es mi amigo, Sebastian! Le gusta ti muy mucho! Sebastian, this is Sylvana Pagán."

"Uh, hi!" he said, with more suspicion than enthusiasm.

"Hey, you guapo!"

"That means handsome." said Blake. "Sebastian es solo. Necesita un novia."

"Oh yeah? Tux, how come you so mean to me? Hey Sebastian, you ride the Crazy Train with me? Is scary." She took him by the arm and pulled him into the line. "We have to sit real close."

"Tux, I..."

"Will thank me later. She's better than Soojee! Wait 'til you meet her dad."

Blake strode down the Midway, spirits restored. He headed for the Ferris wheel, making it just in time to get a seat on the last gondola. The attendant secured his passenger restraint then turned to assist another last-minute rider, apprising them both of the safety rules. As she exited the gondola Blake could finally see who was riding with him.

"Put 'er there Sparky!"

A four letter word passed through Blake's mind. "Hey, how are you

Hunter? Enjoying the festival?"

"Totally! You're having a good time aren't ya?"

"Yeah, oh yeah!'" Blake startled as the machinery engaged and the wheel began to turn.

"Wait 'til you see the lake and the town from up top."

"So, where's Jenny and everybody?"

"She's afraid of heights. Like my sister." He chuckled. "Go on, ask! I know you want to know."

"Why is Mia afraid of heights?" he said, not sure if that was correct question.

Hunter laughed, relishing the memory. "One time, I piled up all of the mattresses in the foyer," He giggled and shook his head. "And I caught her—she was about nine and I dangled her from the third floor balcony by her ankles! Man, could she scream. I dropped her of course—oh boy! She landed on her back but she bounced about ten feet and smacked a big mirror. Man, there was blood everywhere!" He laughed so hard he started coughing. "Is that the best, or what? It wasn't long after that Mom spoiled the ride. Split and took Mia with her. Then squirt started taking Karate." He started to look serious but burst out laughing again. Blake tried to smile agreeably. They reached the top of the arc. The town stretched out like a miniature in a display case, the lake was a lavender mirror.

"You know why I like you, Sparky? I'm sorry, what's your real name?" Hunter slouched in the corner and spread his arms out on the edges of the swaying gondola.

"Blake Barber."

"Barber? I thought it was Urquart."

"That's my mom's side of the family."

"Blake, I like you because I'm sure that if I had you by the throat, crushing your windpipe, you'd still look me in the eye and spit in my face."

Blake swallowed hard. "I'll try not to disappoint you."

"I can respect that. Not these butt-kissers I call my friends. I'd trade a hundred of them for one of you."

"That's nice of you to say. I'm not sure I'm all of that."

"Oh yes you are, pal. You've got it in you. What's your old man do?"

"He's in marketing."

"I'll tell you a secret. See, I'll inherit all my wealth. I'm set. As long as Dad doesn't screw up and let Mom clean him out, I'll never have to work a day in my life. You, you'll have to build your empire from the ground up. But you'll never do it working for the man."

"I see."

"Two little words, Blake. Passive Income. Repeat after me."

"Passive income," said Blake.

"Rental properties. Return on investment. Big Gunn understands it. That's why my old man hates him. That old geezer owns the best properties in town. Tyner's, the Emporium, the antique malls. All that lease money goes right in his pocket, whether he's working or not. That's passive income. Say it again!"

"Passive income."

"That's the secret to building your empire, Blake. Sure, there's a little more to it. You ask Gunn. It's never too early to start!"

Blake spotted Sylvana dragging Deadhorse to the line for the Ferris Wheel. He couldn't help thinking that this was his cosmic reward for that little bit of match-making. Hunter made pleasant conversation, advising him on topics ranging from sailing, to college, to things about girls that Blake never imagined there would be a need to know. They debarked and were met by Jenny and her entourage. She snickered jealously.

"Hey little baker, how's Patty Cakes?"

He ignored her. Hunter slapped him on the back and shook his hand. "Good talking to you young man! You come see me anytime. Remember the magic words?"

Blake gripped Hunter's hand manfully and to bluff the groupies, feigned all the confidence he could muster. "Passive income, rental properties, return on investment. I'll never forget it. And thanks for the sailing tips."

"Remember what I said about women!"

Blake smiled and winked. "How could I forget!"

Sylvana swooped up from behind. "Hey Tux! Hold my Sloshy! Sebastian buy it for me, but I can't take it on the ride." She pressed a big cup full of blue icy-slop into his hand.

"Well if it ain't our little trouble maker!" said Hunter.

"Tux, you gonna let Tio Guapo talk to me like that?"

"What'd she call me?"

"Uncle Handsome. And I'm on his side," said Blake.

"Hey, where my Sebastian go? How come you always dumping me on people, Tux?"

"It's my way of getting even with my enemies."

"Oh yeah? C'mon Tio, let's ride that big wheel. You more fun than Tux, any day." She slid over to Hunter. Jenny didn't defend her territory, opting for a strategic victory.

Hunter shied away in disgust. "What's this Tio stuff all about, Jeanie Beanie?"

"Well, you gonna be an uncle right?"

Jenny bit her lip and grinned.

"Jack and Jill went up the hill to have a little fun!" said one of the Cheer twins.

"But stupid Jill forgot her pill and now they have a son!" said her sister.

"Not funny!" Hunter fumed.

The seemingly random comments of the day began to patter on the tin roof of Blake's mind and flowed into a sudden torrent of comprehension. "What have you been telling people, Sylvana?"

"I don't tell nobody nothing!"

Jenny spoke up. "Just that Patty Cake's got a bun in the oven!"

"I said can it!" chided Hunter.

Jenny flinched, then winked at Sylvana—who slithered back to Blake.

"Hey Tio, you want some of my Sloshy?" She gave Blake's hand a hard underhanded smack, dousing Hunter with a liberal helping of blueberry slush.

"Ugh! I hate blueberry! Oooh Sparky," he said, with a grim smile. "I'm sorry about this!"

"Hunter *she* did it!"

"It's a matter of principle, pal. One!" said Hunter through a lunatic grin.

"Wait!"

"Two"

"But, Hunter!"

"Two and a quarter!"

"Hey, he's counting," said Sylvana, "I think you s'posed to run!"

"Two and a half!"

Blake wasted no more of his head start and sprinted off into the crowd.

Hunter grinned. "Three!" and he was off in hot pursuit.

"Don't worry Tux, I'm coming! You owe me a Sloshy!" yelled Sylvana as she ran after them.

"Tally ho!" cried Jenny and loosed her pack into the chase.

Blake dove and dodged through the crowd like a ball through the pegs on the Emporium's pachinko machine. He burst across Chase Street and tore down the alley between the Lutheran Church and the Funeral home. Hunter was still a good hundred feet behind.

Blake flew into a parking lot where a knot of youths lounged on BMX bikes and teetered on skateboards. Blake broke right and streaked past a greasy-faced fellow in a leather trench coat, leaning against a light-pole. "Get 'im!" cried Voodoo Jack.

Tires buzzed across the pavement, boards rumbled. Hunter poured on the steam to get around them.

Blake hit Second Street. Tyner's Pizzeria and Bar was just a heartbeat away. He dashed in the open door, leapt up and ran down the side of a pool table surrounded by bellowing bikers. Hunter followed two seconds later, down the other side.

"Hey! That's the goose kid!"

"Hell, that's my nephew!" cried Carson.

Blake zipped across the beer garden, boosted off a bench, and over the privacy fence. The Freeman Freaks turned into the alley to cut him off, just as Hunter landed. A half dozen bearded Harley warriors burst out of the gate. Blake looped back around the building and charged straight through Sylvana and the Hellcats. He fled down Main Street toward the heart of the Festival. Hunter dodged them with a curse but was swamped by Freaks and bikers as they surged out of Second Street.

"Make waaaay!" cried Blake, bearing down on the ocean of celebrants. The throng parted like the Red Sea.

The White Hound saw Blake tear past and barked wildly. He made a lap around the pen and rocketed over the fence. Natalie, who had been in the pen all evening, opened the gate. A dozen barking canines poured into the street as the mob thundered by.

"Sister Elizabeth! The dogs! After them!" commanded Sister Solomina.

Mia crouched in the cabin of the *Terrapin*, snapping photos through the porthole. Her father and Brigita were just motoring away from the next dock. "Dang it Tux, where are you?" She looked at her phone. Blake's icon was making a bee line straight down the screen. "This can't be good." She ran to *Sophia* and readied *Cry of the Osprey*. Mia flung the cockpit covers into *Sophia's* stern and untied her.

Hunter fought his way to the front of the herd, now fully thirty-five strong, not including dogs.

Blake cut left through the Emporium parking lot, up the back steps of Saint Gregory's and through the back door. The White Hound and Hunter followed, everyone else went around. Blake opted for the steep banister down the mountain of front steps, with Father Leo closing in.

He cut around the hardware store and passed the thrift shop. The sight of Waterfront Park was all he needed to summon one last burst of energy. He spotted Tripper Gunn ahead. "Mr. Gunnnn!" The old man quickly shuffled aside when he saw Blake surfing the human tidal-wave. "Don't wait up!" Blake gasped, as he whooshed past.

Mia maneuvered *Cry of the Osprey* so that her bow touched the end of the big dock, just as Blake made the landing. He plummeted down the curving steps in three, hip-jarring plunges, the White hound on his heels. Hunter and an unidentifiable flood of shouting, barking, cursing, huffing pursuers poured down behind them.

"Blaaake! Blake I'm here!" Mia shouted, waving her paddle so he could see her over the end of the dock.

"A hundred feet! A hundred feet! A hundred feet!" he panted to himself.

His sides felt like they'd ripped open and his lungs were about to explode. He could feel the throng thundering across the planks, eating up his narrow lead. Then halfway down the dock the White Hound rounded and charged the mob, fangs bared, barking viciously. Hunter, Father Leo, Sylvana, Carson, the Freeman Freaks, six bikers, two Sisters, four Hellcats, six wannabees, and a host of curious thrill seekers dove for the safety of the lake, just as the first shells of the Freeman fireworks shredded the heavens.

Blake made a flying leap off the end of the dock and slammed down on *Osprey*'s foredeck so hard that Mia had to brace-stroke to steady the violently bobbing kayak. She back-paddled furiously as Blake slithered into the foreword cockpit and wilted. Mia turned the *Osprey* and headed for the channel.

"As soon as you feel like helping out, we've got a boat to catch."

"What's this bag under the deck? There's something moving in it."

"Hand it back here. Just some friends I made along the way."

Blake handed her the heavy, wriggling bag. The lights of the *Eclipse* disappeared in the distance. Mia checked her phone. "Fudge. They're in the dead zone. Still, probably headed for Cheater's Cove."

Blake slouched low in his seat, legs out on the foredeck. "If it's all the same to you, can we just go home? I've gotten in more trouble in the last four days than I have the entire time I've been here."

"That's what makes you so much fun to be with. Yeah. I think I have enough dirt to do the job." She let him rest for five minutes. Mia sighed. "So, I'm waiting."

"For what?"

"You to start paddling and fill me in on your harrowing, manly adventure."

"Pick *one*." He pulled his hat down over his eyes to block out the brilliant flashes of bombs bursting in air.

"Tell me a tale of a sailor named Tux."

"Sylvana. Blueberry Sloshy. All over Hunter."

"Ooooh, *blueberry*? That explains a lot. But what about the crazed mob with pitchforks and torches? I thought that was a nice touch, by the way."

"Crazed mob? What crazed mob. Was there a crazed mob?"

"They didn't exactly look like stark raving fans!"

Blake pulled his paddle-halves from under the deck and snapped them together.

"Just some friends I made along the way."

***

They sat on Gunn's ridge, under the setting sliver of July's early moon, and watched the blinding, pyrotechnic finale. Though three miles distant, the thunder from it burst across the lower lake louder than Sunday's storm and rolled into the distance for a full minute after the last shell exploded. Then everything was quiet, save for the insidious whine of mosquito's wings. The night chorus whirred back to life.

"Mia, how do you know if you love someone?"

"I don't. I don't know what love is. But I'm pretty sure I know what it *isn't*." Red and green running lights appeared in the channel as the keel boat fleet made its way to home port. "Write it down if you find out, 'cuz I want to know."

"I'm sorry I hurt your feelings," said Blake.

"Don't worry about it. Horse is a doofus."

Blake let a minute pass in silence. "Mia, are we an item?"

"Look," she said, gently. "I need to set some things straight. I kind of forgot myself at the party. I think I gave you the wrong impression. I let my guard down and as usual, somebody got hurt."

"I'm glad you did. I got to see you happy," he said. "You deserve to be happy."

"I'll never forget *that* night. That's for sure."

"Sooo, we're not an item?"

"Can't we just be Mia and Tux?"

He smiled. "Yeah. That's all I want."

She scooted close, put an arm around him and squeezed. "We're going to stay in touch after you go home, right?"

"I'm not going home. The thought of it makes me feel like I'm turning inside out. This is home."

"I've got to get out of this place. Hey wherever we end up, no matter how bad it gets, we can always remember this crazy summer, right?"

"Do you hear a big dog barking out on the water?" Blake peered through the night-scope. "It's the White Hound—standing up in the bow of the *Terrapin* with his paws on the rail." He handed the scope to Mia.

"It just gets crazier by the minute!" she said

As the *Terrapin* neared Gunn's harbor, the dog dove over the side and swam to shore. He scrambled zig-zag up the ridge and disappeared in the forest. A moment later, he burst out of the underbrush behind Mia and Blake, drenched them with a vigorous shaking of his coat and dashed back into the forest.

"You're welcome!" said Blake.

***

"'Hello, Mr. Gunn?' is that what you have to say, Caduggin?" said the old man, as Blake secured *Sophia's* spring-lines. "It's no enough that I have to face the board tomorrow night, but did we have to add the PD and the Mayor's Office, and the town council, to boot? Give me a hand up, Miss; then put those hatch-boards in. Lad, yeh meet me in the interrogation room in ten minutes."

"I told ya Tripp, Hunter was after him," said Carson.

Mia had just gotten him onto the dock when a small, raspy bark bounced out of *Sophia's* cabin. They stopped and looked at each other. Carson ambled over from the *Terrapin*. Another bark popped out followed by paws and nails scrabbling on fiberglass. A little black dog with bat ears and flat face skated into the cockpit. It stood there staring at them, panting expectantly with its tongue hanging out.

"Will yeh look at that thing! I don' know if I need a leash or an exorcist!"

357

Mia jumped down and made friends with the stowaway. She put the dog on the dock. It farted and made a bee-line for the house.

"Caduggin, we're going to skip interrogation and go straight to execution."

Chapter 34

"What do yeh mean 'can I prove it came from Friends of Saint Francis?'" Gunn shifted the phone to his other ear and gave the little black bulldog wedged next to him a disapproving look. "Yeh lost a pack o' dogs at the festival—they were all over the docks! I get home and there's a flatulent French Bulldog stowed away in my cabin! Where else would it have come from?"

Blake topped the stairs and headed down the hall.

"What do yeh mean by that? She *certainly* is not! And don't you dare repeat that, Sister Psoriasis!" He plunged his thumb into the End button on the handset. He huffed and looked at the dog. "I believe there's a special place in Hell for people like that, what do *you* think?" The dog whimpered and peeped at him out of one eye. Blake returned to the living room. He gave the dog a quick scratch behind the ears.

"What'cha gonna call her?"

"Sooner. 'Cuz I'd sooner no had 'er!"

"Well, the boat's loaded. We're leaving. We could pick up a leash in town on the way back."

"Oh no, yeh will not! Yer no going near town! I've been on the phone with every major official in Freeman this morning and I think I finally got it all straightened out. Yer no going to blow anything up, nor start any riots, sink any boots, nor get anyone pregnant! Yer going up-lake on a job with yer uncle and then down to the meeting tonight!"

"Technically, I haven't blown anything up...yet. And who said anything about...pregnant?"

"That crabby lay-sister, of all people! Where did she get such a notion?"

"If it's the same lady I saw last night, she didn't seem too happy when I mentioned your name. What's that all about?"

"It's tale for which the world is no yet prepared. Now go on, get outta here. Try not to aggravate yer uncle or teach Cezar any bad habits."

***

Carson sat at the helm, on the low side, feet up on the opposite bench. Blake explained the basics of sailing to Cezar in sweeping gestures and very broken Spanish.

"You playing charades or teaching him how to trim the main?"

"No, I understand, sir!" said Cezar.

"Don't call me sir! Me llamo es Carson!"

"You speak Spanish?" said Blake, surprised.

"And a little Arabic, to boot. And some Lakota Sioux, but I can't repeat *that*. Since when do you speak the lingo?"

"I got a book. Cezar and Romero help me. I help them with their English."

"Fair trade. You speak Spanish pretty good, kid!"

"Oh, thank you!" said Cezar. Blake gave him a playful slug on the shoulder.

"Well played, Chico! So," said Carson, "tell me again about that catfish you saw."

"It was just for a second. It was gigantic."

"Three feet?"

"I don't know. Big as me, I guess."

"Could you tell what color it was? Have any markings?"

"It was just huge. I'm just glad it's trapped in that lagoon."

"Odd, it jumping like that when you pushed Ol' Lucky over. Think you..."

"No! No way am I going back there!" interupted Blake.

"Hold on, now!"

"Forget it!"

"On a map, Blake! I just want to see where it is on the map."

"Why do you want to know?"

"Just curiosity, that's all. Cezar, take the tiller! Blake, talk him through a couple of tacks."

It was a long day on Beverly Maitland's backwoods estate. Cezar was on pool duty, Blake picked up limbs and debris while Carson repaired the system of shafts and gears that opened the glass ceiling panels of her decrepit greenhouse. Even under the forest canopy it was hot. Blake wasn't sure which was worse, his mounting anxiety about the impending meeting, Beverly's bitterly bad lemonade, her continual doting, or the way she followed him everywhere jabbering randomly about absolutely anything and everything. When Beverly started to fret about the meeting, even the lemonade didn't seem so bad.

Blake wondered when she'd gone so far around the bend, or if he just hadn't noticed before. He eluded her for a minute and detoured through the greenhouse, if only to give his uncle a roll of the eyes and a forlorn look. Carson snickered. "She's just thrilled to have company, kid. But I haven't had lemonade that bad since Santa Fe back in seventy eight!"

"Would it be rude of me to suggest that most people put sugar in it?"

"There you are!" Beverly crooned. "Blake! I'm ready to mulch the flower beds!"

***

Blake and Carson crept in the front door of the club, careful not to let the door whump shut. They slipped quietly into the middle of the back row, behind Beverly. Gunn was before the officer's table, arguing with Commodore Devlin.

Beverly looked worried. "It's not going so well. They've waived the Minutes and they got their quorum, but Devlin's backers are here in force. I don't know where all the good guys are tonight!" she whispered.

"Hung over," Carson said, as he counted heads. "They've got a majority, by one man."

Mia was nowhere in sight. Things got loud at the officer's table.

"Well he would'na been running if your son had no been chasing him!" said Gunn.

"That's immaterial, Gunn! The damage done to the club's image is what is at stake here," said Devlin.

"And running the lad up a tree and roasting him with a torch, yeh call that good PR?"

"Again, Tripper those *alleged* events are not germane to this meeting. Our first order of business is this glaring breech of club rules perpetrated by yourself and to a lesser extent the Vice Commodore, whom I am sure felt pressured to do so."

"I'd like to address that!" said Trudeau, from his seat next to Devlin.

"You'll have your opportunity to testify during the special inquest."

"Objection!" cried Beverly jumping to her feet. "You know good and well that the parties in question get a chance to explain themselves before *we* decide if an inquest is necessary!"

"Here, here!" grumbled eleven from the assembly.

"Order! Mrs. Maitland, you have not been recognized by the chair. Please reserve your comments," said Devlin. "I think you all know the situation and so..."

"Larry," said Trudeau, "you can't make the motion until you have read the order of business. You *know* that! Seriously, you're going after the lifetime membership of the sole surviving founder of this club? Talk about a scandal."

"Quite right, Bill." Devlin picked up the agenda and read "The first order of business regards the determination of the need for a special inquest relating to a breech of Highland Creek Sailing Club's bylaws and regulations pertaining to prohibited activity on club property, which occurred on Friday night July first, and potential disciplinary actions against members found directly responsible for, or aiding and abetting, or otherwise closely associated to said violation. Those members being named are Daniel Tripper Gunn, William Trudeau, Carson Urquart, Blake

Barber, Beverly Maitland, Raymond and Elsie Rolff, Judy and Griffyn Williams, and Mia Devlin."

"Yeh forgot the Cajuns!"

"Order! Take your seat Mr. Gunn."

Blake was stuck between fuming rage and sinking despair, as Devlin read out the instructions for the motion and the vote. He heard a door squeak, nearby.

"Psst!" Blake's heart leapt when he saw Mia in the doorway of the men's locker-room, just beyond the end of his row.

He started to get up but she motioned him to stay put. She gave him a saucy smile and held up her digital tablet with all of the drama and flourish of a game-show assistant. She swiped a finger across the screen and a photo of Lawrence Devlin kissing Brigita appeared. She tapped on Brigita's face and an envelope-icon popped up. She lifted an eyebrow and with a smug smirk stabbed the envelope with one finger.

Commodore Devlin stood and pronounced "I make the motion that a special inquest be convened to ascertain the culpability of members Daniel Tripper Gunn..."

Mia feigned comic impatience, crossing her arms and drumming her fingers on her biceps.

"...and to determine the appropriate disciplinary actions up to and including expulsion from the club."

Mia looked at her tablet. She held up one hand and began a five-fingered countdown.

"I second the motion," said someone in the assembly.

Mia dropped her pinky. Devlin's phone rang just as the third motion-backer opened his mouth.

"What the! Sorry, I thought I'd silenced it. How embarrassing!" He pulled the phone from his blazer pocket and winced. "I apologize—mayor's staff—I have to take this!"

Devlin turned his back to the crowd and mumbled nervously into the phone for four minutes. The assembly grew restless. He hung up and turned back around, flushed and sheepish.

"Ah, I think you're right Bill. My estimation of this situation was maybe a little disproportionate, ehh, so I think I'll go ahead and withdraw my motion for the inquest."

"Well if you don't have the guts, I'll make the motion!" said the second backer. "I second!" said the third. "Third!" cried another.

Mia's sassiness turned into a panicked grimace.

Devlin drooped into his chair.

"Are you going to call for the vote, Mr. Commodore?"

"All in favor?"

Twelve responded "Aye."

"We've only got eleven!" hissed Beverly over her shoulder. "He's got to vote with us or we're…" she made a slashing gesture across her throat.

"All opposed?"

Eleven raised their hands and granted a vociferous. "No!"

Devlin reluctantly brought up the rear, barley getting his hand off the table. "No. Tie vote, motion not carried."

Blake looked back to Mia in disbelief. She put one fist on her hip and shot him with a pantomime pistol. She blew the imaginary smoke off, tossed her head and strutted out the side door.

"Larry, you alright?" said Trudeau.

Devlin looked as if he were about to spontaneously combust. "Bill, I've got to see to some things. Take over," said Devlin without so much as a glance.

***

Bats tumbled after moths in the gathering twilight and four weary sailors lumbered down the hill toward their yachts.

"I can only assume," said Gunn, "that your little girl had something to do with the bizarre ending to that pathetic fiasco?"

"I'm not sure how she pulled that off, exactly."

"Well who cares how she did it!" said Beverly, in her warbley voice. "It worked! It got us all off the hook—even Griffy!"

"I care! Don' yeh understand? The lad's got to know that any organization is vulnerable to corruption—whether yer Sunday sewing circle or Vatican City. We fight evil, greed, and misguided ambition; but we do so according to the rules, under the color of law—otherwise anything becomes justifiable."

"What about extremism in the defense of liberty?" said Blake.

"What Ray says when he's drunk is no thing to set yer moral compass by!"

"Actually," said Carson, "Senator Goldwater said that during the Nixon administration."

"Even worse! Lad, that girl must be wielding a whopping lot of power to bring her dad to his knees with a single phone call. She's playing a wicked-dangerous game. You don' want any part of it. Mark yeh, it'll go rough for her before it's all over."

"Yes sir," said Blake, contemplating the awful possibilities.

"I'm sending the lot of you back to Beverly's tomorrow whilst I go down to see Maynard and Shelby. Caduggin, clear the moorings! I hope that gruesome cur hasn't widdled and puked all over my house!"

***

Blake stood silently in the bow compartment as the *Terrapin* puttered toward Trespass Island.

"Hey kid, you know Maynard caught a giant red-bellied pacu out of this lake? Couple of years ago. Thirty inches in diameter! He'd been feeding it bananas every morning off his dock. Mueller 'bout peed himself when he found out!"

Blake turned and leaned against the cabin top. He weighed his thoughts for a solid minute. "Uncle Carson, what's love?"

"Big pain in the butt—avoid it at all costs."

Blake turned back to face the looming silhouette of the island. *Too late,* he thought.

Chapter 35

An enormous stick bug poked its spindly way across the high, vaulted timbers of Beverly's family-room. Blake watched it with vacant fascination from a deeply cushioned chair. He struggled against the outgoing tide of post-dinner coma. Beverly had stuffed them with spaghetti. Blake had covertly redeemed his lemonade with several smuggled packets of sugar, but was still wondering what could've been done to save the marinara. Cezar groaned quietly as his eyes finally drooped shut. Carson, one hand on his belly, belched discreetly and stared at the evening-news. "That lady's got a heart of gold but kid, she could burn water."

Blake was on the verge of a swirling vortex of unconsciousness when something on the TV sucked him back to reality. It was Daley Dunright: Action Reporter!

"Thanks Bob. As you know—parents, educators, and law enforcement officials are scrambling to find ways to combat the rising tide of drug use among teens in the Channel Three viewing area, especially following the tragic death of a thirteen-year-old boy from Merlin this week, after he overdosed on psychedelic mushrooms. I spoke with Merlin Police Chief Maxwell Hartley and this is what he had to say:"

The scene cut to a talking-head shot of the chief. "Kids just don't understand how dangerous Psilocybin mushrooms are. Uh, they think since they're natural, and grow in our Indiana forests, that it's not as risky as meth, or cocaine. But, uh, they need to understand that 'magic' mushrooms certainly do pose a serious threat to their lives, and uh, they should be aware that shrooms are a controlled substance and illegal to possess in the state of Indiana."

Daley went on to tell the sad tale of the dead boy. Blake glanced at his uncle, who looked as grim as if he were at the funeral.

"You okay, Uncle Carson?"

Carson looked the other way. He glared at the hummingbirds dipping and zipping after each other outside the sliding glass doors.

"I just take stories like that kind of personal."

"We'll lose the afternoon breeze soon."

"Then wake up sleeping beauty there and we'll say our farewells."

***

Cezar sat by the mast, enthralled in the euphoric mystery of being a young man under sail. Blake tended the helm, looking pensive. "That kid was my age," he said.

Carson flicked the toothpick he'd been chewing over the side. "And we both know where those mushrooms are coming from."

"Two go out, only one comes back."

"That's it."

"Why don't the police…"

"Cuz it's coming out of the park. PD figures it's Buck Mueller's problem. Mueller's understaffed and overburdened. He can barely keep up with lake-traffic and the rec areas, much less launch a one-man war on drugs."

They sailed on in brooding silence for another half hour.

"Here comes the island." said Blake. "Ready to come about and strike sail." He stood up. "Lista amigo! Baja el foque por favor. Y ayuda mi tio con la vela grande."

Carson looked both amused and incredulous. "No crap? What happened to that scared little snot my sister dumped on me this past spring?"

"I heard he drowned on the shoals a few weeks ago. Come about!" He put the tiller over and brought the *Terrapin* straight into the wind. Each man saw to his duty and the canvas came rattling down. Blake gave a fierce yank and the motor sputtered to life.

All three bays were wide open in the workshop as they puttered up to the dock. Blake considered with slight suspicion the mountain of brown boxes that had sprung up in the far bay. He assumed that it was for the cabinetry work but couldn't imagine what they would need *that* much of. Sylvana and Romero met them at the dock.

The brothers conversed excitedly.

"My brother say you got a whole bunch of boxes today!" said Sylvana.

"Yeah, I caught that, thanks. "Por mi? No por su padre?"

"Si. Por Tux y Mia Urquart." said Romero.

Blake leapt out of the boat and ran to the workshop. The stack was taller than he was and twice the size of the boat he'd just abandoned. And every shipping label read as Romero had reported: Blake and Mia Urquart c/o Gunn's Marina. He jerked a box down. It smacked the floor sending a plume of sawdust up in to the slanting shafts of late afternoon sun. He thrust a hand deep into his pocket and grabbed his knife. He opened the top flaps just as Sylvio and his curious children joined him.

"What you got Tux?" said Sylvana.

Blake yanked a spongy green plastic-wrapped cube out of the carton and shoved it into Sylvana's chest.

"You tell me!" he shouted. "You tell me and you tell your dad! Or I will."

Sylvio required no explanation. The rage on Blake's face told him everything he needed to know.

"Sylvanaaaaa!" roared Sylvio.

"I don't know nothing, Poppi!" She tossed the package at her father and ran crying for Abuelita.

Sylvio fumbled the catch. The diapers bounced twice and landed at Tripper Gunn's feet. Sooner appeared from behind his heels and sniffed eagerly at the green bundle. Gunn sucked his lower lip and squinted at the new inventory.

"Must be nigh fifteen hundred cubic feet of diapers there, lad."

"Mister Gonn, I am so sorry." said Sylvio. The UPS just keep bringing more. I thought it was for you. If this is my daughter's doing, I take responsibility."

"Don' worry yourself man. Caduggin, am I to guess she's the source of this rumor I've been hearing?"

"Yup! But I'm betting Hunter's harem took it and ran with it."

"Sylvio, refuse any further deliveries addressed to Blake."

"Wait!" said Blake. "No. Take them. There are two kinds of people in this world, Mr. Gunn. People that things happen to and people who make things happen. We're going to pull a Soojee on them."

"I hope it's as painful as it sounds." said Carson.

"She's that little blue-haired girl what saved the party." said Gunn.

"Look, People spent a lot of money on this. I don't want it to be for nothing. Until we can get it stopped, we'll give it all away. Churches, homeless shelters, we'll stand in front of the Emporium and hand them out, if we have to."

"That would make a good news story." said Sylvio.

"That's even better! We expose the internet prank, prove it's a stinking rumor and help a whole lot of people to boot."

Mia pulled the *Osprey* ashore and strolled up from the waterline. "Is it Christmas in July or are you opening up a FedEx hub? Ugh! Mr. Gunn, your atrocious gargoyle is slobbering on my ankles!"

"No accounting for taste with these creatures!" Gunn said.

Blake shoved the box back up on the pile. "You're not going to like this, but…"

"Explain it to me on the water. Come on. I just heard the half hour gun. I about split a gasket bustin' it over here."

"Where do think yer going Caduggin?"

"I thought we were going to race *Sophia* in the Wednesday night Keel Haul?"

Gunn dismissed the assembly. As soon as they were out of earshot he looked at Mia and said in a low, stern tone. "Miss Devlin, I like having yeh around. I'm glad yeh two have become friends. But I'll no allow Blake nor myself to be dragged into your family's ugly politics. D'yeh understand me?"

She looked at her feet. "Yeah. I hear you."

"Do yeh?"

Mia looked him in the eye long enough to say "Yes. Mister. Gunn."

"Why don' yeh come up where it's cool. Help Caduggin unravel this mystery. Seeing as how all of this super-cargo is addressed to the both of yeh."

***

A torrent of profanity gushed out of Mia's mouth at top volume and surpassed even Griffy's wildest tirade. It coursed into every hall, flooded every room, deluged every ear in Gunn's home.

"All hands and the cook! Do yeh kiss yer mother with that mouth!" said Gunn. "I suppose yeh found what yeh were looking for?"

Blake held up the tablet. There at the top of a new Facebook page bearing his name was a very convincing photo of Blake with his arm around a very pregnant Mia.

She buried her face in her knees and hissed incoherent threats and curses. "This is so embarrassing! I'll never be able to show my face in town again!"

"I already have a plan to deal with that. Have you got Soojee's phone number?"

Mia dug into her pack and tossed Blake her phone. He turned it on and she poked the contacts icon. Blake tapped and swiped his way around until he found it. "Mr. Gunn, may I use your phone?"

"You've got mine in your hand, doofus!" said Mia.

"Sorry, I'd rather use a real phone."

Mia rolled her eyes and slumped back in the couch. Sooner landed in her lap like a snorting cannonball and snuggled down. Mia listened to Blake talking on the kitchen phone.

"Hi Soojee, it's Tux. I need your help. How'd you guess? Yeah we've been pranked on Facebook again. It's still under Tux Urquart. See it? Yeah, no kidding 'holey kamoley!' Totally. She's in the living room recovering from apoplexy. Try five hundred boxes—at least. Got any ideas? Exactly what I was thinking! Wait a minute. Let me write this down. Okay, sure. Thanks! We'll see you on Monday."

He returned to the couch. "Show me how to email." he said, "And how to look up all the churches and homeless shelters around here. And how to contact that reporter you ticked off the other night."

Chapter 36

Daley Dunright had an absolute field day. It was the story she'd been waiting for all summer. She interviewed Blake, Tripper Gunn, and Sylvio. Her cameraman covered the diaper ziggurat from every which way. She squealed in delight when UPS delivered another load. Soojee showed up and subtly insinuated herself into the crew as back-seat director. She stealthily guided Daley to exploit every story angle to Blake's advantage while throwing in plenty of free advertising for the Cabinet Works, sailing club, and Gunn's handyman business. She accomplished this with such finesse that Dunright thought it was all of *her* own devising. Soojee was carrying the reporter's clipboard and touching up her make-up by the time they got to town.

Every move was documented: from the loading of the *Terrapin's* hold, to the over-loading of the Pagán's big green pick-up, the paint on its signage glistening in the sun. She followed Blake and Cezar as they rolled through town delivering the diapers and she interviewed the recipients. She interviewed the mayor, the chief of police, and store owners. She stopped parents and kids on the street and asked them what they thought of social-media pranks and cyber-bullying.

The mobile broadcast van rolled up for live noontime coverage of the booth in front of the Emporium. Sister Elizabeth handed out bundles of diapers each with a flyer about cyber-bullying and Blake and Mia's story. Overhead a bright blue and pink banner proclaimed "Tux and Mia ~ NOT

Having a Baby! Free Diapers!" By one o'clock, the Emporium was swamped. Volunteers were hauling diapers back from Gunn's by the truckload and started two more distribution points at Nick Tyners and the Flea Market.

At Soojee's suggestion, Daley called Facebook on camera and apprised their publicity director about both the party, and the diaper prank. They took the page down immediately and posted an official apology in its place. Then she called UPS and halted the deliveries. And then she showed up on Jenny Hopkin's doorstep.

When dust from the Channel 3 news van finally settled in Tripper Gunn's parking lot, the mountain in bay three had completely disappeared.

"When will we get to see it?" said Gunn, ambling up from the *Terrapin*.

"It?" said Soojee. "*It's* going to be on all week, in ongoing installments! Cyber-bullying is Channel three's scoop of the summer. It'll run at five and ten with teasers on the morning show and noon news. There'll be updates, tweets, emails, Facebook posts, and voicemail polls! She's gonna milk this thing like a—well never mind."

"And yeh laid the groundwork for all that, before ten this morning?"

"I don't sleep much when I get an idea. Daley said she'd write me a referral for film school."

"Yeh kids keep me in continual amazement. I'd like to meet yer folks. Caduggin, yer little girl was conspicuously absent today."

"I don't know if she was more embarrassed by the rumor or our little stunt."

"Who can blame her. I'm going up and take a load off. Thanks again, Missy. See yeh Monday."

Blake and Soojee found themselves alone in the long, hazy shadows that reached across from the forest on the far shore. Blake hoped Soojee's ride wouldn't be long in coming. He had his sights set on a long hot soak.

"Will your parents be here soon?" he said.

"Yeah. You want to go up to the ridge and watch the sun set?"

Blake shifted his weight to one foot and scratched his calf with the other. "Well, we just spent all day fighting one rumor, why start another?"

"How come you don't like making out? Is it because I'm…"

"No, I…didn't say I didn't like it." He walked toward the dock. "I just think it's for people who…plan on staying together for a long time."

"Like engaged or married or something?"

"Yeah."

"My parents have been together since I was born. But they aren't married. Is that a sin?"

Blake detected a little uncertainty, perhaps worry in her voice.

"I don't know. Who married Adam and Eve?"

"I think if two people really love each other they'll just stay together," she said.

Blake watched minnows dart after gnats in the shallows. "Yeah, well I'm still trying to figure out what love is."

"I think it's really, really liking somebody and you want to be around them all the time, and do stuff with them."

Tires crunching gravel and someone trying to play *La Cucaracha* on the horn of a forlorn Toyota brought a welcome interruption to this uncomfortable moment. Blake's immediate sense of relief evaporated, along with his bath, when the motor stopped and people got out.

"Hi sweetie! Did you get your internship?" said a very short woman with very short, spiky hair, and mascara that would have fooled a raccoon.

"Was there any doubt I would? You're looking at Channel 3's new junior intern! Weekends, after school starts."

That explains a lot! thought Blake.

"I'm so proud of you, Kiki! And you're Tux? You have to be! Sweetie, you're right, he does have gorgeous waves!" She walked right up and ran her fingers across his scalp.

"Oop! You've got something in your teeth! Hold still!" To Blake's utter disgust, she delicately scooped something from between his front teeth with the long nail of one of her pinkies and flicked it away. "You look good with this length but you're getting shaggy. Let me get my snippers—don't move!"

"Uh that's alright!"

"Don't worry, Mom's a stylist. She'll fix you up!" said Soojie.

A six year old sprinted straight down the dock and assumed command of the *Terrapin* with shouts of "yo ho ho" and other piratey slang.

A man, far too tall for a Toyota unfolded from the other side of the car, plunked a baby-seat down on the hood, and lit a cigarette. The dark circles under *his* eyes didn't come from Revlon. A very little girl climbed out one window and enthroned herself on the car's roof.

"It's like *Doctor Who*," said Soojee. "Dimensionally transcendental. Bigger on the inside than on the outside."

The bay window swung open. "Is that company Caduggin? Bring 'em up. I want to meet her folks!"

Blake sighed. "You want a haircut?"

Part III

Siluriana

Chapter 37

The second session of Junior Training seemed to get off to a good start. The class topped out at twenty-six, and five of them hadn't shown up. There were as many new faces as there were repeat offenders.

"Okay," said Blake, "let's all gather around the Flying Junior under the big oak tree and Griffy will show you how to rig it up."

"We don't get pirate names, again?" said Scurvy.

There was a murmur of general assent. Griffy, who had been skulking at the margin of the class, smiled to himself.

"I thought you guys didn't like the names?"

"We didn't. We liked complaining about them!" said Rickets.

"Can we throw Griffy off the dock again?" said Natalie.

There was more agreement.

"Alright, everybody to the oak!" said Carson.

As they approached the tree, a familiar rumbling clatter echoed from the boat lot. Two bikes and two skateboarders whizzed around the corner and up to the oak. Blake couldn't believe his eyes. Orangutan, Mohawk, Tattoo, and Ring-lips glided up to the demonstration area like a flock of sinister parrots.

"What do you guys want?" growled Carson.

"Pirates oughta know how to sail; right, dude?" said Ring-lips.

Small pink patches marred Mohawk's arms and legs. Blake remembered escaping that Doberman's fangs by mere inches.

"Where'd they go?" called Gunn, huffing into view with Mia at his side. "Check the list, man. We're paid for!"

Carson scanned the roster on his clipboard. "They're on the list, Tripp."

Gunn lumbered up and got right in their faces. "I d'know what yer up to, but if there's one blessed bit of trouble from any of yeh…"

"Pipe down, ancient mariner! We're here to learn!" said Ring-lips.

Gunn glared at them hatefully then looked to the uneasy class. "Keep track of your valuables. Report any trouble immediately." He stalked away.

***

The Junior fleet was ready to shove off when one of the missing sailors was dropped off in front of the dock.

"Poop Deck!" cried Griffy. "Woohoo!"

Poop Deck trudged down the dock dragging his lifejacket behind him.

You're in the *Darby McGraw*," said Mia, pointing him to the red Lightning. He recoiled with a cry when he saw his shipmates.

"Any last words, cabin boy?" cackled Orangutan.

"Jimmy crack corn!" said Mohawk with an unsettling leer. "Blue tail fly!"

Poop Deck climbed aboard, reluctantly.

"Mia, that was cruel even by your standards," said Blake. "Hey Poop Deck—you want off that boat?"

"What do you think?" he sneered.

"The offer still stands. Learn your knots, you lose the name. Sail to the Island and back and get re-assigned."

"Dude! Like, you've done this before?" said Ring-lips.

Poop Deck folded his arms and sulked.

"Vee have vays of making you talk!" said Tattoo, in a weird falsetto, with maniac eyes and an evil smile.

The command was given to cast off and the fleet crawled away in the light morning breeze; the shepherding safety-patrol boats bringing up the rear.

By lunchtime it had become scorching hot and the wind had quit completely. The closer crews paddled back to the harbor, some swam towing their boats by the bowlines, some pushing. The farther vessels were retrieved by the small *Pontoon Queen* and towed back in a long line.

After lunch they watched a video, had an hour of book instruction, and a round of knot-tying races, after which class was dismissed to swim for the remainder of the afternoon.

Carson cornered Poop Deck by the fireplace. "They give you any trouble?"

"They're scary and weird. They kept poking and pinching me and saying creepy stuff."

"About what? Me? Blake?"

Poop Deck scowled fearfully.

"C'mon buddy, I'll make it worth your while."

"Get me off that boat."

"I kinda need you on that boat for a little while longer."

"Nooo! Please!"

"Kid, I'll make it worth your while. What'd they talk about?"

"They talked weird. The kept saying stuff about the 'victim,' and the 'prince.' All that one guy would say was 'Jimmy crack corn.'"

"Anything about Voodoo Jack?"

"Huh-uh. They said something about the 'plague.'"

Carson stroked his mustache. "I'll have you off that boat by Wednesday. Keep your ears open."

Carson headed for the locker room. Poop Deck went out onto the patio.

Orangutan appeared behind him. "Hey Bloat! Snitches get stitches!" he said, in a sing-song way.

"And wind up in ditches!" continued Tattoo, who leapt up to the railing from the ground below.

Poop Deck hurried for the steps at the far end of the patio, leaving the snickering villains in his wake.

Chapter 38

The next day, the breeze came back and a morning of spirited sailing was enjoyed by all. All except Poop Deck. He pleaded with his mother for fifteen minutes in the car and another five with Blake.

"Look, there are two kinds of people, Vikings and victims," said Blake.

"And dumb-asses, that's what my Papaw says!" added Natalie, happy to be at his side.

"Some by birth, some by choice!" said Carson, as he passed by.

"Be a Viking! Make your mom proud!"

"You're not listening to me!" Poop Deck yelled. "Nobody is listening to me!" He stomped his foot.

Then Gunn tramped onto the dock, jaw set, eyes ablaze. Poop Deck boarded the *Darby McGraw*, took the tiller and headed straight for Trespass Island.

"Caduggin, may I have a word?" said Gunn. "Get aboard yer boat Missy."

Gunn watched Natalie slide into a boat with three other girls.

"That lass, she's no on the roster."

"I noticed that."

"Nor on last session's."

"She lives with her grandfather. The way she talks, they don't have enough money to pay their bills."

Gunn pursed his lips and thought for a moment. "Then it'll be our secret."

Ring-lips and Mohawk hiked and whooped; Orangutan stood on deck, hanging out from the side-stays, while Tattoo rode on the low side by the rushing water, and smoked a foul-smelling cigarillo. Poop Deck was giving the Freaks the ride of their lives and they loved every minute of it.

"This is a trip!" said Ring-lips. "We'll do some trippin' when the master comes back!"

The lunatics hooted.

He tacked hard around the shallow-water buoy, dumping Mohawk off the leeward rail. Poop Deck raced away on a broad reach. He tore straight for a safety patrol boat that puttered near the mouth of the harbor.

Blake smiled in disbelief. "Mia, look at this!"

She stood up and saw the *Darby McGraw* bearing down on them. She grasped the throttle and prepared to throw the wheel over.

The *Darby* swept past their transom and rounded into the wind alongside the patrol boat. Poop Deck boarded them before there was time to protest. He grabbed the bowline and tied it in a knot.

"Figure eight!" He undid it and tied another. "Bowline!" Then he made two overlapping loops and jerked them tight around Blake's forearm. "Clove Hitch! He tied the slack to a fitting on the rail. "Cleat Hitch!" I'm off that boat and my name is Clarence Cornelius Baxter!" he blubbered over the violent rattling of *Darby's* luffing sails.

"I think I'd stick with Poop Deck," said Mia.

Blake grabbed the boathook and gave the Lightning's bow a hard shove. Her sails filled with a thump, she heeled over and began to make way.

"There's a five hundred dollar reward for anyone who turns in Voodoo Jack!" shouted Blake. "And I'll add five hundred to it!"

"Beware the appointed season, little prince!" said Ring-lips. "Hey baby, you're not pregnant?"

Mia grimaced, jammed the throttle forward and spun the wheel. Blake grabbed the chrome safety rail with one hand and seized Poop Deck by the life jacket with the other. The Boston Whaler pitched over on its side and whipped through a tight circle. The savage wake Mia hurled at the pirates rolled over *Darby McGraw*'s afterdeck and swamped her cockpit.

Blake cupped his hands to his mouth and shouted "Grab your tiller, Davy Jones! Open your bailers and fall off on a reach before you broach!"

"Give our Pooper back!" wailed Orangutan.

Poop Deck got his legs under him and shouted "My name is Baxter!"

Chapter 39

Tuesday rolled into Wednesday. Everyone had mastered their boat handling and knot tying well enough. Carson slipped Baxter a twenty-dollar bill and let him stay in the clubhouse as a reward for his service. After a couple of wild jibes and a capsize, Ring-lips and Tattoo gradually emerged as skipper and first mate of their motley crew and began to enforce some semblance of order and seamanship. They were the last ones into the harbor at the end of the afternoon. Blake and Mia chugged along behind them.

Tattoo stood up, his lurid ink sleeves glowing under the blazing sun. "When do we learn to sail real boats?" He pointed to a small cabin cruiser. "Like that one?"

"Sailing is sailing," said Blake. "If you can sail a Pram, you can sail a cruiser. Why?"

"Pirate's gotta have a boat, don't he!" Tattoo grinned, like the Jolly Roger. The crew snickered in low tones and exchanged knowing glances.

***

Carson and Blake sat aboard the *Terrapin* waiting for Gunn. Mia floated languidly in her Kayak just to Starboard.

"They're up to something. They got plans for somebody," said Carson.

"Well duh!" said Mia. "They were asking about keelboats this afternoon."

"A specific Keelboat. That O'Day Mariner," said Blake.

Carson squinted in the direction of the floating docks "That's actually a center-boarder. You can get in fairly shallow with that boat. Same with *Darby McGraw*."

"Two go out," said Mia.

"One comes back," answered the guys, in unison.

"I'll poke around the marina on my way home. See what I can find," said Mia.

"Much obliged, Miss Devlin," said Carson.

She took up her paddle and slipped away.

"You seem to get along with her pretty well."

Blake pretended not to watch her go. "No es mi novia."

***

Blake made his way through the maze of saw horses and lumber racks to Bay 3, where Carson rummaged through the paint locker.

"You gonna to help me paint Garvey's old boat, tonight?" said Carson, matter-of-factly.

"The *Covenant*? You mean *my* boat?"

"*Your* boat?"

"Yeah, my boat! I burned, sank *and* took her as a prize! Mr. Gunn says she's mine by right of conquest!"

"Fine. You gonna help me paint *your* boat, tonight?"

"Green, black, and brown? Ick!"

"It's a camo-pattern. Now get the tractor and drag her in here!"

They sanded the hull and by ten o'clock they had painted it, forgoing the use of primer. The fumes could have knocked out an elephant.

"I suppose you're going to change her name, too?" said Blake, through his respirator.

Carson looked away.

"Is it a secret?"

"*Becky Lynn*." Carson seemed to focus harder on his strokes, as if painting out some ugly spot in his memory.

"Girlfriend?"

"Just the girl next door."

Blake was beginning to catch the slightest taste of the acrid fumes. He noticed that his uncle had stopped painting and stared blankly at the ink-blot-crazy pattern on the boat's side.

"I think my filter is shot. I'm going outside," said Blake.

Carson went back to painting.

Blake left his respirator by the door and decided to go in the house. Gunn and Sooner were watching the latest installment of Channel 3's cyber-bullying exclusive.

"Yeh sure gave'm something to talk aboot!"

"You know he's painting my boat?" said Blake, arms akimbo.

"Is he now? Which one?"

"The *Covenant*, of course. Renamed her, too."

"Did he, now?"

"*Becky Lynn.*"

"Hmm." Gunn looked like he knew something. "Got a nice ring to it."

"He's acting *weird*."

"Must have something on his mind. Try not to piss him off."

Chapter 40

Thursday morning, *Cry of the Osprey* met the *Terrapin* as they reached the mouth of the harbor. Mia tossed Blake her bowline for a free tow.

"What news, little sister?" said Carson.

"There's a ratty—and I mean ratty—O'Day Mariner in slip ninety-nine. Might be the one you're looking for."

"'Captain Ring-lips' *and* Kalijah both said something about the 'appointed season.'" said Blake.

Carson pondered for a minute. "Full moon's tomorrow night. Give me your phone, Miss D." He pulled her up close enough to grab the black slab of glass and plastic. "Uh, how do I use this?"

Blake punched it on. "Who do you want to call?"

"Dockmaster at Devlin's Marina."

"It's in the directory, Tux," she said.

Blake handed it to Carson. "Here, it's ringing."

"Dockmaster? Yeah! Say, I need a favor. I got an old hulk in berth ninety-nine over there and I forgot how far I paid up. Much obliged. November third? Great! Listen, just so I can keep my books straight, who's name's on that? Well there ya go. I thought so. Thanks a lot!"

Blake hung up for him.

"Well?" said Mia.

"Guess."

"Edna Montaine?" she said.

"You got it! Mount Edna! Blake, you still got those walkie talkies? Charge 'em up tonight."

Chapter 41

Carson stood on the point and surveyed the hazy lake, with a suspicious eye. Flat water stretched into the distance like a dull mirage. He swabbed his brow. A single redwing blackbird complained of his intrusion from a parched sapling nearby. Cicadas chattered endlessly in angry crescendos.

"Friday at last, Friday at last, Friday at last," he mumbled.

Dry grass crunching under foot announced a visitor.

"What's the verdict?" said Blake.

"Swimming Party. Water balloons and greased melon. Don't even pull the covers off the boats."

Blake made his way across the limestone riprap to the slimy waterline. A crust of brown algae crumbled off the rocks with each step sending countless, tiny, brown spiders skittering into crevices. "I can't believe how far the lake's down."

"Seen it worse. Back in the eighties, half the harbor dried up. Made a lot of money pulling shorebirds and tourists off shoals, that summer!"

"What's the plan for tonight?"

"Surveillance. You and the girl'll be advanced recon. Radio me when they leave the dock so I can get down the lake ahead of 'em. That little putt-putt I hung on the back won't keep up."

"They'd hear that, anyway."

"That's why I mounted an electric troller on the front. Get down there in a hurry, then switch to stealth mode. It'll be a late night. I'll get some shut-eye this evening while you two keep watch."

"You're not going down the branch are you?"

"Depends on where they go. Here's Miss D!" *Cry of the Osprey* sliced across the glassy blue mirror. "Did you bring it?" he called.

"I don't go anywhere without it!"

***

Blake announced the afternoon activities and, to everyone's relief, the Freaks asked for their tee-shirts and departed for cooler circumstances. In spite of the heat a good time was had by all. Even Baxter's mood seemed lightened by the departure of his warped shipmates and the shedding of his shameful moniker. He took every opportunity to crow about the mortal perils he braved aboard the *Darby McGraw*. Gunn dismissed the class without handing Natalie her shirt.

"Little girl?" he said, as the class departed for their waiting rides.

"Here's yer shirt. And this, too." He handed her a small packet wrapped in silver gift paper.

"That's for yer Papaw. Yeh see that he get's it. And no a word where it came from, d'yeh hear?"

She smiled and waved at him, then trotted off toward the gate. "That was gracious of yeh, Caduggin."

Blake looked to Mia, who fanned herself with the clipboard. "What do you want to do for the rest of the afternoon?"

"Anything but roast."

***

There was still an hour of daylight left as Mia and Blake paddled up the channel. He squinted toward Drascombe Heights. "What do you have in mind for a lookout? I was thinking the fire tower."

"Use your head. Too far from the *Osprey*. We'd be bumbling in the woods after dark."

"Oh, yeah. Duh."

"There's a restaurant that overlooks Daddy's docks. We'll have dinner on the balcony."

They crossed the upper lake and tied up in the cove that served as the eatery's water-borne parking lot. Mia cast a surly glance at the marina's bright blue buildings and headed up the stairs.

"Marco De Bistro?" said Blake, studying the signage. The 'o's' and the 'e' all had seriphs that made them look like three surreptitious sixes. "What's wrong with people."

"What? I grew up eating at this place."

They found the perfect vantage at the corner of the deck. Slip 99 was clearly visible at the end of a two hundred foot dock.

"She's still there" said Blake, focusing his binoculars.

No sooner had the waitress been by with water and menus than someone else greeted them.

"There's the man to watch, right there!"

The mayor and Brigita meandered to their table. Mia's gut cramped.

"This is the young man who's been grabbing all the headlines around town! Gita, this is Blake Barber and this is..."

"Oh Teddy, who doesn't know Mia Laurentia Devlin! She is an aspiring chess player."

"Backgammon" said Mia.

"Yes, a daring gambler!"

"Well come on inside, let me buy you both dinner!" said the mayor, grandly.

"Now, Teddy, they are having a romantic adventure. Look, the boy has field glasses."

"C'mon, how often does the mayor buy you dinner? I insist! Resistance is futile?"

Blake cast a final glance back at the dock. "Well, no sense arguing."

The waitress seated them in the middle of the dining room. In spite of the intrusion, Blake liked the mayor. Tall, silver haired, immaculately shaven, and imminently friendly, he reminded him of the principal at Agatha's school.

"Gita, this is what I've been talking about. This young fellow. When life handed him lemons, not only did he make lemonade but he shared a glass with everyone! That's visionary. That's leadership. That's what this country needs. That's what this town needs! And that's why he won the…"

"Teddy! Don't give it away!"

"Oh, did I let it out of the bag! Sorry, sometimes I forget I'm not on TV!"

Blake smiled sheepishly.

"Well, you might as well know," said the mayor. "Freeman maintains a college scholarship fund. Once in a while a kid comes along and does something outstanding. The town council shows their appreciation with a scholarship."

"Wow!" said Blake.

"No kidding, 'wow!'" said the mayor. "Congratulations! You got yourself a five-thousand dollar head-start on your college career!" He reached across the table and shook Blake's hand.

"Thank you! I'm speechless."

"Teddy, do universities accept home schooled children?"

"How did you know I'm home schooled?"

"I know all sorts of things!" she said, shooting Mia a look. "So you will be in the news, yet again."

"I don't know if you realize it, Blake, but you've brought a lot of positive attention to our town and good publicity for the lake."

"Yes, what is Independence Day without a riot?" said Brigita.

"Gita, it wasn't a riot. And *they* were chasing *him*."

"I'm teasing, you! Don't be so sensitive. "Still," she said, coy in her angelic beauty, "you must protect your image because now you are the face of our little town. Be careful of the company you keep."

Mia smiled disingenuously and wrapped her feet around the legs of her chair to keep from kicking Brigita's kneecaps off.

"It was your brother, wasn't it? Hunter Lawrence?" said Brigita.

"I wasn't there," said Mia.

"Blake, have you ever heard of the DeMolay Club?" interrupted the mayor.

"Uh, no."

"It's a service club. It's the junior chapter of the Masonic lodge. I think you'd be a model candidate. I'd be proud to sponsor you."

Blake noticed the black and gold ring sparkling on the mayor's hand. "Oh, the Freemasons! Ah, well, I'd have to talk to my parents about that."

The waitress brought drinks and a plate full of stuffed mushroom caps.

"Say, how's your dad doing, Mia? Been forever since I've been in the ol' boat shop."

"Just the same old workaholic. But he still finds time for the women in his life."

"Teddy, you should see his son, Hunter Lawrence. Gorgeously athletic. So handsome."

"He takes after Dad. I'm more like my mother: loyal, stable."

"Been a long time since I've seen Priscilla. Beautiful gal, your mom."

"Teddy! You know how I feel when you talk about other women!" whined Brigita.

"Variety's the spice of life," said Mia. "That's what Daddy says. And a picture's worth a thousand words. Whatever *that* means."

Brigita's peachy cheeks flushed rosy red. "That awful vagrant the boy apprehended, what became of him, Teddy?"

"They've got him locked up in a psychiatric hospital, for the time being. Novo Synaptix, or someplace."

She locked her eyes on Mia and smiled sarcastically. "How unfortunate!"

"Say, let me excuse myself before the main course arrives," said the mayor, rising from his seat. Once he was gone it was all fangs and claws.

"How charming. Dinner with the black queen and her little knight. Or should I say blackmailing queen?"

"Don't know what you're talking about," said Mia. "I made you an offer. You opted out. Just wanted to show my appreciation, so I sent you a *candid* photo that I took in a *very* public place. Anyone could have taken that picture."

"You were spying, you dirty little blackmailer!" she hissed. I fired my entire housekeeping staff, today. Did you know *that*? Lawrence has done the same. Your little offer has cost the jobs of twenty people."

Mia shrugged. "So what?" she said, coldly. "They were a security risk anyway, right?"

Brigita smiled. "Maybe I should be a little impressed with you." She looked at Blake. "The little knight—always dodging and jumping. I wonder what you will do when I have captured your queen."

"Leave him out of it."

"Guilt by association. Now, you wait and see what I have in store for you, *Laurentia*."

"Bring it on, *Dragana*!"

"Hey, you'll never guess what I just saw!" said the mayor, returning to his seat. "This shabby keelboat with a four hundred pound lady in the cockpit! Just leaving the dock."

"Um, You'll have to excuse me!" said Blake. "I have to make a call."

Blake hurried outside to the railing and focused his binoculars. He pulled the walkie talkie off his belt.

"Castaway to Uncle Arctica! Uncle Arctica, come in!"

"Uuuncle Arctica, go ahead: over!"

"The sea-cow jumped over the moon. Repeat the sea cow jumped over the moon! Circus is loaded and under motor. Five minutes from the straits. Five minutes from the straits!"

"Copy that, Castaway! Who's aboard?"

"The fat lady of Nirvana, four freaks and…a crate of live chickens?"

"Roger that, Castaway. En route presently. Uncle Arctica out!

***

Cry of the Osprey drifted under the ascending moon.

"I hope your Uncle knows what he's doing." said Mia.

"I hope you know what *you're* doing,"

"What's that supposed to mean?"

"Blackmailing the mayor's wife? With that picture?"

"I did not. I did exactly what I said."

"It's still extortion by any other name," Blake protested.

"It got your butt off the hook and all your friends, too. Man, is that the thanks I get?"

"But what's the cost? That woman is scary. You can see it in her eyes."

"She's just a trophy slut. You overestimate her."

"She's from the Balkans—you don't mess with those people!"

"What *ever*. Your uncle better not lose my night-scope *or* my flash."

"I have the feeling if that's all he loses, he'll be lucky."

Chapter 42

Blake turned under the sheet for the umpteenth time, sure that he had pushed the unlimited refills beyond reason. He shuffled to Carson's room. The silhouette of the dresser was like a low, black tombstone at the end of his empty bed. The digital clock on the nightstand read 3:07. He visited the bathroom and went to the bay window, again.

Near the ramp a long, dark shape lay like a coffin beneath three feet of murky water. The White Hound loped nervously down the dock and disappeared into the *Terrapin*. The refrigerator door creaked.

"Uncle Carson?" Blake rushed to the kitchen. "Uncle Carson?"

"Go back to bed, kid."

Carson stared vacantly into the soft yellow glow of the open fridge, brown bottle in his hand. His breath came in slow, deep swells through his nose. He swayed slightly. He was drenched.

"What are you looking for?"

"Bottle opener."

Blake pulled the magnetized opener off the fridge and handed it to him. He didn't take it.

"You're bleeding!"

"Just a scratch. Go back to bed."

"Just a scratch? There's blood on the *floor*!"

"Shhh! Don't you know by now the old man's a light sleeper?"

"No. I don't go out late at night."

"Just as well. Go check all the doors. Store, shop—all three bays. Lock 'em. Windows too."

Blake gently urged him to the kitchen table. "You need to sit down. You're in shock!"

"You would be, too. I've been around this world twice on a Navy destroyer. I ain't never seen anything like as that."

Blake opened the bottle. Carson took a swig and clunked it down on the table. "Must've been a hundred-fifty of 'em. Stompin' and thrashin' to the drums out on that mud-flat in that flickering firelight, like one writhing mass of naked evil. And I mean naked! They carried the fat woman out in a sedan chair. All decked out in red robes and miter—like the Pope on payday."

Blake turned on the light over the sink and fetched a pair of scissors. Carson took a long drink. Blake pulled the collar of his uncle's tee shirt out and cut straight down the back.

"Then she starts 'em all chanting the name of their god—Bacon! Bacon!"

"Uh, that would be Dagon, actually."

"The water started roilin'n about ten feet out from that stupid catfish statue. Then out comes Jack, all painted white, wearin' his fish-head and cape. And he throws a live chicken out there in the water. Big splash and it's gone. And another, and another. Four *whole* chickens. Nothin' left but feathers on the water."

Blake swallowed hard and gingerly peeled the shirt away from Carson's skin. A shallow, crimson furrow stretched across his chest.

"You've been shot!"

"Shot at. Boat's been shot."

Blake set another beer in front of his uncle and disappeared down the stairs. He returned with the first aid kit.

"Keep talking." He put on gloves, opened a bottle of sterile water and a packet of gauze.

"I was hard against that mud-bar you told me about when I hear whining, and here comes the White Hound out of the underbrush. Jumps right in the boat and starts growlin' at the lake. Next thing, I got a spot light in the face and the dog's barkin' like mad. So I lit off your girl's flash at the guy and went over the side. Bullets started flyin'. I went under his boat and rolled him out. We were strugglin' in four feet of water and I noticed *Becky Lynn* sailin' away. Stupid dog was standin' on the trolling pedal."

Carson winced as Blake patted the wound.

"Well, I hear the drums stop and Jack yells 'infidel,' and then lot of screamin' and people crashin' through the woods to get to us. I dragged the guy under 'til he let go. Swam along the bottom as far as I could and when I came up I was smack in the middle of Satan's swim team. Screamin' and flailin' away in the moonlight; insane devil-dolphins all tryin' to catch *Becky Lynn*."

"They didn't notice you?"

"I was just another body in the water. They all petered out pretty quick. I like to never got the dog off that switch, though. Must've swam a mile. Old man's gonna be pissed."

Blake padded the wound with gauze and wrapped his torso with an ace bandage.

"We gotta get serious about our faith kid. Cuz' those people sure as hell are."

The kitchen light came on. Gunn stood by the breakfast bar, in his robe. He surveyed the gory scene. "Did yeh come back here just to compete with the lad?"

***

"Don't tell me it was some flathead, Buck! It sucked down four whole chickens! No, it wasn't *three or four* flatheads. It was one big fish." Carson protested into the phone. "I saw it with my own eyes!" He sat on the old tractor, the big back-wheels up to the axles in the water. Blake and the Pagán boys manhandled *Becky Lynn* off the bottom and onto her submerged trailer. Sylvio and his uncle supervised from the dock.

"I thought you pulled Lucky out of there? Oh, don't give me that manpower malarkey. Look, at least one wanted man was there, drugs were there, stolen property was there, where were you?"

"Tell 'em you got shot!" said Blake.

Carson covered the phone with his hand. "Shut up! We don't want that getting out! You want 'em to know it was us?"

"Take care yeh haul her out a little at a time," Gunn shouted down from the bay window. "Or yeh'll blow the tires out!"

"Horsecrap Buck! What happens in Mangrave *doesn't* stay in Mangrave! That's the problem!"

"We're ready!" said Blake as he cranked the last tie-down taut.

"Thanks for nothing Officer Mueller. Have a donut for me!" Carson fired up the tractor and jammed it into gear. The *Becky Lynn* came sloshing up from her watery grave like a kraken on wheels. Ten feet up the ramp, the tires went 'boof!'

Gunn set his jaw and shook his head. "This is why we can no have nice things, yeh know!"

The boys stood and watched water stream out of holes in the boat's side and bottom. Blake hardly needed to pull the drain-plug out.

"Is okay, Mr. Gonn!" said Sylvio. "They reseal just fine! Romero, la bomba!" His eldest son jogged to the shop and returned towing the portable air-compressor.

"I assume you lost Mia's flash and night-scope?" said Blake.

"I did not! The scope's still in the boat!"

"I'll let you tell her. We still visiting Korbin this morning?"

"I got some errands to run."

"On Sabbath?" said Blake.

"Is it really Saturday?"

"He said he wanted to see you before he moves on."

"I'll get by there today."

"I think he meant before he dies."

"I said I'd go, now just get off me."

"I'll gas up the *Terrapin*."

The air hose hissed. As soon as the tires plumped up, the tractor grunted to life and Carson rumbled off to bay three, the bullet-riddled boat irrigating the pavement the whole way.

***

Korbin opened his eyes and croaked weakly from the back of his throat. His lips didn't move.

"Young Uh-quot! Where's Caw?"

"He promised he'd be by later."

"Then sit down here, next to me. Give me some encouraging word."

Blake sat down in the wheelchair and rolled over to him.

"That little girl you brought in here, she said her folks don't care about her."

"I'm afraid it's true."

"You read her the twenty-seventh Psalm. Take that Bible there."

Blake cast about and spied a large book on the dresser.

"Now, open those curtains a little. Let a ray of hope in here."

Blake returned with the Bible. He thumbed through the pages.

"You never saw a Bible like *that*," said Dubois. "They took the great name of the Almighty out of there. Put LORD in its place. Shouldn' orta done it. Scripture says there's a heavy price to pay for that."

"And you've gone through and put it back in. That's a lot of correction-fluid!"

"Nigh on seven thousand time! And I put the name of the Son, there too."

Blake flipped forward to the Gospels. "Yeshua?"

"That's his name. Short for Yahoshua. Yahweh's Salvation, that's what it means. Angel told Mary, you call his name Yeshua, 'cause he'll save his people from their sins. Take that book with you, young Uh-quot. I don't need it no more."

"But I…"

"Promise me something! You promise? Don't let 'em burn me," said Dubois.

"I'm sorry, what?"

"Promise me you won't let 'em put me in an oven and burn me up like trash. You make'm put me in the ground like a Christian man."

"What can…"

"You promise me young Uh-quot! I already been in one burning box, that's one too many."

"I think I can get you a nice casket, but I don't know about the rest."

"You go talk to ol' Miss Clydesdale. You tell her you're gonna be my Power of Attorney."

"I'm not old enough. I'm just thirteen."

"Then you gonna have to get Caw. Or they'll burn me up for sure. Promise me you'll get Caw."

"I'm here!" Carson leaned against the door frame. "Go get the paperwork like he told you, kid. We got some business to take care of. Here I am, Korbin."

"I want Sylvio to build him a casket. I'll pay for it."

"Fine, now go on."

Blake headed up the hall.

"Hey wait a second, kid! Her name's Miss Blucher."

***

A few teenagers loitered in front of Haraguchi's Karate Dojo, waiting for rides. Haraguchi spotted Blake through the window of his little office and motioned him inside. The sensei met him in the practice studio.

"Hey, Diapah Man! Come to see *Thee* Haraguchi, huh?" he laughed through the glass. "We like supah heroes!" Blake went in feeling a little more empathy for Mia's constant irritation with the man.

He came out and shook Blake's hand.

"Is Mia…"

"Mia not here! Play hookey, two weeks! Run around causing trouble with her boyfriend, all time! Too busy for Karate. How's old man Gunn?"

"At the flea market this morning. I better get to the Emporium. She's probably there, already."

"You got question for me."

"Nooo?"

"Sure you do. You got lots questions. *Thee* Haraguchi answer all questions, then kick *everybody* ass!"

Blake started to give voice to his query, but stopped short. "Nah, it's a stupid one."

"No such thing as stupid question," Haraguchi said, putting his hand on Blake's shoulder with paternal sincerity.

"Remember when you said some people never change, but we should still try to love them?"

Haraguchi grunted affirmatively and nodded.

"You never actually told me what love is."

"You want me tell you what love is?"

"Yes."

Haraguchi's face warped into the lunatic grin of a kabuki mask. He popped Blake hard on the back of the head with the flat of his hand. "Stupid question! How come you ask such stupid question! You see that wall?" Haraguchi clutched the top of Blake's head and turned it sharply. "That concrete block! Person *you* love on other side of wall. You go bang your head on wall 'til you on the other side too!" He bobbed Blake's head back and forth as if to illustrate via whiplash. "That what love is. Sometime you get through, sometime you don't. But it always give you big headache!" He thoroughly mussed Blake's hair. "Now ask me smart question!" Haraguchi laughed.

"I think that's all the ancient wisdom I can handle for one day."

"Tell old man I say hello! You go home, think of smart question!"

***

Carson found them in the pinball room at the Emporium.

"Hey wolf-man, how'd the gadgets work out for ya?"

"Blake didn't tell you?"

Mia let go of the pinball machine and put her fists on her hips. Blake took her place on the flipper buttons. "You lost my gear?"

"No! I didn't... *lose* it... exactly. It went down with the ship."

"That was like—a three-thousand dollar scope, buddy! It was my dad's!" She looked at Blake. "See, Honey, this is why we can't have nice things." Blake repressed a smile and kept his eyes on the game.

Carson sighed impatiently and rolled his eyes. "I hope we can make some kind of payment arrangements?"

"Tell me you still have it? Please tell me."

"I've still got it."

"Got lens cleaning stuff?" She grinned mischievously.

"What for?"

"The scope's waterproof. But the flash *ain't*."

"*That*, I lost."

"Saved his life though. Show her your wound!" said Blake.

"I said to shut your pie-hole about that!" Carson glanced back warily into the dining room. "There's Buck. I got a little more to say to him. You comin' home with us?"

"Nah. We're going up to the hollow," said Mia.

"Then I'll take this back for you." He held up Korbin's Bible.

"I can't take his Bible!" Blake said.

"You got no choice. You guys take plenty of water. Dang hot out there. Don't know why they didn't cancel training this week." Carson departed.

"What wound? What the heck happened? This is crazy!"

"Crazy doesn't even come close. I'll tell you when we're alone."

"Then let me finish my game, so we can get out of here!" She shoved him aside but he wouldn't let go of the machine. He shoved back. It turned into a giggling, grudge-match until finally the old pinball machine threw in the towel with a flashing 'Tilt." warning.

Mia slugged him in the shoulder. "You owe me a quarter!"

"Add it to my tab."

***

Mia's voice bounced off the stone walls of the hollow. "Holy ka-moley! That's not crazy, that's Satanic!"

"And this from the girl who's never read the Bible," said Blake.

"Look at this, I've got goose-bumps! And they shot him?"

"Grazed him right across here. I patched him up."

"To think we taught those mutants to sail!" She threw a pebble, with an angry flick of the wrist. "That's all we need on top of everything else: A freak-death catfish cult."

"Officer Mueller isn't in any hurry to do anything about it either."

"Hah! No doubt!"

"We ought to figure out a way to pit Brigita and Hunter, Edna and the Freaks, and your dad all against each other."

"They're probably all in cahoots, somehow. I think I *will* let Gunn take me home, from now on."

"Uncle Carson's really fired up about it. I'm worried he's going to do something stupid."

"Oh! That's all we need! And then there's Junior."

"Why? He's been kinda nice to me lately."

"In case you hadn't noticed, Junior's like a roller coaster, Tux. He goes up, up, up; levels off for a while, then wham! Takes the plunge, bottoms out, does a few loops, then up he goes again."

"You know, I think my uncle may be the same way."

"Hunter thinks he's the king of audacity and that's *all* he respects. You've dared to out-do him at every turn. That's sheer audacity in his eyes. Keep it up and he'll start thinking of you as an equal."

"That doesn't sound so bad."

"No, you don't get it. He'll keep upping the ante. It's the thrill of the hunt—it's the one thing that really floats his boat. It's all big fun to him."

"Ohhh," Blake said with sinking comprehension. "Would you be offended if I used a four-letter word?"

Part IV

Terror Novia

Chapter 43

The third session of Junior Training was sparsely attended. Soojee had politely resigned, Deadhorse quit. Gunn decided early on that the class was small enough to not warrant his presence and went home to the air-conditioning. Griffy was missing in action, along with the wind. The heat, however, had shown up with a vengeance. That left the eight unenthusiastic enrollees in the care of Blake, Mia and Carson.

Carson's eye was on the channel, as much as his drifting wards. He had come over on *Becky Lynn*. The day passed without sight of his quarry and ended with the labored packing of boats, and watching the class swim in the listless, green harbor.

Mia and Blake stood by the safety-boat shed, waiting for the water from a spigot to run cold.

"Who's this?" said Blake, as a dowdy dumpling of a white woman with a clownish ginger-colored afro and round glasses approached.

Mia sagged. "Got anymore four-letter words?" she said.

"Well hello Mia Devlin. How are you?"

"Hello Mrs. Suckwind," Mia said, sourly.

"Seguin! Mr. Higgins sent me over to make sure you remember that the first day of school is August tenth." She handed Mia a clipboard.

"What's this? I didn't order any cookies."

"You're to sign that. It's an attendance promise stating that you agree to a semester of early detention to make up for all of the days you missed last year. There's a pen…"

Mia flung the clipboard over her shoulder and waited for the splash. She went back to dousing her face in the cold spray.

Seguin swelled up like a toad. "You're on staff, here, aren't you? Do you have a work permit?"

"Talk to my dad. He's the Commodore. He's responsible for all that crap."

"And do *you* have a work permit?" she said, squinting at Blake, presumptuously.

"Leave him out of it. He's not from around here."

"We'll see what the Labor Board has to say about that."

"Ma'am, wi' all due respect," said Blake, putting on the Scotsman, "Are ye a member o' this club?"

"No, young man, I am not. I am a social worker from…"

"Then will ye no haul yer carcass off the property, before we call the authorities!"

Mia coughed water and clamped her hand over her mouth.

"How dare you!" fumed Seguin.

"Show yer membership card or we call security!" He produced his walkie-talkie and turned it on. It responded with an official-sounding "bee-plonk," and hissed expectantly.

"August tenth, little Miss Devlin. Six A.M." Seguin waddled away.

Mia burst out laughing.

"Wha? Been a hot day. I'm no in the mood for it."

***

Carson spent the night on the point, scope in hand, *Becky Lynn* waiting nearby.

Chapter 44

Tuesday morning brought enough breeze to waft the surly octet of fourth graders around a triad of small spherical buoys. The sky had taken on that shade of slate gray that warned of something severe but brought nothing but heat-lightning in the night hours.

Carson left the flotilla and chugged up the channel far enough to spy Devlin's Marina. He peered through Blake's field glasses. Slip 99 was still occupied. The upper lake leapt and churned with ski-boats and Skidoo's throwing hundred-foot rooster-tails of spray behind them.

Mia and Blake puttered near the point in Safety 2, calling out instructions and tossing bottles of cold water to the juniors.

"Hey you, in the motor boat!" shouted a man, his voice so full of stern authority that everyone flinched. A police officer stood like a drill instructor on the point: jack boots, campaign hat, mirrored sunglasses and all.

"You know there are laws against stalking?" He shouted, angrily. No one knew exactly who he was talking to. Blake was certain he wasn't going to talk back this time. "You better be careful about who you follow around and where you point that camera!" He stabbed a finger in their general direction.

Mia went back to steering, clearly intimidated. "I am speaking to you! You had better get your hands off that wheel unless you have a valid Indiana Drivers license!"

She slapped her hand on her back pocket suggestively, then whipped out her license and waved it in the air.

"I can't see that!"

"Then come get it, Officer Duncan! I'm sorry, is this your jurisdiction?" She turned the transom to him and motored away. When they looked back, he was gone.

"That was the scariest guy I've ever seen," said Blake.

"Officer Duncan Donald Utz. Think's he'll be the next Chief."

"Who's going to show up tomorrow?"

"Hey Dakota! Jibe the boom and get around that mark, you're holding everybody up! I'm sorry, what were you saying? Ping's for dinner, billiards and a show? I'd love to."

When the *Terrapin* arrived in Gunn's harbor, the Pagáns had the grill going and that banged-up Toyota was in the lot. Romero and Cezar carried plates of meat and corn on the cob into the house. Soojee's dad strode down the dock like a walking bean pole with a cigarette. His two youngest chased each other along the gunky waterline.

Mia killed the motor. "This is not what I had in mind."

"Well," said Blake, "like my uncle always says…"

Chapter 45

Mia lurked in the women's room until it was time to hit the water and then took Safety 2 and towed the little fleet well away from the shore—where Buck Mueller found her. *Moby* came along side casually, Buck putting a couple of fenders over and taking hold of Safety 2's chrome handrail.

"What?" said Mia, with a look of exasperated contempt.

"Just a friendly reminder to you two. Indiana has a curfew law for kids your age."

"Are you kidding me?" she sneered.

"One A.M. on weekends for you. Eleven P.M. every night for you Mr. Urquart. 'Til five in the morning."

"Who sent you?" said Mia.

"I'm just doing my job, keeping the lake safe," he said, without an ounce of sincerity.

"Safe from who? Me? Why don't you stop my brother on one of his jail-bait cruises? Or those lunatic shroom-head devil-worshippers down lake? Does Indiana's curfew apply to them?"

"Eleven to five, weekdays. One to five, weekends. Blake eleven o'clock seven days a week."

Mia said something so profane that Blake blushed and felt the urge to apologize.

"Always a pleasure to serve the public, Ma'am," Mueller said as he pushed the boats apart and hummed away.

***

Blake found *Becky Lynn* in the shallows at the foot of Gunn's ridge. Fishing poles stuck out of the stern like the antennae of some giant insect. Fist-sized red and white bobbers lolled a few feet away. In the distance, the ospreys circled above the rippling reflection of Trespass Island. Carson was nowhere to be seen.

Blake waded out and boarded her. Something smelled like vinegar. An overstuffed, canvas rucksack lay against the middle bench. He lifted the flap.

"Just leave that be!" called Carson, as he skidded down the steep face of the ridge.

"What is all this stuff? What are you going to do?"

Carson reached over the side and slapped the flap shut. "Just never mind."

"You're taking my boat, I think...'

"I think we just got things patched up. Let's not ruin it."

"You could have at least asked if you could borrow my boat."

"Can I take your boat, kid?"

Blake hopped out. "Fewer holes. More freeboard."

Carson smiled. "Deal. If I'm not back in three days, you sic Mueller on the Freaks."

***

The muted pink horizon faded to black. Carson settled across the middle bench of the *Becky Lynn*. He didn't have to wait long. The wind picked up slightly. Far off in the channel he could make out a white shape under the starless sky. The scope confirmed it. They were on their way. The newer, slightly larger motor came to life with a harrumph and sped the sixteen foot sharpie around Highland Point, and down the lake.

Chapter 46

"Okay gang, listen up!" said Mia. "We're going to Trespass Island."

When Mia arrived, the club was a ghost town. No Blake, no Carson. No Gunn, no Ray, nor Elsie. She was now solely in charge of eight presumptuous little shorebirds. Mia was not happy.

"First one around the shallow water mark gets to ride back!"

They were halfway there when the *Terrapin* finally appeared out of the shadows of the island. Mia zoomed off to collect her dilatory crew.

Blake leapt aboard.

"Good morning Mr. Gunn!" she said.

His jaw was set and he gave only the slightest nod before turning *Terrapin* for home.

Blake lay down in the bow. He stared into the sky. He was panting.

"Uh oh," said Mia, standing on the seat and looking over the window.

"Yeah, 'uh oh."

"I'm afraid to ask. Who was it this time?"

"Remember that scary cop, yesterday? This was a hundred times scarier."

"Who was it?"

"Department of Immigration and Naturalization. Guns and everything."

"Oh my god, no! Did they,"

"They're perfectly legal. They still gave'm a hard way to go. I got mad and told them if they wanted to hassle wetbacks, they should go to your dad's and the mayor's mansion—if they had the guts."

"You said that to the Feds? Guts and all?"

"I wish I could take it back."

"That's awesome! I can't believe you did that!"

"They're just pawns! Those people didn't ask for trouble. They're just trying to survive. I feel terrible about it."

"They're used to it. They'll all have new ID's in two weeks and switch houses. Nobody'll even bat an eye."

"Well it gets worse."

"Hold on." Mia throttled up a little and puttered toward the shallow water mark. The prams were almost there. She shut the motor off and threw an anchor over the stern.

She returned and sat down on the bench in front of the pulpit. "Tell me."

"That lady with the afro showed up just as INS was leaving. She had Child Protective Services with her."

Mia gave a little gasp.

"I was never so scared. Ever." He plastered one hand against his face and gagged twice. Blake tore himself off the deck and chucked his breakfast over the bow. He plunked back down and sniffled. "I was so scared. They'll take me away from everything. This place. This is everything to me. I'll die before I ever let them take me away." The sobs came on in earnest. "I'll die."

"Miss Mia! I'm first around! You owe me a ride!"

"Alright Hyperion! Wait 'til everyone's around. She slid down to the deck and gathered him up. "I am so sorry, Blake. They won't take you away. I won't let them. Gunn won't let them." He slumped against her.

"They said they were going to take me for examination and observation. You *know* what that means?"

"How the heck did you get out of it?"

"Hey Miss Mia! I know what you guys are doing!"

"We're plotting your woeful demise, Hyperion! Keep it up!" she snarled.

"Can you believe the crap shorebirds name their kids these days?"

"Mr. Gunn showed CPS my guardianship papers. He called the school and laid into the principal right in front of afro-lady. I guess they're old friends."

"That should be the end of her."

"Mr. Gunn's furious. Where's my uncle?"

"Gone. Buddy, I know you don't wanna hear this, but we gotta be Vikings. Starting right now. We've got to hit back hard and do it fast."

Something slammed into the side of the safety-boat.

"Starting with this Gold Coast brat! Hyperion, you're dead meat!" She grabbed his bowline and hauled up with all her might. The boy went over the back of the pram with a wail. She shoved the little eight-foot dinghy away. "There goes your ride, pal!"

Something chimed in her back pack. She checked her phone with a tap, a swipe, and a curse word. It was the picture she'd taken of Brigita and Devlin. But with Mayor Teddy planting the kiss on her cheek instead. "Touché, Dragon Lady." Mia returned to the wheel. "We just lost our leverage. She fixed-up the picture I sent her. Best Photoshop job I've ever seen. Now she can say ours is the phony photo. And who's word do you think they'll take?"

"What do you mean ours?"

"Miss Mia, can you tow us back?" pleaded a small voice as the fleet drifted its way toward Safety 2.

"We're gonna need stronger stuff." She turned the ignition. "Alright, you guys! Boards up and tillers amidships. Tie up bow to stern!" She pulled up the anchor and tossed a towline to the nearest pram.

***

Carson hiked his backpack over one shoulder. The Gunn estate seemed strangely subdued. In Bay 1, the Pagáns worked in uncharacteristic silence. He found Gunn sitting at the dining-room table, two empty bottles before him and a third in hand. Sooner cowered beneath his chair.

"That ain't just for breakfast anymore, you know?"

Gunn glared at him with fuming disdain.

"I know, I heard. INS was here."

"And waving guns, and pushing people around like they were the infernal Gestapo!" Gunn yelled it as if he'd been waiting all day for the chance. "And *then* Child Protective Services showed up! If it had'na been for Gordon Gwinnup at the high school, they would'a taken Blake!"

"And I s'pose it's all my fault?" Carson dropped his pack and shouted.

"I told you this would happen if yeh'd no put any effort into him!"

"I think he was doin' pretty well without me!"

"That girl is nice enough, but she's having an impact. He mouthed off to the Feds and practically attacked that busy-body social worker!"

"He's a pistol when he's riled up!"

"He did'na even tell me she'd been at the club. That's no like him. None of it!"

"Like you said, he's thirteen. He's findin' his way."

"He needs a guide! And Mia Devlin *ain't* it! She's mixed up in something dangerous and he's in the line o' fire. He's losing sight of where the boundaries are."

Carson went to the refrigerator. "You give a kid boundaries, he'll just break 'em."

"That's no true! Even if he does, he'll understand why they were there when he's older and he'll pass that wisdom on."

"You never had kids, how come you're suddenly the expert on parenting?"

"Because I learned a few things from my father!"

"There ya go, throwin' Dad back in my face."

"I suppose yeh'll storm off and pout for another month and leave the lad to think it was his fault?"

Carson returned and picked up his pack. "As a matter of fact, he's had an impact on *me*. I'm gonna follow *his* lead this time and give back to my community."

"Yeh did'na go down lake and kick the hornet's nest did yeh?"

"Nope. I stomped all over it!"

"You fool! What have you done?"

"A little justice, I hope."

"Vigilante justice!"

"Thirty years ago you'd have gone down there and shot 'em all yourself."

"And at what cost, blast yeh!"

"At what cost? What's the cost of doin' nothing, old man? How many more kids have to die?"

"Oh it's about *her* is it? You think this'll quiet all the ghosts of yer past."

"Yeah. It's about Becky Lynn! And it's about that little boy that died last week! And Blake Barber! And his kids! How many more?"

A brief silence fell between them.

"Between you and that girl, I'll have to move before this is all over. Go pick him up. I've got a few things to say to him."

"After you dry out a little."

***

Mia and Blake watched in disbelief as Carson laid into his second steak. They huddled around the table in one of the little side-rooms at Tyner's. A woman appeared in the door. "There's our special guest! Take a seat. What can I get you?" gushed Carson.

"A bowl of blazing hot news!" said Daley Dunright, as she sat down and opened her laptop. "Hi kids."

Carson pushed the little black camera across the table. "Don't burn your fingers!"

She laughed with disingenuous professional courtesy and connected the camera to her computer. Daley turned the screen so they could all see it. Carson reached over and pulled the sliding door closed.

"Give us a little narration here, Carson," she said.

"Okay, here's the notorious ship "*Old Gods*" which was also present at the voodoo orgy I witnessed Friday night."

The reporter cocked an eyebrow.

"He got shot!" said Blake.

"Shot at. Here she makes landfall and the pirate crew goes ashore. And here we are at the campsite with Fearless Leader—Voodoo Jack. Wanted on a host of charges including kidnapping and torture."

The freaks sat around a campfire and passed a couple of odd-looking cigarettes around.

"So, its a pot party," said Daley, unimpressed.

"Oh, it's so much more! We got live chickens!" he said, as the camera zoomed in on a wire crate by a big black tent. "But that's for later. Now it's the next day and we're..."

"Harvesting marijuana. Okay, seen that before."

"Hold on! Now we're off to the magic gulley where grow the biggest patches of psychedelic mushrooms I have ever seen."

Daley Dunright's impatience turned to startled appreciation. She whistled. "Look at the psilocybin and fly agarics!"

"And off they go to process the fruits—or uh, fungus if you prefer, of their labors. And here I am adding my contribution." A black wand appeared in the frame squirting a stream of liquid on the remaining patches.

"What is that, fungicide?"

"Salt and vinegar. Goes great with mushrooms." He winked. "They'll never grow there again." The White Hound trotted into the picture. "And here's a fine specimen cannis albus idiotus magnus! Had to feed him all my grub to keep him from giving me away."

"That explains the steaks," said Mia.

"Now, 'bout those chickens...It's time to feed Monstro!"

Mia and Blake were riveted to the screen.

"Is that Lucky?" said Daley. "This is getting weird."

"Oooh, you have no idea, sister," said Blake.

Ring-lips beat a steady rhythm on a djembe drum right at the waterline. Voodoo Jack appeared in full regalia, chicken in hand. Daley flinched.

"You ought to smell that guy!" said Blake.

Mia curled her upper lip in disgust. The water began to roil about ten feet out. Jack slung the chicken into the lagoon. There was an enormous splash.

"Oh my heck! What *was* that!" yelped Daley.

Carson chuckled with deep satisfaction. "You bring the chopper down on Sunday morning, and I'll show you."

"You are not going back down there! Blake protested. "No way. Not with my boat, anyway!"

"Kid, were gonna need a bigger boat."

Daley watched in rapt horror as the catfish priest dispensed the remaining poultry treats.

Carson poked her in the side. "Boo!"

She jumped with a gasp. "Tell me it doesn't get any creepier."

"Lots creepier. But not on this tape. Now here's the part you've all been waiting for."

The shot switched to a lonely stretch of asphalt road, Jack loitering on the shoulder. A Freeman police cruiser rolled around the bend. An arm snaked out of the driver's window. As the car passed by, they got a clear view of the man at the wheel. Daley's jaw nearly hit the table. Jack held out a green nylon cooler-bag. The cop made the snatch and pulled it into the cruiser.

"Officer Donny Utz?" said Daley. "What do you intend to do with this?"

"I was hoping for a little advice."

"The first thing is, don't show it to *anyone*. Yet."

"I'm listening."

"I've...we... this is huge. Unbelievably huge. Dead bodies in a pile huge. Look, I have a friend in D.C. A senator. He can pull the strings we need pulled. Can I copy this to my laptop?"

"Help yourself!" he said with a wink and a gracious smile.

She pointed at Blake and Mia. "You two! Not! A! Word! Do you hear me? This is deadly serious."

"Yeah, well, we sort of have our own 'deadly serious' going on at the moment, so no problem," said Mia.

"Alright, just what are we doing Sunday, adventure man?"

***

Sooner woofed and dislodged herself from her customary crevice next to Gunn. He stirred from his nap and switched off the TV. Blake and Carson topped the stairs.

"Sit down, Caduggin."

Blake seated himself gingerly on the edge of the couch. Carson went down the hall.

"I'm sorry about…"

"Hush. It is my responsibility to keep you safe and sound. You've gotten tangled up in Miss Mia's troubles and it's my duty to extract you from them. When Junior Training is finished tomorrow, you're to say goodbye to her and come straight home. Do I make myself clear?"

"But,"

"Do I make myself *clear*?"

"Yes sir."

"There'll be none of your sea lawyer loopholes this time. You're no to see her until all of this blows over. Completely. Now, get a bath and go to bed. Yeh've had a big day."

Something suddenly ached in Blake's chest, and tingled behind his eyes.

"Yeh got mail today. On yer dresser. Give yeh something to lift yer spirits."

Blake hauled himself up on wobbling knees, and went to his room.

Chapter 47

Blake plunged the mushroom-shaped anchor back in to the lake a few times to get the sludge off and dropped it next to the gas tank. He went to the bow, leaned on the chrome railing and watched the little fleet bob its way home.

"I won't be sorry to say goodbye to those little hellions," said Mia. "Something eatin' you?"

"Mr. Gunn says I have to say goodbye to you." Blake didn't look back. "At least until things settle down."

"Fudge! Well I guess I can't blame him." She put the motor in gear and throttled up a little. "Why do I always manage to screw everything up?"

"It's not your fault."

"I wreck everything and everybody. Always have."

"Mia, it hurts!"

"Yes it does. And now I have to fight them alone."

Blake returned to the helm and sat on the side-rail. "What will you do?"

"Lay low. Very low."

"Maybe we'll get lucky and they'll all be sucked down by the corruption scandal."

"When and *if* that ever breaks. Can't wait to see what your uncle pulls off down in the branch, though. *That's* bound to be spectacular." Mia sighed. "I'm sorry I got you into all of this, Tux."

"I'm not. Not one bit," he said, defying the universe.

She smiled to herself.

***

Blake picked the last multi-colored shreds of the final water-balloon battle out of the prickly, brown lawn. The harbor stretched like a silent, silver road beneath a featureless gray sky, toward the vast, shimmering misery of the lower lake.

"It all feels empty. The whole world feels empty," he said.

Mia arched her back and groaned. "Be nice if that sky would give us a little rain."

"It's empty, too."

"Look, I'll be around. This isn't 'goodbye forever' goodbye."

"It just makes me mad: this wasn't your fault! What? Are you not supposed to defend yourself? Now what will I do?"

Carson came crunching down the hill. "We're done, kids. Let's get out of here. Old man wants you home and I got some people to see."

"When do I get my new flash, Wolfman?" said Mia.

"Ought to have it by Tuesday," he said, heading for the main dock.

She tugged Blake's shirt-tail. "Give me a hug and get out of here," said Mia. She gave him a good squeeze and headed for the point.

They passed her, just leaving the harbor. She waved long and resumed her journey into the listless afternoon.

***

The cool pillow felt good. Blake contemplated his room. The map. The club pennant. The charred Jolly Roger. The trophy surrounded by a pile of fossils, and Korbin's Bible on the dresser; a collection of feathers taped around the edge of his mirror, his grandfather's dirk hanging over one corner. Sooner gnawed and snuffled frenetically up and down her forelegs.

He picked up yesterday's post card. A painting of two horses on a stormy beach. One reddish brown, with an enormous, wavy, black mane and tail. The other, white, with equally voluminous tresses, sported a narrow gold sash draped across its back. He flipped it over.

Dearest Blake,
I couldn't decide between this, or Angel of Life by
Segantini.
There's an old lady with an antique shop near us.
She doesn't speak a lick of English, but manages to
pantomime her aches, pains and troubles. I leave
Agatha with her and get out by myself whenever I
want.
But then I think of nothing but how I left you
there on the steps.
I am going to make it up to you. All of it.
Please forgive me,
Mom

Dear Mom, he thought. *It had to be done. All of it.*

***

"Carson, you been watchin' *River Monsters* again? Five hundred pounds?" said a tall big-bellied man. He ground his pool cue into a chalk cube until showers of blue powder piled up on his right hand, and rained down on the floor.

"Chalky, you remember that one where the big pacu fishes were biting guys in the…" The triangle of balls clacked and went in all directions.

"Let's don't bring that up!" laughed a man in a leather-vest. He was short and bald, with a five o'clock shadow and hard brow that made him look like he always meant business.

"Tell me Peach, what did Mueller pull out of Maynard's cove a couple of years ago?" said Carson. "Red bellied pacu. Thirty inches in diameter."

"I don't care if it's thirty feet, I ain't goin' to no stinkhole lagoon in Mangrave to hook some urban legend," said an older man sporting a stars-and-stripes bandana on his head.

"Is that the statement of a Ranger, Holly?" said Carson. "Why you bunch of leather-clad sissy-bikers!"

"I ain't goin' in those woods without air-cover," said Holly, white beard brushing the red felt of the billiard table, as he sank the seven ball.

"Got that handled already. You in Hollister?"

"What's in it for us?" said Chalky.

"Your fifteen minutes of glory. Maybe the Cincinnati aquarium will buy it. We'll split the proceeds."

"You ain't told us what it is, yet!" said Holly.

"Gentlemen, I have it on good authority that twenty years ago, a certain Laker with a penchant for exotic pets,"

"A certain Maynard Gilchrest." chuckled the bald man, sipping his beer.

"Obtained a Wels catfish."

"Wels? I seen them on the fishing channel," said Chalky.

"And as soon as it started eating him out of house and home, where do you think it went?"

"Wels catfish? I don't have gear for a fish that size," said Chalky.

"Like I said, leave that to me. Guys, this is about more than a fish. It's about our lake and our community. It's an invasive species. Big enough to take a small child. Holly your grandkids swim in this lake!"

A couple of other guys came over from the bar.

"Carson, you're like the tide, you know that?" said Holly. "Unstoppable when it comes in, low and stinky when it goes out. I don't know which I prefer."

"What's your point? I'll be at the waterfront with the *Terrapin* nine A.M. Sunday morning."

"I'll be there," said the bald man. The two from the bar assented.

"Air cover," growled Holly.

Carson smiled. "Already taken care of."

426

Chapter 48

"You read that psalm to your girl, yet?" said Korbin.

"It's been kind of crazy. Haven't had a chance."

"You read that book I gave you, y'hear me? Won't do you no good sittin' on your chester drawers."

"I promise. I will."

"Don't start in the middle like the preacher tells you to. You start in the beginning and go clean on through to the end."

"How do you feel, Mr. Dubois?"

"Every bit a hundred and eight. You buildin' my box?"

"My friend Sylvio is. No nails!"

"You read that book and you'll have knowledge. Spirit shows you what it means, then you got understanding. When you can apply *understanding* to what you say and do, then it becomes wisdom to you."

"You've taught me a lot, Mr. Dubois. Thank you."

"My pleasure, young Uh-quot. I s'pose my work here is done, as they say."

"No! One more thing, please. What—I feel so stupid every time I ask this. What is love?"

"No greater love has a man than this. That he lay down his life for his friends."

"Right, but what *is* love?"

"I s'pose it's caring. Always havin' a care about how folks are doing.

Seeing to their well-being."

Blake pulled a little notepad and pen from his cargo pocket. Love is the...ongoing...commitment... to care about the welfare and wellbeing... of others."

"It ain't romance and lovey-dovey. Sometimes that figures in, but lot o' time you got to care for folks you don't like at all."

Blake made an addendum on his pad. "Affection... may or may not be... involved."

"Now, you got knowledge *and* understanding."

"You do seem like you feel a lot better today," said Blake.

"Not bad. I recon I'll see another sun-up or two. Hey missy! Bring that ice cream in here! And metal spoons! Can't dig my escape tunnel with those tiny wooden ones!"

***

Blake leaned against the green railing and scanned the waterfront for his uncle. From the vortex of motorized chaos that was the upper lake came the unmistakable sound of *Tantrum II*. The rumble stopped. He spotted the purple and yellow monolith drifting backwards toward the dam. She rumbled again and again, but the engine wouldn't stay lit. *Mia must have been busy last night,* he thought. Hunter appeared to be alone at the helm. Nobody seemed to be offering any assistance to the beleaguered playboy.

Blake ran down to the docks and boarded the *Becky Lynn*.

"Hey, Hunter! Throw me your bowline, I'll tow you in!"

Hunter laughed to see his unlikely rescuer in the little sharpie, rocking in high chop. "Alright buddy, now your talking!" He strutted down the long deck in his Bermuda shorts and wrap-around sunglasses. He tossed the line to Blake, who'd edged closer. "I can't believe you sent that reporter right to Jenny's front door! She hasn't spoken to me since!"

"Sorry!" Blake began to doubt the wisdom of his Samaritan enterprise.

"Are you kidding me? I've been reveling in the bachelor life for a week! She'll simmer down in a few days and be the good ol' ball and chain again."

Blake smiled uneasily and nudged *Becky Lynn* forward to take up the slack, then throttled up. He towed Tantrum to the first dock that had an open stretch big enough. Hunter hung fenders and tied her up.

"I owe you a big one Sparks! Find a slip and come on back."

Blake retuned his boat to her original berth and jogged back to *Tantrum II.*

"Ever been inside one of these bad babes? Come on!"

Blake's curiosity got the best of him. *She's not going anywhere, so abduction's pretty much out of the question,* he thought.

He never imagined that there was anything below deck. Much less leather bench seats, mirrors, a stereo, bar, air conditioning, and far in the bow, a bed.

"Pimped beyond your wildest dreams! Eh Sparks?"

"Now I get the half-million dollar, part."

"Cop a squat man! Sink your buns into that rich Corinthian leather!"

Blake obliged and Hunter stretched himself out on the opposite bench. "Sometimes this boat's worse than the Jag. Whatcha up to?"

"Ah well, I'm having a coffin built for a friend—at the nursing home."

Hunter flinched and chuckled. "No kidding? You are a constant source of amazement to me!"

"As I am to myself," agreed Blake.

"Who's doing the work?"

"My Mexican friends. Working out of our shop."

"Are they legal? INS has been on the prowl. Scary dudes. Cleaned out Mom's, Dad's, and the Mayor's mansion."

"Eeeyeah, they hit us, too. We didn't lose anybody."

"So anyway, you got beaners building coffins out of old man Gunn's. Quality stuff?"

"No nails. Incredible workmanship."

"Awesome! Now this is what I'm talking about. You go around to all the churches, nursing homes, funeral parlors, and you sell 'em on your coffins! Get orders. Skim forty percent right off the top. You got no skin in the game except a little bit of time and travel. Before you know it—bam! You're Blake Barber, the Coffin-Pimp of Freeman!"

Blake laughed both out of nervousness and because it made outrageous sense.

"I'm telling you!"

"That's audacious!" said Blake.

"That's you man! Audacious!"

"So, speaking of the mayor's mansion," said Blake, "What do you know about his wife?"

"Shhhhh!" Hunter sat up in a flash, all traces of merriment gone from his face. "How do you know about that?" He got up, stuck his head out of the companion way, then pulled the double doors closed.

"About what?"

"The Dragon lady." He sat back down.

"I know she's got it in for Mia."

"Then Mia had better look out, little buddy." He went to the bar and poured two drinks.

Hunter returned and handed a tumbler to Blake. He sniffed it. The fumes stung his eyes.

"I rue the day, Blake." He threw his drink back. "I'll be lucky to get out of this one. I've got two words for you, then we speak of her no more. Vicious. Unprincipled."

"You look like you could use another." Blake offered him his tumbler. Hunter gladly accepted it.

"Hear that? Sounds like a bosun's whistle." Hunter cocked his head and looked at his glass as if its contents might not have been a little too potent.

"My uncle! I've got to go. Hope you get the motor started. Good luck with you-know-who!"

"Thanks for the lift!" said Hunter, as Blake burst through the companionway and into the blazing noon. As he made his way back to *Becky Lynn*, a line from *Treasure Island* came floating back, adapted to the present circumstances: *They were all a'feared of Hunter Devlin, but even Hunter Devlin was a'feared of Brigita Dragana Rozik.*

Chapter 49

The rotor blades of the Channel 3 Action Chopper hammered the air. The pilot swept the copter in circles, mere inches above the treetops, as if corralling some quarry below. Branches thrashed and trunks creaked under the tornadic downdraft.

The old ranger grinned through his drab face-paint and sprinted to the next tree. He scanned for bad guys, checked his six and scurried to a boulder. He slid down a slope, dashed through low scrub and saplings. He emerged at the shoreline just as the chopper swung out over the water and put the camera on him. He waved the *Terrapin* in. She charged into the weedy shallows towing Holly's big Jon boat and disembarked her motley crew.

Carson led the charge over the trace to the lagoon. "Alright guys, like I said, this is pure Hollywood. Let's give the lady a good show!" The chopper rose above the lagoon as the half dozen men burst upon the mud flat and froze.

"What's the deal? C'mon!" said Carson.

"What the hell is this place? That's Lucky!" said Chalky. "And what's that stench?"

"Fear and death," said Holly. "Makes a man feel alive!"

"I told you this was about more than a catfish. Now come on, get that netting ready! Sooner we catch it the sooner we're outta here," said Carson.

Carson took up a position in front of the fiberglass effigy and produced a coil of eighth-inch rope from his duffle, threaded it through a large wire leader which sported a hook as long as his thumb. He thrust it into the open end of a whole raw chicken.

"Now, stand by the water and stomp your feet! Altogether! One, two, three, four!"

"You're makin' us look like fools, Urquart!" said Peach.

"Just do it!" said Carson. He swung the chicken in circles as if he were about to lasso a bronco with it. The reluctant stompers did their duty.

From the chopper, Daley Dunright watched in anticipation as the first ripples parted the emerald duckweed, revealing black stripes of inky water. Something big was headed for the stomping bikers. Carson let the chicken fly. A leathery, white belly broke the surface with a slosh as the leviathan rolled over and dove for its prize.

"Did you get that!" she called to her camera man.

"If it gets them do I keep rolling, that's my question?"

"Don't stop tape 'til we're on the ground, McKenna!"

"Get on the line!" yelled Carson. "You guys get the net!"

Holly and Peach joined him in the struggle with the hand-line while Chalky and the others spread the cargo net out.

"Holly, throw a couple of loops around Lucky's head!"

Holly complied, then braced himself in a dramatic stance and glared at roiling water with mock intensity.

"On three, it pulls us all in—Three!"

The trio lurched forward. Lucky went down on his face in the firepit.

The silhouette of the Wels was now clearly visible from the air, as the copter moved directly overhead. The camera man cackled. "Where'd you get these guys? This is like Pro Wrestling meets Wild Kingdom!"

"Will you look at the size of that thing!" said Daley, into her headset. "That's six feet, easily."

"Every bit of nine!" said the cameraman, eyes glued to the monitor.

"Is that a bet, Mckenna?"

"You're on! Crikey! They're gonna wrestle it? These guys are pure gold!"

The fishermen worked their catch into water nearly chest-deep and now Carson tenuously eased his way down the hand-line. He lunged on the beleaguered giant. He was down! He was up! He was thrown off! He went under for thirty seconds! He finally surfaced with his arm in the beast's mouth, past his elbow.

Daley, the cameraman, and the pilot were laughing so hard that it was difficult to keep the shot steady, even with the gyroscopic stabilizers working overtime.

Holly raced to Carson's aid and extracted his comrade's lost limb, bare hook in his grasp. They threw their arms around the gargantuan and fought to steer it toward shore. Peach waved Chalky and the men into the fray. They dashed in, slid the net under the Wels and hauled it triumphantly ashore. They wasted no time in getting it across the trace and aboard the Jon boat. Holly fired up the motor and tore out of the Mangrave Branch, while Carson misted the leviathan's gills with a garden sprayer.

A news crew was ready and waiting when they arrived in Gunn's harbor. The fish was dubbed Jonah and transferred into an empty, inflatable pool laid out in Bay 3. Blake started a pump and the pool filled with lake water, rising quickly from the floor like a giant blue, bean-bag chair.

Terrapin arrived forty minutes later, Daley rolling in shortly after. Interviews were given, the gear packed, and the news crew rushed off to cut it all together for the Live at Five newscast. The pool hall heroes slapped Carson on the back and agreed that a good time had been had by all. They climbed into Holly's boat and headed for town.

Gunn stood on the pool ladder and stared down at the huge fish. He gave a little puff of disapproval through his nose, shook his head, and walked away.

***

They all gathered around the big-screen TV at Tyner's and reveled in the full fifteen minute presentation, featuring unappreciated intrusions into the busy lives of the Police Chief, the Mayor, and Buck Mueller. It ended with the promise of segments revealing shocking occult rituals, government corruption, criminal activity, and a special report on invasive species.

The threatening phone calls began at midnight.

Chapter 50

Carson squatted behind the pool and adjusted the filter system. When he got back up, Buck Mueller stood glaring into the water.

"Got a permit for this fish, Urquart?" he rumbled, coldly.

"She's a beauty, ain't she?"

"I said where's your permit? There are daily fines for keeping dangerous, exotic animals without proper permitting."

"Seriously? Et tu, Bucky?"

"And I want to see your gear. I don't think this fish was caught legally."

"Well it ain't *my* fish, Buck! It came out of *your* lake. Seems like we were doing your job for you!"

"I don't need you to do my job! You've embarrassed me and my staff, and made a mockery of the entire Indiana Department of Natural Resources!" he barked.

A door slammed somewhere in the shop and Blake trotted out, bearing the cordless phone. "Uncle Carson, you've got a call."

"I'm kinda busy here, kid."

"It's the DNR commissioner. He wants to exhibit your fish at the State Fair next month!"

"Well, I guess it *is* my fish, after all!" Carson grinned at Mueller, who turned stiffly and swaggered out of the shop.

***

"Cheer up Caduggin, or I'll send yeh down to Beverly's." Gunn nudged Blake's shoulder as he sat down for lunch. "Pretty neat how the DNR carted ol' Jonah away in that tank truck, wasn' it?"

"Yeah." Blake picked at his beans.

"Mueller's still madder than a boiled owl."

"Yeah."

Gunn sighed. "I know yeh miss her, lad. I must confess, I was getting used to her, myself."

Five days had passed without any word or indication of Mia's welfare.

"I hear yeh've made a business arrangement with Sylvio?"

"We're taking Korbin's coffin around to some prospective customers today," said Blake, unexcited.

"Aye. Fine. Yeh could've asked me first. Why don't yeh call the girl. Meet her for lunch. See how she's doing."

Blake brightened up.

"Ask Charlie for the back room. And yeh don' leave the Emporium, yeh hear me?"

***

At five 'til five, Blake sank into the cool of the couch. Gunn dug the TV remote out of the cushions of the recliner and requested permission from Sooner to sit down.

"Get any orders, did yeh?" He switched on channel 3.

"Seven," said Blake, without enthusiasm.

"Seven? How much a box?"

"Six fifty for the plain one's. I take twenty-five percent. Eleven hundred thirty seven fifty."

"Mother Carey's chickens! I better start charging you rent!"

Blake paid no attention to the news, spending his remaining mental energy speculating on Mia's whereabouts. *Stone Hollow: No, too obvious. Her mom's: too risky. Her dad's: too dangerous. The Emporium: she'd be seen coming and going. No, Nothing in town.*

That mangy cruiser in the boat lot? Maybe. No, too hot. The Club? Empty during the week. Plenty of places to hide. Yes. Either the deep woods, or the clubhouse.

At last came the teaser for Dunright's next installment in the "Old Gods Drug Cult" exposé, and a commercial break.

"I'd have called 'em the Silurians, after the Wels—*siluris glannis*," said Gunn. "And *Dr. Who.*" As angry and skeptical as Gunn was about the entire crisis, Blake couldn't help noticing that Gunn seemed oddly captivated, if not entertained, by the media coverage.

Today's installment featured Carson's footage of Voodoo Jack feeding the monster, Carson's own bloodcurdling tale of the midnight ritual, plus full exposure of the gunshot wound across his hairy chest, and the patched holes in *Becky Lynn*. Daley ran the footage of the pirate camp, and harvest. And to both Gunn's and Blake's surprise, the package ended with Carson giving a tour of his mother's party-trashed garage, including spore syringes and glove bags from mail-order do-it-yourself shroom-growing kits. Finally came Daley's promise to blow open a shocking corruption scandal involving local law enforcement, in the next installment.

"Brilliant. That woman might just give a hoot, after all," said Gunn. "They're flushing them out."

"Who?"

"All of them. You watch: The cop'll break and run first. They'll get him at the border. Then they'll scoop up a couple of Jack's flunkies and grill 'em till they turn State's evidence. Then that'll be it for Edna, Jack, and the lot of them. We better stick close to home, 'til they do."

Blake started working on a pretense to get himself back to the club.

Chapter 51

The cult feature ran again at noon, Tuesday. Gunn could hardly wait until five.

Blake never got his ride to the club. Instead, he spent the afternoon crammed in the roasting cab of Slyvio's truck, frequenting lumberyards and hardware stores. When at last he returned to the comforts of his guardian's estate, he forced himself to call Soojee about a website for the Pagán's business.

Tomorrow, he thought, *I am going over there.*

Gunn's prophecy held true. *Live at Five* broke the news that Officer Duncan Donald Utz had not reported for work and the Freeman Police Department, and City Hall were standing on their heads. Daley's camera harassed every office of local government, queried Joe Public on the street, and finally peered through the big bay window into the dark lair of the Book Nook. But the Fat Lady of Nirvana was not home.

After the excitement was over, he retired to his room and finally finished reading *Treasure Island.*

Chapter 52

The tavern at Tyner's was a dim, cool cave accented with neon endorsements for domestic beer bliss. Carson sat at the bar enjoying lunch, and waiting for the noon news to gush forth from the flat screen television, suspended from the ceiling.

"Be with you fellahs in a minute," said Tyner, drying a shot glass and clinking it under the counter with a dozen others. Carson glanced at the mirrored wall behind the barkeeper. Three Freeman police officers sat down at a nearby table.

The news opened with the latest in the corruption scandal. The rogue officer Utz had been apprehended when the seaplane he'd chartered for Canada made an emergency landing on the American side of Sault Sainte Marie.

"That's one down," said Carson, with a grin.

The policemen got up and left without saying a word. Tyner shot him a dirty look. "Not everybody around here is as tickled with your little stunt as you, Urquart. Stirred up a lot of trouble."

Carson sipped his beer. "Some trouble needs stirring up."

"You'd better be careful what you say, for a while." Tyner finished another shot glass and tossed it under the counter. "Especially in here." He threw the towel down and walked away. The news echoed off the concrete block walls. Carson was alone.

***

The club was not on Wednesday's itinerary, either. Blake spent the day learning to use a circular saw, planer and other dangerous shop tools used in the construction of coffins. It ate at him. Nobody knew where Mia was. Social services paid Treva a visit three days before. Mia packed her gear and vanished that night. But at the moment he couldn't spare her a single thought. A stray memory could cost him an eye, a thumb, or a hand. After a summer of broad liberties, the current precautions seemed like prison. At least Sylvana wasn't around.

At five o'clock, he collapsed on the couch and turned on the TV. He listened to the commercials just to get the feel of English again.

"Mr. Gunn, wake up. It's on."

Gunn roused and sat up. The final shocking installment began with a recap of the week's revelations and culminated with the footage of Utz making the pick-up. Daley's partner ended the epic with corny comments about "im-morel" behavior and Utz's future as a "toadstool-pigeon."

"Now that was cheap," said Gunn. "Well, I won't rest 'til they get Mount Edna and Jack behind bars."

***

Sooner's eyes popped open and glinted like little, black marbles in the dark. Something wasn't right. She lifted her head off Blake and snuffled. Definitely wrong—that smell did not belong to them. She gruffed and sat up, ears pricked—that faint hum was not theirs. Sooner barked twice, vaulted off Blake's back and ran to the living room. Blake pulled on his shorts and followed.

He found her standing anxiously in the bay window. The slightest flicker of orange light danced on the panes. Blake pressed his face to the glass and went pale. He sucked breath in little gasps until he could finally yell, long and loud.

"Fire! Fire! Fire-ship in the harbor!" He bolted down the hall, Sooner barking madly. "Fire-ship in the harbor!"

Carson nearly knocked him over as he dashed to the stairs in his underpants.

"Power washer!" cried Gunn from his bed. "Wear your respirator!"

The angry, boat-borne inferno chugged past the cape and headed toward the dock. The cockpit was a cauldron of roiling orange flame twenty feet high, pumping out stygian, black smoke in a column that went up forever. In the midst of that conflagration could occasionally be glimpsed its hellish Silurian skipper: Lucky the Catfish.

Blake guessed that they had three minutes at best. Carson had already sent the *Terrapin* away under motor. He freed *Sophia's* spring lines and leapt aboard. Blake braced his shoulder against the big bay door and opened it a yard. He heard *Sophia's* motor start, then *Becky Lynn's*. He rushed back out, towing the power washer to the spigot. "Hose, hose, hose!" he panted aloud. The speed-link locked. "Faucet—come on! Turn!" he grimaced. He yanked the starter cord and the engine reported for duty. Blake trundled it to the top of the ramp as fast as the hose reel could pay out.

He looked for the boats. *Terrapin* was grounded across the harbor. *Sophia* had just stuck her keel in the mud, well in the lee of the dock. She'd be safe.

The fire-ship slowed down. It turned the water into a rippling lava flow and in it Blake spotted the silhouette of his uncle, speeding *Becky Lynn* straight for the volcano.

"Are you crazy!" Blake screamed, barely audible above the din of motors. Waves of heat rolled across the harbor. Carson shielded his face with his forearm and to Blake's relief, wheeled the sharpie around and fled before the holocaust.

Then he spotted flames licking up the ridge. He opened his mouth to yell, but the screams came from behind. He turned as a mob of lily-white savages poured out from around the house and came wailing after him. He screamed and clenched the trigger on the wash-gun. It nearly blasted out of his hand. He realized he still had it and took down the first three attackers with a ferocious discharge that hit their faces like a geyser of gravel. Blake raked the punishing torrent in all directions, repelling the crazed barbarians as he backed down the ramp. A pair of headlights crashed out of the wooded drive and tore across the lot. The wash-gun flew out of Blake's hands with a vicious jerk as the rust-streaked pickup careened past, knocking the groaning power washer down the waterfront at forty miles an hour.

Blake saw the crew that leapt out of the bed and the cab. He sprinted for the open door and had it half shut when they put their shoulders to it. Blake leapt over a stack of wood sheets and dashed to the workbench. The big door rumbled open, granting full view of the drifting beacon of doom— now just one hundred feet from the dock. The pirates ran in to the open space of Bay 2 and spotted the deflated pool at the far end of the shop.

"It's gone!" said Ring-lips.

"Get out! Get out!" shouted Tattoo.

They galloped back to the door but stopped cold at the sound of machine-gun fire, directly over head. Brilliant red streaks pierced the burning boat like the shimmering arrows of angels. Something clacked repeatedly in the shop behind them and Orangutan shrieked, then Mohawk. Blake rained pain from a pneumatic staple gun, steadying his aim on Korbin's coffin. The raiders tumbled out the door beneath the stream of machine gun fire and dove into the truck. Ring-lips slammed it in reverse. Gunn switched to full auto and a hail of those tiny meteors ripped through the hood and buried themselves in the engine. The pirates abandoned ship and escaped with the rest of their lunatic throng. All except Ring-lips, who ran face first into Carson's knuckles.

Gunn put another hundred rounds into the hull of *Old Gods*. The last flames flicked out as her molten deck slipped beneath the surface. Her keel touched bottom, her bow but an inch from the dock. The grass fire on the cape burned itself out. Suddenly, everything was dark and quiet again. Sirens began to wail in the distance.

"Took your time, didn't you, old man?" said Carson.

"Had to pee," he said from the bay window. "Where's the lad?"

"I'm okay!" Blake said, peering out of the shop.

"Round up the boots, Caduggin. And you," he said to Carson, who stood over a sprawled-out Ring-lips. "Truss that one up."

Chapter 53

Officers from the Freeman PD, the County Sheriff's department and the DNR had been in and out all night—not to mention the fire department, and TV crews from three different stations. They'd all finally cleared out by eight, except the flatbed tow-truck backing down the ramp.

The winch screeched unbearably as it dragged the charred carcass of *Old Gods* onto the tow deck. Foul, oily water poured like black blood from her punctured belly. Daley taped with her mini-cam and, with Carson and Blake, puzzled over the odd glyphs spray-painted crudely on her sides. It had been a long night—the longest of the summer—so no one noticed when Mia sidled up next to Blake.

"That battle axe looks like a P," she said.

Blake agreed, then did a double take. "Hey! I've been worried about you!"

"Is this what you guys do when I'm not around?"

"You should've seen it. They attacked us! The whole place was on fire!"

"I did see it. The fire anyway—who d'ya think called it in?"

"I think she's on to something," said Daley. "The scythe is an L."

"There's A for good old Anarchy," said Carson.

"The skull's definitely a G," said Mia.

"The severed hand makes a U," said Blake.

"Then the trident thingy is an E," said Daley.

"And a big red X," concluded Carson.

"Plaguex?" said Daley, looking doubtful.

"Try Plague X," said Carson.

"Ahhh!" they all assented in unison.

"Okay, what's the X?" said Daley. It quickly became clear who hadn't had enough sleep that night, as the whole inquiry devolved into punchy silliness.

"X marks the spot?"

"X Lax!"

"eeeeX-cellent!"

"X-Wife!"

"X-tra terrestrial!"

"X-pository!"

"Suppository!"

"Ten," said Blake. Everyone looked at him.

"I think yer kinda missing the pattern, kid," said Carson.

"The Roman numeral X is ten." Everyone looked back at the boat as it slid to a stop on the tow deck.

"Plague Ten," said Carson, coming back to his senses.

Blake sank a little. "Oooh."

"Someone want to clue the girls in?" said Mia.

"Tenth plague of Egypt," said Carson. "Death of the firstborn."

"I'm off the hook," said Mia.

"Me too," said Blake.

"Ditto," said Daley.

"Thanks. I feel so special," said Carson.

"So, it was a death threat then," concluded Daley.

Three black choppers burst over the treetops and swooped westward.

"Looks like I've got an appointment in Mangrave!" said Daley, as she whipped out her phone and sprinted for her car. "Keep your eyes open and give me a call!" She peeled out of the lot.

The driver of the flat-bed secured his load. The truck groaned up the ramp and drove away.

"Got something in the house for ya, girlie. Be right back," said Carson.

"So, where have you been?" said Blake.

"Spent a couple of nights in a hollow sycamore near the rookery. Too hot, so I've been in the utility closet in the women's dorm."

"I knew you were at the club! I couldn't get over there for anything."

"Listen, one night next week we may have a mission."

"I can't, you..."

"I can't do it alone. We can fix this whole thing. But I need your help."

Carson returned and handed her a small box. "As promised. I wouldn't hang around. The old man's had a rough night." He headed back to the house. "We're never gonna get that stench out of this harbor."

"Hey, congratulations by the way," said Mia. "The fish *and* Utz. That's one off my back. Thanks!"

"My pleasure." The storm door hissed shut behind him.

"If they've caught enough of the bad guys by then, maybe Mr. Gunn will let Carson and me sail in the Keel Haul race or camp out or something."

"Be thinking about it." She boarded *Cry of the Osprey* at the waterline. "Give me a shove."

Blake took the bowline and pulled her into knee-deep water. An oily, rainbow sheen slithered and swirled over the surface. "I miss you like crazy," he said.

She smacked him on the behind with her paddle as she passed by.

***

The men of the Gunn estate loafed wearily in the living room. The noon news came on and it was about one thing: Raid on Mangrave.

The pickup truck driven by the invaders traced straight back to Mount Edna's disreputable spouse, Willy Montaine. His two-car garage was packed to the gills with stuff—other people's stuff. His grubby, blue, ranch house was crammed with even more—and drugs to boot. Utz and Ring-lips had squealed—loudly; and the County Sheriff, the FBI, and the DEA were all ears.

Two dozen houses were raided in the Mangrave bust, which yielded:

one shoot out, two crack houses, three meth-labs, forty-thousand dollars in cash, a live collection of deadly arachnids from around the world, and one less-than-coherent old lady with two hundred cats living in her double-wide. Mohawk and Orangutan had been collared at the ER, after Nurse Tamzon pulled the industrial staples out of their shoulder blades. Authorities made forty-eight arrests: fully one third of them identified by their pirate leaders as having taken part in the assault on Gunn's harbor. Ring-lips confessed that Edna herself had given orders for the fire-ship and its malevolent message: Plague X.

"Yeh'll stand to collect a reward for this, like as not," said Gunn.

"What for?" said Carson.

"Providing information leading to arrests and all that. Lad, I saw your girl out there. She doin' alright?"

"Laying low. She's the one who called 911."

"We owe her one for that, then. Sylvio called. Said take the day off. He found a fine little rental in town. Family's moving today."

"One of yours?" said Carson.

"Aye. The Water Street bungalow. Caduggin, I'm thinking we need to get out of town for a while."

"Well, I… uh… Sylvio…we still have a lot of work to do."

"Ah. And yeh no want to leave yer girl?"

"No—it's…"

"Say what yeh like. But that's the heart of the matter."

Carson threw down the gauntlet. "What's wrong with that?"

Blake, with a headache begging for sleep, left them to bicker.

Chapter 54

The big door to Bay 1 rumbled open. It was eight A.M. Friday morning, and the humidity was as clingy and oppressive as Blake's conscience. *Should I? Shouldn't I? I hate this! Of course I shouldn't, but how can I not? But how can I disobey? She got herself into this!* Miserable, he ambled down along the waterline toward the cape. *She didn't deserve to be stuck with parents like that. That adulterer! He hates me and Carson and Mr. Gunn. And what's to stop Brigita from coming after us when she's done with Mia? Who could help us, then? Even Hunter's afraid of her. She has to be stopped. What if she puts CPS on me again? What have I got to lose?*

He reached a winch on a post at the tip of the cape. He removed the padlock, released the catch and let the handle fly. The two hundred feet of chain that stretched across the harbor's mouth went to the bottom with a splash.

I could end up disgracing Mr. Gunn, my family, the club, and Freeman. They could take my scholarship back—oh to heck with Freeman, it's rotten to the core anyway.

The Pagán's pick-up truck rumbled into the driveway. Carson trundled two squat, red tanks of gas down to the *Terrapin* in a wheelbarrow. Blake threw a rock at the open lake and headed back.

I've got everything to lose. And everybody. Mr. Gunn would never trust my word again. He'd probably let CPS have me.

They spent the day at Beverly's estate tending her grounds and cleaning her pool.

Chapter 55

Gunn kept Blake close at hand. They spent Saturday at the flea market. He didn't even get to see Korbin. Gunn gabbed all day with the seemingly endless stream of hungry newshounds, slobbering for a retelling of the 'night of the fire-ship.' In reality it was Blake, under compulsion, who did most of the gabbing. Gunn would lead in with some modest statement such as "I just stood in the window and poured lead into the thing. The lad here was on the ground where the action was." As if it were the dullest, most mundane thing for an eighty-five-year-old man to fire an automatic rifle out of his living room window at a blazing kamikaze. And so, for the umpteenth time, Blake would be obliged to recount his tale of the harrowing melee; after which, Gunn would deliver a lecture on Siluris Glannis, then demand that Blake expound on the Biblical record of Dagon worship, followed by a dissertation on local species of psychedelic mushrooms.

This, compounded with his mounting anxiety over the upcoming "mission," irritated Blake royally. And once again, as angry and rattled as Gunn was over the affairs of the past week, he seemed to relish the glamour of it all. It brought him an odd glory which he fed on, eagerly. In any case, it drew a steady crowd of customers to the booth, who bought lures and everything else with cordial enthusiasm.

***

"Better catch forty winks when we get home, Caduggin. I have a feeling Soojee and company will be by tonight."

That was exactly what Blake did not want to hear. But Gunn called it right. Soojee's gang showed up right about dinner time and he indulged them with a feast of carry-out. There were some things about Gunn that Blake was sure he'd never figure out. How he could have earned such a reputation as a curmudgeonly ogre and yet show such unrepentant hospitality to the most annoying hordes of complete strangers—was beyond Blake.

In fact, annoying didn't begin to describe the Weinhausen family, as far as Blake was concerned. Though it was nice to chat and play cards with Soojee in the bay window, it didn't fill the gap. The gap was now filled with cramped contortions of conscience, interrupted by squealing children and an endless barrage of banality from Soojee's mother, Kat. He eyed her as she slunk along the hearth on her tip-toes, invading Gunn's mementos with her trespassing gaze, and prying him with insipid, personal questions.

"Who's this? Is this your sister?" she said, arriving at the silver frame.

"No, mum. That's my true love. Sophie."

"Awww! What year?"

"Forty-four. We were eighteen."

"Were you in the war?"

"Dunkirk. Nineteen-forty. Sailed a pilot cutter back and forth across the channel with my father."

"You hear that Jamie? Tripper was in the war," she called to her husband.

"Did you say Dunkirk?" he replied, from the pool table.

"Rescued four hundred eighteen soldiers. Day and night, sometimes under fire. Thought for sure that old cutter'd sink like lead, she was so overladen."

"Did you enlist?"

"Aye. Ended up in North Africa with Montgomery. That was a hot dusty affair."

"You fought Rommel? The Desert Fox? Nineteen forty-two, right?"

"You're a history buff, eh?" said Gunn.

"Oh Tripper, he'd watch the History Channel in the bathtub if he could!" Kat cackled obnoxiously, to restore Gunn's focus to its proper place—herself.

Blake perked up. "So wait, you were only sixteen when you enlisted?"

"Ah well, something like that." Gunn struggled out of his recliner and shuffled for the kitchen, post haste. "Can I get yeh another beer, Jamie?"

"Isn't that romantic, Kiki?" crooned Kat. "He lied about his age to fight for his country, then came home and married his sweetheart!"

Blake was on the verge of telling her to shut up and mind her own business when Gunn returned to the pool table with refreshments. "Did'na work out that way, mum. No, Mr. Hitler's rockets ended *those* plans. If I'd no enlisted, we'd undoubtedly been somewhere else and things had turned out different."

"Sorry, man," said Jamie, accepting his bottle. Gunn took a cue from the rack and chalked it industriously.

Well, well. Thought Blake. "Uno!" he said, laying down a yellow card.

"Draw four," said Soojee, "and I'm out!"

Chapter 56

Sunday there was enough breeze to sail, in spite of the beastly heat. Gunn had a hankering for Elsie's cooking, more than any real desire to race. Blake knew that Mia would not be at the club but embraced the idea of going simply for the sake of finally getting there. The race crowd was present in full force. Blake wasted no time in invading the girl's dorm. The utility closet was empty. But In spite of the listless musty air, he could still detect the faintest flowery hint of her shampoo. In the corner, sticking out from a loose strip of baseboard, he spotted a bright orange wedge of paper.

Blake snatched it out. He unfolded it and took it to a window.

> I knew you couldn't resist!
> Think Wednesday night, after 11:00.
> I'll send word.
> I really miss you, too.
> This note will self-destruct in 5 seconds.
> You just counted to 5, you idiot!
> M.

A little giggle rippled through him. It was the first pleasant feeling he'd had since he'd seen her on Thursday. He folded it back up and slipped it in his wallet.

Back on the first floor, Blake headed for the galley. Rounding the corner he almost collided with Commodore Devlin, who was shuffling backwards and gesturing like a tour guide. His audience was none other than Mayor Teddy and the White Queen herself! Blake ducked aside as Devlin said, "So, you can see how repurposing this space to restaurant use and adding shoreline slips for motor yachts would generate added value for the Highland Lake residential and tourist experience and…"

"And there's the man to beat!" said Mayor Teddy, pointing around Devlin

Devlin looked over his shoulder at Blake. "Yeah, he could use a good beating."

"Hey buddy, I hear you had a heck of a barbeque at Gunn's place, the other night?" said the mayor.

"It was life or death on a lee shore, sir." Mayor Teddy shook his hand. Devlin stepped aside and stood next to Brigita.

"Call me Ted, son. Well, you and your uncle sure know how to turn a town upside-down!"

Blake merely shrugged and grimaced sheepishly.

"Sometimes it has to be done, no matter what the cost; what's popular isn't always the best thing for a community. Isn't that right Larry?"

"Oh, yeah. Definitely. As I was saying…"

"Doing what must be done is the burden of a true leader, Blake. Sometimes it means going against the flow. Raising a few hackles. Making a few enemies. But in the long run, people will see the sense in it."

"Oh Teddy!" moaned Brigita, twirling a platinum-blonde lock around her middle finger. "Not another motivational speech? The poor boy wants to go race his little boat with his girlfriend." Devlin shot her a quick, nervous look.

"Speaking of restaurants, Mayor Ted, you ever been to the Tryste? It's a little sidewalk café in town." said Blake.

"Yes! Great little place! Haven't been there in a long time."

"Really? I was sure I saw a picture of you two there, during the Freedom Fest. My mistake, I guess."

Brigita turned that rosy color again. "A very big one." She smiled wickedly at him and drew that finger out of her hair and slowly across her throat. The nail left a thin crimson line that vanished in a second.

"No, it *was* you, ma'am. Without a doubt, no one in Freeman is as pretty as you!" Blake locked eyes with the Commodore for an instant.

"Flattery will get you everywhere, young man! He is taking lessons from you, isn't he Teddy?"

"She has a point!" laughed the mayor. "You better get going, Blake. Let's have lunch sometime, buddy! Talk about colleges." The mayor now took the lead of the procession, spreading his arms as if to embrace the great room itself. "Devlin, you can't be serious? This place is a piece of local history—it's legendary! You'd ruin it for the sake of commercial interest? I was thinking of launching a campaign to get it on the National Register of Historic places!"

"Check!" Blake said to Brigita, as they passed by.

She gave him such a chilling stare that he thought he'd have to go stand in the sun to kick-start his circulation. "Croatian," she countered, deftly.

Chapter 57

Tuesday at sundown, Blake stood on the cape, cranking away at the winch. "Lied about his age!" he groaned as he cranked. "Sailed a century-old boat for nine days—unarmed—into hostile waters! Went to war at sixteen!" The rhythmic clinking of the safety-latch in the braking gear ebbed and surged like a mechanical cicada. Foot by foot, the steel cable snaked out of the water, finally pulling the chain taught, two feet above the surface.

If this isn't war, I don't know what is, he thought, staring at the dripping barricade. *I hope Mia sees this in time.*

The green pickup rumbled into the lot. Cezar and Romero were returning from a pool job.

Blake headed back to the shop. Cezar met him halfway.

"Hey amigo! Aca!" He furtively slapped a cell phone into Blake's hand. It was the one Mia had given him on Independence Day. It went straight into one of his cargo pockets. Cezar winked. "No es su novia, eh?"

"Verdad."

"Su Rica diga mi 'Miercoles, cierto.'"

"Practican en Español?" said Blake.

"Si. Muy bien."

"I *knew* it. She *does* speak Spanish." he shook his head. *Alright Mia. Come what may, it's Wednesday for sure.*

Chapter 58

Cowboys galloped across the canyon floor an flung lassos around the allosaurus's blue neck. An epic struggle ensued. Carson laughed in delight.

"*Valley of Gwangi.* How can you beat cowboys and dinosaurs?"

Sooner wasn't so sure. She huddled close to Blake on the floor. It had all happened as he'd hoped. Gunn had gone to bed early. Carson drifted off toward the end of the movie. Blake switched out the light and went to the bathroom. He checked the phone. Mia was well past Trespass Island. When he returned, Sooner was curled up on Carson's lap. Trembling, Blake slipped out the kitchen door.

He met her at the cape. It was twelve thirty. "How long will this take?" he whispered.

"Nice to see you too! They're about two miles up the lake. A couple of hours, if all goes well."

He dug his paddle into the silt and heaved them off. Blake filled her in on Sunday's encounter.

"You said *that* in front of my dad and the Dragon Lady? I'm impressed!"

"What did I have to lose? Might as well go down kicking."

"Come on, take heart. We end this tonight."

"How? That's what concerns me."

"You'll receive your orders when we're close to the target."

"When it's too late to turn back."

"Exactly. Just think how boring your life was before this summer! Look at all the stories you'll have to tell."

"They don't let you make money on books you write in prison."

They paddled in unison with strong, swift strokes. *Cry of the Osprey* flew over the still water for a half hour. Mia signaled Blake to stop paddling.

"Thar she blows!" she whispered. Blake could barely discern a faint flickering light against the distant black shore.

"Turn off your phone and hand it here." She turned off her own and stowed it. Then she prepared her camera. The flash whined like a mosquito that had just tapped a vein of triple espresso. "There's a bag of cable under your deck. It's got a shackle on both ends. Lose those and we're screwed. There's a nail in there to tighten 'em up with."

Blake pulled the bag up into his lap. Mia pulled a burlap bag from under her knees. Something inside resituated itself, displeased with the commotion. "Okay, here's the deal."

They crossed the lake and sped down the opposite shore. At last, they crept upon their prey. The *Eclipse* lay in a wide cove, with her bow toward the lake. Seductive, foreign music and a pungent smell drifted through the air. Candle light flickered in the porthole, and out of an open hatch on the foredeck. Blake surveyed her with the night scope. Carefully, he nodded to Mia then back-paddled. They turned *Cry of the Osprey* around. Mia pulled dock fenders out of the aft cargo net and deployed them along the starboard side. Blake looped the thin wire cable around the trunk of a leaning tree and shackled it. Mia paddled the kayak in reverse toward the bow of her father's yacht, while Blake paid out cable. He shackled the other end to the ring in *Eclipse's* nose.

They hunkered low and ghosted down the port side, then eased around the stern. They snuggled *Osprey* up with her bumpers against the transom of the big yacht. Mia lifted herself up the swim ladder just high enough to see into the companionway. "Go, go, go!" she whispered, almost silently. Daintily, Blake drew himself up the swim ladder and into the cockpit. Mia handed up the burlap bag, then pushed off. Blake wasted no time getting to the bow, his steps light and even. He could hear murmurs mixed with the bewitching music; and the incense—if that's what it was—made him dizzy. Trembling fingers unknotted the mouth of the bag. He put one hand under it and waited for the signal. He hoped he could hear it over the blood pounding in his ears. An unmistakable wolf-whistle tripped across the cove. Blake dumped the contents of the bag into the hatch, knocked the prop out and dove on the cover. The screaming and commotion below had to be heard to be believed. Brilliant white flashes illuminated the harbor with a light as stark as the terror on the lovers' faces, as they burst over the stern. Before he knew it, Mia was along side.

"Get their clothes!" she said over the splashing and shrieking astern.

"What!"

"Go on, get below! You've got thirty seconds and I'm gone."

"Dang it!" He jerked the hatch cover up, dropped onto the wedge-shaped bed below, and snatched their wardrobe out of a narrow hallway. He shook the wallet out of Devlin's shorts and plucked up Brigita's tennis skirt—to find an enormous black rat snake. The White Queen was still screaming and cursing out there in the dark somewhere. The boat rocked— Blake froze. Someone had mounted the ladder. Mia wolf-whistled. Devlin got his head over the stern just in time to catch the flying serpent across his eyes.

Blake blew out the candles on his way back to the hatch. On deck he chucked the laundry in the lake and dropped awkwardly into the *Osprey*. Mia went into overdrive. Blake pulled his paddle from its straps and laid into it like never before.

They were almost to the far shore when they heard the motor start. "Quick! Give me the scope!" said Mia.

The mucky anchor dangled from the pulpit as *Eclipse* lumbered forward. She went fifty feet before her bow lurched suddenly to starboard. The boat heeled hard and cut a sharp semicircle toward shore, then grounded firmly in a muddy shoal.

Mia switched on her phone and dialed. Blake resumed his stroke. "Yeah, Mitch? *Eclipse* is stuck in the mud. Cheater's Cove. Daddy says hurry!" Mia cackled in delight. "Best. Voicemail. Ever!"

***

The knob didn't turn. No mistake—the kitchen door was locked. A pang of anxiety fermented in Blake's belly. *Seriously? Did I really lock myself out? Okay, Plan B,* he thought.

Blake checked his watch as he slunk around the far end of the workshop. It was 1:55. He wormed his hand into the gap between the big sliding door and its frame. He found the hook and worked it out of the eye. With a little effort, the door grunted open just enough. He made his way through the dark cavern of the shop, expecting Carson to jump out on him at any second. The door to the storefront was unlocked. He retrieved the key to unlock the stairway, and emerged silently in the upstairs hall. Something snuffled and puffed hot breath on his feet. Blake gasped and plastered himself against the door.

Carson snickered in his bed. "Must've been an interesting date. You smell like a fart in a hookah bar!"

Chapter 59

Mia dialed Hunter's phone. Her father answered, "You found it! Finally looked where I told you?"

"Don't hang up now! You're about to hear an important message from your daughter!"

"State your demands."

"Call off the heat."

"Clarify," he said.

"The INS, DHS, CPS, FDS, and the freaking PTA. Whatever that Slavic slut of yours has left in her bag of dirty tricks. That includes Hunter."

"But he's been so good, lately."

"You know that cuckoo clock between his ears is about to strike midnight. It'll be better for us all if that happens in Florida."

"Hunter is as Hunter does. Can't make any guarantees on that one. You want your money, I suppose?"

"Reinstate my trust fund disbursements and my allowance. With back-pay." She could hear him clicking away with the mouse, punctuated with a final 'ding!' from the computer.

"Done."

"Get mom off my back. You'll have to get the school to lay off me first."

"Pretty tall order."

"Let me explain," she said.

"First, let me explain something to *you*. It's a little thing called 'the balance of terror.' I'm going to meet your demands. As long as you lay off me, I'll lay off you. And just to show what a loving father I am, I've made reservations for you at the finest behavioral treatment center in the state. The one with the heavy duty restraints on all the chairs and beds, the compassionate staff and the oh-so-fabulous pharmacy. You know the one?"

Mia's heart skipped a beat and sweat broke out on her forehead.

"Hellooo?" he said.

"I remember."

"You so much as slip up, little girl, and it'll be a one way trip to a lifetime of electrodes and needles. Now, explain this whole thing with the school."

***

Mia crossed the open lake in broad daylight for the first time in almost a week. She tied up across from the *Terrapin* and sought Blake in the shop. He was feeding a wide plank into the planer. Cezar received it as it crawled out the other side of the screaming machine. He waited until Blake released the last few inches of the board, then nodded to Mia. He pulled the board free and shut the Planer off.

"Señor Pagán! Un momento con mi amiga, por favor?"

"Si. You go on. Is dinner time, anyway." He eyed them with paternal concern as Blake escorted her out of the work bay and into the late afternoon swelter.

"Put sails and a rudder on those and you could start a new fleet," she said.

"Huh? Oh, hold on." He pulled neon-pink plugs out of his ears. "What did you say?"

"Never mind."

"Well, I see you're smiling."

"I told you we'd fix it. I'm still keeping my head down until everyone's gotten the word to back off. So, I thought we should celebrate. I brought dinner!"

The bay window squeaked open, above. Gunn leaned out. "Lad, what are yeh up too?"

"Mia brought dinner for the two of us. Is it okay if we eat out on the cape?"

Gunn stared at her for a second. "A'right. Don' keep him out all night. State Fair opens tomorrow—we're leaving bright and early."

"I'd love it if I could tag along!" said Mia.

"No without permission, lass."

"Could you call my dad and ask him, then?" She smiled sweetly. "I mean if you don't mind."

Gunn scowled, then glanced at Blake who already had a wary eye on her.

"A'right." He shut the window.

"Talk about audacious," Blake said.

"You mean that in a good way or a bad way? Come on, dinner's in the boat."

Cumulus clouds piled up in the distance but gave no rain, no flash of lightning, no thunder. Mia piled the table with goodies from the Emporium's deli, which Treva had supplied to her in hiding. Tall bottles of sparkling apple cider stood like green glass towers amid battlements of cheese and salami and a castle of crackers.

Blake watched herds of house boats chugging their way up and down the lower lake.

"I've never seen it this busy, down here." he said.

"It's the last 'hurrah.' School starts next week. That reminds me! Guess what?"

"I'm afraid. *Very* afraid."

"I'm home schooled, now—whatever that means! I can pretty much do whatever I want and call it school, right?"

"Not where I'm from."

"You can fill me in later. So, I backed my camera up onto my tablet. Get your flash drive, I need to give you a copy."

"My what?"

"The little fish-thing Mueller gave you," she said, incredulously.

"I'm not sure what happened to it."

"I'll get mine from Treva's, then."

"Do I have to? I really don't feel right about it."

"Buddy, that's our insurance policy. Anything happens to either one of us and those pictures go straight to the mayor, my mom, and the newspaper."

"But still…"

"Still nothing! We're in this together. Like it or not, we have to depend on each other from here on out."

If I hadn't gone, he thought, *things would have been different.*

"How do you like the sparkling cider?" she said, pouring him another.

"The what?"

"The Martinelli's. The fizzy apple juice?"

"Oh, It's good." He smiled timidly and thought *Just another thing on my father's long list of forbidden fruits. Too bad he forgot extortion."*

Chapter 60

Blake slouched in the bay window and reflected on his day at the Indiana State Fair. It was good to go wander anonymously among the 'great unwashed masses,' as Gunn called the boundless crowd.

He stared for a moment at the pole light by the dock. Bats circled and dove through the insect smorgasbord that clouded around it.

He turned his attention to the postcard in his hand. On one side were scenes from the Fair; on the other, blank space. He mulled over a fading twinge of resentment. *If Mom hadn't gone, things would've been different.* Visions of what that different summer would have been like, had his family not gone to France, played out in his head. He imagined the battles, the confrontations, the boredom, the brow beatings, the misery. He imagined how he would have handled it all with gallant defiance. Then he realized *I wouldn't have handled it that way. Because that's what I would do now. That's not who I was.*

He took up his pen.

Dear Mom,
Sorry I haven't written. It has been an unbelievable summer. The State Fair was amazing! The Chinese Acrobats and DNR Building were my favorites. Huge Catfish named Jonah. Raptor show. 4H Art, and model rockets were a close second. Uncle Arctica

says to tell you "Send lawyers, guns, and money." I concur.
Miss you,
Blake

Chapter 61

Blake and Carson motored *Becky Lynn* up the channel. The nursing home had called and needed Carson to fill out another form of some sort. It was the Sabbath and, after twelve hours of walking around at the Fair the day before, they were ready for a rest.

Blake spotted the stump and chain, and triangulated with the cell tower. "Stay this course and we'll miss the piling!"

Carson grinned and steered straight for the stump. Blake shook his head and leaned over the side to catch sight of the monster. Carson turned back toward the upper lake, then there it was—looming up from the murky depths into clear water: the massive, algae-jacketed monolith of the Yaegerstown bridge piling. It was longer than their boat and four feet wide. Its flat top was scarred with furrows; its edges chipped and chunked away by the props, keels and centerboards of the ignorant and unwary.

"That's no more that two feet down!" said Blake.

"You want to stand on it?"

"No way! It's spooky!"

"Always reminded me of a giant chess piece." Carson leaned out and watched it go by. "Dad wanted to dynamite it, but the Corp of Engineers wouldn't do it for some stupid reason. Took out all the others and left that one. Galled him all his life. He tethered buoy's to it every which way he could think of, but they never would stay. Finally he put just that chain on that stump, there."

464

Blake stared as the stump passed out of sight. "This whole thing has been like a chess game, you know?"

"You play?"

"A little. Know any secrets?"

"Yeah. Don't be afraid to lose your queen. And look out for people who *are*. Most folks lose their queen and think it's all over. It ain't about the queen. It's about using what you got left and forging ahead with your plan. If you can do that, it rattles your opponent."

Don't be afraid to lose your queen? Here was a notion nearly as startling and heretical as Korbin's refusal to answer his phone.

"That and thinking ahead several moves," said Carson. "That's the real lesson chess has to offer."

Blake dug a bottle of cold water out of the cooler and tossed it to his uncle. He opened one for himself.

"Tripp really gave you this boat, huh?" Carson twisted the cap off and drained half the bottle in one swig.

"By right of conquest."

"She has seen some action, hasn't she?" he said, slapping the hull affectionately.

***

Blake left his uncle at the nurse's station and went to Korbin's room.

"You readin' that book, boy?" said Dubois, the motor in his chair whirring dutifully.

"A little. We've been pretty busy, and I'm pretty tired by the time I go to bed."

"S'pose Caw's down there fussin' with Miss Clydesdale?"

"Yeah. Pre-arrangement paperwork, I think he said. Do you know anything about Yagerstown?"

"Heh! They weren't no Christian people, I know that! State paid 'em to relocate when they flooded the valley."

"Let me guess where they went. Mangrave?"

"Sure enough."

"Were they devil worshippers or something?"

"They were settlers, brought their old religion from where ever they came from. Always just bad people, them folks in Yaegerstown."

That gave Blake a chill. "And why do people call me the prince?"

"'Cause they can see it!"

"See what? I mean people who don't even know me call me that."

"Young Uh-quot, there is a spiritual reality behind this *material* masquerade. One great Kingdom—those who love and seek to establish it, and those who hate and seek to destroy it. You read that book. It tells you the story."

"I'm sorry. I'm still not getting the 'prince' part."

"Your granddaddy raised a stronghold for that Kingdom, here. But your uncle abdicated his stewardship and now the enemy runs wild over this place. So the legacy falls to you. Now *you're* the prince."

"All the arrangements are made Korbin," said Carson, sauntering into the room. "The boy here built you a fine box."

"I'm sure he did. Caw, you ought to be teaching this boy the Word on the Sabbath day!"

"His Daddy's a Chet Allworth man, he oughta know it inside and out!"

"You don't learn this boy, Caw, and he'll turn out a drifter just like you!"

"It has it advantages," said Carson, becoming testy.

"So, um, did you hear about the big catfish?" Blake interrupted.

"I'm sure *you* think so!" said Korbin.

"Look, I just came over here to…"

"Say, I turned thirteen!" said Blake.

"I know you're thirteen, had five hundred people over to your party!" replied Dubois.

"Could we talk about something else? I didn't mean to start anything."

"Blessed are the peacemakers, boy; but it's best not to get 'tween two old fellers when they're bickering."

"Who you calling old?" Carson protested.

"You're just a pup!"

"Forty nine and a pup? Whatever you say, Methuselah."

"Show some respect, Uncle Carson, please!"

"I dish it out to whoever hands it out. Don't care if they're nine or nine hundred ninety and nine!"

"I'll meet you at the boat," said Blake, as he stood up. "Good to see you Mr. Dubois."

"You're the prince, now, young Uh-quot! The Book is the house rules for the Kingdom. Don't forget!"

Chapter 62

Sunday morning, Blake and Mia were on their way to Indianapolis, once again. This time in the spacious back seat of Beverly Maitland's Buick battle-cruiser deluxe. Today it would be the State Museum, the Eiteljorg Museum of Native American History, and if anyone was up for it, the Indianapolis Zoo. Mia entrusted Blake with her fish flash drive, and a stern look.

Hunter, too, was cruising on down the road. His phone rang. It was exactly who he didn't want to hear from. "Talk to me, baby!"

"Where do you think you are going, my bronze hero?" said Brigita.

"Oh you know, just got the wander lust."

"I have no doubt it is lust, but not for the road. Get back here. I have something important for you to do."

"Are you kidding? I just crossed the Ohio River!"

"Your sister and her little pet—Sparky, that's what you call him? They have humiliated me and your father for the last time."

"Sounds like a personal problem." The radar detector on the dash of his Porsche bleeped. Hunter braked and shaved twenty-five miles per hour off his speed.

"A very personal problem for us all, I assure you. Your father's empire and your future hang on the pictures in her camera. We get it back, or we all lose everything."

"She's made a thousand copies by now, if that's the case."

"Then you get the camera, her tablet, her computer, all of it!" she shouted. Then regaining her composure said "Meet me tonight. And bring two bottles of that almond champagne." The line went dead. Hunter turned around at the next exit.

***

Tantrum II drifted under the lights of the looming dam. Hunter ducked the empty champagne bottle as it careened off two walls and bounced across the floor.

Brigita screamed like a wounded goddess. "How did she know! How is it possible!"

"Watch the woodwork, sister! This is my old man's boat!"

"You should see his other boat! It's got cobras!" She kicked the bottle straight into the companionway doors. "How could she find us? Twice! How could she know about my tattoo?"

She snatched up a gym bag and thrust her hand into it. Out came a most wicked looking cat o' nine tails, fashioned from eighth-inch steel cable. "Do you know what I will do? I will *whip* the flesh from their bones!" she wailed, thrashing the bench cushion. Shredded leather and chunks of foam stuffing flew everywhere.

"Hey, hey, hey! Enough! Hell hath no fury, but come on! You're making the Devil nervous, here!"

She turned from the mutilated cushions and menaced Hunter with the flail's barbed, metal tentacles.

"She is your sister. Just a little girl. How did she do this?"

Hunter thought for a moment. "Give me your phone."

"What?" She wiped sweat from her brow. "What?"

"Sit down, shut up, and give me your phone. Open that other bottle while you're at it."

Brigita threw the flail down and got her phone. She handed it over, then stood impatiently with her arms crossed. Hunter tapped, swiped, and pinched.

"Here it is. A cute little app called *Traxxum*."

"How did she get that onto my phone? Wait; those vulgar, brown peasants! Isn't it bad enough that they handle my linens, but they touch my personal things?"

Hunter continued to fiddle with the phone's settings. She stared at him with growing envy.

"And they have touched *you*, my bronze hero."

"Call it a weakness. Starts when you're young." He handed her the phone. "All gone. I said open that bottle." She went to the little refrigerator under the bar. Hunter pulled out his own phone, found the spyware, and made a few hasty changes to its settings. The map popped up, with two icons: one for Mia, one Brigita. He double tapped Brigita's image and it faded out behind the little red word 'hidden.'"

There was a loud pop. Brigita returned with the bottle and no glasses. She took a swig and wiped her mouth on her forearm. "How will you do it?"

"Well, this is a good start," he said, holding up his phone.

Chapter 63

Hunter ate a donut and leafed through a sports magazine. His phone dinged softly. Mia's icon was halfway down the channel. He picked it up and dialed the Emporium.

"Yeah, is Treva there? She is? Good. Sure I'll wait." He hung up, then dialed again. "Mitch—the light is green, we are go! Repeat, we are go! Tantrum in one hour." He ended the call. "Just enough time for a little trip to town."

***

Twin Mercury outboards pushed the big pontoon workboat down the channel, *Tantrum II* in tow. Hunter signaled and Mitch cast him adrift in the mouth of Highland Harbor. They had cut it close. Blake and Mia were just on the other side of the ridge, in Thistle Bay. Hunter fired up the engine. The unmistakable thunder paralyzed them mid stroke. Mia was about to give the command to drive for shore when Mitch chugged into view. She shouted and waved frantically. He waved back and slowed down. Paddles whirled like windmills until Blake was close enough to toss him the bowline.

"Mitch, take us back to Gunn's!" said Mia.

He tied them off and continued down lake.

"No! Mitch! Gunn's!" He didn't turn around.

"I don't think he can hear us over those monsters," said Blake, cupping his hands around his mouth.

They went a quarter mile before *Tantrum II* slithered into view behind them. They renewed their efforts to get Mitch's attention, but to no avail. Blake remembered his mini air-horn and gave it several blasts. The skipper glanced over his shoulder. They made wild gestures toward their pursuer. He seemed to understand and throttled up a little. *Cry of the Osprey* was now clipping along at eight miles per hour, widening the gap ever so slightly between them and *Tantrum II*.

Another nerve-wracking mile went by. She looked back. Hunter had edged up on them by two hundred feet. He was talking on his phone.

"I know some people down here. Maybe you could call them?" said Blake. Mia looked back, then to Mitch—who was on his phone, too. Something twinged in her already churning gut. She pulled out her phone and launched the tracker. Tears of sheer terror burst over her cheeks.

"What's the matter, Mia? Mia?"

She turned the phone around slowly, so that he could see.

"Brigita?" It only took a second. "It's a trap!"

Mia's arm went limp as she slumped back and sobbed. The phone slid off the curved deck and spun into their wake.

Blake took his bearings. The mouth of the Mangrave Branch was coming up fast.

"Mia, get ready to paddle for your life!" She only stared and cried.

Blake dug into his cargo pocket. He brought out a buck knife and a flat roll of duct tape he'd made. He slid one end of his paddle through the bungee straps on the bow and frantically swabbed the other end dry with the tail of his shirt. He opened the knife and taped it to the paddle blade, with a half dozen wraps.

He pulled the makeshift spear free and turned back to Mia. "Are you ready? Look at me! We are *going* to make it but you *have* to paddle! You've spent all summer telling me to be a Viking, you're not gonna go victim on me now! Paddle!"

He turned back and whipped the gleaming blade down where the bowline looped through the nose of the kayak. The rope snapped like a rubber band.

"Hard to port!" He yelled, digging his paddle in with all his might. The sudden loss of speed shocked Mia back to reality. She put everything she had left into moving that kayak. They managed to keep most of their momentum, caught up to Mitch's wake and surfed over it. Blake looked over his shoulder, fully expecting to see *Tantrum II* bearing down on them. "He's not following us."

"That worries me even more!"

They reached the mouth of the Mangrave Branch. Hunter, five hundred feet astern, changed course but did not accelerate.

"Here he comes!" said Mia. "What's your plan, Tux?"

"Don't rush me, I'm working on it!"

"Need I remind you where we are?"

"Don't worry, my uncle and I have had some great times here!"

They were well past the lagoon when Hunter entered the branch. The rumble of his engine went up a notch and the cigarette boat came down on them in earnest.

"Blake!"

"Hard to Starboard!"

They swooped into a narrow tributary and dashed for the high wall of cattails at its end.

Hunter made a slow careful turn and crept gingerly up the stream, keeping a nervous eye on the high slopes to either side.

Blake and Mia didn't stop paddling until there was no more water under their keel. They leapt out and dragged *Cry of the Osprey* into the almost impenetrable jungle of bone-dry reeds. They dropped her and pressed on against the slashing, slapping vegetation that turned ankles, tripped and snagged and frustrated every effort to advance. Finally, the adrenalin gave out. They stopped and bent double, trying to catch their breath as the snarling leviathan approached.

Brigita was now on deck. "Why are you stopping?"

"Because I don't have wheels," said Hunter.

"Now how will we get them?"

"The old fashioned way. Go in there and hunt them down."

"In there? Don't be ridiculous!" She stormed back down into the cabin.

"Alright you guys!" he shouted. "You know what we want. Sparky, you just bring me the camera and we'll call it a day."

Blake and Mia looked at each other. "The camera!" Mia started for the kayak. Something popped—a blazing red ball flashed into the cattail forest and broke into a thousand sparking starlets. Immediately the air was filled with the sound of crackling and the smell of sulphur.

"What the hell are you doing?" shouted Hunter, reversing the throttle.

Brigita reloaded the flare gun. "We do not chase vermin. We burn them out!" She fired again.

Blake and Mia wasted no time. They plunged headlong through the unyielding vegetation. As it began to thin Blake grabbed her hand and led her into another ravine. There were no cattails in this streambed.

"What's that smell?" said Mia, taking the lead.

"Smells like when they clean the floors at church."

The chemical stench was almost asphyxiating. She stopped and glanced around. Directly across the ravine, wedged in a hollow twenty feet up the hillside, was an ancient house boat. It had been deliberately shored up and disguised with limbs and vegetation.

"Oh my god! Run!" She scrambled up the opposite ridge.

Every burning fiber of Blake's body screamed for oxygen as he clawed for traction and dodged Mia's heels. A strange sound halted him. He looked back to see a roaring river of fire running up the wash. It turned and went straight up the hill and in the front door of the houseboat. The blast knocked him flat. He rose spitting leaf litter and dirt. And the heat! Searing heat gushed up the slope like a desert wind and stole his breath. Where was Mia? Everything seemed to wobble. Flaming chunks of wood and Styrofoam began to fall through the trees.

He called for her but his voice seemed as if it had been captured in a glass jar and hidden somewhere in the forest. He staggered to the summit. She was nowhere in sight.

Then he heard it. Just a little squeak—no, a scream! There, down the slope! Hands clasping the base of a skinny tree at the ragged edge of a cliff. He dropped on his behind and slid down to straddle the trunk, threw his arms around it and seized her wrists. A hundred miles away she was shrieking pleas to Hunter not to let go.

He pointed his toes up and yelled "step on my feet!" Mia got one foot, then the other onto the human stirrups and worked her way up. He seized her waist band and pulled her around. She was gone in a heartbeat.

"Wait! This way!" She skidded to a stop and reversed direction. She fled past him screaming, the white hound appearing from nowhere and loping after her.

"It's okay! He's alright!" Blake finally caught up to her. "Don't panic! You're gonna get us killed."

She said something to him, but he did not hear her. The hound was barking without a sound. Then it hit him. "I can't hear! Mia I can't hear anything!" Smoke from the ravine was beginning to filter through the trees.

"How do we get out of here?" she said. He looked puzzled. She pointed to her mouth and said it again, slowly. He dug out his compass, thought for a moment, then pointed.

The hound took off in that direction as if to affirm Blake's decision.

***

Maynard and Shelby, along with every other watercraft on Highland Lake, moseyed toward the thinning column of black smoke. Shelby heard it first. The insistent bleating of a little air-horn from the shore. Two kids yelling and waving their arms frantically, as they ran into the shallows.

They slouched behind the low aluminum walls of *Quitcherbitchin*. They were a complete mess: scratched, cut, torn and scorched. And thirsty.

"You must be parched!" drawled the leathery woman. "There's tea in that cooler, but…" She pointed to the blue chest Blake had his arm on. He opened the lid, seized a quart jug and guzzled half of it.

"Not that much! Drink it slow, now!" said Shelby, with a self conscious laugh.

That struck Mia as an odd thing to say. She yanked the plastic decanter away and took a whiff. She shot Shelby a look. "Seriously?"

Blake shook his head like he'd been stung on the nose by a bee. His face glowed like that fireball in the woods. "Give that back!"

"Lady, we're gonna need a bucket!" said Mia.

***

Four coffins leaned against the work bay door, gleaming in the sun. They were the old-fashioned style: wide at the shoulder, tapering toward the head and foot, a small window with a sliding cover in the lid. Gunn admired their workmanship as he came up from the *Terrapin*.

"Business is booming Sylvio!" he said, as he passed by.

"Oh yes! The web site is very good. People are dying for our coffins!"

"Yeh didn'a just say that! The lad home?"

"We see him go upstairs. I think he may be sick."

***

"Lad? Lad?" Blake was passed out on his bed, Sooner curled up under one armpit. Gunn nudged him forcefully. "Caduggin!"

Blake opened one bleary eye. "Stoof it in yer pookits!"

"Yeh smell like a four-alarm fire in a rum distillery!"

"Speak up, man! I'm Deeeef!"

"That ain't all yeh are!" said Gunn. He stepped back into the hall. The bathroom door opened and Mia came out, clad in a luxuriant, white bathrobe, with a towel wrapped around her head.

"Mr. Gunn! Ah, I know this must look bad."

"Look bad? The lad's passed out deaf and drunk, pretty young girl steps out of my shower wearing my robe, all Hell's broken loose down lake, and I've got Mexicans building coffins in my boot shop. No, it's just yer average day around the Gunn estate!"

The phone rang. She shrugged her shoulders and said, "Give you three guesses?" He lumbered off to the living room.

"Gunn! Oh, Officer Mueller? Will the wonders never cease? Explosion? Yeh don't say. Another meth-lab? Aye they're both fine. Why would yeh assume they'd be involved? Anonymous tip, is that all yeh have to go on? And a molten slab of plastic the size and shape of a tandem kayak? What color? Purple! I was sure her's was yellow."

"When can I get it back?" said Mia.

"Girl wants to know when she can claim the charred remains?" He covered the phone with one hand. "He says it's evidence." Her jaw dropped.

"Alright. See yeh 'round five." He hung up.

"I've gotta get out of here." she said.

"Yeh can tell me aboot it on the way."

"I'm worried about Blake. He really is deaf."

"Start at the beginning." he said, grimly.

"We were minding our own business…"

***

Dr. Trudeau returned from the hospital with Blake, long after the Police and Fire Chiefs, Buck Mueller, and Daley Dunright had gone. Blake was now sober enough to fear the impending consequences of the day's adventure. Gunn merely sent him off to the bathtub.

Trudeau fetched a beer from the fridge.

"The hearing loss shouldn't last more than seventy-two hours," said Trudeau. "The hangover, though…" He sat down on the hearth.

Gunn took a swig from his own bottle. He leaned heavily on the armrest of the recliner. The evening had taken a toll. "It's no fair! I can't even give 'im a good haranguing. Seventy-two hours and I'll be over it!"

"So, you believe Mia's story?"

"Every word of it, Bill."

"That's troubling."

"What's troubling to me is what they must have done to provoke it? Hunter and random mayhem with a flare gun—not at all out of the question. But Hunter—and the Mayor's *wife* with a flare gun—*and* Mitch? That's a conspiracy, man! Then there's that kayak—what's in it that she wants it back so badly?"

"Maybe Blake will be more forthcoming."

"It kills me, Bill! I'm gonna have to ship him off to his Grandmother. And his Uncle with him. Those two and that girl have managed to turn this entire lake into a war zone. They've destroyed every shred of clout or goodwill I ever had with the higher-ups in town, except maybe Mayor Ted. Buck Mueller's even turned his back on me."

Trudeau thought for a moment. "How are *you* holding up, Tripp?"

"Tired. But I'm alright."

"For a geezer?"

"*The* Geezer."

Chapter 64

"Not so loud, lad!" said Gunn, as Blake counted his score on the cribbage board. The old man picked up the phone. Blake watched his mouth, but his expression said more. Gunn hung up, wrote a note and handed to it to Blake.

Treva said yesterday someone broke in and stole Mia's tablet and computer.
When the cops showed up, they arrested Mia as a runaway.
Last thing she said was 'get the fish to Soojee.'

"What's that mean Caduggin?"

Blake stared at the note. *Don't Panic...They're coming for me next...Now, think! Where did I put it?*

Gunn rapped his knuckles on the table. Blake felt the vibrations and looked up. "What's does it mean Caduggin?" he pointed at the note.

"It means there's no time!" He ran to his bedroom and rifled through everything. It wasn't there. He went through the hamper in the bathroom. Nothing. *Sunday's shorts!* He flew to the laundry room and dumped the basket in front of the dryer. A lump in a pocket—*That's it!* The little green fish had been through the washer and the dryer. *How could I be so stupid!* He flung it into the trash and went back to the table. "Please ask Buck what happened to the Kayak?" Gunn flinched at the volume of the request. He eyed him suspiciously and dialed the phone. It was a short call. He wrote another note.

Commodore Devlin claimed it. Took it home.

Sooner bolted out from under Gunn's feet and leapt into the bay window barking. Blake's heart leapt. He ran to the window. Ms. Seguin and her ginger afro stood waiting for her passenger to get out of the car. A police cruiser rolled in behind them.

Blake shouted a word that he was glad he couldn't hear and tore off to his bedroom. Gunn heard the bathroom door slam. They rang the doorbell and banged on the storm door glass at the same time. There was nothing Gunn could do. They had a court order and a warrant. They talked to the bathroom door for five minutes before one of the officers lost his patience and prepared to batter it down.

"That kind of lock opens with a screwdriver, yeh know?" said Gunn.

"Go sit down, sir! Now!" said the other officer.

Splinters sprayed the bathroom. The door flew open, knob banging a dent in the wall.

The curtains blew gently in the hot breeze. The officer rushed to the window, Tazer drawn. He scanned the roof of the workshop, which made a T with the house. He spotted Blake's boonie hat twenty feet away, then noted the old radio tower at the far end of the building.

"He's gone down that antenna at the end of the roof!" He pulled his weapon back in the window.

Blake watched the cobra-like shadow retreat across the narrow strip between his toes and the edge of the roof. He was braced hard against the bathroom dormer, trying to keep any bare flesh off of the searing shingles.

"He's in the woods. Yeh'll never find him now," said Gunn.

The other officer spoke into his radio. "Dispatch, Cruller! Send K9 to the old marina."

"Copy!" came the squelchy reply.

"And I told you to sit down and shut up!"

Blake waited five interminable minutes, slid down on his roasting rump and took the slightest glance around the front of the dormer. *Coast clear.* He edged around the corner on his haunches and stole a peek in the window. *Bathroom empty.* He eased himself through and crept to the shattered door. Sooner sat in the middle of the hall staring up at him, looking ready to announce her joyous discovery. He glared at her and put his finger to his lips. There was movement up the hall in the living room. The door to the stairs was wide open. *Now or never!* He eased down the steps. The door to the shop was half open. Sooner licked salty sweat off his ankles. Blake sheltered in the stairwell and watched an officer ordering the Pagáns around Bay 1. Lieutenant Cruller made them open each of the coffins, working their way ever closer. Finding the last one unoccupied, the cop turned and walked back through them, berating the family with menacing gestures. Blake took a deep breath, whisked across the floor, and lay down in the closest coffin. Sooner jumped in on top of him. Romero and Cezar, eyes like saucers, hastily replaced the lid.

The K9 unit arrived just as the old green pickup, laden with caskets, ambled out on to the county road.

***

The phone was already in Gunn's hand when it rang. It was Sylvio.

"Mr. Gonn, I am very sorry about the trouble today. The police come to my house after we make our deliveries. They think maybe we sneak Blake out in one of the coffins."

"I wish yeh had."

"We got the little black dog here. We bring him back tomorrow."

"I wondered where she got to!"

"With all respect, you got to change his food. That little dog is not right!"

Gunn laughed for the first time all day. "I'll take that under advisement."

"I got something else to tell you. I get a special order today. My client, he wants me to carve a greefy on the lid of his coffin. You understand what he means?"

"He means a griffin."

"I tell him that but he say he want a greefy. Is like… he can't *hear* me. You understand Mr. Gonn?"

"Perfectly. You tell him that a griffin is a fantastic beast, but a Griffy is a jackass by any other name."

"Very well, Mr. Gonn. I tell him. Buenas noches."

"And a good night to you, my friend."

Gunn let out a long sigh of relief and sank into his recliner a little deeper. "Carson, your nephew is becoming skilled at intrigue. I'd wager he'll either work for the CIA or the mob."

Carson sat in the bay window, one foot on the bench. He stared at his reflection. "And that all depends on me, right?"

"Yer going take him and go down to yer mother, ASAP."

"How do you propose that, seeing as I don't drive?"

"That suspension expired a long time ago. Get some insurance, get your license, get yer arse to North Carolina. While yer gone maybe my lawyers can fix this."

***

"Wow, I've never known a real fugitive before," said Kaz.

"He's not a fugitive, he's a common criminal," said Griffy, fidgeting and contorting around his game controller.

"Well he saved your bacon—a couple of times!"

"After he fried it to a crisp!" On cue, Griffy's star fighter exploded, extravagantly.

Blake was glad he couldn't hear what they were saying. He lay on the floor, staring solemnly at the ceiling. Kaz reached over the chessboard and poked him. Blake startled.

"Sorry! Go ahead, do it."

Blake rolled over, picked up a black pawn and landed in white's back row. "Give me my queen!" He swapped the pawn for his reclaimed piece. "Check—and mate!"

"Not so loud!" said Griffy. "A deaf man could hear you!"

Blake contemplated his victory. *That's it. Nobody's afraid of a pawn. You drive straight in. Attack from an angle they don't expect. You get your queen back.* He jotted a note on his little pad and handed it to Kaz.

"Again? This is like the five-thousandth time!"

Blake dialed Soojee and handed him the phone. "Do it!"

"Voicemail again." Kaz shrugged.

He wrote another note.

I need a map to Lawrence Devlin's house and floorplans. Now.

"Are you serious?"

Blake drew a skull and crossbones and gave Kaz a scowl Mia would've been proud to wear.

Kaz wilted. "I'll get my tablet." After a few minutes of searching, he held up the device. "Couldn't ask for more than this! Devlin's mansion was featured in the Freeman tour of homes. Lots of interior photos, a neighborhood map and a floorplan."

Blake studied each photo with grim intensity. He wrote on his pad again.

Call Cezar. Tell him we have a pool job tomorrow. Pick me up at 10.

Kaz typed nervously on his tablet. "Hey, this makes me an accomplice, doesn't it?"

"Welcome to my world," said Blake, just above a whisper.

***

He lay awake far later than he wanted. He longed for the symphony of the night lake. Even the freakish squawks of the crowned herons and the eerie cry of the whippoorwills.

The silence made it all too easy to brood over the boiling cauldron of his predicament.

He wondered how hard it would be to learn sign language. It had been two days since the explosion, but all he could hear was the whining polyphony of tinnitus that whistled in his head at a glass-shattering pitch. *Judy has been so nice,* he thought, *and Griffy such a jerk. And Kaz is…who knows. They're downstairs arguing about high-scores and DVD's and whose farts are worse. And here I am guessing about prison terms. I'm about to disgrace everyone whose ever put an ounce of faith or hope in me—even if I get away with it and nobody finds out. I will have to live with that the rest of my life. But how can I just walk away and forget my best friend? Just say 'oh well' and walk away and leave her in the hands of the most evil people I've ever met? I would so feel ashamed of myself, I'd...I could never...be human again.* He picked up the tablet and went through the pictures twice more.

Chapter 65

Graciella Maria Garcia De La Cruz looked down on the two muchachos on her doorstep—one Latino, one gringo in a ball cap and mirrored sunglasses.

"What is the meaning of this?" she said in Spanish.

"We are here to service the pool," said Cezar.

"The pool men were here last week. Be gone!"

"Yes, but we received a call for emergency service. Decontamination."

"You are lying trash! What emergency?"

Blake thumbed through a pad of official looking papers on a clipboard and held it up for her to see. "Decontamination requested by Hunter Devlin!" His tan and his accent were good enough that she thought twice about his origins.

"Why does he shout at me?"

"He cannot hear, Señora."

"Our pool is not contaminated!"

"Oh si!" said Blake. Numero dos! Caca, Cosas Morenas! Mierdo!"

"He is cursing me? The boy is mad! He belongs in a zoo! Go away before I call the police!"

"No, Señora, he is only explaining that someone took a big dump in your pool!"

She went pale and clutched her chest. "Go! Decontaminate the pool. Hurry up!"

"Please open the garage, we'll need electricity—the house current."

"Whatever you want. Just clean the pool!" Graciella Maria Garcia De La Cruz made her errand to the garage then rushed whimpering to the shower. She had taken a secret swim that morning.

Cezar grabbed some necessary-looking equipment from the truck and hustled around the mansion. As promised, the side door to the modest four-car garage was open. Blake entered. Cezar headed to the pool.

The warped plastic slab that once was his old friend *Cry of the Osprey* lay in state across three saw-horses. He felt the same uneasiness he'd had the time he thought Korbin was dead in his recliner. A bulge in the middle gave away the location of Mia's backpack and camera. He inspected a big chain-of-custody tag plastered across the bow. A low pulsing hum and growing pressure arose in his ears. He ignored it and inspected the bulge: there were no signs that anyone had tried to extract the pearl from this enormous charred oyster. *They only got it here this morning. This is going to be easier than I thought!* He turned to fetch Cezar but was startled by the dizzy sensation that he was falling. Harsh sunlight suddenly spilled across his feet. The garage door was going up!

The gull-wing swung up on the red Ferrari and Hunter stepped out. "Hey! Jimmy-Changa! What do you think you're doing?" He strode to the end of the pool. Jenny remained in the car.

"Decontaminacion, Señor!"

"Bullcrap! You're on the wrong estate, now beat it!"

"Very sorry Señor! My mistake!" Cezar pulled up his net and hastened to the truck.

"C'mon baby! Dad sent the goodies home today!"

Hunter selected a heavy-duty Saws-All from the tool cabinet.

"Eew!" said Jenny. "I don't want that crap all over me. You know where I'll be." She headed for the door to the house.

"Be there in a minute, baby!"

"Shower!"

Hunter pulled the trigger and the reciprocating blade chewed its way through the hulk. Blake peered under the gleaming Jaguar at the far end of the garage. He saw what used to be his half of the boat hit the floor. Then another cascade of plastic shavings and Mia's end bounced off the concrete.

Hunter clamped the bulge in a table vise and made an H-shaped cut across the top. He pried the halves open, then took a utility blade and cut through the backpack. He extracted Mia's camera and switched it on. The screen glowed. "Oh baby! Am I glad to see you!" he chuckled.

Blake kept his eyes glued to Hunter's feet. They finally swaggered into the house. He waited three awful minutes before zipping over to the door. He turned the knob ever so slowly and peeked in. The long empty hall reminded him of his church building. He called the map to mind. He'd have to pass the utility room and laundry to reach the next hall, then turn right and pass the kitchen to reach the grand foyer. He clamped his lips between his teeth, took a deep breath and hot-footed it down the corridor. The air was laced with the cozy, humid smell of clothes fresh out of the dryer. He passed the door in a flash. Right turn. Now the kitchen. The laundry made him think. He sniffed the air. Nothing cooking. Slight scent of perfume. He crept to the kitchen archway, got low and scuttled across. He crouched at the next portal and suddenly lost focus. The pictures on Kazdorf's tablet had not come close to capturing the domestic opulence of the grand foyer and it's bold declaration of superiority and wealth. The ceiling was four stories up, capping a wall of glass that admitted the full sun in slanting rays that scattered off the gleaming, black marble floor. Water flowed quietly down a limestone wall, hung with moss and vines, and trickled into a little pond. *The hanging gardens of Babylon,* he thought. Something in his peripheral vision startled him back to the reality that he was an intruder in Nebuchadnezzar's palace.

A young Latina wheeled a housekeeping cart across the foyer, parked it in front of a set of bronze doors and walked away. *The elevator!* He darted behind the cart and pressed the button. The car was all the way at the top. Forty-five eternal seconds later, the housekeeper returned just in time to see the cart wheeling itself into the elevator. She crossed herself and sputtered a prayer against the Devil.

The doors opened on the fourth floor. Blake peered over the top of the cart. There was the dance floor. The master bedrooms would be on the right. The executive sky-lounge at the far end on the left. He wished he could hear: a cough, a thump, a TV; anything to tell him the lay of the land. The doors began to close. He lunged around the cart, stabbed the Open Door button and stumbled out onto the parquet floor. The doors closed. Blake sheltered behind a statue of Poseidon, set amid a jungle of massive peace lilies. It was a good spot, kitty-cornered to the executive playroom across the spacious floor. Its wood framed windows and hanging sign made it look like a main-street tavern. The sign read: "Where Eagles Dare!" The tinnitus shrieked louder and not to be outdone by the mounting pressure in his ears, his bladder decided it had waited long enough. He hurriedly watered the lilies. Just as Blake decided it was time to advance, Hunter appeared from his bedroom and strutted merrily over to the lounge, camera in hand. *Don't shut the door!* he squealed in his mind. *Don't! Oh dirt!*

Blake crossed the planked expanse and slunk below the windows. He looked back to the elevator's bronze door, full of apprehension. *Bronze is a symbol of judgment, in the Bible,* he thought. *No, it's brass, Mr. Professor.* The car was now on the second floor. *How long does it take to clean two floors in this place?* The wooden blinds on the other side of the glass were down and closed. He squinted through one of the small, oval holes where the strings passed through the slats. It afforded an extremely limited view, but he discovered that quickly shifting his glance across the holes tricked the eye and created one long, vertical slit of visibility. So he slipped along from string to string, bobbing his whole body up and down in a sort of demented lizard-dance. He looked back to the elevator. *Are you kidding?* It was now on three. *Someone needs to check her work!*

As far as he could tell, the playroom was still arranged as it had been in the pictures: bar at one end, pool table at the other; a giant leather couch in the middle of it all, in front of a panoramic window. He caught sight of Hunter fooling with some electronics on a long table behind the couch. He vaulted it, landing next to a fluff of red hair on the other side. Blake stopped bobbing and squinted at the dancing lines on the glowing panel. *Loud music! And camera—yay me!* He put the slightest pressure on the door handle. *Locked! Blast! One last chance.* He scurried to the end of the wide hall and tried the door to the library. It was unlocked and, better yet, once inside he found the French doors adjoining the playroom wide open. They were flanked by two bookcases made from the halves of a large green canoe. One that Blake recognized.

He slithered out of the library to the cover of the pool table. Hunter was turned away, apparently in a meaningful conversation with Jenny. Blake scampered to the stereo table. He raised his eyes over its edge, only to see Hunter's hand snake over the back of the couch and seize his prize. Blake ducked, then peeked again. A long, delicate arm craned over and deposited the camera back in front of him. Just as quickly, the hairy limb of her beau snatched it back. Blake scuttled down to the bar. It offered excellent cover as it was situated behind the couch, in the corner. He was able to lay on his stomach, head out far enough to watch openly.

There was some horseplay going on over there. Jenny stood up, laughing and tugging furiously at something. Blake slunk back. Jenny ripped the camera from Hunter's grip and sprung like a gazelle over the back of the couch. He followed for five spirited laps around, which ended in a standoff. He vaulted the couch, she headed straight for the bar. Blake retreated, packing himself into the empty space below the first shelf. He hoped the music was loud enough to cover his breathing, which was now desperately heavy.

Slender bare feet and shins appeared, minced back and forth six inches in from his nose, then disappeared. After a minute, Blake wormed himself out of his cubby and went back to spying. He couldn't see them. The camera wasn't on the table. He went to the other end of the bar and peeked around the end. Oh yes, they were there—but horizontal.

Then it occurred to him. He looked over the top of the bar. There, reflecting his smile back from its big glass eye was his reward. He gathered the camera up as gently and affectionately as if it were the golden goose. The trip back to the library was comparatively effortless.

Blake's boiling blood froze. The housekeeper's cart was in the middle of the dance floor. The stairs would be at the end of the corridor to the right of the cart. *Oh come on! Is this necessary? It's just down the stairs, across the foyer and out the front door!* He weighed his options, which were few, and opted for the mad dash to freedom.

He reached the corner just as the door to Hunter's room began to open. He skidded to a stop instead of plunging ahead for the stairs. He dove through the bedroom door just behind him.

The maid entered and retrieved all of the linen from the master bath, unaware that the mound of sheets and pillows on the bed was watching her. She opened what looked like a linen closet and chucked the towels down, followed by the contents of the hamper. Then she turned and jerked all of the bed linen off the mattress with the flair of a matador before El Toro. It took a second for it to register. There was a muchacho huddled in the middle of the bed. Blake became aware of a new sound, just above the tinnitus, like a mosquito driving its needle-nose into his consciousness, whining ever louder until the pressure in his ears suddenly sucked itself inside-out and he could hear her shriek in all of its petrifying glory. She bolted out the door.

Hunter was on the scene in a hot second. He made a careful search of the room. Jenny peered cautiously out of the executive lounge, then joined him.

"What was that all about?" she said.

"Dunno. She kept screaming about a ghost boy," replied Hunter. Something clunked deep in the wall. A broad grin of anticipation spread across his face. He stuck his head in the laundry chute and burst out in joyful laughter. "Jenny, go stop her from calling the cops."

"What is it?"

"Just go, hurry up!"

Jenny complied.

"Sparky, you do not disappoint! You okay?"

"A little cramped."

"You made it a lot farther than I did! Fire department had to cut out a whole wall to get me. Don't let your legs fold up in front of you. You'll suffocate. Hold on!"

Blake fumbled frantically with the camera. The tail of a linen bed sheet with a big knot in the end whooshed down the chute.

"First things first. I hate to deprive you, but Dragon Lady made off with all Mia's electronics. That camera is my last shot at freedom."

Blake knotted the sheet around the neck strap. "Okay!"

Hunter hoisted it up and cheerfully removed his catch. He tied four more sheets together from the neighboring linen closet. Again the white rope went down the narrow shaft. "Now, keep your feet together and point your toes." He braced his head against the back of the chute, reached in with both arms, and hauled with all his might. Blake straightened his jammed ankles and knees, and held on for dear life.

"You ready?" said Hunter.

"For what?"

Hunter let the sheet slide through his hands. Blake plunged through the next two and a half stories in near-free fall. He bounced off a mountain of dirty laundry at the bottom and sailed—tangled in fluttering white sheets— past the poor maid whom Jenny had just escorted in. Blake shed his spook's apparel and burst through the foyer and out the front door at a dead run. The green pickup screeched to a halt in front of the mansion. Blake dove in the open window, and they were away.

"Where to, now?" said Cezar.

Blake said a quick thank you to the Almighty, then between gasps answered his friend. "Devlin's Marina."

***

Cezar dropped Blake off at the entrance to Devlin's Marine & Sail Supply Showroom, then turned the truck around. Blake headed straight to the service counter.

"I need to speak with Lawrence Devlin, please?"

"May I tell him what it's about?" said the clerk.

"Tell him that I have important information about his daughter."

The man picked up the phone and pressed a button. He relayed the message, and chuckled as he hung up. "Chief says he doesn't have a daughter."

"Sorry, I meant his girlfriend. I have photographic evidence of *that*."

The clerk picked up the phone again. A door jerked open just down the hallway behind the service desk. "Uh, you can go on back." The clerk lifted a hinged section of countertop to allow him through.

Larry Devlin sat back, feet on his desk, trying to look in control. "Any last words before I call the authorities?"

"Let Mia go."

"Oooh, no can do Bucko! Little Miss D has earned herself permanent residency status in the finest lock-up for the baddest of the bad little girls."

"Call them up and get her out of there," Blake said, grimly.

Devlin put his hands behind his head and grinned. "Aren't you forgetting something?"

"Huh?"

Devlin dropped his feet and leaned on his desk. "Or. Else. Let her go *or else*. Just a tip from one businessman to another, seeing as how you *are* the coffin-pimp of Freeman—and how is business, by the way?"

"People are dying for our coffins."

"Oh, boy! That one never goes away does it? Anyway, *Or else* is usually your lead up to putting your chips on the table. Unless you don't have any. And seeing that I possess the camera, I'd say you *don't* have any."

Blake tossed the little square memory card on the desk. "Unless it's the chip that goes in the camera."

Devlin hesitated for a second, looking as if his head might implode. "Nice bluff. You're trembling little boy, cracking under the pressure. You'll never make it in the big league."

"Look at it." *Don't lose it now! Keep it together!* he thought, balling his fists.

"I don't need to. It's blank. You probably stole it. So we can add shoplifting to extortion."

"I never said 'or else.'"

Devlin sniffed. "Are you really *that* sophisticated?"

"If you're not going to look at it, give it back."

"Oh, don't worry. It's going the same place you are."

"Fine. Call the police. They'll look at it, for sure. Erase it first. I have a dozen people with copies of their own. And they know exactly what to do if anything happens to me."

"Yeah, well here's what's gonna happen to you, Bucko: we're going to find you some quality foster care. Maybe a couple of sweet guys and a lonely rotweiler with a passion for little fellahs like you."

"Go ahead, call 'em." He walked out the office. "I'll be waiting out front. Oh, sorry. No I won't."

Blake slammed the truck door. Cezar had just put it in gear when the clerk came jogging up shouting "Hey kid!" He handed him the phone.

"Cracking under the pressure, Mr. Commodore?"

"Don't push it kid. Tell your ditzy waitress friend that they'll drop the runaway off, tomorrow afternoon."

"What about my situation?"

"What about it? That wasn't my doing."

"You got Hunter off the hook. Get CPS and the cops off me."

"How am I supposed to do that?"

"The old fashioned way. Put your lawyers on it."

***

Blake entered the Emporium kitchen through the alley door. Treva spotted him and nearly dropped her tray. Blake delivered the news and was smothered in tearful hugs and kisses.

"How did you ever pull it off, young man?"

"If I told you, you'd have to testify. Do me a favor?"

"Anything. Name it!"

"Call Mr. Gunn and let him know I'm okay. Tell him I'm sorry, but I have to stay out of sight for a little while."

"I'll do it right now."

"I'll come over as soon as I'm sure it's not a trap."

"What is going on in this town?" she said, shaking her head.

"I'd tell you, but you'd have to wash my mouth out with soap."

Charley insisted on sending him off with a feast in a bag. It felt good to know that folks were still on his side.

Part V

Cosmic Fate, Ltd.

Chapter 66

Treva answered her back door. It was Blake. She stepped out and closed it behind her.

"Is she here?"

"Signed, sealed, and delivered just like you said. No cops. Not so much as a drive-by."

"Is she sleeping?" he said, apprehensive about Treva's stalling.

"Honey, you need to understand some things before you see her. She's not going to be herself for a few days. They really drugged her up good in that place. It'll take awhile to wear off. I just want you to be prepared."

A quivering worm of anxiety crawled through his chest. Mia lay on the couch in the fetal position. Her head was enshrouded by the hood of a black sweatshirt. Only her nose and mouth betrayed that this was anything other than a mannequin.

"Hey Sissy, Tux is here to see you!"

She didn't move.

"You awake Mia?" said Blake. He sat down on the sturdy coffee table next to her. "I'm sorry it took so long to get you out. There were a few complicating factors."

She took a single deep breath and let it all out at once.

"Guess what? I can hear again!" Something seemed odd about her head. It was too small, the hood too round and smooth.

He turned to Treva. "What...happened?" he said, pointing to his own head.

"They shaved her head, honey. Don't know why on earth. She gave 'em a hard way to go and got herself a black eye, to boot. That's why they doped her up so heavy."

A sickening tingle gushed into Blake's cheeks and eyes. It warped his face into the image of the most unbearable anguish he'd ever felt. Everything strong, confident, gorgeous, and defiant—everything that was Mia—was gone.

"Those animals!" he wailed. "I will kill those damned motherless savages! I will burn their houses down on top of them! I…"

Treva swept him up and took him down the hall, out of earshot. She wrapped her arms around him. "It's not fair! I went through all of that! I put everything on the line! And this is how it ends? He buried his face in her chest and bawled.

She held him out by the shoulders and looked him in the eye. "Listen to me, honey. Like it or not, we have to face the fact that Miss Mia brought this on herself. All she had to do was show up at that dumb, old school for a few more weeks and her momma and the social workers would've let her be. She didn't have to go all out to disgrace her daddy. She didn't have to take those pictures. None of this would'a happened and you wouldn't be tangled up in all this trouble either. We've got to face that. And so does she."

He wilted, and she gathered him up again and let him cry it all out. He was absolutely spent.

"Listen, Mr. Tripper sent your backpack over with some clothes. You go take a nice hot bath while I get dinner. You just watch. She'll be the same wily rotten ol' Mia in a couple of days."

Indeed, the hot bath did him a lot of good. Outside, It was a scorching one hundred two degrees, but Treva kept her little house a comfy sixty-eight. In Blake's exhausted state, that felt downright nippy.

He was delighted to find not only two changes of clothes in his pack, and his compass, lighter, and multi-tool; but also a couple of DVD's, a Tintin collection, and Korbin's Bible—from which protruded a handwritten note:

Caduggin,   *August* 13
Glad to hear you two are safe and sound.
I sic`ed my 'legal eagles' on Seguin and the rest.
Surprised to find you already had someone on the job!
Carson put your TV lady on them, just for nuisance value.
Stay put. We've just about got this under control.
Enjoy the movie. It's African Queen. Written by the same fellow who did Hornlblower.
As for the Good Book: now that you can hear, you might want to listen!
We'll collect you in a few days.
Gunn
P.S. I'm suing the P.D. for brutality. Anticipating a nifty settlement.

A vicious squall ripped across the lake that night, every bit the demonic storm that drove him to the boiler-room with Soojee. But what distressed Blake the most about it was that Mia didn't even seem to notice.

Treva quartered him on a palette of blankets in her little sewing room. He made sure that the windows and screens opened, and checked below to see what he'd be landing in, should another 'exit stage left' prove necessary. He lay down and considered his surroundings. The sewing room was less than half the size of the library at Devlin's. In fact he was sure the little, yellow cottage would have fit easily into the grand foyer. Of all the weeks that had been 'weeks from Hell,' this one had—hands down—been *the* week from Hell: all caps, bold, underline, italic.

Chapter 67

Treva's diagnosis had been correct. The tranquilizers they'd used on Mia at Novo Synaptix Behavioral Rehab had worn off by the time Blake rose, at the crack of noon. But the fire had not returned to her spirit. She kept the hood drawn tightly around her face and lay motionless on the couch. She was responsive, but not conversational. "Yes" and "no" was as much as she'd say. Hard as it was, Blake followed Treva's advice and didn't push her to talk.

He peered out of the blinds. The patrol car from the private security service Gunn hired sat in the driveway, motor running. Somehow it didn't make him feel any more secure. He was certain Brigita could buy anyone off.

"I know what you're thinking, honey," said Treva. "Read the bumper sticker on my car."

The faded sticker on the little Chevy read *I believe gun control means using both hands!*

Blake settled down with Korbin's Bible.

"Read it to me!" said Treva, drying the breakfast dishes. "Give me a sermon, seeing as I'm skipping church this morning."

He turned to the section entitled *The Proverbs* and read aloud: "The proverbs of Solomon, the son of David, king of Israel: to know wisdom and instruction; to discern the sayings of understanding; to receive instruction in wise behavior, righteousness, justice, and equity; to give prudence to the naïve; to the youth knowledge and discretion."

Chapter 68

Blake had fallen asleep watching *African Queen* for the umpteenth time. He sat on the floor, back against the couch. Mia laid on the cushions behind him. He awoke with her arm draped across his chest and her face mashed against his head. The collar of his shirt felt icky. She'd drooled down the back of his neck.

"So, are you going to put me in a headlock or are you going to kiss me?"

She must have been awake enough, for she closed her arm around his neck and smooched him on the right temple. He took it as a good sign.

"You got the flash drive to what's-her-name, huh?" she said, quietly.

"No, it went through the washer, actually. And dryer."

"Doesn't hurt 'em. Just put it in a bowl of dry rice for a couple of days."

"Oh, really? I wish I'd known." This was the heavily censored version of what he was thinking.

"So how did you do it, if you didn't have the fish?"

"Remember when Hunter got stuck in the laundry-chute and the fire department had to cut out the whole wall to get him?"

"I never told you that story."

"He said I made it a lot farther down than he did." Blake grinned over his shoulder.

"You were... What were you doing in the laundry-chute in my dad's house? Wait, when did you get your hearing back?"

"When the maid screamed."

"The maid was screaming?"

"Because she found me hiding under the blankets on your dad's bed."

"Back up. How did you get past Graciella gorrilla?"

"Cezar and I posed as pool guys. Well, I mean we *are* pool guys. We told her that someone pooped in *la piscina*." Mia shook her head as if she should have known.

"Okay, so you freaked the maid out, jumped in the chute and got stuck…"

"With the camera I just stole out from under Hunter's nose in the big lounge. I think it's called *Where Turkey's Trot?*" Blake had been waiting three days to spring all this on her.

"And you made your daring escape how?"

"Traded Hunter the camera for getting me unstuck."

"I'm officially confused."

"While he was tying sheets together, I got the memory card out of it just like you showed me! Then he let me fall to the laundry room. Where, incidentally, I met the maid again. Then I hot-footed it over to your dad's office and exchanged it… for *you*."

She combed his thick, wavy hair with her fingers and stared into his face. One by one, tears like little diamonds rolled out of her eyes. He waited for her to say something—something in particular. But she did not. She only offered an admiring, little smile.

"You drooled on my head," he said.

She clenched her fingers and gave his mop a few playful tugs. "What else have I missed? What day is it?"

"Tuesday, August 16th. I talked to Mr. Gunn last night. He said they finally have CPS under control. Treva bought you some bandanas, and a sun-proof hat. It's like SPF 50."

"Thanks, but I'm not leaving the house."

"Yes, you are. Don't freak, but Mr. Gunn called your mom. She's stuck in Chicago on business. But she'll be back as soon as she can."

She covered her eyes and rolled on her back, exhaling in despair. "Why did he do that?" she groaned.

"He told her what happened. She's ready to *kill* your dad."

"Yeah well, let me tell you who's number two on her list."

"Don't be so sure! Mr. Gunn said she started to cry and told him to let you know how awful she feels about what you've been through."

"She really said that?"

"Yup! And here's the best part. We're going to the Dunes!"

"Nice. When are you going?"

"Are ye deaf, Lass? I said we! *We* are going. Your mom overnighted Mr. Gunn a permission letter—*notarized*, even—saying you can go with him anywhere in the continental U.S."

They were quiet for a minute.

"You sure he was talking with Priscilla Devlin?"

"Mia, what if God's giving you a chance to start something new with your mom?"

"I dunno," she said, skeptically.

"Just think about it. And the Dunes."

"And a shower. My head feels like an anthill. Ants included."

***

It took the combined nagging and cajoling of Blake and Treva to get Mia back off the couch and to the little table in the kitchen. It was the smell of Treva's cooking that did the real work, though. Mia was gaunt, having eaten only the little yogurt Treva had spoon fed her over the past four days. The black eye was now yellow and green, streaked with purple. She looked unnervingly ready for a body-bag. Blake buried his revulsion in smiling encouragements, as he'd learned to do with Korbin's grave-bound neighbors. But her appetite was anything but dead and there was much rejoicing when the second box of spaghetti went into the pot.

After dinner, Mia headed straight back to the couch. But Blake, impish grin on his face, intercepted her. Treva punched a button on the CD player and a dazzling Cajun two-step by Pour Vous trotted out of the speakers.

Blake took her hand and whisked her into a dance around the little living room.

"No, c'mon guys!" Mia moaned, as her partner handed her off to the cook.

"Happy times, Sissy! Gotta remember the happy times!"

"I'm happiest when I'm unhappy. Let me go!"

"We're not happy unless you're happy!" said Blake, taking custody again.

"Get ready for a life of disappointment."

Blake twirled himself under her arm.

"Did we tell you we love you?" said Treva, clapping and bobbing to the infectious beat of the music.

"Didn't Tux tell you the rules, Blondie?"

"My house, my rules!" She scuttled to the couch and stretched out across its length as the track ended.

"I am *so* not in the mood." A bittersweet waltz began. Blake drew her close and gently lulled her into its haunting sway.

Satisfied with their success, Treva went to dish up the ice cream. They would repeat this little fiasco at every meal for the next two days.

Chapter 69

"I could lay here and look at this all day," said Blake.

Mia adjusted the wide brim of her hat. "That's the extent of my plans."

There wasn't a cloud in the sky, nor a ripple on the infinite blue expanse of Lake Michigan. They lay on a blanket at the crest of a tidal wave of sand.

Blake focused the binoculars on the western horizon. "I can't believe you can see Chicago from here!" Mia remained silent. "I don't get something. Why don't your parents get divorced, like everyone else?"

"Because not everyone else had a grandfather like mine."

"That explains it."

"Gramps was a bit of a nut job. Put a nifty little catch in his will. Any beneficiary of his filthy millions, me included, who gets divorced, has an abortion, or bears a child out of wedlock, loses their inheritance. Period."

"But..."

"Yeah, I know. It probably saved my life. Thanks. Great life, Gramps!" She stretched luxuriantly. Blake thought her purple bandana and white boonie hat needed a gold earring and a cutlass to complete the ensemble. "So, Dad cats around and Mom uses the threat of calling it quits—which she never will, as long as she gets whatever she wants—*which* she always does. And I do mean *whatever*. They're completely addicted to the money. And completely stuck with each other."

A little breeze came up the glaring slope, rustling patches of yellow flowers and long dune grass.

"But, still; maybe you and your mom can start over?"

"You gonna patch it up with your dad when you go home?"

"It's not the same. It sounds like your mom is at least reasonable. Dad's always on me about everything and nothing at the same time. And on top of that, all Agatha has to do is give herself an Indian wrist-burn, run to Dad and it's welcome to Hell-on-earth at the Barber house for the next week."

"Once again, great life, Gramps!"

"I still think Mr. Dubois is right, though. We've still got food and shelter. It could be a lot worse. Maybe you could start over with your mom."

"Oh yes, Mommy and little Mia!" she said. She blew a gnat off her lip with bitter contempt.

""Look, why can't it all start over today and be better?"

"What best seller did *that* come from?"

"C'mon it's true! I didn't ask to be dumped in the middle of nowhere with a crazy uncle on Lunatic Lake! But..."

"I hear ya."

"Until it happened, I'd practically never been out of my own backyard—literally. I had never been sailing, or hiking, or cooked my own meals over an open fire,"

"Or built coffins, or sank a boat," she said.

Blake picked up her challenge. "Or learned to dance and speak Spanish,"

"Or incited a riot, or tortured a devil worshipper!"

"Or become a celebrity, or rescued a friend!" he fired back.

"Or burglarized a million dollar mansion, or blackmailed its owner!" She was grinning wryly now.

He played his trump: "Or kissed a girl!"

"Say what!"

"Well, she kissed me actually."

Mia rolled over and rose up on one elbow, grinning in delight at the rosy shade his tan cheeks had assumed. "Like, on the mouth?"

"Yeah."

"Tongue?"

"Miaaa!"

"Who was it? Greta? I *saw* her grab your butt."

"Never mind." This was embarrassing, but suddenly she was Mia again and he wasn't letting that go for anything.

"That one hairy chick from session two?"

"No! Yikes!"

"Wait a minute…"

"I said never mind." He looked up at the sky.

A look of mock horror spread across Mia's face. "No, not Natalie! Eeeew! I thought you had more self-respect than that!"

"Okay, so it was Soojee! It wasn't my plan. Or hers, actually. Although she's perfectly willing anytime with anybody."

"Wow! Who'd a thunk!" She rolled back over and chuckled at the sky.

"Anyway, the point is that I'm *glad* my parents dumped me. And I'm glad your grandfather put that catch in his will. 'Cuz it landed you on top of a two hundred-foot dune, on the shore of one of the largest freshwater seas in the world, on the most awesome day that ever was. With me!"

"Stick to the rules, buddy."

"Stoof it in yer pookits! I'm no suckin' up!"

"You know what I mean."

"I don't know what 'in love' means, but now I know what love is. I wrote it down, just like you said."

"I really told you to do that?"

He dug his little notebook out of a cargo pocket and leafed through the pages. "Love is the ongoing commitment to the welfare and wellbeing of others. Affection may or may not be involved.'"

"Hey, look at that lizard!" she said. Blake didn't buy it.

"Admit it or not," he continued.

"Look out! Tarantula!"

"By definition,"

She rolled her eyes. "Don't say it…Puh-leez!."

"We love each other!"

"Alright! You win! I love you!" she said with a defeated sigh. "Is it everything you hoped it would be?"

Blake, face aglow, searched carefully for his next words. "Even better."

She hauled herself off the blanket. "I'm going swimming."

Gunn reclined on a folding chaise lounge in the shade of a large beach umbrella and slathered his nose with sunscreen. The beach, which just the weekend before had been packed with bodies like a multitude of sun-worshipping walruses, was only sparsely dotted with mothers brooding over their preschoolers. Like giggling sand-pipers at the waterline, they played catch-as-catch-can with the little surf that had come up with a refreshing breeze.

Gunn glanced up from his book, squinted at the bobbing heads now too far out, and blew three hard blasts on a chrome gym whistle. "Too far!" he shouted. "Mind the rip! Yeh'll end up in the Soo Locks before they find yeh!"

His wards swam back, body-surfing the little breakers. "Fix us some lunch, will yeh?" said Gunn, as they slogged up out of the shallows. Mia spread a blanket and menaced the hoard of expectant seagulls that lurked near the cooler.

"You feel alright, Mr. Gunn?" said Blake.

"Aye. Why'd ye ask?" he snapped.

Mia snuck a glance over her shoulder.

"I'm just hot, that's all," said Gunn.

"You look extra tired."

"Who wouldn't, things as they've been?"

Mia paused in slathering his bread with mustard. *Thanks Gramps. Wily, rotten old Mia at your service,* she thought. She finished his sandwich and opened a cold ginger-ale for him.

"Yeh taking a hike, now?"

"Aye," said Blake. "The long one. And I've got my keys to the van."

They finished lunch, and visited the big brick beach house. Blake bought post cards, a couple of tee shirts, a sturdy hiking stick and a disposable camera from the gift shop.

***

They were three miles down the forest trail and it was now impossible to ignore the fact that heavy weather was not only brewing, but about to pour out of the sky on them. The woods had grown dark and the forest canopy was a swaying, rustling commotion. One beligerent grunt from the sky dismissed any remaining illusion that those distant rumblings were merely jets headed for Chicago O'Hare. At last the trail bent toward the lake and as they neared the ridgeline of the dune-forest Blake jogged ahead to survey their situation.

It looked like Judgment day. The gorgeous, friendly sky was now an inky black void; lightning flicked from cloud to cloud and lanced down to smite the foaming swells. White-capped breakers rose into ten-foot behemoths that crashed on the beach. Something stung his face—wind-whipped sand and the first spitting rain.

Mia joined him and made a sound of despair he'd never heard. "Oh my god!" she cried, bracing herself against the gusts.

"Amazing isn't it? Awe inspiring and completely terrifying at the same time!" Blake shouted above the wind.

"This is not helping my recovery!"

"Hey, let's take a self portrait!" He dug for his camera.

"Are you crazy? I'm scared enough to pee *your* pants!"

"Don't worry. It's just False Evidence Appearing Real!"

"No, that's pretty damn real!"

"Hold on," He turned his back to the storm, threw an arm around her and held the camera out with the other. "Maybe we'll get lucky and see a water spout!"

A crooked river of white fire shredded the heavens directly above them with the sound of a freight train crashing through a thousand exploding meth labs. Blake flinched so hard that he went off the dune backwards, rolling and bouncing down the sandy slope.

Mia jumped off and skidded down on her feet, like a surfer in the pipe, wailing the whole way. Blake had just gotten up when she crashed into him. They tumbled into a shallow blow-out. She rolled him over and seized his shoulders. A barrage of flashes like the Devil's paparazzi lit them up. He yelped in horror at the shuddering, ghoulish creature that shook him and screamed in his face. Rain spattered on its naked head, scalp criss-crossed with scabbed furrows dug by cruel clippers, sickening green smudges of a jaundiced bruise underscored the hollow fear in its sunken eyes. Where was Mia?

"Stop!" He spat sand. "We are not going to die!"

"Do something, Blake! Just do something!"

"Come on! There's a trail-head a half mile up the beach. It goes straight to the nature center. Run!" He grabbed her hand and pulled her along. Over rills, through blow-outs, across slopes they pounded through rain that whipped sideways in cutting sheets. At last they ascended to the tree line. She was crying and begging him to stop. He dragged her, stumbling down the trail until she couldn't run another step. They took refuge under the boughs of a short pine tree. He struggled for breath and any words that might comfort her.

"I keep waiting for the White Hound to show up!" He tried to chuckle bravely. She huddled against him, startling violently with each crash from the stygian abyss, above.

"Mia, listen to me. This forest has taken the worst that Lake Michigan could dish out for at least a couple hundred years, it's gonna make it through this one and we are, too! Do you hear me? Look, I was saving this as a surprise, but I got you a couple of things. A new tablet, for one." He gently fitted her hat back on and put his arms around her. "And what do you think about *Cry of the Osprey II?*"

"You shouldn't have done that," she stammered.

"Don't worry about it. I got it on this thing called EBay. Besides, You know how much money I'm making on the coffin business?"

"No! I mean I'm not going back on the lake. I'm not going back to Freeman. Ever!"

"Then we can take it somewhere else."

"No! I can't, I can't!"

"You're not going back to Freeman, but you can't go anywhere else?"

"No!"

"Why?"

"Because I'm afraid! I'm afraid to stay in Freeman and I'm afraid to leave it."

"It's going to be okay!"

Another white-hot surge blasted over the treetops, as if to disagree. She buried her face in his chest. He was now shaking as hard as she was.

He looked up and cried out to the dark canopy. "Father in Heaven? Yahweh? We've done it all wrong! We've hated our parents! We've lied and stolen! We've blackmailed! Forgive us, please! Save us! We're sorry! Help us, Father! In Yeshua's name, Amen!"

For a moment he just listened to the rain and wind and thunder. Then he saw it. Just briefly—between the waving branches—a light. He ducked his head and squinted. Definitely a light, moving through the gloom.

"Mia, someone's coming! I see a light!" She perked up. "Hey! over here!" They scooted out from under the prickly boughs to meet their rescuer. It looked like a lantern coming up the trail, but as it rounded the bend it was clear that no one carried it. An orb of pale yellow fire the size of a grapefruit, drifted four feet off the ground like a glowing soap bubble on the lightest of breezes. Blake spread his arms and backed Mia up.

"What is it?" she hissed "A will-o-the-wisp?"

"Ball lightning, I think," he said, voice full of cautious wonder.

"Dangerous?"

"Extremely."

She hooked a finger in his belt and towed him back. "Don't make it mad!"

In spite of the wind and rain, the eerie globe of faerie fire stayed over the trail, as it wandered past them. Then, as if finding a sudden updraft, it spiraled through the canopy and returned to the angry sky.

"Blake? Come on, get back under the tree." She jerked his belt insistently.

"Wait, listen," he said.

Something growled between the gusts, in the direction the orb had come from. Beams of light swept through the trees as a big, six-wheeled ATV rounded the bend. They ran back to the trail, yelling their heads off. It was a park ranger. They hopped in the cargo-bed.

"I thought you guys were never going to stop! I must've followed you a whole mile!"

"Follow what? We've been under that tree for a half hour, sir!" said Blake.

"You weren't carrying a lantern?"

"You won't believe this but you were following ball lightning! It went right past us five minutes ago."

"I've seen some crazy things out here, but that beats 'em all. Hold on, back there. It's a bumpy ride!"

***

By the time they rolled up to the beach house the furious tempest had moved on to points south. The sky was still a featureless black vault, tossing the occasional, blazing bolt. In the west the clouds had broken in a single, towering rift—revealing the mountains and canyons of Heaven itself, permitting a few gracious rays of splendor to fall on the gleaming city of glass on the far shore. A cargo ship sat a mile out on the still water, her smoke rising straight up.

The parking lot was deserted except for Gunn's van. The ranger switched the ATV off.

Mia opened the passenger door and climbed in. "Mr. Gunn? Blake, he's not here!"

"Have you seen my…grandfather anywhere? Is he in the building?"

"Old Scottish fellah?"

"Yes, sir."

"Um, well they had to take him to the hospital. He collapsed at the concession stand before the storm rolled in. Hold on." He radioed someone. The radio squawked something barely intelligible. The ranger translated.

"They think it was a coronary. He's at Saint Anthony's in Michigan

City. Just go out to Twelve and go left. About twenty miles and you'll come right into the city. Take a Right on Wabash. Goes straight to the hospital."

Blake sagged. Mia stepped down and put a hand on his shoulder. "How are we going get there?"

"You've got a license," said Blake.

"I'm not insured," she said in a low tone, through clenched teeth.

"Um, do you know Buck Mueller by any chance?" said Blake.

"Mueller? Went to the Academy together. He manages Highland Lake, right?"

"Yes! You know, Mr. Gunn and my real grandfather created that reservoir?"

"How about that! Tell Buck that ol' Couch said 'hi!'"

"Well, now we have to figure out how to get to get to Michigan City without getting arrested. So, thanks for the rescue."

"Look, uh…" The ranger finally took the hint. "Let me get my cruiser and I'll follow you. Nobody'll stop you."

***

Officer Couch tooted his horn and drove on as they turned into the ER lot of Saint Anthony's. Mia pulled into a spot, yanked the keys and stared at the entrance. She flinched when Blake opened his door.

"What's wrong?" he said.

"She's in there." Mia clutched the steering wheel, with white knuckles. "She cut my hair."

"Who?"

"She's in scrubs and a mask. But those eyes, that hair, that voice. It's her. She cut my hair."

"Who are you talking…" suddenly it came to him. "You mean Brigita?" They'd run the heater full blast the whole way there, but all at once he was cold again—from the inside out. "Mia, *this* is Saint Anthony's Hospital, *not* Novo Synaptix. Brigita is not in there. Tripper Gunn is."

"I can't."

"Give me the keys and promise you won't freak out and run off." He held out his hand.

She handed them over and gave him a despairing look.

"Lock the doors. Lay down in the back. Take a nap. I'll be back in a half hour."

He hadn't gone ten parking spaces before he heard the door slam and she was at his side, clinging to his upper arm with an iron grip. They were still damp and the hospital air-conditioning seemed impossibly polar. Mia stuck to him so tightly that walking like sober people became a challenge. A male nurse escorted them though heavy double doors into the depths of the Emergency Ward. They found the great Scot alive and well in his little observation room. He was sitting up in bed watching TV and soaking up all the attention the staff could pour on him.

"Here they are! My children!" he announced, lavishly. "Weathered the storm, I see?"

"I guess you could say that. Are you okay? Was it a heart attack?" said Blake.

"Electrolytes. Just a little dehydrated. Couple of quarts low on Gatorade, that's all." He noted how Mia was still attached to Blake's arm, which was now largely numb. A fine sheen of sweat had broken out on her cheeks. Her eyes flicked from the two IV bags hanging by the bed, to the tangle of multi-colored wires that snaked out of his pale, green gown to a monitor above his head. "Miss Devlin, yeh all right?"

She labored to smile. "Rough day for everyone. Glad you're okay."

"Give me your hand, Missy. Both of yeh." His large hot palms felt wonderful, closed around their own shivering hands. "This was no your fault, yeh hear? Neither of yeh. So put it out of yer heads." They only answered with smiles that couldn't conceal their chattering teeth.

"Yer freezing! Yeh go check into the hotel. Lake Comfort Lodge. Doctors are keeping me overnight and running tests tomorrow. Yeh collect me around four." He picked up his wallet and doled two hundred dollars in twenties to Blake. "Here. Whatever yeh need." He gazed at them a long minute. "I love yeh both. Now, go on, get warm."

***

Blake unloaded their baggage onto a courtesy cart and waited while Mia parked. The sounds of a squabble in a foreign tongue ricocheted out of a little office behind the front desk. Blake rang the bell on the counter. A tall man, brown and largely bald, greeted them with suspicion. They looked like refugees from a tsunami.

"We'd like to check in, please. Reservations for Daniel Tripper Gunn," said Blake.

"Are you Mr. Daniel Tripper Gunn?" said the man. He had a distinct musical, accent. Mia took a deep breath in anticipation.

"He's my ... grandfather."

"Will he be coming in?"

"He's in the hospital until tomorrow."

"I am sorry. Dis is a respectable establishment. Not a haven for immorality."

"What?" said Mia, authentically offended.

"Dere will be no under-age fornication under my hotel roof if I can help it. You will have to go to somewhere else."

Mia couldn't hold back. "Mister, if we were shacking up do ya think we'd have our grandpa pay for two rooms? Look, we have enough luggage here for a freakin' circus!"

"Do not try to reason with me, your protests avail nutting."

She snatched a cable-television guide out of a rack by the cash register and held it up like the damning piece of evidence in a courtroom epic. "Really? You've got cable porn and you're worried about fornication?"

"Blake held out a little card. "Would you please call the hospital? Dial that extension."

The man inspected the card and picked up the phone. "Hello, Mr. Daniel Tripper Gunn? My name is Ranjit, proprietor of de Lake Comfort Lodge... Yes, dey are here. De reason for my call is to verify de legitimacy of your reservation... Very good sir. Get well soon." He put the phone down and smiled smugly. "He said he did not have a coronary just as a cover for your lascivious enterprises! I will not be checking you in."

Mia squinted at his name badge and called out "Mrs. Ranjit!"

"Yes! What is it?" A petit woman came out of the office. She looked at Mia and seemed deeply concerned—not for the worry of any trouble, but for Mia herself. She wore a peacock-blue Sari.

Mia felt the sudden and very unfamiliar need to be respectful. "Namasté," she said.

Mrs. Ranjit cocked her head and smiled, showing off a gold tooth. "How may I serve you?"

"Ma'am, our grandfather is in the hospital. He has a thick accent. I think Mr. Ranjit misunderstood what he said about checking us in. Would you please call him?"

"You are not calling anyone, woman!" said Mr. Ranjit. A heated exchange followed in Hindi, which the little woman won. She took the phone and card, and dialed.

"Mr. Gunn? Dis Mrs. Ranjit. Sorry to hear of your illness, Mr. Gunn. May I have the pleasure of checking de grandchildren in on your reservation? Tank you very much." She hung up and snapped at her husband, then smiled sweetly at Mia. "We will check you in now. Mr. Gunn says you are to have anything you like."

"Thank you ma'am. That's a beautiful sari."

"Tank you. You are a very pretty girl." Mrs. Ranjit returned to the office. Her husband whacked away on the computer, then handed them each a card-key."

"We should get two each," Mia contested.

"You will not be going in and out of each other's room! I will not have it."

"Mrs. Ranjit!"

"Alright! I've got it dear!" He slapped them on the counter. "Do not lose dem. Dere is a fee." he grumbled.

Mia made sure that Mr. Ranjit saw that she took Blake's card and gave him her own.

While they stood waiting for the elevator, Mrs. Ranjit came across the lobby, same happy expression on her face. "Miss Gunn? Dis is for you. For de hot bat." She opened a little jar and a most wonderful and exotic aroma wafted out. "Very relaxing! And dis ointment is for de bruise. It will be gone tomorrow. Read de directions!"

The elevator doors opened. Mia thanked her with another namasté, and a little bow.

The doors closed. Blake was crammed behind the luggage cart. "This seems strangely familiar," he said.

"I feel so ashamed. All the people I grew up looking down on and treating like total crap—they've been the ones that have been the nicest to me."

"Except Mr. Ranjit."

"Yeah, he's definitely a butt," she agreed.

Mia slid the card-key into the electronic lock, fully expecting it to do nothing. But the door to her room opened. Blake was still fiddling with his. "I'm ordering pizza when I get out of the tub," she said. "Oh, and unplug your TV. There's stuff on there that'll make you go blind." Her room was nice. She dropped her bags on the dresser, went straight to the heater and cranked it all the way up. She picked up a red book from the night-stand, a Gideon's Bible. She cracked it open and read *There is a friend who sticks closer than a brother.* "Amen" she said, aloud.

***

Blake awoke in a tub of tepid water. The phone was ringing and someone was knocking on the other side of the shower wall. He grabbed a towel and hustled to pick up the phone.

"You fell asleep in the tub, didn't you?"

"No, huh-uh."

"Liar! I know you did, 'cuz I did too. Idiot!"

"I love it when you call me that."

"You unplug your TV?"

"Yesss," he droned. "I'm sorry I didn't turn back when you wanted to."

"It's alright. It was only the most hair-raising experience of my life." They ended with the inevitable thought, together "If I had any hair."

"Pizza man is here. I need the stash-o-cash," she said. "By the way, did I tell you you're totally awesome?"

"You really think so?"

"No."

Blake smiled and hung up.

Chapter 70

The diesel horns of the South Shore Line echoed in the distance. Blake and Mia walked along the crowded beach toward the jetty. They'd been through the zoo, Washington Park Tower, the Old Lighthouse Museum, had lunch, and inspected the marina. And there was still ample time to explore the final attraction before catching the bus back to the Hospital—the Michigan City Lighthouse.

The jetty was a long concrete pier that snaked out into Lake Michigan and terminated at the red-roofed cube and tower of the white lighthouse. A slant-sided parapet, supporting the black iron piers of the catwalk ran its length like the backbone of a sun-basking sea serpent.

They strolled along the wide promenade past fishermen, romancing couples, and families tossing corn chips to an insistent swarm of seagulls. They were nearly to their destination when a small group of teenagers emerged from the far side of the lighthouse and hopped down from the parapet. Blake's jaw dropped. He lowered his mirrored sunglasses.

"There is no stinking way!"

Mia took stock of the approaching youths: athletic, clean-cut and cocky. She took them for shorebirds. "Is this the part where we forget everything and run? Because that's what F.E.A.R. means now."

"No, this is the part where we hold hands and speak Spanish, mi corazon."

"Who is it?"

"He's the equivalent of Hunter's evil church-twin. C'mon."

The leader signaled and the group of young men fanned out. Blake took her hand and led her to the three iron rungs that went up the parapet.

"I always thought of Hunter as his own evil twin, actually," she said, as she climbed.

The leader went up a set of rungs, as well.

"Blake, I can't knock him off here. He'll crack his head and die."

"Español, mi novia!"

He took the lead and walked gingerly down the right side of the piers. The troublemaker chose that side as well. Blake towed Mia between piers to the other side. The jerk followed suit, with a cocky smile that said *hey guys, watch this!*

"Who is this jackass?" said Mia, in Spanish.

"The pastor's son from my father's church. Pretend to be a furious she-devil."

"Where did you learn Spanish?" she said, sarcastically.

They rounded the next pier and crossed back over. As expected, so did the other. They were now just twenty feet apart. Blake stopped and put on his best Mexican accent. It helped that he was wearing a red tee-shirt bearing the flag of Mexico.

"You gotta problem? We jus' wanna get to de lighthouse."

The rest of the young men gathered at the base of the parapet as if watching a professional wrestling match. Blake recognized his old Sunday-school friend Wolf, among them. He looked like he'd shot up a foot since the last time they'd met. He wondered what he was doing with *this* bunch.

"By all means!" He made a sweeping gesture and planted himself in the middle of the walkway.

"You know, you are acting like a preacher's kid?" said Blake.

"Maybe. What would you know about it?"

"I know a lot of things. I bet you got some church name, like Aleesha. I bet you amigos call you Alice!"

"Elisha! How did you know that?" he shouted, taken aback.

Man, have I changed that much? thought Blake. "Cuz Alice es a good name for a bully!"

"I'll show you some bully!" Elisha took a provocative step forward.

Mia pushed to the fore. "Permisa mi un poco violencia!" she snarled.

"No, mi corazon!" Blake grabbed her arm. "She say she wanna do you some violence! You better be careful!"

The young men were jeering and making mock wagers. Mia caught more than a few racist cracks.

"I bet you gotta fonny last name, too," said Blake. "Like uh, corazon, wha's de name of de little pig in de movie? With de spider?"

She smiled and said with a wicked sneer "Wiiilbur!"

"Yeah, Wilbur! But there's more. Like uh, Wilbur farts?"

"Wilburforce! *How* do you know my name?" Elisha Wilburforce was both angry and intimidated.

"I tell you, I know lots! Dis I know best: my name es Blanco Alonzo Barbarossa Pagán. I don't stop for no bullies. Vamanos, mi amor." They locked elbows and advanced. Wilburforce slid the six feet down the face of the parapet as quickly as he could put his butt on the concrete.

Blake turned. "Hey you! Flaco!" he pointed at his old friend. "What's better or worse? A Christian who acts like a pagan? Or a pagan who acts like a Christian?"

Wolf took a long look and smiled as he recognized the young foreigner. "C'mon novia!" Blake planted a kiss on Mia's cheek and led her away.

Once out of earshot, she said "Taking liberties, aren't we? Or was that all part of the act?"

"What act?" he said, with a saucy smile. "I can't believe those punks were here. Must be a youth-group outing. And I can't believe Wolf was going along with that. We used to be good friends. I wonder where the girls are?"

They were on the other side of the lighthouse, with a chaperone. If they recognized him they didn't say a word. Their fearful, condescending glances said something else.

"Hey!" said Mia, in their general direction. "You looking at my boyfriend? How you like to swim home, huh? I saw you looking at his butt!" Blake was simply elated. The chaperone nervously herded the girls off the riprap and back around to the jetty.

"Were they really looking at me?"

"You wish!" Mia snickered.

"I'd say we've done enough damage to Latino-American race relations for one day," he said, admiring the white tower of the lighthouse.

She stared off into the hazy blue distance. "Whatever, Mr. Professor."

Chapter 71

"So what's in the box?" said Blake. He sat crossways in the front seat so he could see Mia. She sat in back, on the driver's side. Gunn chewed his pipe and drove with one hand, listening to talk radio.

"Since you're going to hound me until I open it, I might as well get it over with." She dragged the flat box over, slipped the ribbon off, then the lid. When the surprise wore off she relaxed in her seat and smiled out the window. She looked truly humble.

"Well?" said Blake.

"I don't believe it. It's Mrs. Ranjit's dress. The blue one." She tilted the box up so he could see. She remembered thinking how close in size she was to that woman, who seemed to beam kindness right into you. How she hurried over with the box on their way out and hugged her; how she whispered her parting wish into her ear, "May de love of Christ fill your heart."

"Can't wait to see you in it," said Blake.

Mia slipped the lid back on the box. "So, what's our next stop on this magical mystery tour?"

"Ludington!" said Gunn.

"We're going to pick up *Cry of the Osprey II*," said Blake.

"Where, may I ask is Ludington?"

"Halfway up the west coast of Michigan!" said Gunn.

"We're going all that way for a Kayak?"

"No," said Blake, "to catch the Badger."

"We d'need no stinkin' badgers!" said Gunn.

"No offence Mr. Gunn, but it really loses something when *you* say it. If we're going to Ludington to catch the badger, where do we go to catch the *Osprey?*"

Blake gave Gunn a sly look and they announced in unison: "Manitowoc!"

"We're going to Wisconsin?"

***

Viscous black smoke roiled out of the S.S. Badger's funnel while her crew deftly packed a veritable traffic jam of cars and trucks into her belly. Blake regaled Mia with all the facts about the ferry as they leaned over the fantail and watched the loading below.

Gunn marveled as an eighteen-wheeler carrying enormous windmill blades was swallowed up by the ship. "If the tree huggers could have their way, they'd shut her down."

"She's the last coal-fired steam ship operating in American waters," said Blake. "Four hundred ten feet long. Originally built to carry railroad cars and stuff. Launched in 1953."

"And you just know this?" said Mia.

"No, I read the brochure on the way up here."

"I thought it would do us good to get away," said Gunn. "Out among normal people, for once. Take a voyage that didn't involve pirates, zombies, or other assorted maniacs. I did'na realize how jacked up our lake's gotten!"

The unexpected turn of phrase made Mia giggle.

"Eh? Yeh don' agree?"

"No, it's definitely jacked up," she said.

"Ha! *Definitively* jacked up! Look, I brought yeh both up here because yeh needed to refocus. See that there's life outside of Freeman—a whole world outside those woods and beyond that big dam. Out here yeh can see the horizon."

The 'all clear' was called, as the last of the vehicles crawled into the ship

524

and her massive transom-gate began to swing slowly into place. Churning foam erupted from beneath her stern as she crawled away from her berth. With two great blasts of her horns, S.S. Badger declared her resolute intent to cross Lake Michigan and, like children on a carousel, all on deck gave a giddy cheer.

"Get yerselves some lunch. I'm retiring to my state room for a little horizontal meditation." He began to sing as he walked away. "Port out! Starboard home! Posh is the life for me! P-O-S-H!"

***

Mia sat at a table in the café, leafing through a cruise guide while Blake waded into the buffet-line.

"Hi!" said a small, but exuberant voice.

Mia looked up. A little girl in a long, floral sundress stood expectantly by the table. She had a silk scarf wrapped tightly around her head. It was evident that she had no hair.

"I'm Fiona. I'm nine!"

"Mia. I'm sixteen."

"Do you have cancer, too?" said Fiona.

"Um, no."

"Oh. When I saw your bandana, I thought that maybe you were on chemo. Chemo sucks."

"I bet." Mia never imagined a conversation with a nine-year-old could be so intimidating.

"Mom was worried I'd get seasick, but this is nothing compared to chemo. So, did you cut your hair just because?"

"It's kind of a scary story," said Mia, scowling in hopes that the urchin wouldn't sit down.

"Oooh, like a fairytale?" Fiona cooed, and slid into the seat opposite Mia.

"See, my Dad fell in love with an evil queen. I got really mad about it and tried to get between them."

"What happened then?" said Fiona, leaning low across the table and whispering breathlessly.

"The evil queen had her secret police kidnap me. They took me to a really bad place, tied me up, and she shaved my head."

"Well I hope you kicked her in the balls!" Fiona grinned ear-to-ear with the tip of her tongue between her teeth. When Mia found herself speechless, the little rascal cracked up in bubbly laughter. "I know! She's a girl! That's why it's so funny. My dad says it all the time. Don't tell my mom, though. She hates it!"

"As a matter of fact, young lady, I did do that. And I got a shiner and a punch in the gut that left me on the couch for three days. Then they drugged me up, strapped me down, and were going to leave me in that hellhole for the rest of my life."

"How did you ever escape? I gotta know!"

"See that guy in line over there?"

"The one in the freaky Hawaiian shirt? Is he your boyfriend?"

Mia considered it for a second. "Better than that. He's my best friend. He pulled some amazing crazy stunts you'd never believe and forced them to let me go."

"*Totally* romantic," said Fiona, with an air of authority. "Were you afraid you were going to die? My mom and dad are afraid I'm going to die. But I just tell them that it'll be okay. I'll be with God and he'll take good care of me until they catch up."

Again, Mia found herself totally stunned by this irrepressibly sunny waif. Fiona pulled a tablet out of an embroidered shoulder bag and jumped out of her seat.

"Hey let's take some selfies!" she declared, pulling the scarf off her gleaming, bald head.

"Oh, Fiona, I don't know."

She crammed in next to Mia. "C'mon, it'll be fun! I'll look at them in the hospital. They'll help me be brave. Take off your bandana." Before Mia could react, she'd snatched it off her head.

"Hey! Freakin' come on!" Mia barked.

Fiona, suddenly still, stared at Mia's fuzzy head. "What are all those scratches? Somebody drop a Siamese on your noggin?"

"I told you. The clippers."

"That was for real? I thought you made that up because you didn't want to talk about chemo."

"All. *Too.* Real. And we're still in danger. That's why we're on this trip."

"Well, it looks like its growing back," said Fiona, regaining her momentum. "Black right?"

"Like midnight."

"Hey, that makes me cue ball and you're eight ball!"

"You gonna take those selfies?"

She mashed her cheek against Mia's and snapped the picture. "Now, let's make crazy faces!"

"Fiona!" Mia protested.

"Do it, or I'll kick *you* in the balls!"

Mia laughed. She didn't want to but she absolutely couldn't help it. Fiona snapped another.

"You are awful!" Mia screwed up her eyes and stuck her tongue out sideways. Fiona took a dozen loony portraits.

"One more!" She planted a big kiss on Mia's cheek and recorded it for posterity. She reviewed the portfolio, glowing with admiration. "Give me your email address. I'll send them to you.

"That's alright," said Mia.

Fiona pulled a business card covered in flowers and ladybugs out of the bag and gave it to her. "Here's mine."

"I think you and my Karate teacher are made out of the same stuff."

"Is your hair curly?"

"Yup."

"Mine too! See, I told you! We're like sisters! Well, I gotta go. Promise you'll write me, sister?"

"I can't promise."

"Promise, Mia!" Fiona pointed a threatening finger. "Or you *know* what'll happen!"

"Okay! Just get out of here, will you? I think I hear your mom calling!"

Fiona laughed with satisfaction and waved, and then she was gone.

Blake plunked turkey sandwiches down on the table. "Who was that?" he said.

"Haraguchi's devil spawn."

***

Blake leaned against the railing at the fantail and stared down into the spreading wake of the ship. He followed it out to the sharp line between sea and sky. There was no land in sight. You could walk all the way around the deck and it was just water and sky: the depths above and depths below. *That's all we are*, he thought. *Ninety-eight percent water, a little bit of dirt, with a breeze blowing through us.*

Suddenly, Mia was at his side. "You'll never guess what I found under the mattress in our stateroom." She held up a postcard that read *Viva Fort Wayne!* in big, yellow letters over a collage of familiar landmarks. "It's blank on the back."

"Give me that." He pulled a pen out of his cargo pocket and wrote as fast as the words would come. Mia strained to read as he scribed.

> Dear Dad,
> I went on a voyage, you went on a trip.
> The boy you don't want went down with the ship!
> You and Agatha made him feel hated fearful hurt useless worthless lost sad confused lonely enraged trapped foolish stupid hopeless. Thank you for making sure I had food, clothes, a house, for marrying Mom, and for ditching me at HCSC.
> Respectfully,
> Blake.

"Are you really going to send that?" she said, amazed at his epiphany.

He looked her in the eyes and smiled from a place newly discovered. "Here it goes." Blake flung the card into air and watched it spin down through the slipstream into the blue-rippled abyss.

"Let me know how that works out for ya," she said.

"I feel better already."

That little voice chimed in from behind. "If you two get married, will you adopt me?"

Mia rolled her eyes and dropped a fist on the rail. "Fionaaa!"

Chapter 72

Carson didn't bother to get up from the couch when Sooner went nuts in the bay window, nor when the front door swooshed open and the stairwell filled with joyful voices and baggage-burdened footfall. Blake dropped his suitcases and scooped the pooch up in a frenzy of snuffley whining and licking.

"We're back!"

"So I hear," said Carson, without enthusiasm.

"Man we had a great time. Went to Manitowoc on the Badger, saw the Maritime Museum, went on a World War II Sub!"

"Glad somebody had a good time."

"Got married, adopted a child, bought a kayak," said Mia, irritated with Carson's passive-aggressive tenor.

Blake sat down on the arm of the couch. "Did you see Korbin last Saturday?"

Carson looked away. "You could say that."

Blake paused. "He died, didn't he?"

"Friday, about three in the afternoon."

Mia gave Blake a consoling look from across the room. Gunn had just topped the stairs. "Friday at three," said Gunn. "I was in the ambulance and you two were in the teeth of that storm. What are the arrangements, man?"

"They've done been arranged."

Blake swelled with indignation. "You mean they went ahead and cremated him? Damn those people!"

"No, they didn't burn him—and you watch your mouth! Somehow Mort Toten and Sons' fridge went out, so we couldn't wait 'til you all decided to come back. Me and the boys from Tyner's put 'im in his box, hauled him over to the bone yard and planted him."

"What a delicate eulogy. Beautiful sentiment," said Gunn.

The bicker-rama commenced without delay, but Blake did not hear. It was as if he were deaf again; their voices on the far side of the ever-present ringing in his ears.

"Did yeh get yer insurance?"

"There were complications."

"There always are. Miss, how do you feel about a jaunt to North Carolina?"

"Forget it," said Carson. Gabby gave up the ghost yesterday."

"So, Clarissa's coming back, then?"

"She's got a dozen friends between here and Charlotte she intends to see."

"Mother Carey's chickens, it'll be Thanksgiving before she turns up!" said Gunn.

Mia touched Blake's arm. "Come on. Let's get you settled back in."

***

Blake flopped down on his bed. She sat down next to him.

"I'm sorry about Mr. Dubois."

He nodded.

"Hey, I like what you've done with the place. Kind of a cross between 'early clubhouse' and Eagle Scout." Mia looked around for a minute, waiting for him to break the insistent silence; but he did not. She stood up, put her hands on her hips and declared "Best. Vacation. Ever."

He smiled. "Want to take *Osprey II* around the Island?"

Mia sent Blake ahead while she tended to necessary things. It was quitting time for the Pagáns. Cezar and Romero helped him get the kayak down from the top of Gunn's van. They also confided that the coffin business was going through the roof, that their father had farmed the landscaping out to some cousins and compelled Sylvana to find regular employment in the housekeeping industry. And, as fate would have it, she landed a position in the mayor's mansion.

***

It was good to be in home waters, again—steadily receding, though they were. They sat on Highland Point as the sun sank behind the far shore.

"I forgot to ask you about the flash drive when we got home," said Mia.

"I'll look for it tomorrow."

"You didn't lose it did you?"

"I said I'll look for it tomorrow," he replied, gently.

"Hey, I'll be right back." Mia went to the *Osprey and* returned with a little bundle of stuff. She laid out an assortment of odds and ends on the picnic table. Birthday candles, white paper lunch-sacks, light-gauge wire, and dry cleaning bags. "While you were getting the *Osprey* in the water, I was shaking Mr. Gunn down for all of this stuff."

"Uh, alright. And this is for?"

"Closure. So you can have some kind of closure on your friend's passing. Find me some small flat rocks. And think of a prayer and some good things to say."

***

Hunter leaned back against the windshield of *Tantrum II* and watched the little lights drifting out from the shoreline. Then, one after another, three flying lanterns ascended like luminous jellyfish into the night sky.

Brigita stood in the cockpit. "We will be so happy together."

"I got news for you, sister," he said, without looking back. "We're done. I'm gone."

"I don't think so, my hero."

"Go bother my dad."

"Lawrence has lost his taste for adventure. He thinks a few pictures will hold me at bay. But there is something he does not know."

"Keep it to yourself."

"Hunter, I am carrying a baby. A *Devlin* baby. Teddy will think it is his. Unless…"

He gave her a look which, even if only for a split second, frightened her.

"A simple DNA test will determine which of you loses it all. Maybe both? And you know I will not be a single mother."

"You are one cold…"

"And you were a fool for letting that little boy take your power! But I cut off his freedom. Then I broke your sister's will and I cut off her hair." She ran her fingers across his scalp. "Yours is too short. I wonder what prized possession I shall cut off of you?"

He jerked away. "Prove it."

She produced her cell phone, tapped the screen a few times and handed it to him. Hunter glared at the close-up selfie: Brigita smiling smugly, holding a white, pregnancy-test stick. There was little a pink plus-sign in its result window.

"You Photo-shopped it."

"We'll see, won't we? Come here my Hero. Show me that you still love me." She popped the cork on another bottle of almond champagne.

Chapter 73

Carson dumped an armload of dirty clothes in front of the washer, and watched with amusement as his nephew excavated the trash can. "What are you looking for?"

"A flash drive. I thought it was ruined. I threw it away."

"I don't even know what that is, kid."

"A computer thingie. It was a little green fish. The head comes off and there's a connector."

"Oh. That?" His voice drained of mirth. "I though it was a practice plug."

"You found it? Where is it? I have to have it!"

"Well, I screwed a treble hook into it and made it into a real lure."

"Tell me it's in the tackle box?"

"It was. I went fishing with it the day after we buried Korbin."

"That's okay, I know how to dry it out." Blake started for the door. "Is it in the boat?"

"It's in a fish, actually. Something huge hit it, and when I set the hook all I got back was the little plastic head of the thing. All makes sense, now."

Blake slumped against the doorframe and stared at the ceiling for a minute. "I'm glad it's gone," he said flatly, and walked off.

***

The custodian parked his cart, entered the dark room, and shut the door behind him. He stood at the foot of the bed and looked long at the sleeping man with the shaggy gray mane and shark-fin nose.

"Master? Master!"

"Why disturbest thou me, by bringing me up?" said the hollow voice through lips that barely moved. "Who art thou?"

"Master Kalijah, it is I."

The man sniffed the air, then let out a long sigh. "My devoted acolyte, Jack! You are free! What of the community?"

"Raided. Imprisoned. Scattered."

"First Yaegerstown, now Mangrave is decimated?" he groaned. "The family lines will fade into the pages of history. Our ways will be forgotten. What of the disciples?"

"Betrayed one another and fled."

"The Great High Priestess?"

"Captured with her husband."

"And the sacred fish of our god?"

"Caught and hauled away."

"The glorious crop of the sacrament?" Kalijah whimpered.

"Trampled by the firstborn infidel."

Kalijah rubbed an itch out of his nose. "What of the Prince?"

"He grows stronger," said Jack.

"And the ancient one?"

"In the ground, where he belongs. The others will join him, soon enough."

"Oh Jack! No ceremony? No ritual? That is not sacrifice but cold blooded murder! All is lost."

"But there are new initiates!" said Jack. "And Jared still serves us. There is a new Adept. He knows much. He got me this job. He's been ditching your meds so you can lead us, again. We can still bring back the old gods."

"No Jack, the one God has triumphed and driven out the old gods. They *are* no gods Jack."

"Don't say that, Master!" he hissed at the blasphemy.

"It is true," he said, hoarsely. He cleared his throat. "And my showers! I get a shower twice a week! Three meals a day, TV in bed! The medicine makes the voices go away so can I concentrate on… Bingo! Think of the money I've won, Jack! A dollar and thirty-seven *cents*!"

Voodoo Jack furrowed his brow and blew a torrent of hot, stinking breath out his nose.

"It's the promised land, Jack. The promised land." Kalijah grinned at the fond thought of his new situation.

Voodoo Jack snatched a pillow off a nearby chair and stuffed it against Kalijah's face with all his might. The scarecrow of a man thrashed and twisted under the blankets. By the merest chance he clutched his call light. Thirty hellish, writhing seconds later he heard a nurse scream. The suffocating weight suddenly evaporated. Somewhere in the distance, a whining alarm buzzer announced that Jack had made his escape through the emergency exit.

Chapter 74

"He's on the other side of that little hummock," said Gunn.

Mia pushed the huge spray of flowers to Blake, who received it out of the back of the van. He couldn't see through the bouquet jungle so she guided him between graves up the gentle rise. She stopped dead at the top.

Blake pulled his face out of the flowers and looked at Mia. "Your expression is somewhere between 'I sense something's wrong,' and 'I wet myself.'"

"Don't look." she said.

He struggled to set the spray down without damaging the tall stems. Halfway down the mild slope was a sizeable mound of fresh dirt with a head, shoulder and one arm sticking out of its base. "Take a picture so we don't get blamed for this," he said.

Mia came to her senses. "Can't. We really gotta get new phones."

Blake approached cautiously. He recognized the grotesque ink-sleeved arm. "It's one of the pirates. Jared Dake!" He knelt down on one knee, out of the arm's reach. Mia kept her distance.

"Hey! Tattoo man!" said Blake. The pirate's eyes popped open. He managed one parched word. "Help."

"Mia! Get Mr. Gunn!" She flew across the hummock. Blake snatched a flower urn off a nearby headstone, chucked its faded plastic blossoms and started dredging like mad. He heard the van rev up and drive away. Soon, the pirate's chest was free to expand and Blake stopped digging.

Mia returned with her new tablet. "He's gone for help."

"Get some video." He looked at the pirate as she started recording. "Help us out here. We're kind of at a loss."

"Got down to the vault, it all caved in. Jack split."

"Why?"

"Trap. He knew you'd come. Says he's gonna kill you."

Mia and Blake both cast about warily.

"Just for the record," said Mia, "what was your name again?"

"Jared Dake."

"And who did you say wanted to kill Blake and left you here to die?"

"Jack Christenson," he croaked bitterly.

Sirens wailed in the distance. Before long the Channel 3 Action Chopper was leering down on the macabre scene with its cyclops-eye, as the tattooed pirate was extracted from Korbin Dubois' grave. Every last emergency vehicle in Freeman choked the lanes of Two Acre Gardens Cemetery. Volunteer responders lined the shoulders of the main road. Finally, the groundskeeper materialized carrying shovels and, with Blake and Mia, erased all signs of desecration. Mia's video and stills made the news, the paper, and went viral on the internet. It was a slow news-day in Freeman, Indiana.

Chapter 75

"Maybe you want to steer the boat now?" said Sylvio, doing a lousy job of sounding casual.

"You're doing fine!" Blake responded in Spanish. He was in the bow compartment, explaining the tabernacle and rigging to Tio Salvador. "Cezar will keep an eye on you."

The *Terrapin* was under full sail, with Blake in command of a crew of Pagán men. The staple gun had blown a seal, so it was off to the hardware store. Romero had taken Abuelita to the grocery, Carson was at Beverly's and Gunn was on his way out the door to visit the doctor. He gave Blake leave to ferry Sylvio to Freeman the old-fashioned way. And like all Pagán enterprises, it turned into a family affair.

Pot-bellied Abuelito sat in the cockpit, enjoying his son's obvious nervousness to no end. Cezar tended the main, jib and mizzen sails. When Blake and Salvador finally returned aft, Sylvio insisted on handing off the tiller.

"Oh, you can let go. She's been steering herself since Cezar trimmed the sails," Blake grinned. "Go ahead. Let go."

Sylvio slowly released his death grip on the tiller. *Terrapin* held her course. Abuelito and Tio were suitably impressed.

"Amazing. Mr. Gonn said he and your grandfather build it, together."

"That's what I hear." said Blake.

"That little boat too." said Abuelito. "*Becky Lynn.* I think maybe I'd like to build a fishing boat like that one."

Tio nodded. "The fishing boats at the marina are no good."

Blake thought for a moment and got a sly look. "Why don't we build ten?" he said. "And rent them out."

The men looked at each other. Slowly, smiles of comprehension turned to nods of assent.

"Perhaps Mr. Gonn will graciously allow us to lease his old store as our rental office?" said Abuelito.

"We could sell bait and tackle" agreed Tio. "I would like that very much."

"There are three recreation areas on the lower lake that don't get used much," said Blake. "You know why? No camp store down here. I'm thinking full service camp store."

"What is your percentage, as the master-mind, Mr.Urquart?" said Sylvio.

"Ten percent. I bet the Mayor, the Park, and the Chamber of Commerce will give us a public endorsement, too!"

"You sure got big plans for a small guy," said Sylvio.

"That's because somewhere along the line, I figured out that the only obstacle between me and what I want to do is usually just me."

***

Blake advised the clerk that anything too big to be carried was to be delivered to the *Terrapin* on Pier 2. He left his crew at the hardware store and set out on an errand of his own.

The flea market was a ghost town. Only a few bargain-hunting tourists and bored locals wandered its shuttered halls. Blake arrived at a secluded booth in the far back corner. He browsed the contents of the glass counter, while the wiry old proprietor sat in the corner, leafing through a magazine and actively ignoring his customer. Blake politely cleared his throat.

"Help you?" croaked the man, without looking up.

"Yes please. I'd like two of the large pepper sprays and two stun guns."

The man merely raised a shaky, nicotine stained finger at a hand-painted sign above the counter.

You must be 18 and show ID

To purchase these items:

Tobacco ~ Dirty Books

Stun Guns ~ Pepper Spray

Blake stared at the sign.

"You old man Gunn's brat?"

"Yes," said Blake, sure that would be the magic word.

"Don't matter. Still gotta be eighteen. Heh, heh!"

Something landed on Blake's shoulder and clamped down like a great horned owl. He recognized the grip. "Not a problem, sir!" said Hunter. "I'd like what he ordered and a signal flare kit, and a brace of pistols.

"Huh?"

"Two flare guns, old timer."

The proprietor eyed them suspiciously as he struggled out of his butt-sprung easy chair. Blake cast a nervous glance at Hunter, who smiled with the creepy confidence of a mugger in a nursing home.

"You want that in a bag or are you planning to rampage directly?"

"Bag please," said Blake.

The man jabbed away at a filthy calculator and announced "One hundred seventy-nine dollars even. He collected two Benjamins from Hunter.

"Stay upwind with that one and don't use the zappers when you're wet," he warned.

"No receipt?" said Hunter.

"I never saw either of you."

Hunter steered his captive out of the booth. "Let's take a walk over to the snack bar," he said, collecting his purchases and handing the bag to Blake.

"Actually..."

"I know—you've got peeps waiting on you. I saw you sail over. Have to admit it, that old shoebox has a charm all her own, under a spread of canvas. We need to talk, buddy o' mine! I need those pix."

"I gave the chip to your dad."

"Well, dear old Dad is throwing me under the bus."

"Because of the will?"

"Bingo. Whenever anyone gets cut out or croaks, it means a bigger slice of the pie for everyone else."

"Thanks, Gramps," said Blake.

"That Balkan bed-beast has my jewels in a vise, while everybody but me seems to have a copy of that digital dragon-bane."

"I don't, um didn't, well…"

"You don't have it?"

"Mia doesn't even know. My uncle mistook the flash drive for something else and lost it."

"Then it's plan B. 'B' for burglary. We're going to pull a repeat performance of your little stunt, over at the mayor's place."

"Wait, give me a couple of days to fish around for it. And I may have a plan C."

"Well, just to show you what a generous guy I am, I'll give you until Labor Day. Hey, you in on the bass tournament?"

"No, sorry. Crewing in the Commodores Cup Regatta."

"Too bad. I could use a partner." He squeezed Blake's shoulder even harder, then released him. "Don't let me down, Blake." Hunter turned and walked out the side entrance by the snack bar. Blake stared at twin posters plastered on the glass doors.

S K Y Z A B L A Z E!

Over

Highland Creek Reservoir

~

Biggest Baddest Fireworks Display

of the Summer

~

Featuring

Mustang Circus! WWII P51 Squadron

~

This Labor Day!

***

Gunn was surprisingly agreeable to Blake's business proposition. He granted permission to begin cleaning up the old boat store immediately, on the condition that they all sit down and draw up a business plan and a lease agreement. Abuelita burst out in a fountain of joyful tears when Blake brought back news that by spring she'd be running a tienda with her husband and brother. "Mi American dream!" was all she could sob, as she embraced them over and over.

Chapter 76

'Swallowed by a fish?" said Mia, pulling her paddle, mid-stroke. "Are you kidding me?"

"Sadly, not," said Blake. "C'mon, paddle, we're almost there."

"And you seriously thought you didn't have *any* backup, but you still gave Dad the chip. Tux, what the?"

"I couldn't get hold of Soojee. I guess I should've had Griffy and Kaz copy it for me. My bad."

"No! Never mind. Point taken."

"Once I had the card I didn't want to chance losing it *and* you! I mean, it's not like anyone would try to kill us for it, right?"

"Ya know, you're really getting the hang of the sarcasm thing. Stop it, by the way."

"I told Hunter I'd look for it. He gave me 'til Labor Day."

"And he really said it has to do with the will?"

"Your dad is throwing him under the bus. His words."

"That can mean only one thing."

Blake stopped the dumb question before it escaped his lips and remembered the terms of the will. "You're going to be the aunt of your half-sister?"

"Tux, I liked you better when you were young and naïve. We have to get my tablet or laptop back. Preferably both."

"If they're not at the bottom of the lake already. And no, I am not setting one foot in the mayor's mansion."

"I wouldn't ask you to."

"And I will not put Sylvana in that kind of danger."

"Then what are we gonna do?" she said, impatiently.

"I think if we keep our heads down long enough, it'll work out."

"Easy for you to say. You're out of here in a few weeks."

Blake stopped paddling and turned around as far as he could. The look of wounded disbelief on his face stung her conscience.

"I didn't mean that. I'm sorry."

"Just give it some time and see what happens. Trust and go forward."

"Okay," she said, reluctantly. "Labor Day. You mad at me?"

He smiled. "Git to paddlin' woman!"

They rounded Trespass Island. Several barges were being rafted together to make a fifty by one hundred foot platform for the SkyzAblaze fireworks and monster sound system. The workers anchored it just north of the island. A modest pontoon cruiser housing the fire-control center would be parked in the mouth of the cove, on the night of the show.

"I can't believe they're doing this. The whole forest is like a tinderbox," said Blake.

Mia shook her head. "Never underestimate what money and tradition can accomplish."

Chapter 77

The three senior Pagáns had set right in to cleaning up the old marina storefront. By mid-week the countertops were paved with blueprints, marine hardware catalogs, and supply lists like a bridge of dreams. And lest the dream quickly become a nightmare, it was decided early that the first vessel in the Pagán fishing fleet would be named *Salma*.

***

Sylvana pushed her cart into the cavernous master-bedroom, glad the lady of the house had finally left for her tennis match. She stripped the adjoining bathroom and tried not to remember how just the week before she'd found her co-worker, Marisol, crumpled in the corner of the sumptuous marble shower—crying in shame. She went about her business but Marisol, and the tales her brothers had told her about Tux and La Rica, haunted her at every step. The mayor was nice enough when he was around. But his wife—and Sylvana considered herself tough—scared the pee out of her.

The bathroom done, she stripped the bed—but found the door to the walk-in closet locked. In fact the knob had been changed to the sort requiring a regular house key. She reported this to the head of staff, who informed her that the bed linens had been moved across the hall to the closet in the guest bedroom. Fear or no fear, Sylvana had always hated a mystery, always hated being denied entry—and this closed door was no different.

Chapter 78

Other than the encounter with Hunter, it had been an unremarkable and sane week. Too sane, Blake thought. He had wrestled with the temptation to grill Sylvana, but he stuck to his resolution to keep her out of it. As far as he knew, Mia had not spoken to her, either. Just when it seemed as if things would be okay, here they were on pins and needles again.

Even the weather had been reasonable, with temperatures in the low eighties. But summer was quietly stoking its furnace for a final torrid blast. It peaked on Saturday, canceling the first day of racing in the Commodore's Cup with a one hundred two degree swelter. No one complained, though, because the club party went on as planned that night. Sunday promised not only to be twenty degrees cooler, but to usher in a favorable wind as well.

The Commodore's Cup shindig was the usual beery barbeque. The band knocked out rock-n-roll classics appealing to the tepid nostalgia of the fifty-something crowd. The instrumentals were good, but the vocals less than stirring.

The junior sailors were positively thrilled to have two local heroes in their midst and swarmed Blake and Mia relentlessly. Then Griffy, Kaz, Soojee and Natalie turned up. Blake could see that Mia had had enough and engineered their surreptitious escape. He rejoined her in their old refuge: the attic dormer.

"This band sucks," she said, pulling off her purple bandana. She scratched her scalp sumptuously. "My head feels like a dirty tennis ball."

"Looks like one, too. I think your dad picked the band." Blake stood and peered around the edge of the window and scanned the deck. The juniors searched the patio for their missing celebrities. "I think they just figured out we're not coming back. And yes, I locked the door."

Mia looked at the peaked ceiling of the dormer and sighed deeply. "What are we going to do?"

"Be ready for peace or for war. That's Mr. Gunn's clan motto. Didn't know he was in the Klan, did you?"

"You idiot. I meant about us."

"What about us?"

"Are you *that* dense? It's really going to suck when we have to go our separate ways."

"I thought I was the little brother you never wanted? You didn't go and break the rules did you?"

"I got used to you. Like body odor."

"We'll stay in touch. I'll come back next summer and we can do it all over again," he said, sitting down beside her.

"It won't be the same."

"Well, we are on a journey, I guess."

Mia scoffed. "Did Haraguchi give you that speech, too?"

"It's true."

"Promise you won't get all mushy-dramatic and cry when the time comes," she said.

"You know what's funny? You use the same shampoo as my mom. Whenever I smell your hair, it reminds me of her."

"That's not funny. That's weird. I *was* going to kiss you, but you can forget that now, pal."

"Really?"

"No."

"No you weren't really going to kiss me, or no you're not going to kiss me now."

"Exactly."

"How 'bout a headlock for old times sake?" He squinted and puckered up with a juicy smooching sound. She shoved him over and turned toward the window in a mock pout.

"But seriously, something's up with my mom. When I read her postcards it's like she's someone I never knew—who'd been there all along. Just waiting to get out. Dad's the same though. He'll come back here and just tell me to get in the car. No 'I missed you, son,' or 'where'd you get that scar?' Just 'get in the car, we're going now.'"

"If he even recognizes you."

"Have I changed that much?"

"Tux, since the last time we sat in this spot you've shot up six inches and put on twenty pounds! Your voice dropped an octave and your hair's different, and your tan is so dark that when you speak-a da Spanish people think you're a Mexican. All you have to do is tell your dad you died and you're home free."

An insistent knocking echoed up the stairwell. Beverly's unmistakable voice warbled through the door. "If you two are up there, we've got homemade ice cream! And don't think putting the key back over the door and locking it behind you is fooling anybody. It never worked for your uncle, either! See you downstairs!"

Mia cocked an inquiring eyebrow. Something irresistible welled up in Blake, not so amorous as it was mischievous. He lunged forward to steal a kiss, but clacked his teeth against hers.

"Owww! Craaap!" she cried, cupping a hand over her aching mouth. "My orthodonture!"

He bolted for the stairs. "Not sorry!"

She stumbled to her feet in hot pursuit.

Chapter 79

Blake opened the front door to get the newspaper, expecting to be robbed of breath by the oppressive furnace of summer. To his surprise, he was embraced by a wonderfully chilly gust. He stepped out, smiling in disbelief. A cool gale rolled through the treetops, which seemed to dance with relief.

He picked up the paper and perused the headlines. *Special Labor Day Edition*

Mustang Roundup! WW2 Warbirds Return for 14th Annual SkyzAblaze! Celebration...Record Bass Hooked by Freeman local Hunter Devlin: "This bad fish is going straight to the trophy room!" Fireworks Show Will Go On: 400+ Boats Expected on Upper and Lower Lakes. Mangrave Properties Seized by State to be Auctioned. 75% of Town on the Block. Break-in at Devlin's Marina: Office Ransacked.

Blake shivered and trotted upstairs. He smiled at the new second-place trophy gleaming on the mantel. Gunn sat at the breakfast table stirring his coffee. "Forgot to tell yeh. Got a card Friday. Got lost in the shuffle."

He took it to the bay window. It was a long, narrow, hexa-fold affair that opened up to make a bizarre, black-and-white mural a yard long. The picture began with a field of gray parallel lines increasingly interrupted by the word Metamorphose. The word repeated at right angles and eventually formed a grid, which turned into a checkerboard; which morphed into reptiles; which became hexagons; which changed into a honeycomb; then into bees; then into mutant butterflies; into fish which became birds; which stretched into stacked cubes that grew into a towering city on the shore of a chessboard, a cluster of pieces in one corner; then back into a flat checkerboard that faded into a grid of Metamorphose, in a sea of gray lines.

He studied the chess pieces. The black knight, queen, and bishop had white in checkmate. A good omen, he thought. He folded it back up and turned it over.

Metamorphosis II, M.C. Escher.

Dearest Blake,
I was sooo excited to get your card. It made my whole week! I left a message on Nanna's machine, but please tell her that we will pick you up on Sept. 30th, in the afternoon, at the sailing club. I wish I could visit with Tripp and take a cruise, but Daddy and Agatha will want to go home. You know, we have never been apart since you were born? You can't imagine how strange and scary it has been without you. You are my hero! I am counting the days.
Love,
Mom

A strange smudge marred the corner of the address. The single droplet that had landed there spoke more than the sum of her words.

Dear Mom, he thought, *visiting the grave of a friend and finding someone else in it—alive—was strange and scary without you. Being in a meth-lab explosion and going deaf—was strange and scary without you. Being chased by homicidal maniacs from one end of this lake to the other—on a regular basis— is strange and scary without you. Having a girl friend who isn't my girlfriend but is my girlfriend but isn't—is strange and scary without you. I can't imagine how strange and scary it will be without her. I guess I'll get used to it—like I did with you.*

Somewhere in the house, a ring-tone played faintly. Blake sought it out. It was Mia. "Leave your phone at the far end of the shop, again?"

"Ha ha. Where have you been?"

"Had to buy a flippin' jacket if you can believe that. I'm thinking your boat was made for days like this. Find a spare harness and see if your uncle will go out with us."

"Really! When?"

"Sooner the better. By four there'll be so many boats on this lake you'll be able to walk from your place to mine. I'll be there in an hour."

The wind howled over the sails as *Seven Thunders* leapt across the whitecaps, the forward half of the hull out of the water. She threw a curtain of spray from her bow. They spent the afternoon planing up and down the lower lake. Everyone got a ride on the wire and a trick at the helm, five miles at a time. Then came lunch, siesta, and the passage to the club for the grand Labor Day soirée.

It was seven o'clock and, as packed as the club was, the crowd still didn't come close to the numbers seen at Blake's birthday bash. A floating city had sprung up between the point and Trespass Island, and the smell of charcoal grills swirled together with boat exhaust that wafted in from the water.

Out of the midst of the armada came the *Becky Lynn*, chugging along with Abuelita Salma proudly ensconced on the middle bench like Lord Admiral Nelson—little Marcelo clamped firmly between her knees. A little Flag of Mexico fluttered smartly from an ensign pole in her stern. Blake waved them to the last dock, where *Cry of the Osprey II* was berthed. He made them fast, fore and aft, and offered the grand matriarch a supporting arm as she disembarked. She smiled deferentially and waddled regally off the shimmying dock. Cezar and Romero were next, then Sylvio with Marcelo on his shoulders.

"Hola, Tux! long time no see!" said Sylvana as she manhandled a heavy cooler onto the dock.

"Hi! Hey how's the job?"

She piled folding camp chairs like logs. "Weird, Tux. *Real* weird."

"Sylvana! Sillon! Ahora!" shouted Abuelita.

"Si! Momento!" She snatched up a chair and headed for shore.

Blake grabbed two and followed. "Weird how?"

"Like the wife, she put a big lock on her closet. Where the linens was."

"Where are the linens now?"

"Who cares? I wanna know what's in the closet!" They caught up to the family, who had settled in the grove. Sylvana unfolded a chair for her grandmother. Abuelita settled into it imperiously, then got up and indicated a superior location. Sylvana moved the seat. The process went on for ten minutes. *Terrapin* entered the harbor and reluctantly Blake excused himself.

He met them at the main dock and berthed them in the commodore's favorite spot. After he'd gotten Gunn on the planks, he hurried back to interrogate Sylvana. Tripper received the cart from Carson and, item by item, loaded it with their supercargo of picnic necessities. He paused for a moment, as if listening to a familiar voice whispering in his ear. Carson took note and smiled. Gunn strapped the stuff down with bungee cords, then paused again. He closed his eyes and pursed his lips.

"They're coming," he announced.

"Ten bucks, as usual?"

"Certainly." Gunn opened his eyes.

"How many?"

"Twelve. Four Mustangs, four Zeroes."

"Zeroes? Not Messerschmitts? And that's only eight."

Gunn closed his eyes again and held his breath. "I don' believe it. They brought the Flying Fortress! B-17, man!"

"Twenty bucks," said Carson, with a confident grin. "How long?"

"Fifteen minutes. Double or nothing."

Carson, sure that the wind was playing havoc with his friend's clairvoyance, took the wager. "Forty dollars. You're on!"

***

Mia slouched in a low-slung camp chair, wrapped in a blanket, and fiddled with her tablet. She heard dry grass crunching behind her.

"Hey, Rica!"

"Que pasando, Chica!"

"I got a name, you know?"

"Me too," said Mia, indifferently.

"I wanted to tell you I'm real sorry about what happen to you. Especial you hair. It was *real* nice. I wish I had hair like that," said Sylvana.

Mia considered for a moment and decided to smile. "Thank you, Sylvana. That means a lot."

"You see Tux?"

"Not for a while. How's the job?"

"That's what I want to tell him. Is weird. I mean really loco. The mayor's wife, she force my friend to take a pregnant test,"

Mia sat up. "Was she?"

"Hell yes she pregnant! She's do for the baby next month! And that lady, she keep the test!"

"Sylvana, I think I might like you after all. What else?"

Sylvana recounted the case of the locked closet.

"You know how to pick locks?" said Mia.

"What! You think I'm a freakin' criminal?"

"It's a skill, just sayin'. Look, she's got my tablet and my laptop. Tux didn't want me to say anything, but if you could get those back I'd...I mean it would really help us out."

"What was you gonna say the first time?"

"I was going to offer you a reward, but I thought it would be insulting."

"You can insult me all you want! Real big! Go ahead!"

"You get my tablet and you'll be helping Tux, me, and even my jackass brother. And not a word of this to Tux, okay?"

When Blake returned to the grove, Sylvana was long gone on another errand. He found Mia on the point. She was recounting her new tales when Blake's two spies, Scurvy and Rickets, materialized and advised that Hunter was indeed in the clubhouse and that Rexroat and Hopkins were lurking on the grounds.

"That's great news!" he said to Mia. "She's powerless now."

"Don't bet on it," said Mia. "Let's get out of here."

He shelled out a dollar to each of his informants. She packed her tablet away and began folding her blanket.

"I'm going to tell Hunter, now," he said, jogging away.

"If you insist," she said. "I'll get the *Osprey* ready."

Blake took the bluff trail back up the peninsula, to approach the clubhouse by stealth. When he reached the place of ascent he was surprised to encounter a motley band of stoners loafing in a beat-up Jon boat, grounded at the shoreline.

"Hey honey, where ya going?" said a chubby girl in an embarrassingly sheer tank top.

"I'm sorry, are you club members?"

"Oh, yeah," said one of the young men. "Members! Hey you wanna join our club?"

"This is private property. I'll have to ask you leave."

"We're picking someone up. Hey, you're that kid, aren't you?"

"C'mon, get psillie with us! We'll hook you up! You like tripping on shrooms?"

Blake realized who the missing captain must be, and who they were there to pick up. He snapped a suitable branch from a downed tree and leapt into the boat swinging in earnest. Yelping stoners hit the water. Blake shoved the boat out into Thistle Bay.

He went up the slope, tree by tree, searching for any sign of Voodoo Jack. He emerged on Ray's patio. The groundskeeper's apartment was the lowest level in the clubhouse, the fan-shaped patio set into the hillside. Blake was about to scale the retaining wall when something jerked him backward, spun him around and threw him against it.

"Shoulda checked behind the trash cans, genius!" hissed Jack. Blake felt a cold, sharp line pressed against his throat. He held his breath and tried not to move. Or pee. "I ought to cut your head off right here." He got right in Blake's face. He thought his breath smelled exactly like the time the toilet overflowed, back home. "I *want* to cut your head off right here. But that would be murder. So I'll save you for the sacrifice and murder your uncle like we planned all along."

Suddenly, Jack flew back and then slammed straight into the wall, with tremendous speed and force—not once, but twice. The big black Bowie knife clattered across the concrete as Voodoo Jack crumpled.

"Denied," said Hunter.

"Wow, am I glad to see you!"

"I hope you have good news for me, Sparky. It's been a disappointing week," he said, voice grave, gaze as sharp and cold as the blade that just crossed Blake's Adam's apple.

"Yes! You won't believe this but…"

"It had better be incriminating pictures of my enemies."

"No, its better than that. Brigita's not pregnant!"

"Oh Sparky," Hunter clapped his hands on Blake's shoulders and looked him in the eye. "I am *so* disappointed in you."

"Brigita's not pregnant. Listen to me!" The look on Hunter's face made it clear that he wasn't listening, because he wasn't there. "We're going to pay the mayor's mansion a little visit while everyone's at the big event."

"Couldn't we try the Marina again? Your dad probably has the chip in his safe or locked up in his desk."

"Safety deposit box. The bank."

"I could call your mom. She likes me. She could put pressure on your dad."

"You don't understand, Sparky. Now we're going to have to do things the hard way."

"He'd have to give you a copy. Hunter, Brigita is not pregnant! You can call her bluff!"

Hunter shook his head. He seemed to be steeling himself up for something terrible. Jack groaned and crawled toward the woods.

"Hey, he's getting away. He's wanted. We gotta call the cops!"

"You were my greatest creation. I'm sorry it has to end this way." Blake definitely didn't like the sound of that. Hunter began to rock him back and forth. Blake scrambled for anything he might say. Then he remembered Griffy on auto-pilot.

"That's true! You made me everything I am. I owe it all to you, Hunter."

"Yes, you do."

"You made me the 'Coffin Pimp of Freeman for cryin' out loud!"

"Yes, I did." The rocking deepened.

From the distance, the trilling fanfare of *Ride of the Valkyries* came rolling in from the lake. An ominous growling arose far in the northern sky.

"People just don't get it Hunter. It's all about *you*, man!" The rocking slowed and he began to nod, as if the wave had worked its way up his arms and into his head.

"Yes it is. It is all about me."

"You are a *great* guy. People just don't see how generous you are."

"I *am* generous!" he said, upper lip a tight sharp line.

"Give me a count of three, Hunter. For old time's sake. One last run, man?"

"Hunter stared vacantly for a moment then turned Blake around. "On your mark." He steered him to the low end of the opposite retaining wall. "Get set." He had barely lifted his hands and said "Go," before Blake was over the wall, around the club's patio-deck and on his way down the harbor side of the hill. The brass kicked in on *Valkyrie*. The growling in the sky grew louder.

"One, two, three." Hunter put two fingers in his mouth and whistled. Then he ripped down the hillside to the bluff trail, rebounded off Voodoo Jack at the bottom, and tore for the point at top speed. The battered diabolist landed in a lavish briar patch.

Blake had just hit the bottom of the hill when Hopkins came roaring up behind him. As he flew down the gravel path, *Lemon Drop* came plowing out of the back of the harbor. He burst through the grove, shouting for Mia as he passed the startled Pagáns. She was already afloat just off the rip-rap, having backed up to get a running start. Hunter burst out of the brush, dodging picnickers and straight-arming Sylvana as she jumped in his way. She flew over the fire pit and took out Abuelita. Cezar and Romero were on their feet instantly. Hunter went straight for the pile of kayaks, snagging a paddle and slinging the sleekest hull into the water. He was a stroking fury when the Pagán boys hit the waves in a commandeered canoe, Hopkins just behind. Mia timed her run perfectly—Blake made the leap into his seat with practiced precision. They headed for the chaos of the Freeman flotilla with a good forty second lead on Hunter. *Lemon Drop* went wide of the armada and disappeared.

They charged into the shuffling traffic jam, dodging and fending through ever-shifting avenues which formed and vanished with each passing vessel. Motorboats and sail-cruisers stretched as far as the eye could see. Blake shouted warnings, Mia shouted instructions back. Being right down on the water among the big boats was intimidating enough, but the booming music made it all the more disorienting as it bounced though the ever-morphing maze.

"There! I saw him to starboard!" said Blake.

"Edge port!" Mia leaned and used a rudder stroke while Blake powered the turn. They banged over a rough wake and sprinted a hundred yards. "Crap, there's Hopkins! Edge Starboard!" Hopkins gave a shrill whistle.

"Where are we?" said Blake.

"Trapped in Frogger Hell! Go!"

They slithered between two big-bellied Bay Liners approaching each other head on and caught sight of Hunter crossing their path fifty feet ahead. He spotted them just as a modest pontooner passed between them. Then like magic, they were gone.

The driver looked over the side to see the big, blue parasite he'd picked up. Blake and Mia clung to his dock fenders.

"Home, Jeeves!" sniped Mia.

The man doused Blake with his beer. "No modockin!"

They released their host and crossed his wake. The growling in the north turned to a roar like a hundred *Tantrum II's* in the sky. Over the treetops of Highland point burst four sleek planes, their silver sides glinting in the evening sun. They ripped over the fleet and passed Trespass Island in seconds.

"That was awesome!" said Blake, in delighted exhilaration. They made two hundred yards before another whistle pierced the air behind them. Hopkins was on them and gaining fast. He cleared a ponderous houseboat which obscured two Mexicans in a big aluminum canoe. They t-boned and rolled him. Mia arced *Osprey* around a drifting cabin cruiser whose skipper was cursing over its silent motor. Four more propeller-driven fighters, green with red disks on their sides and wings, rumbled overhead.

Hunter sliced over a wake behind them with a clear lane for pursuit. "Use the fogger!" cried Blake.

"Its in my pack, in the hatch!"

"We need it!"

"Then come back and get it! Paddle!"

Blake screamed as a wayward Skidoo swerved and side-swiped them with a hard jolt. He snatched its short bowline out of the water.

"Watch where you're going, idiot! Turn loose!" shouted the driver.

"Take us to the Island and we won't report you! Buck Mueller is my dad!" Blake shouted back. The Skidoo pilot bought it and throttled up. They left with Hunter sitting a mere forty feet behind.

The reeling, insistent music got brassier and was joined by a chorus of four more engines as the B-17 Super Fortress swept over the club and out across the lower lake. The Skidoo launched them fifty yards into the clear zone and abruptly broke away. They were completely exposed. To the left stretched more than a hundred yards of open water to the island—and *Lemon Drop* was barreling around to cut them off. To the right, Hunter bobbed at the edge of the armada, leveling two bright orange pistols at them.

"Roll the boat!" cried Mia. She grabbed the lip of the cockpit and threw all her weight over the side. Blake lurched as well. *Cry of the Osprey II* showed her belly as Hunter grinned and pulled the triggers. The first blazing shot bounced off the kayak, but the second went high and landed in Rexroat's lap, as *Lemon Drop* swooped by. He jumped straight up, shrieking and flailing. He kicked the wheel and the throttle as he dove over the side. *Lemon Drop* banked toward the island, shoving a leviathan wall of water at the fire-control boat. The skipperless juggernaut slashed through the shallows clipping one submerged stump after another. Like a giant pachinko machine of cosmic fate, chance and nature locked *Lemon Drop* into a collision course with the floating launch pad.

The tsunami threw the fire-control boat almost on its side and the captain's bathtub-sized margarita sloshed over the control panel. *Lemon Drop* slammed into the barge, knocking the hundred-and-fifty odd launch tubes into skewed disarray.

"Brace up!" Mia's shout was barely audible over the music, boat motors, and the entire squadron of planes now circling in parade formation. They righted the *Osprey* and the world exploded.

Shells streaked randomly in every direction, bursting low over the heads of the Labor Day mariners. The stampede was instant. Two of the fighter pilots peeled off and dove straight into the shimmering inferno, barely a hundred feet over the water. Blake and Mia accelerated to top speed in record time. Clouds of thick, sulphurous smoke rolled over them as they made for the sheltered-side of Trespass Island. Another Mustang chased a Zero right over them, followed by an exploding shell.

"I love this!" coughed Blake. "It's like the *Covenant* and the meth-lab rolled into one, with theme music!"

"You're crazy!" she screamed. "You've turned into an adrenalin junkie! I hate you!"

"Are you kidding me? I am sooo buying this CD!"

A sixteen-inch shell crashed into the woods on the island and blasted multi-colored ribbons of glittering fire through bone-dry underbrush and crispy canopy. A carpet of flame rolled across the ground and snaked up into a burning tornado, kicking off a mass exodus of island residents. *Osprey II* had just rounded onto the lee shoal when the breakers from the frantically scattering flotilla rolled in.

"We gotta get to deep water!" yelled Blake. He was pretty sure Mia replied with affirmative profanity. They crested several three-footers deftly. Blake noticed that swells seemed to be alive with all sorts of odd wriggling and splashing. They goofed their timing on the next wave and it washed over the deck, leaving an assortment of waterlogged varmints clinging to cargo nets, gaskets and anything else their little claws could dig into. They blew the following wave, too; completely exchanging the selection of critters for a new set of refugees. Blake found himself faced with a cat-sized, black and white beastie which clung tenaciously to the bow.

"You don't want that!" cried Mia.

Blake scooped up the bewildered skunk with his paddle and flung it away. *Osprey II* dipped into the next trough and banged hard on the bottom.

"Dammit! We're getting swamped!" yelled Mia.

As they surged up on the next ridge of water, Blake saw something huge burst out of the next wave and screamed, "Duuuck!" He bent double and covered his head as a half dozen deer vaulted the kayak. And then came the bees, motivating the most desperate stroking yet. As they cleared the shoals a ski boat charged up from behind and tossed Blake a tow rope. They joined the fleeing herd of motor yachts headed up the lake. Two P51 Mustangs wheeled around the island on their wingtips and roared into the distance, executing a triumphant barrel-roll as *Die Valkyrie* crashed through its bombastic finale.

"Hey, we passed Mr. Gunn's!" said Blake.

"That's the first place they'll look." She was working the mini pump like mad, stopping only to snatch sundry small animals out of the bilge. "You *do* realize we just demolished a couple of hundred *thousand* dollars worth of fireworks, right?"

"They were gonna shoot them off anyway," he said, looking back at the column of flame and black smoke that made Trespass Island look like Krakatoa. "I guess they'll call it Fire Island, now."

Mia shrieked as a weasel darted across her thigh and out of the boat.

"That wasn't our fault. Directly, anyway. He wouldn't listen. He was like totally someone else," said Blake.

"I warned Daddy a month ago. And I tried to stop you. But does anyone ever listen to Mia? Noooo!"

They released the tow and paddled for an hour to a little tributary, far east of the bridge. Mia steered them up the stream as the sun sank below the horizon. "Of all the nights to spend in the woods, drenched to the bone, we pick the coldest, windiest one of the summer," she said.

They pulled the *Osprey* ashore and hid her in the woods.

Blake was shivering. "You've got emergency blankets in your pack, right?"

"One."

"We need shelter and a fire, or we'll end up with hypothermia."

"No kidding? You wanted to see Thompson's Cave, that's where we're going." She wrung out her jacket and put it back on. "I stashed a survival kit in the bottom of that cave a couple of years ago. Let's see if it's still there." She pulled a flashlight out of her pack and led the way up a narrow trail.

***

The entrance to Thompson's Cave was a ragged, musty crag at the bottom of a small, misshapen sinkhole. And it wasn't easy to find in the dark. They searched for an hour and a half.

"Wouldn't it be better just to build a nice fire?" said Blake.

"You saw what happened to the Island and you want to build a fire?" Mia eased into the little pit.

"Doesn't spelunking require special safety gear?"

"Yup. You got any?"

"C'mon," pleaded Blake.

"C'mon nothing! They will hand me over to my dad and you gave up our only bargaining power *and* told my brother. I can't go back."

"I'm sorry." Blake was trying to sort out whether she was angry at him and if he should be defensive.

"It is what it is. There's food in the kit and I'm hungry. Don't sweat it. It's a beginner cave. Like going to Stone Hollow, only in reverse."

Mia climbed into the crag, flashlight between her teeth. Blake carefully followed suit. It *was* like Stone Hollow. Thirty feet down, the crag opened up to a roughly hemispherical chamber. Their little lights only illuminated a small wedge of the room at a time. Beyond that it was a solid wall of absolute darkness.

"Careful, there's sort of a trench along that wall. Big enough to fall in."

"I'm freezing," said Blake. He hated the cold, gritty, webby feel of the place.

"Down here. Scoot on your butt." They went down a steep incline that seemed to dead end. "Now we crawl," she said.

"This is your revenge for today, isn't it?" said Blake as she disappeared into a horizontal crack, only two feet high. He followed the soles of her feet. She stopped in a place where the ceiling rose a little and wormed her way up into a crack. All he could see was her legs. He felt completely disoriented. Pangs of panic began to twinge in his chest. Mia worked her way back down and lay on her back. She was fuming.

"It's gone—all of it. Crap."

"Mia, I'm really scared. Can we go."

She pointed her light in his face. He looked like he did when he had the rat snake in his lap.

She sidled back enough to lay her hand on his cheek. "You're okay, Tux. C'mon, let's go build a fire."

To his great relief the ceiling continued to rise and the walls drew in to make a tunnel—and that tunnel was headed for the surface.

"What's that smell?" he said.

"Wasn't me!" She sniffed the air. A pungent, herbal stench wafted down the passage. "Wait!" she whispered. She stopped and turned out her light, Blake reluctantly followed suit. "Listen." Low, murky echoes, as of distant conversation bounced through the air. "Grab my belt loop." She crept forward, feeling her way along the wall. Blake guessed that they must have ascended twenty feet. The echoes became distinct voices and the stench stronger. He remembered it. He had smelled it in the *Eclipse* the night they took the pictures—marijuana.

He followed her around a corner and saw little orange lights floating here and there. They flew up and glowed brighter, drifted down and dimmed. People were talking in worried tones. He unzipped her backpack and pulled out the stun gun.

Mia switched on her light. Seven stoners huddled together along the wall of a long gallery. They held up their hands and groaned at the brightness.

"Man you found the light! We thought we were gonna die down here!"

Blake recognized the kids from the boat. He switched on his light.

"Hey," said one, who's that?"

Mia pointed the light at the wall, then the ceiling, then the other wall. They were painted in a freakish, blood-red mural. "What have you morons done to my cave?" she said.

Blake scanned the psychedelic designs, fiendish catfish swallowing people, severed body parts and other unspeakable things. At the far end of the gallery stood a pile of stones topped with a shrunken head and a framed photo of Lucky the Catfish.

"That ain't Jack!" whispered one.

"That ain't our doin', that's Jack's trip, there. We're just here for the herbal remedies."

"Yeah, we don't know nothin' about no human sacrifice!" said another, without thinking.

They got to their feet. Mia turned out her light, as did Blake. "Hey, wait! Can you help us outta here? The candles didn't last. We don't know where Jack's gone."

"We'll die if you leave us down here!" said the girl from the boat, sobbing in terror.

"Yes you will," said Blake. "Because you're on the list." He shined his light on the wall above them. Those glyphs are your names, written in the ancient Phonecian alphabet. Jack plans to kill us all." Blake switched out his light. "Let's go mi corazon." She crept back into the passage as fast as she dared. But the cries of pleading terror were too much for Blake's conscience. "Mia, we have to help them."

"Seven less maniacs in the world, Blake. I can live with that."

"I'm giving them my light. How long does it take to get out of here?"

"Five minutes. Up this passage to the entry room, then into the crag. Here, don't give'm your flippin' light!" She pulled three chemical glow-sticks out of her pack. "Give'm those."

He activated them and tossed the glowing green sticks into the gallery.

"Straight up this passage, into the main room, up the crack. Can you handle that?"

There was a unified clamor of appreciation. They switched their flashlights on and hustled up the passage. Mia was finding her footing in the crag when Blake turned loose of her belt loop.

"What are you doing?"

"I gotta make sure they get up here." He returned to the mouth of the tunnel. "Hey! You coming!"

"Yeah! You're awesome! We're good man!"

Mia stepped back to retrieve him. He turned to follow her and in the waxing green glow behind him there seemed to unfold a monstrous silhouette, a shadow preparing to fall on him like a life-consuming avalanche of hate. "Duck!" she sprang forward, throwing a punch that parted his hair. It landed solidly against a greasy forehead. The shadow tumbled backwards into the passage way, bowling down half the stoners on their way up.

"Oh my god! Jack!" wailed one of the girls. Blake scurried to the bottom of the tunnel. There lay Voodoo Jack, his nose bleeding, face already black, blue and swelling.

Mia brought up the rear. "Oh crap, is he dead? He can't be dead!"

"Calm down!" Blake knelt down, stun gun at the ready. He held his hand over Jack's mouth. "He's breathing. I can feel it. You have to call for rescue."

"I can't! They can't find me here! If he dies…"

"You have to!" Blake shouted. "We can't leave him to die. I could never live with myself."

"We can't get reception up here in the woods, anyway."

"Then go get the *Osprey* out on the lake, get a signal, and call for help. Then go home. I'm the only one who knows how he fell. I'll cover for you."

She hesitated, then pulled the emergency blanket out of her pack and unfolded the paper thin mylar. "Cover him up. He's in shock. You have to keep him warm. I love you." She kissed his forehead and left on her mission.

***

The great horned owl on Buck Mueller's wall glared down at Blake with angry authority.

Blake was still damp and cold.

"The old man knows you're okay," said Mueller, taking his seat. "Now listen up. I'm going to tell you what I know, and you're going to tell me what you know. I know there was a violent altercation on the groundskeeper's patio, at the club. We found blood on the wall and a Bowie knife. We know that Hunter Devlin chased you to the end of the point, where you escaped into the spectator fleet in a kayak with your girlfriend. We know that Hunter pursued you, aided by Lance Hopkins and possibly Thad Rexroat. The next thing we know is that we had an unscheduled D-Day reenactment with live fire."

"Pearl Harbor, actually."

"Whatever!" shouted Mueller. "Your butt is in so much hot water, you can't imagine it! And then three hours later you turn up in a cave with Freeman's most wanted, with his head bashed in."

"He fell backwards down the passage."

"Start at the patio. Your knife."

"Jack's knife."

"Oh, right."

"I never touched it. Dust it for prints."

"Don't get smart. Why were you on the patio to begin with?"

"I was looking for Hunter."

"Why?"

"Because the Mayor's wife isn't pregnant."

"Stop screwing with me, kid!" He slapped his hand on the desk.

"I'm not, sir."

"Why does she matter?"

"Because of the will."

Mueller stared blankly at the far wall for a few seconds. "Am I to assume that Jack Christenson was on the patio with you?" And if so, please explain."

"He was looking to kidnap me and…well use me as a sacrifice to Dagon, the Phoenician fertility god. Oh, and then murder my uncle."

"Did he so much as tell you this?"

"Oh, yes. He did. That's what Plague Ten was all about."

"Plague…Ten?"

"The fire-ship. It had Plague X painted on the side. It means 'death of the first born.' My Uncle Carson is the firstborn and I'm the Prince."

"I think Gunn owes me a drink," said Mueller.

"Hunter—who isn't even supposed to be on club property—saved me. That's Jack's blood on the wall. I know what you're thinking. Why was Hunter chasing me if he just saved me from Voodoo Jack?"

"You think so?"

"I tried to tell him but he was pretty much out to lunch, because of Brigita."

"The mayor's wife?"

"Right. She's blackmailing him. He needed the flash drive you gave me."

"Hey, don't you implicate me in this!"

"The flash drive had incriminating pictures of his dad and Brigita on it, but my uncle lost it. Commodore Devlin won't give Hunter a copy of the one *he* has, so that Hunter will be cut out of the will and Commodore Devlin will get a bigger slice of the pie."

Mueller stopped writing and held his breath. "An anonymous caller gave us a tip that two kids in a kayak fired signal flares into a passing motor boat, causing it to veer off course and create the mayhem that endangered hundreds of panicking people and destroyed a quarter-million-dollar fireworks show."

"Sounds familiar. I'd wager it was the same caller who framed us for the fire in Mangrave."

"Thad Rexroat positively ID'd you both."

"Sure he did. He's Hunter's lackey."

"You're going to need more proof than that, Blake."

Mia appeared at Mueller's door. "Then come here and look at my boat," she said.

"How did you get in here?" he demanded.

"It was a no-brainer. Some moron left the front door unlocked."

"I have had it up to here with you kids making a fool out of me!"

"Don't give me the credit. You're a self-made man."

"Mia," said Blake, "please don't antagonize the nice man who happens to have our future in his hands."

"I'm just sayin look at my boat." She handed Mueller her tablet. He swiped through a dozen views of *Osprey II*'s belly. "Note the scorch mark."

"So what. You were hit by a stray shell."

"On which side."

"Looks like starboard. Traveling centerline to the edge."

"We were headed toward the south shore."

"That checks out with the Fire Boss."

"We rolled the boat when Hunter fired. Sooo?" She planted her fists on her hips and gave him an impatient look that said *figure it out you idiot.*

"The starboard side was out of the water." He wasn't giving in.

"Which means what?"

He scowled and reluctantly deduced "If your bow was pointing south and the starboard side of the hull was up, the shot hitting center and going to the edge of the hull..."

"Then?"

He handed the tablet back. "The shots came from the flotilla, not the barge."

"Thaaank you," she said.

"Oh," said Blake, "Hunter bought the flares from that booth in the far corner of the flea market last Monday. You can check the security tapes. Just ask Mr. Gunn."

Mueller looked at the ceiling. "I'm afraid to ask, but what do you know about the mayor's wife?"

"Other than kidnapping me, punching me in the gut 'til I puked blood, and shaving my head, I hear she forced a mega-preg housekeeper to take an EPT test and kept the whiz stick for herself."

"Stop there!" cried Mueller, tossing up a hand. "Look, here's where things stand. The evidence is swinging in your favor but you're not off the hook, yet. Until we can talk to your brother, or some slam-dunk evidence materializes, you're still officially suspects. Don't kid yourselves—people are going to jail over this. I'll call your folks to come get you."

"Don't bother," said Mia. "Carson's out front. C'mon Tux."

Blake looked to Mueller. He tilted his head toward the door. Blake exited.

Mueller went to his door and called out to the empty lobby. "Hey! I really *do* want to exonerate you two."

Mia's voice drifted back from the stairwell. "We'll lock the door on the way out, Buck."

"You do that, smart-ass!"

They took the stairs down to the lobby. "You came back?" said Blake.

"Don't remind me. I have one question. Where did you learn to read ancient Phoenician? Is that a home school requirement or something?"

"Who said I did? I just told them that's what it said."

She shot him a wry look with more than a hint of admiration in it.

Carson was singing to a tune on the CD player when the passenger doors opened: "Brothers will desert you when you're down and all out of luck…"

"I guess Mr. Gunn's furious?" said Blake, climbing into the front seat.

"If you got any last words, I'd write 'em down."

"Actually," Mia said, "the only thing he's miffed about is that there weren't more planes and no boats sank."

Carson laughed. "We didn't have the faintest idea you were involved until your Mexican cutie filled us in."

"I'm sure it crossed someone's mind," said Blake.

"Well, yeah. The old man's words were: "They'll expect a trip to Cancun for this!" Carson put the van in gear and pulled out of the lot. "You're both unofficially under house arrest. Mostly for your own safety. They've got a warrant out for Hunter."

Sooner met them at the top of the stairs, shivering with excitement. The room was cozy, courtesy of a cheerful blaze in the fireplace. Gunn was in his recliner watching Daley Dunright's gonzo coverage of the great fiasco.

"Caduggin! Glad to see yer well!"

"Glad to be home. I don't know what to say."

"Yeh vanquished another of yer enemies, yeh crushed the Silurian cult for good *and* yeh kicked off the greatest spectacle this lake has ever seen. What more is there to say?"

Blake considered it for a moment. "I'm cold, tired, and hungry."

"Miss Mia, there's Ping's in the fridge. Will yeh warm it up while the lad gets a hot shower?"

"There'd better be some left when I get out!" said Blake.

"Oh, Miss! Yer mother returned my call. She'll be back as soon as the Chicago deal closes. Yer to stay with us until yer brother's apprehended. And she called the PD and advised them that under no circumstances are yeh to be remanded into the custody of yer father."

"No kidding?" Mia was truly astounded.

"I told you," said Blake.

***

They sat close together in front of the glowing fireplace, Sooner wedged tightly between them. Blake had brought out his collection of postcards and allowed her to read them.

"I'd like to meet your mom," she said.

"September 30th you will. You think *your* mom will like me?"

"If my dad hates you, my mom will cherish you forever—just because."

They were quiet for a minute. "Mia, where do you think we'll be in a year?"

"In South America, fighting a revolution."

Chapter 80

Tuesday, Doctor Trudeau was called to the Gunn estate to investigate Abuelita's feelings of ill health, born out of the previous evening's festivities. Trudeau diagnosed it as the strong desire for the prestige of having a personal physician at her beck and call. He humored her with his stethoscope and blood-pressure cuff. He also let Blake know that he'd arranged for an impromptu Laser II regatta on the upcoming weekend.

The good news came Thursday morning. Someone finally accepted the burden of their civic duty and offered up their cell-phone footage to the authorities. It was blurry and unstable, but definitely documented two blazing streaks zipping *out* of the spectator fleet. Blake and Mia were officially off the hook. Hunter was now the hunted. Voodoo Jack was undergoing surgery for the subdural hematoma he suffered during his fall in the cave. Garvey "Kalijah" Woodhead survived the attempt on his life by his former disciple, and went on to win $3.98 in the monthly bingo tournament. Daley Dunright's exhaustive reporting—so called by Carson for its ability to wear one out—went on all week, to Tripper Gunn's delight. The climactic package included a tour of the cave and its lurid gallery.

It was still wonderfully chilly and though a far cry from Cancun, Gunn took Blake and Mia for a daytrip to the historic canal village of Metamora. It was there that Mia casually took Blake's hand as they strolled quietly along the green canal.

***

Sylvana pushed her cart into the guest bedroom and shut the door behind her. The head of staff was off for the day, so she was able to dawdle in the laundry room to delay her rounds. Brigita was berating someone in the foyer downstairs. Sylvana hoped it wasn't Marisol. She went into the bathroom and turned on the water. The mayor's mansion, she had learned, had many secrets. One of them was that the shower in the master suite ran like Niagara Falls—literally—and killed the water pressure in all of the taps on the second floor. She cleaned the bathroom and dusted the suite until finally the tap snorted and sputtered. She watched it dwindle to a pathetic trickle.

She slipped across the hall. Brigita's tennis clothes were strewn in a trail to the bathroom door, her keys and purse thrown carelessly, if not angrily, on the bed. Sylvana had the closet open in ten seconds. She tossed the keys back on the bed, locked herself in and found a place to hide.

***

Carson chalked his pool cue as Peach took his shot. Holly returned from the bar with another pitcher of cold draft and a sour look.

"What's eatin' you?" said Carson.

"Aw, Peeler's in there shootin' his mouth off, again."

"What about, this time?"

"How we gotta keep our eye on the news tomorrow. Says something big's gonna break and he's gonna be famous."

Carson filled two glasses and headed for the bar. Delden "The Beast" Peeler: Taxidermist to the Stars, stood at the bar making ostentatious pronouncements to anyone who cast so much as a stray glance his way. The stools to either side of him were empty, much to the annoyance of the barkeep. He combed his well oiled pompadour in the mirror behind the bar and smiled at himself. He looked like a fat-faced woodchuck. Peeler spotted Carson in the reflection, holding up two glasses and motioning to a corner booth. Peeler followed him, much to the barkeep's relief. He sent a complementary pitcher over, for insurance.

"So Del, what's new?"

"Shoot! You wish you knew what's new, Urquart!" He drained half his glass. Carson filled it right back up to the foamy brim.

"Must be awful big?"

"Hah! You don't know big! People gonna forget all about your stupid catfish and that kid. People gonna know my name from coast *to* coast. Del "The Beast" Peeler: Taxidermist to the stars!" Carson filled him up again. Peeler had dubbed himself with the lofty title in 1972, after Johnny Cash visited his booth at the State Fair and jokingly asked for a quote on stuffing an escaped coatimundi that had assaulted him in a Porta Potty.

Carson leaned in and spoke in a low tone "Big like seventy-two?"

Peeler sat up straight and scoffed "Forget seventy-two! That's a blip on the radar compared to this. This goes right to the top!"

"How far up?"

"You got manure in your ear? I said the top!" Peeler slammed his glass down, indignantly. Carson dispensed more of the bubbly yellow truth serum and snapped his fingers in the direction of the bar. Another pitcher appeared on the table, almost instantly.

"Justice will be served. Heads gonna roll. The first shall be last and the last shall be first. And that's all you're gonna get outta of Del Peeler 'til tomorrow." Carson filled him up again.

Peeler belched. "You takin' that pitcher with ya?"

"All yours chief!" He returned to the pool hall and borrowed Holly's phone. "Yeah, kid? I've got a hunch you and the girl need to keep your heads down tomorrow. Way down."

Chapter 81

Sylvana ate a gigantic breakfast, held a mug of hot coffee to her forehead for five minutes, brushed her teeth with mint toothpaste, then returned to the kitchen and downed a glass of orange juice in front of the sink. The gastric geyser erupted with such soul-curdling violence that Sylvio ran out of the house and the cat, usually highly interested in the fallout from such acts of nature, cringed and slunk away. Abuelita put Sylvana to bed and called Dr. Trudeau.

***

The mayor woke up scratching his neck and face.

"What is the matter, Teddy?" said Brigita, from the bathroom. "You kept me up with your tossing all night. You know I must have ten hours of sleep, or I am ruined!"

"Don't know, Gita. Maybe they changed fabric softener." Something icky tickled the back of his throat. He gagged, then extracted a long, black hair from his mouth. He studied it with disgust, as if it were a tapeworm. Then he noticed his pillow. It was oddly lumpy. He reached through the slit in the satin case and pulled out a long hank of curly, black hair. There was a price tag tied to the end. He put on his glasses and looked down his nose to read it. He flipped the tag over. Printed in a hand he did not recognize were the words *Property of Mia Devlin*.

"What are you doing with that!" screamed Brigita, from the bathroom door. "What were you doing in my closet?"

"It was in my pillow case. What on earth is this?"

"Give it to me!" She lunged at him but he deflected her grab. She ran to the closet and found it locked. "Those filthy, brown people have been in my things again!" She unlocked the door and dashed in as if expecting to catch one in the act of desecrating her inner sanctum.

His phone rang. "Bayer, here. Hey Phil! No, I haven't seen the paper. The girl that brings me my breakfast is out with the flu. Page two? Alright. Come in the back way? Uh, oh."

He dug under the bed with one foot to find his slippers but instead ran across something cold, metal, and wickedly prickly. He yelped and drew back bloody toes. "Thanks for the heads-up." He tossed the phone on the bed. Teddy got down on one knee and pulled out Brigita's homespun cat-o-nine-tails.

She emerged from her vault of secrets to see Teddy contemplating the weapon, in baffled horror. She pounced across the bed on all fours, tackling her husband. She wrested the flail from his grip. He jumped up, grabbed his pillow and shielded himself. The cruel cables whistled as Brigita's best backhand filled the air with a blizzard of little feathers, like a goose through a jet engine.

Teddy threw the remains of the pillow in her face and slammed his hand on the panic button above his nightstand. He escaped across the mattress and bolted to the safe room in his boxers.

***

"Good news!" said Carson, knocking on Blake's door. "Found the flashdrive!"

Blake had his shorts on and the door open in an instant. Carson held the morning paper up. The front page was a tawdry collage of Mia's café pictures bearing the headline SCANDAL AT THE TRYST! Carson revealed page two: a minimally censored shot of Devlin and Brigita leaping out of the *Eclipse*.

"Ohhhh dirt! They printed that?"

"It's good to have friends in high places. Enemies, not so much," said Carson, looking very pleased.

Mia came out of her room and snatched the paper. She read silently, then aloud. "Astoundingly, the humiliating images were discovered by a local taxidermist, on a flash drive lodged in the gullet of a prize winning bass. The fish was taken by local resident Hunter Devlin, during the Labor Day Fishing tournament. The Office of the Mayor will release a statement later today. Lawrence Devlin, owner of Devlin's Marina was unavailable for comment." She was stunned. "That's it for my dad. The estate lawyers watch the paper like a hawk. Mom'll file divorce in a hot second."

"That's what you wanted, wasn't it?" said Blake.

Mia was struggling to stay afloat in a flood of memories. "At first, I just wanted them to stay together. Then I just wanted to know that Daddy loved me. When I couldn't get that, all I wanted was for him to show me some attention. And when he didn't and I couldn't make him, I just wanted to hurt him."

For a moment Blake tried to gauge his own position along that spectrum.

"Mission accomplished!" said Carson. He swaggered away. "He-who-must-be-obeyed has breakfast on. Best not keep him waiting."

"I don't feel so hungry," she said.

Gunn had spread a sumptuous table. He filled Mia's plate and sat down. He made a blessing, then sighed. "So, this is what it was all aboot, then?"

Mia couldn't look him in the face. Blake explained Hunter's involvement.

"I feel like I need a shower after that story," said Gunn.

"I'm sorry," said Mia, still staring at her plate. "I never meant to get Blake tangled up in this. Things didn't quite go as planned."

"They rarely do, Mia. Still, what are the odds?" he said, looking at Blake. "Yeh throw the thingamabob in the trash, your uncle finds it and goes fishing with it—of all things! And the very fish that swallows it is hooked by the very man seeking it and put into the hands of a taxidermist with a vendetta who, finding it, hands it over to a vindictive newspaper editor. I'd almost dare to say—almost dare, mind yeh—to say that it was meant to be."

"Peeler had a vendetta?" said Carson, tending the coffeemaker in the kitchen.

"Devlin and Ted were instrumental in blocking a zoning variance Peeler needed to put his shop on Main Street. The denial wasn't without merit. The man's a vulgar embarrassment to the community. But he's got a right to have a business just like everyone else. I'd no be surprised if heads roll at the Gazette. They've never printed trash like this. It's a disgrace."

"Must gall Hunter to no end, to know he had it in his hands," said Carson, returning with the fresh pot of coffee.

"Gall ain't the word for it," said Mia. "If we're lucky, he's in Bermuda by now."

"Eat up you two, yeh've got a regatta to win!" said Gunn.

***

Winds were light and shifty as six crews performed their starting-line rituals. Mia and Blake cruised confidently past the Committee boat in *Seven Thunders*. Carson liberated Griffy from the shackles of his grounding, and resurrected the *Wild Man of Borneo*, an abandoned hull from the boat lot. Trudeau and his teenage daughter and two junior crews from Cincinnati rounded out the field of competitors. It was a one day regatta consisting of three short triangle courses of two laps each, followed by a long windward-leeward course that ended, uncharacteristically, in a spinnaker run to the finish line. Trophies were awarded along with sailing club tee-shirts. Carson and Griffy, in their hideous derelict, won the day.

Preparations were made to roast brats over the fire pit on pram point, next to the beach.

The kids played Frisbee and got to know each other on the sand while Trudeau deflated buoys by the safety-boat shed. Mia and Carson went to the clubhouse to fetch ice and drinks. Blake rummaged in the boat house looking for a bolt to fix a loose leg on the picnic table. He was poking through the tool cabinet on the work bench when he glanced out the window and saw Hunter standing at the edge of the beach. Griffy passed him on the way to the waterline and casually quipped, "Oh! Hey, Hunter. You tell your mom that you're gay, yet?"

"No," said Hunter, vacantly. The guest crews didn't know better and snickered. Then it registered. "Hey Cowboy, where's Sparky?" he demanded. Everyone froze, Blake included.

Griffy cackled. He turned around and continued to walk into the lake, backwards.

"How would I know? He's your girlfriend, not mine!"

"Your number's up, Cowboy," said Hunter, as he strode resolutely into the water.

Griffy was in up to his waist and about to dive away when a sharp rock gouged the sole of his foot and buckled his knee. Hunter seized him by the throat and plunged him under. He dragged him back up, Griffy clawing at his bronze forearm, his eyes bulging. The kids on the beach screamed and yelled frantically. Hunter plunged him under again. Blake snapped to his senses and thought to grab a paddle from the corner, but instead found the pitchfork Ray used to spread straw on grass seed.

He snatched it and ran for the beach, hefting it over his shoulder like a javelin. He hit the water ready to loose his lethal missile, when something pounded across the wide dock to his right and flew in front of him like a human cannonball. Carson crashed Hunter into the lake. Griffy popped up immediately, choking and vomiting. Blake rushed forward and got him to his feet. Carson and Hunter did not reappear.

Griffy looked at the pitchfork in amazement. "Were you really gonna...use that?"

Blake glanced at the sharp tines. "Oh, this little thing?"

"From now on you're my body guard." He gurgled and spat blood.

Hunter exploded out of the water with a moaning gasp, back arched in pain. Carson propelled his captive forward, right arm wrenched savagely behind his back and shouted, "You don't mess with Aquaman!" He wrestled Hunter to the beach and slammed him on the coarse sand. "I assume someone called the police?"

An emergency meeting of the board of directors was convened within the hour. Commodore Devlin was deposed in absentia and his membership permanently revoked by unanimous vote. Dr. Trudeau was sworn in as Commodore four months ahead of schedule.

Griffy was taken to the ER by ambulance and diagnosed with a strained larynx. He was ordered not to use his voice for two weeks.

Gunn was on the front steps of the clubhouse, lighting his pipe. Blake stepped out and stood silently beside him. "Too bad we could'na got this out the way at the beginning," said Gunn. "But then who would you be now, Caduggin?"

Chapter 82

Blake was on the way down the stairs to fetch the Monday morning gazette, when Gunn stopped him. "No paper this morning, lad." Mia poured his coffee. "Seems that Peeler's shop burned to the ground last night. And while the Fire Department was fighting *that* fire, someone set the torch to the *Freeman Gazette*. Ms. Rozik is being sought for questioning."

Mia put the pot down and went pale. "It just doesn't stop!" She covered her mouth with one hand and teared up. Gunn took her by the arm. "Listen to me lass. Those people made their *own* choices. Peeler did'na have to go public. And the news chief didn'a have to print those photographs. Every step of the way, there's been an opportunity to stop this. An old clergyman once said that if yer planning revenge, yeh best dig two graves. One of them for yerself. Now, remember the Badger. There's life beyond this." Mia bit her lip and nodded.

***

The Pagáns were relaxing after the day's work by doing a little fishing and talking about their future fleet. Mia and Blake were standing on the dock contemplating a trip to survey the damage on Trespass Island, when a silver Lexus rolled into the lot. It was Mayor Ted. He got out of his car holding a long, narrow, white box. Blake thought it might be roses.

Gunn appeared at the front door. "Mr. Mayor. You honor us!"

"Tripper Gunn, how are you? I was just dropping by to speak with Mia

Devlin, if you don't mind."

Mia and Blake came off the dock and greeted him. He handed her the box with both hands. "Mia, I don't know what to say."

She took it and lifted the lid. It was her hair. Cezar came up from behind and looked over her shoulder, as she read the tag.

"That's Sylvana's writing," he said.

"I am so sorry, Mr. Bayer."

"Well," he said, searching for his oratorical footing.

"I took the pictures. I'm sorry. It's no excuse, but I was so angry at my dad."

He cleared his throat, clearly taken aback. "While this has been a tragic and challenging time… for all of us, um… I am confident that we will be able to find the positive in it and… joining hands in the spirit of forgiveness, move forward to forge a brighter, better future for our community, together."

"Thank you, Mr. Bayer." *That's Mayor Teddy Bayer,* she thought. *Stuffed with fluff.*

"Might I offer yeh something to drink, Theodore?"

"Wish I could stay, Gunn. Having a working dinner with my legal team. Blake, Mia, your kids are going to be unstoppable! See ya around!" The mayor got back in his car and drove away.

Blake looked at Mia. "Did he say…?"

"Shut up, Tux."

"What will you do with your hair?" asked Cezar.

She pondered the question and only smiled. "Let's go see Fire Island."

Chapter 83

The officer behind the counter looked up from yet another stalemated game of computer solitaire. "You've got a lot of gall coming in here!"

"I'd like to see Hunter Devlin," said Blake, intimidated.

"Gotta be eighteen to go down to the lock up. Now get lost."

Blake dialed his phone and put it on speaker. "Mayor Bayer, here. What can I do for you Blake?"

The officer's eyes got big, his jaw slackened.

"Mayor Bayer, I'm over at Police Headquarters. I know I'm not old enough to go down to the lock-up, but I really need to see Hunter Devlin. I've got some information that may give him some peace of mind. Maybe help his attitude, make him easier to handle."

"Barclaw giving you a hard time?" Blake squinted at the officer's badge. "As a matter of fact, he is."

"Now, wait a minute!" said Barclaw, trying to maintain his composure.

"That's his job, Blake. Let me call the chief and I'll have you downstairs in a minute."

"Thanks Mayor!"

Blake rocked on his heels and stared at anything except Officer Barclaw, who started another game of solitaire and tried not to look like his head was about to explode. Two minutes later, the phone on his desk rang. "Barclaw. Yes sir. Affirmative," was the extent of the conversation. "You got five minutes and not a second more, smart-ass."

He led him to Hunter's cell and returned to lean against the door to the stairs. "I'm watching you!"

Hunter lay on his hard bunk, staring up at the patchy gray ceiling.

"Hello, Hunter."

"Sparky. Come to gloat about your victory?"

"No! I tried to tell you on Labor Day, but you weren't exactly in the mood to listen."

"I'm all ears now, pal."

"Brigita's not pregnant."

"Say that again."

"Brigita's. Not. Pregnant. She forced one of the housekeepers to take a pregnancy test and I'm guessing that's what she showed you."

"Blake, if you could prove that, I'd name you my heir and fake my own death."

"A DNA test and fingerprints ought to do it."

"Four minutes!" echoed through cinder-block hall, at top volume.

Hunter sat up. "Are you intimating that you actually have the EPT in your possession?"

"No."

Hunter sagged.

"I gave it to your lawyer."

A grin spread across Hunter's face and he fell back on his bunk, laughing. "God does have mercy on babes and fools!"

"Three Minutes!" boomed Barclaw, sternly.

"Hunter, no offense but…I hear there are medicines that…help balance things out."

"I hear ya, Blake. I'll look into it. I promise."

"And speaking of God, um… you should talk to him. No matter what."

"I'll have to think about *that* one. Hey, if you find my keys, let me know?"

"Sure. I'm leaving in a couple of weeks. I probably won't see you for a long time. Thanks for teaching me about passive income. If you ever wonder if you've done anything good in your life, remember that."

"You bet, pal. Hey, I hear I jacked Cowboy up pretty badly."

"Two Minutes!" bellowed Officer Barclaw.

"Tell him…I'm sorry. Very sorry."

"Thanks. I'll do that."

"You better go before the drill instructor splits a gasket."

Blake wished him luck and returned to the world of the free, thinking about those gray steel bars and his own impending captivity.

Chapter 84

Saturday was another spectacular day for sailing. Blake and Mia ran into Griffy and Judy at the club. Upon learning of their plan to sail, Griffy entreated his mother with incorrigible, pantomimed pleading and the most hilarious expressions. And, of course, she gave in.

They sailed into the upper lake and across the base of the giant dam. When they passed the Freeman waterfront, up went the chute and they took off on a broad reach, bound for home. They crossed the upper lake and rocketed into the channel. Griffy rode the trapeze, breeze in his hair, spray in his face. Mia and Blake hiked for their lives, screaming and hooting with delight as *Seven Thunders* dashed across the waves on a fire-hose plane.

They did not notice the huge cigarette boat that roared into the channel behind them, cutting its engines precisely at the idle-zone buoy.

"What are you doing?" Brigita sneered at Rexroat, who was driving.

"Idle zone, lady! *Moby'll* get us!"

"What are you babbling about! They're getting away! Go on!"

Rexroat reluctantly eased the throttle forward, the motor rumbled louder, and the bow lifted a bit.

"Give it the gas, damn you!" Brigita screamed, brandishing the wicked flail at him. She climbed out onto the deck. "You are mine now, you little turds! I will cut out your hearts and eat them!" She carried on until she was in an absolute, shrieking frenzy of profanity. Rexroat began to feel very nervous. She had shanghaied him at knifepoint and forced him to steal

Tantrum II using Hunter's keys. He would have abandoned ship, were he not certain that she would take the helm and run him down.

Blake and his crew were still ripping along in ecstasy when Mia began to hear something familiar and troubling. She looked back and froze. Blake stopped laughing and looked as well. Griffy, perceived the sudden silence and checked his six. *Tantrum II* was bearing down on them, much less than a quarter-mile away. Blake headed up to a beam reach and *Tantrum II* changed course to intercept.

"She'll kill us all, this time," said Mia, flatly.

In that instant, Blake's cold fear boiled into seething anger, pointed straight at the ranting maniac on the deck of the approaching juggernaut. A look of cunning determination spread across his face. He turned *Seven Thunders* down to a run and yelled "keep her flat!" He scanned the shore ahead and then the far shore to windward.

Brigita was still raving and motioning Rexroat to change course. They had closed the gap to 500 feet but Rexroat had managed to ease off the throttle, a little. "You son of a whore! We're losing them, again! Idiot!" Rexroat pushed it up a little and Brigita resumed her mad bellowing.

"What are you thinking?" Griffy croaked. He could barely hear himself. Blake didn't answer. He kept his gaze fixed on the far shore, occasionally glancing ahead and adjusting course. "We'll never make it!" Blake, answer me!"

"Tux, what are we going to do?" asked Mia, hoping he knew.

Blake looked aft to check on the pursuers, then to the far shore. Satisfied, he turned once again onto a broad reach. "Mia, trim! Hike for your lives!" *Seven Thunders* surged ahead once more as the big, cigarette boat loomed up from behind, like the four horsemen of the apocalypse. Brigita's shrieking was now close enough to be intelligible.

Suddenly, Blake took the mainsheet from Mia and let it go. The boom swung all the way out and the sail shook wildly. The little boat slowed quickly. "What are you doing!" she screamed in disbelief. Blake stood up, steadied himself and shouted to Brigita: "Hey psycho-girl! Do you kiss your Serbian mother with that mouth? Double your dosage, you Bosnian freak!"

Brigita paused in her frenzy, momentarily stymied by this last, great act of defiance. Quickly, however, her bewilderment returned to rage and she signaled Rexroat to go full-steam-ahead and run them down. He gave Brigita a look that brought her and the flail back down into the cockpit. She scourged him out of the driver's seat and over the side.

Blake dropped back down to his spot, shoved the mainsheet at Mia and yelled, "trim it! Now!" He jerked the tiller hard to windward. The sail snapped taut, Griffy pushed out over the water and the *Seven Thunders* sprang to life once again.

He dipped her to leeward, then arced back up to her original heading, carefully steering for the cell tower on the far shore. Mia couldn't help noticing that Blake looked like he had a secret.

Then a sound, like a dragon with a belly full of thunder, shook the air as Brigita seized the throttle and thrust it forward. She leapt to the deck to watch the kill. A wall of spray erupted from the stern of *Tantrum II*, its whole hull surged up from the waves like the angel of death taking flight. She went exactly fifty feet before striking the top of the submerged Yaegerstown bridge piling. The behemoth boat lurched up out of the water with a terrific scraping-cracking sound, the force of the impact launched Brigita like a blonde bombshell. She bounced hard off the waves and landed in *Seven Thunders'* wake. *Tantrum II's* mighty, roaring engine gurgled to a stop as the disemboweled monster slid diagonally off the piling, like a crocodile shot dead on a sunny bank.

Blake steered across the wind and eased the main until it luffed. Now they could more comfortably enjoy the success of his daring plan. Griffy swung inboard, grabbed the mast and hissed "Yesss! Yesss! Ohhhh Ye-heh-heh-hessss!"

Blake remained silent and did not take his eyes off of *Tantrum II*. Rexroat, covered in bleeding stripes, swam to the pilling and stood on it, looking for anyone to wave down for help. The lake barely came halfway up his shins. Brigita bobbed in stunned silence nearby.

"You sank my dad's boat!" said Mia, in delighted disbelief. Blake did not respond. He savored every moment as the garish hull gradually and inexorably slid beneath the waves. The hot engine hissed and spat as the flood lapped over it. At last, Highland Creek Reservoir swallowed up *Tantrum II's* purple and yellow bow, leaving only steaming bubbles to mark the place of its final rest.

"You *sank* my dad's boat!" Mia chuckled in mock protest and slugged him in the arm.

"Yes, I did," said Blake, plainly, confidently—still without turning.

"Ho ho! Here comes *Moby Dick*!" wheezed Griffy! "Lights and all!"

Blake smiled, deeply satisfied and said, "Take that, you damned swabs."

Chapter 85

Mist drifted over the calm waters of the channel, where *Terrapin* and *Becky Lynn* were anchored. A rigid blue-and-white flag swung from a short pole on the stern of each boat and a buoy sporting a red flag with a diagonal, white stripe bobbed nearby. Carson was treading water next to *Becky Lynn* as Cezar and Romero fed what looked like a long, canvas bag over her side. He pulled his goggles up, put the SCUBA regulator back in his mouth and dove. He resurfaced ten minutes later by the *Terrapin* and took an air hose from Mia. She fed it over the side as he dragged it to the bottom. Blake yanked the starter cord on the compressor they'd stashed in the bow compartment, and it roared to life. The hose jerked as it filled with air. They waited and watched for another ten minutes. "There!" said Gunn, pointing to a slight unsettling of the lake's surface, thirty feet away. "Get your harpoon, Ahab! She breaches!"

The water seemed to mound up, then a shadowy form appeared below the surface like leviathan rising. The yellow and purple bow broke the surface, followed by the deck and cockpit.

"Kill the compressor," said Gunn. "Alright, Mueller wants this environmental hazard out of his lake. Let's accommodate the man."

They helped Carson aboard and out of his SCUBA gear. "That was fun! I forgot how much I love diving."

Anchors were pulled up and a towline secured. They delivered *Tantrum II* to the launch ramp at Devlin's Marina. Gunn presented the harbor master with an invoice. He balked not only at the amount, but Gunn's demand of *cash only*.

The old Scot thumped his fist on the counter and got right in the harbor master's face. "Not only did you hire my services, but Mueller will fine you five hundred dollars for every day that oil-dripping hulk lays on the bottom. And we're the only outfit for a hundred miles who can do this job. I can drop her where she sits and leave you to figure it out, if you like—but yeh will still pay for the job."

They sailed away with six-thousand dollars in cash, which was divided evenly among the recovery crew.

Mia emailed the video she took of the raising of *Tantrum II* to her mother, along with a note that she was moving back in with Treva. To her surprise, she received a reply that afternoon thanking her for the heads-up, that she was glad she was okay and that yes, her father's goose was totally cooked.

***

Cry of the Osprey II floated silently below the night ocean. Blake slouched in his cockpit, legs out on deck. Mia zipped her jacket up and pulled its hood over her head. She flicked a little water at Blake and giggled when he flinched. At last, the lake was theirs.

Chapter 86

They had agreed to meet at the sailing club and paddle to the Nature Center. Carson dropped Blake off at the point. As he came up the riprap he spotted her. She was leaning against the tree by the last dock, retching. "Did you hear?" she panted.

"Apparently not," said Blake, trying to imagine what possibly could have happened now.

"Treva texted me. Lance Hopkins died."

"Oh... wow..." Blake hesitated. "How? What happened?"

"Something in his brain. Blood vessel burst or something. I gotta get out of here."

"Why? It's not *your* fault!"

She shook her head and heaved again.

"That was months ago! The hospital did tests and stuff. They sent him home. He was okay!" Blake protested.

"You don't understand," she groaned, clutching her belly.

"No! Even if it was you, it was self defense, anyway. He *chose* to attack you. He had it coming."

She spat a ribbon of thick goo. It stuck to her chin and defied all of her efforts to be rid of it. "You don't get it, Tux. It doesn't matter. Freeman is Smallsville. I will always be known as the girl who killed Lance Hopkins."

He got her water bottle from the *Osprey*. She rinsed her mouth and washed her face and hands. "Come here." She wrapped her arms around him and squeezed. "Tell Mr. Gunn and your crazy uncle I said thank you. You guys taught me so much. And don't worry, I'll be in touch. I gotta go." She tenderly pressed a kiss into his cheek and left him. He watched her paddle back toward the channel. There were a thousand feelings begging for expression, but he couldn't find the words for any of them. He agreed that mushy drama and crying would be an embarrassing disgrace to everything they'd done together—to the glory they'd won. Puke and an argument were much more in line with things.

She was almost to the far side of the harbor when he called, "Are you my girlfriend?"

"I don't know, Tux. Am I?"

Seriously? he thought. "I love you, Mia!"

As she disappeared around Boy Scout Point, her voice echoed back across the water. "I love you, too, Blake!"

He smiled. Then it struck him. She had changed her shampoo.

Chapter 87

Blake sat at the bottom of Gunn's back steps and watched the sun rise. Mia had been gone for three days, with no word. Her phone wasn't even accepting voicemail. Purple twilight gradually warmed into flames of orange and red, and soon the sky was a glorious conflagration.

This had become one of Blake's favorite places and times of the day. There on the bottom step in the cool morning, he felt peace and wonder in witnessing the world's quiet waking. But this week had been different. The White Hound had appeared twice in the woods at the edge of the boat lot. No sooner had the sun topped the trees and laid its first rays of splendor across the sleeping sailboats, than came a baleful howl from the woods.

He jumped to his feet and began scanning the trees for the big dog. Another pained howl came, but no creature. Finally there was rustling and panting and the hound emerged from the underbrush. He loped along in the weeds between the woods and the gravel, pausing here and there to sniff around, and lick the dew. At last he stopped, looked at Blake and howled again. The hound vanished back into the woods.

The eerie moment evaporated with the morning mist and Blake retreated back up the stairs. At breakfast, they discussed the day's itinerary. Blake mentioned having seen the White Hound several times that week.

"Have you checked the weather?" said Carson.

"Becoming cloudy. Chance of Storms," said Gunn. "Was he lurking or howling?"

"Lurking the first two times, but he howled this morning."

"Did you see that sunrise?" said Carson

"It was like the sky was on fire!" said Blake.

Gunn gave Carson a serious look. "Red sky at morning…"

Carson and Blake finished the sentence together. "Sailors take warning!"

"Why does he howl like that?" said Blake.

"Old dog," said Gunn. "Joints probably ache when the weather changes. Like mine."

"I never did find out what his name was."

"I've just always called him Bruce." said Gunn.

The clouds did roll in, though the breeze was light. The lake was silver, and the sky was as gray and sullen as Blake's mood. The *Terrapin* ran west under motor. Gunn and Carson discussed the Pagán's fishing fleet: how many yards of fiberglass cloth, how many gallons of epoxy, how prices for materials were through the roof and so on.

"Alright, Caduggin. We've got a little plumbing gig. One of the Cliff Side Cottages. Yer job will be to stay with the boat and keep your eyes on that haze in the west. See how it looks, now?"

"Aye."

"When yeh see it change, yeh let us know, yeh hear? It may be subtle— the color may shift just so slightly, or it may just feel wrong. Yeh'll sense it more than yeh'll see it."

Blake stared at the gray pall above.

"Yeh miss her, don't yeh?"

Blake nodded.

"So do I," said Gunn.

He helped lug the tools up to the worksite then returned to the *Terrapin*, beached on the gravelly shore. He tried to get comfortable on the hard cockpit bench, with a dock fender for a pillow. He moved to the cabin roof and leaned against the mast. He sat in the cramped bow and swiped through pictures on his phone until the battery died. He still wasn't used to charging it regularly. He stood up and looked around. A dozen herons moped in the mucky shallows like shades of the dead. It was just one of those hard, gravelly, bleak days he had not known since leaving Fort Wayne. And it was becoming stuffy. The heat had broken on Labor Day, but there was still the odd spike in temperature and today was going to be one of them. He returned to the cockpit, stretched out on the starboard bench and shut his eyes.

He wakened when a huge carp jumped. By the way his head felt, he guessed he'd napped for two hours. Blake gathered his senses and rose sluggishly to his feet. The breeze had come up and the sky was definitely darker. He waited for the fog in his brain to clear. Then he saw it. Just like Gunn said—the slightest shift in the dreary pallet of the gray sky. With a malevolent gust, the wind kicked up another notch. Indeed, something felt wrong. He ran for the cottages.

Gunn sat on a folding chair by a tiny crawlspace window in the cottage foundation. The treetops swayed in the portentous breeze.

"It's coming!" Blake gasped, as he rounded the corner of the small house.

"Drag yer carcass out of there, Urquart! Weather's on the way."

Carson slithered out into the light. "I hate to leave a job half..." His lungs cleared of the musty crawlspace stench and he smelled the fresh air. "Nevermind. Get the tools kid."

Carson yanked the starter cord until he thought his arm would come out of its socket. The motor was not cooperating.

"Forget it!" said Gunn. "Make sail!" Blake shoved *Terrapin* out and climbed in over the bow. Carson unfurled the mizzen so the boat would weathercock. Blake took the jib up, then with his uncle hoisted the main. The sky was now a roiling black cauldron, thunder hammering their nerves. "Ease out, we'll run before it."

"We won't make the club, Tripp, we gotta shelter!" said Carson.

"For once I'm in agreement. The Castle, then! Drop the starboard leeboard!"

Blake braced his feet against the bench on the low side and uncleated the preventer line. The massive leeboard swung into the whitecaps and the boat seemed to roll a little less. He struggled back to the high side as they turned downwind and ran wing-and-wing before the gale.

Raindrops the size of jumbo olives thumped the deck. Lightning flashed into the hills around them. Blake remembered his comment about not wanting to be caught out in weather like this and began to appreciate Mia's anxiety at the Dunes. He wished that his phone was charged and that she was answering. "Father in Heaven," he whispered. "Yahweh, have mercy on babes and fools."

"There's eleven hundred pound of lead weight in the bottom of this boat. We broach and we're done," said Gunn above the howling wind.

"Then don't broach!" said Blake. As if on cue, the wind shifted. Everyone ducked as the boom crashed across the boat and slammed to a stop. *Terrapin* heeled over hard and Blake fell through the companionway into the swiftly tilting cabin. The boat arced sharply toward the wind but lost momentum halfway through. She was almost on her side. Blake pulled himself into the companionway and beheld Carson and Gunn bellied over the high side, clinging for dear life. Dark green water sloshed into the cockpit in rhythmic surges. Something was wrong. The main wasn't paying out and luffing like it should. He spotted a tangle in the mainsheet—it had pinched in the pulley-block. He found his footing and launched himself into the swamped cockpit in a sort of stumbling lunge. He dove for the thick line and snatched it with one hand as the rolling hull heaved him off balance and plunged him into the churning lake. Blake jerked the mainsheet with all his might as he was swept aft of the *Terrapin*. The tangle cleared and the boom carried the mainsail to the end of the sheet, reeling Blake back in through the transom in the process. Carson jerked the jib sheet loose. The sail danced violently, whipping the lines against the cabin-top in its fury. The mizzen now did its job and cocked them into the wind. They dropped the mainsail in a fluttering mess. Blake pulled the spring loaded pin in the tabernacle and Carson struggled to drop the mast with some measure of control—but it was too much—it slammed down over the cockpit, missing Gunn by inches. Gunn turned and threatened the old outboard, pounding it with his fist. He yanked the cord and it sputtered to life. He gave it full throttle and steered back downwind.

"There it is!" yelled Carson, pointing to a small inlet along the shore ahead.

"Pull the bowsprit!" said Gunn. A nickel-sized ball of ice exploded on the cabin roof, then another.

"Never mind, get below!" said Carson, taking the tiller out of Gunn's hand. "Go on!" Blake helped Gunn down the companion way. Carson sheltered below the mast and folds of mainsail, as the hail battered the boat. Then amid the deafening clatter came loud bangs and flying ice as the storm began to serve up hail the size of tennis balls. In spite of the leeboard, *Terrapin* rocked hard as Carson took her parallel to the waves in his bid for Castle Cove. The noise in the cabin was unbelievable.

Then a startling bang—louder than the rest—sent splinters flying from the cabin ceiling. Blake shielded his face. Another crash fractured the planks above their heads. Water dripped from the jagged shards that jutted down like daggers. He stole a quick glance out the companionway. It was gloomy night. The cockpit looked like an ice chest. Hail the size of grapefruit battered the *Terrapin* like cannon shot, denting, cracking and splintering everything. Carson trimmed the boom amid ships and, hunkering beneath its meager shelter, pulled several layers of canvas over himself like a tent. Blake realized his uncle was driving blind for the narrow entrance of the safe harbor, if it was that. The motor took a direct hit and conked out, just as black walls loomed up on both sides of the boat. The violent tossing eased, but now branches and leaves were falling along with the devastating ice, as the *Terrapin* drifted. The merciless avalanche of hail ceased suddenly, as if the sky were waiting on the cosmic icemaker in Heaven's Frigidaire to kick in. The trees on the ridge began to sway violently. Drowning rain poured down through the canopy.

Carson emerged from his shelter and pulled up the leeboard. He dashed to the bow and unrigged the bowsprit. It was a pole of sturdy spruce, eight-feet long, three inches in diameter. He stood in the bow and propelled *Terrapin* forward with it, punting her along like a gondolier on a Venice canal. The tall, moss-streaked walls of an abandoned foundation loomed out of the darkness ahead. Carson returned to the tiller and pointed them at the arched opening at its bottom. They coasted into the bunker-like structure, bumping to a stop at its far wall. Carson pitched the anchor over and joined them in the dark cabin. "My feet are colder than a well digger's kiester in the Klondike!"

"Damned fine job, Urquart." said Gunn, lighting his pipe. Blake found the warm glow of his lighter and familiar, acrid aroma comforting.

"Thank you kindly, but the kid saved the ship." he tapped a splintered plank with a hammer from the tool bucket. "You won't fix that with duck tape!"

"It's *duct* tape, if yeh must know." said Gunn, with a sidelong glance.

Blake switched on a solar powered lantern. "It's both!" he chided, shivering. He couldn't believe that those two were ramping up for yet another bicker-fest.

"I'll accept that." said Carson. "You saved the ship kid! Now, get that shovel and clear the cockpit."

Blake stepped out into frigid water deeper than his ankles. He wasted no time sluicing the arctic swash out through the transom. The whole forest swayed and cracked, the wind and thunder roared. He had just finished bailing the cockpit with a bucket, when a deep and monstrous rumbling rose above the howling tempest. Large branches began to split and fall outside.

"Guys, it sounds like a freight train out here!"

"There's only two things in Indiana that make *that* noise and *that* ain't the three-ten to Yuma!" said Gunn.

Blake hopped back into the cabin. "I can't feel my feet either!"

"This is, hands down, the worst storm I have ever seen, or care to see." said Gunn.

The rumble grew louder and everyone's ears popped. Gunn looked grave and prayed "Mighty and merciful Father in Heaven, forgive us our errors and deliver us from this present danger!"

Blake and Carson followed with a sincere "Amen." They listened in uneasy silence as the mighty rushing wind passed into the distance.

"Yer one brave lad." said Gunn.

"I don't feel brave." he replied, rubbing his feet.

"Bravery is no aboot being fearless. On the contrary. It's aboot doing what must be done, *in spite* of yer fear." He switched on another lantern and pulled a ratty deck of cards out of the tool bucket. "Your crib, Caduggin."

The storm raged for another hour. The first golden shafts of sunlight seemed unreal as they pierced the forest and dispelled the nightmarish darkness.

Carson pushed the *Terrapin* out of the Castle using the bowsprit, Blake steering her backwards through the arch. Floating hail clunked against the hull as they made their way out of the narrow inlet. On the open lake the breeze was fresh, the western sky clear and blue. To the east the majestic cumulonimbus, like Mount Everest in the sky, lumbered onward; scourging the earth with wind, water, ice, and electricity.

Blake felt robbed. What seemed like a lifetime of hell on earth was suddenly all sunshine and a fair wind, as if nothing had ever happened. *Nature,* he thought, *might not be indifferent, but it is most certainly unapologetic.*

Gunn stared at the storm bank. "Now that, lad—is a threatnin' nimbus!"

The mizzen mast was re-stepped, the mainmast raised, the bowsprit rigged. All canvas was hoisted and they made for home.

"I may as well tell yeh now, Caduggin." said Gunn. "I'm pushing eighty-six. I've got no one to leave my properties and assets to. And I have'na worked all my life just so the State can have it."

Blake saw Carson grinning.

"I've been in touch with my lawyers and named yeh heir to my modest estate. Should I kick off before yer eighteen, it'll be put in trust for yeh."

"Tell him what it's worth." said Carson.

"Ahh, in today's dollars, roughly a, ehhh…a crap-load."

"I don't even know what to say." said Blake.

"Yeh'll think of something. I wonder where yer little girl is. Hope she's safe."

Chapter 88

Sooner buried her head under Blake's pillow, annoyed by the dissonant hum of a generator somewhere in the workshop below. Gunn's Marina was one of the few places on the lake with electricity that Saturday morning. The news confirmed it—an F3 tornado had come down the lake, cutting a ragged gash through the forest. It peeled the roof clean off Devlin's Marina, lifted *Tantrum II* from its trailer and hurled it through Marco De Bistro's dining room. Freeman proper was spared major damage, owing largely to the woods of Waterfront Park.

Blake rolled over, pulled his phone off the nightstand and dialed Treva.

"Hi honey!" she answered in her ever-sunny tone. "I know what you're calling about. I've got like two minutes charge left on my phone, so I gotta make it quick!"

"Speak, Blondie!" said Blake.

"Little Miss Mia is okay. She took her stuff back to her mom's on Tuesday and left town the next morning. Don't know where she went. You all got power over there?"

"Oh yeah! Generator."

"I should've known Tripp would. Whole town's out. They say it won't be back on 'til…" That was it. *I guess I'm not the only one who doesn't charge their phone when they should.* he thought.

Carson knocked on his door. It was nice being able to close the door. At home it was forbidden to him; but not Agatha, of course.

"Kid, wake up. We gotta go to Mom's and Make sure the basement didn't flood, or anything."

***

Blake stood on the hearth and restored his grandfather's trophy to its rightful place on the mantel and carefully positioned the portrait next to it. He returned the Urquart clan dirk to its cradle in the book case. He gazed around the cozy living room, feeling that somehow things were complete—that at last, order had been restored to the universe.

He found Carson in the kitchen, listening to the answering machine. "Anyone call for me?" said Blake.

"Nope. Only one message and it's for me."

"So Nanna *has* been getting Mom's messages," Blake said to himself. "Who called *you*?"

"My old buddy Barry. Becky Lynn's big brother." Carson headed down the basement stairs, Blake followed. "Got himself a little schooner down in the Bahamas. Doin' ecotourism. Said he needs a dive master."

"You should do it!" said Blake.

"Gotta get recertified. It'd be kind of a commitment."

"It'd be the Bahamas! Where can *I* get certified?"

Carson reached the bottom of the steps. Well, this ain't too bad! Not bad at all."

"It's spooky, is what it is." said Blake. "Like a dungeon."

"It could use a light or two. Otherwise a little going over with a mop to get the dirt up and it'll be fine. Let's go see if Mrs. Haraguchi needs anything. Then we'll grab lunch and finish up here.

***

The Empress Haraguchi had a punch-list a mile long and supervised every facet of its completion with exasperating attention to the smallest detail, such that Blake longed to be swabbing the floor in the basement of the brown bungalow.

And at last, he was. Thankfully, it was a light job; but it would be well

601

after dinner before they got home to Gunn's. Blake lugged the string-mop clumsily out of the bucket and lodged the handle into a joist-brace above. Something fell out in a cascade of dust and landed behind him. Even in the dim light from the small, basement window, it only took a moment to realize what it was—a sort of cocoon with a shriveled rat's tail protruding from one end. Anxiety swept through his body like a cold wave that started at his scalp, ran down the back of his neck. It washed over his heart, plunged through his viscera and pooled in his knees and bladder. He fought for the breath to scream. And when he finally did, it came out like a long, moaning crescendo of pure revulsion as he fell back against a shelf of clinking preserve-jars.

Carson came around the corner in a hurry. "You all right?"

Blake remained plastered against the pantry shelves, quivering. "You— you lied to me!"

"What are you talking about, Blake?" Then he spotted the rat-mummy between them on the floor. His insides likewise turned to chilled liquid.

"Old Hairy!" he said, almost groaning. "I didn't lie to you, Blake. I've never owned a spider."

"How can you stand there and say that?" demanded Blake, tears rolling down his cheeks.

"Old Hairy belonged to Jack! I never dreamed he'd make it through the winter. I counted on it, as a matter of fact! I had no idea Jack left him rats."

" *That's* why he was living in his car and why you've been living in a shack and a tent and at Mr. Gunn's and anywhere but here!"

"Hold on, Sherlock! It's twenty miles to the lake. Had no wheels 'til last week. You know that. Well, that certainly explains Miss Margaret's poor Chihuahua! Old Hairy must be coming and going through the..." Something metal squeaked in the direction of the wood-burner. "Stove. Blake, did you turn that damper open?"

Blake swallowed hard. "What's a damper?"

"Opens and closes the stovepipe." Carson took a step back. "Listen!" he hissed. After a moment there came a distinct tapping sound from behind the door of the squatty rectangular stove. Tink, tinka tink-tink...Tink, tinka tink-tink…Another wave of distilled dread flooded their veins.

"Find something to throw. Now." Carson whispered. "Just in case it *ain't* the wind."

Blake's gaze landed on a box of old-fashioned, magnesium flash-bulbs on the workbench. The tapping stopped. The square door of the stove creaked slowly open. Blake tenderly gathered the box of flash-bulbs to his bosom. "Cover me!' said Carson, creeping tenuously toward a shelving unit which stood next to the stove. Old Hairy popped his thorax and four fuzzy front legs onto the black hearth, pin-head eyes gleaming. He was one huge tarantula.

Blake screamed, and loosed a volley of blinding, blue bombs. The spider backed into his iron fortress, just as stunned by the white-hot magnesium flashes as the invaders were. Carson seized a dusty case from the top shelf and retreated.

Old Hairy charged out across the hearth and down to the floor. At the same instant, the air erupted with crackling like a thousand Black Cat firecrackers. Sparks blossomed across the stove and concrete floor, chasing the giant arachnid halfway up a shelving unit in the pantry. Old Hairy escaped from sight over the top of the canned peaches.

"What the heck is that?" exclaimed Blake.

"You like that? Hand cranked .22 machine gun with folding stock. Highly exotic! Your Grandpa got it from a fellah named DeArmond," beamed Carson, as he slapped another clip into the gun. "Now, where is that eight-legged abomination?"

Blake sheltered behind his uncle, ready with the last half of the flash-bulbs and an old softball he found in the bottom of the box. Minutes passed like hours. They could hear the spider creeping somewhere behind the shelves, but Carson held his fire. There wasn't a can of beans, soup, or fruit below the fourth shelf that wasn't bleeding fatally. A little cascade of dust poured down from between the joists just in front of the shelves.

"The braces!" cried Carson, as he loosed another deafening barrage. Dust poured down from the joists, heading in the direction of the wood-burner. Splinters sprayed in his wake as Carson tracked and cranked. Old

Hairy dropped onto the horizontal pipe that connected the stove to the chimney, scrambled down it and across the stovetop. He skittered back into the stove upside-down. And all under a hail of gunfire and bombardment that would have gotten him a medal in most branches of the armed forces.

Blake grabbed the softball and threw it at the open stove door with all the arm he had and nailed it. It flew open to its limit, then recoiled shut. Carson leapt forward and kicked the latch with his foot. "Flippin' A! Throw me that red spray-can over there and take cover!"

Blake tossed Carson the can of ether. He opened the draft-vent on the stove door and sprayed it full. Blake got behind the water softener, confident that the least he could expect from this experience would be flash burns and temporary blindness. There was a clattering in the vertical pipe. "Ohhh no you don't!" said Carson, and bounded back to his nephew. "Gimme one!" He snatched a bulb out of the box. "Fire in the hole!"

He zinged the bulb at the stove door. The pop and flash were followed by a crashing explosion that rattled everything in the house, embedded the iron burner plates into the kitchen floorboards above, and belched fire across the south half of the basement. Packages of toilet paper burst into flames, ten feet away.

Carson snatched a fire extinguisher from the workbench, to put out the flaming TP, and residual fumes in the stove. Blake stood up from behind the water softener. "Holey Kamoley!"

Eyewitnesses later recounted how a jet of fire thirty feet high had blown out of Nanna Urquart's chimney, launching a flaming ball the size of a melon, skyward. It landed in Mr. Haraguchi's koi pond a quarter mile away. It was instantly consumed by fifty of the most beautiful carp in the world. Thus perished Old Hairy, the evil with eight legs.

Blake spent the next three days downstairs, prying little lead bullets out of practically everything. He also learned how to repair sub-flooring and lay tile in the kitchen. And though the last curse of Voodoo Jack had been dispelled, they continued to discover Old Hairy's grisly mementoes—which didn't help the basement's dungeon ambiance in any way.

Chapter 89

Just about everyone came to the Bon Voyage party; from the mayor down to little Marcelo Pagán. After all the speeches, gifts, toasts and well wishes, Blake stood and gathered his courage. "You know, you're treating me like a hero, but I still just feel like a kid who came to your town and caused a lot of trouble."

"Seven hundred sixty-eight thousand dollars worth and some change," said Gunn.

"But who's counting?" said Mayor Teddy.

Carson stood up, amid the laughter and applause. "I have something to announce as well. My obstreperous nephew here has inspired me to finally make something of myself. As soon as I renew my SCUBA certification, I'm packing my bags for the Caribbean. I've signed on as Dive Master aboard the schooner Tarshish."

There was more applause and glad-handing. Blake slipped out through the locker room door. As things were winding down, Gunn found him at the patio railing looking out over the lake.

"Yeh throw quite a wake, for a little boat."

"How's that?" said Blake.

"Look at all the people in there. They would'na otherwise have come across one another, but for being stirred together by your passing through. Even Sister Psoriasis is here! That's what you call 'sphere of influence.' You never know the impact yeh really have on people."

Blake surveyed the crowd milling behind the clubhouse windows.

"She was right, yeh know. She *had* to leave, at least for a time."

"I guess so," said Blake. "I do, too."

"For a time." Gunn put his hand on Blake's shoulder. "Your grandfather would be insufferably proud of you." Blake threw his arms around the old man and they exchanged a long hug. "And I am, too."

Chapter 90

Seven Thunders slipped quietly down the lower lake under full sail. It had become a point of daring with Blake, in lighter weather, to manage the main, jib, and spinnaker while sailing solo. Pale light tumbled down from the faded blue sky; a gentle, chilly breeze blew across the sparkling water. There was a strange and bittersweet serenity that seemed to permeate the day. Somewhere between solitude and loneliness—it tugged at Blake's heart, this feeling. He searched for words to describe it. Then it came to him. Change. Sooner than he thought, everything had changed—and would never be the same. Mia was gone. Griffy was back in school. Carson would soon be headed for the Caribbean. He trimmed his sails and gazed at the forest.

"This is all going to change," he said to a solitary gull, bobbing nearby. "Those leaves are going to fall. This lake is going to freeze over and I'll be back in Fort Wayne where nothing is different."

Today was the day. After one hundred fifty-four days, the Barbers would return to claim their lost baggage.

The surviving leaves on Trespass Island were becoming a brilliant orange now, its scorched trees spotted with white egrets assembling for their yearly exodus to warmer climes. As he approached the harbor, the wind began to kick up a little and *Seven Thunders* yawed unexpectedly. He instinctively dropped the spinnaker and let go the jib. He brought his boat into the wind and recovered the sail from the lake. He dropped the main and ran in on the jib, alone. He waved to Carson, who was driving the big orange tractor down the ridge.

***

Blake sat drowsing in Mia's favorite sunny spot by the windows—feet on the ledge, chair rocked back on two legs. The front door swooshed open and squeaked shut. He breathed deeply and did not turn around.

Then behind him, he heard the last voice he ever wanted to hear again. It was Agatha's. "Hi, I'm looking for Blake Barber. Have you seen him around?"

Blake summoned the Mexican within. "Blake Barber? Um, He es no… weeth us…anymore.

"Say what? He's not here?"

"No, eh, he…You must be—how to say? Next of keen?" Blake put the chair down flat and stared hard down the hill. It took every shred of concentration to hold himself together. Was she really there, standing right behind him?

"Next of kin? What do you mean, next of kin?"

"We…well…" He stood and leaned against the window. "I'm so sorry señorita, but you miss his memorial. We bury him last month! I'm sorry! Is too much! Escuse me, Por favor!" Blake covered half his face with one hand. He whimpered and hurriedly pushed his way between tables to the side exit. The large window in the door caught Agatha's reflection, as he whipped it open—and what a glorious picture of stark shock Blake beheld. In an instant he was outside and the image of his demon sister was banished for ever.

He jumped the patio railing and trundled down the hill. He was half way to the dock when another voice called. One he could barely ignore.

"Young man? Young man? I'm looking for my son. Can you help me?"

He pretended not to hear. His heart was pounding. *Keep going,* he thought. *Just a little farther. Just keep going.*

"Young man?" She was pursuing him. He reached his boat, berthed at the dock by the beach. Keeping his back to the shore, he untied the bowline. Deck-boards creaked behind him.

"Young man, I'm looking for my son, Blake Barber. Do you know where he is?"

He kept his back turned and again, the Mexican answered for him. "He's over at Gonn's Marina. I take you to see him. You pull up the sails."

"Alright." There was a little apprehension in her voice as she sat down on the dock and slid into the boat. Blake couldn't believe she was buying it.

***

The orange tractor chugged to a stop by the front door and snorted defiantly when Carson pulled the key out of the ignition. He made his way up the steps, weary and numb from a day's mowing.

"Carson! What is going on here?" barked James Barber. He stood by the windows, Agatha bawling into his chest.

"I'll bite, what?" said Carson, caught absolutely off guard. "And howdy do to you too, James!"

"How can you just stand there like nothing has happened?"

"Um, could you give me a hint?"

"There was young Mexican man who told Agatha that Blake…That Blake…" His voice cracked. Carson thought the man might puke with his next word: "*passed.*"

Carson's confusion quickly congealed into complete, delicious, comprehension. "*Mexican?* Not Scottish?"

"That's what I said!"

"Red Hawaiian shirt, collar turned up?"

Agatha turned her face from her father's snot-drenched shirt and sniffled "Yes."

"Kind of wavy reddish-brown hair?" Carson said, grinning. Again, she turned her head and gave an affirmative sob.

Carson chuckled. "I know that kid! He's got that accent down to a tee, don't he? Can't believe he didn't go with the Scots, though."

"Urquart, what has happened to my son? Where is he!" James blubbered.

"Well, James, if you're talking about the angry little boy you dumped here four months ago, he *is* dead—*and* gone. If you mean the young man that just pulled the wool over your eyes," he said, leaning to the side to look past them, "I'd say he's probably halfway across the lake with his mother, by now. Probably gonna go see his girlfriend."

James stared blankly. Agatha caught her breath long enough to comprehend that last sentence. "Girlfriend?" she gulped. She tore from her father's embrace and flung herself at the window.

"Creep! Miserable little creep!" she hissed, eyes locked on *Seven Thunders* as it caught the wind and sprinted out of the harbor.

James, finally catching up, squinted lakeward in disbelief. "You let him take a boat out by himself?"

"Why not? Earned the money and paid for it!"

"Earned the money? Just… Just exactly what has he been doing all summer?"

***

"Señora, you see that island, there? All them white birds?" said Blake.

"Yes, I see them."

"You know why they all together like that?"

"Tell me, why?" his mother replied, smiling dreamily.

"They gonna leave and fly away for the weenter. Then they gone."

"But they won't be gone for ever," a tear rolled down Ava's cheek. "You know why?"

"No Señora, you tell me."

"Because, they know this is where they belong." She turned to Blake, all beaming smile and wet cheeks. "Like you!"

In one swift maneuver, Blake eased the main and brought the boat across the wind, then threw himself into his mother's arms.

***

"Now, this'll take a minute." Carson eased into a deck chair, leaned back and put his feet up on the table. "I don't know where to begin. Let's see, between working odd-jobs on the lake with me and Tripp, he started a couple of businesses with a family of Pagáns, he survived a tornado, brought smiles to a lot of lonely faces, battled a giant spider in his grandmother's basement, and convinced me to make something of myself. And that's just the recent stuff."

The mention of the spider drew Agatha's immediate attention.

"You bet it was real, honey. Shave and a hair cut! Oh, and on top of all that: he turned thirteen, deposed the commodore, stole his daughter's heart and outwitted his psychopathic son. And, lest I forget—I think this is the crowning achievement—sank the old crook's half-million-dollar motor boat."

Agatha slipped around her gaping father and straight out the back door. She ran full tilt to the point. Carson dropped his feet back on the floor and slapped his hands on his thighs. "James, you've got a fine young man on your hands. I suggest you get to know him." He got up and walked to the front door. "This might be your last chance," he said, as it closed behind him. The tractor snorted back to life and chugged down the hill.

***

Agatha watched from the point as the little boat zig-zagged its way back from the island. It veered to the left and up went the spinnaker, round and colorful. Agatha couldn't believe her eyes—Mother was steering! Blake had slipped into the harness, snapped to the trapeze, and was flying over the water waving his arms above his head and shouting for joy.

"Free as a bird!" said Agatha in disgust. As if summoned, a huge white gull swooped past so startlingly close that she jumped backwards and fell down. She knew she would never be able to dominate her little brother again.

***

The back door to the clubhouse wheezed open and the room filled with the happy chatter of mother and son. Carson trailed in behind them. Agatha squinted around the edge of one of the wingback chairs near the fireplace.

611

Father stood up from his. "At last, the prodigal pirate returns! Get your things, so we can go home," he sniveled, loudly.

"James!" said Ava, in a pleading tone. You haven't seen *your* Blake in four months and that's what you want to say? Not even 'Hello, son! Glad to see you?'"

"I'll be glad to see him back in decent clothes, looking like a proper *little* boy again! Mother you can get him a haircut tomorrow. Now, let's get on the road." Agatha grinned her Siamese grin.

Blake took a step forward. "I am *not* a little boy. And I am *not* a pirate. I spent all summer *fighting* pirates. You can drag me back to Fort Wayne if you want, but I am a *laker* and *this* is *my* home."

Agatha's grin deepened. She bit her lower lip in anticipation and turned slowly to look at her father.

James drew a huge breath and shouted "Get your things and get in the car this instant! I will not tolerate this insolence!"

"Jameson!" Ava sing-songed, in a raised but polite voice. "Blake is not going back with us!"

"He's not?" said Agatha.

"I'm *not*?" Blake repeated, looking back at his uncle, who only smiled cross-wise and winked slyly.

"What do you mean he's not? Of course he is!" said James.

"Mom is back home in Pemberton, now. She wants him to come stay with her."

"Out of the question! We don't have the time or money to drive all the way back down there! And he's missed too much schooling already."

"James, Mom is sending Blake to Pemberton Academy, isn't that wonderful?"

Agatha's self-satisfied smile began to melt into a slack-jawed mix of confusion and envy. Blake was beginning to feel the way he had on the night things started going sour for Commodore Devlin.

"Have you all gone crazy? We can't afford anything like that! That's why he's home schooled!"

"James, Mom is going to pay for it. She has a room fixed up and all ready for him. Think about it, honey. Can't you see the advantages?"

"Uprooting him and moving him like that would be detrimental to his personal development."

"I think I'll adjust, somehow." Blake dead-panned. "You know, I only managed to hold down three jobs this summer?"

"And a girlfriend!" Agatha said.

"She's not… Yes! *And* a girlfriend!"

"Is she pregnant?"

"Agatha!" James barked.

"We don't know, yet!" retorted Blake.

"Blake!" gasped his mother.

"Kidding! Just kid-ding!"

"Well, I guess if you want to abandon your family like that, so be it."

"Dibs on his room!" said Agatha, throwing a hand in the air.

"Abandon?" shouted Blake, "*Abandon*? You might as well have tied me up in a garbage bag and thrown me in the Saint Joe River! You never pay *any* attention to me, you *never* wanted me!"

"I have never seen such a shamefully ungrateful little boy!"

"Nobody is abandoning anyone, let's all calm down!" cried Ava.

"I am *not* a little boy! All I *ever* wanted…"

"James! Blake! Please!"

The angry words rebounded off the windows and walls like cannon shot, clashing and splintering in an unintelligible cacophony of rage.

"You're not a Barber, you're a barbarian!"

"My name is *Urquart*!" howled Blake, so hard he thought his throat would collapse.

It ended as suddenly as it had begun, when James stalked out and slammed the door behind him. The air quivered with the energy of the battle. It took a moment for the spirit to dissipate. Ava covered her mouth with one hand and cradled Blake's face with the other. She drew him close. Agatha slunk out the door without a sound.

Carson sat down and stroked his moustache.

"I'm sorry mom. I didn't want it to be this way. I thought I had changed. But it's all still the same."

Ava gazed down at him and smiled. "You're right about one thing. You *are* an Urquart."

Chapter 91

Blake sat in a big, comfy chair with his new laptop, at the spacious Pemberton Public Library. He pondered the latest email in his inbox. It was from blue_sari@manitowoc-exchange.com, sent October 22nd. *Three days ago? Who is that? I really have to check my SPAM settings,* he thought. He clicked on the title 'Whassup?'

The email loaded, filling the screen with a close-up selfie. His heart leapt! It was a little girl wearing an ebony cascade of natural curls, laughing her head off. Mia's smirking face occupied the rest of the picture. A short mop of curls stuck out from under her purple bandana. The caption read:

> Yes, that is the little fiend from the Badger. And yes, that's my hair on her head. Sorry it's been so long, Tux. I know you've been wondering where I disappeared to. Would you believe a wigmaker in Manitowoc? Fiona's parents are the nicest people in the world. I hope things calmed down after I left. I heard about the tornado trashing the marina and the bistro. BTW I get it about the name, now... No wonder, right?
>
> So, I'll be staying with my crazy Aunt Serena and going to some private academy, starting in the spring. Uh oh! Guess who's home from school? Ready about, hard a'lee!
> Miss you!
> Love,
> Mia

A wonderful, ticklish feeling fizzed his brain and ran down to his chest. Then everything went dark, as somebody clamped their hands over his eyes.

"Hey, you gotta girlfriend?" said a familiar Latina voice.

"I don't know, do I?" he said.

"You do now!" Mia put him in a headlock and gave him a big kiss on the cheek.

"I hear you need a crew for the Long John Regatta?"

"Give it up, woman," he said, squeezing her arms affectionately. "You know I don't sail. So, where's this Aunt Serena live?"

She slipped around to the side of his chair and rested her chin on its arm. "About a half mile up the street."

"Curious! I live a half mile down the street. I start Pemberton Academy in January."

"How odd, so do I! Five bucks says we get kicked out before school even begins."

"It's okay. I have a crazy uncle in the Bahamas. He'll take us in."

"Maybe he should meet my Tia Serena?"

"Great, then we'd have Aunt *and* Uncle Arctica."

"You lost me there, Tux."

Blake closed his laptop and slid it into his backpack. "I'll explain it later. Come on, I want you to meet my grandmother. And I've got an old, hairy story to tell you."

He took her hand as they passed through the sliding doors, out into the delicate autumn light. As they walked he returned the kiss to her cheek, while red and yellow leaves clattered along the sidewalk.

Weather the Storm!

Sign up for email updates on the upcoming
sequel to Uncle Arctica!

www.trespassislandbooks.com

Glossary of Sailing Terms

You don't have to know anything about sailing to enjoy *Uncle Arctica*, but it will help if you become familiar with a few of the following sailing terms.

Aft Toward the rear of a boat.

Astern Behind the boat.

Backstay A cable which runs from high up on the mast, down to the stern of the boat. Often used to bend the mast back, to take power out of the sail.

Block A pulley.

Boom A horizontal pole attached to the mast, and to which the bottom of the main sail is attached. Also the sound it makes when it hits you in the head during a wild jibe.

Bow The front end of a boat.

Bowsprit A pole or spar attached to the bow of some boats, to which jib sails and the forestay are attached.

Buoy A floating marker. Some folks say "boo-ee," some say "boy."

Centerboard A keel which can be retracted into the hull of a boat.

Cleat A device used for securing a line. There are many styles of cleat.

Some resemble two horns, around which a line is wrapped in a figure-eight fashion; some have spring-loaded jaws through which the line passes; "pinch-cleats" trap the line in a tight wedge-shaped groove.

Companionway A ladderway leading through a hatch to the next deck below, or above.

Daggerboard A small, blade-like keel which is removable.

Deck The top of the boat covering the hull.

Ease To loosen or let a sail out.

Forestay A cable which runs from high up on the mast, down to the bow of the boat. The jib is often attached to the forestay.

Forward Toward the front of a boat.

Guy A line used to control the end of a pole, specifically a spinnaker pole.

Halyard A line and/or cable used to raise and lower a sail.

Hard a'lee The warning given by the skipper that he is turning the boat (by pushing the tiller hard to the leeward side.) Usually preceeded by the call "ready about!"

Heeling When the sailboat leans over as the wind speed (and boat speed) increases. This is usually when the crew hastens to sit on the rail and hike out.

Hike To lean out of the boat to hold it as flat as possible. Boats are usually equipped with straps to wrap your legs around, or toe rails to keep you from falling out!

Hull The body of a boat.

Jib The sail forward of the mast. In some older boats the jib had a boom, too.

Jibe Changing the direction of the boat while sailing with the wind coming from behind the boat. Same as a Tack, but the wind passes from one side of the stern to the other. This results in the boom swinging—often with dangerous force—to the other side of the boat. Jibing is a "duck or die" proposition.

Leeboard A retractable keel fastened to the side of some boats.

Leeward The direction which the wind is blowing to. If the wind is blowing right in your face, then your back is facing to leeward. Your back is then on the leeward side of your body.

Line On a boat, ropes are called "lines." A line is any rope with a specific purpose.

Luff The forward edge of a sail. Also, when a sail collapses because the boat is pointed too close to the wind, the sail is said to be "luffing." Also, a maneuver where one forces a competitor into the wind, causing his or her sails to luff.

Keel A stationary fin or ridge attached to the bottom of the boat which provides stability.

Mainsail The large triangular sail attached to aft side of the mast. Usually, the mainsail is also attached to a boom, along its bottom edge.

Mast The vertical pole to which the mainsail and stays are attached.

Mizzen Mast On a boat with multiple masts (like the Terrapin,) the mizzen mast is the next mast aft of the main mast.

Port If you are in a boat facing forward (toward the bow,) port is left side of the boat. Remember: port and left both have four letters.

Rail Not actually a rail, but that part of the deck along the sides of the boat where crew members may sit and hike out.

Rigging The arrangement of sails, sheets, halyards, control lines, and other gear. Often divided into the running rigging (the previous stuff,) and the standing rigging (the mast, boom, shrouds, and stays.)

Rudder A flat piece of wood or metal used to steer the boat.

Sheet A line used to control the trim of a sail. Main sheet, jib sheet, spinnaker sheet.

Spinnaker A large, parachute-like sail used when the wind is coming from behind the boat.

Spinnaker Pole A removable pole which attaches to the mast at one end, and the spinnaker guy at the other. It is used to control the position/angle of the spinnaker in relation to the boat.

Shrouds Cables which stabilize the mast. also called side-stays.

Spreaders Short horizontal bars which spread the shrouds out as they come down from higher up the mast.

Starboard If you are in a boat facing forward (toward the bow,) starboard is the right side of the boat.

Stern The rear end of a boat

Tack Changing the direction of the boat while sailing with the wind coming from the in front of the boat. The bow of the boat passes through the wind so that it changes from blowing onto one side to the other. For example, if the wind is blowing onto the port side of the boat, you are on "port tack." You turn the boat so the bow passes through the wind (momentarily pointing straight into the wind) until the breeze now blows onto the starboard side of the boat. Now you are on "starboard tack." The sails shift to the other side of the boat as the tack is completed.

Topsides The sides of a boat between the waterline and the deck

Transom The back end of a boat which has a square-stern.

Tell Tale Streamers that indicate the direction the wind is coming from. Often made from old video/audio cassette tape!

Tiller A long handle attached to the rudder for steering the boat.

Trapeze A cable attached high up the mast, by which a crew member may suspend him/herself so as to be able to hike his/her body completely out over the water.

Trim To tighten or pull a sail in.

Windward The direction the wind is coming from. If the wind is blowing right in your face, you are looking to windward. Your nose is then on the windward side of your head.

www.ingramcontent.com/pod-product-compliance
Lightning Source LLC
Chambersburg PA
CBHW022231020726
47496CB00004B/855